JUDITH TARR

THE
HOUND
AND THE
FALCON

ORB
A TOM DOHERTY ASSOCIATES BOOK
NEW YORK

THE HOUND AND THE FALCON

Copyright © 1993 by Judith Tarr

All rights reserved, including the right to reproduce this book, or portions thereof, in any form.

This book is an omnibus edition consisting of the novels *The Isle of Glass*, originally published by Bluejay Books in 1985; *The Golden Horn*, originally published by Bluejay Books in 1985; and *The Hounds of God*, originally published by Bluejay Books in 1986.

This book is printed on acid-free paper.

An Orb Edition
Published by Tom Doherty Associates, Inc.
175 Fifth Avenue
New York, N.Y. 10010

Orb® is a registered trademark of Tom Doherty Associates, Inc.

ISBN: 0-312-85303-3

First Orb edition: June 1993

Printed in the United States of America

0 9 8 7 6 5 4 3 2 1

CONTENTS

THE ISLE OF GLASS 5

THE GOLDEN HORN 223

THE HOUNDS OF GOD 429

The Isle of Glass

For Meredith

"Quis est homo?"
"Mancipium mortis, transiens viator,
loci hospes."
    —Alcuin of York

"What is a man?"
"The slave of death, the guest of an inn,
a wayfarer passing."
    —Helen Waddell

1

"Brother Alf! Brother Alfred!"

It was meant to be a whisper, but it echoed through the library. Brother Alfred looked up from his book, smiling a little as the novice halted panting within an inch of the table. "What is it now, Jehan?" he asked. "A rescue? The King himself come to drag you off to the wars?"

Jehan groaned. "Heaven help us! I just spent an hour explaining to Dom Morwin why I want to stay here and take vows. Father wrote to him, you see, and said that if I had to be a monk, I'd join the Knights Templar and not disgrace him completely."

Brother Alfred's smile widened. "And what said our good Abbot?"

"That I'm a waste of good muscle." Jehan sighed and hunched his shoulders. It did little good; they were still as broad as the front gate. "Brother Alf, can't anybody but you see what's under it all?"

"Brother Osric says that you will make a tolerable theologian."

"Did he? Well. He told me today that I was a blockhead, and that I'd got to the point where he'd have to turn me over to you."

"In the same breath?"

"Almost. But I'm forgetting. Dom Morwin wants to see you."

Brother Alfred closed his book. "And we've kept him waiting. Someday, Jehan, we must both take vows of silence."

"I could use it. But you? Never. How could you teach?"

"There are ways." Just as Brother Alfred turned to go, he paused. "Tomorrow, don't go to the schoolroom. Meet me here."

Jehan's whoop made no pretense of restraint.

There was a fire in the Abbot's study, and the Abbot stood in front of it, warming his hands. He did not turn when Brother Alfred entered, but said, "The weather's wild today."

The other sat in a chair nearby. "Fitting," he remarked. "You know what the hill-folk say: On the Day of the Dead, demons ride."

The Abbot crossed himself quickly, with a wry smile. "Oh, it will be a night to conjure in." He sat stiffly and sighed. "My bones feel it. You know, Alf—suddenly I'm old."

There was a silence. Brother Alfred gazed into the fire, seeing a pair of young novices, one small and slight and red as a fox, the other tall and slender and very pale with hair like silver-gilt. They were very industriously stealing apples from the orchard. His lips twitched.

"What are you thinking of?" asked the Abbot.

"Apple-stealing."

"Is that all? I was thinking of the time we changed the labels on every bottle, jar, and box of medicine in the infirmary. We almost killed old Brother Anselm when he took one of Brother Herbal's clandestine aphrodisiacs instead of the medicine he needed for his indigestion."

Brother Alfred laughed. "I remember that very well indeed; after Dom Edwin's caning, I couldn't sit for a fortnight. And we had to change the labels back again. In the end we knew Brother Herbal's stores better than he did himself."

"I can still remember. First shelf: dittany, fennel, tansy, rue. . . . Was it really almost sixty years ago?"

"Really."

"*Tempus fugit,* with a vengeance." Morwin ran his hands through his hair. A little red still remained; the rest was rusty white. "I've had my threescore years and ten, with three more for good measure. Time to think of what I should have thought of all along if I'd been as good a monk as I liked to think I was."

"Good enough, Morwin. Good enough."

"I could have been much better. I could have refused to let them make me Abbot. You did."

"You know why."

"Foolishness. You could have been a cardinal if you'd cared to try."

"How could I have? You know what I am."

"I know what you think you are. You've had the story of your advent drummed into your head so often, you've come to believe it."

"It's the truth. How it was the winter solstice, and a very storm out of Hell. And in the middle of it, at midnight indeed, a novice, keeping vigil in the chapel, heard a baby's cry. He had the courage to go out, even into that storm, which should have out-howled anything living, and he found a prodigy. A babe of about a season's growth, lying naked in the snow. And yet he was not cold; even as the novice opened the postern, what had been warming him took flight. Three white owls. Our brave lad took a long look, snatched up the child, and bolted for the chapel. When holy water seemed to make no impression, except what one would expect from a baby plunged headlong into an ice-cold bath, he baptized his discovery, named him Alf—Alfred for the Church's sake—and proceeded to make a monk of him. But the novice always swore that the brat had come out of the hollow hills."

"Had he?"

"I don't know. I seem to remember, faint and far, like another's memory: fire and shouting, and a girl running with a baby in her arms. Then the girl, cold and dead, and a storm, and three white owls. No one ever found her." Brother Alfred breathed deep. "Maybe that's only a dream, and someone actually exposed me as a change-ling. What better place for one? Here on Ynys Witrin, with all its legends and its old magic."

"Or else," said Morwin, "the Fair Folk have turned Christian. Though I've never heard that any of them could bear either holy water or cold iron."

"This one can." Brother Alfred flexed his long fingers and folded them tightly in his lap. "But to take a high place in the Church or in the world . . . no. Anywhere but here, I would have gone to the stake long ago. Even here, not all the Brothers are sure that I'm not some sort of superior devil."

Morwin bristled. "Who dares to think that?"

"None so bold that he voices his doubts, or even thinks them, often."

"He had better not!"

Alf smiled and shook his head. "You were always too fierce in my defense."

"And a good thing too. I've pulled you out of many a broil, from the first time I saw the other novices make a butt of you."

"So much trouble for a few harmless words."

"Harmless! It was getting down to sticks and stones when I came by."

"They were only trying to frighten me," Alf said. "But that's years past. We must truly be old if we can care so much for what happened so long ago."

"Don't be so kind. It's me, and you know it. I've always been one to bear a grudge—the worse for my soul." Morwin rose and stood with his hands clasped behind his back. "Alf. Someday sooner or

later, I'm going to face my Maker. And when I do that, I want to be
sure I've left St. Ruan's in good hands." Alf would have spoken, but
he shook his head. "I know, Alf. You've refused every office anyone
has tried to give you and turned down the abbacy three times. The
more fool you; each time, the second choice has been far inferior. I
don't want that to happen again."

"Morwin. You know it must."

"Why?"

Brother Alfred stood, paler even than usual, and spread his arms.
"Look at me!"

Morwin's jaw set. "I'm looking," he said grimly. "I've looked
nearly every day for sixty years."

"What do you see?"

"The one man I'd trust to take the abbacy and to keep it as it
should be kept."

"Man, Morwin? Do you think I am a man? Come. You alone
can see me as I truly am. If you will."

The Abbot found that he could not look away. His friend stood
in front of him, very tall and very pale, his eyes wide with something
close to despair. Strange eyes, palest gold like his hair and pupiled like
a cat's.

"You see," said Alf. "Remember what else had the novices
calling me devil and witch's get. My way with beasts and with men.
My little conjuring tricks." He gathered a handful of fire and shadow,
plaited it into a long strange-gleaming strand, and tossed it to Morwin. The other caught it reflexively, and it was solid, a length of cord
at once shadow-cool and fire-hot. "And finally, Morwin, old friend,
how old am I?"

"Two or three years younger than I."

"And how old do I look?"

Morwin scowled and twisted the cord in his hands, and said
nothing.

"How old did Earl Rogier think I was when he brought Jehan to
St. Ruan's? How old did Bishop Aylmer think I was, he who read my
Gloria Dei thirty years ago and looked in vain for me all the while he
guested here, only last year? How old did he think me, Morwin? And
what was it he said to you? 'That lad has a great future, Dom Morwin.
Send him along to me when he grows a little older, and I promise
you'll not regret it.' He thought I was not eighteen!"

Still Morwin was silent, although the pain in his friend's face and voice had turned his scowl to an expression of old and bitter sorrow.

Alf dropped back into his seat and covered his face with his hands. "And you would make me swear to accept the election if it came to me again. Morwin, will you never understand that I cannot let myself take any title?"

The other's voice was rough. "There's a limit to humility, Alf. Even in a monk."

"It's not humility. Dear God, no! I have more pride than Lucifer. When I was as young as my body, I exulted in what I thought I was. There were Bishop Aylmers then, too, all too eager to flatter a young monk with a talent for both politics and theology. They told me I was brilliant, and I believed them. I knew I was an enchanter; I thought I might have been the son of an elven prince, or a lord at least, and I told myself tales of his love for my mortal mother and of her determination that I should be a Christian. And of three white owls." His head lifted. "I was even vain, God help me; the more so when I knew the world, and saw myself reflected in women's eyes. Not a one but sighed to see me a monk."

"And not a one managed to move you."

"Is that to my credit? I was proud that I never fell, nor ever even slipped. No, Morwin. What I have is not humility. It's fear. It was in me even when I was young, beneath the pride, fear that I was truly inhuman. It grew as the years passed. When I was thirty and was still mistaken for a boy, I turned my mind from it. At forty I began to recognize the fear. At fifty I knew it fully. At sixty it was open terror. And now, I can hardly bear it. Morwin—Morwin—what if I shall never die?"

Very gently Morwin said, "All things die, Alf."

"Then why do I not grow old? Why am I still exactly as I was the day I took my vows? And—what is immortal—what is elvish—is soulless. To be what I am and to lack a soul . . . it torments me even to think of it."

Morwin laid a light hand on his shoulder. "Alf. Whatever you are, whatever you become, I cannot believe that God would be so cruel, so unjust, so utterly vindictive, as to let you live without a soul and die with your body. Not after you've loved Him so long and so well."

"Have I? Or is all my worship a mockery? I've even dared to serve at His altar, to say His Mass—I, a shadow, a thing of air and darkness. And you would make me Abbot. Oh, sweet Jesu!"

"Stop it, Alf!" Morwin rapped. "That's the trouble with you. You bottle yourself up so well you get a name for serenity. And when you shatter, the whole world shakes. Spare us for once, will you?"

But Alf was beyond even that strong medicine. With a wordless cry he whirled and fled.

Morwin stared after him, paused, shook his head. Slowly, painfully, he lowered himself into his chair. The cord was still in his hand, fire and darkness, heat and cold. For a long while he sat staring at it, stroking it with trembling fingers. "Poor boy," he whispered. "Poor boy."

2

Jehan could not sleep. He lay on his hard pallet, listening to the night sounds of the novices' dormitory, snores and snuffles and an occasional dreamy murmur. It was cold under his thin blanket; wind worked its way through the shutters of the high narrow windows, and rain lashed against them, rattling them upon their iron hinges.

But he was used to that. The novices said that he could sleep soundly on an ice-floe in the northern sea, with a smithy in full clamor beside him.

For the thousandth time he rolled into a new position, on his stomach with his head pillowed on his folded arms. He kept seeing Brother Alfred, now bent over a book in the library, now weaving upon his great loom, now singing in chapel with a voice like a tenor bell. All those serene faces flashed past and shattered, and he saw the tall slight form running from the Abbot's study, wearing such a look that even now Jehan trembled.

Stealthily he rose. No one seemed awake. He shook out the robe which had been his pillow; quickly he donned it. His heart was hammering. If anyone caught him, he would get a caning and a week of cleaning the privy.

Big though his body was, he was as soft-footed as a cat. He crept past the sleeping novices, laid his hand upon the door-latch. A prayer had formed and escaped before he saw the irony in it.

With utmost care he opened the door. Brother Owein the novice-master snored in his cell, a rhythm unbroken even by the creak of hinges and the scrape of the latch. Jehan flowed past his doorway, hardly daring to breathe, wavered in a turning, and bolted.

Brother Alf's cell was empty. So too was the Lady Chapel, where he had been all through Compline, prostrate upon the stones. St. Ruan's was large and Alf familiar with every inch of it. He might even be in the garderobe.

Jehan left the chapel, down the passage which led to the gateway. Brother Kyriell, the porter, slept the sleep of the just.

As Jehan paused, a shadow flickered past. It reached the small gate, slid back the bolt without a sound, and eased the heavy panel open. Wind howled through, armed with knives of sleet. It tore back the cowl from a familiar pale head that bowed against it and plunged forward.

By the time Jehan reached the gate, Alf had vanished into the storm. Without thought Jehan went after him.

Wind tore at him. Rain blinded him. Cold sliced through the thick wool of his robe.

But it was not quite pitch-dark. As sometimes happens in winter storms, the clouds seemed to catch the light of the drowned moon and to scatter it, glowing with their own phantom light. Jehan's eyes, already adapted to the dark, could discern the wet glimmer of the road, and far down upon it a blur which might have been Alf's bare white head.

Folly had taken him so far, and folly drove him on. The wind fought him, tried to drive him back to the shelter of the abbey. Alf was gaining—Jehan could hardly see him now, even in the lulls between torrents of rain. Yet he struggled onward.

Something loomed over him so suddenly that he recoiled. It lived and breathed, a monstrous shape that stank like Hell's own midden.

A voice rose over the wind's howl, sounding almost in his ear. "Jehan—help me. Take the bridle."

Alf. And the shape was suddenly a soaked and trembling horse with its rider slumped over its neck. His numbed hands caught at the reins and gentled the long bony head that shied at first, then pushed against him. He hunted in his pocket and found the apple he had filched at supper, and there in the storm, with rain sluicing down the back of his neck, he fed it to the horse.

"Lead her up to the abbey," Alf said, again in his ear. The monk stood within reach, paying no heed to the wind or the rain. Warmth seemed to pour from him in delirious waves.

The wind that had fought Jehan now lent him all its aid, almost carrying him up the road to the gate.

In the lee of the wall, Alf took the reins. "Go in and open up."

Jehan did as he was told. Before he could heave the gate well open, Brother Kyriell peered out of his cell, rumpled and unwontedly surly. "What goes on here?" he demanded sharply.

Jehan shot him a wild glance. The gate swung open; the horse clattered over the threshold. On seeing Alf, Brother Kyriell swallowed what more he would have said and hastened forward.

"Jehan," Alf said, "stable the mare and see that she's fed." Even as he spoke he eased the rider from her back. More than rain glistened in the light of Brother Kyriell's lamp: blood, lurid scarlet and rust-brown, both fresh and dried. "Kyriell—help me carry him."

They bore him on his own cloak through the court and down the passage to the infirmary. Even when they laid him in a cell, he did not move save for the rattle and catch of tormented breathing.

Brother Kyriell left with many glances over his shoulder. Alf paid him no heed. For a moment he paused, buffeted by wave on wave of pain. With an effort that made him gasp, he shielded his mind against it. His shaking hands folded back the cloak, caressing its rich dark fabric, drawing strength from the contact.

The body beneath was bare but for a coarse smock like a serf's, and terrible to see: brutally beaten and flogged; marked with deep oozing burns; crusted with mud and blood and other, less mentionable stains. Three ribs were cracked, the right leg broken in two places, and the left hand crushed; it looked as if it had been trampled. Sore wounds, roughly tied up with strips of the same cloth as the smock, torn and filthy and too long neglected.

Carefully he began to cleanse the battered flesh, catching his breath at the depth and raggedness of some of the wounds. They were filthy and far from fresh; yet they had suffered no infection at all.

Alf came last to the face. A long cut on the forehead had bled and dried and bled again, and made the damage seem worse than it was. One side was badly bruised and swollen, but nothing was broken; the rest had taken no more than a cut and a bruise or two.

Beneath it all, he was young, lean as a panther, with skin as white as Alf's own. A youth, just come to manhood and very good to look on. Almost too much so. Even with all his hurts, that was plain to see.

Alf tore his eyes from that face. But the features haunted him. Eagle-proud, finely drawn beneath beard and bruises. The cast of them was uncanny: eldritch.

Resolutely Alf focused upon the tormented body. He closed his eyes, seeking in his mind for the stillness, the core of cool fire which made him what he was. There was peace there, and healing.

Nothing. Only turmoil and a roiling mass of pain. His own turmoil, the other's agony, together raised a barrier he could not cross. He tried. He beat upon it. He strained until the sweat ran scalding down his sides.

Nothing.

He must have groaned aloud. Jehan was standing beside him, eyes dark with anxiety. "Brother Alf? Are you all right?"

The novice's presence bolstered him. He nodded and breathed deep, shuddering.

Jehan was not convinced. "Brother Alf, you're sick. You ought to be in bed yourself."

"It's not that kind of sickness." He reached for a splint, a roll of bandages. His hands were almost steady. "You'll have to help me with this. Here; so."

There was peace of a sort in that slow labor. Jehan had a feeling for it; his hands were big but gentle, and they needed little direction.

After a long while, it was done. Alf knelt by the bed, staring at his handiwork, calm at last—a blank calm.

Jehan set something on the bed. Wet leather, redolent of horses: a set of saddlebags. "These were on the mare's saddle," he said. "And the mare . . . she's splendid! She's no vagabond's nag. Unless," he added with a doubtful glance at the stranger, "he stole her."

"Does he look like a thief?"

"He looks as if he's been tortured."

"He has." Alf opened the saddlebags. They were full; one held a change of clothing, plain yet rich. The other bore a flask, empty but holding still a ghost of wine, and a crust of bread and an apple or two, and odds and ends of metal and leather.

Amid this was a leather pouch, heavy for its size. Alf poured its contents into his hand: a few coins and a ring, a signet of silver and sapphire. The stone bore a proud device: a seabird in flight surmounted by a crown.

Jehan leaned close to see, and looked up startled. "Rhiyana!"

"Yes. The coins are Rhiyanan, too." Alf turned the ring to catch the light. "See how the stone's carved. *Guidion rex et imperator.* It's the King's own seal."

Jehan stared at the wounded man. "That's not Gwydion. Gwydion must be over eighty. And what's his ring doing here? Rhiyana is across the Narrow Sea, and we're the breadth of Anglia away from even that."

"But we're only two days' ride from Gwynedd, whose King had his fostering at Gwydion's hands. Look here: a penny from Gwynedd."

"Is he a spy?"

"With his King's own seal to betray him?"

"An envoy, then." Jehan regarded him, as fascinated by his face as Alf had been. "He looks like the elf-folk. You know that story, don't you, Brother Alf? My nurse used to tell it to me. She was Rhiyanan, you see, like my mother. She called the King the Elvenking."

"I've heard the tales," Alf said. "Some of them. Pretty fancies for a nursery."

Jehan bridled. "Not all of them, Brother Alf! She said that the King was so fair of face, he looked like an elven lord. He used to ride through the kingdom, and he brought joy wherever he went; though he was no coward, he'd never fight if there was any way at all to win peace. That's why Rhiyana never fights wars."

"But it never refuses to intervene in other kingdoms' troubles."

"Maybe that's what this man has been doing. There's been fighting on the border between Gwynedd and Anglia. He might have been trying to stop it."

"Little luck he's had, from the look of him."

"The King should have come himself. Nurse said no one could keep up a quarrel when he was about. Though maybe he's getting too feeble to travel. He's terribly old."

"There are the tales."

"Oh," Jehan snorted. "That's the pretty part. About how he has a court of elvish folk and never grows old. His court is passing fair by all I've ever heard, but I can't believe he isn't a creaking wreck. I'll wager he dyes his hair and keeps the oglers at a distance."

Alf smiled faintly. "I hope you aren't betting too high." He yawned and stretched. "I'll spend the night here. You, my lad, had better get back to your own bed before Brother Owein misses you."

"Brother Owein sleeps like the dead. If the dead could snore."

"We know they'll rise again. Quick, before Owein proves it."

*   *   *

Jehan had kindled a fire in the room's hearth; Alf lay in front of it, wrapped in his habit. Even yet the stranger had not moved, but he was alive, his pain gnawing at the edge of Alf's shield. But worse still was the knowledge that Alf could have healed what the other suffered, but for his own, inner confusion. How could he master another's bodily pain, if he could not master that of his own mind?

If I must be what I am, he cried into the darkness, *then let me be so. Don't weigh me down with human weakness!*

The walls remained, stronger than ever.

3

As Alf slept, he dreamed. He was no longer in St. Ruan's, no longer a cloistered monk, but a young knight with an eagle's face, riding through hills that rose black under the low sky. His gray mare ran lightly, with sure feet, along a steep stony track. Before them, tall on a crag, loomed a castle. After the long wild journey, broken by nights in hillmen's huts or under the open sky, it should have been a welcome sight. It was ominous.

But he had a man to meet there. He drew himself up and shortened the reins; the mare lifted her head and quickened her step.

The walls took them and wrapped them in darkness.

Within, torchlight was dim. Men met them, men-at-arms, seven of them. As the rider dismounted, they closed around him. The mare's ears flattened; she sidled, threatening.

He gentled her with a touch and said, "I'll stable her myself."

None of the men responded. The rider led the mare forward, and they parted, falling into step behind.

The stable was full, but a man led a horse out of its stall to make room for the mare. The rider unsaddled her and rubbed her down, and fed her with his own hands; when she had eaten her fill, he threw his cloak over her and left her with a few soft words.

Alone now, he walked within a circle of armed men, pacing easily as if it were an honor guard. But the back of his neck prickled. With an effort he kept his hand away from his sword. Fara was safe, warding his possessions, among them the precious signet. He could defend himself. There was no need to fear.

The shadows mocked his courage. Cold hostility walled him in.

It boded ill for his embassy. Yet Lord Rhydderch had summoned him, and although the baron had a name for capricious cruelty, the envoy had not expected to fail. He never had.

They ascended a steep narrow stair and gathered in a guard-room. There the men-at-arms halted. Without a word they turned on their captive.

His sword was out, a baleful glitter, but there was no room to wield it. Nor would he shed blood if he could help it. One contemptuous blow sent the blade flying.

Hands seized him. That touched his pride. His fist struck flesh, bone. Another blow met metal; a sixfold weight bore him to the floor, onto the body of the man he had felled.

Rare anger sparked, but he quenched it. They had not harmed him yet. He lay still, though they spat upon him and called him coward; though they stripped him and touched his body in ways that made his lips tighten and his eyes flicker dangerously; even though they bound him with chains, rusted iron, cruelly tight.

They hauled him to his feet, looped the end of the chain through a ring in the ceiling, stretched his arms taut above his head. His toes barely touched the floor; all his weight hung suspended from his wrists.

When he was well-secured, a stranger entered, a man in mail. He was not a tall man, but thickset, with the dark weathered features of a hillman, and eyes so pale they seemed to have no color at all. When he pushed back his mail-coif, his hair was as black as the bristle of his brows and shot with gray.

He stood in front of the prisoner, hands on hips. "So," he said. "The rabbit came to the trap."

The other kept his head up, his voice quiet. "Lord Rhydderch, I presume? Alun of Caer Gwent, at your service."

"Pretty speech, in faith, and a fine mincing way he has about it." Rhydderch prodded him as if he had been a bullock at market. "And a long stretch of limb to add to it. Your King must be fond of outsize beauties."

"The King of Rhiyana," Alun said carefully, "has sent me as his personal envoy. Any harm done to me is as harm to the royal person. Will you not let me go?"

Rhydderch laughed, a harsh bark with no mirth in it. "The

Dotard of Caer Gwent? What can he do if I mess up his fancy-boy a little?"

"I bear the royal favor. Does that mean nothing to you?"

"Your King's no king of mine, boy."

"I came in good faith, seeking peace between Gwynedd and Anglia. Would you threaten that peace?"

"My King," said Rhydderch, "will pay well for word of Rhiyana's plotting with Gwynedd. And Anglia between, in the pincers."

"That has never been our intent."

Rhydderch looked him over slowly. "What will your old pander pay to have you back?"

"Peace," replied Alun, "and forgiveness of this insult."

Rhydderch sneered. "Richard pays in gold. How much will Gwydion give for his minion? Or maybe Kilhwch would be more forthcoming. Gwynedd is a little kingdom and Kilhwch is a little king, a morsel for our Lion's dinner."

"Let me go, and I will ask."

"Oh, no," said Rhydderch. "I'm not a fool. I'll set a price, and I'll demand it. And amuse myself with you while I wait for it."

There was no dealing with that mind. It was like a wild boar's, black, feral, and entirely intent upon its own course.

Alun pitched his voice low, level, and very, very calm. "Rhydderch, I know what you plan. You will break me beyond all mending and cast me at my King's feet, a gauntlet for your war. And while you challenge Rhiyana, you prick Gwynedd to fury with your incessant driving of the hill-folk to raid beyond the border. Soon Anglia's great Lion must come, lured into the war you have made; you will set the kings upon one another and let them destroy themselves, while you take the spoils."

While he spoke, he watched the man's face. First Rhydderch reddened, then he paled, and his eyes went deadly cold. Alun smiled. "So you plan, Rhydderch. You think, with your men-at-arms and your hill-folk and all your secret allies, that you are strong enough to take a throne and wise enough to keep it. Have you failed to consider the forces with which you play? Kilhwch is young, granted, and more than a bit of a hellion, but he is the son of Bran Dhu, and blood kin to Gwydion of Rhiyana. He may prove a stronger man than you reckon on. And Gwydion will support him."

"Gwydion!" Rhydderch spat. "The coward King, the royal fool. He wobbles on his throne, powdered and painted like an old whore, and brags of his miraculous youth. His so-called knights win their spurs on the dancing floor and their titles in bed. And not with women, either."

Alun's smile did not waver. "If that is so, then why do you waste time in provoking him to war?"

A vein was pulsing in Rhydderch's temple, but he grinned ferally. "Why not? It's the safest of all my bets."

"Is it? Then Richard must be the most perilous of all, for he is a lion in battle—quite unlike my poor Gwydion. How will he look on this plot of yours, Rhydderch? Rebellion in the north and a brother who would poison him at a word and the dregs of his Crusade, all these he has to face. And now you bring him this folly."

"Richard can never resist a good fight. He won't touch me. More likely he'll reward me."

"Ah. A child, a warmonger, and a dotard. Three witless kings, and three kingdoms ripe for the plucking by a man with strength and skill." Alun shook his head. "Rhydderch, has it ever occurred to you that you are a fool?"

A mailed fist lashed out. Alun's head rocked with the force of the blow. "You vain young cockerel," Rhydderch snarled. "Strung up in my own castle, and you crow like a dunghill king. I'll teach you to sing a new song."

The fist struck again in the same place. Alun choked back a cry. Rhydderch laughed and held out his hand. One of his men placed a dark shape in it.

In spite of himself, Alun shrank. Rhydderch shook out a whip of thongs knotted with pellets of lead. Alun made one last, desperate effort to penetrate that opaque brain.

No use. It was mad. The worst kind of madness, which passes for sanity, because it knows itself and glories in its own twisted power. Alun's gentle strength was futile against it.

He felt as if he were tangled in the coils of a snake, its venom coursing through his veins, waking the passion which was as deep as his serenity. As many-headed pain lashed his body, his wrath stirred and kindled. He forgot even torment in his desperate struggle for control. He forgot the world itself. All his consciousness focused upon the single battle, the great tide of his calmness against the fire of rage.

The world within became the world without. All his body was a fiery agony, and his mind was a flame. Rhydderch stood before him, face glistening with sweat, whip slack in his hand. He sneered at his

prisoner. "Beautiful as a girl, and weak as one besides. You're Rhiyanan to the core."

Alun drew a deep shuddering breath. The rage stood at bay, but
it touched his face, his eyes. "If you release me now, I shall forgive this
infamy, although I shall never forget it."

"Let you go?" Rhydderch laughed. "I've hardly begun."

"Do you count it honorable to flog a man in chains, captured by
treachery?"

"A man, no. You, I hardly count as a villein's brat; and you'll be
less when I'm done with you."

"Whatever you do to me, I remain a Knight of the Crown of
Rhiyana. Gwydion is far from the weakling you deem him; and he
shall not forget what you have done to him."

"From fainting lass to royal lord in two breaths. You awe me."
Rhydderch tossed the whip aside. "Some of my lads here like to play
a little before they get down to business. Maybe I should let them,
while you're still able to enjoy it."

The rage lunged for the opening. Alun's eyes blazed green; he
bared his teeth. But his voice was velvet-soft. "Let them try, Rhydderch. Let them boast of it afterward. They shall need the consolation, for they shall never touch another: man, woman, or boy." His
eyes flashed round the half-circle of men. "Who ventures it? You,
Huw? Owein? Dafydd, great bull and vaunter?"

Each one started at his name and crossed himself.

Rhydderch glared under his black brows. "You there, get him
down and hold him. He can't do a thing to you."

"Can I not?" asked Alun. "Have you not heard of what befalls
mortals who make shift to force elf-blood?"

The baron snarled. "Get him down, I say! He's trying to scare us
off."

One man made bold to speak. "But—but—my lord, his eyes!"

"A trick of the light. Get him down!"

Alun lowered his arms. "No need. See. I am down."

Eyes rolled; voices muttered.

"Damn you sons of curs! You forgot to fasten the chain!" Rhydderch snatched at it. Alun dropped to his knees. He was still feral-
eyed. A blow, aimed at his head, missed.

He tossed back his hair and said, "Nay, I was firm-bound. Think
you that the Elvenking would risk a mortal on such a venture as this?"

"You're no less mortal than I am." Rhydderch hurled Alun

full-length upon the floor. Swift as a striking snake, his boot came
down.

Someone screamed.

Pain had roused wrath; pain slew it. In red-rimmed clarity, Alun
saw all his pride and folly. He had come to lull Rhydderch into
making peace, and fallen instead into his enemy's own madness. And
now he paid.

That clarity was his undoing; for he did not move then to stop
what he had begun. Even as he paused, they were upon him, fear
turned to bitter scorn.

After an eternity came blessed nothingness.

He woke in the midst of a choking stench. Oddly, he found that
harder to bear than the agony of his body. Pain had some pretense
to nobility, even such pain as this, but that monumental stink was
beyond all endurance.

Gasping, gagging, he lifted his head. He had lain face down in
it. Walls of stone hemmed him in—a midden with but one barred
exit. The iron bars were forged in the shape of a cross. Rhydderch was
taking no chances.

A convulsion seized him, bringing new agony: the spasming of an
empty stomach, the knife-sharp pain of cracked ribs. For a long while
he had to lie as he was. Then, with infinite caution, he drew one knee
under him. The right leg would not bear his weight; he swayed, threw
out a hand, cried out in agony as the outraged flesh struck the wall.
His other, the right hand, caught wildly at stone and held. Through
a scarlet haze he saw what first he had extended. It no longer looked
even remotely like a hand.

His sword hand.

He closed his eyes and sought inward for strength. It came slowly,
driving back the pain until he could almost bear it. But the cost to his
broken body was high. Swiftly, while he could still see, he swept his
eyes about.

One corner was almost clean. Inch by inch, hating the sounds of
pain his movements wrenched from him, he made his way to it. Two
steps upright, the rest crawling upon his face.

Gradually his senses cleared. He hurt—oh, he hurt. And one
pain, less than the rest, made him burn with shame. After all his
threats—and empty, they had not been—still—still—

He found that he was weeping: he who had not wept even as a
child. Helpless, child's tears, born of pain and shame and disgust at

his own massive folly. All this horror was no one's fault but his own.

Even Kilhwch had warned him. Wild young Kilhwch, with his father's face but his mother's gray eyes, and a little of the family wisdom. "The border lords on both sides make a fine nest of adders, but Rhydderch is the worst of them. He'd flay his own mother if it would buy him an extra acre. Work your magic with the others as much as you like; I could use a little quiet there. But stay away from Rhydderch."

Kilhwch had not known of the baron's invitation to a parley. If he had, he would have flown into one of his rages. Yet that would not have stopped Alun.

His shield was failing. One last effort; then he could rest. He arranged his body as best he might, broken as it was, and extended his mind.

The normal rhythm of a border castle flowed through him, overlaid with the blackness that was Rhydderch and with a tension born of men gathering for war. Rhydderch himself was gone; a steward's mind murmured of a rendezvous with a hill-chieftain.

Alun could do nothing until dark, and it was barely past noon. Thirst burned him; hunger was a dull ache. Yet nowhere in that heap of offal could he find food or drink.

He would not weaken again into tears. His mind withdrew fully into itself, a deep trance yet with a hint of awareness which marked the passing of time.

Darkness roused him, and brought with it full awareness of agony. For a long blood-red while he could not move at all. By degrees he dragged himself up. As he had reached the corner, so he reached the gate. It opened before him.

How he came to the stable, unseen and unnoticed, he never knew. There was mist the color of torment, and grinding pain, and the tension of power stretched to the fullest; and at last, warm sweet breath upon his cheek and sleek horseflesh under his hand. With all the strength that remained to him, he saddled and bridled his mare, wrapping himself in the cloak which had covered her. She knelt for him; he half-climbed, half-fell into the saddle. She paced forward.

The courtyard was dark in starlight. The gate yawned open; the sentry stood like a shape of stone. Fara froze. He stirred upon her back. He could not speak through swollen lips, but his words rang in his brain: *Now, while I can hold the man and the pain—run, my beauty. Run!*

She sprang into a gallop, wind-smooth, wind-swift. Her rider clung to her, not caring where she went. She turned her head to the south and lengthened her stride.

Only when the castle was long gone, hidden in a fold of the hills, did she slow to a running walk. She kept that pace hour after hour, until Alun was like to fall from her back. At last she found a stream and knelt, so that he had but little distance to fall; he drank in long desperate gulps, dragged himself a foot or two from the water, and let darkness roll over him.

Voices sounded, low and lilting, speaking a tongue as old as those dark hills. While they spoke he understood, but when they were done, he could not remember what they had said.

Hands touched him, waking pain. Through it he saw a black boar, ravening. He cried out against it. The hands started away and returned. There were tightnesses: bandages, roughly bound; visions of the herb-healer, who must see this tortured creature; Rhuawn's tunic to cover his nakedness. And again the black boar looming huge, every bristle distinct, an ember-light in its eyes and the scarlet of blood upon its tusks. He called the lightnings down upon it.

The voices cried out. One word held in his memory: *Dewin*, that was *wizard*. And then all the voices were gone. Only Fara remained, and the pain, and what healing and clothing the hill-folk had given.

Healing. He must have healing. Again he mounted, again he rode through the crowding shadows. At the far extremity of his inner sight, there was a light. He pursued it, and Fara bore him through the wild hills, over a broad and turbulent water, and on into darkness.

The fire burned low. Soon the bell would ring for Matins. Alf rose, stiff with the memory of torment, and looked down upon the wounded man. No human being could have endured what he had endured, not only torture but five full days after, without healing, without food, riding by day and by night.

Alf touched the white fine face. No, it was not human. Power throbbed behind it, low now and slow, but palpably present. It had brought the stranger here to ancient Ynys Witrin, and to the one being like him in all of Gwynedd or Anglia, the one alone who might have healed him.

Who could not, save as humans do, with splint and bandage and simple waiting. He had set each shattered bone with all the skill he had and tended the outraged flesh as best he knew how. The life that had ebbed low was rising slowly with tenacity that must be of elf-kind, that had kept death at bay throughout that grim ride.

He slept now, a sleep that healed. Alf envied him that despite its cost. His dreams were none of pain; only of peace, and of piercing sweetness.

4

Consciousness was like dawn, slow in growing, swift in its completion. Alun lay for a time, arranging his memories around his hurts. In all of it, he could not see himself upon a bed, his body tightly bandaged, warm and almost comfortable. Nor could he place that stillness, that scent of stone and coolness and something faint, sweet—apples, incense.

He opened his eyes. Stone, yes, all about: a small room, very plain yet with a hearth and a fire, burning applewood, and a single hanging which seemed woven of sunlight on leaves.

Near the fire was a chair, and in it a figure. Brown cowl, tonsure haloed by pale hair—a monk, intent upon a book. His face in profile was very young and very fair.

The monk looked up. Their gazes met, sea-gray and silver-gilt; warp and woof, and the shuttle flashing between. Alf's image; the flicker of amusement was the other's, whose knightly hands had never plied a loom.

As swiftly as fencers in a match, they disengaged. Alf was on his feet, holding white-knuckled to the back of his chair. With an effort he unclenched his fingers and advanced to the bed.

Alun's eyes followed him. His face was quiet, betraying none of his pain. "How long since I came here?" he asked.

"Three days," Alf answered, "and five before that of riding."

"Eight days." Alun closed his eyes. "I was an utter and unpardonable fool."

Alf poured well-watered mead from the beaker by the bed and held the cup to Alun's lips. The draught brought a ghost of color to the wan cheeks, but did not distract the mind behind them. "Is there news? Have you heard—"

Alf crumbled a bit of bread and fed it to him. "No news. Though there's a tale in the villages of a mighty wizard who rode over the hills in a trail of shooting stars and passed away into the West. Opinions are divided as to the meaning of the portent, whether it presages war or peace, feast or famine. Or maybe it was only one of the Fair Folk in a fire of haste."

A glint of mirth touched the gray eyes. "Maybe it was. You've heard no word of war?"

"Not hereabouts. I think you've put the fear of Annwn into too many people."

"That will never last," Alun murmured. "The black boar will rise, and soon. And I . . ." His good hand moved down his body. "I pay for my folly. How soon before I ride?"

"Better to ask, 'How soon before I walk?' "

He shook his head slightly. "I'll ride before then. How soon?"

Alf touched his splinted leg, his bound hand. Shattered bone had begun to knit, torn muscle to mend itself, with inhuman speed, but slowly still. "A month," he said. "No sooner."

"Brother," Alun said softly, "I am not human."

"If you were, I'd tell you to get used to your bed, for you'd never leave it."

Alun's lips thinned. "I'm not so badly hurt. Once my leg knits, I can ride."

"You rode with it broken for five days. It will take six times that, and a minor miracle, to undo the damage. Unless you'd prefer to live a cripple."

"I could live lame if there was peace in Gwynedd and Anglia and Rhiyana, and three kings safe on their thrones, and Rhydderch rendered powerless."

"Lame and twisted and racked with pain, and bereft of your sword-hand. A cause for war even if you put down Rhydderch, if knights in Rhiyana are as mindful of their honor as those in Anglia."

Alun drew a breath, ragged with pain. "Knights in Rhiyana pay heed to their King. Who will let no war begin over one man's folly. I will need a horse-litter, Brother, and perhaps an escort, for as soon as may be. Will you pass my request to your Abbot?"

"I can give you his answer now," Alf replied. "No. The Church frowns on suicide."

"I won't die. Tell your Abbot, Brother. The storm is about to break. I must go before it destroys us all."

* * *

Dom Morwin was in the orchard under a gray sky, among trees as old as the abbey itself. As Alf came to walk with him, he stooped stiffly, found two sound windfalls, and tossed one to his friend.

Alf caught it and polished it on his sleeve. As he bit into it, Morwin asked, "How is your nurseling?"

"Lively," Alf answered. "He came to this morning, looked about, and ordered a horse-litter."

The Abbot lifted an eyebrow. "I would have thought that he was on his deathbed. He certainly looked it yesterevening when I glanced in."

"He won't die. He won't be riding about for a while yet, either. Whatever he may think."

"He sounds imperious for a foundling."

"That, he's not. Look." Alf reached into the depths of his habit and drew out the signet in its pouch.

Morwin examined the ring for a long moment. "It's his?"

"He carried it. He wanted you to see it."

The other turned it in his hands. "So—he's one of Gwydion's elven-folk. I'd wondered if the tales were true."

"Truer than you thought before, at least."

Morwin's glance was sharp. "Doubts, Alf?"

"No." Alf sat on a fallen trunk. "We're alike. When he woke, we met, eye, mind. It was painful to draw back and to talk as humans talk. He was . . . very calm about it."

"How did he get here, as he was, with his King's signet in his pocket?"

"He rode. He was peacemaking for Gwydion, but he ran afoul of a lord he couldn't bewitch. He escaped toward the only help his mind could see. He wasn't looking for human help by then. I was the closest one of his kind. And St. Ruan's is . . . St. Ruan's."

"He's failed in his errand, then. Unless war will wait for the winter to end and for him to heal."

"He says it won't. I know it won't. That's why he ordered the horse-litter. I refused, in your name. He wanted something more direct."

"Imperious." The Abbot contemplated his half-eaten apple. "The border of Gwynedd is dry tinder waiting for a spark. There are barons on both sides who'd be delighted to strike one. And Richard would egg them on."

"Exactly. Gwydion, through Alun, was trying to prevent that."

"*Was?* Your Alun's lost, then?"

"For Gwydion's purposes. Though he'd have me think otherwise."

"Exactly how bad is it?"

"Bad," Alf answered. "Not deadly, but bad. If he's careful, he'll ride again, even walk. I don't know if he'll ever wield a sword. And that is if he does exactly as I tell him. If he gets up and tries to run his King's errands, he'll end a cripple. I told him so. He told me to get a litter."

"Does he think he can do any better now than he did before?"

"I don't know what he thinks!" Alf took a deep breath. More quietly he said, "Maybe you can talk to him. I'm only a monk. You're the Lord Abbot."

Morwin's eyes narrowed. "Alf. How urgent is this? Is it just a loyal man and a foster father looking out for his ward, and a general desire for peace? Or does it go deeper? What will happen if Alun does nothing?"

When they were boys together, they had played a game. Morwin would name a name, and Alf would look inside, and that name would appear as a thread weaving through the world-web; and he would tell his friend where it went. It had been a game then, with a touch of the forbidden in it, for it was witchery. As they grew older they had stopped it.

The tapestry was there. He could see it, feel it: the shape, the pattern. He lived in it and through it, a part of it and yet also an observer. Like a god, he had thought once; strangling the thought, for it was blasphemy.

Gwydion, he thought. *Alun. Gwynedd.* In his mind he stood before the vast loom with its edges lost in infinity, and his finger followed a skein of threads, deep blue and blood-red and fire-gold. Blood and fire, a wave of peace, a red tide of war. A pattern, shifting, elusive, yet clear enough. If this happened, and this did not; *if . . .*

Gray sky lowered over him; Morwin's face hovered close. Old— it was so old. He covered his eyes.

When he could bear to see again, Morwin was waiting, frowning. "What was it? What did you see?"

"War," Alf muttered. "Peace. Gwydion—Alun— He can't leave this place. He'll fail again, and this time he'll die. And he knows it. I told him what the Church thinks of suicide."

"What will happen?"

"War," Alf said again. "As he saw it. Richard will ride to Gwynedd and Kilhwch will come to meet him; Rhiyana will join the war for Kilhwch's sake. Richard wounded, Kilhwch dead, Gwydion broken beyond all mending; and lords of three kingdoms tearing at each other like jackals when the lions have gone."

"There's no hope?"

Alf shivered. It was cold, and the effort of seeing left him weak. "There may be. I see the darkest colors because they're strongest. Maybe there can be peace. Another Alun . . . Rhydderch's death . . . a Crusade to divert Richard: who knows what can happen?"

"It will have to happen soon."

"Before spring."

Morwin began to walk aimlessly, head bent, hands clasped behind him. Alf followed. He did not slip into the other's mind. That pact they had made, long ago.

They came to the orchard's wall and walked along it, circling the enclosure.

"It's not for us to meddle in the affairs of kings," Morwin said at last. "Our part is to pray, and to let the world go as it will." His eyes upon Alf were bright and wicked. "But the world has gone its way into our abbey. I'm minded to heed it. Prayer won't avert a war."

"Won't it?"

"The Lord often appreciates a helping hand," the Abbot said. "Our King is seldom without his loyal Bishop Aylmer, even on the battlefield. And the Bishop might be kindly disposed toward a messenger of mine bringing word of the troubles on the border."

"And?"

"Peace. Maybe. If an alliance could be made firm between Gwynedd and Anglia . . ."

"My lord Abbot! It's corrupted you to have a worldling in your infirmary."

"I was always corrupt. Tell Sir Alun that I'll speak to him tonight before Compline."

Alun would have none of it. "I will not place one of your Brothers in danger," he said. "For there is danger for a monk of Anglia on Rhiyana's errand. Please, my lord, a litter is all I ask."

The Abbot regarded him as he lay propped up with pillows, haggard and hollow-eyed and lordly-proud. "We will not quarrel, sir. You may not leave until you are judged well enough to leave. Which will not be soon enough to complete your embassy. My messenger will go in your stead."

For a long moment Alun was silent. At length he asked, "Whom will you send?"

Morwin glanced sidewise at the monk who knelt, tending the fire. "Brother Alfred," he answered.

The flames roared. Alf drew back from the blistering heat and turned.

"Yes," Morwin said as if he had not been there. "The Bishop asked for him. I'll send him, and give him your errand besides."

"Morwin," Alf whispered. "Domne."

Neither heeded him. Alun nodded slowly. "If it is he, then I cannot object. He shall have my mare. She frets in her stall; and no other horse is as swift or as tireless as she."

"That's a princely gift."

"He has need of all speed. How soon may he go?"

"He'll need a night to rest and prepare. Tomorrow."

Alf stood, trembling uncontrollably. They did not look at him. Alun's eyes were closed; Morwin stared at his sandaled feet. "Domne," he said. "Domne, you can't send me. You know what I am."

The Abbot raised his eyes. They were very bright and very sad. "Yes, I know what you are. That's why I'm sending you."

"Morwin—"

"You swore three vows, Brother. And one of them was obedience."

Alf bowed his head. "I will go because you command me to go, but not because I wish to. The world will not be kind to such a creature as I am."

"Maybe you need a little unkindness." Morwin turned his back on Alf, nodded to Alun, and left.

The Rhiyanan gazed quietly at the ceiling. "It hurts him to do this, but he thinks it is best."

"I know," Alf said. He had begun to tremble again. "I'm a coward. I haven't left St. Ruan's since—since—God help me! I can't remember. These walls have grown up round my bones."

"Time then to hew your way out of them."

"It frightens me. Three kingdoms in the balance; and only my hand to steady them."

Alun turned his head toward Alf. "If you will let me go, you can stay here."

The other laughed without mirth. "Oh, no, my lord! I'll do as my

Abbot bids me. You will do as I bid you, which is to stay here and heal, and pray for me."

"You ask a great deal, Brother."

"So does the Abbot," Alf said. "Good night, my lord of Rhiyana."

5

" 'She'—that is, the Soul of the World—'woven throughout heaven from its center to its outermost limits, and enfolding it without in a circle, and herself revolving within herself, began a divine beginning of ceaseless and rational life for all time.' So, Plato. Now the Christian doctors say—"

Jehan was not listening. He was not even trying to listen, who ordinarily was the best of students. Alf broke off and closed the book softly, and folded his hands upon it. "What's the trouble, Jehan?"

The novice looked up from the precious vellum, on which he had been scribbling without heed or pattern. His eyes were wide and a little wild. "You look awful, Brother Alf. Brother Rowan says you were praying in the chapel all night."

"I do that now and again," Alf said.

"But—" Jehan said. "But they say you're leaving!"

Alf sighed. He was tired, and his body ached from a night upon cold stones. Jehan's pain only added to the burden of his troubles. He answered shortly, flatly. "Yes. I'm leaving."

"Why? What's happened?"

"I've been here too long. Dom Morwin is sending me to Bishop Aylmer."

"Just like that?"

"Just like that," Alf replied. "Don't worry. You won't go back to Brother Osric. You'll take care of Alun for me; and he has a rare store of learning. He'll keep on with your Greek, and if you behave, he'll let you try a little Arabic."

The hurt in Jehan's eyes had turned to fire. "So I'm to turn paynim while you run at the Bishop's heel. It's not so easy to get rid of me, Brother Alf. Take me with you."

"You know that's not my decision to make."

"Take me with you."

"No." It was curt, final. "With reference to Plato's doctrine, Chalcidius observes—"

"Brother Alf!"

"Chalcidius observes—"

Jehan bit back what more he would have said. There was no opposing that quiet persistence. Yet he was ready to cry, and would not, for pride.

It was the first lesson with Alf which had ever gone sour, and it was the last Jehan would ever have. When he was let go, having disgraced all his vaunted scholarship, he wanted to hide like a whipped pup. For pride and for anger, he went where his duties bade him go.

Alun was awake and alone. Jehan stood over him. "Brother Alf is going away," he said. "He's been sent to Bishop Aylmer. Bishop Aylmer is with the King. And it's the King you want to get to. What did you make him go for?"

Jehan's rude words did not seem to trouble Alun. "I didn't make him go. It was your Abbot's choice. A wise one in his reckoning, and well for your Brother. He was stifling here."

"He doesn't want to go. He hates the thought of it."

"Of course he does. He's afraid. But he has to go, Jehan. For his vows' sake and for his own."

Jehan glared at him. "Alone, sir? Do his vows say he has to travel the length and breadth of Anglia by himself, a monk who looks like a boy, who doesn't even know how to hold a knife?"

"His vows, no. But he will have my mare and such aid as I can give him, and he has more defenses than you know of."

"Not enough." Jehan tossed his head, lion-fierce. "I came here for him. If he goes, I'll go."

"And what of your Abbot? What of your God?"

"My God knows that I can serve Him as well with the Bishop as at St. Ruan's. The Abbot can think what he likes."

"Proud words for one who would be a monk."

"I was a monk because Alf was!"

Jehan fell silent, startled by his own outburst. Slowly he sank down, drawing into a knot on the floor. "I was a monk because Alf was," he repeated. "I never meant to be one. I wanted to be a warrior-priest like Bishop Aylmer, but I wanted to be a scholar too. People laughed at me. 'A scholar!' my father yelled at me. 'God's

teeth! you're not built for it.' Then I rode hell-for-leather down a road
near St. Ruan's, with a hawk on my wrist and a wild colt under me
and my men-at-arms long lost, and I nigh rode down a monk who was
walking down the middle.

"I stopped to apologize, and we talked, and somehow we got
onto Aristotle. I'd read what I could find, without really knowing what
I was reading and with no one to tell me. And this person *knew*. More:
he could read Greek. There in the middle of the road, we disputed
like philosophers, though he really was one and I was a young cock-a-
whoop who'd got into his tutor's books.

"Then and there, I decided I had to be what he was, or as close
as I could come, since he was brilliant and I was only too clever for
my own good. I fought and I pleaded and I threatened, and my father
finally let me come here. And now Brother Alf is going away and
taking the heart out of St. Ruan's."

Alun shifted painfully, waving away Jehan's swift offer of help. "I
think, were I your Abbot, I would question your vocation."

"It's there," Jehan said with certainty. "God is there, and my
books. But not—not St. Ruan's. Not without Brother Alf."

"Jehan." Alun spoke slowly, gently. "You're startled and hurt.
Think beyond yourself now. Alfred is much older than he looks, and
much less placid. He has troubles which life here cannot heal. He has
to leave."

"I know that. I'm not trying to stop him. I want to go with him."

"What can you do for him?"

"Love him," Jehan answered simply.

Alun's eyes closed. He looked exhausted and drawn with pain.
His voice when he spoke was a sigh. "You can serve him best now by
accepting what your Abbot says must be. Can you do that?"

"And leave him to go alone?"

"If such is the Abbot's will. Can you do it, Jehan?"

Very slowly the other responded, "I . . . for him. If it's right. And
only if."

"Go then. Be strong for him. He needs that more than anything
else you can do for him."

Alf regarded Alun with sternness overlying concern. "You've been
overexerting yourself."

The Rhiyanan's eyes glinted. "In bed, Brother? Oh, come!"

"Staying awake," Alf said. "Moving about. Trying your muscles." He touched the bandaged mass of Alun's sword hand. "The

setting of this is very delicate. If you jar it, you'll cripple it. Perhaps permanently."

"It is not so already?" There was a touch of bitterness in the quiet voice.

"Maybe not." Alf continued his examination, which was less of hand and eye than of the mind behind them. "Your ribs are healing well. Your leg, too, *Deo gratias*. If you behave yourself and trust to the care in which I leave you, you'll prosper."

He folded back the coverlet and began to bathe as much of the battered body as was bare of bandages. Alun's eyes followed his hands. When Alf would have turned him onto his face, there was no weight in him; he floated face down a palm's width above the bed.

The monk faltered only for a moment. "Thank you," he said. After a moment he added, "If you take care not to let yourself be caught at it, you might do this as much as you can. It will spare your flesh."

Alun was on his back again; Alf could have passed his palm between body and sheet. "I've been this way a little. There's more comfort in it."

"My lord." Alf's compassion was as palpable as a touch. "I'll do all your errand for you as best I can. That I swear to you."

"I'll miss you, Brother." The way he said it, it was more than a title. "And I've had thoughts. It will look odd for a monk to ride abroad on what is patently a blooded horse. With her I give you all that I have. My clothing is plain enough for a cleric, but secular enough to avert suspicion. Come; fetch it, and try it for size."

"My lord," Alf said carefully, "you're most kind. But I have no dispensation. I can't—"

"You can if I say you can." Morwin shut the door behind him. "Do what he tells you, Alf."

Slowly, under their eyes, he brought out Alun's belongings. The ring in its pouch he laid in the lord's lap. The rest he kept. It had been cleaned where it needed to be and treated with care. Indeed the garments were plain, deep blue, snow white. When the others turned away to spare his modesty, he hesitated.

With a sudden movement he shed his coarse brown habit. There was nothing beneath but his body. He shivered as he covered it with Alun's fine linen. In all his life, he had never known such softness so close to his skin. It felt like a sin.

The outer clothes were easier to bear, though he fumbled with them, uncertain of their fastenings. Alun helped him with words and

Morwin with hands, until he stood up in the riding clothes of a knight.

"It fits well," Alun said. "And looks most well, my brother."

He could see himself in the other's mind, a tall youth, sword-slender, with a light proud carriage that belied the brown habit crumpled at his feet.

As soon as he saw, he tried to kill the pride that rose in him. He looked like a prince. An elven-prince, swift and strong, and beautiful. Yes; he was that. The rest might be a sham, a creation of cloth and stance, but beauty he had.

It would be a hindrance, and perhaps a danger. His pride died with the thought. "I don't think this is wise. I look too . . . rich. Better that I seem to be what I am, a monk without money or weapons."

Both the Abbot and the knight shook their heads. "No," Morwin said. "Not with the horse you'll be riding. This way, you fit her."

"I don't fit myself!"

Morwin's face twisted. A moment only; then he controlled it. "You'll learn. It isn't the clothes that make the monk, Alf."

"Isn't it?" Alf picked up his habit and held it to him. "Each move I make is another cord severed."

"If all you've ever been is a robe and a tonsure," snapped Morwin, "God help us both."

The other stiffened. "Maybe that is all I've been."

"Don't start that," Morwin said with weary annoyance. "You're not the first man of God who's ever set aside his habit for a while, and you won't be the last. Take what's left of the day to get used to your clothes, and spend tonight in bed. Asleep. That's an order, Brother Alfred."

"Yes, Domne."

"And don't look so sulky. One obeys with a glad heart, the Rule says. Or at least, one tries to. Start trying. That's an order, too."

"Yes, Domne." Alf was not quite able to keep his lips from twitching. "Immediately, Domne. Gladly, Domne."

"Don't add lying to the rest of your sins." But Morwin's glare lacked force. "See me tonight before you go to bed. There are messages I want to give to Aylmer."

In spite of his promise to Alun, Jehan dragged himself through that long day. No one seemed to know that Brother Alf was leaving, nor to care. Monks came and went often enough in so large an abbey.

But never so far alone, through unknown country, and against their will besides.

At last he could bear it no longer. He gathered his courage and sought the lion in his den.

By good fortune, Abbot Morwin was alone, bent over the rolls of the abbey. He straightened as Jehan entered. "This is stiff work for old bones," he said.

Jehan drew a deep breath. The Abbot did not seem annoyed to see him. Nor did he look surprised. "Domne," he said, "you're sending Brother Alf away."

Morwin nodded neutrally. That, in the volatile Abbot, was ominous.

"Please, Domne. I know he has to go. But must he go alone?"

"What makes you think that?"

Jehan found that he could not breathe properly. "Then—then—he'll have company?"

"I've been considering it." Morwin indicated a chair. "Here, boy. Stop shaking and sit down." He leaned back himself, toying with the simple silver cross he always wore. Jehan stared, half-mesmerized by the glitter of it. "It's as well you came when you did; I was about to send for you. I've been thinking about that last letter from your father."

The novice almost groaned aloud. The last thing he wanted to hear now was his father's opinion of his life in St. Ruan's.

But Morwin had no mercy. "Remember what Earl Rogier said. That your life was your own, and you could ruin it by taking vows here if that was what you wanted. But he asked you first to try something else. He suggested the Templars. That's extreme; still, the more I think, the better his advice seems to be. I've decided to take it in my own way. I'm sending you to Bishop Aylmer."

Bishop Aylmer . . . Bishop Aylmer. "I'm going with Brother Alf!" It was a strangled shout.

"Well now," Morwin said, "that would make sense, wouldn't it?"

Jehan hardly heard him. "I'm going with Brother Alf. He told me I couldn't. He's going to be surprised."

"I doubt it. I told him a little while ago. He was angry."

"Angry, Domne?"

Morwin smiled. "He said I was hanging for the sheep instead of for the lamb—and brought you these to travel in."

On the table among the heavy codices was a bundle. Jehan's fingers remembered the weight and the feel of it—leather, cloth, the long hardness of a sword. "My old clothes . . . but I've grown!"

"Try them. And afterward, find Alf. He'll tell you what you need
to do."

Miraculously everything fit, though the garments had been made for
him just before he met Brother Alf upon the road, over a year ago,
and he had grown half a head since. But Alf's skill with the needle was
legendary. The boots alone seemed new, of good leather, with room
enough to grow in.

It felt strange to be dressed like a nobleman again. He wished
there were a mirror in the dormitory, and said a prayer to banish
vanity. "Not," he added, "that my face is anything to brag of."

"Amen."

He whipped about, hand to swordhilt. A stranger stood there, a
tall young fellow who carried himself like a prince. He smiled wryly
as Jehan stared, and said, "Good day, my lord."

"Brother Alf!" Jehan took him in and laughed for wonder. "You
look splendid."

"*Vanitas vanitatum,*" Alf intoned dolefully. " 'Vanity of vanities, all
is vanity!' Though you look as if you can use that sword."

Jehan let his hand fall from the hilt. "You know I've had practice
with Brother Ulf. 'Ulf for the body and Alf for the brain; that's how
a monk is made.' "

"So you're the one who committed that bit of doggerel. I should
have known."

Although Alf's voice was light, Jehan frowned. "What's the matter, Brother Alf?"

"Why, nothing. I'm perfectly content. After all, misery loves
company."

"It won't be misery. It will be splendid. You'll see. We'll take
Bishop Aylmer by storm and astound the King; and then we'll conquer the world."

The hour after Compline found Alf in none of his usual places: not
in his cell where he should have been sleeping; not in the chapel
where he might have kept vigil even against Morwin's command; and
certainly not in the study where the Abbot had gone to wait for him.
He had sung the last Office—no one could miss that voice, man-deep
yet heartrendingly clear, rising above the mere human beauty of the
choir—and he had sung with gentle rebellion in his brown habit. But
then he had gone, and no one knew where.

It was intuition more than either logic or a careful search that brought Morwin to a small courtyard near the chapel. There in a patch of sere and frostbitten grass grew a thorn tree. Ancient, twisted, stripped of its leaves, it raised its branches to the moon. Under it crouched a still and shadowed figure.

With much creaking of bones, Morwin sat beside him. The ground was cold; frost crackled as the Abbot settled upon it.

"I've never liked this place," Alf said, "or this tree. Though they say it grew from the staff of a saint, of the Arimathean himself . . . when I was very small I used to be afraid of it. It always seemed to be reaching for me. As if St. Ruan's were not for the likes of me; as if I were alien and the Thorn knew it, and it would drag me away, back to my own people."

"The people under the Tor?" Morwin asked.

The cowled head shifted. From here one could see the Tor clearly, a steep rounded hill wreathed in frost, rising behind the abbey like a bulwark of stone. "The Tor," murmured Alf. "That never frightened me. There was power in it, and wonder, and mystery. But no danger. No beckoning; no rejection. It simply was. Do you remember when we climbed it, for bravado, to see if the tales were true?"

"Madness or great blessings to him who mounts the Tor of Ynys Witrin on the eve of Midsummer. I remember. I don't think either of us came down mad."

"Nor blessed." Alf's voice held the glimmer of a smile. "We did penance for a solid fortnight, and all we'd found was a broken chapel and beds even harder than the ones we'd slipped away from." His arm circled Morwin's shoulders, bringing warmth like an open fire. The Abbot leaned into it. "But no; that wasn't all we found. I felt as if I could see the whole world under the Midsummer moon, and below us Ynys Witrin, mystic as all the songs would have it, an island floating in a sea of glass. *There* was the mystery. Not on the windy hill. Below it, in the abbey, where by Christmas we'd be consecrated priests, servants of the Light that had come to rule the world."

"But the Thorn always knew. I was—I am—no mortal man."

"So now you come to make your peace with it."

"After a fashion. I wanted to see if it was glad to be rid of me."

"Is it?"

Alf's free hand moved to touch the trunk, white fingers glimmering on shadow-black. "I think . . . It's never hated me. It's just known a painful truth. Maybe it even wishes me well."

"So do we all."

Alf shivered violently, but not with the air's cold. "I'm going away," he said as if he had only come to realize it. "And I can't . . . Even if I come back, it won't be the same. I'll have to grow, change—" His voice faded.

Morwin was silent.

"I know," Alf said with unwonted bitterness. "Everyone grows and changes. Even the likes of me. Already I feel it beginning, with Alun's fine clothes waiting for me to put them on again and the memory of all the Brothers at supper, staring and wondering, and some not even knowing who I was. Even Jehan, when he first saw me, took me for a stranger. What if I change so much I don't even recognize myself?"

"Better that sort of pain than the one that's been tearing you apart for so long."

"That was a familiar pain."

"Yes. Plain old shackle-gall. I'm chasing you out of your prison, Alfred—throwing you into the sky. Because even if you're blind and senseless, everyone else can see that you have wings."

The moon came down into the cup of Alf's hand, a globe of light, perfect, all its blemishes scoured away. Its white glow caressed his face; Morwin blinked and swallowed. Familiar as those features were, the shock of them blunted by long use; sometimes still, with deadly suddenness, their beauty could strike him to the heart.

Alf's hand closed. The light shrank with it, snuffing out like a candle flame; taking away Morwin's vision, but not his remembrance of it. Slowly, wearily, Alf said, "I won't fight you any longer, Morwin. Not on that account. But must you send Jehan with me?"

"He has no more place here than you do."

"I know that. I also know that I may be riding into danger. The message I'll carry is not precisely harmless. I could be killed for bearing it, Alun for passing it to me—"

"And St. Ruan's could suffer for taking him in. Don't you think I'm aware of all the consequences?"

"Jehan isn't. To him it's a lark, a chance to be free."

"Is it, Alf?"

"He's a child still for all his size. He doesn't know what this errand might mean or how he may be forced to pay for it. The game we play, the stakes we raise—"

"He knows," Morwin said with a touch of sharpness. "So he's

glad enough about it to sing—that's not blissful ignorance, it's simply youth. When the time comes, if it comes, he'll be well able to take care of himself."

"And also of me," said Alf.

"Why not?" the Abbot demanded. "He's only been cloistered for half a year; and he grew up in the world—in courts, in castles." His eyes sharpened to match his tone; he peered into the shadow of Alf's hood, at the hint of a face. "Maybe you're not concerned for a young lad's welfare—pupil of yours though he is, and friend too. Maybe you don't want to be looked after by a mere boy."

Alf would not dignify that with an answer.

Nor would Morwin offer any apology. "I've done as I thought wisest," he said. "I trust you to abide by it. In the end you may even be glad of it."

The voice in the shadow was soft, more inhumanly beautiful than ever, but its words were tinged with irony. "Morwin my oldest friend, sometimes I wonder if, after all, I'm the witch of us two."

"This isn't witchcraft. It's common sense. Now stop nattering and help me up. Didn't I give you strict orders to get some sleep tonight?"

Morwin could feel Alf's wry smile, distinct as the clasp of his hand.

"Yes, grin at the old fool, so long as you do what I tell you."

"I am always your servant, Domne."

Morwin cuffed him, not entirely in play, and thrust him away. "Go to bed, you, before I lose my temper!"

Alf bowed deeply, the picture of humility; evaded a second blow with supernatural ease; and left his Abbot alone with the moon and the Tor and the ancient Thorn, and an anger that dissipated as swiftly as it had risen.

It was a very long while before Morwin moved, and longer still before he took the way Alf had taken, back into the warmth of St. Ruan's.

6

They left before dawn. Only Morwin was there to see them off. Morwin, and Alun's consciousness, a brightness in Alf's brain. They stood under the arch of the gate, Jehan holding the bridles of the two horses: Fara like a wraith in the gloom, and the abbey's old gelding standing black and solid beside her. He shivered, half with cold, half with excitement, and shifted from foot to foot. The others simply stood, Alf staring rigidly through the gate, Morwin frowning at his feet.

At last the Abbot spoke. "You'd best be going."

Swiftly Jehan sprang astride. Alf moved more slowly; as he gathered up the reins, Morwin touched his knee. "Here. Take this."

Light flashed between them, Morwin's silver cross. Alf hesitated as if to protest. But Morwin's eyes were fierce. He took the gift and slipped the chain over his head, concealing it under his tunic. It lay cold against his skin, warming slowly. He clasped the hand that had given it, met the eyes behind. "Go with God," Morwin said.

The gate was open, the road clear before them, starlit, aglitter with frost. Only once did Alf glance back. Already they had come far enough to see the whole looming bulk of the Tor, and the abbey against the wall of it, and mist rising with the dawn, turning the Isle to an isle indeed. Small and dark upon it, nearly lost beneath the great arch, the Abbot stood alone.

A wind stirred the mist, raising it like a curtain. Gray glass and silver and a last, faint flicker of moonlight, and of St. Ruan's, nothing at all save the shadow of a tower.

Fara danced, eager to be gone. Alf bent over her neck and urged her onward.

From St. Ruan's they rode northward, with the sun on their left hands and the morning brightening about them. Jehan sang, testing his voice that was settling into a strong baritone; when it cracked, he laughed. "I'm putting the ravens to shame," he said.

Alf did not respond. Here where the road was wide, they rode side by side; Jehan turned to look at him. His face was white and set. Part of that could be discomfort, for he had not ridden in a long while, yet he sat his mount with ease and grace.

Jehan opened his mouth and closed it again. For some time after, he rode as decorously as befit a novice of St. Ruan's, although he gazed about him with eager eyes.

At noon they halted. Alf would not have troubled, but Jehan's gelding was tiring. Already they were a good four leagues from the abbey, in a wide green country scattered with villages. People there looked without surprise on two lordly riders, squires from some noble house from the look of them, going about their business.

They had stopped on the edge of a field where a stream wound along the road. Jehan brought out bread and cheese, but Alf would have none.

The other frowned. "Dom Morwin told me you'd be like this. He also told me not to put up with it. So—will you eat, or do I have to make you?"

Alf had been loosening Fara's girths. He turned at that. "I'm not hungry."

"I know you're not. Eat."

They faced each other stiffly. Alf was taller, but Jehan had easily twice his breadth, and no fear of him at all.

Alf yielded. He ate, and drank from the stream where it settled into a pool. When the water had calmed from his drinking, he paused, staring at the face reflected there. It looked even younger than he had thought.

A wind ruffled the water and shattered the image. He turned away from it.

Jehan was busy with the horses, yet Alf could feel his awareness. Jehan finished and said, "Brother Alf. I've been thinking. We're riding like squires, but I'm the only one with a sword. I know you don't want one, but maybe you'd better know how to use it in case of trouble."

Alf tried to smile. "I'd probably cut off my own foot if I tried."

"You wouldn't either." He unhooked the scabbard from his belt. "Try it."

"No," Alf said. "If it comes to a fight, you're the one who knows what to do with it. Best that you keep it by you. I can manage as I am."

"That's foolish, Brother Alf." Jehan drew the good steel blade and held it out.

Alf would not take it. "Jehan," he said. "It's enough for me now that I dress as a worldling. Don't try to make me more of one. If you do, God alone knows where it will end."

"In a safer journey for us, maybe."

"Maybe not. You don't know what I am, Jehan."

"Do you?"

"I know enough. Put up your sword and ride with me."

Jehan sheathed the weapon, but did not move to mount. "Dom Morwin talked to me last night. He told me about you."

"He did?"

"Don't go cold on me, Brother Alf! I'd guessed most of it already. People talk, you know. And it was obvious early on that you had to be the one who wrote the *Gloria Dei*. You knew too much, and thought too much, to be as young as your face."

"How old am I, then?"

"As old as Dom Morwin," Jehan answered calmly.

"And you scoff at the tales of Gwydion of Rhiyana?"

"That's hearsay. You're fact."

"Poor logic, student. I should send you back to Brother Osric."

"You can't," Jehan said. "Dom Morwin won't let you."

"Probably not." Alf rose into the high saddle, wincing at his muscles' protest. Before Jehan was well mounted, he had touched the mare into a trot.

They rode at a soft pace to spare their aching bodies. After some little time Jehan said, "You don't have to be afraid of me. I won't betray you."

"I know," Alf murmured as if to himself. "You and Morwin: fools of a feather. I could be a devil, sent to tempt you both to your destruction."

"*You*, Brother Alf?" Jehan laughed. "You may be a changeling as people say, or an elf-man, but a devil? Never."

For the first time Jehan saw the other's eyes, direct and un-blurred. It was more than a bit of a shock.

He faced that bright unhuman stare, firm and unafraid. "Never," he repeated. "I'd stake my soul on that."

Alf clapped heels to Fara's sides. She sprang into a gallop.

They raced down a long level stretch. At the end, where the road

bent round a barrow, Alf slowed to a canter and then to a walk. Jehan
pounded to a halt beside him. "There," he panted. "Feel better?"

Alf bit his lip. "I'm being foolish, aren't I?" He essayed a smile.
It was feeble, but it would do. "Yes, I do feel better. My body is glad
to be under the open sky. I'll train my mind to follow suit."

By night they had traversed close on eight leagues, fair going for riders
out of training. They slept in an old byre, empty and musty but still
sturdy, with ample space for themselves and their horses.

Tired though he was, Jehan did not go to sleep at once. He
prayed for a while, then lay down with his cloak for a blanket. Alf
knelt close by him, praying still. Moonlight seemed to have come
through a chink in the walls, for though it was pitch-dark in the barn,
Jehan could see Alf's face limned in light, his hair a silver halo about
his head.

But there was no moon. Clouds had come with the sun's setting;
even as Jehan lay motionless, he heard the first drops of rain upon the
roof.

He swallowed hard. In daylight he could accept anything. But
darkness bred fear. He was alone here with one who was not human,
who shone where there was no light and stared into infinity with eyes
that flared ember-red.

They turned to him, set in a face he no longer knew, a moonlit
mask white as death. But the soft voice was Alf's own. "Why are you
afraid, Jehan?"

"I—" Jehan began. "You—"

Alf raised his hands that shone as did his face. The mask cracked
a little into a frown. "This happens sometimes. I can't always control
it. Though it's been years . . ." He closed his eyes.

The light flickered and went out.

Jehan sat bolt upright. "Brother Alf!"

Hands touched him. He started violently and seized them. They
were warm and solid. Keeping his grip on one, he reached into
blackness, finding an arm, a shoulder. Like a blind man he searched
upward, tracing the face, the smooth cheek, the flutter of lids over
eyes, the fringe of hair round the tonsured crown.

"Bring back the light," he said.

It grew slowly, without heat. He stared into the strange eyes. "I'm
not afraid anymore."

"Why?"

Jehan paused a moment. "You're still yourself. For a while I was afraid you weren't. You looked so different."

Alf leaned close. They were almost nose to nose; their eyes met and locked. It seemed to Jehan that he could see through Alf's as if through glass, into an infinity the color of rubies.

"Jehan."

He rose to full awareness, as from water into air, and sat staring. He still held Alf's hand; it tightened, holding him fast.

He shivered convulsively. "How? How could I see like that? I've never—"

Alf looked away. "I did it. I'm sorry. I was looking at the mettle of you; you saw behind my looking."

"Has—has it ever happened before?"

Already Jehan had regained most of his self-possession. "Pure gold," Alf murmured. And, louder: "A few times. I think . . . some humans have in them the seeds of what I am."

Jehan's eyes went wide. "I? Brother Alf, I'm no enchanter!"

The other almost smiled. "Not as I am, no. But something in you responded to my touch. Don't worry; I won't wake it again."

"Of course you will. I said I wasn't afraid, and I'm not. Show me what you can do, Brother Alf!"

Most of it was bravado, and they both knew it. Yet enough was true desire that Alf said, "I can do many things, which probably will damn me, if I can die, and if I have a soul to give over to perdition."

"Dom Morwin said that you can do what saints do. That you can heal hurts, and walk on air, and talk to people far away."

"I can do those things. Though by them I may defy the Scripture which commands that you shall not suffer a witch to live."

"He also said that you could never use your powers for evil."

"*Would*, Jehan. Not *could*. I can heal, but I can also kill."

There was a silence. Jehan searched the pale face, although the eyes would not meet his. "*I* can heal, Brother Alf. And I can kill." He lifted his hand. "This can stitch up a wound or make one, wrap a bandage or wield a sword. Is it any different from your power?"

"Other men have hands, Jehan."

"And others have power."

Alf cuffed Jehan lightly. "Out upon you, boy! You're death to my self-pity. Though it's true I'd no more threaten the powerless than you would attack a handless man. There'd be no fairness in it."

He drew back, and his light died. His voice was soft in the darkness. "Go to sleep now. We've talked enough for one night."

Jehan delayed for a moment. "Brother Alf?"

The other paused in lying down. "What?"

"I'm really not afraid of you."

"I know. I can feel it in you."

"So that's how you'd get around vows of silence."

"Good night, Jehan," Alf said firmly.

The novice wrapped his cloak about him and grinned into the night. "Good night, Brother Alf."

On the second day the travelers could barely move, let alone ride. Yet ride they did, for obstinacy; with time and determination, their bodies hardened. By the fourth day Jehan had remembered his old sturdiness. Even Alf was beginning to take a strange, painful joy in that ride, even to sing as he rode, to Jehan's delight. Hymns at first; then other songs, songs he had learned a lifetime ago, that rose to the surface of his memory and clung there. The first time or two, he stopped guiltily, as if he had been caught singing them in chapel; then, with Jehan's encouragement, he let his voice have its way.

Sometimes they met people on their road, peasants afoot or in wagons, who looked stolidly upon their passing. Once there was a pilgrim, who called for alms and blessed Alf for what he gave, not seeing the tonsure under the hood. And once there was a lord with his meinie, inviting the strangers to spend the night in his castle. Since it was early still, Alf refused, but courteously. Their camp that night seemed rough and cold, even with a fire; and it had begun to rain.

Open land gave way to forest, dark and cheerless. More than ever Alf regretted his refusal of the lord's hospitality; though Jehan laughed and said, "Don't be sorry. If someone had known me there, there'd have been a huge to-do and we'd never have got away."

"Maybe," Alf said. "But our food is running low, and we won't find any here. More likely, what we have will be stolen."

"Do you want to go around?"

"It would add two days to our journey. But maybe we'd better."

"Not I!" Jehan cried. "I'm no coward. Come on; I'll race you to that tree."

He was already off. After an instant, Alf sent the mare after him.

* * *

It was quiet under the trees, all sounds muted, lost in the mist of rain. Leaves lay thick upon the track; the horses' passing was almost silent to human ears. The travelers rode as swiftly as they might, yet warily, all their senses alert. Nothing menaced them, though once they started a deer, to Fara's dismay. Only the high saddle and Alf's own skill kept him astride then.

The farther they rode, the older the forest seemed. The trees were immense, heavy with the memory of old gods. Elf-country, Alf thought. But the cross on his breast made him alien.

Wild beasts moved within the reach of his perception, numerous small creatures, deer, a boar going about its dark business; even the flicker of consciousness that was a wolf. Nothing to fear.

Night fell, early and complete. They found a camp, a cluster of trees by a stream, that afforded water and shelter and fuel for a fire.

When they had tended the horses and eaten a little, they huddled together in the circle of light.

"I wonder how Alun is," Jehan said after a while.

Alf glanced at him, a flicker in firelight. "Well enough," he answered. "Brother Herbal has had him up and hobbling about a little. And he's had Morwin bring him treasures from the library."

"You talk to him?"

"Yes."

Jehan tried to laugh. "What's he wearing? You've got his clothes!"

"He borrows mine. Though he says he looks a poor excuse for a monk."

"Does he fret?"

Alf shook his head. "Alun never frets. He simply follows me with his mind."

"Is he watching now?"

"No. He's asleep."

Jehan glanced about uneasily at the whispering dark. "Are you sure?"

"Fairly." Alf smiled. "Come, lad! He can't see any secrets. He's a man of honor."

"But he *follows* us!"

"Me, to be more precise. Sometimes he borrows my eyes."

Jehan's had gone wild. When Alf touched him, he started like a deer. Those were Alf's eyes upon him: Alf's own, strange, familiar eyes. No one else lived behind them.

They flicked aside before he could drown. He swayed; Alf held him. "Jehan. Alun is like me. My own kind. As you and I share speech, so we share our minds. It comforts him. He gave me all he had; should I refuse to let him be with me?"

The other battled for control. "It's not that. It's . . . it's . . . I can't *see* him!"

"Would you like me to tell you when he's here?"

"Please. I'd rather know."

"Then you will. Sleep, Jehan. I'll keep the first watch."

He would have argued, but suddenly he could not keep his eyes open. Even as suspicion stirred, he slid into oblivion.

The road wound deeper into the forest, growing narrower as it proceeded, and growing worse, until often the travelers were slowed to a walk. Jehan rode with hand close to swordhilt; Alf's every sense was alert, although he said once, "No robber, unless he's desperate, will touch us: two strong men, well-mounted, and one big enough for two."

Jehan laughed at that, but he did not relax his guard. Nor, he noticed, did Alf. Even as that disturbed him, it brought comfort.

The second night under the trees, they camped in a place they could defend, a clearing which rose into a low hill, and at the top a standing stone. Jehan would not have chosen to stop here; but he glanced at his companion and grimaced. Here he was, riding with an elf-man, a proven enchanter, and he was afraid to sleep on an old barrow.

It did not seem to trouble Alf. He made camp quietly and ate as much as he would ever eat, and sat afterward, silent, fixing the fire with a blank, inward stare.

When he spoke, Jehan started. "Alun is here."

The novice shuddered and closed his eyes. For a moment in the fire he had seen a narrow hawk-face, a glint of gray eyes, staring full into his own.

Alf's voice murmured in his ear. "Alun sends greetings."

Jehan opened his eyes. There was no face in the fire. "Is he still . . ."

"No." Alf rose and stretched, arching his back, turning his face to the stars. Below, in the clearing about the mound, the horses grazed quietly.

He laid his hand upon the standing stone. It was cold, yet in the core of it he sensed a strange warmth. So it was in certain parts of St. Ruan's: cold stone, warm heart, and power that sang in his blood. The power hummed here, faint yet steady. It had eased the contact with Alun, brought them mind to mind almost without their willing it.

Yet there was something . . .

Jehan; the horses; a hunting owl; a wolf.

He called in all the threads of his power, and looked into Jehan's wide eyes. The moon was very bright, turning toward the full; even the novice could see almost as well as if it had been day.

Alf cupped his hands. The cold light filled them and overflowed. Slowly he opened his fingers and let it drain away.

"What does it feel like?" Jehan's voice was very low.

He let his hands fill again and held them out to Jehan. The other reached out a hand that tried not to tremble. "It—I can feel it!"

Again Alf let the light go. It poured like water over Jehan's fingers, but he could not hold it. "I could make it solid, weave a fabric of it. I tried that once. Moonlight and snowlight for an altar cloth. It was beautiful. The Abbot wanted to send it to Rome. But then he realized that it was made with sorcery."

"What did he do with it?"

"Exactly what he did with me. Blessed it, consecrated it, and put it away." Alf lay down, propped up on his elbow. "But now I'm out. I wonder what will happen to the cloth."

"Maybe," said Jehan, "Dom Morwin should send it to Rhiyana. The Pope wouldn't appreciate it, but the Elvenking would."

Alf considered that. "Maybe he would."

"He'd certainly appreciate you."

For answer Jehan received only a swift ember-glance. They did not speak again that night.

7

The third day in the forest dawned bleak and cold. They ate and broke camp in silence, shivering. Jehan's fingers were numb, his gelding's trappings stiff and unmanageable; he cursed softly.

Alf moved him gently aside and managed the recalcitrant straps with ease. Jehan glanced at him. "You're never cold, are you?"

"Not often," Alf said. The task was done; he took Jehan's hands in both his own. His flesh felt burning hot.

Startled, Jehan tried to pull away. Alf held him easily. "You don't need to add frostbite to your ills."

Jehan submitted. The warmth no longer hurt; it was blissful. "You're a marvel, Brother Alf."

"Or a monster." Alf let him go. "Come, mount up. We've a long way to go."

The cold did not grow less with the day's rising. Jehan thought the air smelled of snow.

Alf rode warily, eyes flicking from side to side. More than once he paused, every sense alert.

"What is it?" Jehan asked. "Bandits?"

The other shook his head.

"Then why do you keep stopping?"

"I don't know," Alf said. "Nothing stalks us. But the pattern isn't . . . quite . . . right. As if something were concealing itself." His eyes went strange, blind.

Jehan looked away. When he looked back, Alf was blinking, shaking his head. "I can't find anything." He shrugged as if to shake off a burden. "We're safe enough. I'd know if we weren't."

That was not particularly comforting. But they rode on in peace, disturbed only by a pair of ravens that followed them for a while, calling to them. Alf called back in a raven's voice.

"What did they say?" Jehan wondered aloud when they had flapped away.

"That we make enough noise to rouse every hunter but a human one." Alf bent under a low branch. The way was clear beyond; he touched the mare into a canter. Over his shoulder he added, "We should leave the trees by tomorrow. There's a village beyond; we'll sleep tomorrow night under a roof."

"Is that a solemn promise?"

"On my soul," Alf replied.

Which could be ironic, Jehan reflected darkly. His gelding stumbled over a tree root; he steadied it with legs and hands. Ahead of him, Alf rode lightly on a mount which never stumbled or even seemed to tire. Elf-man, elf-horse. Maybe this was all part of a spell, and he was doomed to ride under trees forever and never see the open fields again.

He was dreaming awake. His hands were numb; the sun hung low, and it was growing dark under the trees. He would be glad to stop.

Alf had begun to sing softly. *"Nudam fovet Floram lectus; Caro candet tenera . . ."*

He stopped, as he often did when he caught himself singing something secular. And that one, Jehan thought, was more secular than most. "Naked Flora lies a-sleeping; whitely shines her tender body . . ."

When he began again, it was another melody altogether, a hymn to the Virgin.

That night, as before, Alf took the first watch. The air was cold and still; no stars shone. Nothing moved save the flames of the fire.

He huddled into his cloak. He heard nothing, sensed nothing. Perhaps he was a fool; perhaps he was going mad, to watch so when no danger threatened.

Sleep stole over him. He had had little since he left St. Ruan's, and his body was beginning to rebel. He should wake Jehan, set him to watch. If anything came upon them—

Alf started out of a dim dream. It was dark, quiet.

Very close to him, something breathed. Not Jehan, across the long-dead fire. Not the horses. A presence stood over him.

He blinked.

It remained. A white wolf, sitting on its haunches, glaring at him with burning bronze-gold eyes.

A white girl, all bare, glaring through a curtain of bronze-gold hair.

"What," she demanded in a cold clear voice, "are you doing here?"

He sat up, his hood falling back from a startled face. Her eyes ran over him; her thought was as clear as her voice, and as cold. *God's bones! a monk's cub. Who gave him leave to play at knights and squires?*

His cheeks burned. Unclasping his cloak, he held it out to her. She ignored it. "What are you doing here?" she repeated.

Suddenly he wanted to laugh. It was impossible, to be sitting here in the icy dark with a girl who wore nothing but her hair. And who was most certainly of his own kind.

"I was sleeping," he answered her, "until you woke me." Again he held out his cloak. "Will you please put this on?"

She took the garment blindly and flung it over her shoulders. It did not cover much of consequence. "This is his cloak. His mare. His very undertunic. Damn you, where is he?"

Alf stared at her. "Alun?"

"Alun," she repeated as if the name meant nothing to her. Her mind touched his, a swift stabbing probe. "Yes. Alun. *Where is he?*"

"Who are you?" he countered.

She looked as if she would strike him. "Thea," she snapped. "Where—"

"I'm called Alf."

She seized him. Her hands were slender and strong, not at all as he had thought a woman's must be. Her body—

The night had been cold, but now he burned. Abruptly, fiercely, he pulled away. "Cover yourself," he commanded in his coldest voice.

His tone touched her beneath her anger. Somewhat more carefully, she wrapped the cloak about her. "Brother, if that indeed you are, I'll ask only once more. Then I'll force you to tell me. Where is my lord?"

"Safe," Alf replied, "and no prisoner."

Thea was not satisfied. "Where is he?"

"I can't tell you."

She sat on her heels. Without warning, without movement, she thrust at his mind.

Instinctively he parried. She paled and swayed. "You're strong!" she gasped.

He did not answer. A third presence tugged at his consciousness, one for which he could let down his barriers. Slowly he retreated into a corner of his mind, as that new awareness flowed into him, filling him as water fills an empty cup.

Thea cried a name, but it was not Alun's.

Alf's voice spoke without his willing it, in a tone deeper and quieter than his own. "Althea. Who gave you leave to come here?"

She lifted her chin, although she was very pale. "Prince Aidan," she answered.

Alf sensed Alun's prick of alarm, although his response was quiet, unperturbed. "My brother? Is there trouble?"

"Of course there's trouble. He's not had an honest communication from you in almost a month. And I'm not getting one now. What's wrong? What are you hiding?"

"Why, nothing," Alun said without a tremor. "If he is so urgent, where is he?"

"Home, playing the part you set him and growing heartily sick of it. He would have come, but your lady put a binding on him. Which he will break, as well you know, unless you give him some satisfaction."

"I'm safe and in comfort. So I've told him. So you can tell him."

Thea glowered at the man behind the stranger's face. "You're a good liar, but not good enough." Suddenly her face softened, and her voice with it. "My lord. Aidan is wild with worry. Maura has been ill, and—"

For an instant, Alun lost control of the borrowed body. It wavered; he steadied it. "Maura? Ill?"

"Yes. For no visible cause. And speaking of it to no one. So Aidan rages in secret and Maura drifts like a ghost of herself; I follow your mare and your belongings, under shield lest you find me out, and come upon a stranger. Why? What's happened?"

Alf watched his own hands smooth her tousled hair and stroke her soft cheek. "Thea, child, I'm in no danger. But what I do here is my own affair, and secret."

She did not yield to his gentleness. She was proud, Alf thought in his far corner, and wild. "Tell me where you are."

"Inside this body now," he answered her.

"And where is yours? What is this shaveling doing with all your belongings? Have you taken up his?"

He nodded.

"Why?" she cried.

"Hush, Thea. You'll wake Jehan."

She paid no heed to the oblivious hulk by the fire with its reek of humanity. "Tell me why," she persisted.

"Someday." He touched her cheek again, this time in farewell, and kissed her brow. "The bells are ringing for Matins. Good night, Althea. And good morning."

Alf reeled dizzily. His hands fell from Thea's shoulders; he gasped, battling sickness. For a brief, horrible moment, his body was not *his:* strange, ill-fitting, aprickle with sundry small pains.

She fixed him with a fierce, feral stare. But it was not he whom she saw. "You dare—even you, you dare, to bind me so . . . Let me go!"

His eyes held no comprehension. She raised her hand as if to strike, and with a visible effort, lowered it. "He bound me. I cannot follow him or find him. Oh, damn him!"

In a moment Alf was going to be ill. He had done—freely done—what he had never dreamed of, not even when he let Alun use his eyes. Given his body over to another consciousness. Possession . . .

He was lying on the ground, and Thea was bending over him. She had forgotten the cloak again. He groaned and turned his face away.

"Poor little Brother," she said. "I see he's bound you, too. I'd pity you if I could." Her warm fingers turned his head back toward her. His eyes would not open. Something very light brushed the lids. "I'm covered again," she told him.

She was. He looked at her, simply looked, without thought.

Thea stared back. She was the first person, apart from Alun, who had seen no strangeness in him at all. His own kind. Were they all so proud?

"Most of us," she said. "It's our besetting sin. We're also stubborn. Horribly so. As you'll come to know."

"Will I?" He was surprised that he could speak at all, let alone with such control. "Since you can't approach Alun, surely you want to go back to his brother."

She shook her head vehemently. "Go back to Aidan? *Kyrie eleison!* I'm not as mad as all that. No; I'm staying with you. Either Alun will slip and let his secret out, or at least I'll be safe out of reach of Aidan's wrath."

"You can't!" His voice cracked like a boy's.

"I can," she shot back. "And will, whatever you say, little Brother."

He rose unsteadily. He was nearly a head taller than she. "You can't," he repeated, coldly now, as he would have spoken to an upstart novice, "I'm on an errand from my Abbot to the Bishop Aylmer. I cannot be encumbered with a woman."

To his utter discomfiture, she laughed. Her laughter was like shaken silver. "What, little Brother! Do I threaten your vows?"

"You threaten my errand. Go back to Rhiyana and leave me to it."

For answer, she yawned and lay where he had lain. "It's late, don't you think? We'd best sleep while we can. We've a long way still to go."

No power of his could move her. She was not human, and her strength was trained and honed as his was not. Almost he regretted his reluctance to use power. She had no such scruples.

Like a fool, he tried to reason with her. "You can't come with us. You have no horse, no weapons, not even a garment for your body."

She smiled, and melted, and changed; and a white wolf lay at his feet. And again: a sleek black cat. And yet again: a white hound with red ears, laughing at him with bright elf-eyes.

He breathed deep, calming himself, remembering what he was. In the shock of her presence, he had forgotten. He picked up his cloak and stepped over her, setting Jehan and the fire between them, and lay down.

He did not sleep. He did not think that she did, either. With infinite slowness the sky paled into dawn.

Jehan had strange dreams, elf-voices speaking in the night, and shapes of light moving to and fro about the camp; and once a white woman-shape, born of Alf's song and his own waking manhood. When he woke, he burned to think of her. He sat up groggily and stared.

A hound stared back. Her eyes were level, more gold than brown, and utterly disconcerting.

Alf came to stand beside her, brittle-calm as ever. "What—" Jehan began, his tongue still thick with sleep. "Whose hound is that?"

"Alun's," Alf answered.

The novice gaped at her. "But how—"

"Never mind," said Alf. "She's attached herself to us whether we will or no."

Jehan held out his hand. The hound sniffed it delicately, and permitted him to touch her head, then her sensitive ears. "She's very beautiful," he said.

Alf smiled tightly. "Her name is Thea."

"It fits her," Jehan said. Something in Alf's manner felt odd; he looked hard at the other, and then at the hound, and frowned. "Is she what's been following us?"

"Yes." Alf knelt to rekindle the fire.

Jehan fondled the soft ears. She was sleek, splendid, born for the hunt, yet she did not look dangerous. She looked what surely she was, a high lord's treasure, bred to run before kings.

He laughed suddenly. "You're almost a proper knight now, Brother Alf! All you need is a sword."

"Thank you," Alf said, "but no." The fire had caught; he brought out what remained of their provisions, and sighed. "What will you have? Moldy bread, or half a crumb of cheese?"

8

The trees were thinning. Jehan was sure of it. The road had widened; he and Alf could ride side by side for short stretches with Thea running ahead. Like Fara, she seemed tireless, taking joy in her own swift strength.

By noon a gray drizzle had begun to fall. They pressed on as hard as they might, following the white shape of the elf-hound.

At last they surmounted a hill, and the trees dwindled away before them. Jehan whooped for delight, for there below them in a wide circle of fields stood a village.

It was splendid to ride under the sky again, with no dark ranks of trees to hem them in and the wind blowing free upon their faces. Jehan's gelding moved of its own accord into a heavy canter; the gray mare fretted against the bit. Alf let her have her head.

They did not run far. A few furlongs down the road, Alf eased Fara into a walk. He smiled as Jehan came up, and stroked the mare's damp neck. "We'll sleep warm tonight," he said.

The village was called Woodby Cross: a gathering of houses about an ancient church. Its priest took the travelers in, gave them dry clothes to wear after they had bathed, and fed them from his own larder. He was rough-spoken and he had little enough Latin, and the woman who cooked for him had at her skirts a child or two who bore him an uncanny resemblance. But he received his guests with as much courtesy as any lord in his hall.

"It's not often we see people of quality hereabouts," he told them after they had eaten and drunk. "Mostly those go eastaway round Bowland, to one of the lords or abbots there. Here we get the sweepings, woodsfolk and wanderers and the like."

"People don't go through the forest?" Jehan asked.

He shook his head. "It's a shorter way, if you don't lose yourself. But there's bad folk in it. They're known to go after anybody who goes by."

"They didn't bother us."

The priest scratched the stubble of his tonsure. "So they didn't. But you're two strong men, and you've got good horses and yon fine hound."

Thea raised her head from her paws and wagged her tail. Her amusement brushed the edges of Alf's mind.

He ignored her. He had been ignoring her since he had turned in his bathing and found her watching him with most unhoundlike interest.

"The King," Father Wulfric was saying. "Now there's someone who could sweep the outlaws out of Bowland, if he'd take the trouble. But he's away north, chasing those rebels who broke out while he was on Crusade. You'll have a fine time finding him."

"Actually," said Jehan, "we're looking for Bishop Aylmer; but that means we have to look for the King. They're always together. Two of a kind, people say. Fighters."

"That's certain. But I think my lord Bishop ought to pay a little more attention to his Christian vows and a little less to unholy bloodletting."

Jehan carefully avoided saying anything. The woman and the children had left, ostensibly to return to their own house. The children had looked surprised and fretful; one had started toward the curtain that hid the priest's bed from public view, before her mother dragged her away.

He shrugged a little. Alf had not spoken, either. He was gazing into the fire, eyes half-closed. Something in his face spoke to Jehan of Alun's presence.

The novice yawned. "Whoosh! I'm tired. It's a long ride from the Marches."

"And a fair way to go yet," said Father Wulfric. "Me, I'm a lazy man. I stay at home and mind my flock, and leave the traveling to you young folk." He rose from his seat by the hearth, opening his mouth to say more.

He never began. Alf stirred, drawing upright, taut as a bowstring. Firelight blazed upon his face; the flames filled his eyes. "Kilhwch," he whispered. "Rhydderch." It was a serpent's hiss. "He rends the web and casts it to the winds of Hell."

Thea growled. His eyes blazed upon her. "War, that means. War. I can delay no longer. I must go to the King."

"Tomorrow." Jehan's voice was quiet, and trembled only a little.

"Tonight." Alf reached for his cloak, his boots. "War comes. I must stop it."

Jehan held his cloak out of his reach. "Tomorrow," he repeated, "we ride like the wrath of God. Tonight we rest."

The wide eyes scarcely knew him. "I see, Jehan. I *see.*"

"I know you do. But you're not leaving tonight. Go to bed now, Brother Alf. Sleep."

The priest backed away from them, crossing himself, muttering a prayer. He remembered tales, demons in monks' guise, servants of the Devil, elf-creatures who snatched men's souls and fled away before the sunrise. Even solidly human Jehan alarmed him: soul-snatched already, maybe, or a changeling mocking man's shape.

They signed themselves properly and prayed before they went to bed, Latin, a murmur of holy names. He was not comforted.

They slept to all appearances as men slept. He knew; he watched them. The novice did not move all night. The other, the pale one with the face like an elf-lord, dreamed nightlong, murmuring and tossing. But Wulfric could not understand his words, save that some of them were Latin and some might have been names: Morwin, Alun, Gwydion; and often, that name he seemed to hate. Rhydderch.

When they roused before dawn, he had their horses ready. They acted human enough; stumbling, blear-eyed, yawning and stretching and drawing water to wash in though they had bathed all over only the night before. They helped with breakfast, and ate hungrily, even Alf, who looked pale and ill. Nor did they vanish at cockcrow. In fact it was closer to sunrise when they left, with a blessing from the monk and a wave from the novice. Well before they were out of sight, the priest had turned his back on their strangeness and gone to his work.

9

Alf rode now for three kingdoms. Jehan had caught his urgency, but the old gelding, for all its valiant heart, could not sustain the pace they set. In a village with a name Jehan never knew, Alf exchanged the struggling beast for a rawboned rake of a horse with iron lungs and a startling gift of speed—a transaction that smacked of witchery. But it all smacked of witchery, that wild ride from the borders of Bowland, errand-riding for the Elvenking.

Three days past their guesting in Wulfric's house, they paused at the summit of a hill. Fara snorted, scarcely winded by the long climb, and tossed her proud head. Almost absently Alf quieted her.

This was a brutal country, empty even of the curlew's cry: a tumbled, trackless waste, where only armies would be mad enough to go. An army in rebellion and an army to break the rebellion—hunter and hunted pursued and fled under winter's shadow. Rumor told of a hidden stronghold, a fortress looming over a dark lake somewhere among the fells; the rebels sought it or fought in it or had been driven out of it, always with the King's troops pressing close behind them. Fifty on either side, people had whispered in the last village, no more; or Richard had a hundred, the enemy twice that; or the rebels fought with a staggering few against the King's full might.

Truth trod a narrow path through all the tales. The rebels had taken and held the town of Ellesmere, and the King had laid siege to them there; driven forth, they had fled away southward, pursued by four hundred of Richard's men. Neither force could have gone far, for this was no land to feed an army. The enemy were starved and desperate, ready to turn at bay, the King eager to bring the chase to its end.

Alf gazed over the sweep and tumble of the moor, casting his other-sight ahead even of his keen eyes. "They're close now," he said: "to us, and to each other."

Jehan's nostrils flared, scenting battle. "Do you think they'll fight before we get to them?"

"More likely we'll arrive in the middle of it."

The novice loosed a great shout. *"Out! Out!"* The echoes rolled back upon him in hollow Saxon. *Out! Out! Out! Out!* He laughed and sent his mount careening down the steep slope.

Before he reached the bottom, Fara had passed him, bearing Alf as its wings bear the hawk, with Thea her white shadow. The rangy chestnut flattened its ears and plunged after.

In a fold of the hills lay a long lake, gray now under a gray sky. Steel clashed on steel there; men cried out in anger and in pain; voices sang a deep war-chant.

A jut of crag hid the struggle until the riders were almost upon it. There where the lake sent an arm into a steep vale, men fought fiercely in the sedge, hand to hand. Those who were lean and ragged as wolves in winter would be the rebels, nearly all of them on foot. The King's men, well-fed and -armed, wore royal badges, and mailed knights led them, making short work of the enemy.

Alf found the King easily enough. Richard had adopted a new fashion of the Crusader knights, a long light surcoat over his mail; royal leopards ramped upon it, and on his helm he wore a crown. He of cross and keys in the King's company, wielding a mace, would be Bishop Aylmer.

A hiss of steel close by made Alf turn. Jehan had drawn his sword; there was a fierce light in his eyes.

Battle sang in his own blood, gentle monk though he was, with no skill in weapons. It was a poison; he fought it and quelled it. "No," he said. "No fighting, Jehan."

For a moment he thought Jehan would break free and gallop to his death. But the novice sighed and sheathed his sword. Reluctantly he followed Alf round the clash of armies, evading stray flights of arrows, seeking the King's camp.

When they had almost reached it, a roar went up behind them. The rebels' leader had fallen.

Alf crossed himself, prayed briefly, rode on.

Richard had camped on a low hill above the lake, open on all sides and most well-guarded. But no one stopped a pair of youths on hard-ridden horses, errand-riders surely, trotting purposefully toward the center of the camp.

They sought the horse-lines first and saw to their mounts. There again, no one questioned them.

Folly, Thea decreed, watching Alf rub Fara down. *A thief could walk in, take every valuable object here, and walk out again as peaceful as you please.*

Alf glanced at her. *What thief would come out here?*

Who knows? She inspected a bucket, found it full of water, drank delicately. *What are you going to do now?*

Jehan asked the same question aloud at nearly the same time. "Wait for Bishop Aylmer," Alf answered them both. He shouldered his saddlebags, laden with books and with Morwin's letter to the Bishop, and slapped the mare's neck in farewell.

They walked through the camp. It was nearly deserted, except for a servant or two, but one large tent seemed occupied. As they neared it, they heard screams and cries, and Alf caught a scent that made his nose wrinkle. Pain stabbed at him, multiplied tenfold, the anguish of men wounded in battle.

He had meant to wait by the Bishop's tent, but his body turned itself toward the field hospital. Even as he approached, a pair of battered and bloody men brought another on a cloak.

There were not so many wounded, he discovered later. Thirty in all, and only five dead. But thirty men in agony, with but a surgeon and two apprentices to tend them, tore at all his defenses.

"Jehan," he said. "Find water and bandages, and anything else you can." Even as he spoke, he knelt by a groaning man and set to work.

He was aware, once, of the master-surgeon's presence, of eyes that took him in from crown to toe, and marked his youth and his strangeness and his skillful hands. After a little the man left him alone. One did not question a godsend. Not when it was easing an arrow out of a man's lung.

The power that had forsaken him utterly with Alun rose in him now like a flood-tide. He fought to hold it back, for he dared work no miracles here. But some escaped in spite of his efforts, easing pain, stanching the flow of blood from an axe-hewn shoulder. He probed the wound with sensitive fingers, seeing in his mind the path of the axe through the flesh, knowing the way to mend it—so.

He raised his hands. Blood covered them and the man beneath them—young, no more than a boy, wide-eyed and white-faced. There was no wound upon him.

Thea touched Alf's mind. *You'd better make him forget, little Brother, or one of two things will happen. You'll be canonized, or you'll be burned at the stake.*

"No," Alf said aloud. He forced himself to smile down at the stunned face. "Rest a while. When you feel able, you can get up and go."

The boy did not answer. Alf left him there.

Little Brother—

He slammed down all his barriers. Thea yelped in pain, but he did not look at her. The shield not only kept her out; it kept his power in. There were no more miracles.

Somewhere in the long task of healing, word came. The battle was over. The last few men who came, grinned beneath blood and dust and told proud tales while their wounds were tended.

Alf caught Jehan's eye. The novice finished binding a sword-cut and joined Alf near the tent wall. They washed off the stains of their labors and slipped away.

Weary though the King's men were, they prepared to consume the night in wine and song and bragging of their victory. Even the King drank deep in his tent and listened as one of his knights sang his triumph: a mere hundred against a thousand rebels, and the King slew them by the ten thousands. Legends bred swiftly about Richard.

Bishop Aylmer did not join in the carousing. When he had seen to the dead and dying, he sought his tent, close by the King's and but little smaller. His priest-esquire disarmed him and helped him to scour away the marks of battle, while his monks waited upon his pleasure. That was to pray and then to eat, and afterward, to rest alone.

Alf waited until the Bishop was comfortable, half-dreaming over his breviary but still awake, with the lamp flickering low. There was no guard in front of his tent, for trust or for arrogance. Alf raised the flap and walked in, with Jehan and Thea behind.

The Bishop looked up. They were a strange apparition in the gloom, two tall lads and a white hound, yet he showed no surprise at all. "Well?" he asked, cocking a shaggy brow. "What brings strangers here so late?"

Alf knelt and kissed his ring. "A message from the Abbot of St. Ruan's, my lord," he answered.

Aylmer looked him over carefully. "I know you. Brother . . . Alfred, was it? And you there, would you be a Sevigny?"

Jehan bowed. "The second son, my lord."

"Ah. I'd heard you'd turned monk. Not to your father's liking, was it?"

Something in the Bishop's eye made Jehan swallow a grin. "Not really, my lord."

"It doesn't seem to have hurt you," Aylmer observed.

Alf held out Morwin's letter. "From the Abbot, my lord," he said.

The Bishop took it and motioned them both to sit. "No, no, don't object. Humility's all very well, but it wears on the exalted."

As they obeyed, he broke the seal and began to read. " 'To my dear brother in Christ'—he's smoother on parchment than he is in the flesh, that's certain. Sent to me . . . plainly . . . What's this? You have urgent business with the King?"

Alf began to reply, but Aylmer held up a hand. "Never mind. Yet. I've inherited you two, it seems; I'm to treat you with all Christian kindness and further your cause with His Majesty, 'as much as my office and my conscience permit.' " He looked up sharply. His eyes were small, almost lost beneath the heavy brows, but piercingly bright. "Your Abbot plays interesting games, Brothers."

"Of necessity," said Alf. "He didn't dare write the full tale in case the letter fell into the wrong hands. But there's no treason in this. That I swear."

"By what, Brother? The hollows of the hills?"

"The cross on my breast will do, my lord."

Aylmer marked his coolness, but it did not abash him. "So—what couldn't be written that needs Morwin's best young minds and such haste that even a war can't interfere?"

For a moment Alf was silent. Jehan's tension was palpable. Aylmer sat unmoving, dark and strong and still as a standing stone.

Alf drew a breath, released it. "It's true that Jehan and I have been . . . given . . . to you. You asked for me. Jehan was never made to live in the cloister. But our haste rises from another cause. Some while ago, on All Hallows' Eve, a rider came to the Abbey. He was badly hurt; and we tended him, and discovered that he was the envoy of the King of Rhiyana."

The Bishop's expression did not change, but Alf sensed his start of interest.

"This knight," Alf went on, "had been in Gwynedd with the young King, and had ridden into Anglia to speak with a lord there, seeking peace among the kingdoms. The lord with whom he spoke was preparing war; he meant to use our knight as a gauntlet to cast in Rhiyana's face. The knight escaped to us, though in such a state that even yet he can't leave his bed, and the Abbot took it on himself to send us with his messages to the King."

"What sort of messages?"

"Kilhwch has no desire to go to war with Anglia. But a lord of Anglia has begun to raid in Gwynedd. If our King will refuse to join in the war and will take steps to punish his vassal, there can be peace between the kingdoms."

Aylmer sat for a long while, pondering Alf's words. At last he spoke. "But your man is from Rhiyana. Why is this struggle any concern of his?"

"Gwydion of Rhiyana fostered Kilhwch in the White Keep; he still takes care for his foster son's well-being."

Again Aylmer considered, turning his ring on his hand, frowning at it. "I think you'd better talk to the King. But not tonight. He's celebrating his victory; he won't want to hear about anything else. Tomorrow, though, he'll be sober and in a mood to listen to you. Though peace is never a good sermon to preach to Coeur-de-Lion."

"I can try," Alf murmured.

"I was right about you, I think. You were wasted in the cloister."

"I was happy there. And I was serving God."

"And here you aren't?"

"I never said that, my lord."

"No. You just meant it."

"One may serve God wherever one is. Even in battle."

"Would you do that?"

Alf shook his head, eyes lowered. "No. No, my lord. Today, I watched for a moment. That was enough."

The Bishop nodded. "It takes a strong stomach."

Jehan stirred beside Alf. "My lord," he said with some heat, "Brother Alf is no coward. He spent the whole day with the wounded. And it takes a good deal more courage to mend hurts than it does to make them."

Aylmer looked from one to the other, and his dark weathered face warmed into a smile. "I see that you two are somewhat more than traveling companions." He rose. "You'll sleep here tonight. Tomorrow you'll see His Majesty. I'll make sure of that. But I'm warning you now: Don't hope for too much. War is Richard's life's blood, and he's had his eye on Gwynedd for a long time. One man isn't going to sway him."

"We'll see," said Alf. "My lord."

10

Alf was up before the sun. The Bishop had not yet stirred; Jehan lay on the rug with Alf, curled about Thea's slumbering body. It was very cold.

He rose, gathered his cloak about him, and peered through the tent flap. The camp was silent, wrapped in an effluvium of wine and blood, the aftermath of battle. A mist lay like a gray curtain over the tents.

The horses were well content, with feed and water in plenty. Alf left them after a moment or two and went down to the lake.

The wide water stretched before him, half-veiled in fog. There was no one near to see him; he stripped and plunged in, gasping, for the water was icy. But he had bathed in colder in the dead of winter in St. Ruan's.

When he was almost done, the water turned warm so suddenly that it burned.

He whipped about. Thea stood on the bank in her own shape, wearing his shirt. It needed a washing, he noticed.

She walked toward him, her soles barely touching the surface of the lake. A yard or two away from him, she sat cross-legged on air. "What are you scowling for?" she asked him. "Hurry and finish your bath. I can't keep the water warm forever."

"If anyone sees you," he said, "there will be trouble."

"Don't worry. I'm not easily raped. Even by King Richard's soldiers."

Alf flushed. That was not what he had meant, and she knew it.

"You do blush prettily," Thea remarked. Still wearing his shirt, she let herself sink. "Ah—wonderful. Somehow a bath feels much better on skin than on fur." She wriggled out of the shirt, inspected it critically, rolled it up and tossed it shoreward before Alf could stop her. She was chest-deep, as he was; he averted his eyes and waded past her.

Between one step and the next, the water turned from blood-warm to icy cold. He ran to the bank and fumbled for his clothes. His shirt was warm, dry, and clean, as were the rest. Thea's gift.

Once safely clad, he should have returned to the camp. He stayed where he was, not looking at Thea but very much aware of her.

She emerged at length and accepted his cloak. "Thank you," she said, not entirely ironically. "I suppose I should turn into a hound again and give you some peace."

He glanced at her. She was very fair, wrapped in the dark blue cloak. He remembered what lay beneath; the memory burned. His body kindled in its fire.

So this is what it is, he thought in the small part of him which could still think.

Thea stared. Beautiful eyes, golden bronze, burning. "You mean you've never—"

He turned and fled.

Once he had left her, he cooled swiftly enough. But he could not still his trembling. So long, so long— Other novices had groaned and tossed in their beds or crept to secret shameful trysts with girls from the village, even with each other. Monks had confessed to daylight musings, to burning dreams, to outright sin; accepted their penances; and come back soon after with the same confessions. Alfred had lived untroubled, novice, monk, and priest; had pitied his brothers' frailty, but granted it no mercy. A man of God should master his body. Had not he himself done so?

He had been a fool. A child. A babe in arms.

Was he now to become a man?

He drew himself up. A man was his own master. He faced what he must face and overcame it boldly. Even this, torment that it was, but sweet—honey-fire-sweet, like her eyes, like her—

"No!"

His mind fell silent. His body stilled, conquered.

But he did not go back. Nor did she follow him, as a woman or as a hound.

He was calm when he returned to the Bishop's tent, to find Aylmer awake and dressed and surrounded by his monks. Jehan stood among them, conspicuous for his lordly clothes though not for his size; one or two of Aylmer's warrior-priests easily overtopped him.

There were curious glances as Alf entered. One man in particular fixed him with a hard stare, a small dark man in a strange habit, gray cowl over white robe. Something about him made Alf's skin prickle.

"Brother Alfred," Aylmer greeted him. "I'm getting ready to say Mass. Will you serve me?"

Alf forgot the stranger, forgot even the lingering shame of his encounter with Thea. He had not gone up to the altar in years. Ten years, nine months, four days. Not since he had found himself unable completely to reconcile his face with his years; when he had ceased to doubt that he would not grow old.

But Aylmer had not asked him to say Mass, did not know that he had taken priest's vows. Surely he could serve at the altar. That was no worse than singing in the choir.

Aylmer was waiting, growing impatient. Alf willed himself to speak. "I'll do it, my lord."

Aylmer nodded. "Brother Bernard, show Brother Alfred where everything is. We'll start as soon as the King is ready."

Dressed in alb and dalmatic and moving through the familiar ritual, Alf found that his fear had vanished. In its place had come a sort of exaltation. This, he was made for. Strange, half-human, elvish creature that he was, he belonged here at this altar, taking part in the shaping of the Mass.

He was preternaturally aware of everything, not only the priest and the rite, but the Bishop's tent about him, the high lords kneeling and standing as the ritual bade them, and the King.

Richard was difficult to pass by: a tall man, well-made, with a face he was proud of and a mane of gold-red hair. He heard the Mass with apparent devotion, but the swift fierce mind leaped from thought to thought, seldom pausing to meditate upon the Sacrament. His eyes kept returning to Alf, caught by the fair strange face, as Aylmer had known they would be.

When the Mass was ended, the celebrants disrobed swiftly. Alf paused with Alun's knightly garments in his hands. "My lord," he said to Aylmer, who watched him, "if you would allow me a moment to fetch my habit—"

The Bishop shook his head. "No. It's better this way." A monk settled his cloak about his shoulders; he fastened the clasp. "Alfred, Jehan, come with me."

Richard sat in his tent, attended by several squires and a knight or two. "Aylmer!" he called out as the Bishop entered. "Late for breakfast, as usual."

"Of course, Sire," the Bishop said calmly. "Should I endanger my reputation by coming early?"

The King laughed and held out a cup. "Here, drink. You've taken unfair advantage already by going to bed sober last night."

As Aylmer took the cup and sat by the King, Richard noticed the two attendants. "What, sir, have you been recruiting squires in this wilderness?"

"They've been recruiting me, Sire. Brother Alfred, Brother Jehan, late of St. Ruan's."

One of the knights stirred. "Jehan de Sevigny! They've thrown you out of the cloister?"

"Alas," Jehan replied, "yes. I outgrew it, you see."

"Like Bran the Blessed," Alf said, "he grows so great that no house will hold him."

The King's golden lion-eyes had turned to him and held, as they had during Mass. The others laughed at the jest, Jehan among them; the King was silent, although he smiled. "And you, sir monk-in-knight's-clothing? Wouldn't the house hold you?"

"No, Sire," Alf responded.

They were all staring now, at him, at the King. Their thoughts made him clench his fists. Richard had found another pretty lad, the prettiest one yet.

That was not what Richard was thinking of. He had been trying since Mass to put a name to that cast of features, but none would come.

"Alfred," he said, "of St. Ruan's on Ynys Witrin. Are you a clerk?"

"Of sorts, Sire."

"Pity. You look as if you'd make a swordsman in the Eastern fashion. Light and fast." With an abrupt gesture, Richard pointed to a seat. "Sit down, both of you. While we eat, you can tell us a tale or two we haven't heard before."

It was the first time Alf had sat at table with a King, though he had waited upon royalty once or twice, long ago. Those high feasts had been not at all like this breaking of bread upon the battlefield. Richard was at ease, standing little upon ceremony; no one paid much heed to rank.

Afterward, as they all rose to go, Richard gestured to Alf. "Sir monk. Stay."

Aylmer's satisfaction was palpable; as was the sudden interest of the others. Jehan frowned and wavered. But the Bishop's cold eye held him; he retreated.

One was not precisely alone with a king. Squires cleared away the table; another sat in a corner, polishing a helm. But those in Richard's mind were nonentities. He relaxed in his chair, eyes half-closed, saying nothing.

Alf was used to silence. He settled into it and wrapped himself in it.

The King's voice wove its way into the pattern of his thoughts. "Brother Alfred. Alf. What are you?"

He regarded Richard calmly. His God, a white elf-woman, himself—those he feared. A king troubled him not at all. "I'm a monk of St. Ruan's Abbey, Sire."

"Noble born?"

He shrugged slightly. "I doubt it."

The King's eyes narrowed. "Don't you know?"

"I was a foundling, Sire."

"A changeling?"

"Some people think so."

"I can see why," Richard said. And, abruptly: "What does Aylmer want?"

"Aylmer, Sire?" Alf asked, puzzled.

"Aylmer. Why is he thrusting you at me? What's he up to?"

This King was no fool. Alf smiled without thinking. "The Bishop is up to nothing, Sire."

"So now he's corrupting his monks in the cradle."

Alf's smile widened. Richard's eyes were glinting. "Don't blame him for this, Sire. I asked him for an audience with you."

Richard frowned; then he laughed. "And he didn't even ask. He simply placed you where I'd fall over you. Well, Brother Obstacle, what do you want?"

The mirth faded from Alf's face. He spoke quietly, carefully. "I've been sent to serve the Bishop. But I've also been entrusted with another errand."

"By whom?"

"The King of Rhiyana, on behalf of Kilhwch of Gwynedd."

The drowsing lion tensed. "One monk, with only a boy for company. Are they trying to insult me?"

"No, Sire. They honor you with their trust."

"Or taunt me with it. I know what Gwydion is like. He lairs in his White Keep and spins webs to trap kings in. How did I stumble into this one?"

"You didn't. One of your vassals did. A baron of the Marches, named Rhydderch."

The King stroked his beard and pretended a calm he did not feel. "Rhydderch. What has he done?"

"You know that there's been trouble on the Marches."

There was a dangerous glint in Richard's eye. "I know it," he said.

"Rhydderch is behind it. He's sent forces into Gwynedd and is ravaging the lands along the border."

"Are you implying that I don't keep my lords in hand?"

"I'm implying nothing, Majesty," Alf said.

If Richard had had a tail, it would have been lashing his sides. "You tell me that one of my barons foments a major war, and that the King of Rhiyana will concern himself with it. Gwydion's a meddler, but even so, in this he's going far afield."

"Of course he's concerned. Kilhwch is his foster son. A war with you would end in disaster."

"For one side. Kilhwch is a boy, and Gwydion's no soldier."

"For both sides, Sire. Kilhwch is nineteen, which isn't so very young, and he takes after his father. And Gwydion, I think, would surprise you. Isn't his brother said to be the best knight in the world?"

"His brother is as old as he is. Which is ancient."

Alf shook his head. "The Flame-bearer has no equal, nor ever shall have. Not even Coeur-de-Lion."

That barb had sunk deep. Richard's eyes blazed. His voice was too quiet, almost a purr. "You're very sure of that, little monk. Do you even know which end of a sword to hold onto?"

"I can guess, Sire."

"And you guess at the prince's prowess?"

"The world knows it. I believe it." Calmly, boldly, Alf sat on a stool near the King, his long legs drawn up.

The other did not react to this small insolence in the face of the greater one. "Do you know how to convince me that I ought to go to war? Aylmer could have told you. Anyone could. It's ludicrously simple. Tell the brawn-brained fool the other man is a better fighter than he is."

To Richard's utter amazement, Alf laughed. It was a light free sound, with nothing in it but mirth. "You, Sire? Brawn-brained? Far from it. But you have an alarming passion for fighting, and you want Gwynedd. Unwise, that. You'd do better to send ambassadors to Kilhwch and tell him you want peace. Else you'll have Gwynedd on your left and Rhiyana on your right, and all Hell between."

"A small kingdom whose King is barely in control of his vassals, and a greater one which hasn't fought a war since before I was born. But Anglia is strong, tempered in the Crusade."

"And tired of fighting, though you may not be, Sire. Surely it will be adventure enough to quell Rhydderch."

Richard looked him over again, slowly this time, musing. "Why are you doing this? Are you Rhiyanan?"

"No, Sire. It was entrusted to me by someone else. A knight of Rhiyana who fell afoul of Rhydderch."

"Dead?"

"No, though not for Rhydderch's lack of trying."

"So Gwydion already has a reason to be my enemy."

"Rhiyana doesn't know yet. And won't, if you help us, Sire. Send word to Rhydderch. Order him to withdraw from Gwynedd on pain of death. And let Kilhwch know what you're doing."

The King was silent. Alf clasped his knees, doing his utmost not to reveal his tension. Richard hung in the balance, debating within himself. War, and winter coming, and troops to deal with who fretted already at campaigning so late in the year. To stop Rhydderch, to beg Kilhwch's kind pardon—no. But a truce now, and in the spring . . .

He nodded abruptly and stood. "I'm bound to ride now for Carlisle. By the time I get there I'll have an answer for you."

Alf rose as the King had and bowed, slightly, gracefully. "As you will, Sire."

The lion-eyes glinted upon him. "But it's not as *you* will, is it?"

"I don't matter, Majesty."

Richard snorted. "Stop pretending to be so humble. You're as proud as Lucifer."

Alf nodded. "Yes, I am. But I try. That's worth something."

"A brass farthing." Richard tossed him something that glittered; reflexively he caught it. "I have work to do if we're to ride out of here by night. You'll wait on Aylmer. But I may steal you now and again. You're interesting, sir monk."

Alf bowed low without speaking. Metal warmed in his hand, the shape of a ring, the sense of silver, moonstone.

A simple monk had no business with such things. He knew he should return it with courtesy; half-raised his hand, opened his mouth to speak.

When he left, he had not spoken. The ring was still clenched in his fist.

11

The King broke camp shortly after noon and turned his face toward Carlisle. His men, recovered from the ravages of battle and of drink, set forth in high spirits, singing as they went, songs that made no concessions to the small somber-clad party about the Bishop. The more pious of those pretended not to listen; the rest beat time on thigh or pommel and at length joined in.

Alf rode in silence. He had been silent since he returned from the King's tent.

Jehan frowned. He had hoped that, once Alf had delivered his message and given himself over to Bishop Aylmer, he would be his old self again. But he seemed more moody than ever. He did not even answer when Jehan, looking about, asked, "Where's Thea?"

A little after that, Alf left his place behind the Bishop. Others were riding apart from the line, young knights impatient with the slow pace, bidden by their commanders to patrol the army's edges. He did not belong with them, unarmed and unarmored as he was, but no one rebuked him. He had an air about him, Jehan thought, like a prince in exile.

"An interesting young man," a voice said.

Someone had ridden up beside him, the man in the gray cowl on a bony mule. Jehan swallowed a sharp retort. He did not like this Brother Reynaud—not his face, not his eyes, and not at all his high nasal voice.

The monk did not seem to notice Jehan's silence. He was watching Alf with a peculiar, almost avid stare. "Very interesting," he repeated. "I understand that he's a churchman?"

Jehan had his temper in hand. "Yes, Brother," he said easily enough. "He has a dispensation to wear secular clothes. So do I. We thought it would be less dangerous to travel this way."

"Oh, yes. Yes. It might be. Certainly he looks most well in that guise. Though one so fair would look well even in sackcloth." Brother Reynaud smiled a narrow, ice-edged smile. "Does he come of a princely family?"

"Not that anyone knows of. But he doesn't need to be a lord's get. He's princely enough as he is."

"That," said the monk, "is clear to see. His parents must be very proud of such a son."

"He's an orphan. He was raised in the abbey."

"Oh? How sad." Brother Reynaud's eyes did not match his words; they glittered, eager. Like a hound on the scent, Jehan thought.

Hound. Gray cowl, white robe. Jehan remembered dimly a name he had overheard, a word or two describing a habit and an Order. Hounds. *Canes. Canes Dei.* Hounds of God.

He went cold. His fingers clenched upon the reins; the chestnut jibbed, protesting.

He made himself speak calmly. "Tell me, Brother. I can't seem to place your habit. Is it a new Order?"

Reynaud glanced at him and smiled again. "New enough. The Order of Saint Paul."

The Paulines. They were the hunting hounds of Rome, seekers and destroyers of aught that imperiled the Church. Heretics. Unbelievers. Witches and sorcerers.

Alf rode unheeding, his white head bare, the gray mare dancing beneath him. Someone called out to him, admiring his mount; he replied, his voice clear and strong and inhumanly beautiful. No one could see his eyes as they were—those, he blurred, by subtle witchery—but that was a small thing to the totality of him. He looked what he was, elf-born, alien.

The King had summoned him. The mare wheeled and fell in beside the red charger. They rode on so, horses and men matched in height, but the King heavier, slower, earthbound.

"The King has taken to him," Reynaud observed.

Jehan's heart hammered against his ribs. He could smell the danger in this man, a reek of blood and fire. "I'm not surprised," he said. "He was quite the most brilliant monk in our abbey. And the most saintly."

Reynaud did not react at all to that thrust. "Your Abbot must have been sorry to see him go."

"He was. But Bishop Aylmer asked for Brother Alfred, and it was best for him to leave. He needed to stretch his wings a little."

"Strong wings they must be, to attain a King in their first flight."

"That's what the Abbot thought. And Dom Morwin's right about most things."

"Was it your Dom Morwin who admitted this paragon to the abbey?"

"Oh, no. Dom Morwin's only been Abbot for five years. Brother Alf came when he was a baby."

The gleam in Reynaud's eye had brightened. "Alf, you call him?"

Jehan swallowed and tried to smile. "There are a lot of Saxons in our abbey. And of course there's the great scholar, the one who wrote the *Gloria Dei*. With two Alfreds in the place, one had to have his name shortened."

"Ah, yes. Alfred of St. Ruan's. I hadn't noticed the coincidence. Is he still alive?"

"Still. Though he doesn't go out anymore, nor write much. He's getting quite old, and his health isn't very good."

"That's a pity. Your young Brother is named after him, then?"

Jehan nodded. "Takes after his scholarship, too. He hated to see Brother Alf go. But the Abbot insisted. There are other teachers, he said, and one of them is the world."

"True enough," Alf said.

Jehan drew his breath in sharply. Intent upon the fabric of truth and falsehood, he had not heard the approaching hoofs.

Alf's eyes looked darker than usual, more gray than silver. He smiled at Jehan and said, "I heard you talking about me. Base flattery, all of it. I'm really quite an ordinary young nuisance; my Abbot decided he'd had enough of me and inflicted me on the poor Bishop."

"Both of us," Jehan put in. "What did the King say, Brother Alf?"

Alf shrugged. "A word or two. He wanted to buy Fara." He smoothed the mare's wind-ruffled mane.

"Did you say yes?"

"Of course not. I said she was only lent to me; he said that he understood; we both agreed that she's the most beautiful creature afoot." She arched her neck; he stroked it and laughed a little. "Aye, you are, and well you know it."

Reynaud had withdrawn in silence. But his presence remained, like a faint hint of corruption; surely he strained to hear what they said. Jehan wanted to shout a warning, but he dared not.

Their horses moved together; knee brushed knee. Alf gripped Jehan's shoulder for an instant, as a friend will, saying something meaningless. But Jehan caught the thought behind, the surge of comfort. Alf knew. He was on guard. And the Hounds of God, for all their fire and slaughter, had never caught one of the true elf-blood. That he was sure of, with Alun's surety.

Alf started awake. It was very late, with a scent of dawn in the air. Jehan's warm body lay against him, dreaming boy-dreams. His own had been far less gentle, a wild confusion of fire and darkness, Alun's black boar and a pack of ghost-white hounds, and a lion transfixed with a flaming sword.

He lay still as the cold sweat dried from his body. He had not cried out; no one had awakened.

Thea crouched close in hound-shape, glaring as she had glared on that first night.

"Thea," he breathed. "I thought you'd gone back to Rhiyana."

Her lip curled in a snarl. She was exhausted and in a foul temper. *I set out for St. Ruan's, and traveled all this black day and half the night, and found myself outside this tent. With Alun in my mind all the while, telling me about the book he read today, and chanting the Offices.*

You knew it would happen, Alf said in his mind.

Her hackles rose; she bared her teeth. *I put up every barrier I had. I went down to the very bottom of my power. And I hunted a trail that led me in a long arc back to you.*

Alf sighed. *I hoped you'd be wise enough to go home.*

No!

He winced. Her anger was piercing. *I'm sorry,* he said.

Don't pity me!

I don't. He drew the blanket up to his chin.

She lay down beside him. He went rigid. Her body was beast-warm. But her mind was a woman's.

Her annoyance pricked him, less painful than her anger but more shameful. *Don't be so ridiculous. You never minded it when I slept with Jehan.*

But he doesn't know—

No more do you. She rested her chin on his chest and closed her eyes. All her barriers had firmed against him.

A test, Brother, he told himself. *Think of it as a test.*

By infinite degrees he relaxed. She was only a hound. A sleeping hound, worn out with her long fruitless chase.

Boldly he stroked her ears. She did not respond. With the air of a man plunging into deadly peril, he laid his arm over her flank. It was sleek-furred, wholly canine; her heart beat as a hound's will, swift, slow, swift, slow, in time with her breathing.

He loosed his breath in a long sigh. He had done it. He had mastered her, and himself.

Perhaps.

12

Alf rode most of the way to Carlisle at the King's side. It was not the place he would have chosen, but Richard would not let him ride in obscurity behind the Bishop. "You interest me," the King would say when he protested. "Tell me another tale, Brother!"

And Alf would obey. Or Richard would tell tales of his own: accounts of his travels and of his many battles, of the sea, and of the lands of the East. "Have you ever traveled?" he asked.

"A little," Alf replied. "I went to Canterbury once, and to Paris to the schools."

"Paris! Why, you've never been out of the dooryard. When I get these troubles out of the way, I'm going Crusading again. This damp, dripping land—pah!" He spat. "I'm hungry for the hot sun and the dust and the bare hills of Outremer."

Alf could see them in his eyes, a fierce pitiless country, yet beautiful. He yearned after it as a man yearns after a woman.

"Jerusalem!" he said. "They kept me out of it, those fools and cowards who called themselves my allies; and I had to take a craven's peace, and smile, and bow to the Infidel. But I'll take the city yet. I told him that, the Sultan Saladin. He's a black heathen, but he's a knight and a gentleman. He laughed and said that I could try, and then we'd know who was the better general."

"I'd like to see Jerusalem," murmured Alf. "And Byzantium."

"That city I never saw. The Great City they call it, because its proper name is so much of a mouthful."

"Constantinopolis. Constantine's City, Jewel of the East. I've always wanted to see the dome of Hagia Sophia and the Golden Horn; the caravans coming in from Cathay, and the ships sailing west with the wealth of the Indies."

"Why, Brother! You're a dreamer, too."

Alf laughed a little, surprised. "I suppose I am. That's why I learned Greek, to read about the East."

"You know Greek?"

"Yes, Sire. A little."

"And Arabic?"

"A few words. Maybe."

"God's bones! I've found myself a wonder. When I go back to Outremer, my friend, I'll take you with me. We'll take Jerusalem, and we'll visit the Emperor in Constantinople, and we'll be lords of the East."

When Richard was delighted, he reminded Alf of Jehan. Alf smiled, and blinked. For a moment he had seen a strange thing, the flash of sun on blue water; and scented an air that had never known the gray chill of Anglia. Then the image was gone. Richard had looked back, inspecting the line of march; their speech thereafter turned to other things.

They reached Carlisle in the evening after a day of bitter rain. To Alf it seemed a grim city, walled about with dark red stone, dripping with wet. Its people had come out to greet the King, but their welcome was muted, the dour welcome of the North; they gave their liege lord precisely his due, no more and no less.

The Earl of the city met them at the gate of the castle, with a sour smile; it little pleased him to play host to four hundred of the King's men, and many more besides, come from all about to attend Richard's court.

Richard's smile was wider and brighter, but with more than a hint of malice. "Hugo," he had told Alf, "has been paying me tribute with one hand and stroking my beloved brother with the other. One fine day I'll catch him between the jaws of the trap he's made. But meanwhile, I'll clean out his larder and use up his hoard, and make him thank me for the privilege."

Yet to all appearances the Earl received his King with proper courtesy, and the army dispersed itself about the town. Aylmer lodged in the Bishop's palace near the cathedral. Bishop Foulques loved Aylmer no better than the Earl loved the King, but he had had the grace to withdraw to the abbey near the walls; his dwelling was somewhat more spacious than the castle and considerably more comfortable. Aylmer's attendants, Alf among them, were not forced like the King's to settle as best they could about the great hall; rooms were allotted them, and beds.

Alf shared a cell with Jehan and with a tongue-tied young priest, and with the Pauline monk. Reynaud's doing, Alf was certain. There were others of his Order about, pale shapes in gray cowls, with watchful eyes.

I feel like a cat in a kennel, Alf thought.

Thea made herself comfortable on one of the cell's two beds, to Father Amaury's great discomfiture. *Hounds have only teeth,* she pointed out. *You have teeth and claws.*

If I dare to use them, said Alf.

Reynaud approached her. She showed her teeth; he retreated hastily. She laughed.

They did not keep monastic hours here. But Alf's body, attuned to waking in deep night for Matins, could not lie sluggishly abed until dawn. In the black dark before it, he slipped carefully from the bed he shared with Jehan, gathered up a small bundle, glided out of the cell.

Only the cooks were awake, baking the new day's bread. The bath behind the kitchen was deserted. Alf lit the lamp over the nearest wooden tub and took up the yoked buckets by it, passing through the warm rich-scented kitchen to the well. He was seen but not remarked, a monk in cloak and hood indulging in the eccentricity of a bath.

It was not Thea alone who could warm water without fire, though this was far easier, a mere tubful. He folded himself into it, sighing with pleasure. Let the saints have their holy filth; this ill-made monk would be clean.

He washed swiftly but with fastidious care, rose and dried himself, and took up the bundle he had brought. For a long moment he regarded it. The brown habit was his better one, almost new, yet the near-newness only made it the harsher to the touch.

Slowly Alf drew it on. Without tunic or trews to cushion it, it was nigh as galling as a hair-shirt; and his skin, once inured to it, yearned for the caress of princely linen.

He bound the cincture tightly, settled the cowl over his shoulders, let the hood fall back. On the floor lay the last of the bundle's contents, a fine sharp razor. A stroke or six, and Brother Alfred would have returned wholly, from bare feet to bare crown.

He did not know he sighed until he had done it, and then he did not know why. Kneeling by the tub, he groped for the razor.

It eluded his hand. At length, piqued, he turned to look for it. He had gained a companion, a slight figure in a habit like his own, but within the deep cowl shone a smile he knew all too well, full of dancing mockery. "Returning to the womb, little Brother?" asked Thea.

He held out his hand, tight-lipped.

She folded her arms. The razor glittered in her hand, close to the merest suggestion of a curve.

Alf's breath hissed between his teeth.

Her head tilted; her smile retreated to the corner of her mouth. "It's a pity, you know. To make yourself ugly for God—as if He could care for such trifles."

"It's done, as you say, for God, whether He heeds it or no; and to mark me as the Church's own."

"A slave of Rome. How dramatic. It's still ridiculous, little Brother. Why not make a real sacrifice? Like the pagan priests—or like the monk, the one they all call a heretic—"

"Origen."

"Origen," she agreed lightly. "God's eunuch. Now that is an irrevocable choice."

Alf spoke with care. "I should like to finish what I have begun. If you please—"

"If you insist," she said, "I'll help you. Or are my hands too foul to perform so sacred a rite? Schismatic Greek that I am, unconsecrated by any vows, and—ah, horrors!—a female."

She would prick him into a rage, and only laugh the harder. He struck on his own account with all his native sweetness. "I should not touch a woman, nor she touch me. But in the circumstances, I hope you have a light hand."

Light as air, and as gentle as her tongue was cruel. "What lovely skin you have. Soft as a child's. And your hair—I know women who'd kill to have hair half so thick or half so fine."

"Including yourself?"

She could even mock his self-possession, won as it was through bitter battle. "Why, little Brother! My touch hasn't struck you speechless. You've even mustered a tiny bit of wit. If I were a proper woman, I'd swoon with astonishment."

"If I were a proper monk, I'd exorcise you as a devil."

She was done, the razor secreted somewhere within the pilfered habit. She laid her cool hands on his shaven crown, a touch light almost to intangibility, yet it held him rooted. "Believe me, Brother Alfred of Ynys Witrin, you are a very proper monk. Now you even look it, though I never needed the proof."

His head came up with the swiftness of temper. But she was gone, vanished. There remained only a brown habit, crumpled on the floor.

"*I* need it!" he cried.

The air returned no answer.

Since that first morning in the camp, Alf had served Aylmer each day at Mass. The Bishop called upon him to do the same in Carlisle in the small chapel. Its walls were of that grim red stone which seemed to have been dyed with blood, but arras of eastern work concealed them, and the furnishings were rich, treasures from the first Crusade. Alf sensed both their age and their foreignness; the silver chalice with its graven Apostles held a flavor of old Rome.

As he aided Aylmer in disrobing, a very small page in royal livery slipped through the door. His eyes upon Alf were wide and rather frightened, though it was to the Bishop that he bowed and said, "My lord, His Majesty wishes to borrow Brother Alfred."

"His Majesty knows that he doesn't need to ask," said Aylmer. "Tell him Brother Alfred will be along directly."

The child bowed again, shot Alf a last glance, and fled.

Alf smiled a little, wryly, and laid the Bishop's alb in the press. Aylmer watched him with narrow eyes until he straightened and turned.

"Brother," the Bishop said, "what would you do if I gave you to the King?"

Alf stood still. "In what capacity, my lord?"

"As a clerk, to begin with. Richard needs a good secretary. And," Aylmer added, "a friend."

"Am I competent to be the King's friend?"

"You've been doing well enough at it. He likes you, Brother. Richard deals well with men and knows how to make them love him; but he seldom returns the favor."

"You know what people are saying."

Aylmer snorted. "Of course I know. And I'll be frank with you;

there's substance in it, as far as Richard is concerned. He has a weakness for a fair face. But he doesn't stoop to force. He'll do no more than you let him do."

"My lord," Alf said, "I've only felt desire once. And that . . . that was for a woman." His cheeks were flaming, but he kept his head up. "I don't think the King will endanger me. Not that way. But I had thought—I had hoped—I am a simple monk, cloister-bred. My Abbot sent me to be your servant. Not to become a King's favorite."

"You think so?" Aylmer asked. "I give Dom Morwin a shade more credit. He entrusted you with the Rhiyanan's message. I doubt he expected your errand to end with its delivery."

Alf bowed his head. No. Morwin would not have expected that, old fox that he was, knowing Richard's nature and the nature of the message.

And that of the messenger.

"With whip and spur he drives me into the world." Alf looked up. Aylmer's gaze was unsurprised, understanding. "He drives me straight into the lion's den."

A smile touched the Bishop's eye. "This Lion only devours the weak. And that, Brother, you are not. I'm not afraid for you. If you fear for yourself—" He lifted the silver cross from the other's breast and held it in the light. "This is stronger than armor. Trust in it." He let it fall. "You'll sleep here and you'll serve me at Mass, but you belong to the King. Stay with him. Serve him. Be his friend."

Alf knelt to kiss Aylmer's ring. "As my lord wishes."

Before he could leave, Aylmer stopped him. "Brother. Be wary. This isn't your cloister; people here can be dangerous, especially around the King. If you sense trouble, come to me at once. Do you understand?"

"I understand," Alf said very low.

Aylmer frowned. "Do you? You're not a spy, Brother. Nor are you a watchdog. But I'm the King's Chancellor and your protector. I don't want harm to come to either of you."

"Yes, my lord."

"Go then. The King's waiting."

Alf bowed. As he departed, he felt Aylmer's eyes and mind upon him and shivered. The Bishop saw far more than Alf wished him to see. And Alf did not trust him. Not yet, and not quite.

When Alf presented himself at the keep, the Earl's guards eyed his face and his habit and his newly tended tonsure, and sneered. Yet they let him pass, following him with leers and not-quite-inaudible remarks.

So too the King's own squires, though there was no mockery in their eyes and voices, but black hostility. Alf dressed as their equal and mounted on a horse fit for a prince, and always in the company of the King or the Bishop or the outsize novice, had been hard enough to endure. But Alf alone and afoot and in monk's garb was unbearable. They glared as they admitted him to the solar, and one spat, although he was careful to miss.

The King was deep in converse with several men with the garb and the bearing of noblemen. Alf effaced himself, a silent figure in a brown cowl, settling by the wall. No one noticed him.

The audience was long and tedious. At last Richard brought it to a close, dismissing the barons with courtesy that was a thin veil over irritation. Even as the door closed upon the last, he stretched until his bones cracked, and grinned at Alf, a lion's grin with a gleam of sharp teeth. "Well, Brother. You took your time."

"I'm sorry, Sire," Alf murmured.

"Never mind." Richard looked him over, fingering the rough fabric of his habit. "Hideous stuff, this. Where are your other clothes?"

"They were only to travel in, Sire," said Alf.

"You should have kept to them. They suited you."

"This is my proper habit, my lord. And it's an excellent disguise. Who notices a monk in a cowl?"

Richard laughed with one of his sudden changes of mood. "Aye, who does? And monks hereabouts are ten for a ha'penny. Don't tell me you're about to vanish among them."

"No, Sire. Bishop Aylmer has set me at your disposal. He asks only that I sleep and serve Mass with his people."

"Does he feel that he needs a spy?" Though the King's tone jested, his eyes did not.

"You know my lord needs no such thing. You also know that you were about to ask him for me. So, he anticipated you. What will Your Majesty have of his servant?"

"First," answered Richard, "the truth."

"That is the truth, Sire."

The King pointed to a chair. "Sit." As Alf obeyed, he paced, restless. "I call Aylmer friend. We owe each other our lives many times over. But a King can never trust a friend. God's feet! He can't even trust his own family."

Richard stood in front of Alf, hands on hips. "When my older brother was as young as you are, he tried to throw my father down and make himself King. He died for it. And I learned something. Blood-ties mean nothing. Friendship means even less. All that matters is myself. And winning, Brother. And winning."

"I don't believe that."

"Tell me so when your beard has grown."

Alf did not know that he smiled, until Richard glared and said, "You laugh at me. What do you know that I'm so ignorant of?"

"That the world is a cruel place," Alf responded, "but that it's not as cruel as you think. Aylmer cares for you, as his King and as his friend; I'm his free gift. Even though I look as if I were about to deliver a sermon."

That won laughter; Richard relaxed visibly. "Ah, but you just have." He sat by a table laden with sheets of parchment. "There's a promise I made to you when you were playing at royal ambassador."

"Yes, Sire?"

"Yes, Brother." He shuffled the written sheets, frowning at them. "When I came here, there were messages waiting. You've told me the truth about Rhydderch's raids. Bitter ones they've been, too, for Gwynedd. And Rhydderch's neighbors are worried that he'll bring down reprisals upon them all, for there's word of resistance, and forces gathering along the Marches. There's a war in the making, and no small one either."

"So I told you, Sire."

"It's a bad time for it," Richard said. "Winter's begun and the harvest's in; everyone's laid his sword away and hung his shield on the wall. A sitting target for a man who's not only reckless but clever."

Alf watched the King steadily, with a sinking heart. Richard moved restlessly in his chair, tugging at his beard, contemplating a winter campaign: snow and cold and long grim nights, and the swift heat of battle. Perhaps there would be glory, a contest with Kilhwch, King against King, with a crown for the winning; or with the elven-prince, the Flame-bearer of Rhiyana, who had raised his scarlet shield in all the lands from the sunrise to the sunset.

The King turned his eyes to Alf, only half-seeing the white tense face. "As soon as I can escape, I'm riding south. But I'll do this much for you: I won't take my army with me. Only my own knights, and whoever else pleases to come. Rhydderch will learn that he can't start a war without involving his King in it."

"Sire," Alf said, "this is madness. To destroy three kingdoms for a few days' pleasure—Sire, you can't!"

The lion-eyes glared. "Do you gainsay your King?"

Alf opened his mouth, closed it again. He knew how Alun had felt before Rhydderch. Helpless, and raging. And he could not loose his sorceries upon this madman as Alun had upon Rhydderch.

His head drooped. He had failed. He would have to tell Alun.

If he closed his eyes, he could see the Rhiyanan knight hobbling down a passageway, aided by a crutch and by a sturdy monk— Brother Edgar, who was simple but strong. Alun was intent upon his body's struggle, only dimly aware of the mind-touch. Alf withdrew. Later would be soon enough.

"Come now, Brother! Don't look so grim."

For a moment Alf recognized neither the voice nor the face. His own face had gone cold; Richard checked a moment, then slapped his shoulder. "We've both had enough of this. Ride out with me."

Alf rose slowly. Richard grimaced at his habit. "You can sit astride a horse in that?"

"Try me," Alf said.

The King grinned. "So I will. But boots you'll have—you won't gainsay me there." He turned away, calling for his own riding gear. "And boots for the Brother, Giraut; and mind you bring a pair that will fit!"

After the riding there was work to do, a charter to copy and a letter to write; and after that, a feast in the Earl's great hall. Richard kept Alf by him, although there were stares and murmurs at this blatant display of a new favorite; and such a fair one, with so grim an expression, who ate little and drank less and spoke not at all.

The Earl feasted his guests well though unwillingly, and regaled them with all the wealth of the North. His triumph was a minstrel who knew not only the latest airs from Languedoc, but the old songs of Anglia in the old tongue. "For," said the jongleur, tossing back his yellow mane, "my father was a troubadour in the court of the Court of Poictesme, but my mother was a Saxon; and she swore by King Harold's beard, though he was dead a full hundred years. She told me tales of the old time and my father taught me the songs of the south, and between them they made a jongleur. What will you have, then, my lords? Sweet tales of love?" His fingers lilted upon the lutestrings. "Deeds of old heroes?" A stirring martial tune. "A call to the path of virtue?" Stern didactic chords. "A drinking song?" An irresistibly cheerful and slightly drunken air. "Only speak, and whatever you ask for you shall have."

"War," the King said promptly. "Sing about war."

The minstrel bowed and began to play.

Alf toyed with his wine-cup, half-listening. He knew that Richard watched him. As did many another: Aylmer farther down the high table, and Jehan below among the squires, and Thea forgetting to play the proper hungry hound. He looked at none of them. *War,* he thought, hating it and all it meant. *War. Blood. Three kings, three kingdoms. I have to stop it. I have to.*

But how, he did not know.

Richard's voice rang out suddenly, cutting off the singer. "Enough of that! Sing us something new, man. With a moral in it that a priest would like to hear." As he spoke, he caught Alf's eye; the monk looked away.

The singer bowed in his seat and said, "His Majesty commands; I obey. There's a tale my mother used to tell me that's so old, maybe it's new again." He struck a sudden ringing note and intoned, *"Hwæt!"*

The listeners started; he laughed. "That's the Saxon for *Oyez!* Once on a time, my lords and ladies, which was in the old Angla-land, there was an abbey. There lived a cowherd named Caedmon. He was a gentle man, was Caedmon, but rather slow in the wits; everyone loved him, but everyone laughed at him, too: for that is the way people are, as we all know, sieurs.

"It was the custom then when there was a feast for the revelers to pass the harp round, and for each person to sing a song. Poor Caedmon dreaded that harp's coming, for he couldn't sing a note and he had never learned a song. When the harp drew near to him, he would get up and slink away to his byre, and hide in the dark and the silence and the warmth of the cows.

"One night, when he had fled from the singing and gone to his bed in the hayloft, he dreamed that a man came and greeted him and said, 'Caedmon, sing me something.' Caedmon was bitterly ashamed and like to weep, and he said, *'Ne con ic noht singan'*—'I don't know how to sing.' But the man, who was an angel of the Lord, insisted that Caedmon sing. Then Caedmon stood up, and lo! music came pouring out of him, the most beautiful song in the world. This is what he sang:

> '*Nu sculon herigean heofonrices Weard,*
> *Meotodes meahte ond his modgeþanc,*
> *weorc Wuldorfæder, swa he wundra gehwæs,*
> *ece Drihten, or onstealde.*
> *He ærest scop eorðan bearnum*
> *heofon to hrofe, halig Scyppend;*
> *þa middangeard moncynnes Weard,*
> *ece Drihten, æfter teode*
> *firum foldan, Frea ælmihtig.*'

And that in our feeble tongue is to say: 'Now must we praise the Guardian of heaven's kingdom, the might of the Measurer and His mind's thought, the work of the Father of glory, as He, eternal Lord, ordained the beginning of all wonders. First He shaped for the children of earth, heaven as a roof, a holy shaping; then afterward for men He created Middle-earth, the earth's surface—He, Guardian of Mankind, eternal Lord, almighty King.' "

The singer fell silent. There was a pause; then all at once the feasters began to applaud. He bowed and smiled and bowed again, and accepted a cup from the King's own hand. "Splendid!" Richard cried. "Wonderful! It's a pity we've let the old custom lapse. We ought to revive it." He paused, struck by his own words. "Well, and why not? Walter, fetch my harp! We'll all try our hand at it."

Several of the higher lords looked mildly appalled; their inferiors either feigned interest or answered sudden and urgent calls of nature. Alf saw one man's lips move as he struggled to recall a song.

By Richard's will they all tried the game, some well, some badly, with the aid of a free flow of wine. One dour-faced elderly knight startled them all with a bawdy drinking-song; Bishop Aylmer countered it with an *Ave Maria*.

At last there was only one who had not sung. "Come now," said the King, holding out the harp. "Are you a Caedmon, Brother Alfred? Sing me something!"

Alf took the harp slowly and set it on his knee. It had been a long lifetime since he had learned to play such an instrument from old Brother Æthelstan, who had been a gleeman in his youth. He tightened a string which had gone out of tune three songs ago and met the King's stare, his own level, almost defiant. His head bent, his fingers flickering through a melody. Down the hall, he sensed Jehan's start of recognition.

" '*Ut quid iubes, pusiole,*
quare mandas, filiole,
carmen dulce me cantare,
cum sim longe exsul valde
intra mare?
O! cur iubes canere?'"

" 'Why do you bid, beloved child, why do you command, my dearest son, that I should sing a sweet song, when I am an exile afar upon the sea? O! why do you bid me sing?' "

Richard was no scholar, but he knew enough Latin to understand Alf's meaning. His expression darkened as the song went on; then little by little it lightened. For the lament turned to a soaring hymn, companion to that which had begun it all, and Alf's eyes above the harp were bright, challenging.

His own eyes began to dance, amused, admiring. Here at last was one who could both obey him and gainsay him, yet who bore no taint of treachery.

Alf silenced the harp and returned it to the King, and slowly smiled.

13

The rain which had buried the town in mire gave way to a heavy blanket of snow. Richard cursed it and his court, which held him back from his war, though he prepared with as much speed as he might. "I'll be King of Gwynedd by spring," he vowed to Alf, "or I'll have Rhydderch's head on a pike and your I-told-you-so's in my ears from dawn until sundown."

"King Winter may prove stronger than Richard of Anglia," Alf said. "Why not yield to him and spare yourself a struggle?"

"Am I to turn craven before a flake or two of snow? I'll ride south before the month is out, you and winter and all the rest of it be damned."

*   *   *

So might they well be, Alf thought as he made his way from the castle to the Bishop's palace. It was late, and dark, and it had begun to snow again; he huddled into the cloak Richard had given him.

All at once he realized that he had fallen into the midst of a small company, youths with the King's livery under their cloaks, three of Richard's squires escaped from their duties. He tensed and walked more quickly.

But they had seen and recognized him. "Hoi!" one called out. "It's Pretty-boy!"

They surrounded him, solid young men, battle-hardened. Their eyes glittered; they hemmed him in, wolves advancing upon tender prey.

He had averted his own eyes instinctively, lest they catch the light and flare ember-red. Wherever he turned stood a squire, grinning. He stopped. "Please, sieurs," he said. "It's late and I have no time to spare."

They laughed. " 'Please, sieurs. Pretty please, sieurs. Oh, prithee, let me go home to my cold, cold bed!' " One took his arm, friendly-wise. "Poor little Brother. I'll wager you've never had a proper good time. We'll have to fix that, won't we, lads?"

The others chorused assent. Alf stood still. Perhaps, if he pretended to play their game, they would let him go.

They herded him toward an alehouse. The ringleader, a handsome dark-curled fellow whom the others called Joscelin, held still to his arm. "Come, little Brother," he said. "Join us in a mug or two. Or three. We all know how well a priest can hold his ale."

They reached the tavern's door and swarmed through it. The room was crowded; it reeked of smoke, of sour ale, and of unwashed bodies. The three squires and their unwilling guest elbowed their way to a table, put to flight the townsmen who had occupied it, and shouted for ale.

Joscelin clung close to Alf, stroking-close. The other two were content to laugh; he shot small barbs meant to draw blood. "It isn't sacramental wine we get here, but it's not refectory ale either. Drink up, pretty Brother. I'm paying."

Alf stared at a brimming mug. It was not clean, he noticed. Abruptly he swept it up and drained it in three long gulps.

Another appeared, and another. He felt nothing but a heaviness of the stomach, although his companions, having matched him mug for mug, were beginning to wax hilarious. He measured the distance to the door, considered all the obstacles between, and waited for his chance.

After the fourth round, as the serving girl withdrew, Joscelin seized her plump wrist and pulled her back. She came with but a token protest, giggling on a high note. "Here, Bess," he said. "What do you think of our clerkly friend?"

Her eyes flicked over Alf, once, twice. Cold clear eyes, shrill titter. "Oh, he's *handsome!*"

"Handsomer than I?"

She tittered. "Well, sir, I really couldn't—"

"Of course you could. Because he is. And do you know something?" Joscelin's voice lowered, but it was no less penetrating. "He's never been with a woman." He stressed the last word very slightly.

Again that swift appraisal. Alf kept his eyes lowered, but he heard her maddening giggle. "He *hasn't?*"

Suddenly she was in his lap. She was warm and soft, flowing out of her tight bodice; and she stank.

He shrank a little, fastidiously. She took it for shyness and pressed herself close, nuzzling his neck.

For all her squirmings, he felt nothing but disgust. Gently but firmly, with strength that made her stop and stare, he set her on her feet and handed her his mug. "May we have more ale, please?"

"Bravo, Brother!" Joscelin cried. "Another triumph for Holy Church. Or maybe we've made the wrong offer. Perkin! Perkin lad, where are you?"

Alf rose. "I have to go."

All three united in pulling him down. "Oh, no, Brother," Joscelin purred. "It must get monotonous to spend all your time with men. You need a change."

"All beds look alike," hiccoughed the youngest squire. "So do all backsides."

"Sirs," Alf said carefully, "I wish you a pleasant night. But I must go."

"He can wait, can't he?" Joscelin smiled at him, all sweetness. "He'll have to wait until we've made a man of you."

The others held him down, one on either side, grinning at his white-lipped silence. At last he gritted, "You will tire of waiting before I will."

Joscelin shook his head. "We won't wait. Come on, lads. And hold tight."

Alf felt as if he were trapped in a nightmare. Memories flashed through his brain, a thin pale child set upon with stones and cudgels and cries of changeling and witch's get; a young novice baited by his fellows, mocked for his strangeness; a man with a boy's face, taunted in the schools of Paris for his beauty and his shyness, and made a butt of cruel pranks. And helpless, always helpless, until Morwin or another came to his rescue.

The room to which the squires led him was as fetid as the one below, and occupied. It was not fragrant Bess who lay on the bed there but a younger woman, thinner, almost pretty under the dirt. He could see that very well, as she had nothing to cover it. He looked away.

His captors laughed. He knew what they would do to him, but his struggles had no strength. They tore his habit from neck to navel, baring his upper body. Morwin's cross glittered on his breast; Joscelin snatched at it. There was a brief sharp pain; the squire held the broken chain and smiled. "Pretty," he said, slipping it into the purse he wore at his belt. "Let's see what the rest of you is like."

Alf lunged toward him. The squires tore at him, rending skin with cloth, stripping off his habit. He snatched in vain; they gripped him with iron fingers. He hung there gasping.

"Well." Joscelin whistled softly. *"Well.* Aren't you a beauty? Look, Molly; see what Rome and Sodom claim for themselves. A mortal shame, that."

There was a point beyond shame; a cold calm point, that was not numbness, nor even acceptance. Seventy years, Alf thought. Seventy years, and he had never struck a blow. Such a good Christian monk he had been.

Deep within him, darkness stirred. *Enough,* it whispered. *Enough.*

He stood erect. A shrug: he was free. One of the squires wore a sword; swifter than human sight he swooped upon it. Cold steel gleamed in his hand.

They were not afraid. He had no skill with weapons—they all knew that. "My, my," warbled the youngest. "Look at the Church Militant. The cross is mightier than the sword, you know."

"And if that fails, take a Bible and throw it," the second added.

"Or at the last," Joscelin said, third in their chorus, "waggle your white behind."

He barely heard. His hand knew the sword; knew it as it knew its own fingers. His arm balanced easily with its weight of steel; his body crouched, ready for battle.

"Oh, come," Joscelin chided him. *"That's* not the sword you'll use. Put it down like a good lad and stop frightening poor Molly."

"Molly is not afraid." Alf's voice was cold. "Molly is excited. She thinks that she will have me when I am done with you. She is a fool. I do not fornicate with animals."

He felt her anger as a burning pinprick, and heeded it not at all. The squires had begun to tremble. His face was white and set; his sword flickered swiftly, darting toward each in turn. They had stripped a meek monkish boy and found a beast of prey.

But Joscelin, being clever, was slowest to understand. He laughed and drew his own sword. "Why, sir! You want to duel? It's a little cramped here, but I'll be happy to oblige you."

The others had scrambled out of the way. Alf measured the one who was left. They were nearly of a height and nearly of a weight, but the squire wielded a heavier weapon. His own blade was shorter and lighter, balanced for a single hand; a mere sliver against the great two-handed broadsword.

Joscelin circled; Alf followed. The door was at the squire's back; he backed through it, leaped and spun, and bolted down the stair.

Alf read him clearly. Either the priest would remember his nakedness and shrink from pursuit, or he would forget and run full into the laughter of the crowd below.

Alf snatched at shadows, fingers flying, and wrapped them about his body. They clung and grew and made a robe like dark velvet, girdled with a flare of sword-light.

Joscelin clattered still upon the stair. Alf sprang after him.

They met at the bottom, dark eyes wide to see him so well and swiftly clad, pale eyes lit with a feral light. This game was not ending as Joscelin had planned it. He essayed a light, mocking smile, playing to the large and fascinated audience. "Come now, friend," he said. "I told you you could have her."

Alf said nothing, but his blade flickered like a serpent's tongue. There was a wicked delight in this skill that seemed to grow from the muscles themselves, inborn, effortless. If he had known what he had when he was a boy, no one would ever have dared to torment him. If he had known what a wonder it was, he would have plunged gladly into the heart of Richard's battle. But he knew now, and he knew what he was. Kin to the great cats, the leopard, the panther, swift and strong and deadly dangerous.

The prey, baited, had become the hunter; and now at last Joscelin knew it. The blood had drained from his face. He glanced about, searching desperately for an opening. There was none. Cold steel wove a cage about him. With each pass it drew closer, until its edge flickered a hair's breadth from his body.

His blood would taste most sweet. But his terror was sweeter. Alf smiled into his eyes, and neatly, with consummate skill, sent each of his long dark curls tumbling to the floor. He dared not even breathe lest his ears follow, or his nose, or his head itself.

When he was shorn from crown to nape—laughter erupting behind, and cheers, and wagers laid and paid—Alf leaned close. "Am I a man?" he asked, very softly.

The squire's eyes were rimmed with white. Yet some remnant of pride made him laugh, a hideous, hollow sound. "Not yet, Sir Priestling, though you're not an ill barber."

A panther, prodded, strikes without thought. Alf struck, but not, in some last glimmer of sanity, with the sword's edge. The flat of it caught Joscelin beneath the ear and felled him without a sound.

Slowly Alf turned. The cheering died. Someone offered him a mug, grinning.

Still gripping the sword, he ran from them all.

The snow had stopped; a bitter wind was blowing, scattering the clouds. Alf welcomed the cold upon his burning face. He stumbled against hard stone and vomited. Even after his stomach was empty, he crouched heaving, soul-sick. People passed with no pity to spare for a drunken soldier. At last he staggered erect. His robe was heavy with sorcery; he tore at it until it melted away, leaving him bare in the cold.

His fingers were numb, frozen about the sword hilt. He dragged it behind him, stopping again for illness, and yet again. He had hated and he had used sorcery and he had almost killed. He had given torment for torment and thirsted for blood.

What does it matter? a small voice taunted. *You'll never die. You have no soul. Nothing you do can damn you.*

"My conscience can!" he cried.

The voice laughed. *How can you have a conscience if you have no soul?*

"I do. It torments me." He fell into a heap of snow, and lay there. No owls would come to warm him now. If he was immortal, could he freeze to death?

Try and see. His second self sounded as if it already knew the answer. *You and your delusions,* it went on. *You think you have a conscience, because your teachers said you must have one. It's all delusion. You have no soul. You cannot sin.*

"*No!*" he shouted. "That's black heresy."

How can it be? You can be neither damned nor saved. Your mind is your only standard. Your mind and your body. You were a fool to refuse that woman and to let that boy live, for fear of what does not and cannot touch you.

"God is," he countered. "He can touch me."

How? And if He can, what sense is there in anything? He created you, if He exists, to live forever. He denied you the reward He dangles before humans. He gave you a body with beauty and strength and potent maleness; yet He would have you deny it all, and worship His arrogance, and thank Him for forbidding you to be what you were made to be.

Alf twisted, struggling to escape from that sweet deadly voice. "I serve Him as best I may, whatever the cost."

Do you? Look at you. Your face tempts humans away from virtue; your body incites even your own kind to active lust. If you would serve your paradox of a god, take that sword you clutch so tightly, and scar your face, and maim your body, and cut away your useless manhood.

He shuddered. "I can't destroy what God gave me."

Laughter rang, cold and scornful. *Can't, can't. Pick yourself up, and let your body do what it wants to do. The woman, the boy, even the King: take them all, and rule them. They're but human. They'll kiss your feet.*

"No," he gasped. "No."

The elf-maid, the voice purred. *She is yours for the asking. And she is no foul-scented animal. She is of your own kind, and most fair: and she yearns after you. Go. Take her.*

He clapped his hands over his ears, but it was useless. The voice was in his brain, teasing, tempting, luring him down into darkness. He was immortal, he was beautiful, he was powerful. He could be lord of the world, if he but stretched out his hand.

He raised his head. The sword lay beside him, half-hidden in snow. Death dwelt in it; death even for one who would not grow old. And after, nothing. Was he not soulless?

He set the hilt in the snow and turned the point toward his body, leaning forward until it pricked his breast above the hammering heart.

14

"Have you gone mad?"

Alf recoiled, dropping the sword. A swift hand snatched it up and hurled it away. He never knew where it fell, for Thea had seized him and held him with strength greater than any man's. Her face was white and her eyes were wild; she looked fully as uncanny as she was.

His hand moved to cover himself. She was clad, for once, in his own spare habit and Gwydion's cloak. "Even in that," he said, "you're far fairer than the other was."

She threw the cloak over him and made him walk with her, half-leading, half-dragging him.

"I didn't want her," he went on. "She disgusted me. She was an animal; and she stank. She made me realize something. I'm truly not human, and I have no tolerance for those who are."

She did not speak. She had drawn up the cowl; he could not see her face.

"No tolerance," he repeated. "I almost killed someone tonight. In the end I don't know why I didn't. I humiliated him terribly, but I let him live. I *let* him live. I had that power, Thea. And I wanted it. I delighted in it."

"That's no excuse to throw yourself on your sword."

He pulled away from her with sudden violence. "You don't understand."

"Unfortunately," she said, "I do."

She was speaking to his back. He had fled from her.

Jehan sat late in the Bishop's library, peering at a very old text by candlelight. It was in Greek, and strange, crabbed, difficult Greek at that; he wished that Brother Alf would come to help with it as he had promised. The candle had burned alarmingly low, and still there was no sign of him. The King had never kept him quite so late before.

Jehan rubbed his eyes and yawned. He would wait a little longer; then he would go to bed. He had Mass to serve in the morning and arms-practice after, and lessons with Father Michael, who had just come back from Paris.

The door opened upon a familiar brown habit. He half-rose, framing words, welcome, rebuke.

Alf looked pale, almost ill. When he spoke, cutting off what the other would have said, his voice was faint. "Come with me. Quickly."

Jehan rose fully. "What's wrong?"

"There's no time," Alf said. "Just come."

After a moment's hesitation, Jehan followed him. He moved swiftly and in silence, cowl drawn up. When they left the Bishop's palace for the outer darkness, Jehan could not see him; a thin strong hand gripped his wrist and drew him onward.

He knew where he was by scent more than by sight. Hay and horses and leather: a stable. A dim light glowed at the far end, shining upon a white shape. Fara. Alf led him to her.

There was something in the straw at her feet; from it came the light, welling through folds of dark fabric. Jehan discerned a human shape drawn into a knot, arms wrapped about its head.

He knelt. The figure was naked under the cloak, drawing tighter as he touched it; and he knew it. He turned to his guide, wild-eyed.

Alf's habit. But not his stance nor his height, nor ever his face, that pale oval within the cowl, with its frame of dark hair and its dark winged brows and its eyes gleaming green. Nor was that his voice. His was golden; this was shaken silver. "Yes, I tricked you; but I brought you here without a fuss."

"But how——" he began.

She cut him off. "Later. That really is your little Brother, and he needs a strong dose of common sense."

Jehan looked from her to Alf, seeing the likeness between them. "What's happened to him? Why is he like this?"

She told him, succinctly. His fists clenched and his face hardened. "You," he said when she was done, his voice level, controlled. "Are you the woman?"

She laughed aloud. Fara snorted at the sound. "Dear God, no! If I had been, he'd be there still, and the better for it too."

"Who are you then? What are you doing here?"

Her eyes danced, mocking him. "Don't you know me yet? I've run at your heels for close upon a fortnight."

He stared thunderstruck. "Thea?"

"Thea," she agreed with but little patience. She knelt beside

Jehan and contemplated Alf's still body. "He's more than half mad, you know. After a lifetime of self-delusion, he's had a very rude awakening; he doesn't want to face it."

"Why?" Jehan demanded harshly. "What has he awakened to?"

"The truth. Your monks raised him to think he was a gentle little ringdove, but he's grown into an eagle. And he's just discovered that he has talons."

"No wonder he's terrified." Jehan touched the tense shoulder gently. "Brother Alf. It's all right. I'm here."

There was no response. Thea frowned, but Jehan sensed concern beneath her impatience. "I couldn't do anything with him, either."

"Did you really try?" Again Jehan touched Alf's shoulder. "Brother Alf, it's late, and I've been waiting for hours for you to help me with Dionysius. Won't you come back and go to bed?"

Alf was still for so long that Jehan feared he had failed again. Then the knot loosened, and Alf lay on his back, open-eyed, staring at nothing. "No," he said. "I can't go back. I've sinned mortally. I tried to kill a man, and I tried to kill myself."

"You were provoked," Jehan pointed out steadily, though he wanted to cry. "I'd have tried to kill that son of a sow too."

"It was still a sin. If I can sin. I may not have a soul, Jehan."

The other shook his head firmly. "I don't believe that."

Alf did not seem to have heard. "I wrote the *Gloria Dei*. Even in Rome they sang its praises: the jewel of theological works, the triumph of orthodoxy over heresy. I wrote it in a grand fire of arrogance, in utter certainty of its truth. It is true; I know that, and Rome knows it. But if I am a creature of darkness, a soulless one whose other self is a sword, then what does that make all my pretensions to piety?"

"Logic," said Thea, "is a wonderful thing. But you carry it too far. '*Mouse* is a syllable,' you say. 'A mouse eats cheese. Therefore, a syllable eats cheese.'"

In spite of himself, Jehan laughed. "She's right, Brother Alf. So you're different; so you've never got old. God made you, didn't He? He let you see enough of Him to write your *Gloria*."

Alf closed his eyes. "And people say that I was a changeling, a demon's get; and when I was anointed a priest, the oil cast a spell on me, holding me as I was then, a boy of seventeen."

"Nonsense," snapped Thea. "Get up and face the truth. You are wallowing. You have been wallowing for most of your life. And tonight you found out that you had a temper, by God and all His angels, as if the lowest human cur didn't have one too. Why, even the Christ got angry once and whipped the money-changers out of his Temple. Have you been trying to outdo him?"

He leaped up, eyes blazing. "How dare you speak so?"

"There now. A little honest anger—though your piety is false. You should get angry more often and less piously. Then you won't be tempted to barber brats of squires with a sword."

Alf sank down, head in hands. "Go away," he muttered. "Go away."

"Brother Alf," Jehan said. "She's right. You're taking this too hard. You had to leave St. Ruan's, and the King wouldn't listen when you asked for peace, and those idiots of squires treated you too foully for words. Of course you went a little wild. Come to bed now and get some sleep. In the morning you'll feel better."

Alf let Jehan draw him to his feet again, but he would not go. "The cross," he said. "Morwin's cross. Joscelin took it. And I—I forgot—"

"Poor little Brother." Thea held up a glimmer of silver. "This was much too precious to waste on the likes of him. I rescued it. Mended it, too." She slipped the chain over Alf's head and settled it on his breast.

His hand sought the cold silver as if for comfort. She smiled at him, half in mockery, half in something else, and melted. The white hound wriggled out of the habit under Jehan's wide eyes, and nosed it disdainfully. *Here's something to preserve your modesty. Put it on and go to bed.*

Alf fumbled into the robe, gathered up the cloak, and shook straw from them both. He paused to stroke Fara's neck and to quiet her concern for him; and followed the others.

Some moments after they had gone, a shadow slipped from a host of its fellows and glided after them.

15

Alf did not wake all at once as he usually did, but sluggishly, reluctantly. Long before he opened his eyes, he sensed that he was alone.

He sat up slowly. His hands stung; he stared at them. Each palm bore two thin, parallel cuts. He closed his fingers over them and rose.

The air tasted of full morning, with a touch of incense, and of bread for the day-meal, and of smoke from the kitchen fires. Mass was long since over; everyone had gone about his work. Even Thea was out, pursuing her own business; her mind-touch was sharp, swift, preoccupied.

He bathed with exaggerated care, as if water could wash away the memory of the night. When he dressed, it was in the garments Alun had lent him.

The King was looking for him. But something within him had broken when he took up the sword and had not yet mended. When he left, it was to the stable that he went.

He rode out alone by ways he knew from his riding with the King. The moors rolled away before him, lands that had been empty since the legions marched along the Wall of the Emperor, white now and still, dazzling in fitful sunlight. Away from the town in a hollow of the hills, a small glassy tarn reflected the changeful sky. There he halted, stripped off the mare's saddle and bridle, and hid them in the heather. She stood still, head up, breathing deep of the free air. "Go," he said to her. "Run as you will."

She bent her head and nuzzled his hands. Would he not go with her?

He smoothed her forelock. "I need to think," he said. "I can't do it back there. But you needn't linger with me. Go; be free."

His words made no sense to her. She turned and knelt, inviting him to mount.

He framed a protest, thought better of it. Even as he settled upon her back, she straightened and sprang into a gallop.

* * *

The sun hung low when they returned to the tarn. A white hound guarded the saddle, rising as a woman and inspecting them both with approval. "You look well," Thea said.

Alf slid from Fara's back and stood with his hand on her neck. "I've shirked all my duties."

Thea wrapped his cloak about her and helped him to saddle and bridle the mare. "The King is yelling for you," she said as he tightened the girths.

"Is he angry?"

"Upset. He's already heard about your adventure with his squires. The two boys are riding home as soon as he can spare escorts for them. He wasn't even going to do that, but Aylmer talked some sense into him. As for Master Joscelin, he's locked in a cell. He'll get his sentence as soon as Richard cools down enough to pass it. It will be dismissal at the very least; Richard can't decide whether to strike his head off or to condemn him to keep it as you've left it."

Alf turned to her, dismayed. "He can't do that! Those children have already suffered enough, between the fear I put into them and the ridicule they've won themselves. They don't need any more punishment."

"Except a good whipping."

"They didn't know what they were doing." He gathered up the reins. "I'd better go back and talk to the King."

Thea caught his arm. "Wait." He stopped. Her face was pale, and more serious than he had ever seen it. "Brother, Richard's not the only one who's upset. The tale has grown in the telling. You're the hero of it still in most places—but not in all. Some people are saying that you did more than prove your prowess with a sword. That you used sorcery."

"I did," Alf said.

She shook him hard. "Haven't you got your wits back yet? Reynaud and his Hounds have been closeted with Bishop Foulques. Who's no friend to either Aylmer or the King. And whose brother is assistant to the Pauline Father General."

Alf nodded calmly. "I know that. Will you let me go? I have to see the King."

"You *are* mad." But she released him. He mounted and turned the mare's head toward Carlisle.

Even as Fara moved forward, a weight settled on the crupper; arms circled his waist. "Now," Thea said in his ear. "Tell me what you know that I don't."

He looked back and started. It was still Thea, but Thea changed, dressed as a farmgirl, with a brown freckled face. She laughed at him. "I had to give you a reason for being out all day, didn't I?"

"No," he answered. "You didn't. Get down and run as a hound."

"Oh, no. I won't give you the pleasure. I think I know what you're up to, little Brother, and it's rampant folly."

"What am I up to?"

"Self-sacrifice. Holy martyrdom. Giving your all to the cause of the Elvenking." He said nothing. "See how well I know you. You rode out in a great passion of despair; you cast that despair to the winds; you prayed and you meditated, and you rediscovered serenity. And then, behold! a revelation. Fiends and false prophets are plotting against you. What to do? Flight is wisest. But wisdom has never been your great virtue. Why not stand and face the consequences of your own foolishness? You'll win the delay you've prayed for, bind Richard until spring and give Gwydion time to plan another embassy. And last but far from least, put an end to your dilemma. The Hounds will burn you if you tell them the truth."

"Yes," he said. "They will."

"What did you tell Alun about suicide?"

"He had something to live for. His lady, his brother, all his people. And I . . . I was an innocent. I didn't really understand what I'm capable of. Nor was I sure that there wasn't some way to reconcile the two halves of myself. Now I know better. I can't be both monk and enchanter; I can't be only one of the two. Even when I try to be a plain man, my power slips its chain and betrays me. I'll destroy myself whatever I do. Why not to some purpose?"

"Noble," she said. "Stupid. You may be as old as most humans ever get, little Brother, but you're the merest child."

"Are you any more?"

"Probably not. But I didn't grow up in a cloister. I've been hunted as these Hounds hunt you."

"You weren't caught."

"I didn't mean to be."

He was silent, his eyes fixed upon the walls of Carlisle. Yet he was very much aware of Thea's presence. Strange, he thought. The women in the tavern had roused only disgust; and they had set themselves to seduce him. Thea, fully clothed and decorously riding pillion, and calling to mind all his troubles, made him want to abandon his vows.

Why not? his dark self asked in the deep cell to which he had banished it. *You seek your own death. You know you cannot be either damned or saved. What would it matter if you had your way with her?*

And she would welcome it. But he could not. He was a fool, as she had said, and a coward. That would be his epitaph.

Just within the city's gate, the mare halted. Thea slid to the ground in full view of the guards. "Thanks to you, sir," she said in the broad accent of the North.

Alf flushed. People were staring; most knew who he was. He wheeled the mare about without speaking.

"Thank you for the ride!" she shrilled behind him. Somewhere, someone laughed.

16
🌿

Jehan was at arms-practice when a monk brought a summons from Bishop Aylmer. He had been tilting at the quintain with two or three of the younger warrior-priests; and he was more than a year out of practice. Misaimed strokes or over-slow reactions had brought the wooden Saracen spinning round more times than he could count, to return his own blows with ones at least as heavy. He ached all over; he was glad to stop.

Stripped of his heavily padded practice armor and bathed and dressed, he presented himself at the door of the Bishop's library. Lamps glimmered there, for the high narrow windows let in little light; Aylmer stood near the far wall, listening as a secretary read from a charter. When Jehan entered, he dismissed the man and beckoned. "Ah, Jehan. How went it with the quintain?"

Jehan grinned ruefully. "Terrible," he answered. "I think my father's right. I've gone soft."

"Give yourself time," Aylmer said. "I hear you're doing somewhat better with the sword."

"A little, my lord."

Aylmer nodded toward a chair. He sat carefully to spare his bruised muscles; the Bishop watched with amusement. "How old are you now?" he asked.

"Just sixteen, my lord."

"So?" Aylmer's brows rose. "You'll grow rather more, I think."

"My father's a big man. So is my brother Robert. The others are too young to tell, but they're all robust little monsters. Even my sister Alys."

The Bishop smiled a rare warm smile. "Yes: I've heard of the Sevignys. A proper pride of lions, those."

"We hold our own," said Jehan.

"You do," Aylmer agreed. "Father Michael speaks well of your scholarship. Very well, in fact."

Jehan rubbed a callus on his sword hand and sighed involuntarily. Father Michael had not been pleased to see his new pupil. Quite the contrary. Was he, who had sat at the feet of the greatest scholars in Christendom, to be condemned to teach grammar to this great ox of an Earl's son?

He had made no secret of his contempt. "Do you know Latin?" he had demanded in the vernacular.

"Yes," Jehan had answered in the same language.

"So." The priest had barely concealed his sneer. "Say in Latin: 'The boy sees the dog.' "

Jehan had obliged. And continued to oblige because it amused him, though his good humor had begun to wear thin. At last, as Father Michael framed yet another simple sentence, he had said in the Latin which Master Peter had taught him and Brother Osric refined and Brother Alf perfected, "Father, this is very pleasant, but isn't it rather dull? Could we do a little Vergil? Or maybe a bit of Martianus?"

He smiled even yet to remember Father Michael's face. Skeptical at first, but breaking into incredulity and then into joy. "God in heaven!" he had cried. "The ox has a brain!"

Aylmer had marked both sigh and smile. "Troubles, lad?"

"No," Jehan answered. "Not really. By now I should be used to the way people react to me. I've got such a big body and such a stupid face. But actually, inside, I'm a skinny little rat with his nose in a book."

Aylmer laughed aloud. "Hoi, lad! you're good for me. Here, have an apple. They're from your own St. Ruan's, the Isle of Apples itself."

"Are they?" Jehan took one from the bowl on the table. "They call it Ynys Witrin, too, you know. Though I've heard that the real Isle isn't even in the world."

"The Land of Youth. Yes." While Jehan nibbled at the apple, Aylmer wandered down the line of books, pausing now and then to peer at a title. At the end, he turned. "Do you think there's such a place?"

"There's a lot in the world I don't know, and a lot out of it. Maybe there is a real Ynys Witrin, or Tir-na-n'Og, or Elysium. Or maybe they're all just other names for Heaven."

"Maybe," said Aylmer. He came to sit by Jehan across the table. "Some people say that the mystic realm is right across the water in Rhiyana."

"I've heard that."

"Your mother is Rhiyanan, isn't she?"

"Yes, my lord. She's the Earl's daughter of Caer Dhu."

"Kin to the King, I hear."

Jehan finished the apple and set the core upright on the table. "Distantly. She never went to court. She was fostered by a lord and lady in Poictesme, and married my father when she was barely out of childhood." His eyes upon Aylmer were wide, blue, and guileless. "Are you curious about Gwydion, my lord?"

The Bishop's cheek twitched. "Somewhat," he admitted. "When you were in St. Ruan's, did you talk much with the Rhiyanan knight?"

"I took care of him," answered Jehan. "He slept a lot. Sometimes he talked. He wasn't the talkative sort. He was very quiet, actually, unless he had something to say."

"What did he look like?"

Jehan shrugged. "Rhiyanan. Tall, black hair, gray eyes. Face like a falcon's."

"Young?"

"Rather. Old enough to be a knight, but not much older."

"Well-born?"

"Yes." Jehan tipped over the apple core, and rolled it from hand to hand.

"Was he one of the elven-folk?"

The apple core stopped. "Do they exist?" Jehan asked with a touch of surprise.

"So it's said." Aylmer shifted in his chair and sighed. "So it's said. Did you know that the Monks of St. Paul are forbidden to preach or to found abbeys in Rhiyana?"

"Are they? Why?"

"It's the King's command. The old Orders are sufficient, he says, and the Church in his kingdom is thriving. It needs no Hounds to hunt its heretics."

"Or its Fair Folk? If they exist," Jehan added.

"If they do," agreed Aylmer. "Tell me. Where was Brother Alfred born?"

Jehan went cold. Brother Reynaud he could deal with; for all his cleverness, the man was an idiot. But Bishop Aylmer was another matter altogether.

"He was born somewhere near St. Ruan's," he said. "I don't know where. He was one of the abbey's orphans. There are always a few about. Most grow up and take some sort of vows—by then they're used to the cloister, you see. They tend to forget exactly where they were from, and so does everybody else." He paused. "Brother Alf isn't Rhiyanan, if that's what you're wondering. I think maybe he's Saxon."

"You and he are close friends."

"I don't know about that," Jehan said. "I used to bother him to help me with my books. He was my teacher for a while. Then we came here."

"He taught you?"

"Well. Somebody had to."

Aylmer did not smile, but his eyes glinted. "Isn't it odd that he should have been teaching you? You must be almost of an age."

"Not really. He'd been there all along, and he's brilliant."

"Like his namesake, the other Alfred? I used to dream of sitting at the great scholar's feet and being his disciple. But I never had the chance; and when I was in St. Ruan's last year, he was ill and seeing no one."

"I remember," Jehan said. "I'd just come to the abbey."

"Had you? I never saw you. Though I saw young Brother Alfred. He struck me as a remarkable boy."

"And he doesn't now? Is that why you're asking about him?" Jehan's fists knotted. "That's not true, my lord! He's all you thought he was. But he's having troubles. He's not used to living in the world, and he never wanted or expected to be the King's friend, and people are cruel to him. They can't stand someone who's good and brilliant and handsome, all at once."

The Bishop's smile won free. "Now, lad, there's no need to shout at me. I like to think that I can judge a man by those who love him; and by that reckoning, he doesn't have many equals."

"He doesn't by any reckoning," Jehan muttered.

"I think not. But there's another side to this. Brother Alfred has friends of very high quality indeed. Unfortunately, his enemies are at least as powerful, and more numerous besides."

"The Hounds!"

Aylmer's eyes narrowed. "You know of them?"

"They've been after me about Brother Alf. Who is he, what is he, what do I know about him?"

"Last night," Aylmer said, watching him under heavy brows, "there was an uproar in one of the alehouses in the town. Brother Alfred, it's said, was in the middle of it."

Jehan sat still, his face blank.

"There were unusual circumstances," the Bishop continued. "Alarming ones, some think. Have you ever tried to shave a man with a sword?"

"Shave him? With a *sword?*" Jehan laughed. "It's hard enough to land a proper blow."

"According to the tales I've heard, our frail young Brother, who was raised from infancy in an abbey, barbered a man with a sword as well as any surgeon with a razor."

There was a long pause. "My lord," Jehan said slowly. "I saw Brother Alf last night. He was awfully sick. Not drunk. Just very sick. It was inside more than out. He wanted to die, my lord."

That caught Aylmer off guard. He leaned forward. "What!"

"He wanted to die. A—a friend found him. Stopped him, and came and got me."

Jehan thought he could decipher Aylmer's expression. Deeply shocked, and—concerned? "Why? What happened?"

"I'm not absolutely sure. I do think . . . the stories may be true. But he's no devil, my lord. Nor any devil's servant."

"God knows," Aylmer muttered, "I want to believe that."

"You're learning to love him," Jehan said. "The best people always do. But the rest hate him. It's that hate that makes the Hounds want to hunt him."

"It's more than that, lad."

"Not much more," Jehan said fiercely. "He's so much more God's creature than any of the rest of us. The world scares him witless. Last night he tried to run away from it. He still wants to. And now the hunt is up. He'll run right into the middle of it." He struck the heavy table with his fist, rocking it upon its legs. "Why can't people leave him alone?"

"Because," Aylmer answered, "he isn't like anyone else. I'll shield him if I can. But I may not be able to."

"No one will. And he'll die, and I—I'll kill the man who does it to him!" Jehan leaped up and ran blindly for the door.

The apple core had fallen to the floor. Aylmer set it on the table, carefully upright; and sat for a long while unmoving.

17

Alf paused in the doorway of the King's bedchamber. It was a small room, little more than a cell, dominated by a great carved and curtained bed; Richard had concealed the bare walls with several layers of hangings, and set in it a brazier from the East that did what it could to dispel the northern cold.

The King sat near the coals in hose and fur-lined cotte, playing at chess with Earl Hugo. A lamp hung above them, swinging slightly in the draft that lifted the heavy tapestries, casting its uncertain glow upon the board and the carven pieces. The white knights were warriors of Allah, the black heavy and lumpen in chain mail upon Frankish chargers; the white king a Saracen sultan, the black a Christian with a crown of crosses and leaves.

Richard set a black castle before the ivory sultan. "Checkmate, my lord," he said.

Earl Hugo glowered at the board. "Checkmate," he agreed at last. "Sire."

The King smiled at him, a deceptively gentle smile. "A good game, sir. And," he added, "a good night."

Alf stepped aside to let Hugo pass. The Earl glanced at him and started, and crossed himself.

The poison was spreading rapidly. Alf entered the room, letting the door-curtain fall behind him.

Richard stood by the chessboard. His eyes were very bright. "Well, Brother," he said. "You're later than usual."

Alf bowed slightly and said nothing. His gaze rested upon the chessboard, where a mitered bishop stood beside the Frankish king.

"Sit," the King commanded him.

He obeyed, taking the chair the Earl had left. Richard took up the ebony king and turned it in his hands. "I'm fond of this," he said. "The Sultan Saladin gave it to me, a token of our battles and our truce."

"Are you at war with me now?" Alf asked quietly.

Richard set the chessman in the center of the board and took from a cabinet a flask and two silver cups. He filled them both and gave one to Alf. "You were out all day," he said. "Why?"

"I needed to be alone."

"Longing for your cloister?"

Alf shook his head.

"Liar." Richard sat at his ease, sipping from his cup. "It's quieter there, isn't it? No wars. No kings. No drunken squires."

Under the King's keen eye, Alf sat very still. "They didn't know what they were doing."

Richard spat a curse. "They knew, plague take them. They knew exactly what they did."

Alf looked up, a startling, silver flare. "No," he said. "They didn't. Or they would never have dared."

The King paused. This was an Alf he had never seen, bright, brittle, dangerous. "They told me a fine tale," he said, "of swords and sorcery, and a monk turned demon. Are you an elven-knight in disguise?"

"No knight, I."

"But a master of the sword. Twenty men swear to that—and one is my own master-at-arms."

Alf's fingers clenched about the cup. "I . . . avoid weapons. They tempt me."

"Sweeter than women, aren't they? I wish I'd seen you. Thierry was almost crying. That sweet touch, that perfect control, wasted on a pious shavepate."

"Not wasted," Alf said very low. "Buried deep, and well buried. I think . . . I think I am a killer by nature."

"Aren't we all?"

With an effort Alf unlocked his fingers. They had bent the cup's rim into a narrow oval. He set it down and wiped his hands on his breeches. "All men may be," he said, "but I am worse than most. Or would be, if God's grace had not set me in St. Ruan's."

"God's grace." Richard snorted in derision. "God's japery. With ample help from Mother Church. Look what they've made of you—a butt for every snot-nosed brat who happens by. You who should be out in the lists, daring the Flame-bearer himself to throw you down."

"Whatever I should have been, this I am. And I regret that I ever let my temper destroy my reason. It was unpardonable."

"So was what caused it."

"No." Alf dropped to one knee. "Sire. Pardon the boys who mocked me. One night's hell-raising is not worth three noblemen's disgrace."

The King's brows drew together. "It isn't?"

"Never, Sire. They won't trouble me again. I can assure you of that."

"When they attacked you, they attacked me. They knew it. And they know that they're getting off lightly in only being sent home."

"In dishonor, my lord; and one is in fetters now. Would you make enemies of all his kin, simply because he failed to carry off a prank? Isn't it enough that all Carlisle is laughing at him?"

"By God, no!"

Alf stood. "Then, Sire, you are a fool."

As he reached the door, the King seized him and spun him about.

The hand on Alf's arm was cruelly tight. He glanced from it to the furious face. "Pardon them," he said.

Richard's jaw worked. His fingers tightened, and suddenly sprang free. He stood still, fists clenching and unclenching, battling to master his voice. "You," he said thickly. "You damned, pious, preaching priest."

Alf smiled faintly. "All of that," he agreed, "I may well be. Let the squires go."

"I'll sentence you as I sentenced them. They started the fight, but you brought steel into it."

Alf said nothing. They were eye to eye, almost body to body; he could feel the King's anger as a physical thing, a wave of white heat.

Abruptly Richard spun away, stalked back to the chessboard, began to set the pieces in their proper places. Alf watched him. He paused, balancing the king and his ebony bishop. "Two of them I'll give you. But not the worst of them."

"All three," said Alf. "Especially Joscelin."

Richard glanced over his shoulder, a swift, vicious, lion's glare. "Don't abuse my generosity, priest."

"All three," Alf repeated. "Pardon them."

The King ignored him, setting down a double rank of pawns,

ebony men-at-arms, ivory Saracens. When all stood in their places, he regarded them, arms folded.

A long step brought Alf to stand beside him. "I take your gift of the two boys with gratitude. But give me Joscelin."

"No."

"What will you do with him?"

His gentle persistence drove Richard through rage to a quivering calm. "I'll keep the fool's head shaved and give him to a monastery." The King bared his teeth. "That ought to satisfy you."

"No," Alf said. "It does not. Set him free."

"Priest," purred Richard, "you've got as much as you'll get. Get out of my sight before I take it all back again."

Alf did not move. "Joscelin," he said. "Let Joscelin go."

The King's hand flew up, swifter than thought. Swifter still, Alf blocked it, held it. There was a moment of frozen stillness.

In Richard's eyes, a spark caught. With all his great strength he fought to break the other's grip.

Alf swayed slightly, but did not let go. Richard stopped, panting, staring at the thin white fingers. They looked as if they would break at a word. They held like bands of steel.

The spark grew. Richard looked from the hand to the body behind, and to the pale face. "Let me go," he said, neither commanding nor pleading.

Alf obeyed.

Richard rubbed his wrist, still staring, as if he had never seen Alf before. "Two go free," he said. "You've won that. But the third has to pay."

"How?"

"Either he humbly craves your pardon for his sins, and escapes; or he goes into the cloister."

Alf opened his mouth; Richard cut him off. "No more! That's as far as I'll go."

Slowly Alf bowed his head. "Yes, Sire," he murmured. "Do I have your leave to go?"

"Go, damn you. *Go!*"

The King's wrath had not confined Joscelin to the Earl's dungeon. The squire rested in relative comfort in a dark box of a room behind the kennels, with a straw pallet to sleep on and only a single ankle-chain to bind him.

He lay in a huddle upon the pallet, his cloak drawn over his shorn head, nor did he respond when his guard thrust a torch into a wall niche, flooding the cell with light. The man nudged him with an ungentle foot. "Wake up, handsome. You've got company."

"I'll speak with him alone," Alf said. Joscelin started a little at the sound of his voice, and peered through slitted eyes, seeing only a hooded shadow behind the smaller, broader shape of the guard.

The man withdrew with a coin in his hand and a blessing on his head, fair wages for the night's work.

Alf settled beside the pallet and waited for Joscelin to focus. The squire looked little like the elegant young man who had sought to torment a helpless monk, dirty and disheveled, his dark curls gone. Yet as his sight cleared, he knew the face within the hood; his lip curled. "Well, pretty Brother," he said. "Come to gloat over the victim before he goes to the block?"

"No," Alf said. "I've spoken to the King. He's promised to let you go. On one condition."

Hope leaped high in the dark eyes, though the voice was mocking. "Oh, yes. There's always a condition. What is it? Do I have to kiss your fundament?"

In spite of himself, Alf flushed. "You have to ask my pardon."

"Same thing," said Joscelin. "What if I won't?"

"You'll go into the cloister."

Joscelin yawned and stretched and rattled his ankle-chain. "Is that all? And here I was, saying Paternosters for the repose of my soul. His Majesty's getting soft."

"I don't think so."

"You wouldn't."

"If you fulfill the King's condition," Alf said, "you go free. Completely free."

"And back to my family in disgrace."

"No."

"He really has gone soft. Pity. There was a time when he'd have cropped my ears for getting into a fight with a lily maid, and losing."

"You choose the cloister, then?"

Joscelin lay back and closed his eyes. "Maybe," he said. "It's not a bad life. Wine and song and a woman here and there, and boys whenever I want them."

"Do you think it's like that?"

One eye opened, dark and scornful. And in its depths, a black fire of hate. "Pretty Brother. I *know* it's like that. Don't pretend to be so much holier-than-thou."

"If you only beg my pardon, you can return to your old place and be as you were before."

A tremor ran through Joscelin's body. "Oh, no," he said. "It won't be the same."

"You can live down your disgrace."

"If you don't shut your mouth," Joscelin said quietly, reasonably, "I'll shut it for you. Go away and let me sleep."

"Joscelin—"

"Joscelin," he echoed bitterly. "Joscelin! Be a good lad, Joscelin. Smile nicely, Joscelin. Bow to the handsome Brother, Joscelin. And never mind the King, Joscelin. He's found a new darling and he doesn't need you any more." He laughed, a harsh strangled sound. "There now. I've let it out. I'm jealous, by God's left kneecap! My lord's got a new boy, a beautiful boy, and when he deigns to notice the old one, all he has is a smile and a pat on the head, and a penny for sweet charity."

Alf reached for him without thinking, as he would have reached for Jehan, to comfort him.

Violently Joscelin struck his hands away. "Get your filthy claws off me!"

For an instant they faced each other, deadly pale, Alf with horror and pity, Joscelin with hatred.

"Joscelin," he said gently, "I'm not the King's boy."

Again, that terrible, mirthless laughter. "Don't tell lies, pretty Brother. We're all good Sodomites here."

Alf shook his head. "Believe me. I'm not."

"Lies, lies, lies. Go away and take them with you."

"I will pardon you for all you have said and done to me, if you will only ask."

"*That* for your pardon!" Joscelin spat in his face.

Slowly, carefully, Alf wiped the spittle from his cheek. Equally carefully he said, "If you reconsider, send for me."

Joscelin laughed. His laughter followed Alf for a long while after.

18

When Aylmer could not sleep, he often found peace in the lofty quiet of the cathedral, winter-cold though it was, dim-lit by the vigil lamp above each altar. That night he had lain awake, listening as the great bell tolled each hour, until at last he rose and drew on the brown habit of his old Order, stepped over the novice-page who slept across his door, and went quietly out.

The cathedral was deserted in that dark time between Compline and the Night Office. He bowed low before the central altar, murmuring a greeting and a prayer, and turned toward the Lady Chapel.

In the dimness, he did not see the figure which lay prostrate upon the stones in front of the altar until he stumbled over it. A gasp escaped it; it rolled over swiftly, half-rising.

He knew who it was even before he saw the face; that feline grace was unmistakable. He held out a hand; Alf hesitated, then let the Bishop draw him to his feet. He looked very pale, shadow-eyed.

Aylmer heaved a mental sigh. This had kept him awake, and it seemed determined not to let him go. "Come into the sacristy," he said. "It's warmer there."

For a moment he thought Alf would refuse. But when Aylmer turned, the other followed.

As the Bishop lit a lamp in the sacristy, Alf stood among the holy things, his cloak drawn about him. At that moment, in that light, he did not look entirely human: a creature of the wild hills, trapped in a net of iron and of sanctity.

Aylmer sat on a low stool. "Well, Brother," he said. "You've been living hard, from the look of you."

Alf shivered, though not with cold. "Not living hard, my lord. Just—just living."

"Hard enough, from all I've heard. Were you fighting with the King tonight?"

Alf's lips tightened. "How did you know?"

"He sent me a message."

"I'm not to serve him again?"

"The message was: 'Brother Alfred is to ride with the King tomorrow morning at terce. And tell him to leave his damned skirts at home!' "

For all his troubles, Alf could not help but smile. It was a thin smile, almost a grimace of pain. "He forgives as swiftly as he condemns. And I gave him much to forgive."

Aylmer leaned against a richly carven chest. "First the King's squires, then the King himself. You're trying hard to make enemies."

"They make themselves."

"It takes two to start a war, Brother."

"True, my lord. It needs an attacker. And a victim."

"Do you see yourself as the victim?"

"Better that and dead, than living and a murderer."

"You have an urge to kill someone?"

For the first time Alf looked at him directly. His eyes had a strange gleam. "I could, my lord. I could commit every act that could possibly damn a man."

Aylmer rose and opened the chest. Amid its contents he found a violet stole. As he lifted it, Alf's hand stopped him. It felt thin and cold and not quite steady. "No, my lord. Don't put the seal of the confessional on this."

"Whether I wear the stole or not," Aylmer said, "the seal is there. Though I can't promise absolution."

"I ask no absolution. And no silence."

"Let me decide that for myself."

The Bishop returned to his seat with the stole in his hand. After a moment, Alf knelt facing him.

"I think," said Aylmer, "that I can spare you the agony of telling me a truth or two. St. Paul's monks have a reason to be after you. Don't they?"

Alf nodded tightly.

"A good reason, by their lights. You aren't exactly circumspect about yourself."

"You know," Alf whispered. "You know——"

"Enough," the Bishop finished for him. "If you'd wanted to protect your secret, you'd never have let yourself be sent on an errand for the King of Rhiyana. Especially to me. I've waited on Gwydion in Caer Gwent. I've seen his court. I know what the Fair Folk look like. And," he added, "a little of what they can do."

"Then," Alf said, "you think I'm one of them."

"I know you are."

Alf drew a shuddering breath. "How—how long?"

"Since I first saw you."

"But you never—" Alf stopped. He was seldom at a loss; yet Aylmer had never betrayed that he knew. Not even in his mind.

Carefully Alf mastered himself. "I meant to confess to you," he said. "I was gathering courage for it; but you came before I expected."

"What made you decide to tell me?"

The Bishop's face was stern, his gaze forbidding. And completely unafraid, though he knew what powers Alf had. Knew very well indeed. In their own country, Gwydion's people had few secrets.

Alf faced him with all disguises gone; he met the pale unhuman stare without flinching.

"My lord," Alf said, "I'm tired. I could lie and hide and pretend to be human, but I'm weary of it."

"Weary unto death?"

Alf caught his breath as if at a blow. Yet he answered with the truth. "Yes. Unto death."

"You're young to be so sure of that."

"No," Alf said. "Young, I am not."

Aylmer paused. A breath only, but long enough for a swift train of thought, a flare of recognition. He was not surprised, Alf realized. "Alfred of St. Ruan's," he said slowly. "Alfred of St. Ruan's. I was so proud that I knew what you were, and too blind to see . . . But if the *Gloria Dei* is yours . . ."

"It is mine." Alf's fists had clenched at his sides. "I wish to God that I had never put pen to parchment."

He looked up. To his amazement, Aylmer was laughing silently, a convulsion of pure delight.

The Bishop wiped his streaming eyes, struggling to regain his composure. "Your pardon, Brother. But if I were the Lord God, and I wanted to show the whole herd of theologians and canon lawyers what utter asses they are, I would have done exactly what He has done. Given them you."

"It was sheer hubris for me to dare to write what I did. But I never meant it to be a mockery."

"Nor did I. But the hair-splitters wax haughty in their conviction that man is the measure of all things, the center of the universe, the Macrocosm in microcosm. You show them that there's more in creation than they've ever dreamed of." Aylmer shook his head and coughed. "Brother, Master, you've restored my faith."

For a long moment Alf could only stare. "My lord, I don't understand you."

The Bishop's eyes gleamed upon him. "What! You can make clear the mysteries of Paradise, and you can't impose some sense on a lump of clay?"

"On strictly canonical grounds, you should be blasting the accursed witch-spawn to perdition."

Aylmer shook his head. "No, Brother. I'm a Bishop; I'm God's man; but thanks be to Him and all His angels, I'm no canon lawyer. I judge by what I see and hear, and not by what some mummified authority says I ought to."

"I have practiced witchery."

"Dark rites? Invocations of demons? Curses and black spells?"

"Dear God, no!"

"Not even a stray love-philtre?"

Alf wanted to laugh; he wanted to weep. "My lord, I'm a poorer judge of men than I am of mummified authorities. But I know how you should be regarding me; and how others will regard me if the truth is known."

"Not if," Aylmer said. "When. Brother, I'm minded to send you away. Back to St. Ruan's if you want it, though you're not likely to be safe there. Or to Rhiyana, where God's Hounds can't go."

"I won't go, my lord. And if you know my kind, you know that nothing will hold me when I don't want to be held."

The Bishop's brows knit. "I do know it. I know that there's no arguing with a master of logic, either. What if I command you?"

"I'm afraid," Alf said gently, "that I will have to disobey you."

"Why? Why are you doing this?"

"I told you. I'm tired. And a trial and a burning, if burning there must be, will hold the King here until it's too late for him to destroy himself on the Marches."

"Do you really want to die?"

"I want to break this deadlock. With the King, with the Hounds, with myself. If I have to die to do it, yes. Yes, I want to."

"And if not?"

Alf was silent for a long moment. "If not . . . so be it."

"I understand you," Aylmer said. "I think you're a fool, but I understand you. I'll also do everything in my power to keep you from getting yourself killed."

"No, my lord. You'll do everything you can to assure that the King stays here and that he makes no effort to protect me. You will even support my enemies if necessary, for the King's sake. He must not go to war with Gwynedd."

"And you must not go to the stake."

"I don't matter. All Anglia hangs upon Richard's life and death."

"Have you ever considered what he might do to the men who condemn you? And what they might do to him?"

"There's no death for him in that, and no doom for his kingdom."

"You look like an adolescent angel. But you're as crafty as a Byzantine courtier. And somewhat colder-blooded." The Bishop rose with the violet stole still in his hands. "I've heard your confession. I grant you no absolution."

"You know I want none."

Aylmer kissed the stole and laid it away, and remained with his back to Alf. "Go to bed," he said.

Alf hesitated. Aylmer did not move. After a moment, he rose and bowed, and withdrew.

19

Alf burrowed in the box he shared with Jehan, searching amid their common belongings for the books he had brought from St. Ruan's. They lay on the bottom, lovingly wrapped in leather: the five treasures he had kept out of all that he had gathered. He uncovered them carefully and separated one from the rest.

"Brother Alfred."

He glanced over his shoulder. Reynaud stood in the doorway, smiling as he always smiled, without warmth; on the surface, all friendliness, and beneath, the eagerness of the hunting hound.

Alf took his time in setting the contents of the chest in order and in lowering the lid. When he turned, book in hand, Reynaud had come within arm's reach.

The Pauline monk nodded at Alf's habit. "Not hunting with the King today, Brother?"

"No," Alf said. "I'm to wait on him when he comes back. Meanwhile"—he tucked the book under his arm—"I have leave to amuse myself."

"Blessed freedom," sighed Reynaud. "And you'll do no more than read?"

Alf's smile was a wintry likeness of Reynaud's. "I'd rather read than hunt; I always find myself siding with the quarry."

"Even the wild boar?"

"Why not? In the end he lies on the table with an apple in his jaws, no more or less dead than the stag or the coney."

"But he gives a good account of himself before he dies."

"You expect him to turn Christian and bare his breast to the spear?"

Reynaud spread his hands in surrender. "I can't compete in words with a philosopher. My talents, such as they are, lie elsewhere."

"And where," Alf asked, "is that?"

He shrugged expressively. "In areas far from philosophy, or from serving kings. I preach God's word in my poor way; I serve His servants; I go where He bids me."

"So do we all." Alf glanced significantly at the door. "Do you have duties, Brother?"

"Nothing pressing. The weather is splendid for once. Come and walk with me."

Alf inhaled sharply. Danger always walked with Reynaud—surrounded him, wrapped him about. But that quiet request struck Alf like a blow to the vitals. For an instant he had seen through the veiled eyes; had caught a flare of raw emotion. Hate and hope and burning excitement. The mind of the beast before it springs for the throat.

It had come. So soon. The trap was laid; the quarry had only to walk into it.

Alf relaxed with an effort. "My thanks, Brother, but I promised myself a quiet morning."

Reynaud shook his head in reproof. "You'd mew yourself up in a cold library? For shame! Come out and let the sun warm you. Then you can go to your book with a clearer head."

But Reynaud's mind saw a barred cell and chains, and the stark shadow of the stake. Alf shrank from the horror of it.

Five days hence, Richard would depart for Gwynedd with a hundred knights at his back, and the Marches would burst into a fire of war.

Alf battled to still his trembling. His decision was long since made. Was he to retreat now, when it came to the crux?

He sighed and shrugged. "Very well," he said. "A short walk."

Reynaud smiled. "A very short one. Yes. Come, Brother."

*   *   *

Jehan peered around a corner. The courtyard was empty, its much-trodden snow melting into puddles under the fitful sun. He kilted up his habit and sprinted along the wall into the shadow of a doorway. Still no pursuit. After a moment he eased open a door, slipped down a passage, paused in the stableyard. The hound chained there wagged its mangy tail; he greeted it and offered it a bit of cheese. As it devoured the bribe, he walked boldly into the stable.

A day or two before, he had discovered that, if one settled into a corner of the hayloft near the dovecote, one could pass unnoticed by any who entered; there was light enough to read by, and warmth enough for comfort if one burrowed deep into the hay. And no one would ever think to look there for a truant.

He settled into his hiding place with a sigh of content, armed with Father Michael's precious copy of the Almagest and a pocketful of dried figs. With luck, he could read until it was time for arms-practice, and talk his way out of the punishment for evading kitchen duty.

"You'd better be able to, or what's an education for?"

Jehan choked on a fig. Thea sat astride a beam, dressed like a farmgirl, laughing at his startlement. As he remembered how to breathe again, she dropped down beside him and pilfered a fig. "Ah! these are good. Where'd you find them?"

"Stole them at breakfast." He frowned at her. "You're hardly ever about. Where've you been?"

She shrugged. "Here and there. Keeping people guessing. Whose dog am I, whose wench am I, and what am I up to?"

"Everyone was sure you belonged to me till I said you didn't. I made up a story about how you'd followed us from the lake; maybe you belonged to one of the rebels."

"I am a rebel."

"I never would have guessed."

She laughed again and shook her hair out of its rough knot. "I like playing country maid. It's market day today; I sold a basket of eggs and got a penny, and gave it to the beggar under Westgate. He told me all that's happened hereabouts. Amazing how much the kerns know. The King should ignore his lords and messengers and listen to people in the town."

Jehan watched her, and sighed a little. She was almost unbearably beautiful, yet her speech was as solid and earthbound as her ragged smock. She had no trouble accepting what she was. She simply *was*.

"I wish Brother Alf were like you," he said.

She paused, head tilted, half-smiling. "He is. But he's spent all his life trying to be something else."

"Why aren't you as confused as he is?"

"I wasn't brought up in an abbey, for one thing. My mother was a Greek, a doctor. My father was a Levantine merchant. The whole world used to pass through our house."

"And you left it?"

"One day we guested a prince from Lombardy. He was the ugliest man I'd ever seen, and he stank like one of his own goats, but he was wise and he was clever, and I was tired of living in one place. I ran off with him."

"Did he marry you?"

"Of course not. He had a wife already. And three mistresses and a round dozen of children. After a while we parted on the best of terms, and I wandered about, taking whatever shape pleased me; and I came to Rhiyana, and to the King."

"Gwydion?"

"For us," she said, only half in mockery, "there is only one King."

Jehan lay on his stomach, chin in hands. "Brother Alf should go to him. I wager he'd know what to do with a monk who's also an elf-man."

"He might," she said. She ran her fingers through the splendor of her hair, that was as fine as Chin silk, rippling to her waist. "If the little Brother has his way, there'll be an end of all his troubles in fire and anathema."

"I'll stop him," Jehan muttered fiercely. "I'll make him stop."

She tilted her brows at him. "Will you now? Then you'd better hurry. The Hounds took him this morning."

Jehan sprang to his feet. The doves fled in a flurry of wings. *"What!"*

Thea caught a drifting feather. "He went voluntarily," she said.

"They'll kill him!"

"It's likely," she agreed.

He dragged her up as if she had been a wisp of hay, and shook her. "Where is he? *Where is he?"*

"You're not going to his rescue."

"God's feet!"

"God," she pointed out, "as First Cause, has no material shape. Therefore——"

"Shut up, damn you!"

She was silent. So, for a long moment, was Jehan. With great care he unclamped his fingers from her shoulders. "Where is he?" he asked at last, quietly.

"You will not go to find him. You will go and tell Bishop Aylmer what has happened, and do as he tells you."

"Bishop Aylmer can't—" Jehan stopped. Slowly he said, "I'll go. Where is Brother Alf?"

"In St. Benedict's Abbey," Thea answered him.

He bent and picked up the book which had fallen from his lap. It was open; he closed it gently, running his fingers over the worn cover. "Come with me," he said.

When he left the stable, the white hound trotted behind him.

"This is the man?"

"If man you may call him."

Fingers touched Alf's chin, turning his head this way and that. They were gentle, without malice, like the soft voice. "Certainly he has the look of the elf-brood. And yet . . ."

"Brother?" the other asked with a hint of tension.

"And yet. He let you take him on the first attempt."

"*Let*, Brother? He fought like a very demon!"

"He let you take him," the other repeated.

"Not until Brother Raymond struck him with an iron-shod cudgel. Then we managed to get a grip on him."

Alf lay very still, hardly breathing. His head felt as if he had caught it between a hammer and an anvil; his body ached. He could remember, in snatches—a deserted street, men in dark clothing; a battle, swift and fierce, and a swooping darkness.

And voices. One he knew, nasal, obsequious. In a moment, when it hurt less, he would remember a name.

The soft voice spoke again. "Guard him with all your skill. But be gentle with him."

"Gentle!"

"Yes. Gentle. Send me word when he wakes."

Only when the voices were long gone did Alf open his eyes. He lay on a pallet in a small cold room, no dungeon for it had a slit of window to let in the light, but bars blocked the opening, new-forged iron, newly set into the stone. The door too was new, heavy, bound with iron bands; as iron bound him, wrists and ankles, incised with crosses.

With great care he sat up. He still had his habit and his silver cross; beside him lay a jar and the familiar shape of his book.

The jar held water, touched with sanctity, which did not speak well of his captors' intelligence. Surely, if a demon could wear a cross next to his skin and handle the holy vessels of the Mass, then no sacred precautions could hold him.

He drank a little to quench his raging thirst, and splashed a drop or two upon his face. Gingerly he explored his aching skull. A great knot throbbed at the base of it, the worst of his hurts, though all his body bore the marks of battle.

He rose slowly, dizzily. Chained though he was, he could move as he pleased about the cell, even to the door. Through its iron grille he saw a stretch of stone passageway and the back of a man's head, turning as if startled to reveal a stranger's face. A blast of fear and hostility struck Alf's reeling brain; he cried out and stumbled backward, half-falling against the wall.

The fear receded. He huddled upon the pallet, trembling violently, battling nausea.

Iron grated upon iron. The door opened.

Alf raised his head. Reynaud smiled at him. "Awake at last, Brother? How do you feel?"

"Betrayed," Alf said.

He winced. The blow upon his head had shattered his inner defenses; he could not shield against the other's anger.

Reynaud smiled through clenched teeth. "Do you think I betrayed you?"

"Is the price still thirty pieces of silver?"

"That," said Reynaud, "could be construed as blasphemy."

Alf swallowed bile. "I take a walk with you out of courtesy, and face an ambush. And when I wake I'm in chains. Is this how you demonstrate your friendship?"

It was some comfort to see Reynaud look uneasy. Yet righteousness flooded over the seeds of his guilt and drowned them. "I did as I was commanded."

"By whom? The Sanhedrin?"

Reynaud's hand flashed out. Alf darted away, but the blow caught him sidewise. His ears rang; his stomach heaved.

Reynaud's anger turned to disgust, and then to dismay. A firm yet gentle presence ministered to Alf, while a quiet voice said, "Go to my cell, Reynaud. I will come to you later."

The Pauline monk was gone. The other held Alf until he had

recovered somewhat, cleaned him and dressed him in a fresh habit, a black one. "Your pardon, Brother," the man said, "but we have only Benedictine robes here."

Yet he wore Pauline white and gray: a tall thin man with the face of a Byzantine saint. His face was smooth, his skin as fresh as a boy's, but his hair was white; Alf sensed a great weight of years upon him.

He followed Alf's glance to his habit, and smiled. "And Pauline," he amended. "But I thought you would not want those."

"Nor would you," Alf said.

His smile faded. "Say rather, it would not be proper."

"No. The captive should not assume the garb of his captors."

"You speak wisely and well, young Brother. Though somewhat bitterly."

"You think I should not be bitter?"

The monk shrugged slightly. "I can understand, though not condone it."

"If our positions should ever be reversed, I'd like to hear you repeat that."

The monk's smile returned. "Perhaps I may not. I am human, after all." He paused; seemed to remember a thing he had forgotten; said, "My name is Brother Adam."

"You know mine."

"Do I?"

Alf sighed. "Ah. So the game begins. I'm called Alfred."

"Or Alf?"

"That, too," he admitted. "Reynaud has kept you well-informed. He's not going to welcome the need to treat me gently."

"You heard?"

Alf began to nod, decided against it. "Yes," he said. "I heard."

Brother Adam smiled again, wryly. "I see that I shall have to watch you more carefully."

"Reynaud was not happy. But he did try to obey you, until I provoked him. Don't be too harsh with him."

"And why did you provoke him?" Brother Adam asked, interested.

"I was angry. Inexcusably, but understandably. No one welcomes betrayal."

"Ah," said Brother Adam, "but if he had told you what he meant to do, then you would not have come."

"Maybe I would have," Alf said.

"Even into chains?"

Alf shook one. "They aren't pleasant," he said. "If I promised to behave, would you let me out of them?"

Adam's eyes were sad. "No, Brother. I would not. Certain sufferings are necessary, you see; those I cannot spare you."

"At whose orders? Why am I a prisoner?"

"Two questions," said Brother Adam. "Perhaps you know the answers to both."

Alf sat up. His head throbbed, but he would not lie still. "You have me, and this habit is Benedictine. Is this Bishop Foulques's doing? Is he holding me for ransom?"

"Brother," Adam said, gently chiding, "your innocence rings false. The Bishop knows and sanctions our actions here, but what those actions are, surely you know."

Alf regarded him with wide, gray, human eyes. Not all of the fear there was feigned. "I'm no heretic!"

"That, we will test."

"Sweet Jesu!" Alf knelt at his feet, a proud boy wakened suddenly to full knowledge of his peril. "Please, Brother, Domne. I'm a monk, a priest. I've loved God and served Him with all the faith that is in me. Would you make me suffer because two Bishops are at odds, and an Earl and a King have no love for one another?"

"We do not play the games of the world," Adam told him as gently as ever. "Lie down, Brother. You are not well enough yet to walk about."

Alf let himself be put to bed again, but he clutched the other's hand, his own frail and trembling. "I'm not a heretic, Brother. By all the saints I swear it."

"That may well be," Adam said. "But heresy is not the major charge." He disengaged his hand from Alf's. "Rest now. Later I shall return."

"Brother!" Alf cried. "For God's sake—what else can I be guilty of?"

The dark eyes were quiet. "Sorcery," answered Brother Adam. Even as he spoke, the door closed upon him.

Alf lay on his back, then, after a time, on his face. He no longer felt ill, only aching, and tired.

He rested his cheek upon his arm above the manacle. The fabric of the black habit was finely woven, soft. It lay lightly upon his bruised skin.

Brother. Light too that touch upon his bruised mind. He saw Alun sitting in an angle of sunlight in the cloister of St. Ruan's, hale to look on save for the bound hand and arm. His leg Alf could not see beneath the borrowed brown habit, but two knees bent for his sitting; he touched the right one. *This came out of its bonds yesterday,* he said. *Sooner than you predicted, Brother.*

Alf smiled in spite of his troubles. *Are you running races yet?*

Not quite yet. The lightness left Alun's thoughts. *Are you well?*

Well enough, Alf responded.

Weak as his barriers were, Alun slid past them with ease. His inner voice was almost harsh. *What is this? What has happened?*

Something I brought on myself, answered Alf. *Have you sent word to Kilhwch?*

Yes. Alun stood, balancing upon the strong leg and the weaker one, gray eyes stern. *So this is how you would delay the war until our messenger can reach Richard. Who has you? The King himself?*

The Hounds of God.

Alf reeled. Alun's serenity had shattered, baring for an instant the furnace-fires beneath. *God in heaven! Are you trying to destroy yourself?*

After a long moment, Alf found that he could think again. *My lord,* he said, *I'm doing what I have to do. Richard will be here when your messenger arrives.*

If Morwin discovers what he has sent you to, said Alun, *the knowledge will kill him. He meant for you to be healed, not to be slain.*

Maybe they're both the same. Alf knotted his fists. *My lord, promise me. Don't tell him what's happened. If I live, it won't matter. If I die . . . it's not his fault. It's not anyone's. Not even God's, though He made me what I am.*

Alun reached out through the otherworld. *Alf. Come to me. Now.*

His command was potent. Yet Alf resisted. *No. Be well, my lord. Recover quickly. And give my love to the Abbot.* He gathered the tatters of his shield and firmed them as best he might. Fear rose strong in him that the Rhiyanan would break them down and compel him to forsake his intent.

But Alun did not attack. When Alf ventured a brief probe, he was gone. No trace of his presence remained.

20

The narrow slit of window let in just enough light for a man to read by, more than enough for Alf's eyes. He sat under it, book in hand, reading as quietly as if he had been in the library in St. Ruan's.

Brother Adam watched him for a long while through the grille. He did not seem to notice that he had an observer, although when the monk entered he revealed no surprise. He did not even look up.

"Good morning, Brother," Adam said. "Did you sleep well?"

Alf raised his eyes. They were shining, remote. "Good morning," he said.

Adam's glance found a bowl of food by the pallet, its contents untouched. "You did not break your fast."

"I'm not hungry." Alf bent to his book again.

The other stood over him. "What are you reading?"

With a sigh, Alf shifted his mind fully from his book to his jailer. "Boethius," he answered.

"The prisoner and the Lady Philosophy. Very apt."

"Yes," Alf said. "It is apt. Too apt, perhaps. The prisoner was executed."

"But Philosophy consoled him most completely before he died."

"Did she? In the end . . . I wonder."

"If you are innocent," Adam said, "you will not die."

"I'm not sure I believe you."

"Do you deny that you have practiced sorcery?"

Alf stared at the page, not seeing the words written there, seeing his choices, truth or falsehood, death or life, and Kilhwch's messenger riding hard through the hills of Gwynedd. "What do you mean by sorcery?" he asked.

"You do not know?"

With his thumb Alf traced the cross graven upon one of his shackles. "People say I've bewitched the King. I haven't. He likes to look at me; he likes to listen to me. There's no sorcery in that."

"Except the old one of Venus."

"Jove had his Ganymede," Alf said, "and Achilles his Patroclus, but Richard has never had his Alfred. By witchery, or by any other way."

"Yet you could have cast a spell upon him if you had wished it."

"How, Brother? Have you found a grimoire under my pillow?"

Brother Adam sat on the pallet. "There are two types of sorcerers," he said. "Sorcerers proper, men of human blood and breeding, whose spells are the work of art and of skill, aided by the grimoires you speak of and by sundry devices of human or demonic construction: astrologers, alchemists, soothsayers and herb-healers. These are common and easily found out, and often converted to the path of righteousness. Yet there is a second, rarer brood, whom we call witches, elf-wights, people of the hills. Power does not come to these by study and by art; they need no books of magic, no powders or philtres or chanting of spells. No; the power is born in them, and fills them from the moment of their conception."

Alf laughed a little, incredulously. "You think I'm—what? Hob o' the Hill? Are you mad?"

From a pocket of his robe Adam brought out a disk of silver no larger than his palm. When he held it up, Alf saw his own face reflected there. "Look," Adam said. "What do you see?"

"Myself."

"Have you ever seen such a face before?"

Alf blushed. "I—I'm not ugly. But I can't help that."

"Is your beauty a common, human beauty?"

Alf turned away from the mirror. "Must I be condemned because I look like this?"

"Not for that reason, but for what it indicates. God has marked the elven-folk that they may not be lost among the race of men—has made them surpassingly fair, as fair without as their hearts are black within."

"I am a priest," Alf said tightly. "A man of God."

"Truly?"

"The water of baptism did not sear the flesh from my bones; nor did the chrism of my ordination send me howling into the dark. I have raised the Host in the Mass, aye, more times than I can count; and never once have I been stricken down."

"For that, I have only your word."

Alf rose, trembling. "Test me. Give me the consecrated bread; make me drink of the wine. Say the Mass before me—say the very rite of exorcism over me. I am neither witch nor demon; I am simply Alfred of St. Ruan's."

Adam nodded slowly as if to himself. "So you say. You were a foundling, I am told."

"My mother died; I don't know who my father was. I was given to the abbey as a hundred other children have been, before and since."

"By three white owls?"

Suddenly Alf was very still. "Owls? Who told you that?"

"We have heard tales, round about."

"Owls." Alf shook his head. "That's absurd."

"You came to this city in the company of a hound. A wondrous hound, white yet with red ears, such as the old people say runs at the heels of the Lord of the Otherworld or on the trail of the Wild Hunt."

"Because," Alf said with taut-strung patience, "such beasts are bred all over Anglia. Of course Arawn or Herne the Hunter would have a pack of them."

"Then whence came yours?"

"She's not mine. She followed us; she might have belonged to one of the rebels the King's men slew. She comes and she goes, depending on whether one of us is disposed to feed or pet her."

"Indeed," Brother Adam said. "Do you deny that you have practiced sorcery?"

Alf lifted his chin. "Yes," he answered. "I do deny that I have practiced the black arts."

Adam stood, unruffled. "So. I am sorry that I interrupted your study of Master Boethius."

The other stared at him. "You won't let me go?"

"I cannot." Brother Adam sketched a blessing in the air. *"Dominus vobiscum."*

"Et cum spiritu tuo," Alf responded, signing himself with more defiance than reverence.

Adam smiled and took his leave.

The axe swung skyward; poised for a moment against the sun; flashed down. Its victim fell, cloven neatly in two.

"That for the cursed Hounds," Jehan muttered.

He set another log upon the block and sent it the way of its fellow. There was an odd, crooked comfort in that labor. At least it was action, if not the action he wanted.

He scowled at the block, seeing upon it Reynaud's thin sharp face, and smote with all his strength.

"Well smitten!"

He gritted his teeth. Company, he neither needed nor wanted. He reached for a log, hitched his habit a little higher, and raised the axe.

"Again," said his observer, "well smitten."

He turned, glaring, and stopped short. The King stood there in the mud of the kitchen garden, alone and unattended, and laughing at his expression.

He dropped the axe and knelt, bowing his head. "Sire," he said. "Majesty. I didn't know—"

The King cut him off. "Get up. You're not at court here." Although his words were sharp, amusement danced still in his eyes.

Jehan rose. Only one thing could have brought the King alone to this place; that knowledge turned his startlement to something very much like fear. With care under the other's eye, he rolled down his sleeves and let his habit fall properly to his feet. But there was no concealing his face. He arranged it as best he might and said, "You gave me a start, Sire. I thought you were one of the Brothers."

"I don't look much like a priest, do I?" Richard inspected the heap of new-cut wood and took up the axe, testing its balance. "So this is how Aylmer trains his knights. Practical. I should try it with my own men."

"Only if you want axemen, Sire," Jehan said.

"True enough. It's no good trying to hew wood with a sword. Though if I could set the swordsmen to harvesting grain and the mace-men to slaughtering sheep . . ."

Jehan laughed. "And the lancers could practice on cows, and what would Bishop Aylmer do for penances?"

"You're being punished, are you?"

"Yes, Sire." Jehan looked down, shamefaced. "I was reading in the hayloft instead of working in the kitchen. So I hew wood and draw water until my lord sees fit to let me go."

To his credit, Richard neither frowned nor smiled. "And when will that be?"

The novice shrugged. "When he pleases, Sire. But that's fair enough as penances go. I could have got a caning. Would have if I'd been in my old abbey."

"You sound singularly unrepentant."

Jehan raised his eyes. "Why, Sire! I'm most repentant—that I have to spend my days here instead of in the tilting-yard."

The King grinned and placed a log upright upon the block. He measured it with his eye and raised the axe. It was not an ill stroke,

Jehan thought, both amused and shocked that a King should want to try his hand at a villein's work.

"Sire," he said. "You really shouldn't—"

"I really shouldn't be here." Richard essayed a second blow. "In fact, I'm not here at all. I'm closeted with Bishop Aylmer."

Jehan was silent. The King set down the axe and dusted his hands on his riding-leathers. "This is easier work than hewing heads. A log can't hit back."

"The worse for the log," Jehan said. He did not move to resume his task. "Did Bishop Aylmer send you here, my lord?"

"Bishop Aylmer is cooling his heels in my workroom." The good humor had vanished from Richard's face; his eyes were fierce. "And what's His Majesty of Anglia doing running his own errands? Is that what you're thinking?"

After a moment Jehan nodded.

The King nodded also, sharply. "Some things even a King can't pass on to underlings. Or he passes them on and they disappear, and he never sees them again. That, boy, is called 'humoring the King.' "

"It's also called 'burying the evidence.' "

Richard laughed shortly. "So. You're smarter than you look. Are you too clever to tell the truth?"

"That depends on what you want to know, Sire."

"Nothing theological. Not even anything personal. Just a simple thing. It's so simple that I've spent a full three days trying to find it out, which has done my war no good at all. I've been sent by proxy from pillar to post, till I've had to set my own hand to it or never know at all." The King leaned close, so close that Jehan could see nothing but the glitter of his eyes. "Where is Brother Alfred?"

Jehan blinked. "Brother Alfred, Sire?"

"Brother Alfred," Richard repeated as to a witless child. "The tall one, with no color in him. Do you remember him?"

"Sire," Jehan said, "you came here just for him? But why to me?"

The King stepped back, scowling. "Just for him. Yes. And to you, you young fox with an ox's face, because he called you his friend. Which is more than he would do for me. Where is he?"

"You haven't seen him, Sire?"

"Boy," Richard said very softly, "I have not seen Alfred since he promised to attend me after I hunted, three days ago, and he never came. I thought it was one of his moods. But he didn't come the next day when I called for him, and the page I sent was told that he couldn't see the Brother, even at the King's command. And so the next messenger I sent, and the next. This morning I heard a whisper that Brother Alfred couldn't come because he wasn't there. More: he went out walking three days past, and never came back." The King spoke more softly still, a near-whisper. "Where has he gone?"

Jehan ran his tongue over his lips. "Sire. He is gone. But I can't tell you where."

"Can't? Or won't?"

"Can't, my lord. He went out, as you've heard. No one's seen him since. We—we think—someone took him."

"And why couldn't he simply have run away?"

"Sire," Jehan said hotly, "if you know him, you know that's not his way. He gets moods and he does strange things, but he'd never run off without telling anybody. Especially not on foot, with nothing on but his habit and a book in his hand."

Richard's eyes narrowed. "You saw him go?"

"No, Sire. Would to God I had! But I was playing truant, and when I came back, he—he was gone." Jehan struggled to keep his voice steady. "I know someone took him. I know it."

"Taken," Richard muttered. And, louder: "He's sent you no word?"

"No, Sire." Jehan's calmness shattered altogether. "Sire, don't you think I've tried everything I can? I even went to Bishop Aylmer and tried to get him to send out searchers. When he told me to wait, I yelled at him. That's why my penance isn't limited to a day or two. He—he told me to be patient and to let him do what he could, and—and not to talk to anyone about it."

"Did he?"

The King's tone made Jehan cry out, "He's no traitor! I'm sure of it. But he said, if Brother Alf's been taken, his takers must be your enemies. They haven't asked for a ransom; they must want you to go after him and fall into a trap, and maybe get killed. That's why my lord hasn't let you know the truth. He wants to find Brother Alf himself and spare you the danger."

"Fool," Richard said. "He'll find a corpse or nothing at all, and likely get his death by it."

"Sire!"

Richard hardly heard him. "I'll find him. As God is my witness, I'll find him, alive and whole and telling me I was mad to have tried it."

"Your Majesty," Jehan said, shaking but determined, "you can't do that. Your court—your war with Gwynedd—"

"Damn the court! Damn the war! Damn the world! I'll have that boy back, or I'll cast my crown in a dungheap."

"He's only one man."

"He's only my friend."

Long after he was gone, Jehan stood, trembling uncontrollably.

When at last he could command his body, he sat on the block and breathed deep. Now the King would ride out, searching for a traitor. Bishop Aylmer had wanted that; had all but challenged Richard to try it. But he would not search in St. Benedict's. That, the Bishop would make sure of. With the King abroad upon a fruitless chase and the war in Gwynedd forgotten, the Church would look after its own.

And the least of its novices would wait and pray, and try not to think of what the Hounds might be doing to Brother Alf. Jehan rose and took up the axe, and returned grimly to his penance.

Brother Adam sighed wearily. "Will you not confess?"

"No," Alf said with equal weariness. "I am not the Devil's minion. I know nothing of the black arts."

"But more of dialectic than any man ought, let alone one of the Night's brood." Adam shook his head. "Brother, I have done all that I can. There are those who urge me to resort to force. Is this what you would have?"

This too Alf had heard before. Without a tremor he said, "The answer would be the same."

Adam looked down at him where he sat upon his pallet, a dim figure by candlelight. He stared back without expression. He had eaten nothing since he was taken; he felt light, hollow, almost heedless. It has become a game, this constant resistance, four days and four nights of fruitless questioning. The other was haggard, unshaven, shadow-eyed; when he touched his own face, he could feel the jut of bones beneath the skin.

"Brother," he said, "I won't confess to a crime I haven't committed. Not even to spare you pain."

"Not even to spare yourself?"

Alf shook his head.

"I will not be your questioner in that extremity," Adam warned him. "Brother Reynaud will have the honor. He is well known for his skill."

"I'm not surprised," Alf murmured.

"That was not charitable."

"Neither is he." Alf lay back.

There was a pause. As it stretched to breaking, the other laid an icy hand upon his brow. "You are very warm. But you do not look fevered." He held the candle close. Alf turned his face away from it.

"Strange," Adam said. "In this room, in this season, you should be blue with cold. Yet I have never seen you shiver."

Alf shivered then; but Adam shook his head. "Too late, Brother. Your Master has shielded you well against the banes of your kind, cold iron and sacred things. Why, I wonder, has he omitted to take away the fire of Hell which warms you?"

"If it were Hell's fire," Alf said through clenched teeth, "it would sear your hand."

"Could it, Brother?"

"It is not Hell's fire."

"Then, pray, what may it be?"

"My own body's warmth. That is all."

"So simple a thing, to be so inexplicable."

"Inexplicable?" Alf asked. "Hardly. My fiery humors are in full blaze. I'm being held against my will; I'm charged with black sorcery; now you threaten me with torture. Can you wonder that my anger keeps me warm?"

"If all men were so made, we would have no need of clothing. Wrath alone would suffice."

"Though not for modesty," Alf said.

Adam was silent, his eyelids lowered, but he continued to watch Alf from beneath them.

"St. Ruan's Abbey," he said at last. "You were raised there, you say. Have you considered that if you persist in your obstinacy and are punished for it, your Brothers will suffer? For since it is what it is, where it is—surely its monks knew what dwelt among them: a creature of that elder race which ruled there before Christ's Gospel was borne into Anglia."

"My Brothers are guilty of no fault. They have seen nothing, recognized nothing, for I am no more and no less than any one of them."

Adam shook his head slowly, half in denial, half in sorrowful rebuke.

Alf sat up. "They are not guilty. There are no Elder Folk."

"There, Brother, you lie outright. For I have seen them. With my own eyes I have looked on them."

"But not in Ynys Witrin, Brother Adam. That I know. They do not haunt St. Ruan's cloister. Christ is ruler there; his cross rises above the Tor." Alf smote his hands together. "Accuse me if you must. But in the name of the God who made us both, let my Brothers be!"

Again Adam paused, pondering. "If you will confess, I may be able to keep St. Ruan's out of the tribunal's consideration."

"I do not bargain with lies," Alf said. "Nor would you be wise to threaten more than my mere self. Remember that your Order is a new one, not yet as powerful as it would wish to be, and St. Ruan's is very large, very wealthy, and very, very old. Would you dare to set yourself against so great a power?"

"Would you dare to call upon it?"

The chill left Alf's voice to lodge in his bones. "I am the least of its children. I will not beset it with this shame."

"No shame to it if you are innocent."

"So am I condemned. I protest my innocence—I am commanded to confess. I speak of shame—it must be guilt, and not a foul and envious lie. Wherever I turn, whatever I say, I cannot be exonerated. My very face is held as evidence against me."

"So it is," Adam said. "So it must be until all the truth is known."

"The truth as you would have it."

"The truth of God." Adam signed himself and his prisoner. "May He keep you, and loose your tongue at last."

For that, he gained only silence and the turning of Alf's back.

Alf lay in the dark, luxuriating in his solitude, in quiet unbroken by that gentle deadly questioning. It would resume all too soon, to wear him down, to search out his weaknesses.

In the end he would confess. But not easily, and not soon.

You may not be able to choose.

Thea's voice. He closed his mind against her.

There was a long stillness. Outside, his guard snored softly.

The bolt slid back. The snoring did not pause. Alf turned, for that was not Adam's slow sandaled tread. This was silent save for the faint rustling of cloth. He could see no more than a dark shape, clad and cowled in black.

"Thea!" he whispered fiercely. "Will you never learn—"

Her hand covered his mouth. "Hush, little Brother. You wouldn't talk to me the safest way, and I won't be put off."

"If anyone comes and sees you—"

"I'll be invisible, inaudible, and intangible." She knelt beside him. There was light enough from the guard's cresset outside for their eyes to see, but her fingers explored his face. "You're down to bare bone. But"—she examined the rest of his body, despite his resistance—"they haven't harmed you yet. I suppose you regret that."

Her hands had ended on his shoulders. He wanted to shake them off, but he did not. *Better there,* he thought, *than elsewhere.*

She laughed very softly. "Why, little Brother! Prison's been good for you. It's chipped off a layer or two of prudery."

"Is that all you came to see?"

"No." She released him and sat on her heels. "I've been eavesdropping. You haven't used power much, have you?"

"Only with my questioner, and only a little."

"That's what I was afraid of. I don't suppose you know what's been happening."

"The King is looking far afield for me. Bishop Aylmer is waiting for the Hounds to betray themselves. Kilhwch's messenger is coming."

"You're better-informed than I thought," Thea said. "Did you know that you're to be tried on St. Nicholas' Eve?"

Alf drew his breath in sharply. "Two days—but they were waiting for my confession!"

"The Hounds were. Earl Hugo and his imbecile of a Bishop have been getting nervous. They want you safely tried and burned before the King gets back. Aylmer they'll tell of the trial—far too late for him to gather any resistance. Then when Richard appears they can say that it was an ecclesiastical matter; that Aylmer was notified; and that the sentence was carried out promptly to prevent a public outcry against the terrible sorcerer. All in due and proper form. And you'll be a heap of ashes, and he'll have lost what he loves most."

"No," Alf said. "He doesn't love me. He loves my face. He lusts after my body."

"He loves you," said Thea. "God knows why."

Alf clenched his fists. "You are doing your best to talk me out of this. You won't succeed. I know what I'm doing; I've considered all the consequences; I won't be shaken."

"You," she said in a thin cold voice, "are the most selfish being I've ever known."

"Why? Because I won't walk out with you now and forget both my duties and my troubles, and let you seduce me as you've tried to do since first we met?"

"Seduce you? *You*, you pallid, spineless, canting priest?"

"You sound exactly like the King," he said. "Do you fancy that you love me?"

When he could see again, she was gone. He lay where she had felled him, his brain reeling. Women, he thought foggily, were frail vindictive creatures, given more to tears than to blows. But this one had a heavier hand then Coeur-de-Lion.

Almost he called her back. He had meant to wound her; and yet, he had not.

Better for both of them that they not meet again.

He lay on his side, hand to his throbbing cheek, and tried to make his mind a void.

21

The Chapter House of St. Benedict's was a wonder of the north: a ring of pale gold stone, its vault held up with many pillars, and on each pillar a carven angel. Between St. Gabriel and St. Michael, beneath a gilded arch, sat Bishop Foulques. Robed and mitered, with an acolyte warding his jeweled crozier, he seemed no living man but an image set upon a tomb. His long pale face had no more life or color than one molded in wax.

On his right, beneath arches smaller and unadorned, sat figures cowled in black or gray, monks of St. Benedict and of St. Paul. On his left, somewhat apart, was Bishop Aylmer, dressed as he had come from Mass, in the brown habit of a monk of St. Jerome. Set against the splendor of his brother-Bishop's garb, his simplicity was a rebuke.

Jehan, beside him, felt even larger and more ungainly than usual, crowded into a narrow niche with no more than a finger's breadth to spare on either side. He battled the urge to make himself as small as he might and sat erect and still, shoulders back, hands upon his knees. Opposite him, the monks stared and whispered. They had not expected Bishop Aylmer to appear on an hour's notice. Nor, Jehan suspected, had they thought to see himself.

Reynaud was not among them. After that first swift glance, Jehan ignored them.

A man in Pauline garb entered and knelt before Bishop Foulques, murmuring in his ear. The Bishop nodded once, imperially.

There was a pause, then a stir at the door, echoed round the hall. Jehan went rigid.

Four monks of St. Paul paced into the hall, burly men with hard grim faces. In their midst walked their solitary charge.

Jehan drew a shuddering breath. Brother Alf moved with the same light grace as always despite the chains which bound his hands; he bore no mark of violence. Yet he was alarmingly thin, his eyes black-shadowed, his skin so pale that it seemed translucent.

His guards brought him to stand apart on the Bishop's left, facing outward. If he saw Jehan, he did not show it. His gaze was strange, blurred, exalted, as if he walked in a trance.

Bishop Foulques rose slowly. The acolyte placed the crozier in his hand; he settled it firmly and straightened his cope. "My brothers," he intoned, "we are met in Christ's name by the authority of Holy Church. The Lord be with you."

"And with your spirit," the monks responded.

"Oremus," the Bishop bade them. "Let us pray."

Jehan barely heard the long ritual, prayer and psalm and prayer again, blessing and invocation and calling of Heaven to the labor of justice. His eyes and his mind fixed upon the tall slight figure of the prisoner.

The prayers ended; a monk came forward, he who had spoken to Bishop Foulques, with a parchment in his hand. He began to read from it in a voice both soft and clear.

"We gather here, my most noble and august Lord Bishop, to seek your judgment. Before you stands one anointed with the sacred oil of the priesthood, consecrated upon the altar of God most high, yet accused of crimes most terrible and most unholy, forbidden by all the laws of God and man. By the testimony of many witnesses and by that of the prisoner himself, we have found due and proper cause to call him to this trial. Therefore, with God as our witness, we contend that this prisoner, known in this world as Alfred, once of St. Ruan's upon Ynys Witrin and now of the following of His Majesty's Lord Chancellor, is in fact a thing unholy and unclean, a changeling, a sorcerer, and a servant of the Lord of Hell; that he has knowingly and blasphemously profaned his sacred vows; and that he has cast a glamour upon His Majesty the King and upon His Majesty's Chancellor, blinding them to his demonic origins and shaping them to his infernal ends."

Jehan ground his teeth. Aylmer's hand had clamped about his wrist, else he would have risen. Perforce, he sat motionless and help-less, while the gentle voice wove its net of lies and half-truths.

As the monk went on, Jehan's wrath turned cold. In that grim clarity he became aware of a strangeness, a faint, maddening rever-beration at the end of each pause. At first he did not trust his ears; yet with each brief silence he heard the echo more clearly. When at last the speaker ceased, there was no echo but a faint, distinct *"Amen!"*

Brother Alf had heard the charges without expression. But his eyes had focused slowly; had flickered about as if he searched for something. Others too cast uneasy glances round the room; one of the monks crossed himself.

Bishop Foulques seemed oblivious to the ghost-voice. "We have heard the charges," he said. "We will now hear the witnesses."

Was that a ripple of eldritch laughter?

The Pauline monk laid aside his parchment, genuflected to the Bishop, nodded to the man who guarded the door. He opened it to admit a young man at once arrogant and afraid. His eyes flicked at once to Alf and flinched away. He bowed low before Bishop Foulques, hesitated, bowed likewise to Aylmer.

As he straightened, the monk smiled at him. "Ah, sieur, you come in good time." He gestured; an acolyte brought a stool and set it in front of the Bishop. As the young man sat upon it, the monk said, "You would be Sir Olivier de Romilly, would you not?" The knight nodded; again he smiled. "And I am Brother Adam of Ely. My lord Bishop you know; it is to him that you should speak, although it is I who will question you."

Sir Olivier smoothed a wrinkle in his scarlet hose. "And the rest?" he asked.

"They will only listen," said Brother Adam. "I will speak and my lord will judge."

The other nodded.

Adam paused. After a moment he said, "Some days ago you told me a tale. Perhaps it would be best for my lord if you told it to him now, just as you told me."

Olivier obeyed. He would not look at Alf or at the silent Bishop; he spoke to the likeness of St. Michael with his flaming sword, in a high rapid voice as if reciting a lesson.

"A fortnight and more ago, I was riding with the King against

Earl Rahere and his rebels. We fought in the hills by Windermere; a hard fight as they all are, though we had the victory. I was one of those who paid for it. I met a man with an axe—a Viking he must have been, as they tell of in old tales, a great blond giant of a man. I broke my sword on his axe; he dragged me from my horse and hewed me down.

"I was badly hurt. Very badly hurt, Brother, my lord. My yeomen carried me to the tent where the doctors were. There were strangers there. They were helping the doctors."

Olivier stopped. The listeners leaned forward, intent. Bishop Foulques frowned.

"They were helping the doctors," Olivier repeated. "I didn't think much of it. One doesn't when one's had an axe in the shoulder.

"One of them came to me. He gave me water. I was very glad of that. Then he . . . he touched me."

"Yes?" murmured Adam as the pause stretched beyond endurance.

"He touched me. I remember, he was looking at me—not at my face, but at my shoulder. I thought he must have been a clerk, but he was dressed like a squire. Then I thought it was strange that I could think at all. And then . . . then I knew." Olivier shivered. "I didn't feel any pain. None. Only a sort of warmth, like a patch of sun."

"And your wound?"

Olivier touched his shoulder and flexed it. "I was all over blood. But there was nothing there."

"No scar?"

"Brother, you know full well—" He stopped, composed himself. "There was a scar. My lord. But no wound. That, I've sworn to, on holy relics."

"May my lord see?"

Jehan had felt the blood drain from his face as the young knight told his tale. When he bared his shoulder and the deep livid scar there, the novice swallowed bile. He had not known of that healing; Brother Alf had never spoken of it. Which was most damnably like him. Had he been trying even then to get himself killed?

He seemed unmoved, although the eyes which turned to him held now a kind of horror.

"Prisoner," Bishop Foulques said, no name, no title. "Have you aught to say?"

Alf drew a breath to speak. In the silence, a thin eerie voice chanted: *"Kyrie eleison!"*

His lips tightened. "No," he said. "No, my lord. I have nothing to say."

Adam turned to him. "No, Brother? Is it true then as Messire has said? Did you work your sorceries upon him?"

" 'And He healed them,' " sang that voice without breath or body: " 'and the multitude wondered, when they saw the dumb to speak, the maimed to be whole, the lame to walk, and the blind to see: and they glorified the God of Israel.' "

Alf threw up his head like a startled deer.

Laughter rippled through the hall. Bishop Foulques half-rose; Olivier drew his dagger and spun about, hunting wildly for the enemy.

Brother Adam alone seemed unperturbed. "The air is full of sorcery," he said. He sketched a blessing over Olivier's head. "Go, and have no fear. No evil can touch you."

Olivier withdrew, white and shaking, his dagger still in his hand. One by one the monks settled back into their seats. The Bishop sat once more; his acolyte straightened his cope and crowned him again with the miter which had fallen from his head.

Brother Adam considered them all, so quietly certain of his victory that Jehan wanted to strike him down. "You have heard, Brothers," he said, "true and certain proof that we contend here with the work of the Enemy. For it is the way with demons that they make mock of what is holy. I would have you hear now of a night not long ago, when our prisoner revealed his nature for all to see."

The new witness was a stranger to Jehan, a man in the garb of a Benedictine novice. He had a handsome languid face and the air of a nobleman, but some ruthless barber had cropped his hair to stubble.

By that Jehan knew him. He took in the stranger's lazy grace, his expression of worldly ennui, and detested him, instantly, utterly.

He performed an obeisance which was proper to the point of parody and sat where he was bidden, enduring Brother Adam's introduction with every evidence of boredom. When he spoke, it was to Alf. "So, Brother. You look well in chains."

"And you," Alf said, "look ill in that habit."

Joscelin smiled. "Maybe it's your ham-handed barbering."

"Brother," Adam said, with the first small hint of sharpness Jehan had heard from him, "you are here to tell your tale."

"So I am," Joscelin agreed, unruffled. "Well now. How shall I begin?"

"At the beginning," Adam suggested.

Joscelin settled more comfortably. "So. The beginning. A good enough place, isn't it, pretty Brother?" He caught Adam's eye and grimaced. "Very well. I'll begin. I was the King's esquire then, and proud of it too. A little more than a sennight past, I walked out with friends for an evening's pleasure. On the way we met with yonder beauty."

Jehan clenched his fists. Olivier had told the truth as much as he might, but this was truth twisted out of all recognition. As Joscelin told it, he and his fellow squires had taken Alf with them out of sheer goodwill, with a touch of censure for his most unclerical fondness for ale.

"And for the serving-wench," said Joscelin with a wry look, half the admiring young squire, half the new-hatched cleric.

Alf had gone upstairs with them, though reluctantly, Joscelin conceded; but then, he had been with the King not long before. No one mistook the implication. Alf stared at his feet, fists clenched about his chains.

"He was even more reluctant when he saw the woman," Joscelin said. "We did wrong, I'd be the first to admit it, my lords, but we were drunk, and so was he. We got him out of his habit." He paused, shook his head and sighed. "Brothers, before God, it was perilous to look at him. Nakedness of course is a sin, and when you couple it with such a body . . . *pardieu!* He looks a pretty fool, like a girl with her hair cut off, but the rest of him—"

"You stripped him," Adam broke in. "And then?"

One or two of the listeners sat back in ill-concealed disappointment. Joscelin sighed and resumed his tale. A sword had appeared in Alf's hand; Joscelin had tried to dissuade him; he had threatened, and the squire had lured him down to the common room, where the public eye might shock the monk back to his senses.

It did not. He covered himself in a robe of darkness and worked his magic with the sword, and before half a hundred startled men, he vanished.

Adam nodded as he finished. "We have found and questioned a number of the witnesses," he said, taking from his wallet a folded parchment and placing it in the Bishop's hand. "This, my lord, is their assembled testimony. All have sworn, separately and similarly, that he clothed his body with nothing more substantial than shadows, and that he disappeared from the midst of them all. We have his habit and his cloak, taken from the room in the inn, certain proof of his presence there."

"And from thence he was taken up to heaven, alleluia."

Not a few of those there had expected it; but that uncanny voice roused them to superstitious terror. Brother Adam raised his arms. "In the name of Father, Son, and Holy Spirit, be thou still!"

For a long moment no one breathed. The voice was silent. Slowly each man relaxed, although he looked about uneasily, signed himself, and muttered a prayer.

Adam let his arms fall.

Eldritch laughter mocked all their folly.

A flush stained Adam's pale face. "Brothers," he said, "my lord Bishops, surely it is clear to you all that the Evil One lurks among us. One of his servants stands before you. The other you have heard; and of that one I have somewhat to say. For I have learned from witnesses that the accused is not alone in his sorcery. A familiar serves him, a creature of darkness which takes most often the shape of hound. It is a clever being, more clever if I may say it than its master, for we have been unable to capture it. Yet there are many who have seen it, and one man has observed it in its sorceries." He nodded to Joscelin, who retired to a seat among the monks, and raised his voice. "Brother! You may come in."

It was Reynaud who took his place before the judge, that hated face, that hated smile. Olivier had borne witness for fear, Joscelin for malice, but this man testified for the love of it. He had found Alf, he had begun the pursuit; now he bent to rend the throat of his quarry.

He spoke calmly, distinctly, with none of the false friendliness Jehan had known. From the first day of Alf's arrival in the camp, he had watched and recorded and judged, and he had missed very little. His tale took in Olivier's and Joscelin's and the accounts of many witnesses, and shaped from them a larger whole, the portrait of a sorcerer.

And of his familiar. "A white hound," he said, "with red ears like the beasts of the pagan superstitions, and in its eyes the intelligence of a child of Hell. But when it chooses, it walks erect in human form."

"In what likeness?" Adam asked him.

"A shadow-shape, cowled like a monk but speaking with the voice of a beautiful woman."

And he told of the night in the stable, word for word. Eyes turned to Jehan as he spoke; the novice glared back. "Yes!" he wanted to shout. "I was there. I knew it all. Burn me, too!"

He could not speak. His tongue felt enormous, leaden; when he tried to form words, his mind blurred. He sat in silence, raging.

Reynaud ended at last. The monks stirred and murmured. "The *Gloria Dei,*" someone said in a stunned voice. "He wrote the *Gloria Dei?*"

"Demonic mockery," Reynaud answered firmly, "intended to lead the young novice astray."

Jehan leaped to his feet.

The door burst open. A battle raged through it. Pauline white and gray, Benedictine black, and in the midst of it a whirlwind.

The struggle parted. Its center hurled itself forward, full upon Reynaud. Together they toppled.

Jehan plunged into the fray. A wild blur of faces—Bishop Foulques's beyond, crumbling into terror—a white shape, a tangle of bronze-gold hair. Jehan stared into Thea's wide feral eyes.

Adam's voice rose above the tumult. "What is this?"

The battle resolved into individual shapes. Reynaud sagged in his fellows' arms, groaning, his face bleeding from a dozen deep scratches. No one else had come to harm.

Jehan let Thea go and backed away. She stood breathing hard, her hair falling about her face. Her gown was rent and torn; white flesh gleamed beneath.

She tossed back her hair. Some shrank from her; others started forward. She froze them all with her glare, her great eyes like a cat's, golden, wild. Her beauty smote Jehan's heart.

Again Adam spoke. "What is this?"

It was she who responded. Her voice they all knew, though this was born of throat and tongue and lips, a living voice as that other had not been. "I am not *what.* I am *who.* Is it a work of your famous Christian charity to wound a harmless woman?"

One of the monks called out, "It's a demon! It appeared before us; it tried to lure us away; Brother Andreas pretended to yield, and I struck it with the flat of my knife." He held it up, a small blade, too blunt for aught but cutting bread.

She whirled upon him. He raised the knife; she recoiled. "Aye," she cried, "he struck me, damn him to his own Hell; he burned me horribly." Across the palm of her hand spread a long red weal. She cradled it against her breast. "I shall demand redress."

Adam regarded her with an uncanny mingling of triumph and horror. "What sort of creature is this, that the flat of a blade will burn it?"

"The blade was iron," she said, shuddering, holding her

wounded hand close. "Cursed iron. I would have gone free if he had not struck me with it."

"You should never have come!"

All eyes turned to Alf. He had fought his own battle to escape from his guards; two gripped him still, although he no longer struggled. "You should never have come," he repeated.

"What! and miss such a splendid game?"

"It is no game for me, nor now for you. For God's sake, escape while you still can."

"I can't," she said. "I'm bound."

"You're no more bound than——"

"Little Brother," she said to him, half in scorn, half in tenderness, "there's honor even in the hollow hills."

"That doesn't mean you have to die with me!"

"No?" She turned away from him to Brother Adam. "Yon holy saint, sir, is as witless as he is beautiful. My grief, for I saw him as he rode in the wood, and he was as fair as the princes of my own people; I set my heart upon him. But a greater fool never left an abbey. Would he dance with me? Would he let me sing to him? Would he be my paramour? No, and no, and no: and Lord have mercy, and begone, foul fiend, and back to his prayers again. Prayers, forsooth! and he so fair that the Goddess herself couldn't ask for better."

Adam's thin nostrils flared. Here was a gift to lay at the feet of the Pope himself: no mere witch or heretic, but a true child of old Night. "Are you aware that this is a trial, and that Brother Alfred is accused of serious crimes against the Church?"

"Crimes? He doesn't even know how to sin!"

"He stands accused of sorcery, for which the penalty is death."

"He?" She laughed, that same wild laughter which had run bodiless to the vaulted roof. "That child could walk among us and pass for one of us, but he's altogether a son of Earth."

"The evidence——"

"Lies," she said. "Lies and twisted truth."

Bishop Foulques moved suddenly to strike his crozier upon the floor. "This is a mockery! Brother, rid us of this creature."

She regarded him in amazement. "What! The stones can speak?"

A flush suffused the Bishop's waxen cheeks. "Adam! Do as I say."

Aylmer rose. Through all of that turmoil, he had not moved or spoken, had shown no fear or surprise. When he stood, it was as if one of the carven angels had stepped down from its pillar. "My lord

Bishop," he said, "it is my understanding that you wish to determine the guilt of a sorcerer. The Brothers have gathered their evidence scrupulously enough, although I find certain of their methods somewhat questionable and their motives disturbing. It concerns me particularly that no attempt has been made on the part of this court to defend the innocence of the accused. Yet it seems to me that this lady, however unorthodox her arrival and her origins may be, has undertaken to do precisely that. Will you prevent her from doing so?"

Foulques seemed close to an apoplectic fit. "She has invaded the precincts of the Church's justice, has—"

"Justice?" Aylmer asked. "Is it justice to refuse to consider evidence of a person's innocence? In the court of His Holiness in Rome, even the Devil has his Advocate."

As Aylmer spoke, Adam had approached Foulques and whispered urgently in his ear. He shook his head, glowering; Adam persisted; at length, with obvious reluctance, he nodded.

Adam faced Bishop Aylmer. "My lord will permit her to testify. Yet she should be aware that her testimony may lead to her own trial and possible conviction; for we are committed to the destruction of all of Satan's works and creatures."

"Then," said Thea, "you would do well to burn your King."

Aylmer considered her for a long moment. "Maybe it will come to that, my lady," he said. "When the King's friend is in danger, can the King himself be safe?"

"The King has been bewitched," Adam said sharply. "We seek to protect him from such evil and to destroy the source of it."

Aylmer nodded to himself. "Ah, yes. I'm bewitched, too. Well then, continue with your mummery." He beckoned. "Come here, Jehan. Sit and let them entertain us."

Adam chose to ignore him. He glanced about, saw that a man guarded the door with drawn sword, faced Thea. "You say that you are bound. How so?"

She gestured toward the monk with the knife. "He touched me with iron, and it has a stronger magic than mine. I can't leave unless he bids me."

"Indeed." Adam indicated the stool. "Sit."

"I prefer to stand."

He did not press her. "Very well. First, your name."

"Oh, no," she said. "Iron binds me tightly enough. I won't give you that power besides."

Reynaud shook off the hands which had supported him. "Thea. They called you Thea."

Her lip curled. "Jackal. Vulture. I scented you upon our path. Would to Annwn I had done as my heart bade me and torn out your throat."

"Your name is Thea?" Adam asked her quietly.

Her eyes burned upon him. "Yes. But you gain no power by it. It's not my true-name."

"Thea, then. Not a name of this land."

"And not the truth."

"So." Adam looked her up and down. "You are of the Fair Folk?"

"Haven't I said so? I saw your Brother Alfred as he rode through Bowland; I followed him."

"In the likeness of a white hound?"

"A hound!" She tossed her head. "Should I so degrade myself? I followed him; now and then I let him see me. He would have nothing to do with me. Such a little saint, he is. Either he tried to exorcise me, or he tried to make a Christian of me. I tempted him with enchantments; he prayed them away."

"Enchantments?" asked Adam. "How so?"

"So," she shot back. "One night three young hellions trapped him in a tavern. I want him to be a man and not a mumbling priest—but the Gray Man can have us both before I let any mortal woman have him. I gave him a sword and the skill to use it; I clothed him in spells; and he escaped. Did he thank me for it? No, before all the gods! He cursed me and bade me begone."

"That's not so!" Alf cried.

She raised her hand. He gasped and swayed. "Love is a blind god," she said, "and an utter fool, else why do I endure this? See how he tries to save me, who never had a kind word for me when I begged him to love me."

"You contend that he has practiced no sorcery?" Adam demanded of her.

"So does he," she pointed out.

"The sorceries ascribed to him are in fact yours."

"Sorceries," she said, "no. We don't traffic with the Dark. But the spells were mine. I was abasing myself to win that iron heart. I made his way easy for him. I warmed the water he washed in, I healed the man he tended, I set a hound to guard him. All useless. He's as cold as ever."

He stood mute as Jehan had stood, white with the strain of his resistance. She regarded him sadly. "Little Brother, I didn't know the humans would try to burn you for what I did."

"You say he is of mortal descent."

"Entirely."

"We have gathered certain evidence—"

"Nonsense," she said. "Look at him! No one of the true blood could wear a cross or bear such chains. All your so-called evidence is a travesty."

"So is your testimony!" Reynaud burst out. "I say that you are both witches and sorcerers; that you aided and abetted each other, and that you both should go to the fire."

She spat at him. "Cur! You would give your soul to gnaw our bones."

"Silence!" Adam commanded them. To Foulques he said, "My lord, I am inclined to support Brother Reynaud. I was not aware of this woman's existence or intervention, both of which alter the charges somewhat. That she may have worked her witchery as she has told us, I believe, yet I am not convinced of the other's innocence. Surely he yielded to her to some extent; he made use in the inn of the gifts she gave him, whatever he may have told her afterward."

"The stable," Reynaud said. "Their speech—"

"Devilish mockery, you said yourself," she broke in. "You can't have it both ways, jackal. If our little Brother, our beardless boy, is the greatest of your theologians, then surely he must be of our blood, for the book he wrote is twice as old as his face. But that can't be possible, can it? You didn't hear what you thought you heard, what you wanted to hear in your lust for his death."

"Witch!" he hissed.

"I madden you. You can't bear it that I should want him and not you. If I promised to take you, you would do everything in your power to have me set free. You'd even promise to free him—but that would be a lie."

Beneath the livid marks of her nails, his face was a mask of fury. "Demon! Tempter!"

"But not a liar," she said. "It's you who lie. You want him to die, for your own glory and for the King's grief. You haven't deigned to mention all the accomplices who must have known what our Brother was, raised him and trained him and made a monk of him—they're too many and too far away, and much too powerful. You haven't even called Master Jehan to account for his guilt, though in your tale he's as much at fault as the rest of us, for he doesn't matter to you and he has kin who could avenge him. The King's kin are his enemies and urge you on, and the little Brother has none."

Adam stepped between them. "We do not act as the bidding of any temporal power. Our part is to search out and destroy the enemies of the Church; here in this court we judge by that Law which commands, 'There shall not be found among you any one that maketh his son or his daughter to pass through the fire, or that useth divination, or is an observer of times, or an enchanter, or a witch, or a charmer, or a consulter of familiar spirits, or a wizard, or a nec-romancer. For all that do these things are an abomination unto the Lord.' And in speaking of punishment, the Law is most simple and most strict: 'Thou shalt not suffer a witch to live.' "

There was a silence. Thea seemed at last to have understood what she had confessed. A tremor ran through her body; she drew back a step, shying as her guard raised his knife. She stopped and stood very still. "Brother Alfred is not a sorcerer. If anyone is to die, it must be I, though life on this earth is very sweet, and since they tell me I have no soul, Heaven is barred to me."

"Hell will take you gladly," Reynaud muttered.

She hissed at him. "The Dark Lord is my bitter enemy, as he is of all my people. We've thwarted him too often and too thoroughly. But you he would welcome with open arms."

She turned to the Bishop. "This is not a trial. This is a gathering of the King's enemies to destroy the one thing he cares for. That one"—she indicated Adam with a toss of her head—"believes in what he does, which is all the worse for him. But the rest of you would kneel to a crucifix, and then spit on it." Through gasps of horror and cries to seize her and cast her down, she laughed without mirth. "Ah, you mortal men! The truth sears you like cold iron. Shall I strike you again? You'll burn the little Brother. The stake is ready; you have only to tie him to it and light the fire. And then the King will come. What then, Lord Bishop? While you kept to the abbey and plotted in secret, he suffered you. But now you declare open enmity."

"He will not touch a man of God," Adam said. "He dares not."

Again she laughed, freely now, almost joyously. "Don't be a fool. He'll tear down this abbey stone by stone and drive you Hounds into the sea, and rend yon puppet of a Bishop limb from limb and cast him to the dogs."

"Interdict—anathema—"

"You're babbling, pious Brother. Ask Bishop Aylmer if Anglia or its King will suffer for vengeance taken upon traitors."

"*Silence!*" Bishop Foulques was on his feet, quivering with passion. "The trial will resume. And I will hear no further word from you, witch; or as God is my witness, I will cast you out."

"My lord Bishop," Adam said soothingly, "she will not speak again. We, for our part, have presented our case. We contend that the prisoner is guilty as charged, and we submit him to your judgment."

For a long while, Bishop Foulques did not respond. He had mastered himself; his face had returned from livid wrath to its former pallor. He seemed deep in thought, frowning, shooting swift glances at Alf, at Thea, at Aylmer: glances compounded of hatred and of cold terror. Slowly, repeatedly, his thumb traced the intricate carving of his crozier.

When at last he spoke, it was to no one and to everyone, in a firm voice. "I have heard both attack and defense. I have reached a conclusion."

He paused. Jehan found that he could not breathe. Alf was absolutely still, death-pale; Thea had turned toward him, holding him fast with her burning gaze.

The Bishop resumed. "No one has denied that witchcraft has been practiced in and about this city and the King. The doubt seems to lie in the identity of its practitioner. Either it is a woman of unknown origins and overweening arrogance, and a flagrant disregard of the dignity of the Church, its court, and its Scriptures; or it is a monk in the habit of the holy Order of St. Jerome, an ordained priest and an acknowledged favorite of His Majesty the King." Again he paused. Most of those there listened in puzzlement. But Adam's face had paled and Reynaud's gone livid. "The charges are grave. The penalty, as Brother Adam has informed us, is death."

Alf tore his gaze from Thea's and turned toward the Bishop.

Foulques raised his voice slightly. "It is my belief that both the accused and the woman are guilty of witchcraft, of sorcery, and of black enchantment. Yet in view of the evidence, it is also my belief that the guilt is not evenly apportioned. The prisoner has not confessed to his crimes, but has denied them; the woman . . ." He steadied himself with a visible effort. "The woman has admitted her guilt freely, insolently, and most unrepentantly. She also denies that the other shares that guilt; of this I am not convinced. In my judgment, she was the instigator, he the accomplice; she the cause, he the sharer of their sorceries.

"Therefore," Foulques proclaimed, "I sentence them both. You," he said to Alf, avoiding the pale stare, "as a priest of God, have sinned most grievously. Yet you are young, of an age when the beauty of a woman may overcome the strength of your vows; the passion of your blood has tempted you to do what is most direly forbidden. You have not fallen wholly, as this woman has testified; yet for your transgressions you must pay the due and proper penalty. Here before the court of Holy Church, by her authority vested in me, I suspend you from your sacred vows. You shall not go up to the altar of God, nor perform the functions of a priest, nor admit yourself into the company of priests or of monks, until such time as you may have proven by the purity of your life and actions that you have atoned fully for your sin. Furthermore, to remind you that you are but dust and ashes in the face of the Lord, I command that you submit to the punishment of twenty lashes upon your bare back; and that with each stroke, you cry to Him for His mercy."

Alf stood rigid. His face was terrible, wholly inhuman.

The Bishop turned to Thea, his eyes glittering. "And you," he said. "You have cast your mockery in the face of Holy Church. You have given voice to lies born of the Devil your sire. And yet, in coming to this place, in crying your defiance, you have submitted yourself to our power. That power I invoke to its fullest extent. Woman of the hills, nameless one, corrupter of priests, you shall die by sacred and cleansing fire, and your bones shall be cast into a pit, and the curse of God's wrath shall lie upon them."

Alone of all those who listened, she seemed unmoved. Alf broke away from his guards. "No!" he shouted. "*No!* Let her live. I lied; I deceived you all. It is I who am the sorcerer. *I* worked the spells; I pretended innocence to confound you. *I* should go to the fire. Let me die in her place!"

"So completely has she corrupted him," the Bishop said, half in pity, half in satisfaction, "that he will defend her unto death. It grieves me to see such virtue turned to evil." He raised his hand. "I have spoken. So be it. *Fiat. Fiat. Fiat.*"

22

Early in the morning of the Feast of St. Nicholas, the townsfolk of Carlisle began to gather near the east gate. In the space before St. Benedict's Abbey, a new growth had appeared in the night, a tall stake hung with chains. Heaps of brushwood stood beside it.

By full day, a sizable crowd had taken shape. A newcomer, ignorant of the cause, might have thought that they kept festival under the rare cloudless sky and despite the winter chill. They laughed and jested; among them moved peddlers and pickpockets, a traveling singer and a troupe of jugglers. On the fringes a huddled circle, a chorus of shouts and jeers, proclaimed a cockfight.

Only the space about the stake remained clear. Pauline monks guarded it, interspersed with men-at-arms who wore the blazon of the Bishop of Carlisle.

Beyond the throng in the lee of the abbey's wall, workmen had erected a canopied platform. Figures began to take their places there as the hour approached terce: Benedictines, Paulines, a layman or two. Earl Hugo appeared with his lady and half a dozen attendants, settling on the right of the vacant high seat. Not long after, Bishop Foulques swept in to take the chair of honor, escorted by the Abbot of St. Benedict's. Servants saw them settled and wrapped in warm robes against the cold.

The crowd boiled. Bishop Aylmer strode through it on foot and simply dressed, with a troop of monks at his back. Eyes widened and grew wise. Not one of the escort was armed or armored, and none wore spurs on his sandaled feet, but the smallest overtopped the burly Bishop by half a head.

Aylmer bowed curtly to the dignitaries on the dais, and paused a moment. The high ones exchanged glances; one or two half-rose as if to make room for him.

The King's Chancellor turned on his heel and took his place close to the stake, with his monks in a half-circle behind him.

* * *

At the stroke of terce, the great gate of the abbey swung open. A hush fell; eyes stared, necks craned, fathers swung children onto their shoulders.

It was a small procession for so great a matter. A tall thin Pauline monk carrying a book and a scroll; a pair of novices, thurifer and crucifer; monks chanting a psalm. And behind, guarded by mailed men with drawn swords, the prisoners. The first stood taller than his guards, a familiar pale face ravaged now with fasting and with sleeplessness, and beneath it a thin white tunic which afforded little protection from the biting wind. Chains bound his wrists, but he walked with his head up, seeing nothing and no one.

But the second made the crowd jostle and crane, straining to see. She was harder to catch a glimpse of, tall but not as tall as the other, her long tangled hair half-hiding her face. Her tunic was much like his, but her chains were far heavier, of black iron, weighing down her slender body.

A growl rumbled in a hundred throats, swelling swiftly to a roar. A stone arced over her head; others followed it. Men-at-arms surged forward, striking with fists and flattened blades.

Thea paid them no heed. Nor did she heed Alf, who continued his nightlong mental barrage. For each shield he had battered down, she had erected another; he could not reach her mind. *Thea!* he cried. *Thea, for the love of God, answer me!*

Her shield held fast. And he had nearly exhausted his mind's strength. A last desperate shaft struck not at her mind but at her chains.

It rebounded to pierce his own bruised brain. He staggered; a hard hand held him up.

Out of madness and frustration and sheer perversity, Alf let fall the illusion which shielded his eyes. The guard gasped and crossed himself.

With a small tight smile, Alf walked on. He had not restored the seeming. If enough people saw soon enough, he would go to the stake with Thea.

It loomed before him now, half again his own height, a great lopped treetrunk. Beside it stood a hooded man, in his hand a long whip. He wore lay garb, but Reynaud's mind laughed within the hood. Adam had not let him touch the precious prisoners, but Bishop Foulques had been more amenable, had let him take the executioner's place. In that much, he would have his revenge on them all.

The procession arrayed itself round the empty circle. Adam performed obeisance to the high ones, and at Bishop Foulques's nod, mounted the dais. In a clear voice he began to read the charges.

Alf did not listen. The stake held his gaze and his mind. They were economical, these people. He would be flogged first at that stake, and afterward they would bind Thea to it, heaping high the fuel. And then—

They were dragging him forward. Adam had come down from the dais; he met the monk's eyes. The mind behind them mingled regret, compassion, a touch of genuine liking; and a fire of zeal for his calling, that leaped high as the truth struck his consciousness.

Denounce me, Alf willed him. *Make them burn me. Make them!*

Adam's deep eyes hooded. He stood aside as the men-at-arms chained Alf to the stake, back to the air, face to the rough bark. It was sweet-scented, seasoned pine; it would burn well and swiftly.

Hands tore at his tunic, baring his back. Vulgar jests rang in his ears. He pressed his cheek to the wood, aware of Morwin's cross caught between breast and stake. Adam had let him keep it. Gentle, cruel Brother Adam.

There was no gentleness in Reynaud. The whip whistled as he whirled it about, teasing, taunting him with the anticipation of pain which never came.

Pain. A trail of fire across his shoulders. Remember the discipline. Remember. *Pie Jesu, miserere mei:* sunlight upon apple boughs, chanting in the choir, a child bathing in both up in the oldest tree, the Lady Tree, that had once been sacred. Remember sweet scent, sweet singing, sweet freedom-from-pain. Ride on scent, song, light, up and up to Light. *Lux. Fiat lux,* and light was made; and He looked upon it and saw that it was good.

Far below in the dark place, a small soft thing clung to a stake. Red weals marred its back. A black ant labored, striking and striking and striking again. Voices cried out to him: to stop, to slow, to go on, to beat, to strike, to kill. He laughed.

Men ran forward, small robed shapes, to seize the hand as it swung upward yet again, to wrest the whip from it, to hurl the madman laughing and struggling to the ground.

Alf plummeted. Agony—agony—

He gasped and gagged. Blood lay heavy upon his tongue. He had bitten it through.

They loosed his hands. His knees held him. Control, yes. It took control. He turned. The faces nearest him held horror. "Fifty lashes," someone said. "I counted fifty."

"Sixty," another insisted.

"More. It was more."

He dared not breathe, nor move hastily. He shook off the hands which reached to aid him, walked slowly forward. Reynaud was gone, his laughter silenced.

He stopped where his guards bade him stop. Dimly he was aware that they did not wear mail or the Bishop's blazon, but dark robes; they were tall, as tall as he or more. One face he knew, but he could put no name to it. A strong bony face, a great Norman arch of a nose, a tousle of straw-colored hair.

It blurred. Beyond it men heaped faggots about the stake, taking their time, letting the crowd work itself to a frenzy. The words and rituals of the Church sank into that uproar and vanished.

Thea stood in the center of it, very pale, very still. Tall though she was, as tall as most men, she seemed terribly frail. She tossed back her hair and turned her face to the sky; upon it, a look almost of ecstasy. When Adam made the sign of the Cross over her, she smiled. Her lips moved. "Lord of Light," she said, *"Christos Apollo, chaire, Kyrie . . ."*

It seemed an incantation. But Alf understood. She prayed in her own Greek tongue, entrusting her soul to the Light.

Her soul.

She believed that. He tried to spring forward.

She bound him with power, bonds he did not know how to break.

They chained her to the stake—face outward, she, so that all could watch her die. She was smiling still; and she changed her speech to Latin. In sudden silence, her voice rang silver-pure. *"Deum de Deo, lumen de lumine*—God from God, light from light . . ."

Alf's hand sought the silver cross. With a swift movement, he broke its chain and hurled it flashing and glittering across the wide space.

Bound though she was, she caught it. Kissed it for all to see—all those who thought her the Devil's kin. One of her guards thrust a torch deep into the fuel at her feet. Drenched with oil, it blazed up.

The flames coiled about her, caressing her with a terrible tenderness. She stretched out her hands to them. Her face was rapt, serene, untouched by pain or fear.

A howl welled from the center of Alf's being. He tensed to break free of the hands that gripped him.

And cried aloud; but not with the beast-roar that had been born in him. For the fire had enfolded her; she had melted like mist in the sun.

Out of the pyre rose a white bird with a cross in its bill. It soared up and up into the vault of the sky, winging for heaven.

The fire licked hungrily at an empty stake.

23

Alf lay on his face. His body rested in blessed comfort, but his back was a fiery agony. He had a dim memory of fire and shouting, swift-moving shadows, the call of a trumpet, a thunder of hoofs. And Jehan's face, drained of all color, with eyes that held death. *No*, he had tried to tell him. *No vengeance, Jehan. For your soul's sake, no vengeance!* But his voice would not obey him; darkness closed in.

For yet a while longer he rested. There was someone with him, and someone fretting at some little distance; he did not extend his inner senses more than that. It was too pleasant simply to lie still and know that he was well, and more, far more, that Thea lived.

He opened his eyes. The King stared back, surprise turning to relief so sharp it was like pain. "Alfred?" he asked, trying to soften his voice. "Brother?"

Alf smiled. "Good—day? Sire."

"It's night."

"Is it?" Alf raised himself on his hands. He was clean, naked but for trews of fine linen, his back salved and bandaged. As he sat up, the King reached for him in protest, but shrank from touching his hurts.

He drew a breath carefully. Movement had awakened new pain, the price of his folly. He set his teeth against it and looked about. "Sire! This is your own bed. How did I come here?"

"I brought you," Richard answered. "You shouldn't be moving about."

"I'm healthy enough. What's a stripe or two to a born eremite?"

The King's eyes glittered. "It was a lot more than two. And a lot more than twenty."

"Sire," Alf said, "don't harm anyone for my sake."

"They were eager enough to harm you for mine."

"I started it, Sire. I sought it out."

Richard fixed him with a steady amber stare. "I know you did. I should hang you up by the thumbs. Do you have any conception of what it did to me to be chasing wild geese all over Cumbria, and to find out too late that you were right under my nose? If you weren't half-flayed already, I'd have your hide for that."

Alf's head drooped; his eyes lowered, shamed. "I'm sorry, Sire. Most sorry."

"You ought to be. While I was out hunting will-o'-the-wisps like the scatterbrained fool I am, half my knights decided they'd rather spend Yule at home by the fire than fight in the snow on the Marches. It's paltry satisfaction that I smoked out a nest of rebels and got an excuse to hamstring those cursed Hounds."

"Sire!" Alf cried. "What did you do to them?"

"Little. Yet. They and their traitor Bishop are locked up safe and sound in the abbey. Tomorrow Aylmer and I will give them a somewhat fairer trial than they gave you."

Alf staggered to his feet, heedless of pain and of gathering darkness. "My lord. I beg you. Don't punish them."

The King swept him up with ease. Yet even when he had been set in bed again, he would not be quenched. "You must not!"

"Boy," Richard said, half in affection, half in exasperation, "I seem to spend a great deal of precious time fighting off your Christian charity. But this time you won't extort a surrender. His two-faced Excellency is going to discover that he didn't divert me by burning the wrong prisoner; and the Hounds have had this coming to them for a long, long while. It was their mistake to let Foulques talk them into going after you."

"It wasn't Foulques. They would have pursued me no matter who I was."

"Would they?"

"Yes," Alf said. "I told them the truth, Sire. I'm no demon nor any demon's servant. But that was only half of the truth they looked for. The woman they tried to burn . . . was no less human than I."

Richard's face did not change. "The holy angel? So she was like you. I thought so. Clever of her to make such a spectacular exit."

Alf was speechless.

Richard laughed. "Thought I was just another mortal fool, didn't you? I grant you, for a long time I was. But while I was combing the

Fells for you it all came together. Even the most dutifully Christian monk doesn't take a foreign king's command to heart unless he has good reason. Such as that that King is his kinsman."

"My ancestry—"

"Probably it's as low as you want to think it is. But you're one of Gwydion's kind. They hang together, those Fair Folk in Rhiyana. Did he send the woman to help you?"

"She came of her own accord."

"Ah," said Richard. "Was she as beautiful as you?"

"More so."

"Impossible." The King stretched. "Rather interfered with your attempt at martyrdom, didn't she?"

Alf's cheeks burned. "I was acting like a fool, my lord. She knew it. And so, at last, do I."

"Someday I'll find a way to thank her for that. When I realized what you were, I knew where you had to be. Nigh killed a good horse getting back here—just too late. If you'd had your way, by then you'd have been a pile of ashes."

Alf shivered. Richard struck his brow with his fist. "What am I doing, wearing you out with things you'd rather not hear? Wailter! Food and drink, and water the wine!"

It was not the King's servant who brought the meal, but Jehan. Richard scowled at him but said nothing. He set the cups and bowls upon the table by the bed with such admirable self-control that Alf smiled. He did not even look at the invalid, although he bowed to the King, every inch the royal page.

"Jehan," Alf said, "are you angry with me?"

The novice spun about. His face had the stiff haughty expression it always wore when he was fighting back tears. "Angry, Brother Alf? *Angry?*"

"I've made you suffer terribly."

"Not as much as you've made yourself."

"Ah, but I wanted it."

"I know. Idiot." Jehan looked him over with a critical eye, only a little blurred with tears. "You look ghastly. When's the last time you ate?"

Alf could not meet his gaze. "I don't remember."

"*That* long? *Deus meus!*" Jehan sat on the side of the bed and reached for a bowl. "Broth then and nothing else, till we've got your stomach used to working again."

"But I'm not—"

"You're never hungry. That's most of the trouble with you. Will you eat this yourself or shall I feed you?"

Beyond Jehan's head, Alf could see Richard's broad grin. With a sigh he took the bowl and raised it to his lips.

"He rode into Carlisle like the wrath of God," Jehan said when Richard had gone to contend with his court, "galloped through the crowd, scattering them right and left, and stopped dead in front of Bishop Foulques.

"Odd," the novice went on. "I expected him to blister our ears with curses. But he just sat there on his heaving horse with his men straggling up behind him, and stared. The Bishop turned the color of a week-old corpse and started to babble. The King put up his hand; old Foulques lost his voice altogether.

"The Hounds were howling like mad things about witches and sorcerers and spells; the kerns were yelling about saints and martyrs and miracles. Some people were fighting, the guards who were Hounds against a bravo or six from the town.

"The King had his man blow his trumpet. That quieted people down a little. 'Aylmer,' he said and pointed to the people on the platform, 'take these men into custody.' Bishop Aylmer did, except for Earl Hugo and his lady, who'd scampered for cover as soon as they heard the King's trumpet.

"The King didn't stop to watch. He took you up on his saddle—had to fight me for you, too, till I saw the sense in it—and carried you to the keep. Nobody got in his way." Jehan shivered. "I hope I never see anyone look like that again. He was almost as white as you, and he looked as if he wanted to cry but couldn't, and the not being able to made him want to tear the world apart."

Alf rested his forehead upon his arm. His voice was soft, muffled. "Did he curse me?"

Jehan hesitated. Then: "Only after his doctor said you'd be all right. He has an impressive vocabulary." After a moment, when Alf made no response, he added, "He stayed with you all day. He wouldn't go out at all, for anything."

There was a long silence. Jehan thought Alf had fallen asleep, until he said, "Thea is gone."

"As soon as it's safe, she'll be back."

"No. She's gone. She's kept me from getting myself killed; she's had enough of me. She's gone back to her own people."

"I suppose you're relieved," Jehan said. "You never liked her much, did you?"

Alf did not answer.

The King did not submit Bishop Foulques and his allies to the disgrace of a public trial. His revenge was more subtle. He spoke privately with the Bishop, with the Earl, and with the Paulines; and each emerged in somewhat worse state than when he had entered.

"It's what we intriguers call a 'settlement,' " Aylmer explained to Alf afterward. "Foulques has changed his allegiances rather than find himself Bishop of Ultima Thule. Hugo has become the most loyal of the King's men, with his eldest son for a surety. And our Brothers of St. Paul have found sudden and urgent reasons to leave the kingdom."

Jehan laughed. *"Urgent* is the word. None of them dares to show his face out of doors. The kerns are in a rage, that the priests of holy Church have tried to burn one of God's own angels; they'd gladly put a Hound or two in the fire."

"I'd gladly oblige them," the King said, "but I know I'd never have any peace if I tried."

Alf smiled. He had managed to bathe with Jehan's help and dress in a cotte of Richard's, and sit propped carefully with pillows. With the King and the Bishop and the novice about him and a page waiting to serve him, and half a dozen servants hovering within call, he knew how a prince must feel.

"You're the people's darling now," Jehan told him. "Everyone who said you were a sorcerer is swearing up and down that you're a saint, and that God sent His angel to save you from the fire. Sir Olivier's been going about declaring that you healed him with divine power, and promising every farthing he has to charity because he testified against you."

Alf's smile turned to a look of dismay. "I'm anything but a saint. I'm not—even—" His voice died.

"You are," said Bishop Aylmer. "I've revoked your suspension."

They waited for him to wake to joy. But he shook his head. "My lord, I'm most deeply grateful. And yet . . . No. I haven't functioned as a priest for a long while. Not since I became fully aware of what I am. But I couldn't bear to give up the duties and offices of a simple monk, mockery though they were, performed by one who was not a man." All three moved to speak; he silenced them with a glance. "I know; you think I'm wrong. Like Abbot Morwin, you think a child of the Fair Folk can be as good a priest as any mortal man. Maybe one can; maybe I can. But I know what the Church says—know it as well as the Paulines knew. Until I'm certain of the truth, I can't call myself a man of God."

"You are," Jehan said. "You *are!*"

Alf touched the other's knotted fist, lightly. It tightened; then it sprang open to grip his hand with painful force.

"Brother Alf," Jehan said, though he shook his head at the title. "You'll always be that to me. But . . . if this will help you, or heal you . . . then do it. Only, don't tear your soul apart for a few empty words."

"Sometimes one has to be torn apart in order to grow." Alf smiled his familiar wry smile, that Jehan had not seen in a long while. "See: I'm even getting wise in this my old age. There may be hope for me yet."

Alf promised to sleep if he were left alone. That won suspicious glances, but at length even Jehan withdrew.

He did sleep a little despite a rebirth of pain. In his dreams he endured again the stroke of the lash; and suddenly he held the whip, and the prisoner chained to the stake had a woman's white body and a fall of bronze-gold hair. He dropped the whip in horror; she turned in her chains. Her eyes held the old familiar mockery. "What, little Brother! Can't you even flog me properly?"

"I'm not a priest anymore," he said.

She laughed and stretched, sinuous as a cat. The chains fell away. "Not a priest? You? I don't believe it."

"I decided I needed to grow up. They were right in St. Ruan's, you know. The sacrament cast a spell on me; I stayed a boy, mind as well as body. But I've broken the spell. I'll be a man now."

"Truly?" She approached him. He stood his ground, although he trembled violently. Her hands tangled themselves in his hair, that had grown thick and long, shoulder-long; she drew his head down. He felt his body kindle. Only with her, he thought. Only, ever, with her.

"Such a handsome boy," she said. "Will you be a man?"

"Yes," he whispered. "Yes."

He started awake. No warm woman's body stirred beneath him; no wild pale mane brushed his shoulders. He staggered up and groped for the watered wine Jehan had left for him.

A deep draught steadied him somewhat. He sat on the bed, head in hands. "Poverty," he said. "Chastity. Obedience. Poverty, chastity, and obedience. Three vows, little Brother. Only three. And she is gone away and will never come back."

He drained the cup. Again he stood, swaying. Among the King's belongings he found a voluminous dark cloak. He settled it about his shoulders, flinching as the weight of fabric roused his back to pain.

No one saw him leave the King's chamber. He went slowly, concealing his face from those he passed; thronged to bursting as the castle was, he passed unnoticed.

It was raining without, a gray cold rain. He bent his head beneath it and made his way through the town.

Brother Adam paced the length of St. Benedict's cloister, heedless of the wind which swirled round the carved and painted columns to fling rain in his face. No one else had braved the weather, save one latecomer who paused in an archway, wrapped from crown to ankle in a dark cloak. Yet, swathed though he was, the stranger wore neither shoes nor sandals; his feet were bare, spattered with mud as if he had walked a distance in the wet.

He let his hood fall back. Adam regarded him without surprise. "Brother Alfred," he said.

" 'Brother' no longer," said Alf.

"No?"

"You of all people will admit that it is fitting."

"Perhaps."

Alf drew nearer to him, undisguised. He shivered slightly but stood his ground. His mind was a wondrous thing, elegantly ordered, shaped for the glory of God. Yet its foundations had begun to crumble.

Adam's voice was very quiet. "Get out of my mind."

"You know what I am," Alf said.

Still quietly, without malice, Adam responded, "You walk as a man, you pass as a man. But a man you can never be."

"You didn't denounce me."

"Perhaps I should be damned for it."

"For mercy?"

"For suffering a witch to live."

"It's a strange thing," Alf said. "We deny the power of the Old Law; we revile those who follow it still. But when it suits us, we follow it to the letter."

"A witch," said Adam, "has set the keystone upon our theology.

Alfred of St. Ruan's, you are such a creature as would drive Rome mad."

"Rome, and you, and myself. I'm learning, slowly, that sanity lies in acceptance. The world the Church has made is a world of men, but does it encompass all of the world that God has made?"

"You tread upon the edges of heresy."

"Don't we all? When you defined yourself to me, you implied that evil had created me, that God had no part in it. And that, Brother, is the error of the Manichees."

"It is a dilemma," Adam said. "You are a dilemma. It is a sin and it is a child's folly, but I would that you had never been born."

"Or that I had truly been evil?"

Adam's face was drawn as if with pain. "Yes. Yes, God help me. There are priests who live lives far less pure than yours, witch-born though you are, and no one censures them. And I knew this, and I kept silence in despite of the Law."

"You are a compassionate man."

"I am a fool!" He controlled himself with a visible effort. "I shall do penance. I am leaving my Order; I shall set sail over sea to Hibernia and dwell there in solitude, far from any man. Perhaps I shall learn to forget you."

Quietly Alf said, "I can make you forget."

Adam threw up his hands as if to avert a blow. "No!"

Alf bowed his head.

The Pauline monk drew a breath, struggling to steady himself. At length he managed a faint, bitter smile. "You were a far better prisoner than am I. Does it amuse you to see how low I have fallen?"

"No."

Adam shook his head in disbelief. "Come now. Surely you came to taste your revenge. You have overthrown a great Order in Anglia and driven Reynaud mad beyond all healing, and cost the King's enemies two of their strongest supporters. Are you not human enough to be glad of it?"

"No," Alf repeated. "You called me. I came as soon as I could."

"I never—" Adam fell silent. He looked his full age, sixty years and more. Hard years, all of them, and this the hardest of all.

Alf laid light hands upon his shoulders. He shuddered and closed his eyes, but did not draw away. "Brother. Alone of all my enemies, you did what you had to do, for the love of God and of the Church, and never for yourself."

"That I should hear such words from one of your kind . . ." Again

Adam shuddered. "Yet you mean them. Soulless, deathless, inhuman—you mean them."

"Perhaps I have no soul, but I am as much God's creature as any other being upon this earth."

" 'Let all the earth proclaim the Lord . . .' Ah God! You torment me."

Alf let his hands fall. "I meant to heal you."

"I think I may be beyond any healing but God's."

"Then I pray that He will make you whole again."

"Perhaps," Adam said, "He will hear you."

The other drew up his hood and gathered his cloak about him. "If I were a man, I would want to be your friend. Since I am not, may we at least part without enmity?"

Slowly Adam nodded. "That . . . I can give you. I too regret that we are what we are."

Alf bowed to him as if he had been a great lord. "The Lord be with you," he murmured.

For a long while Adam stood where Alf had left him. At last he raised a trembling hand and sketched a blessing in the air. Very softly he whispered, "And with your spirit."

24

"The Devil's Crown." Richard held it up to the light: the great Crown of Anglia, set with rubies like drops of blood. "That's what my father used to call it." He set it on the bed beside Alf, rubbing his brows where the weight had plowed deep furrows in the flesh. "He used to call us the Devil's brood, and say that his grandmother would be delighted to see what we'd turned into."

"There's no taint of evil in you," Alf said, venturing to touch a point of the crown with his fingertip. "Nor in this," he added, although he sensed power in it, the power almost of a sacred thing.

"I'm the great-grandson of a devil," Richard said.

"The Demon Countess? Maybe she was one of us."

"Hardly. She'd sit through Mass just up to the Credo, no more. The day her lord made her stay longer, she held on until the Consecration; then she grabbed up the two closest of her offspring and flew shrieking out of the window. No one ever saw her or the boys again. Likely enough, when Father went to his well-deserved place in Hell, he found his uncles there already, stoking the fires."

"I think you're proud of it."

The King grinned at him. "Why not? It's a noble ancestry, though it's come down a bit in the world."

"My lord!"

Richard laughed aloud. "You look like a virgin in a guardroom."

"I *am* a—" Alf bit his tongue. "Sire, I'm learning to live as a worldling, but couldn't I do it slowly?"

"All at once, or not at all," Richard decreed. He tilted a jar, found it still half full of spiced wine, poured a cupful for each of them. "Consider it a punishment. Because of you, I'll be riding to war with half the men I need and with winter breathing down my neck."

Alf held the cup but did not drink. "You persist in this madness?"

"In spite of all your tricks," Richard answered, "yes."

"When?"

"Tomorrow."

Alf took the crown and laid it on his knee. It was very heavy, too heavy, surely, for a mortal head to bear. "Take me with you," he said.

The King paused. Alf did not look at him. "What would you do on a winter campaign?"

"Ride," Alf answered. "Tend the wounded."

"And browbeat me into surrender. No. You'll stay here and mend. When the court goes to Winchester for Yule, you'll go with it."

"I would rather go with you, Sire."

"You'd rather I didn't go at all." Richard drained his cup and retrieved the crown from Alf's lap. "When I get back I'll have another of these for you to play with."

"You'll have a wound that will drain your life away, and two kingdoms in revolt, and the Flame-bearer ravaging your coasts."

Alf's eyes were blurred, unfocused, his voice too soft to be so clear. The King shivered with a sudden chill. Yet he spoke lightly. "So. You're a prophet, too."

"No. I see the patterns, that is all."

"My pattern has two crowns in it and Jerusalem at the end of it."

"Two hundred years ago," said Alf, "there was a very learned man who rose to the Papacy. He had been promised that he would not die until he had seen Jerusalem. Being a clever man, he decided to live forever, for he would never leave Rome. But one day he fell dead upon the steps of a church within sight of his palace. The name of the church was Jerusalem."

"I should put you in a bottle like the old Sibyl, and never uncork you."

Alf smiled faintly, set his untouched cup aside, and rose.

"You're not supposed to get up until tomorrow," the King said.

"Really?" Alf asked. "I walked to St. Benedict's this morning to see Brother Adam, who was my questioner. I've shaken his faith very badly; I wanted to give him what comfort I could." He sighed and took up his tunic. "I didn't give him much."

"Was there ever anyone like you?" the King demanded of him.

Carefully Alf drew on the tunic, and then the cotte. As he fastened the belt he said, "If you're leaving tomorrow, I'd best get all your letters done today. There must be a week's worth to do."

"You'll do nothing of the sort. Get back into bed and stay there."

"Not to mention your mother's letter, which you've put off answering. And the matter of the estate in Poitou—"

"Alfred."

"Yes, Sire?"

"Go to bed."

"Saving your grace, Sire," Alf said, "no. I suppose my writing case is still in the solar?"

Richard snarled in exasperation and let him go.

Alf set down his pen. He had finished his third letter, and he was more weary than he cared to admit.

He looked about the solar. The King conversed quietly with one or two of his knights, considering matters of the war. The usual complement of servitors moved about or stood at attention. No one glanced at the clerk in his corner, although there had been stares enough when first he came. He had disappointed them by seeming the same as ever but for his hollowed cheeks and his secular dress, and by settling quietly to his old task of writing letters for the King. They had expected more of one charged with witchcraft and proven a saint.

He reached for a new sheet of parchment. His back twinged; his half-smile turned to a grimace. He moved more carefully to sharpen his worn quill.

A disturbance drew his eyes to the door. The guard within conferred with the guard without and turned. "Sire!" he called out. "Owein of Llanfair, courier of the King of Gwynedd, asks grace to converse with Your Majesty."

Alf crossed himself. *"Deo gratias,"* he murmured, no more than a sigh.

The man entered with dignity, although he was wet to the skin and plastered with mud. He wore no livery nor any sign of rank, but the brooch which clasped his cloak bore the dragon of Gwynedd and the eyes which scanned the room were proud, almost haughty. They fixed without hesitation upon Richard; the messenger limped forward to sink to one knee before the King.

"Your Majesty," he said in a clear trained voice, "your royal brother of Gwynedd sends his greetings and his respect."

Richard's amber glare had passed him by to burn upon Alf. *Your doing,* it accused him. *Damn you!*

Alf smiled. A vein pulsed in the King's temple; it took all of his control to say, "Anglia responds with similar sentiments."

The envoy bowed his head and raised it again, and took from his wallet a sealed letter. "My royal lord bids you accept this epistle, and with it his goodwill."

Richard took the letter but did not break the seal. "What is his message?"

" 'To our dear brother of Anglia,' " responded the messenger, " 'we have held our throne now for two years and two seasons, since the lamented death of our father, whom God cherishes now among His angels; in our poor fashion we have endeavored to govern his kingdom as he desired it to be governed. In particular, we have attempted to maintain relations with our neighbor and dear friend in Anglia, for whom—' "

Richard cut him off. "Never mind the bombast! I can read it easily enough myself. What does Kilhwch want?"

Owein's face did not change, although his eyes flickered. Amusement, Alf realized, and reluctant admiration. "Your Majesty, the words he spoke to me were blunt and without embellishment. But he bade me couch them in the terms of courtesy."

"Courtesy be damned. What did he say?"

Alf had come quietly to stand behind the King. The messenger's eyes widened a little; he closed his mouth upon his protest and bowed slightly, yet with more respect than he had shown the King himself. "His Majesty of Gwynedd said to me, 'Pretty it up, Owein. But make sure you let him know that his barons are raising hell on my borders, and that my barons are like to raise hell in return; and that's no good to either of us. I'll see him and talk to him in any place he chooses;

maybe we can put out this fire that's threatening to burn us both out of our kingdoms.' "

Richard's brows had drawn together until they met; his eyes had begun to glitter. "Kilhwch won't fight?"

Owein maintained his serenity. "My liege desires a conference. The place is to be of your choosing; he asks that you come as he will, with no more than twenty knights in attendance, and in certainty of his friendship."

"He wants peace? Bran Dhu's son wants peace?"

"The King of Gwynedd desires what is best for his kingdom."

Richard broke the seal and skimmed the letter, muttering to himself. " 'Kilhwch of Gwynedd to Richard of Anglia, greeting . . . Conference . . . alliance . . . friendship . . . Given in Caer-y-n'Arfon, four days before the Calends of December.' " He looked up sharply. "It took you this long to ride to me?"

The messenger nodded briefly. "Yes, Sire. My horse was shot from under me as I passed the border; I walked until I found another; there were other difficulties."

"Pursuit," Alf said softly. "Battles. A wound. And cold and famine and this deadly rain."

Again Owein bowed, with respect which came close to reverence.

Richard looked from him to Alf, tugging at his beard. At length he said, "I'll consider my reply. Giraut, take this man and see that he's well cared for. I'll call for him later."

For a long while after the messenger had gone, escorted by the King's page, no one moved or spoke. Save the King, who paced like a caged beast.

He came to a halt in front of Alf. His glare swept the solar. "All of you. Out."

They obeyed swiftly. One or two shot pitying glances at Alf. The King's wrath looked fair to break upon his head.

When the last small page had passed the door, Richard smiled sweetly. "Now, my fair young friend," he said. "Suppose you tell me exactly how you managed to concoct this plot with the King of Gwynedd."

"To concoct what plot, Sire?"

Richard shook his head. The rubies flashed and flared upon his crown. "No, Alfred. Don't play the innocent here. Just tell me the truth."

"Very well, Sire," Alf said calmly. "The truth is that Kilhwch of

Gwynedd is a wise man, and he sees no profit in a war between your
kingdoms. And you, Sire, are furious, and ready to force a conflict for
pride and for folly."

The King's breath hissed between his teeth.

Alf nodded as if he had spoken. "Yes. I dare much. Overmuch,
perhaps. But only because I wish you well."

"You wish me hamstrung and unmanned."

"I wish you strong upon a strong throne." Alf sat at the King's
worktable with grace which concealed his growing weakness. "Sire, if
you agree to this meeting you suffer no disgrace. Your friends will be
glad that you don't try to sap the kingdoms' strength with a useless
war; your enemies will be mortified. They're relying on your falling
into the trap."

"Weaselling words. Maybe you're my enemy."

Alf held out his hands, the wrists bearing still the marks of chains.
"I won't contend with blind anger that knows full well that I speak the
truth. For Anglia's sake, Sire. For your own. Agree to meet with
Kilhwch."

"You take a lot on yourself, for an unfrocked priest."

"Yes," Alf agreed. "I do."

"Damn you!"

Richard raged about the room, fists clenching and unclenching,
jaw working. Alf watched him and tried to forget the pain which
darkened the edges of his vision. He could not faint now—must not.
He gathered all of his waning strength and held it tightly, waiting for
the King's temper to cool.

It calmed long before Richard wished it to, nor would it rouse
again. Cold reason dulled the fire; calculation slew it altogether. The
King stopped and glared at Alf, who seemed intent upon a letter. He
looked pale, haggard; a dark stain was spreading over the back of his
cotte. The hand which held the letter trembled just perceptibly.

Richard snarled and cursed him. He did not look up. But Richard had seen enough men on the edge of endurance to recognize
another.

And he had done it all with quiet, monkish obstinacy, to get what
he wanted.

"Damn you," Richard said again, little more than a whisper.
"You're worse than a woman. Or is that what you are?"

Alf smiled and shook his head. "In the words of your former
squire, I have a face like a girl's. But the rest of me . . ."

"The rest of you ought to be roasted over a slow fire."

Alf had gone back to his reading.

Richard snatched the letter from his hand and dragged him to his feet. "All right, damn you. I'll go to meet this wonder-child, this wise old sage of seventeen."

"Nineteen, Sire. Nearly twenty."

"What! So ancient?"

"So ancient," Alf said. "I'm glad you've come to your senses."

"I think I've lost them altogether."

Alf smiled again, but his lips were white. "Sire, if you don't mind . . . may I sit down?"

"You're going back to bed."

And Richard carried him there, past staring faces and in spite of his protests. When he lay in the royal bed with the King's surgeon tut-tutting over his reopened wounds, Richard said, "You've won. It's cost you your vocation and half your hide, but you've won."

Alf winced as the surgeon probed too deeply, and blinked away tears of pain. But he spoke as clearly as if he had been lying at his ease. "Sire. If you really want to do this, I know where you can meet with Kilhwch."

"Of course you do. You plotted this months ago."

"Days, Sire. There's a place not two days' ride from Gwynedd across Severn's mouth, with room enough to house two kings and their escorts; the Abbot there—"

"Abbot, sir?"

Alf nodded. "I'm speaking of St. Ruan's, Sire."

"I suppose the Abbot's in the plot, too?"

"If plot you choose to call it. The man whose errand I took on myself is still there, a lord of Rhiyana who can speak for the Elven-king. Think of it, my lord! Three kings and three kingdoms united in amity, with the Church as witness. Your enemies will gnash their teeth in rage."

"You can play me like a lute," Richard said. "God knows why I stand for it."

Alf smiled. "Because, Sire, you need my meddling. Your reputa-tion forbids you to be sensible, but if you can blame it on my plotting, you can do whatever is wisest, and confound your enemies without awakening them to the truth."

"Flatterer. Go to sleep and leave me in peace."

Obligingly Alf closed his eyes. Richard stood for a while, watching the surgeon's deft gnarled hands, flinching from the sight of the outraged flesh. "Goddamned martyr," he muttered.

The pale face did not change. Richard's hand crept out to touch it; stopped short; withdrew. He turned on his heel and strode out.

25

Kilhwch's messenger left at dawn, well-fed and newly clothed, with the King's horse under him and the King's letter in his satchel, and gifts of gold and food and safe-conduct to ease his way to Gwynedd.

Richard rode out well after sunrise with twenty knights at his back, and among them, Aylmer and a grim-faced novice. And, falling in behind as they left the keep, a rider in blue on a gray mare. His hood was drawn up against the cold, the rest of him well-muffled.

The King's men exchanged glances. One or two dropped back; two more fell in on either side of him, concealing him from the crowd which had gathered to see the King go.

It was the wind which betrayed him. As they neared the south gate—as the King passed beneath its arch—a gust blew back his hood, baring his head. A flash of sunlight caught it and broke into rays about it.

A shout went up. A single voice at first above the cheering for the King: "The saint! The saint!" Two joined it, three, a dozen, a hundred; the crowd surged forward. Voices, faces, minds beat upon all his senses. "Let me touch you—don't go away—my baby's sick—my eyes, my sore eyes—my leg—my arm—my hand—it hurts—oh, God, I hurt—"

The gate arched above him. The voices thundered in the hollow space, beating him down.

And suddenly he was free. The mare moved into a canter, keeping pace with the beasts about her. The shouting faded behind them.

Alf did not look back. His protectors moved away; the mare lengthened her stride. She ran as lightly as a deer among the heavy destriers.

Just behind the King, she slowed. Richard rode between Aylmer and Jehan; only the novice acknowledged Alf's presence. He reined back his mount to keep pace with the mare, and regarded Alf with a wild mingling of joy and anxiety. "Brother Alf! You weren't supposed to come."

"Should I have stayed behind in *that?*"

Jehan glanced back. Carlisle huddled within its red walls, crowned with its red keep; about its gate seethed the crowd which had sought to overrun Alf. He looked at his friend, who rode with eyes fixed forward, face white and strained. "I am not a saint," Alf said. "I am—*not*—a saint."

"You're ill," Jehan said.

Alf shook his head sharply. "I'm somewhat battered, and I'm a little weaker than I should be. That's all."

"A *little* weaker!"

"Would you be able to keep from shaking if you'd just been canonized?" Alf stared at his hands. In spite of his words they were almost steady. "She said it would happen. They would canonize me, or they would burn me. They tried both."

"Brother Alf—"

He straightened in the saddle. "Don't call me that."

"Brother Alf," Jehan said stubbornly, "you're trying to uncanonize yourself by proving just how nasty, disobedient, and downright human you can be. Don't you know by now that you don't have to prove anything to me?"

"Maybe," murmured Alf, "I need to prove it to myself."

Richard looked back, a fierce amber glare. "Take my word for it. You are nasty, disobedient, and downright human. And damnably clever. I should send you back to Carlisle and make you find your own way out of the mess you made there."

"Sire! I—"

"Look at that," Richard said to Aylmer. "Injured innocence, done to perfection. Should I send him back? Or should I let him find out for himself that he's not half strong enough to keep the pace I'll set?"

Aylmer met Alf's glance with a dark steady stare. To the King he said, "He was determined enough to come over your express command. Let him stay. He can pay whatever penalty he has to pay."

Alf nodded. "Just because I've been a priest, Sire, doesn't mean you have to treat me as if I were a woman or a child. I can do whatever I have to do."

"Do you mean that?" Richard demanded.

"Yes, Sire."

"Well then. You've cost me an esquire. Take his place. That means you'll be treated exactly like any other squire—the good and the bad. You'll be bowed to, but you'll have to work; if you slack up you get a beating. And you'll be exercising at arms whenever you get the chance. Do you still want to ride with me?"

"Yes, Sire," Alf replied without flinching.

"That's a commitment, boy. From the moment you take my hand and swear on it, you're mine until I see fit to let you go." Richard held out his mailed hand. "Will you take it? Or will you go back?"

Alf hesitated only briefly. He clasped the King's hand and met the King's eyes. "I shall try not to disgrace you."

"You'll do more than try. I'll give you till evening to learn what you've got yourself into." Richard turned his back on him and clapped spurs to the red stallion's sides. *"Allez-y!"*

Jehan dropped back with Alf to the rear of the column. "I think he planned that," the novice called over the thunder of hoofs.

"I know he did. Look—not a single royal squire in all this riding."

"And you *let* him?"

"I came, didn't I?"

Jehan shook his head. "It's a long leap from saint to squire, and you started as a monk. You've got a lot to learn."

"Then you'd best teach it to me. I've only got till evening."

"Thank all the saints you're clever, then."

To Jehan's amazement, Alf laughed. "Too clever, maybe. Come now, Master, your pupil's ready. Will you keep him waiting?"

By nightfall the travelers had found lodgings in a baron's drafty barn of a castle, driving that provincial notable to distraction with the honor and the terror of playing host to the King. In such confusion, any number of errors could have gone unnoticed. But Alf labored to do exactly as Jehan had taught him. He won no reward for his effort, not even a glance from Richard, but he had expected none.

The lord and his lady boasted the luxury of a chamber to themselves, an airless cell behind the hall, nearly filled with a vast featherbed. This Richard was given as his due, nor in courtesy could he refuse it. He sought it soon enough, if none too soon for his newest squire, who had served as cupbearer through an interminable feast. Alf had locked his knees with an effort of will, else he would have collapsed in the hall with every eye fixed upon him.

But Richard, it seemed, had not yet forgiven his disobedience. Even as the King rose from the high seat, he crooked a finger. "Alfred. You'll wait on me."

Alf bowed as deeply as he could. He knew he looked stiff, arrogant; he was past caring. His sight had begun to narrow. Grimly he focused it on the King and on the path he must take. Across the dais, up a steep railless stair, through a heavy curtain. Somehow he had acquired a lamp, a bowl filled with tallow, its wick a twisted rag. As if his eyes needed—

They fixed before him. Not far. Not far at all. Slowly. They would take it for stateliness, the proper gait of a servant before his King. The lamp's smoke was rank; oddly, the stench revived him a little. He set his foot upon the stair.

Richard inspected the bed and pulled a face. "Fleas in the mattress for sure," he muttered, "and lice, and worse things yet, I wager. And this sheet hasn't been washed since King Harold's day."

Alf set the lamp in a sooty niche. However cramped this chamber was between two tall men and a bed as broad as a tilting-yard, it lacked at least the press of bodies below. He could see again; he could speak, though not strongly. "There are no vermin here now, Sire."

The King's eye flashed upon him. "Don't like you, do they?"

"Like you, I prefer to live without them."

"And you, unlike me, have the means to assure it. Would you happen to have a similar predilection for clean sheets?"

Alf granted him half a nod, the bowing of the head but not the raising. Gently, completely, his knees gave way beneath him. At least, he thought, it was a clean bed he fell to.

Would have fallen to. Richard had caught him, eased him down, pulled off his surcoat. "You're bleeding again. Idiot."

Alf tried to shrug free, but for once Richard's hands were too strong. "I'm strong enough still; I can serve you. Later—Jehan can—"

"You're weak as a baby. Where'd those fools put—ah. There." Richard had Alf's own baggage, opening it, searching swiftly through it. In a moment he brought out the rolled bandages and the salve the doctor had made, that Alf had made stronger with his own healer's skill.

"Sire," Alf said, "how came these to be—"

"A squire stays with his lord. Particularly if he doesn't want the world to know that he's out on his feet." Richard began to ease the slid from Alf's shoulders. Here and there it had clung where blood had dried, fusing linen to bandages and bandages to torn skin.

"Majesty. You can't wait on me like this. I won't allow it."

"A squire allows anything his King commands. Hand me the basin. Ah, good. Clean water at least. Hold on, boy. This will sting."

Like fire. But it was a clean fire, and Richard was surprisingly skillful. With a small sigh Alf accepted the inevitable. He let his body rest, sitting upright, eyes closed. Richard's voice was a soothing rumble in his ear. "Well now. I haven't lost much of my skill. I used to be a good hand at field-surgery—from necessity at first, then I rather liked it. It's a good thing to know when you're on the field and your men are falling everywhere, and you need every hand you can muster."

If the water had stung, the salve was agony. Alf's jaw clenched against it. With infinite slowness it passed, bound beneath the clean bandages.

Carefully but firmly Richard completed the last binding. Alf mustered the will to move, at least to turn his head. The King had fallen silent, sitting very close, his gaze very steady.

Alf's throat dried. Between exhaustion and pain, he had closed his mind against invasion—and against perception. He had only done as he was bidden, gone where he was sent, endured until he might rest. Bringing himself to this.

The King would not ask. Not openly. Nor would he compel. Yet, at ease though he seemed, every muscle had drawn taut.

Richard laid his hand on Alf's brow as if to test for fever. "You're burning," he said. But his palm was hotter still.

Alf swallowed painfully. He was not afraid, but he could have wept. Should have, perhaps. Richard hated tears; they put him in mind of women.

Alf forced himself to speak in his wonted voice, light, cool, oblivious. "It's not a fever I have, Sire. I'm always so. My power causes it." He managed the shadow of a smile, moving as if to seek comfort for his back, sliding as by chance from beneath the King's hand. "It's a very great advantage in a monk. All those cold vigils . . . I make a wonderfully effortless ascetic."

That shook laughter from Richard, though it held less mirth than pain. "There's no need for a vigil tonight. I'll look after myself. Lie down and sleep—the bed's big enough for my whole army."

"Sire—"

"Lie down."

There was a growl in Richard's voice, the hint of a warning. Mutely Alf obeyed him. It could not matter now what people thought or said, and the bed was celestially soft.

Richard stripped with dispatch and without modesty, took his generous half of the bed, and fell asleep at once. There was a royal secret, to lose no sleep over what could not be mended.

Alf had no such fortune. Now that he was almost in comfort, laid in the bed he had longed for since midmorning, his strength had begun to repair itself; it grew and spread, filling him, driving back the mists from body and brain.

For a long while he lay awake, now on his side, now on his face. The lamp sputtered and died. Richard snored gently. In the hall, a hound snarled; a man cursed; the hound yelped and was abruptly still.

At last Alf rose, moving softly lest he wake the King. He drew on his shirt, gathered his cloak about him.

The stair from the hall continued upward to emerge upon the barbican. The wind smote Alf's face, clear and cold; the stars blazed in a sky from which all clouds had fled. He turned his eyes to them and breathed deep. His exhaustion had vanished, and with it his heart's trouble. He felt as light and hollow as he had in the trial, stripped of his vows and of his sanctity, made anew, squire-at-arms of the King of Anglia.

His hand went to his head. His hair was growing with speed as unhuman as his face; in a month or a little more, no one would know that he had ever been a priest. Even here, even now, his host had regarded him with interest but no curiosity, taking him for a young nobleman whose family had recalled him from the priesthood. Such men were common enough.

And could he play that part as he had played the other? Fifty years a priest and a scholar, fifty years a squire, a knight, a lord of the world. And then—what then? Priest again, or something else?

The stars returned no answer. They were older than he and wiser, and content to be what they were. They did not need a flogging to shake them into their senses.

Carefully, gingerly, he flexed his shoulders. With time and patience he would heal; the pain was his penance. The pain and the scars. His vanity had suffered nearly as much as his flesh itself.

Someone mounted the steps. He moved away, pricked irrationally to annoyance. The newcomer paused as if to get his bearings, then turned toward him. He leaned upon the parapet and pretended to be absorbed in his thoughts.

"Little Brother," said a voice he knew very well indeed, "are you so sorry to see me?"

Thea regarded him with eyes that caught the starlight, turning it to green fire. He had forgotten how very fair she was.

"Thea," he said through the thundering in his blood. "Althea. I thought you weren't coming back."

"I? I'm not so easily disposed of. Besides," she added, "I had this." She held out her hand. Silver gleamed in it. "I knew you'd want it back."

He did not move to take the cross. "Keep it."

"It's yours."

He shook his head. "I gave it to you. You can sell it if you don't want it."

"Of course I want it!" she snapped. "But it belongs to you. Will you take it or do I have to throw it at you?"

He kept his hands behind his back. "I'm not a priest now. I'm the King's squire. I want you to keep the cross."

"That is supposed to be a logical progression?"

The blood rose to his cheeks. "Will you please keep it?"

Thea's fingers closed over the cross. "All right. I will. Though I know what your Abbot will say."

"Morwin will say that I had a noble impulse, and leave it at that."

"Will he?"

Alf turned outward, letting the wind cool his face.

"I've met him," she said. "I like him. He's wise and he's sensible, and he's not at all afraid of the female race."

"All that I lack, he has." Alf glanced at her. "Alun let you find St. Ruan's."

"Finally," she said. Her voice changed, hardened. "And no wonder it took him so long. Prince Aidan is going to raise Heaven and Hell when he sees what's been done to his brother."

"Not if Alun can help it."

"Alun is going to have his hands full. And since he's only got one he can use, he's likely to lose the fight."

"He didn't lose it to you."

"I'm not Prince Aidan."

"So I noticed."

She laughed. "Why, Brother! You've grown eyes."

"My name is Alf. I'd thank you to call me by it."

"Pride, too," she said to herself. "The monk's becoming a man."

"I was always proud, though maybe I was never much of a man."

"Don't say that as if you believed it." She stood very close to him, almost touching; the wind blew a strand of her hair across his face. "What did you think of my miracle?"

He could hardly think at all. Yet words came; he spoke them. "We're part of local hagiography now. The saint, and the angel who saved him from the fire. The Paulines are furious."

"I meant them to be. But what did *you* think?"

"I thought you were blasphemous, sacrilegious, devious, and splendid."

"Not hateful?"

"Maybe a little," he admitted.

"Swiftly and virtuously suppressed. Alfred of St. Ruan's, I don't know why I endure you."

"I'm afraid I do."

"Afraid, little Brother?"

"Afraid, little sister."

"Now I know how to break you of your bad habits. Peel you out of your habit, clap you in chains, and whip you soundly."

"And threaten to burn the woman I—a woman of my own kind."

"The woman you what?"

He would not answer.

She made a small exasperated noise. "It's the tender maid who's supposed to blush and simper and pretend to be modest. Why don't you come out and say it?"

"Why don't you?"

For the first time since he had known her, he saw her blush. Brazen, shameless Thea, who had cast defiance in the face of holy Church and set out coolly to seduce a priest—Thea blushed scarlet, and could not say a word.

Her confusion gave him more courage than he had ever thought he had. "It was easy enough when I only a pretty innocent, to tease me into tears. Then you realized that I mattered. I, not the diffident little Brother, not the fool who tried to fall on his sword because he discovered that he could use one, and to be put to death because he couldn't face himself. When you flew out of the fire, you mocked all my pretensions; you made me see them for what they were."

"I'd have done that for anyone," she said sharply.

With breathtaking boldness he touched her cheek. It was very soft. "Would you have come back for anyone?"

"The cross——"

"Morwin could have kept it for me. It was his, first."

"You are the worst possible combination of divine wisdom and absolute idiocy."

"And you are as prickly as a thorn tree and as tender as its blossom." He laughed a little, breathlessly. "Thea, you make my head whirl; and I'm still in Orders though I've suspended myself from my title and my duties. What are we going to do?"

"You can go and pray and mortify your flesh. I——" She tossed her head proudly. "I'll find myself another Lombard prince and run away again."

"Maybe that would be best."

She whirled upon him. "Don't you even care?"

"I care that I can't be your lover, and that we would only torment one another."

"You're not a gelding."

"No. I'm worse. I'm a priest who believes in his vows. And you care now for me, or you'd have seduced me long since. Your thorns are thick and cruel, Thea, but your heart is surpassingly gentle."

"It's black and rotten, and it damns you."

"I think not."

"You bastard!"

"Probably."

She struck him, a solid, man's blow that sent him careening to the stones. As he struck them, he cried out.

Her own cry echoed his. He rolled onto his face; she dropped beside him, reaching for him. Without warning the pain was gone. She knelt frozen, her face a mask of agony.

He dragged himself to his knees and shook her. "Thea," he gasped. "Thea, for the love of God, *don't!*"

The pain flooded back, almost welcome in its intensity. Thea sagged in his hands. "I tried to heal it," she said faintly. "I don't have the gift. I can't even— Oh, how can you bear it?"

"Not easily. But I provoked you."

"I didn't have to hit you. Now it's all opened again, worse than before, and you—how you hurt! Let me take some of it. Just a little. Just what I added to it."

"You didn't add much." He drew a breath carefully. "It's passing. You took the worst of it."

"I had to. I always hurt what I care for. Always. Always."

"Thea, child——"

"I'm not a child!"

"Nor am I so very little a Brother; and I'm much older than you."

"Not where it matters."

"Maybe not. But, Thea, you see what I can do to you."

"And I to you." Her composure had returned, ragged but serviceable. She shook her head. "Little Brother, after you a Lombard prince is going to be very dull."

"Peaceful."

"No. Dull. What will people say if your white hound comes back?"

"That my familiar has found me again."

"That won't do," she said. "I'll think of something else."

"You could wait with Alun in St. Ruan's."

"I could." She stretched as high as she might and kissed his brow, lightly. "Good night, little Brother."

He bowed so calmly that he might have seemed cold, but his heart was hammering. "Good night, little sister," he said.

26

They rode hard from castle to castle, round Bowland and its shadows to the dark hills of the Marches and the flood of Severn, swollen with rain; and at last, the dim and misty country about the Isle of Glass. Only a month ago, Alf had left it, yet he looked on it with the eyes almost of a stranger. Literally indeed when his mind touched Thea's, flying with her on falcon-wings, soaring high above him. *I was a monk when I left,* he thought, *driven into exile. Now I'm—what?*

An eagle learning to fly, she answered him.

I feel like a roast swan. Plucked, gutted, and done to a turn.

Her laughter was both an annoyance and a comfort.

The last day began in a driving rain, but toward noon the downpour eased, freeing the sun. Jehan pushed back his hood, shook his sodden hair, and laughed. "There!" he cried. "St. Ruan's!"

The King wrung water from his cloak and sneezed. "The first thing I'll ask for is a draught of their famous mead."

"Roast apples," Jehan said. "Warm beds. Baths."

"No more water for me!" cried the knight behind him. "I've had enough to last me a good fortnight."

Richard grinned. "Come on. First one to the gate gets a gold bezant!"

The gray mare was swifter by far than any of the heavy chargers, but she ran far behind. Jehan held in his own mount in spite of his eagerness, looking back with troubled eyes. Now, if ever, Alf's brittle new mood would shatter.

He seemed calm enough, although he kept Fara to a canter. He even smiled and called out, "Won't you race for the bezant?"

"Won't *you?*" Jehan called back.

He shook his head.

Jehan hauled his destrier to a heavy trot and waited for the mare to come level with him. "Are you going to be all right?"

Alf's smile turned wry. "Poor Jehan. You're always asking me that. What will I do when I don't have you to look after me?"

"Fall apart, probably. Are you sure you're up to this?"

Alf looked ahead to that race which was like a charge of cavalry, and to the abbey waiting beyond. It floated before them on its Isle of mist and light, but solid itself like the bones of the earth. Its gate was open; he could see figures within, brown robes, faces blurred with distance. "It's odd, Jehan," he said. "I thought I'd hardly be able to stand it—that I'm here, and I don't belong anymore. But it all seems very far away, like something I knew when I was a child."

"I know what you mean." Jehan's gelding snorted and fought his strong hand on the bit. "I'll race you for a bath. Loser gives the winner one."

"Done," Alf said, and gave the mare her head.

They passed the slowest of the knights running neck and neck. Jehan grinned; Alf grinned back and leaned over Fara's neck. She sprang forward, running lightly still, taunting the big gelding with her ease and grace. Jehan had a brief and splendid view of her flying heels.

She thundered through the gate half a length ahead of the King and wheeled within, tossing her head. The monks had scattered before the charge, slowed though it was, the more prudent arriving at a trot. Richard laughed and tossed Alf a coin; he caught it, face flushed, eyes shining.

The monks stared openmouthed as he slid from the saddle with the bezant still in his hand.

"Well, Brothers," the King said in high good humor, "I've brought back your prodigal."

"In grand style," Morwin observed, stepping from behind a pair of tall monks. "Welcome to St. Ruan's, Your Majesty."

The King knelt to kiss his ring, as was proper even for royalty in the Church's lands, and turned to present his followers. Novices took their horses; others led them, once presented, to the guesthouse.

Alf stood apart with Jehan hovering behind him. None of the Brothers approached them, although Brother Osric half-moved toward them and stopped. The King's presence, and their own air of the world and its splendors, made them strange.

Morwin completed his courtesies. It was odd to watch him as if he had been a stranger, a small elderly man in an Abbot's robe, very clean but somewhat frayed.

At last he looked at Alf, a quick encompassing glance, measuring this falcon he had cast from his hand. Suddenly he scowled. "This is a fine way to greet an old friend. What are you hanging back for?"

Alf came to his embrace. He was as thin and fragile as a man made of sticks, but he was still wiry-strong. He grinned at Alf, blinking rapidly. "The good Brothers will never get over it. Gentle Brother Alf who used to have to be dragged bodily out of the library to see what the sun looked like, roaring in at the head of a troop of cavalry. The next thing we know, Brother Edgar will be reading Aristotle."

The other laughed with a catch in it, for Morwin's tight embrace had kindled sparks of pain.

The Abbot held him at arm's length. "You look as if you've got a lot to tell me. As soon as I've settled things here, come and talk." He glanced beyond him, at Jehan. "You make a pair of bashful maids, to be sure. Or are you so used to rubbing elbows with kings and bishops that you can't spare a good-day for a mere abbot?"

"Good day, Dom Morwin," Jehan said obediently, with a glint in his eye.

"That's better." Morwin flung his arms wide. "Welcome back, you two. Welcome back!"

The Brothers crowded round them then, reticence forgotten. In that babble of greeting and of gladness, none but Jehan noticed Alf's pallor. With each hearty embrace it increased; although he smiled and spoke cheerfully enough, his face was drawn with pain.

"You should rest," Jehan said in his ear.

Alf shook his head almost invisibly. "Yes," he said to Brother

Osric, "I had a look at some new Aristotle. And a copy of Albumazar in Arabic, from the Crusade. . . ."

"So," said Morwin. "You're the King's squire."

Alf stood by the window of the Abbot's study, gazing at the orchard, bleak now and gray, fading into the early darkness. "Nothing's changed," he murmured. "Nothing at all."

"But you have."

Alf did not answer. Morwin prodded the fire, rousing the embers to sudden flame. He fed it with applewood; the sweet scent crept through the room.

"It's so quiet here," Alf said. "Nothing happens from year's end to year's end, except what's always happened. The trees bloom; the apples ripen; they fall, and the winter comes. The world races past, but no one heeds it, except to spare it a prayer."

"Do you think I shouldn't have sent you out into it?"

Alf sighed. "I've been like a man from the old tales, taken away to the Land of Youth for a night, but that night was a lifetime long."

"It's all too easy to stay a child here, even if your body can grow old."

"I know. Oh, I know!" Alf faced him. "I've been seventeen years old for half a century. And suddenly I feel as if I could advance to eighteen if I tried hard enough."

"So," the Abbot said with a wicked glint, "you've finally caught on."

"God knows, it took me long enough."

"Sit down and tell me about it," Morwin commanded him. "How did you get from monk to royal squire in a little over a month—and half of it spent traveling?"

Morwin listened to Alf's tale, standing by the fire, neither moving nor speaking. When Alf spoke of the trial and of his punishment, the Abbot's face grayed; his eyes glittered. "Show me," he said.

Alf did not move to obey. "There's no need. I'm mending; I'm content."

"Let me see."

"No."

"Alfred," Morwin said, "I want to know what you paid for your foolishness."

"Less than Alun paid for his, and more than you would like." Alf shifted in his seat, and shook his head as the Abbot began to speak.

"Let it be, Morwin. It's part of my growing up; you can't protect me from it."

"You don't deserve to be protected."

"Everyone seems to agree with you, myself included."

The Abbot glared at him. He smiled back. Little by little Morwin softened. "Well. You haven't done so badly since. The King seems fond of you."

"I'm fond of him. He reminds me of Jehan. Hot-headed, impetuous, and exceedingly wise when he has to be."

"And fond of letting people underestimate him," Morwin said. "Are you going to stay with him?"

"I'm sworn to it."

"But do you want to?"

Alf stared into the fire. Slowly he answered, "I don't know what I want. I'm a little afraid to take up a career of arms—it's so alien to all I've ever been or taught. And yet I have a gift for it. Weapons fit my hands."

"You aren't carrying one," Morwin said.

His hand went to his belt where a sword should have hung. "Not yet. But I will. If I continue."

"You doubt it?"

He closed his eyes and shook his head. "I don't know what I'm saying. Of course I'll go on. The King has bound me; I've made up my mind to it."

"It's going to be odd to see you riding about in mail with some lady's sleeve on your helm."

Alf rounded upon him.

Morwin laughed. "That's part of the world, too, Alf. Don't tell me you're that innocent!"

"I'm no more innocent than you."

"Nonsense!" Morwin snorted. "Remember the year in Paris? Every girl we met sighed after you, and you didn't even know what it meant."

"Of course I knew. I was the one who explained it to you. Horrified, you were. *People* did that? But that was for animals!"

"You blushed furiously all the while you told me, too, and swore you'd never stoop so low." Morwin's eyes danced upon him. "You're blushing now. What will you do when you get to court?"

"Nothing," Alf snapped. "I wouldn't want to do anything. I've discovered something horrible, Morwin. I can't bear the thought of . . . making love . . . to human women. They revolt me."

"Whores and sluts would revolt me, even if I weren't under vows—and I'm as human as they are."

Alf shook his head sharply. "It's all women. All human women. And men too, if it comes to that. I can love my fellow man, but not—not carnally."

"And what led you to that sweeping conclusion?"

He would not answer.

Morwin shrugged. "Talk to me again when you're a made knight, and we'll see if you say the same."

"I will."

"We'll see," Morwin said. Even as he spoke, he glanced over his shoulder; his eyes lighted. "My lord! Come in."

Alf had been aware of the listener for some time; he turned, rising, bowing with new-learned grace.

Alun left the doorway, walking unaided although he limped noticeably. His eyes smiled upon Alf; his mind touched the other's, the familiar gentle touch. Alf clasped his good hand and would have kissed it, had not his glance forbidden. "Brother," he said. "Well met."

"Well indeed," Alf responded, looking him up and down. Even lame and with his hand still bound in a sling, even in the brown habit Alf had left him, he looked strong and proud, a knight and a prince.

The smile found its way to the corner of his mouth. "I make a very poor monk, my brother, though I've done my utmost, short of actually taking vows."

"He has," Morwin agreed. "Brother Cecil is almost resigned to the loss of his best tenor from the choir since he's gained a splendid bass-baritone in exchange. When you go, God only knows what I'll do to pacify him."

Alf smiled. "And have they put you to work elsewhere?" he asked of Alun.

"No, but not for my lack of trying. Apparently I'm still an invalid."

"Almost," Alf said, "though if you asked, I might let you ride."

"I wasn't going to ask. I was going to do it."

"Fara will be glad to have you back again."

The Rhiyanan shook his head. "I gave her to you, and she has come to love you. Keep her, my brother; in your new station, you need her."

"But—" Alf began.

"It's her wish as much as mine. Take her, Alf."

"My lord, I can't."

Alun sighed. "You can't, but you shall." He sat by the fire, warming his good hand. "Now. Tell me what your King will do."

"Won't you see him yourself?" asked Morwin.

"Not until tomorrow, when Kilhwch comes." Alun's gaze crossed Alf's, held for a moment, flicked away. "Then we'll meet, all three of us."

"Gwynedd and Anglia and Rhiyana," Alf said. "That will be an alliance to reckon with."

"It will indeed," said Alun.

27

The King of Gwynedd rode into St. Ruan's in the late morning, his dragon banner leaping and straining in a strong wind, the sunlight flaming upon his scarlet cloak. Richard waited in the courtyard with his knights about him, vivid figures among the brown-robed monks.

Kilhwch reined his mettlesome stallion to a halt and sprang down. At first glance he seemed ordinary enough, a short stocky young man with a heavy, almost sullen face. But the eyes under the black brows were striking, steel-gray, piercing; flashing over the assembly, taking in each face. They paused several times, at Richard, at the Abbot, at Aylmer. And, for a long moment, at Alf.

He stepped forward, stripping off his gloves and thrusting them into his belt. "Well, my lord of Anglia, you're here before me." His voice was harsh, clipped, his manner abrupt.

Richard's eyes were glinting. "I left as soon as I saw your messenger off. He arrived safely?"

"Safely and in good time, with plenty of good to say about you." Kilhwch's eyes flicked to Morwin. "My lord Abbot, you're generous to lend us your hospitality. If your Brothers would see to my men, we could get to our business."

The Kings ate at the Abbot's table with Bishop Aylmer and one or two of the knights, attended by their squires. In spite of his impatience, Kilhwch seemed content to debate the merits of Frankish and

Alemannish chargers and to tell long tales of the hunt and of the joust. He did not move to speak of either war or peace.

He watched Alf steadily, with a look almost of puzzlement. He glanced from the strange face to the royal leopards ramping on the tabard, from the hands which poured his King's wine to the head which bent to catch a comment from the hulking lad in the Bishop's livery. With each glance his frown deepened.

At last he leaned toward Richard. "Your esquire. Who is he?"

Richard bit off half a leg of capon and chewed it deliberately. "Why? Have you seen him before?"

Kilhwch shook his head impatiently. "How long has he been with you?"

"Not long at all. Less than a month."

Kilhwch sat back. His bafflement was turning to anger. "He's been tonsured. Did you snatch him out of a monastery?"

"Yes. This one, in fact." Richard grinned at Morwin. "The Abbot's generosity is legendary."

The young King turned toward Alf, who stood with the other squires by the wall. "You, sir! Come here."

Alf came quietly, with that calm of his which could have passed for haughtiness. "My lord?" he asked.

"What is your name?" Kilhwch demanded.

"Alfred, Sire."

"Alfred? Is that all?"

"Of St. Ruan's, Sire." Alf smiled a very little. "I have no lineage to speak of. If it's that you're looking for, you should talk to my lord Bishop's esquire. He has pedigree enough for both of us."

"Your pedigree doesn't concern me," snapped Kilhwch. "I had a message from one of the Folk, who gave me to think that he was with my lord of Anglia. But you're not he. Where is he?"

"Here."

Kilhwch leaped up. Aylmer too had risen, his face as unreadable as ever.

The young King all but vaulted over the table, and dropped to one knee. "My lord!" he cried. "What have you done to your sword-hand?"

"Little," Alun answered him, raising him and embracing him as a kinsman.

He pulled away, eyes blazing. "You went to Rhydderch. After all my warnings, you went to Rhydderch. And he well-nigh killed you, from the look of you. I'll have his hide for a carpet!"

"You will do no such thing." Alun's soft voice had a startling effect. The King of Gwynedd subsided abruptly, like a child rebuked by his father.

Richard watched them with great interest. "So," he said, "you're the one who ran afoul of my baron."

Alun nodded, bowing slightly. "My lord of Anglia. I am glad that at last we meet."

"I've you to thank for my new esquire—and for the fact that I'm here and not waging war against Gwynedd. You're a shameless meddler, sir Rhiyanan."

Kilhwch whipped about. "Keep a civil tongue in your head, sir!"

Richard's teeth bared. "I may be rough-spoken, but I don't run like a dog at some hedge-knight's heel."

"Damn your insolence! Would you speak so of a king?"

"King?" Richard laughed. "King of what? Rags and patches?"

Aylmer stirred. "No," he said. "Rhiyana."

While his King stood speechless, he approached the man in the brown robe and knelt as Kilhwch had knelt. "Your Majesty, I thought perhaps it was you."

"And why did you think that?" asked Alun, who was Gwydion. The hand with which he raised the Bishop flamed with the blue fire of his signet.

Aylmer shrugged. "It was like you to do something of the sort."

"Nonsense!" Richard burst out. "Gwydion of Rhiyana is unspeakably ancient. This is a boy with his first beard. How old are you, lad? Twenty? Twenty-two?"

"Eighty-one," said the Elvenking, limping forward. Jehan, closest of the squires, leaped to offer him a chair at the end of the high table.

Richard shook his head stubbornly. The gray eyes rested upon him, quiet, amused, and uncannily wise in the smooth youth's face.

"Sire," Alf said. "He is who he says he is."

Richard glared at him. "You knew?"

"From the beginning."

"And you never said—"

"I did not wish it." Gwydion accepted a cup of mead from Alf's hand and sipped it. "It's one thing for the King of Rhiyana to ride abroad alone and under a false name, and another altogether for him to suffer violence at the hands of a foreign king's vassal."

"That," growled Kilhwch, returned now to his place, "it surely is. Before God, that swine shall pay for it."

Richard tugged at his beard, scowling fiercely. "Did he know who you were?"

"Only that I was Rhiyana's ambassador," Gwydion answered.

"And in Rhiyana, do they know?"

"No." Gwydion set down his cup. "My brother's face is the image of mine. I left him holding the crown and the throne; those of our people who saw me go thought I was Aidan, fleeing the peace of Caer Gwent. They think so still."

"Not for long," Kilhwch muttered. "Wait until Aidan finds out that you've been stirring up scorpions' nests on the Marches of Anglia. Half the exploits he's known for are yours—but this one was harebrained even for him."

Gwydion's face grew stern, although his eyes glinted. "Hush, lad! You're giving away state secrets. As far as anyone knows, I sit serenely and pacifically on my throne, and Aidan rides far and wide upon his errantries. Would you ruin the reputations we've labored so hard to build?"

"You've already done it. Spectacularly. And it will be even more spectacular when Aidan gets wind of it."

"Not if we turn failure to success," Gwydion said. "Here we sit all together, which is a thing Lord Rhydderch never looked for. Shall we thwart him further?"

"How?" demanded Richard.

"That's for us to decide. Shall we begin?" He glanced to Morwin. "By my lord Abbot's leave."

Morwin bowed his assent. "Alf—bring out the best wine, the Falernian. And see if Brother Wilfred has any cheese."

Jehan followed Alf on his errand. In the odorous dark of the wine cellar, he gave himself free rein. "Brother Alf! Is Alun really Gwydion?"

"Yes." Alf blew dust from an ancient jar and peered at the inscription upon its side. "Greek wine," he muttered.

"You really have known all the time?"

"Almost." The second jar was Greek also; he frowned.

"How did you know?"

"I was in his mind. He thinks like a king. High, haughty, and most wise." Alf sneezed. "Pest! where is it?"

Jehan held up a small cask. "Here."

Alf glared, and suddenly laughed. "Why didn't you tell me?"

"I wanted you to talk to me. What do you think the kings will do?"

"Kilhwch and Richard will squabble and drink and squabble some more. Gwydion will keep them from each other's throats."

"And then?"

"With luck they'll come to an agreement."

Jehan tucked the cask under his arm and followed Alf among the cobwebbed shelves, past the great tuns of ale. As he mounted the steps to the pantry he said, "They ought to bring Rhydderch here and make him answer for all he's done."

"That's not an ill thought."

Jehan almost dropped his burden. "Thea, for the love of God! Can't you ever come on gradually?"

She laughed and stepped back. Alf closed and locked the door, not looking at her, but Jehan could not tear his eyes away. She stood resplendent in the garb of a high lady, a gown of amber silk embroidered with gold and belted with gold and amber; a golden fillet bound her brows. Rather incongruously, she carried a great wheel of cheese wrapped in fine cloth.

"Where did you get the gown?" Jehan asked her.

"From the air," she answered. "Where else?" She set the cheese in Alf's unwilling hands and pirouetted in the narrow space of the pantry. "Do you like it?"

"You look beautiful," Jehan said sincerely.

Her eyes danced from him to Alf, who had said nothing at all. "You don't agree, little Brother?"

He met her gaze. "Lady, you are beautiful, and you know it."

"And you." Her mockery was brave but shaky. "You make an extraordinarily handsome young squire."

"And an extraordinarily dilatory one. Many thanks for fetching the cheese; will you let me by to take it to Their Majesties?"

"Better yet, I'll go with you."

He opened his mouth to protest, closed it again. "Come then."

The kings were deep in converse with the Abbot and the Bishop, but Thea's arrival silenced them abruptly. Kilhwch grinned a sudden, startling grin. "Thea Damaskena! What are you doing here?"

"Waiting on my liege lord," she replied with a flash of her eyes, "since he won't let me give his game away to his noble brother."

"And performing an occasional miracle on the side," Richard

put in, rising. "Demoiselle, you have my deepest gratitude for saving the life of a certain worthless cleric."

She sank down in a deep curtsey, but her eyes were bright and bold. "You are welcome, Majesty."

Alf had set the cheese on the sideboard and begun with great diligence to cut it. Richard looked from him to Thea, and smiled with a slight edge. "May I ask you something, Lady?"

She inclined her head.

"Why did you do it?"

"Why not?"

Richard laughed. "I can see you're a match for him."

"She's a match for any male alive," said Kilhwch.

"What woman isn't?" She settled between Gwydion and the young King. "Well, sirs. How goes the battle?"

Kilhwch sat back with folded arms, glowering at the table. "Nowhere," he muttered, "and to no purpose. I won't have Anglia's army on my lands, even to round up Rhydderch's troops."

"And I can't control him if I can't get at him," snapped Richard. "If he's not in his castle, I'll damned well have to go after him."

"Take his castle and hold his people hostage."

"That won't be enough. He'll raise the whole Marches around me."

"Then take the whole Marches! Or aren't you king enough for that?"

Richard rose, hand to dagger hilt.

Thea laughed like a clash of blades. "Don't be such witlings! There's a better way than that."

"And what may it be?" Gwydion asked.

"It's not my idea," she said. "Come here, Jehan. Tell them."

The novice started and nearly poured wine into Aylmer's lap. Deftly the Bishop relieved him of flask and cup and said, "Speak up, boy. What would you do if you were a king?"

He swallowed. For the merest instant, he hated Thea cordially. But they were all staring, even Brother Alf; and something in Thea's eyes made him forget fear.

"It's just a simple thing," he said. "You talk about armies and invading each other's lands and stopping uprisings. Why can't you send for Rhydderch and make him come here? He'll have to obey a royal command, especially if it comes from three kings at once."

Gwydion nodded, for all the world like Brother Alf when he had just asked a question and got the answer he wanted. "A point well taken. How could you be certain that he wouldn't destroy your messenger, and claim afterward that none had come?"

"I'd be very careful to send someone with rank enough that his loss would be noticed. And I'd give him a strong escort—half from Anglia maybe, and half from Gwynedd. With a binding on him that if he weren't heard from within a certain length of time, then both kings would fall on him with all the power they could muster."

There was a silence. Jehan's palms were damp; he wiped them surreptitiously on his hose. Both Richard and Kilhwch were frowning. Gwydion, who seldom wore any expression at all, was staring into his cup.

It was he who spoke. "Well, my lords? Would it please you to bring Rhydderch face to face with his crimes?"

"The one against you most of all," Kilhwch said fiercely. "Yes, by God. Yes!"

Richard arranged crumbs in careful order on his trencher, line by line. "One would almost think," he said idly, "that my lord of Rhiyana had had this in mind all the while."

"And if he had," asked Thea, "would it matter?"

He added another line to his army, and over it a banner of rosemary. "I suppose not. Who would go if we agreed to do this? One of us?"

Thea rested a light hand on Gwydion's bandaged one. "That would be tempting fate. It has to be someone whose life isn't vital to the survival of the kingdom. And," she added, for Alf had started forward, "who isn't one of our people. Rhydderch has learned to hate us; we want him to come as quietly as possible, not bound and raging. But since he's madder than a wild boar, his keeper had better be strong enough, and clever enough, to handle him."

Richard nodded slowly. "If I agree, will you give me the right to choose the messenger?"

"Whom would you choose?" Kilhwch asked sharply.

"The best man I know of: well-born, strong as a bull, and clever as a fox."

They were all staring at Jehan again. He stared back and tried not to shake.

Kilhwch's black brows met. "He looks more than strong enough; he seems clever. But he's only a boy."

Thea laughed. Kilhwch's scowl grew terrible. "My ancient lord," she said, "even children have their uses. You were one once. Remember?"

He flushed darkly. "I wouldn't have entrusted myself to Rhydderch's tender mercies."

"Wouldn't you? Who was it who went after a boar with his bare hands? Give in, Kilhwch. Just because you can't go doesn't mean you have to hold him back."

"If he wishes to go," Gwydion said.

Jehan drew a shuddering breath. "Of course I want to. Though I don't deserve the honor."

"Why not?" asked Richard. "You're a Sevigny; you're trained in arms and a scholar besides; and no one who looks at you could possibly think you have a brain in your head. If anyone can lure Rhydderch out of his lair, you can."

He bowed low, unable to speak.

Richard struck the table with the flat of his hand. "Well. That's settled. Alfred, wine for everybody, and double for our ambassador."

As Alf filled Jehan's cup, he met the wide blue stare. His own held fear for the other's safety, but pride also, and deep affection. The novice smiled crookedly and toasted him with a remarkably steady hand, and drank deep.

28

Night was falling with winter's swiftness, but what light clung still to the low sky cast into sharp relief the castle upon its rock.

Jehan muscled his red stallion to a halt; behind him his escort paused. A thin bitter wind tugged at their banners, Gwynedd's scarlet dragon, Anglia's golden leopards.

He stared up at Rhydderch's fortress, his face within the mail-coif grim and set. He liked the sight of the castle as little as Gwydion had. Less.

But Gwydion had not ridden up to it with a dozen knights behind him and two kings' banners over him. Jehan turned in his saddle, scanning the faces of his company. Strong faces, a little disgruntled perhaps to be under the command of a half-grown boy, but warming to his gaze. He grinned suddenly. "Well, sirs. Shall we see if the boar's in his den?"

The drawbridge was up, a chasm between it and the track. Jehan rode to the very edge of the pit, so close that the stallion's restless hoofs sent stones rolling and tumbling into space. No light shone above the gate, nor could he discern any figure upon the battlements.

He filled his lungs. "Hoi, there!" he bellowed.

No response.

Again he mustered all of his strength and loosed it in a shout. "Open up for the King's messenger!"

After an intolerably long pause, a torch flickered aloft. A voice called out: "Which King?"

"Anglia," he shouted back, "and Gwynedd."

Rhydderch's man raised his torch a little higher. Jehan could see a sharp cheekbone, an unshaven jowl. "Take your lies somewhere else and let us be."

One of the knights urged his mount to Jehan's side. Light flared, illumining a thin nondescript face, a straggle of brown beard. But the eyes were Thea's. She raised her brand high, casting its light upon the banners that strained in a sudden blast. Dragon and leopards seemed to leap from their fields toward the guard upon the battlements.

"Open up," Jehan commanded, "and take me to your lord."

"He isn't here," the man said harshly.

Jehan's mount snorted and half-reared. "Then by Saint George and Saint Dafydd, let me in to wait for him!"

The torch wavered. After a moment it dropped from sight.

With a groaning of chains, the drawbridge lowered; the iron portcullis rose. Light glimmered within. Jehan sent the red stallion thundering to meet it.

Jehan sat in the high seat in Rhydderch's hall, his mail laid aside for a princely robe, Kilhwch's gift as the stallion had been Richard's.

Gwydion's gift contemplated the array of dishes which the cook had hastened to prepare for them, and nibbled fastidiously on a bit of bread. "Barbarians," she said in her own voice, although her face remained that of the young knight from Gwynedd.

He nodded, holding his breath as a squire leaned close to refill his cup. The youth had not encountered soap or water in longer than he cared to think. He looked about, surveying Rhydderch's domain. Caer Sidi was a fortress above all; upon the bare stone walls of its hall

hung neither tapestries nor bright banners but ancient shields black-
ened with smoke. The men beneath them, the servants who moved
among the tables, had a dark wild look, ever-wary, like hunted beasts.

"I've seen such faces elsewhere," Thea said in Jehan's ear. "In
Sicily in the cave of a bandit chieftain. In Alamut among the Hashishayun."

He shivered and set down his new-filled cup.

She laughed softly. "All men who follow madmen have the same
look. But this is only a petty madman and a fruitless madness. You're
easily a match for both."

"I'm not so sure," he muttered under his breath.

As the hour grew late, Rhydderch's men waxed boisterous with wine.
But Jehan's knights clustered together near the high table, drinking
little and eating less, casting longing glances toward the weapons
heaped just outside the door. The air about them was heavy with
hostility, the servants' conduct hovering on the edge of insolence.

The knights endured it grimly, for they had been chosen with
utmost care. But they had their pride. The youngest of them bore
with fortitude the wine poured down his rich tunic, but when the
offender grinned at him, he struck the man down. The servant leaped
up with a long knife gleaming in his hand.

Jehan sprang to his feet. What he felt, he realized later, was not
fear but cold fury. His voice cracked through the hall. "Put down that
knife!"

Silence fell abruptly. Among Rhydderch's men, eyes rolled
white. Half a dozen blades clattered to table or bench or floor, the
servant's among them. Jehan caught the knight's blazing eye and
willed him to return to his seat. Slowly he obeyed.

Jehan sat himself, trying not to shake. With reaction, or with
laughter that was half hysteria. He pushed his cup aside and gathered
himself to rise again, to put an end to this mockery of a feast.

And froze. Men had come and gone often, as always during a
banquet, but those who strode in came armed and helmeted, their
cloaks dabbled with mud.

A short broad man walked at their head, clad in mail with no
surcoat. But once one had seen his eyes, one forgot all else—strange,
almost as light as Brother Alf's, but red-rimmed and glaring like a wild
boar's.

He halted in front of the high table, his men fanning out behind
him. Eight, Jehan counted, no more than an escort. But there were

five times that in the hall, watching him as the hound watches the huntsman, with hate and fear and blind adoration.

Jehan leaned back, running a cold eye over him. "Is it the custom to walk armed into hall?"

"In my hall," Rhydderch answered, "I make my own customs. Who are you, and what are you doing, lording it in my castle?"

"*Your* castle?" Jehan's eyes were wide, surprised. "Are you the Lord Rhydderch then?" He rose and bowed as equal to equal. "Jehan de Sevigny, body-squire to the Lord Chancellor of Anglia and ambassador from the Kings of Anglia and of Gwynedd, at your service, sir."

Rhydderch's nostrils flared; his knuckles whitened upon his sword hilt. "Anglia?" he demanded. "Gwynedd? Anglia *and* Gwynedd?"

"You heard me rightly," Jehan said. "Come, my lord. Share the feast. Your cook's outdone himself tonight by all accounts."

The baron did not move. "Gwynedd and Anglia together?" He seemed stunned. "What do they want with me? I'm but a poor Marcher lord."

"Let's say," said Jehan, "that you're not as insignificant as you'd like Their Majesties to think you are."

"But not so significant that I'm worth a made knight."

"Well," Jehan said. "There are twelve of them with me, and I'm bigger than any. And the alternative was war." Rhydderch's eyes gleamed; he smiled. "The two kings against you and your men. But they've been feeling compassionate lately. It must have hit you hard when Sir Alun escaped."

It was a long while before Rhydderch could master his voice. "Sir Alun?"

"Of Rhiyana. A remarkable man, that."

"A spy," grated Rhydderch.

"An ambassador," Jehan countered. "Like me, but not quite so well-attended. Nor so well-treated. Through sheer stubbornness he found his way to an abbey. The Abbot sent word to the King, and the King met with Kilhwch of Gwynedd."

"Peaceably?"

"Perfectly so. They're two of a kind, after all."

Rhydderch did not sneer. Not quite. "And why have they honored me with your august presence?"

"Out of longing for your own. You're bidden to attend them on Ynys Witrin as soon as you can ride there."

"I?" Rhydderch asked. "What can I do for Their Majesties?"

"You can go to them and ask."

"And if I don't?"

"If you don't," Jehan said, "they come and get you."

"Am I to be punished for arresting and dealing with a spy?"

"I don't know about punishment, but my lords would like to talk to you," answered Jehan. "You have a day or two to think about it."

"And then?"

Jehan's smile was affable. "If I'm not back in St. Ruan's by the third day from now, in your company, both kings will come to find us. On the other hand, if you ride with me, Richard might be disposed to be friendly. Even if he can't exactly condone his vassals' warmongering in his absence and without his consent, he can understand it."

Slowly Rhydderch shrank in upon himself. He had planned for every contingency but this one, that the kings would ally against him; his swift mind raced, seeking wildly for an opening.

He bowed his head as under a yoke, fierce, hating, yet apparently conquered. "I'll do as my King commands. We ride out tomorrow at dawn."

Jehan nodded. "Excellent. You may take one man. Be sure he has a good horse."

As Rhydderch turned away, Thea left her seat beside Jehan and followed him. She paused only once, to retrieve her sword from its resting place near the door and to meet Jehan's eye. Her own was bright and fierce. With the slightest of bows, she strode after the baron, silent as his shadow and no less tenacious.

Jehan released his breath slowly and beckoned to the hall steward. "More wine," he commanded.

Somewhat to his surprise, the man obeyed him. He returned to Rhydderch's seat and sat there, lordly, unconcerned, and shaking deep within where no one could see.

29

Half a mile from St. Ruan's, where three days ago Richard's knights had begun their race for the gold bezant, a figure stood alone. From a distance he seemed a lifeless thing, a stone or a tree-trunk set upon the road, dusted with the snow which had begun to fall a little after noon. Now and then a gust of wind would snatch at his dark cloak, baring a glimpse of brightness, scarlet and blue and gold, or plucking the hood away from a white still face that turned toward the north and west.

The snow thickened. He paid no heed to it, nor tried after the first time or two to cover his head, although the flakes clung to his hair and lashes, half-blinding him.

He heard them long before he saw them, the pounding of hoofs, the jingle of metal, the harsh breathing of horses driven fast and hard over rough country. Through a gap in the swirling snow burst a company of knights.

Their leader well-nigh rode over him. The red stallion reared, its iron-shod hoofs seeming almost to brush his face. Its rider cried out, "Brother Alf! For the love of God!"

The stallion stood still, trembling and snorting. Alf laid a gentle hand upon its neck and regarded the company, and Rhydderch a shadow in their midst. He shivered slightly. "You're back," he said, looking from Jehan to Thea. "We've all been waiting for you."

"Obviously." Jehan held out his hand. "Come up behind me."

He shook his head. "Your poor beast has all the burdens he needs." Yet he clasped Jehan's hand, a brief, tight grip, fire-warm, and smiled. "I'm glad to see you safe." He turned away too quickly for Jehan to answer, and swung up behind Thea on the gray mare of Rhiyana.

The kings received the arrivals in the Abbot's hall, in royal state. Even Gwydion had put aside his brown robe for a cotte which seemed made of the sky at midnight, a deep luminous blue worked with

moonlit silver in the image of the seabird crowned. Both Richard and
Kilhwch, to his right and his left, blazed in scarlet and gold.

Through all the journey from his stronghold, Rhydderch had
spoken no word. When royal guards relieved him of his weapons and
monks bathed him and trimmed his hair and beard and clothed him
as befit his rank, he offered no resistance. He seemed half-stunned by
the failure of all he had plotted.

He came before the kings as docilely as an ox led to slaughter,
following Jehan blindly, hardly aware of the guards about him.

Before the three thrones they drew away to leave him standing
alone. The ambassador named each of the kings for him, and each
bowed a high head: Kilhwch of Gwynedd, Richard of Anglia, Gwydion of Rhiyana.

The Elvenking regarded him with a level gray stare, and deep
within it a flicker of green fire. Rhydderch started as if struck. For an
instant the mute submission dropped away, revealing the black rage
beneath.

"Well met, Lord Rhydderch," Gwydion said softly, "and welcome."

Rhydderch's eyes hooded; he bowed low. "I came as you commanded, Your Majesties. What will you have of me?"

"Your company," Richard said, toying with the heavy chain he
wore about his neck. "I'm glad you came so quickly. It would have
been uncomfortable for us to have to go after you."

"I've always labored to do as my King commands."

"I'm pleased to hear that." Richard gestured; Alf brought a
chair. "Sit down and be comfortable. We're all friends here."

Rhydderch sat quietly enough. He had not looked at Gwydion
since that first terrible glare. "It pleases me to see Your Majesties so
friendly."

"Your doing," Kilhwch said. "Sir. We'll have to thank you
properly when there's time."

"My doing, Sire?" Rhydderch asked, as if incredulous. "How
can that be?"

"You don't know, my lord?" Kilhwch smiled. "Perhaps my lord
of Rhiyana can enlighten you. He's tasted your famous hospitality,
has he not?"

Rhydderch frowned slightly. "I can't recall, Sire, that I've ever
had the honor of guesting a King."

"Not even the Dotard of Caer Gwent?"

Gwydion stirred. "Kilhwch," he said very low. The young King's mouth snapped shut. He himself leaned back, cradling his broken hand as if it pained him. "I'm not what you expected, am I, Lord Rhydderch?"

"You are precisely what the tales say you are."

"Then you'll admit that you knew who he was?" demanded Kilhwch.

The Elvenking raised his hand. "This is not a trial," he said. "Lord Rhydderch has ridden hard and far, and he has not slept well of late. He is hungry and weary, and much bemused, I am sure, by the suddenness of our summons. Let us eat and sleep; in the morning we may turn to deeper matters."

"I don't like this," Jehan said. "I don't like any of it. I wish I'd never brought that man back!"

It was very late. The kings had long since gone to their beds, but he sat with Alf and Morwin in the Abbot's study. Of all the praise he had had for a task well and swiftly done, theirs was the sweetest. But he had not earned it.

"He came too easily," he went on, "without even trying to fight. Either he's a complete fool—or we are, and he's about to prove it."

Morwin shook his head. "He's a clever man and a vicious one, but he knows better than to set himself against three kings. He planned to prick them into killing each other, without letting them know who was responsible. Unfortunately, one of his provocations turned out to be the very King he wanted to provoke."

"True enough," Jehan agreed, "but you're forgetting something. He looks sane and ordinary, but he's neither. He's had a terrible blow, and he knows he doesn't have much to hope for. The best he can expect is to get his lands back, with a ruinous tax on them and a knight's fee he'll have to struggle to meet. He'll die a pauper, who wanted to be a King. Who knows what he'll do if he breaks?"

"He's here and very well guarded, not in Caer Sidi hatching war. And tomorrow—"

" 'And seven alone returned from Caer Sidi.' "

Alf's voice startled them both. He had been sitting quietly, apparently drowsing; his eyes were half-shut, blurred as if with sleep. He sighed deeply and shivered. "He calls his castle by the name of the Fortress of Annwn. Death walks in his shadow. How cold it is!"

Jehan opened his mouth to speak, but Morwin hushed him.

Again Alf shivered. His eyes cleared; he looked about as if bewildered. "I must have been dreaming. I thought someone had died, and Rhydderch had killed him."

Morwin laid a hand on his brow. It was burning hot, yet he shivered violently. "No one's dead, and no one's going to die, least of all at his lordship's hands. Look, Alf. Jehan is back safe and sound, and Rhydderch's surrounded by every guard the kings or the abbey can spare. There's nothing to be afraid of."

Jehan brought him a cup of mead. He drank a little; his shivering stilled. He tried to smile. "I shouldn't stare into the fire; it makes me see horrors. And Rhydderch isn't a pleasant man to think of. Even Gwydion can't see very far into his mind. It's too dark and too twisted and too wild, like the black heart of Bowland."

"Don't talk about him," Morwin said sternly. "Don't even think about him. That's for the kings to do."

"Low station can be a refuge, can't it?" Alf drank the last of his mead and stood. "We all need our sleep. Come, Jehan."

Morwin had risen with him. "I'm not sleepy yet. I'll walk with you."

"There's no need for you to—"

"What's the matter, Alf? Do you expect me to be waylaid in a passageway?"

Jehan laughed. Alf paled and shuddered, but did not speak.

When Alf lay on his pallet near Richard's door, Morwin drew Jehan aside. "Watch out for him," he said. "When this mood is on him, he's apt to do anything." Jehan nodded, understanding; he smiled. "Good night then. God be with you."

"And with you, Domne," Jehan murmured.

The Abbot blessed him and turned away, walking as lightly as a boy.

30

Rhydderch lay motionless and sweating under thick blankets. Across his door, his own liege-man snored softly. Outside in the passage, two knights slept deep, clasping their swords to their breasts. One was of Anglia, one of Gwynedd.

Carefully he opened his eyes. The moon escaped from its wall of cloud and hurled a bright shaft across the room, transfixing the hilt of his sword. He was not a prisoner. No one had chained him or bolted his door; the guards were for his honor and protection.

His lip curled. They mocked him, those fools of kings. Richard, cheated of a war, turned weakling and woman-heart. Kilhwch, who thought himself so clever and so cruel, who set his man to watch the guest and to kill him—by accident—if he ventured to escape.

And Gwydion. Gwydion, with his bandaged hand which he kept always in sight, and his cold gray eyes, and his too-handsome face. Huw had had orders to break that eagle's beak of a nose; he would lose his own when Rhydderch won free of this gilded trap.

Rhydderch growled deep in his throat. Gwydion had brought him to this. Gwydion, who refused to age as a man ought, who looked on his enemy with cool and royal scorn. He had not been so haughty when Dafydd plied the hot iron; his blood, royal and immortal though he was, had flowed as redly and as readily as any villein's.

With infinite caution Rhydderch rose. He had kept on his tunic and hose against the cold. Soundlessly he crossed the room.

His hand eclipsed the moonlight upon his sword hilt. He froze for an instant; his guards did not stir. Taking up the sheathed sword, wrapping himself in his cloak, he crept toward the door.

The Lady Chapel glimmered softly by the light of the vigil lamp. It was the fairest of the abbey's chapels, Morwin thought as he paused in its doorway, and the most wonderful, walled with a tracery of pale stone, its altar of white marble inlaid with lapis lazuli. When Morwin was young, some forgotten artisan had painted the curving ceiling the color of the sky at night and set it with golden stars.

He knelt in front of the altar and contemplated the face of the carven Virgin behind it. A gentle face, a little sad, as if it looked upon the ills of the world and mourned for them. But beneath the sadness lay a deep serenity.

He did not pray in words. Somehow the Lady of Comfort was beyond them.

Instead, he remembered. Good things, ill things. Apple blossoms in the spring; plague in the village. The Brothers chanting the *Te Deum;* soldiers chanting a war chant and men screaming. The day of his ordination, he and Alf taking their vows side by side, each serving the other at his first Mass; the day he realized that his hands were twisting and stiffening with age, and that the hairs which fell from the

barber's shears were more gray than red; and that his friend, who had
been a boy with him, had not changed and would never change.

He sighed. The hands on his knees were like the branches of an
ancient apple tree, gnarled and almost sapless. "And I still don't have
a likely successor," he said to the Virgin. "Alf's wings have spread too
wide and he's flown too high. *Mea culpa,* Lady, *mea maxima culpa.* I sent
him out, knowing what would happen; that the world would claim
him—and heal him a little."

Has it? the calm eyes seemed to ask.

"I don't know. I think it's too early to tell. The scars are still too
deep."

For a while longer he remained there, head bowed. The lamp
flickered. It needed refilling, he thought inconsequentially, and smiled
at himself. That was age and power, to worry about lamp oil when
his mind ought to be on the Infinite.

The abbey was a labyrinth, vast and unlit and stone-cold, and apparently deserted. Rhydderch's nose wrinkled at the holy stink of it,
rotting apples, long-dead incense. Once or twice a monk prowled the
empty passages; he hid until the shadow passed, itching to test his
blade on priestly flesh. But he had promised it a better offering.

Light at once alarmed and attracted him. He inched toward it.

A heavy door stood ajar. The light shone beyond it, dim and
unsteady, hanging over an altar. He had found a chapel. From his
vantage point he could see a kneeling figure, a dark robe, a bowed
white head. An elderly monk at prayer, all alone.

Rhydderch drew his cloak over the hand which held the sword
and advanced boldly.

"Excuse me, Brother," he said, softening his voice as much as he
might. "I got up to go to the privy, and I seem to have taken a wrong
turning."

The monk turned. Rhydderch did not pay much heed to the
sharp-featured old face. They all looked alike, these shavepates; he
had another face before his mind's eye, quite another face altogether.

"Lord Rhydderch," the monk said. He did not sound surprised.
"Your room has its own garderobe. Don't tell me your guard forgot
to remind you."

Rhydderch ground his teeth. Thwarted, always thwarted. The
damned witch. He picked a man's mind clean and told the world
what he had found.

The sword gleamed naked in Rhydderch's hand. The monk

regarded it almost with amusement. "Isn't that a little excessive, my
lord? A simple request will do. Shall I take you back to your room,
or do you have somewhere else in mind?"

"You," Rhydderch growled. "I ought to know you."

The monk smiled. Small and sharp-nosed and deep-wrinkled as
he was, he looked like a bogle from an old nursery tale. "We've been
introduced, my lord, though the light's not good here. Just call me
Brother and tell me where to take you."

Rhydderch raised his sword and rested the point very lightly
against the withered throat. "Take me to the Witch-king."

It did not seem to trouble the monk in the least that death pricked
his adam's apple. "Well, my lord," he said, "that's a hard thing to do.
We're inundated with royalty here, I grant you, but there's none who
answers to the name of—"

"Gwydion," snapped Rhydderch. "He calls himself Gwydion."

"And what do you want with His Majesty of Rhiyana at this hour
of the night? I can tell you now, my lord, that he's long since gone to
sleep and that he oughtn't to be disturbed. Unless, of course," the old
babbler added, "it's deathly urgent."

"Urgent. Yes, it's urgent. Take me to him!" A red film had drawn
itself over Rhydderch's eyes; his tongue felt thick, unwieldy; his fingers
trembled on the sword hilt. The point wavered; the monk winced. A
minute, glistening droplet swelled from his throat.

"Now, sir," he said reprovingly. "There's no need to hurt anybody. Why don't you put your sword down and say a bit of prayer
with me? Then we can decide if your message is important enough
to break into a King's sleep."

"If you don't do as I say," Rhydderch said very low, "I'll hack
off your head, tongue and all."

"It's a mortal sin to shed blood in a sacred place, my lord. Not
to mention the fact that you'll have to get past three kings and their
men to escape. And then where will you go? Come, sir. Let me take
you back to your bed, and we'll both forget we ever met each other."

He was smiling. Smiling, damn him, as if he were the one who
held the sword, and as if he pitied the poor misguided victim. The
witch had smiled so with those cat's-eyes of his, not hating, only
pitying. Poor Rhydderch, with his ragged army and his hovel of a
castle and his mad dreams of kingship.

The sword retreated. The monk's smile widened. "Ah, my lord,
I knew you'd—"

The bright blade whirled in an arc and flashed down.

* * *

Jehan spread his pallet next to Alf's, undressed and settled on it. His friend seemed to have fallen into a restless, tossing sleep. He moved as close as he could without actually touching, and tried to think calmness into the other's mind.

After a while it seemed to work, or else Alf had relaxed of his own accord. Jehan dared to close his eyes.

He drifted lazily between sleep and waking, not quite ready to let go. A dream hovered just out of reach.

He started awake. Alf sat bolt upright, his face so terrible that for an instant Jehan did not even know it.

The novice reached for him. "Brother Alf," he whispered. "Brother Alf, it's all right."

The body under his hands was rigid, the eyes all red. "Rhydderch," Alf hissed. "Murder. Sword. Morwin." His lips drew back from his teeth. They were very white and very sharp, the canines longer and leaner than a human's. Jehan had never noticed that before. "Chapel—chapel—*Morwin!*" It was a cry of anguish.

Even before Jehan had scrambled to his feet, Alf was almost out of sight. The other bolted after him.

Rhydderch stood over the crumpled body, breathing hard, the sword dangling loosely from his hands.

A whirlwind swept him up. The blade flew wide; he fell sprawling. His head struck the floor with an audible crack.

Alf dropped beside Morwin. Blood fountained from the deep wound in the Abbot's breast. Desperately he strove to stanch it, but it spurted through his fingers.

"It's no use, Alf."

In the gray and sunken face, Morwin's eyes were as bright as ever. He grinned a horrible, death's-head grin. "Well, old friend, Cassandra was right after all. I'm sorry I laughed at you."

Alf shook his head mutely. All his strength focused upon the gathering of his power. Slow, so slow, and Morwin's life was ebbing with the tide of his blood. Yet the power was there, as it had not been for Gwydion's healing. It was ready to gather, to grasp—

"*Alf!*"

Morwin's cry brought him to his feet. Rhydderch's sword clove the air where his head had been; madness seethed behind it, a black fire of hate. Kill the monk, kill the witch, kill—

Alf's eyes flamed red. Without a sound he sprang.

Rhydderch fought like a wild boar. But Alf was a cat, too swift to catch, too strong to hold. They swayed back and forth, twined like lovers, battling for the bloody sword.

It fell with an iron clang. Swifter than sight, Alf seized the hilt.

For an instant, the world stood still. So one held the sword. So one raised it, beyond it the hunched black shape, fury turning to fear, fear to blind terror.

In that timeless moment, Alf was completely sane and keenly aware of all about him. The chapel with its gentle Virgin and its golden stars; the Abbot drowning in his own blood; the huddle of stunned figures in the doorway, Jehan foremost, white as death. And Rhydderch.

Rhydderch, who had killed Morwin. Coolly, leisurely, with effortless skill, Alf hewed him down.

31

Very gently Alf cradled Morwin in his arms. The Abbot's body seemed light and empty as a dried husk, but a glimmer of life clung to it still.

He tried to speak. Alf laid a finger on his lips. Already they were cooling. "In your mind," he whispered, "the old way."

The old way, Morwin thought. *Not long now . . . Alf. Promise me something.*

"Anything," said Alf.

The Abbot smiled in his mind, for his grip on his body was loosening swiftly. *Say my funeral Mass.*

Alf flinched. Quietly, steadily, he said, "I murdered a man in cold blood in God's own sanctuary. I am in the deepest state of mortal sin. I can't say Mass for you. It would be blasphemy."

No! Morwin snapped with a ghost of his old vigor. *You said you'd do anything.* Anything, *Alf.*

"Morwin—before God—"

Before God, Alfred, ego te absolvo. . . .

"Morwin!"

Friend, brother, son, thy sins are forgiven. Say the Mass, Alf. For love of me, for love of God. And for your soul's sake, see to his rest the poor creature who killed me.

Morwin's eyes were fading; he blinked, peering through the shadows. *Such a fair face, to be the last thing I see. Are there tears on it? Poor lad. When you've laid this bag of bones in the ground and made your peace with Rhydderch, find your own peace in the City of Peace. What is it that the Jews say? "Next year, in Jerusalem."*

"You—you bid me make a pilgrimage?"

For peace, Alf. To Jerusalem. The darkness was almost complete. But on the very edge of sight glimmered a light. Morwin reached for it. *So far, so fair . . . Alf! Alf, look. It shines. It shines!*

Alf raised a tear-stained face. Jehan was standing over him. "He's gone," he said. His voice was soft, level. "I couldn't follow him. It was too bright." Suddenly, luminously, he smiled. "But he went on; I saw. I felt. There was joy, Jehan. *Joy!*"

The novice stared at him as he crouched there with the Abbot's lifeless body in his arms, his hands red with the blood of the man he had slain and the man he had defended—and on his face, pure joy.

Jehan swallowed hard. Others crowded behind him, an alarming number, the kings, Aylmer, Thea, a handful of knights, several monks, all in various states of undress. Their faces were white with shock; even the kings seemed frozen with the horror of it, a chapel turned to a charnel house, an Abbot foully murdered.

Jehan frowned. Three crowned kings—and not one had the wits to act. He singled out the solid dark figure of Aylmer. "My lord Bishop, you'd best take over the abbey and see that the Brothers know what's happened. Brother Osric, Brother Ulf, take Dom Morwin to the mortuary; you, sir knights, had better see to Rhydderch. Brother Owein, roust out a party of novices to clean up the chapel; it will have to be purified later. And if you please, my lord Gwydion, would you take care of Brother Alf?"

Jehan hesitated at the stair's foot. Gwydion had left Alf in his old cell, by Alf's own choice, for it was quiet and isolated, and it had a door which could be bolted against the world.

With sudden decision, Jehan strode forward. The door was shut; he knocked softly.

"Come in," Alf said.

He sounded like his old self. Jehan lifted the latch and stepped into the cell.

It was the same as it had always been, very plain and very bare. Alf sat cross-legged on the hard narrow bed in his shabby old habit, as if he had never left St. Ruan's at all.

Jehan found that he had nothing to say. Alf looked quiet, serene; he even smiled. "Have they finally let you go?"

"I let myself go." Jehan sat on the bed and looked hard at him. "Brother Alf, are you bottling yourself up?"

Alf shook his head. "I've been talking with Gwydion. That's all."

"But you're so *quiet.*"

"Ah," said Alf. "I should be raving and trying to find a sword to fall on." He turned his hands palm up and flexed his long fingers. "Yes. I should be. I killed a man. He killed one who was dearer to me than a brother. And I have to say Morwin's funeral Mass, witch and murderer that I am, suspended from my vows."

"You're none of those things."

He sighed deeply. "Am I not? It's very strange, Jehan. I've tormented myself for so long for so little; now that I have a reason, I find that I can't. I am what I am; I've done what I've done; I can't change any of it."

"Is that acceptance or indifference?"

"I'm not sure yet. Gwydion says it's part of my healing. Thea says I'm finally coming to my senses. I think I'm numb. Either I'll come burning back to life again, or I'll mortify and fall away."

Jehan swallowed, but could not speak.

" 'I am the Resurrection and the Life; he who believes in me will never die.' " Alf spoke softly, wonderingly. "To believe that, and to *know* it . . . When I looked into the middle of the Light, Jehan, for a moment I saw Morwin. He was a boy again; and he was laughing."

Jehan could not bear it. "Brother Alf! Don't you understand? It's my fault he's dead. It was my idea to bring Rhydderch here; I brought him; and he—he killed—"

So young, so strong; he had borne all that Alf had borne, and been a shield and a fortress, and never wavered or fallen. "Jehan," Alf said. "Jehan. It was none of your doing."

"It was!" he cried.

Alf shook him. "Jehan de Sevigny, Rhydderch's coming put an end to the war and to the quarrel between kings. When he died, when no one else could move or think, you did both, splendidly."

"I started the whole thing. The least I could do was put an end to it."

"Which you did, most well. You're fit to walk among kings, Jehan."

"I'm not fit to walk with a dog." Jehan dashed away tears, angrily. "I wish people would stop praising me and see what an idiot I am."

"You are yourself. That's enough."

Jehan's brows contracted. "Here you are, giving me my own advice. And you're barely in any condition to bear your own burdens, let alone mine."

"No," Alf said. "I think I'm stronger than I ever was." He settled his arm about the tense shoulders. At first they tightened, but little by little their tautness eased. Jehan drooped against him.

He smoothed the unruly hair, gently. "Just before Morwin went to the Light, he paused. He turned back to me with the joy already on his face, and said, 'Don't mourn for me, Alf. And don't mourn for yourself. I'm not leaving you alone; you have Jehan to be friend and brother and son. Love him, Alf. Love him well.' "

Jehan buried his face in Alf's robe and wept.

Alf held him until he had no more tears to shed, and for a while after as he lay spent, without speech or thought.

When he stiffened, Alf let him go. He sat up, scrubbing his face with the backs of his hands, sniffing hard. "A fine great booby I am," he said. "You must be mortally ashamed of me."

Alf smiled and shook his head. His own cheeks were wet. "We both needed that. Do you feel better?"

"Yes. Yes, I do." Jehan tried a smile. It wobbled, then steadied. "Thank you, Brother Alf."

The other looked down. Gratitude had always embarrassed him.

Jehan's smile warmed. "You've changed completely, and yet you haven't changed at all. If you're going to say Mass again, does that mean you're going back to being a priest?"

"I—" Alf's fingers knotted; he stared at them as if their pattern held an answer. "I don't know. Morwin left certain things for me to do. For atonement. The Mass was one. And I'm to go to Jerusalem as a pilgrim. Whether I'm also to go as a priest, he didn't say."

"But of course you should. Isn't that what you are?"

"That's the trouble. I'm not sure I am. I'm still Richard's squire. And Gwydion—Gwydion and Thea—talked to me for a long while. Gwydion will be going back to Rhiyana very soon now, before his brother comes raging into Anglia. He's asked me to go with him as a kinsman."

"Do you want to?" asked Jehan.

Alf raised his eyes. "When I'm with him or with Thea, I feel as if I've come home. I'm no longer a witch or a monster or even a peculiar variety of saint; I'm only Alf. They could set me free to be what I was truly meant to be. Maybe even, still, a priest. A priest of the Fair Folk." His lips twitched. "The theologian in me is going to have to do some very agile thinking."

"You'll do that then," Jehan said.

"Maybe." Alf unlocked his fingers, one by one. "Maybe not."

Jehan shrugged. "It doesn't matter to me. I don't care in the least where I go, as long as it's with you."

For a long moment Alf was silent. His face was very still, his eyes at once clear and impossible to read. "Jehan," he said at last, "I love you as a brother. As a son. When I had fallen as low as I could fall, you lifted me up again and showed me how to be strong. You've been living your life for me." Jehan opened his mouth; Alf raised a hand. "Jehan, you're young. You have a whole life to live, a life of your own. You'll be a warrior, a scholar, a prince of the Church. You'll walk with kings; you'll counsel Popes; you'll even win the respect of the Infidels, who deny the Christ but who know what a man is."

"You can do all that," Jehan said. "We can do it together."

"No, Jehan. Maybe our paths will cross. Maybe they'll even converge for a space as they have now. I pray they will. But whatever you do, you must do on your own, for yourself. If I go to Rhiyana or to Jerusalem or to Winchester with the King, you must not follow me, unless your own path takes you there."

"It will—because it's yours."

"Child," Alf said, though he bridled at the word. "Your way lies for now with Bishop Aylmer."

"He'll free me if I ask."

"Don't."

Jehan glared at his feet. Great ugly feet, like all the rest of him. And in the center of him, a terrible ache.

"Jehan." He refused to look up. Alf went on quietly. "I'll tell you the truth. If we have to part, it will not be easy for me to bear. But I want you to go your own way, wherever that is, without regard for me. Please, Jehan. For my sake as much as for yours."

Jehan's shoulders hunched; his head sank between them. His

voice when he spoke was rough. "If you go one way and I go another, will I ever see you again?"

"Yes," Alf answered him. "I promise."

Muscle by muscle Jehan relaxed. He drew a deep breath. "All right then. I'll grow up, and stop dangling at your tail."

Alf smiled.

He scowled. But Alf's smile was insidious. It crept through the cracks of his ill-humor, and swelled, and shattered it, for all that he could do. He found himself smiling ruefully; then more freely, until they were both laughing like idiots over nothing at all.

32

Rhydderch's body rested in the room in which he would have slept, guarded as he had been while yet he lived. Even now he seemed to scowl, hating those who had tended him and made him seemly, clothing him as a lord and according him due honor.

Alf stood over the bier, too still and too pale. He did not respond when Richard came to stand beside him; his eyes were fixed on the dark furious face.

"If ever a man looked like the Devil's own," Richard said, "this one does."

Alf shuddered.

The King clapped him on the shoulder; he winced, for his back was still tender. "There now. He was damned long before you put the seal on it, but he'll get the Christian burial you wanted for him. There's no need to shed tears over him."

"I'm not weeping for him," said Alf. "I'm praying for his soul."

"God knows he needs it."

"Who doesn't, Sire?"

Richard laughed. "Aylmer says you have the face of an angel, and the Devil's own wit."

"A fair face and a black heart. That, say the Paulines, is the essence of elf-kind."

"Your heart is as pure as a maid's and somewhat softer." He met

Alf's bright strange gaze. "We've decided to be kind to this carrion. After you've buried your Abbot, it goes back where it came from, with a company of knights to keep off the birds and bandits and a good man to hold the lands and the folk until I find a proper lord for them. One who's loyal, and who'll wait for me before he starts any wars."

"Are you going to turn against Kilhwch after all?"

Swift anger flashed across Richard's face. "Kilhwch is a splendid fellow. So is His Majesty of Rhiyana. And I'm not such a scoundrel that I'll break up a pair of noble friendships. There'll be no fighting on either side of Anglia while those friendships hold." His anger faded. "Imagine, Alfred. A King who can ride wherever he likes and leave his brother with crown and throne, and who knows that he can come back and take both without having to shed even a drop of blood. And I'm going to have a chance to see this prodigy. There's to be a tournament in Caer-y-n'Arfon in the spring, and Gwydion says the Flame-bearer will come; I'll have a chance to see which one of us is stronger."

Alf smiled. He was no longer quite so pale.

"And you," Richard said. "Aylmer's trying to steal you back from me. Anyone can see, he says, that you belong in the priesthood. You and that great clever ox of a Sevigny—you'll be the right and left hands of the Church Militant, and half the body besides."

"I know," Alf murmured. "He came to talk to me this morning. He wants me to resume my vows in full and to take up knightly training, and to teach theology to one or two of his priests."

"Will you have time to eat or sleep?"

"Occasionally."

Richard stood squarely in front of him. "Tell me now," he said. "Tell me the truth. If you were free to do whatever you chose, would you go with him?"

"Once upon a time," said Alf, "two men disputed the ownership of a fine hound. One had raised it from a pup; the other had found it wandering in the wood, and taken it and fed it and trained it to hunt. They took their case to their liege lord. He heard each side of the story, and deliberated for a long while; at last he had his men draw a circle on the floor of his hall and place the hound in it. The owners stood on opposite sides and called to it."

He stopped. Richard frowned. "So? What happened?"

"The beast lay down," Alf replied, "and calmly went to sleep."

The King glared, then laughed. "The Devil's wit, indeed! Who's calling you?"

"Aylmer, for one. Gwydion wants me to go with him to Rhiyana.

My Abbot, when he died, bade me make a pilgrimage to Jerusalem. And you, Sire." Alf smiled wryly. "I haven't forgotten the promise I made to you, though you've been most kind to let me see my Abbot to his rest as if I were still one of his monks. When his Mass is over, if you command me, I'll put on your livery again."

"And if I don't command you? If I leave you free to choose?"

Alf was silent. Richard could find no answer in his face, nor in his eyes that were the same color as the winter sun.

The King's voice roughened. "When you have a hawk, there comes a time when you have to set it free. If it comes back it's yours. If not . . ." He drew a breath. "I'm freeing you. You can go with your priests or to your Fair Folk. Or you can rule Anglia with me. In Winchester I'll make you a knight and give you lands and riches, and set you among my great lords. And in the spring after the tournament in Gwynedd, we'll start planning a new Crusade. You'll have your pilgrimage to Jerusalem, Alfred, and a kingdom there if you want one. And after that we can travel to Constantinople, just as we said we would when we were riding to Carlisle." His face was flushed, eager, lively as a boy's. "Tell me, Alfred. Tell me you'll do it. With you by me, there's no one in the world who can conquer me."

"Sire," Alf said. He moved away from Rhydderch's body, that weighed like a stone upon heart and mind. Richard followed him until they stood together by the cold hearth. "Sire, I've been offered so much. Aylmer promises to set the Church at my feet; Gwydion opens the realm of the Fair Folk to me. And you spread before me all the kingdoms of the world."

A shadow crossed Richard's face. "Is that all I am to you? A tempter?"

"My lord, you know that's not so."

"Do you realize that you've never called me by my name?"

"You're my King, Sire. I wouldn't presume—"

Richard struck the wall with his fist. "Damn you! You've presumed to rule me, heart and soul, since the day you met me."

"Richard," Alf said. "Richard, my lord. You see so much, can't you see that I look on you as my friend?"

"I see it," Richard answered harshly. "I wanted to hear it."

Alf, who spoke as much with touch as with words, had never touched Richard. He laid his hand very lightly upon the King's shoulder. "You never once tried to overstep the boundaries I set. For that I learned to love you."

Richard trembled under his hand.

He did not draw it away. "Richard. I have so many choices, who never had any, who needed to have no thoughts of my own but only to do as I was bidden. Each choice is one I would make gladly. But I can't have them all. Only one."

"And that's not mine."

"No!" Alf cried. "Don't you see? I don't know. I can't choose. Bishop Aylmer thinks I should go back to Winchester for Yule and do my thinking there; then I can go where I will."

"That makes sense."

"Do you think so?" Alf let his hand fall from Richard's shoulder. His eyes were troubled. "Sire, I have to think. I have to pray. But whatever I choose, remember. Remember that I'm still your friend. Your brother, even, if you will."

For a long moment the King stared at him, as if to commit to memory every line of his face. Suddenly, swiftly, Richard embraced him, and let him go, stepping back. "I'll remember," he said. He turned away, striding past Rhydderch's body, paying it no heed.

Alf drew a shuddering breath. "There," he whispered to the empty hearth, the dead shape, "truly, is a King."

> *"Sing praise to the Lord, you His faithful ones, and give thanks*
> *to His holy name.*
> *For His anger lasts but a moment; a lifetime, His good will.*
> *At nightfall, weeping comes in, but with the dawn, rejoicing."*

Such a contrast, Alf thought, between Rhydderch and his victim. Morwin lay in state in the chapel, surrounded with candles and incense and the chanting of monks. He seemed strange, lying so still, who had been lively and restless even in sleep; the robes of a Lord Abbot had displaced his old brown habit. But his face bore a hint of his wicked smile.

Almost Alf could hear his dry humorous voice. "All this fuss for a silly old fool. I should sit up and grin, and give them all a proper fright."

Alf smiled and touched the cold hand. Something glittered beneath it upon his breast. Alf's fingers found the shape of a cross, the cool smoothness of silver, and a memory of Thea's presence.

> *"To you, O Lord, I cried out; with the Lord I pleaded:*
> *'What gain would there be from my life-blood, from my going*
> *down into the grave?'"*

The chanting rolled over them both, living and dead. From where Alf stood, he could see the shadow that was the doorway of the Lady Chapel, a faint glimmer as of painted stars. The lamp there was extinguished, the chapel forbidden until it should be cleansed of the stain of murder. Bishop Aylmer would do that tomorrow after the funeral Mass.

> *"You changed my mourning into dancing. You took off my sackcloth*
> *   and clothed me with gladness,*
> *That my soul might sing praise to You without ceasing; O Lord,*
> *   my God, forever will I give You thanks."*

Alf knelt beside the bier and bowed his head over his folded hands.

"Brother? Brother Alfred?"

The chapel had been silent for a long while. Alf straightened slowly, stiffly. Several monks stood near him, watching him: Brother Osric, Brother Owein, and old Brother Herbal.

Looking into their faces, he realized that they had always thought well of him. The younger ones had been his pupils; Brother Herbal had taken vows a year or two before he had. Familiar, all of them, and yes, beloved.

Brother Osric cleared his throat. A bright lad, he had been; aging now, his eyes, never good, peering myopically through the dimness. "Brother," he said again. "We've met in Chapter, all of us, to elect our new Abbot. Some of us wanted you to be there. But . . . well . . . you were sent out and you came back a layman, and there's the matter of—of—"

Osric had always lost all fluency when he was agitated. Alf finished the sentence for him. "Murder," he said. "I know, Brother. I understand. And I appreciate your coming here to tell me." He looked from face to face. "Whom shall I congratulate?"

They would not answer. Yet they had chosen someone; that much Alf could read, even without witchery. Someone important, and someone controversial, from the gleam in Brother Owein's eye and the set of Brother Osric's jaw.

Brother Herbal frowned. Like Morwin, he had never had much patience. "Well, Brothers? Isn't anybody going to tell him?"

Alf stood. His knees ached; his back was twinging. He had lost the knack of kneeling for long hours on hard stones. "What's the trouble?

It can't be anyone I'd object to very strenuously; I'm not such a fool that I'd demand another Morwin."

"Good," said Brother Herbal. "Because Morwin, you're not."

"What do I have to do with—" Alf broke off. He knew. God help him, he knew.

He wanted to burst into wild laughter. Four times now. Would they never learn? And five choices, it made. Five. He would go mad.

"Now look here," Brother Owein said sternly, as if he had been a stubborn novice. "This is becoming a ritual. Elect Brother Alfred; argue with him; lose the argument; and go through the whole foolish process again to elect someone less able but more willing. I know Dom Morwin wanted you to be Abbot after him—and so did Dom Andreas, Dom Willibrord, and probably Dom Lanfranc, too. Haven't you got the message by now?"

Alf sank down upon the altar steps, so pale that Brother Herbal hastened to him. He waved the old man away. "I'm not going to faint. I'm not going to shout at you, or howl, or even weep. I'm not even going to remind you that I'm still recovering from trial for witchcraft, or that I killed a man on sacred ground."

He held out his hands to them. "Brothers, you honor me more than I can say. To gather, all of you, and to elect me your Abbot, even knowing what I am and what I've done . . . I think I shall weep, after all."

Brother Herbal grimaced. "Go ahead. But tell us first. Yes or no?"

Alf looked at each in turn. "You know that I have a charge from Morwin to seek absolution in Jerusalem."

"We know," Osric answered. "If you go now, you go as Abbot, and some of us will go with you. By your leave, of course."

He wanted to laugh again, for pain. "Oh, Brothers! Do you know what torment this is? I stand upon a peak in the desert with all of heaven and earth spread about me, and voices whispering in my ear, bidding me look and choose. A warrior-priest in the Bishop's train, a lord of Anglia, an elven-knight of Rhiyana—and now, Abbot of St. Ruan's. Dear God! What shall I do?"

Brother Orwein stood over him, hands on hips. "All of a sudden your worth is catching up with you. I don't doubt you'd make a good knight or lord or priest; you'd certainly make a better Abbot than most." He glanced at his companions. "We had orders to make you accept, by force if necessary. But we didn't know how many others had been at you. The abbey can manage as it is for a day or two. Take the time. Meditate. Pray. Say the Mass and ask for guidance. Then tell us. Yes, or—God forbid—no."

They left him then, with many glances over their shoulders. The last, as they passed the door, found him upon his face before the altar. His shoulders shook. Weeping, they wondered, or laughter?

33

Reverently, lovingly, Alf lifted the vestments from the press where he had laid them away, so long ago. They bore a sweet red-brown scent, for the press was of cedar of Lebanon. Amice and alb, white linen of his own weaving; the cincture from his first habit, soft with age; maniple and stole; and the chasuble of black Chin silk, embroidered with silver thread, heavy with pearls.

He laid out each garment as an acolyte would have done, but the novices who would serve him, and the Bishop and the priests of St. Ruan's who would concelebrate the Mass, had busied themselves elsewhere in the sacristy, leaving him alone with his priesthood and his God. He found that his hands were shaking, nor could he stop them; his heart pounded. To say the Mass, and this Mass of all others, with such burdens as weighted his mind and his heart, and perhaps also his soul, if soul he had . . .

He leaned against the wall, breathing deep again and again. *Dear God*, he thought. *Morwin, make me strong. It's been so long, so long; and I am not worthy. I am—not—*

Jehan's concern pierced through his barriers. He forced himself to straighten, to take up the amice. His hands, his mind, remembered. He touched the garment to his head and laid it about his shoulders, murmuring a prayer.

He reached for the alb. Jehan held it out to him. For a moment their hands touched. Alf smiled. "My bulwark," he said. "Thank you, Jehan."

The novice bowed, smiling back; Alf drew the white robe over his head. There was comfort in this ritual of robing, each movement prescribed, each thought foreordained. For so long he had only served and watched; he had forgotten the quiet joy at the center of the rite.

One of the novices peered round the door. "Almost time," he said.

They were all without, the monks, the kings and their men, even Thea, schismatic Greek that she was. Her mind brushed Alf's for an instant, bright and strong.

The procession had taken shape while he paused. He moved into his place, walking slowly beneath the weight of his vestments.

As he passed Aylmer, the Bishop touched his arm. "Remember," he whispered. " 'Thou art a priest forever, in the order of Melchisedec.' "

Forever.

He lifted his chin. The chant had begun, slow and deep. *"Requiem aeternam dona eis, Domine . . . :* Eternal rest grant unto them, O Lord, and let perpetual light shine upon them. . . ."

Morwin lay before the altar dais, as for three days he had lain with Alf as his constant companion. The procession moved slowly past him, Alf last of all, and divided, each man or boy taking his place as the ritual commanded.

Alf bowed low to the Abbot on his bier and lower still to the altar. In the silence after the antiphon, his voice was soft and pure. "I will go up to the altar of God."

"To God who gives joy to my youth," the acolytes responded.

He gathered all of his courage, and went up.

Richard watched him as he had watched on that first day in the camp by the lake. Then Alf had been only an acolyte; now he was the priest, Abbot-elect of St. Ruan's. Yet he looked the same, too fair to be human, rapt in the exaltation of the Mass.

As the rite continued, it seemed to the King that all light gathered about the slender figure on the altar. The priests about him, the novices moving about their duties, the chanting monks, faded to shadows. When he raised the Host, it blazed like a sun; his splendid voice rang forth: *"Hoc est enim corpus meum:* For this is my body."

Richard covered his eyes with his hands. Mass had always been a duty, and a dull one at that. But this was different. God, the God he had ignored or given only lip service, had entered into this place and shone through the priest, the sorcerer, the manslayer, soulless and deathless.

He is a priest, the King thought, too certain of it even to despair. *Aylmer will have him. Aylmer or the abbey. What a fool I was to think that I could ever make a lord of him!*

Looking up, he found Gwydion's gray eyes upon him. The Elvenking shook his head very slightly. *Wait,* his gaze said. *He has not
chosen yet. Wait and see.*

At the height of his exaltation, Alf looked again upon the Light to
which Morwin had gone; approached it and almost touched it. In that
moment he felt again Morwin's presence, like a warm hand in his, a
quick smile, a murmured word. *Well done, Alf. Oh, well done!*

The young face within the Light, the old one upon the bier,
merged and became one. His voice lifted. " 'May angels lead you to
Paradise; at your coming, may the martyrs receive you, and lead you
into the holy city of Jerusalem. May a choir of angels receive you, and
with Lazarus, who was once a beggar, may you find eternal rest.' "

Strong monks took the bier upon their shoulders and paced
forward. In a cloud of chanting and of incense they bore it through
the chapel, down a long stair into the musty dark of the crypt. There
they laid it down, the chanting muted now, the incense dimming the
flicker of candles. With gentle hands they raised the Abbot's body and
set it in a niche, among the bones and the rotting splendor of the
abbots who had gone before him.

The chanting faded and died. Alf bent and marked the cold brow
with the sign of the Cross, and kissed it gently. "Sleep well," he
whispered.

He turned. The lights and the candles departed one by one,
leaving Morwin to his long sleep.

Alf took off his vestments as reverently as he had put them on. No one
spoke to him, not even Jehan who served him, for the light lingered
still in his face. When at last he stood in his brown habit, Jehan
glanced aside, intent upon his duties; Alf slipped away.

The Thorn of Ynys Witrin slept its sleep which was like death, its
boughs heavy with snow as with blossoms in spring. Alf stood beneath
it, brown as it was, crowned with white.

He laid his hand upon the gnarled trunk. The power glimmered
in it as in the stone of Bowland, rising drowsily to touch his own—a
warmth, a green silence. It no longer wished him ill, if indeed it ever
had.

"Choices," Alf said to it. "So many choices. 'A priest forever.' I
am; yet I'm so many other things besides. What shall I do? Shall I be
the Lord Abbot? Can you endure that? Shall I be rather a soldier of

God? An elven-knight, or a prince of Anglia? What shall I be? What can I be?"

The wind whispered in the branches, yet without words. The gray sky bent over him. High above him a hawk wheeled, crying.

He turned his face to it. It was no common hawk, merlin or kestrel, but a splendid bird, the hawk of princes, the peregrine. Even as he watched, it turned upon its great wings and sped away eastward.

His breath caught. An answer, after all, and so simple. "I forgot," he said. "Dear God, forgive me for being a fool. I forgot, that abbot or priest or knight, I remain myself. Alfred. Alf. Not Sir or Lord or Father or Brother. Only Alf. Myself."

Himself—with all the world before him and choices without number, and freedom at last. Freedom to choose as he would.

A moment longer he hesitated. He was afraid. To choose, who had never chosen—what if he chose ill?

What if he did not choose at all?

All of St. Ruan's gathered in the hall for the Abbot's funeral feast. Even Brother Kyriell had left his post at the gate, freed for once from his duties.

But a lone figure stood under the arch, wrapped in a cloak, waiting.

Alf regarded her without surprise, as she regarded him. "You've chosen," she said.

He nodded.

She looked him over from cowled head to sandaled foot. "You're going away."

"To Jerusalem."

"Alone?"

He nodded again. "Morwin thought I'd find peace there. Or at least that the journey would show me how to accept myself for what I am."

"And the kings? The Bishop? The monks?"

"They all want me to be a great lord. But how can I be great or high or lordly, if I don't even know myself? I'll be Alfred now, and only Alfred. I think they'll understand."

"They'll try," she said.

There was a silence. Alf stared at his feet. "Tell Jehan. The books in my cell are for him. With my love. The ring with the moonstone in it and the gold bezant, I'm keeping; but all the rest of his gifts my lord Richard can dispose of as he wills. Aylmer must have my vest-

monts that I wore in the Mass. And Gwydion . . . tell him to look in
the coffer in the Abbot's study. The altar cloth there is my gift to him.
And Fara—Fara he must have again. Tell him."

"I'll tell everybody."

"The Brothers will have to elect someone else. I hope they choose
Owein. He'd make good Abbot, better than I."

She said nothing.

"And for you," he said. "For you I have this." He took her face
in his hands. Lightly, awkwardly, he kissed her.

He drew back. Her eyes were wide, all gold; he could not meet
them. "Good-bye," he said. "God be with you."

Still she did not speak.

He shot the bolts and pushed open the postern. A thin cold wind
danced about him, blowing from the east. He turned his face to it and
his back to the abbey, and left the gate behind.

Thea stood for a long moment as he had left her. He did not look back
with eyes or mind.

Where a woman had stood lay a crumpled dark cloak. A white
hound ran down the long road.

Her four feet were swifter than his two, and lighter upon the
snow. She drew level with him, leaped ahead of him, bounded about
him.

He stopped. "Thea," he said. His voice was stern, cold.

Jehan was a fool, she said in her mind. *He asked if he could come. I'm
not asking.* She trotted ahead a yard or two and paused, looking
bright-eyed over her shoulder. *Well, little Brother? Are you coming?*

He drew breath as if to speak. All that he might have done or said
raced through his mind. Thea watched it all with dancing eyes. Did
he think that any man, even an elf-priest, could gainsay her?

Suddenly he laughed. "Not even a saint," he said.

She ran before him, and he followed her, striding to Jerusalem.

The Golden Horn

For my parents

O City, City, jewel of all cities, famed in tales throughout the world, leader of faith, guide of orthodoxy, protector of learning, abode of all good! Thou hast drunk to the dregs the cup of the anger of the Lord, and hast been visited with fire fiercer than that which in ancient days descended upon the Five Cities. . . .

—Nicetas Choniates

. . . And therefore I have sailed the seas and come
To the holy city of Byzantium.

—W. B. Yeats

1

Rain and sun and thirty years' neglect had faded the tiles of the courtyard and softened the curves of the marble dolphin in the center. But the fountain played still, though half choked with weeds and leaves and verdigris. The pilgrim sat on its rim, letting her veil fall, here where there was none but her companion to see her face. She was very pale, her gold-bronze eyes enormous, staring at the fall of water without truly seeing it.

"Thea," the other said softly. When she did not respond, he knelt by her and took her hand. "Althea. Was it wise to come back?"

She blinked and shook herself. "What? Wise? That's a virtue neither of us has much of. Are you still determined to watch the Frankish armies overrun Byzantium?"

"Are you still determined to stay here and be reminded over and over again of what time can do to the rest of the world?"

"Aren't both our follies actually the same thing?"

He bowed his head. His hat's broad brim hid his face; she took it off, uncovering his hair. It was thick and long and very pale, silver-gilt like the eyes he raised to her, just touched with gold. "Do you know," she said, "if I'd left here even a season later than I did, I would have been caught in the plague."

"Would it have made any difference?"

"Who knows?" She spoke easily, lightly, as if it did not matter. "I promised you a bath and a good supper and a soft bed, and the best company east of Anglia. Will you forgive me if all I can offer you is a roof over your head?"

"You know there's nothing to forgive."

"Such a good Christian Brother." She rose. "Shall we sample the hospitality of House Damaskenos?"

The fountain gave them water to bathe in, and Thea's wallet yielded an ample supper. They settled for the night in a wide cool room where the painted walls retained much of their splendor: a wild garden full of fierce golden beasts.

"I did that," Thea said, sitting in a corner, clasping her knees. "Miklos wanted lions, and I gave him lions, eight of them, one for each of his birthdays. He was delighted, though not everyone else was. Father used to test people here. He'd ask them what they thought of the painting, and if they said it was outrageous, he knew they were honest."

The other smiled. "Do you remember the lion of Saint Mark? Poor bedraggled creature, shut up in a cage for people to stare at. I like your lions better."

"They're not very good ones. I wasn't a very good painter. It was easier to become a lion, though it upset people if they caught me at it."

"Only upset them?"

Upon her mantle lay a great tawny lioness with Thea's eyes. He regarded her in neither surprise nor fear. And, as she returned to her own shape: "I'm of your own kind," he said. "And I know you."

"Do you?" asked Thea.

"I know you shouldn't stay here. Let's go to Constantinople. Now. Tonight."

"Why? The house is empty and so are our purses. We can stay here for a while, rest, tell a white lie or two; and when we're well ready, go to the City in proper style."

"With nothing but bare floors to sleep on, and no bread but beggars' bread, and the chance of being stoned as witches."

"Food and furniture are easy enough to come by."

"And the other, Thea? What of that?"

She sat on her heels near him. "What of it? Are you afraid, little Brother?"

"Someone is bound to remember your face."

She shook her hair away from it. "And if someone does? Althea Damaskena ran away thirty years ago. She's an old woman now. And how old am I?"

"Ancient. Newborn." He leaned toward her, not quite touching her. "Thea, no good will come of it if we stay here. I know that."

"As you know you have to go to the City?"

He nodded.

"So," she said calmly, "you go and watch the spectacle. I'll stay and be one."

"I haven't been with you for so long to leave you now."

"I thought it was I who'd been with you through no choice of yours. Now you can be free. I'm back where I came from; you can go on with no one to threaten your holy purity. Think of it, Brother Alfred of Saint Ruan's Abbey. Or should I call you Abbot Alfred? You would have been that if the Brothers had had their way. Now you can go back to it."

"No." His voice was barely audible. "I asked for my vows to be dissolved, and they were. I'm neither monk nor priest nor abbot. I'm only Alf." He drew a breath. It helped the pain, a little. "I won't let you face this alone. You went to the stake for me; should I do any less?"

"Little Brother," she said, "I knew exactly what I was doing. And I had, and have, no scruples at all about using witchery. You do all you can to make yourself human. You won't even shape-change as I did to fly away from the fire."

"I can't."

"You could if you would. But it's too uncanny. Who ever heard of a man, or even a saint, who could be any living thing he wanted to be?"

"That's not my gift. But I can do what a friend must do. A kinsman. A brother."

"You don't look anything like Miklos." She traced the shape of his face with a light finger and let it continue down his cheek to his jaw, along the line of his neck to his shoulder. "I wish Father could have met you. He admired genuine innocence. It was the last thing a merchant could want, he said, but it was the first requisite of a saint."

"A saint must also be human. Not—what I am. Whatever I am."

"Changeling. Enchanter. Elf-wight. Demon, daimon, one of the Jann. Pilgrim from Anglia, healer in the hospital of Saint Luke beside the Holy Sepulcher, traveler to the Queen of Cities. And a very handsome—young—man." Her arms circled his neck. "Do you love me, Alf?"

He was as stiff as a stone, and as still, but no stone had ever burned as he burned. "Yes," he answered, "I love you. As a sister."

"I've been that to you, haven't I? Once I started to care enough about you to respect your vows, even Brother Alfred, famous for his chastity, couldn't rebuke me. And I've held to it. Five years now, Alf. There are people who'd say I was lying if they knew how long I'd traveled with you, lusty wench that I am, and never came closer than you'd allow. And you with a face like an angel and a body to drive a woman mad."

Only her arms touched him, but he felt the rest of her as if she had pressed close. Her face, tilted upward, was painfully beautiful, her voice low and piercingly sweet. "Your vows are gone. No need now to be poor or chaste or obedient. You can be the man you were meant to be. Swift and strong and fair, and as alien to a monk's meekness as a hunting leopard." Her arms tightened. They were body to body now with only threadbare linen between; their hearts hammered just out of rhythm.

With a sound between a gasp and a sob, he broke free. His robe lay draped over a broken bench; he lifted it with shaking hands. Once it had been the habit of a monk of Saint Jerome. He drew it on with fumbling haste. It felt heavy, constricting, damp from its rough washing in the fountain.

Thea knelt where he had left her. There was no anger in her. Not yet. Only shock, and a deep, tearing pain.

In a low dead voice she said, "You poor, innocent, pious priest."

He said nothing.

She rose slowly. "Go to the City. Sing in the angels' choir in Hagia Sophia, and wait on emperors, and be as pure as your saintly heart desires. The wild witch-woman won't trouble you anymore."

"Thea—" he began, but she paid him no heed.

"She'll leave you alone. Her family is dead; she can run off again and find another victim. One who knows what a man is for."

"Althea." This time she did not silence him. He went on steadily, "You expected to find your kin alive and well and not much older than they were when you left them. You've found only an empty house and a market tale; and it's struck you at last what price we pay for what we are. Beauty and strength and great power; life without age or sickness or death. And with it the reckoning: to love what must die."

"Or what must not," she said through clenched teeth, "and what will not give love in return."

"You're bitter. The house you loved is empty. The humans you loved are dead."

"The man I loved is a preaching priest." Her eyes blazed upon him, green as a cat's. "If God is just, Brother Alfred of Saint Ruan's, He will damn every one of you who ever cursed the love He made for man and woman. That is the sin, little monk. That is the horror which feeds the fires of Hell."

"Is it love, Thea? Or is it grief and anger turned to desire?"

"If that were all it was, would I be flinging myself at you, knowing

what you are?" She stopped and shook her head. "But no; you're
used to that. Everyone stares, gasps, and falls at your feet. And you
step over them in pious disdain and walk on undefiled. Saint Alfred
of Ynys Witrin, saved from burning by an angel, rapt up to Heaven
before the eyes of his King. Who was just as besotted with you as I
am, and just as incapable of understanding why."

"You aren't—"

"Don't tell lies, little Brother. Just look at me. Once on a time I
was the Lady Althea of the Court of Rhiyana, renowned for her
beauty, her valor, and her pride, and proud not least of her strength
of will. Nothing frightened me; I could laugh at Death himself if he
came too close to me. As for priests with their lice-ridden robes and
their shaven crowns, what were they? Mumbling fools, as lecherous
as any under the cant and the chanting. Then I saw you. There you
lay by the fire under the trees, with your vows upon you like chains
of silk and steel. But under them, fire and magic, asleep but easy
enough, thought I, to wake. *You* were never meant for a monk, you
who could promise so much with a glance or a smile or a turn of your
shoulder." She hunched her own, then flung them back. "The rest
pretended to be chaste. There was no pretense in you. I learned it
soon enough, but by then it was too late for me. I was bound. When
I tried to escape, I couldn't. When you fled your vows and your
strangeness, I followed. All the long way to Jerusalem, through all the
places between. Leagues. Years. Now as a woman, now as a hound,
now as a falcon—and never as your lover."

Mutely he reached for her with healing in his hands. She eluded
him to stand with her back to the wall, the center of her pride of lions.
"Oh, no, Alf. No witcheries. Only stand and tell me the truth. Do you
love me?"

"As a sister," he answered again.

Her eyes were all green, her white teeth bared, her face more cat
than woman. "Sister!" she spat. "I am no man's sister. I am no man's
kin. They are all dead. *Dead!*"

Again he tried to touch her, to heal her. Claws raked his hand.
He snatched it back. A cat crouched by the wall, ears flat to its head,
tail lashing its sides. Its mind was a fierce cat-hiss. *I have no kin. I have
no friend. I walk alone.*

"Thea." He was almost weeping. "Thea, beloved—"

Her tail stilled save for its restless tip. *Beloved?* She flexed her
claws. *Your soul is a cold cloister full of chanting and incense. Love to you is but*

a word, a spell to keep the mad witch quiet. And mad I was to follow you so far for so little. That is ended. I encumber you no longer. I encumber no one. I love no one. I want no one.

"Althea—"

She arched her back and spat and sprang up to the window ledge. The cat-shape blurred and melted; a falcon spread its wings, glaring at him with a mad golden eye. Even as he cried out, it took wing into the night.

2

The Lady Sophia Chrysolora yawned and wished that there were a better way for a lady to travel. This jolting carriage was worse than a ship in a storm, and hotter than a smithy in summer. Her maid dabbed at her brow with a scented cloth; she pushed it away irritably. Her mounted guards looked hot and discontented, but at least they had the wind on their faces.

She settled a little less uncomfortably on the cushions. So close to noon the road was less crowded than it had been earlier although thronged still, little disturbed it seemed by the invaders in the city across the Bosporus.

Once again she brought out her husband's letter, although she knew it by heart. The City was quiet, the children well; she was not to worry, she could remain in Nicaea until her mother was recovered, surely the Latins would be gone by then. Irene had written a poem in the pastoral mode, which was enclosed; Anna had had a touch of fever but was well again and teaching her pony to jump in the garden; and Nikki had outgrown another set of clothes. Sophia smiled at that last with a touch of sadness and let her veil fall a moment to fan her streaming face.

The walls and towers of Chalcedon had begun to rise before her. The countryside, never rich, now seemed more barren than ever, all dun and dust with no gentling touch of green. The Franks' mark, she thought darkly, straining to look ahead. The land's rising hid the sea and the City on the other side. The changes would be greater the closer she came to it, and in the City itself the greatest change of all.

Latin barbarians would be swarming everywhere, with two new emperors on the throne and a wide swath of the City leveled by fire. Their own house was safe, Bardas had written, although others nearby had been all but destroyed.

She wished she had wings to fly to see, or at least that she could ride like one of the imperial messengers, racing swiftly into Constantinople. But she was a lady, and a lady sat in hard-won patience with her veil modestly concealing her face and her hands folded in her lap.

The mules slowed from a trot to a walk and then to a halt. A laden wagon had stopped short some distance ahead; the oxen would not advance for all the driver's whipping and cursing. Opposite them milled a mounted company, the riders struggling with their horses. There seemed to be a space between, filled with something terrible.

Without thinking Sophia gathered up her skirts and stepped down from the carriage. Her maid's protests passed unheard. She walked calmly past the startled faces of her guards, one or two of whom had the presence of mind to dismount and follow her, and threaded her way through a herd of sheep, milling and bleating, and a cluster of pilgrims doing much the same, and a group of mounted Turks who stared and murmured as she walked by. The curses were clear now, and inventive.

The wagon reeked of onions. She skirted it and paused. In the road lay the cause of it all: a huddled shape, no more than a bundle of rags. As she stared it stirred, resolving into a huddled form, a long narrow body in a pilgrim's mantle rent and torn and covered with dust. Ignoring the sudden silence as farmer and riders stopped to gape at her, she knelt beside the fallen man. Carefully she turned him onto his back.

She caught her breath. His face was horribly burned and blistered as if he had stood in a fire. Yet his brows and lashes remained intact, very white against the livid skin.

His lips moved. They were cracked and bleeding, his voice no more than a whisper, breathing words she could not understand. "Hush," she commanded him as if he had been one of her children. Her eyes flashed to the men on horseback. "You, sirs. Your water flasks, if you please."

She received them, and promptly. She poured a little into the pilgrim and soaked her veil to bathe the terrible face. In doing it she had to loosen his mantle; the skin under it was the whitest she had ever seen, and smooth, no old man's. Nor was there any age in the hands which tried to fend off her own: long hands, burned not as badly as his face but beginning to blister. One bore deep parallel scratches like the marks of claws.

He could not lie in the road in that merciless sun. She beckoned to the guards who had followed her; they raised him in spite of his feeble struggles. As she led them to the carriage, horses and oxen started forward docilely; the traffic of the empire began to flow again.

The keeper of the best inn in Chalcedon received the travelers with becoming courtesy and sent at once for a doctor. Servants, meanwhile, ministered to milady and her escort and most especially to her guest who had been taken ill upon the road; undressed him and bathed him in cool water from the well, and laid him in bed covered with a sheet. His face seemed all the more terrible against his white smooth body, that in his robe had looked light and slender, even frail. But under it he had proved panther-lean, smooth-muscled, surprisingly broad in the shoulder.

And very young. Little more than a boy, Sophia thought as she sat beside him waiting for the doctor. His hair, water-darkened, was not white as she had thought, but palest gold.

Yet he was no child. His hat lay in her lap, brushed clean; its band was a braid of palm fronds, mark of the greatest of all pilgrimages, the journey to Jerusalem. And she had seen a terrible thing when the servants lifted him. His back was a sight more tormented even than his face, a mass of ridged and twisted scars, white with age.

She laid his hat aside and took up his wallet. It was very worn, patched here and there, like all he owned. It held very little. No money, no food. A water flask, empty. A book as worn as the wallet but beautiful within, illuminated with gold and silver and myriad colors, written in Latin letters. A small wooden crucifix, exquisitely carved, the suffering Christ so real that he seemed almost to breathe. A heavy ring of silver and moonstone wrought in intricate fashion. And a folded parchment with seals which, with a belated stab of conscience, she did not pause to examine. That was all.

She folded each treasure away again. Penniless Latin pilgrims were common enough, and sun-sickness their eternal companion. But she had never seen one so young or so pale or so badly burned.

The doctor arrived as she sat wondering: a stately Arab, very grave and very learned, escorted by a boy with a box of medicines. He frowned when Sophia revealed her knowledge of the patient's condition, frowned more deeply when it became apparent that she knew neither his name nor his nation, and scowled blackly at the suffici himself, who had begun to stir and murmur. Grimly he bent to his examination.

At length he straightened. His eyes were cold.

"Can anything be done?" Sophia asked of him.

"You may summon a priest."

Her breath caught. "He's dying?"

The man's thin lips tightened. "He will not die."

"Then why—"

"To be rid of him." He bowed stiffly, conveying with eloquence his opinion of a woman who traveled about without husband or kinsman to ward her, and who took up from the roadside such a creature as this. "By your leave, madam . . ."

"You do not have it!" She startled herself with her own sharpness. "This boy is ill. Can you treat him or can you not?"

She had angered him, but she had also touched his pride. "I can heal him. But I am bound only to the care of men. This—" he made a sign over the pilgrim, as if to avert some evil "—can better be dealt with by a man of God."

"I shall see to that. You," she said coldly, "may do your office."

For a moment she thought that he would leave. But he bowed even more stiffly than before, and did as she bade.

When he had gone, Sophia left her chair to stand over the pilgrim. His face was salved and lightly bandaged; his breathing seemed to have eased. He did not look evil.

She slipped the carven crucifix from his wallet and crossed herself with it. Half in apprehension, half in defiance, she laid it on his breast. After an interminable moment he stirred. His groping hand found the cross, closed over it. He sighed a little and lay still.

Sophia remained with him. They brought her supper there; she ate only enough to quiet hunger and set the rest aside.

Perhaps she dozed. She was stiff and her head ached, and something had changed. She glanced about, puzzled. It was dark, the lamps lit, but that was not the strangeness.

From amid the bandages his eyes watched her. Great calm eyes the color of silver-gilt.

She smiled. "Good evening," she said. "How do you feel?"

"Foolish." His Greek was accented but excellent. "You're most kind to me, my lady."

"Sophia Chrysolora."

"Alfred of Saint Ruan's in Anglia."

"You've come a long way, Alfred of—Saint Ruan's?"

"Alf." His eyes took in the room. "And this?"

"The Inn of Saint Christopher in Chalcedon."

"Ah." It was a sigh. "Then I'm deeply in your debt."

"It's nothing," she said. "I shouldn't be tiring you with talking."

He shook his head slightly. "I want to talk. I don't remember much. How did I come here?"

"I found you in the road." There was water in a jar by the bed; she supported his head and helped him to drink. "Are you hungry?"

"No. Thank you." He lay back. His hands explored the bandages, fumbling with them. Before she could stop him, he had them off.

It was not a pleasant sight. He must have seen it in her face, for his hand half lifted as if to cover it. But he did not complete the gesture. "The air will heal it," he said, "if you can bear to look."

"I can bear it. It's only . . . the doctor . . ."

"He knows his trade, I'm sure, and he concocts an excellent salve. But his wrappings will strangle me and do my skin no good at all."

She looked at him: the young man's body, the flayed mask, the bright eyes which seemed to know so much. Under the swollen and blistered skin, she thought his features might be very fine. "You know a little of healing?" she asked.

"A little," he admitted. "I worked in Saint Luke's hospital in Jerusalem."

"Then you know a good deal more than a little."

He shrugged, one-sided. "It didn't keep me from making a fool of myself." He inspected his hands, raw and red as they were, and on one palm the deep scratches. His eyes flinched; he closed them. Yet his words were quiet. "You must be very tired with caring for such a great idiot as I am, and you an utter stranger. Please don't let me keep you from your rest."

"I don't mind," she said. "I have a daughter who's not so very much younger than you. She'll be fourteen next month."

There was no way to read his face. "I'm . . . somewhat . . . older than that. Is she living in the City?"

"With the rest of my family. My husband would find you interesting; he's His Imperial Majesty's Overseer of the Hospitals."

"Is he a doctor?"

She smiled. "Bardas? No, only a bureaucrat. He sees to it that the doctors have places to work and people to work on and the wherewithal for both."

Was that an answering smile? "A most essential personage."

It did not seem weary, but she rose briskly, smoothing her skirts. "I've been keeping you awake. Would you sleep better if I left?"

"If I knew that you yourself would sleep."

This, she reflected as she left him, was a very pleasant young man. Clever certainly, and old for his years. But no demon's get. The doctor was a superstitious fool.

When she looked in later, he lay deep in sleep, his cross on the pillow next to his cheek. She withdrew softly and went to her own bed.

Sophia was up with the sun, but she found Alf awake before her. Up, in fact, and dressed in his rags that the servants had cleaned and mended as much as they might, and eating with good appetite. In the morning light his face seemed much better, the swelling subsided, the blisters broken or fading. His smile was recognizable as such, as he rose and bowed and offered her his cup. "Will you eat with me? There's enough for two."

For a moment she could do no more than stare. At last she managed a smile and sat where she had sat in the night. "You seem to have mended very quickly," she said.

He paused in filling a plate for her. "Sometimes a hurt can look worse than it is. And you cared for me well and promptly. So you see, I've learned a much-needed lesson and am only a little the worse for it."

"A lesson?"

"About walking unprotected in the sun. About Greek charity. And," he added, setting the plate before her and lowering his eyes, "about my own vanity. If my face were my fortune, I'd have lost it yesterday."

"You'll get it back," she assured him.

His smile turned wry, but he only said, "Please eat. I've had all I need."

She discovered that she was hungry. Between bites she said, "I've arranged for you to stay here until you've recovered. The innkeeper has orders not to let you go without a doctor's approval, and to tend you like a prince."

He seemed taken aback. "Lady . . . you're most generous. But I can't accept so great a gift."

She waved that away. "Call it my debt to God and man."

"You've paid that in full already." He stood close to her, so that she had to tilt her head back to see his face. As if he sensed her discomfort, he dropped to one knee, setting his head lower than hers. "My lady, I'm most grateful for what you've done. I'll pray for you if you'll accept the prayers of a Latin heretic. But I can't take your gift."

She looked hard at him. He moved with striking grace, but he was not quite steady; his breath came a shade too rapidly. And there was his face. "You're not as well as you pretend."

"I'm well enough to travel."

"I don't think so." She regarded him sternly. "You were dangerously ill when I found you. You're shaking now though you think you can hide it. Go back to bed."

He sat on his heels. "I'm sorry, my lady. I can't."

If he had been one of her offspring, she would have fetched him a sharp slap to teach him sense. "You are a stubborn boy. Must I call my men to put you to bed by force?"

"It wouldn't be very wise," he said.

"Arrogant too."

His head bowed. "I'm sorry. But I have to go to the City."

"Why? Are you one of the Crusaders?"

"God forbid!" His vehemence startled her; he went on more quietly, "I'm as filthy a Latin as any. But not . . . of that kind. No; I want to see the City and learn from its wise men and worship in its holy places. While there is time. There's so little left. So very little."

She shivered though the morning was already hot. His eyes were wide and luminous, the color of water poured out in the sun, his voice soft and rather sad. "Understand," he said. "Those are not monsters camped across the Horn, but men like any others. Most of them think they've only paused on their way to free the Holy Sepulcher. They can't see what must happen now they've come so far into such hostile country, led on by a foolish prince's promises. Both greed and honor will have their due. And then—" He stopped. Perhaps, at last, he had seen her fear.

"And then?" she asked through a dry throat.

He turned away, fists clenched at his sides. "Nothing. Nothing. I've been listening to too many doomsayers."

Her voice came hard and harsh. "You *are* mad. And you're coming with me. We'll be sailing well before noon; we'll be sheltered from the sun; and you can rest a little. And when we come to the City—have you a place to stay?"

"I'll find one."

"The lilies of the field . . ." she murmured. "You need a keeper, do you know that? You'll stay with us."

He faced her. "What will people say?"

"That I'm as much a fool as ever."

"And your husband?"

"Precisely the same."

"But I can't—"

"Do you object to the hospitality of the perfidious Greeks?"

She was half jesting. But only half. He spread his hands. "I could be a thief, or—or a murderer. I could slay you all in your beds and make off with everything you own."

"I'll take my chances."

"Oh, Lady!" He seemed caught between laughter and tears. "The doctor was right, you know. You'd do well to be rid of me."

"Are you a demon?"

He shook his head. "But—"

"So," Sophia said brusquely. "I've things to see to. I'll send for you when it's time to leave."

3

The sun danced and blazed upon the blue waters of the Bosporus; a brisk wind filled the sail, lightening the oarsmen's work, carrying the barge toward the Golden Horn. Under a striped canopy on the deck the passengers sat at their ease, even the guards relaxed in their vigilance.

Alf had been docile enough when they left Chalcedon, lying quietly on the pallet Sophia had ordered spread for him in the deepest shade. But as they drew nearer to the City he grew restless, until at last he rose and settled his hat firmly upon his head and stood like a hound at gaze, his face toward the wonder across the water. Slowly, as if drawn by the hand, he moved to the rail. He stood full in the sun, though with his back to it.

Sophia sighed and came to his side. "Don't you think—" she began.

He seemed not to have heard. "Look," he said, his voice soft with wonder. *"Look!"*

All the splendor of Byzantium spread before them: the long stretch of the sea walls set with towers, guarding the Queen of Cities; and within their compass rank on rank of roofs and domes and pinnacles. Gold glittered upon them, crosses bristled atop them, greenery cooled the spaces between, rising up and up to the summit of the promontory that was Constantinople. There on its prow shone the dome of Hagia Sophia with its lesser domes about it like planets about the moon, rising above the gardens of the Acropolis, crowning the Sacred Palace with all its satellites.

"The walls of Paris on the banks of the Seine," Alf murmured. "The citadel of Saint Mark on the breast of the sea; Rome herself in her crumbling splendor; Alexander's city at the mouth of the Nile; Cairo of the Saracens; Jerusalem, Damascus, Ephesus; Antioch and holy Nicaea: I've seen them all. But never—never in all my wanderings—never such a wonder as this."

Yet it was a wonder touched with death. The ship had turned now, sailing past the Mangana, striking for the narrow mouth of the Horn. A city spread over its farther shore, once rich, now much battered, guarded by a charred and broken tower.

"Galata," the ship's captain said, coming up beside them. "All that shore is infested with Franks, though they've camped farther up in the fields beyond the wall. Most of the ships you see there are theirs."

Sophia's hands clenched on the rail.

The captain spat. "They broke the chain. Clear across the Horn it went, from Galata to Acropolis Point, thick as a man's arm and strong enough to hold back a fleet. But they broke it. Hacked at the end on Galata shore and sent their biggest war galley against the middle with wind and oar to drive her, and snapped it like a rotten string."

"Couldn't our own fleet do anything?" demanded Sophia.

The man laughed, a harsh bark. "Our Emperor that was, bless his sacred head, called up the fleet, sure enough. Only trouble was, there wasn't any. A couple of barnacle-ridden scows was all he had. The rest of it was in the Lord Admiral's pocket. The cursed Franks sailed right over them."

"And then?" she asked. "What then?"

"Well," said the captain, "then everybody decided to do some fighting. The Frankish horseboys headed northward to the bridge past Blachernae. Saint Mark's lads took the sea side. Between them they flattened a good part of the palace up there before the real fight began. The Franks got a drubbing, but the traders got the Petrion and set it afire. Burned down everything from Blachernae hill to Euergetes' cloister, and as deep in as the Deuteron on the other side of the Middle Way."

"What of our people? Where were they?"

He shrugged. "They fought. Drove off the Franks, thanks mainly to the Varangians. But the Emperor turned tail and bolted. The mob dragged old Isaac Angelos out of his hole and put the crown back on his head, and the Franks brought in the young pup Alexios and crowned *him,* and now there's two Emperors, father and son, as pretty as you please, with the Franks pulling the boy's puppet-strings and the old man roaming about looking for his poor lost eyes."

"If I had been Emperor," Sophia said fiercely, "this would never have happened. The shame of it! All the power of the empire laid low by a mere handful."

The captain shrugged again. "It's fate, some people say. Fate and sheer gall. The traders' leader, what do they call him, the Doge; he's ninety-five if he's a day, blind as a bat, and there he was in the lead ship, giving his men what for when they wouldn't let him off first. They say he fights better, blind as he is, than most young sprouts with two good eyes."

"He ought to." It was one of the passengers, a wine merchant from Chios. "I've heard that he masterminded the whole affair for revenge, because his city had been slighted when the Emperor was handing out favors."

"If that were all it was," the captain said, "he'd have stayed home and pulled strings. The way I've heard it, he was in the City twenty years ago when the mob burned down the Latin Quarter, and he was blinded then by the Emperor's orders. Now he's making us pay for it in every way he knows how."

"With Frankish help at least, that's certain. They're barbarian fools, but when they're up on those monstrous horses of theirs in all their armor, they're impossible to face. A troop of them, I heard once, could break down the walls of Babylon if they were minded to try."

"If the Emperor hadn't been a coward, they'd never have got into the City. They were in terror of Greek fire and of the Varangians' axes."

"But not in such terror that they turned and fled." Sophia glared at a galley moored among a hundred lesser vessels near the sands of

Galata, its sides hung with bright shields, its lion banner snapping in
the breeze; and turned to glare even more terribly at the walls which
loomed out of the sea. "The City could have held forever if there had
been men to hold her."

The men shifted uneasily. After a little the captain said, "You
should have been a man, Lady."

"Such a man as sold my city to the Latins?" She tossed her head.
"I'm better off as a woman. At least my sex can claim some excuse
for cowardice." She stalked to her seat under the canopy, to cool
slowly and to begin to regret her show of temper.

Alf remained by the rail, unconscious of aught but the sight
before him. The wind had borne the barge into the teeming heart of
the empire. Warehouses clustered all along the shore, thrusting
wharves into the Golden Horn; steep slopes rose beyond to the white
ridge of the Middle Way, clothed in roofs as a mountain is clothed in
trees. Even from so far he could hear and smell the City: a ceaseless
roar like the roar of the northern sea; a manifold reek of men and
beasts, flowers, spices, salt brine and offal, with an undertone of
smoke and blood. At the far end of the strait he could see the battered
walls and beyond them great gaps in the roofs and towers, or charred
remnants thrusting blackly toward the sky.

He hardly noticed when Sophia spoke to him until she tugged
sharply at his sleeve. "Come. Up. Into my litter."

With an effort he brought himself into focus. A litter stood on the
pier, its bearers waiting patiently. None of the many officials standing
about, inspecting cargo, peering at lists, interrogating passengers,
seemed at all interested in him, although one bowed to his companion. "Come," she repeated. "It's all been seen to. Get in."

He looked down at the woman. She was small even for an
easterner; her head came barely to his shoulder. "I'll walk," he said.

"You'll do no such thing. Get in."

"But—"

"Get in!"

She was small, but she had a giant's strength of will. He smiled
his wry smile, bowed and obeyed. She settled opposite him. With a
smooth concerted motion the bearers raised the litter to their shoulders and paced forward. The escort fell into place about it with
Sophia's maid trudging sullenly behind.

The house of Bardas Akestas stood at the higher end of a narrow
twisting street in the shadow of the Church of the Holy Apostles, a
bleak forbidding wall broken only by a grating or two and a gate of

gilded iron. Even as the bearers paused before it, the gate burst open, releasing a flood of people.

There were, Alf realized afterward, less than half a dozen in all: three children of various sizes and sexes, an elderly porter, and a mountainous woman with a voice as deep as a man's. They overwhelmed the arrivals with shouts and cries, sweeping them into a sunlit courtyard. The light was dazzling after the high-walled dimness of the street, the children's joy dizzyingly loud. Alf made himself invisible in his corner of the litter and waited for his head to stop reeling.

"Come now," a new voice said over the uproar, deep and quiet. "What is all this?"

At once there was silence. The speaker came forward, a short broad man in a gray gown. The servants stepped back; the children leaped to attention. Sophia stepped from the litter, smoothed her skirts, and said, "Good day, Bardas."

"Sophia." He was as unruffled as she. "How was your journey?"

"Bearable," she replied.

The smaller of the two girl-children wriggled with impatience. "Father," she burst out at last. "Mother's home. *Mother's home!*"

Sophia swayed under a new assault. Over the children's heads she smiled at her husband; he nodded back briskly, but there was a smile in his eyes.

The elder girl had greeted her mother with a warm embrace, but dignity forbade her to join in the others' exuberance. While Nikki clung tightly to his mother's skirts and Anna babbled whole months' worth of happenings in one breathless rush, she stood aloof, trying to imitate her father's lofty calm. Her eyes were taking it all in, litter, bearers, and escort; the servants coming from everywhere to greet their mistress; plump Katya the maid deep in colloquy with the towering nurse; and if that was not she sitting in the litter, then—

"Mother," she said suddenly, "who is this?"

Sophia nodded in response to Anna's flood of news, lifted Nikki in her arms, and turned toward the litter. Its occupant emerged slowly and somewhat unsteadily: a tall thin figure in pilgrim's dress, with a terribly ravaged face and clear pale eyes gazing out of it. Irene forgot her dignity and loosed a little shriek; Nikki hid his face in his mother's shoulder.

"My guest," said Sophia. "Alfred of Saint Ruan's in Anglia, who has come up from Jerusalem to see our City."

They all stared, save Bardas who bowed and said, "Be welcome to House Akestas."

Alf returned the bow with grace and precision; straightened and swayed. Several of the servants sprang to his aid. Gently but firmly they bore him into the cool shade of the house.

4

Anna opened the door as quietly as she could and peered around it. The room was dim and cool and smelled of the roses that grew up over the window from the garden outside. There was no one there except the stranger in the bed.

He seemed to be asleep. She edged into the room, her bare feet silent on the carpet that had come from Persia, and tiptoed to the bed. Her heart was hammering. But curiosity was stronger than fear, even fear of her father's reprimand.

She looked at the pilgrim's face. It glistened with the salve the servants had spread on it over a patchwork of purple and scarlet.

His eyes opened in the midst of it and stared at her. She almost turned and ran. But they were very quiet eyes, and very kind, and that was a smile on the blistered and bleeding lips. She winced to see it. "Does it hurt?" she asked.

"No more than it ought."

She liked his voice. It made her think of one of the bells in church, the deep clear one that rang on holy days. "Then it must hurt a great deal," she said, "because it looks horrible."

"It will heal." He sat up. He was wearing a linen tunic; it was too wide, a little in the shoulders, much more in the middle. "I'm glad you came to visit me. I'm not nearly as ill as everyone seems to think."

His eyes invited her; she perched on the edge of the bed. "I'm not supposed to be here. I just wanted to look at you without everybody pushing and shoving."

"Why?" he asked.

She shrugged and looked at her feet. "I don't know. I guess because I've never seen a Latin up close before."

"Do I disappoint you?"

"A little. You're so clean. And you speak Greek. And you're not wearing a mail-shirt. Don't you own one?"

He shook his head. "I'm only a poor pilgrim. Armor is for knights."

"You aren't a knight?"

"Oh, no. I was a monk before I was a pilgrim. Never a knight."

"Oh." She was disappointed. "You're hardly a barbarian at all."

He laughed. His laugh was even better than his voice, like a ripple of low notes on a harp. "But surely," he said, "I look like one."

"You won't when it heals. The statues on the Middle Way have noses just like yours. Are you handsome under the burns?"

He would not answer, except to shrug a little.

"Mother says you are. Irene wants you to be. Irene is thirteen and getting silly. She's always looking at this boy or that, and sighing, and quoting poetry."

"That seems silly to you?"

"Well, isn't it? She tells me to wait. Three more years and I'll know what she's feeling." She shuddered. "I hope not."

"Maybe you'll escape it. I did for a long time."

"Well. You're a man. Men are slower, Mother says." She looked at him, narrowing her eyes until he blurred. "Do you quote poetry at girls?"

"Not . . . quite." He sighed. "I haven't got that far yet. Maybe I never will. It was only one woman, you see. I lost her."

"Because you burned your face?"

"It's the other way about. She went away, and I stopped caring what happened to me."

"Irene should hear you. She'd write a poem." Anna brought her eyes back into focus. He had stood up and gone to the window. His tunic was too short as well as too wide. It showed a great deal of him; she observed it with interest. "Why did the woman go away?"

He spoke mostly to the roses and partly to her. "She'd just learned that all her kin were dead. I couldn't comfort her as . . . as she wanted. We quarreled. She left. I left soon after. That was all. Life is like that. Love is like that, I suppose."

"I wouldn't know," she said. "But I'm sorry she left."

"Thank you," he said, turning back. He had plucked a rose; he gave it to her. She buried her nose in it.

When she looked up, Nikki was standing just inside the door with his thumb in his mouth and his big eyes fixed on Alf.

Alf stood very still. Anna opened her mouth to say something,

and shut it again. Nikki hesitated. After a long while he left his place
by the door and inched toward Alf, sidling, stopping, never taking his
eyes from the other's face.

Very slowly Alf sank to one knee. Nikki stopped as if about to
bolt; Alf was still; he edged forward again. Alf hardly breathed. Once
more Nikki stopped. His hand crept out. It halted just short of Alf's
face. Drew back a little. Darted out, a quick, frightened touch. It must
have hurt; Alf's eyes winced. But he did not flinch away, even by a
hairsbreadth.

More boldly now, Nikki explored him with hands and eyes, nose
and tongue. He knelt patiently even when Nikki pulled his hair. He
did not try to say anything, except with his eyes.

Suddenly Nikki froze. His eyes were wide, his mouth open
slightly. Alf had not moved. Nikki made a small hoarse sound. All at
once he flung himself at Alf, clinging as he had clung to Sophia. Alf
held him and patted him and looked at Anna over the tousled dark
head.

She stared back. "He likes you. He doesn't like anybody except
Mother."

"And you," said Alf, "and Irene, and your father."

"Sometimes. He can't talk, you know, though he's almost five.
It's because he can't hear; God closed his ears before he was born.
We're all sinners, Uncle Demetrios says, and he's our punishment. I
almost hit Uncle Demetrios once for saying that. Father gave me a
tanning, but afterward I heard him say that I had more sense in one
eyelash than Uncle Demetrios had in his whole head."

"I think I would agree." Alf sat on the floor with Nikki in his lap.
"There's no sin in your brother. Only God's will, for His own reasons;
who are we to ask what they are?"

"That's what Mother says."

"Your mother is a very wise woman."

"She has to live up to her name, doesn't she?"

"And you try to live up to her."

"I don't do very well. She's a great lady; I, says my nurse, am a
perfect hellion. Someday I'd like to forget I'm a girl and travel about
and see all the things I've heard about in tales."

"Maybe you will."

"You have, haven't you? Did you walk all the way from Anglia?"

"Sometimes I rode. Sometimes I went by sea."

"Where? When? What was it like? Tell me!"

Her eagerness made him smile. He sat on the bed; she sat beside

him, and he began to talk. He was better than any storyteller in the
bazaar; she forgot time and duties and even old terrors in listening to
him.

The light in the window had shifted visibly westward when Alf
paused. Anna waited for him to go on, but his eyes were fixed on the
doorway.

She turned to look, and paled. A dreaded presence loomed there.
"Anna Chrysolora!" thundered her nurse. "What did your father tell
you about intruding on our guest?"

Alf rose with Nikki in his arms. "But, madam, she was not—"

"You, my boy, were told to rest; and look at you." Corinna drew
herself up to her full height. She was somewhat taller than he and
thrice as broad. She planted a fist on each massive hip and glowered
at them all. "Just look at you. What the master will say, I don't like
to think. Anna, Nikephoros, come here." They came, even Nikki,
dragging their feet. Alf stood alone and defenseless in his ill-fitting
tunic.

"To bed with you," Corinna commanded. Her tone would have
done justice to a sergeant-at-arms. He went meekly, to suffer the
indignity of her tucking him firmly in. "There now. You stay put until
you're given leave to get up. Do you understand?"

He nodded.

"Good." She swept up the children and bore them away, leaving
him alone, half stunned, and beginning to shake with uncontrollable
mirth.

5

The dome of Holy Wisdom hung weightless in the air, held to
earth by columns of light. Beneath the dome and among the pillars
swirled a sea of people, overlaid with a manifold mist of incense,
perfume, and humanity, eddying here and there as a priest or a
potentate swept by.

At this hour between services, most of those in Hagia Sophia
were pilgrims and sightseers. Hawkers of relics moved brazenly
among them, offering for sale splinters of the True Cross, threads

from the Virgin's robe, and bits of bone and hair from the bodies of innumerable saints. The few Latins in the throng were fair prey for these, wide-eyed barbarians that they were, and ignorant of Greek besides.

One walked alone, a clear target: a burly young man, cleaner and better kempt than most, gazing about with a child's pure wonder. Under the great dome where Christ the King sat on his throne, he stood with his head thrown back in rapture.

"Twigs from Saint Bacchus' vine, Saint Andrew's fingernails, a lock of the Magdalen's hair—cheap, holy Father, cheap at the price!"

The man was like a buzzing fly, barely noticed at first but maddening in his persistence. His victim tumbled headlong from heaven into the world's mire, and crouched there stunned.

"Relics, holy relics, more precious than gold. Filings from Saint Peter's chains—a chip from Simon Stylites' column—"

The lion in repose is a great, slow-seeming, indolent beast. But aroused, he is terrible. The young Latin woke all at once to a roar of Greek, both fluent and scathing.

When his tormentor had fled, taking his wares and his ragged *langue d'oeil,* the young man stood a moment shaking with fury. Slowly his tension eased. His face regained its amiable, slightly foolish expression; he sighed and shrugged. The house of light had turned to mere stone, and no force of will could change it back again.

That was the way of the world. And since heaven was denied him, he focused upon earth: the ebb and flow of people through the wide space, the flow of light and line about and above them. He began to walk slowly, aimlessly, as a sightseer will. His size won him easy passage; his race and his priestly tonsure won him hard looks and hostile gestures and once a muttered curse.

Beneath one of the four lesser domes, under a haloed angel, he paused again. These easterners were small people; he, tall even for a Norman, could see easily over their heads. But not far from him stood a Greek quite as tall as himself though considerably less broad. He could see no face, only a long body robed in silver-gray, and a gray hat beneath which he glimpsed long white-fair hair.

The Greek shifted slightly, tilting his head back as if to gaze at the ornamented ceiling. Even from behind he seemed rapt yet not solemn, glowing with awe and wonder and heartfelt delight.

The watcher drew a slow breath. That turn of the head—that lift of the shoulder—surely he was dreaming or wishing, as he had dreamed and wished for so long, and seen what he longed to see in every tall pale stranger. And yet—

"Alf?" he wondered aloud. "Brother Alfred?"

The other turned with swift, feline grace. A fair strange face, a flash of silver eyes, a sudden brilliant smile. "Jehan de Sevigny!" Even the voice was the same, and the touch, the hands much stronger than they looked, holding him fast.

He knew he was grinning like an idiot; paradoxically, his eyes had blurred with tears. "Brother Alf. I never thought—how did you—I thought you were in Jerusalem!"

"I was." Alf drew him away from the jostling crowd into the quiet of a side chapel. Jehan's eyes cleared; he looked hard, drinking him in, incredulous still. But—"God in heaven! what ever did you do to your face?"

Alf raised a hand to it. "I did battle with the sun," he replied, "and he won."

"I'll wager he did." Jehan scowled formidably at his old friend and teacher. "Have you been in agony ever since you left Anglia?"

"Only this once," Alf said.

"But—"

"I have my defenses, as you well know. A few days ago I forgot them. Foolish, and dangerous besides, but in the end it led to good fortune. I'm a guest now in the City, and I'm most well tended."

"You look it," Jehan admitted. "Except for your face."

"Another day or two and you'd never have noticed anything at all."

"Oh, I would have." Jehan took him in again and felt his grin return, wider than ever. "Brother Alf. Brother Alf. It's so good to see you!"

"And you." Alf measured him with an admiring eye. "You've grown."

"I'm as tall as you now."

"But wide enough for three of me. I see they knighted you."

"Last year. Bishop Aylmer did it before I left for the Crusade. He made me a priest, too. Might as well get it all done at once, he said."

Alf smiled, remembering the dark grim-faced bishop who had accepted an elf-priest with no reservations at all. "Is he well?"

"Well enough, though he's gone a bit gray. Grief, I think. We were with my lord Richard when he died." Jehan spoke quietly, but his eyes were dark with old sorrow. "Magnificent fool that he was, to take an arrow in the vitals fighting for a treasure that wasn't there. As soon as he realized that he wasn't going to get up from his bed, he told us to stay well out of brother John's way and sent us to Rome to bring Anglia's greetings to the new Pope. We've been serving Innocent ever since. A great man, that. Young too, for a Pope, and a bit more of a politician than a priest ought to be. Though I should talk, when I've been squire to Anglia's infamous Chancellor."

"Infamous only in the new King's eyes. Is it true that John has weeded out all of Richard's old friends?"

"Most of them. The last I heard, Father was in Rhiyana visiting Mother's family. Purely for courtesy, you understand. But it's been a long visit. Years long."

"Like yours in Rome."

Jehan nodded. "We were in Rhiyana ourselves for a while. The King sent you his love. Now how did he know I'd be seeing you?"

"Witchery, of course."

"Of course," Jehan said with a crooked smile. "His court is even more wonderful than legend makes it. All those Fair Folk . . . there's magic everywhere and a wonder at every turning, and Gwydion on his throne above it all, looking not a day over twenty-two. He told me he'd been cured of errantries, at least until he could think of a better one than peacemaking between Gwynedd and Anglia."

"And, I trust, until he was cured of the wounds he took on that venture."

"Well. His leg had knit by then and he'd lost his limp. His hand was taking longer. He could use it, but only just; it was stiff, and twisted a little. So, he'd say when people looked at it, at least he still had it, thanks to a witch-priest from Anglia; and he was learning to be a right-handed man. His brother would scowl whenever he said that, and thunder would rumble away somewhere. They're twins, you know, as like to look at as two peas. But Prince Aidan is as wild as his brother is quiet. Only Gwydion and that splendid Afreet princess Aidan brought out of Alamut can even begin to control him."

"Is he as wonderful a warrior as you thought he was?"

"Wonderful? More than wonderful! I followed him about like an overgrown pup; he condescended to teach me a little now and then. I've never seen a better swordsman. But do you know what he said? He was nothing; I should have seen his brother. Imagine; modesty, in the Flame-bearer."

Alf smiled.

Jehan smote his hands together. "What are we doing, talking about somebody you don't even know? Tell me about yourself!"

"Tell me first how you came to be here."

"They were preaching a Crusade; my head was full of grand ideas; I begged and I threatened, and Bishop Aylmer sent me to the Pope, and the Pope let me go with his legate." Jehan paused for breath. "Now, Brother Alf, stop evading and tell me. Why did you come here? How did you manage to get yourself up as a Greek gentleman? Where's Thea?"

"I came to see the City," Alf answered. "I'm dressed as a Greek because it was a Greek who took me in after my clash with the sun, and the servants burned my old clothes. They weren't even fit for rags, it seemed, although they covered me well enough."

He was keeping a tight rein on his vanity, Jehan could see. But he knew how very well he looked. "And Thea? Is she here?"

"No," Alf said, "she isn't here."

Something in his voice brought Jehan about sharply. "What's wrong? She hasn't—she's not dead, is she?"

Alf laughed more in pain than in mirth. "Thea? Dear God, no! She was with me until a few days ago. She was the best of companions, too, whatever shape she chose. A hound most often. In Jerusalem when I worked in the hospital, she used to sit at my feet and laugh in her mind when people petted her and admired her beauty. Sometimes she'd put on a gown and be herself and walk about the city. She marveled at it, though she pretended to be cool and worldly-wise, that she was there in the holiest place in the world."

The other gripped his arm. "What happened? Where is she now?"

"I don't know. We . . . disagreed. She went away. I've searched, but I can't find her. She doesn't want me to."

Jehan was young and a priest, but he was neither a child nor an innocent; and he had been as close to Alf as a brother. He read the quiet voice and the expressionless face, yet he offered no pity. "She'll come back."

"Will she?" Alf asked, but calmly. "In some things we were never well matched. I only wish . . . I would be more at ease if I knew where she was."

"Is that what you've been telling yourself when you want to cry?"

"I never cry."

"You should. It would do you good."

Alf shook his head slightly. "Come, explore the City with me. And after, if there's time, you can meet my hosts." His smile was no more than half forced. "I wasn't even to leave my room for a day or two yet. But I escaped this morning and left a message to assure my benefactors that I hadn't abandoned them. Maybe, if I come back with a friend—a very old and very dear friend who also happens to be very large—they'll be inclined to forgive me."

"Will they welcome a Latin?"

"They'll be mildly disappointed. Like me, you know what hot water is for, and you speak Greek. And you aren't wearing your armor."

"My squire's cleaning it, poor lad. Should I go back and get it?"

Alf laughed and shook his head, and led the other away.

Jehan was not, after all, a disappointment. Pound for pound and inch for inch, he was as close a match for Corinna as any man could be; when he promised to show Anna his armor, she clapped her hands with delight. But she was far from content. She watched him warily all the while he set himself to charm the household. Nikki, she noticed with satisfaction, eyed him in deep distrust. But everyone else seemed completely smitten.

"He's not at all handsome," Irene whispered to her, "but he has beautiful eyes. I love blue eyes. And his voice. I wonder if he can sing?"

Anna glared at her, but she was too far gone to notice. Could no one even see? He was sitting side by side with Alf. Every now and then he touched his friend lightly, familiarly; or Alf would lay an arm about his shoulders, holding him in a brief half-embrace. They were like brothers long parted, not quite believing yet that they had met again.

Her throat felt tight. This was a man from Alf's own country. He talked about Anglia, and about a king named Richard whom people called Lionheart and whom they both had loved; he talked about Rome and Saint Mark's citadel and the Latin princes camped across the Horn; and when he smiled, Alf would smile back, as proud as a cat with its lone kitten. Then, when Jehan had begun to think of leaving, he said it. "Alf, why don't you come with me? There's always a place among us for a good man."

"What would I do?" Alf asked, not in protest but as if he truly wanted to know. "I'm neither knight nor priest."

"You've been a clerk and a healer and a king's squire. Any of those, even the last, we've dire need of. And . . ." Jehan hesitated, suddenly shy. "I . . . I'd like it very much if you could be with me."

Anna held her breath. Irene, she noticed, had caught on at last; she was looking stricken. Mother looked merely interested, watching their faces as they talked.

Alf was tempted. She could see it. He wanted to see his own people again and to live with his friend.

"I'll come," he said. Jehan began to grin; Anna gathered to fling herself at one of them, she was not sure which. But Alf was not done. "I'll come," he repeated, "to visit you. For a little while. But not today. I'm in trouble enough as it is for being out when I should have been in bed."

Jehan's face fell. Anna hurtled into Alf's lap, though Nikki was there already, and hugged the breath out of him. He smiled. "You see why I have to stay."

Slowly Jehan nodded, battling a sudden, fierce, and irrational jealousy. "I see," he said a shade coldly. With an effort he returned Alf's smile. "I'm singing Mass in camp on the Sabbath. Will you come and hear me?"

"Gladly," Alf answered. Jehan had risen from his seat; he rose likewise, setting Anna on her feet. But Nikki's arms had locked about his neck. He was still so the last Jehan saw of him, standing in the gateway with the dark-eyed child in his arms and the rest of the household a blur behind.

6

"Now, mind you," Bardas said as the litter bore the two of them through the crowds of the Middle Way, "Master Dionysios is the best physician in the City, and he knows it. He'll give you this one day's trial; if you can satisfy him, he'll put you to work. It might be menial labor, boy, be warned of that. I'm only His Majesty's overseer, not Saint Luke himself, to tell Master Dionysios what to do with you once he has you."

Alf watched as a troop of Varangians swung past, fair-haired giants in scarlet and gold with great axes on their shoulders. One or two, younger than the rest, looked very much like Jehan. "I don't mind servants' work. I did it in Saint Ruan's and in Jerusalem."

"You'll do it for Dionysios. A rare thing, Dionysios: a doctor who can look after his own hospital. He works his people like slaves, from the brat who sweeps the kitchen all the way to the senior surgeon—and himself harder than any."

"I think I shall admire him."

"Or hate him," Bardas said.

Master Dionysios took Alf's measure with the air of an officer inspecting a raw recruit. "This," he snarled at Bardas, "is your prodigy of medical erudition?"

Bardas bore his wrath with unruffled calm. "This is Alfred."

Dionysios circled Alf slowly, lip curled. "You. Boy. What do you know?"

"Little," Alf answered, "but of that, enough."

The Master had come round to face Alf again. "So. You fancy yourself clever. Let me see your hands." He examined them, turning them in fastidious, surgeon's fingers. "Soft as a girl's. Have you been cut, boy?"

Alf's lips tightened. "No, sir," he replied levelly, "I have not."

"Pity. You'd please the women." Abruptly Dionysios turned his back on him. "Come with me.

"We tend anyone who can be treated," Dionysios said as they walked, "and some who can't, but who have nowhere else to die in peace. Poor, most of them. Filthy. Are you afraid of dirt, boy?"

Alf shook his head.

"Well then," the Master said, pausing in a doorway. In the room beyond, many ragged figures sat on benches against the wall or squatted on the floor. At the far end a man in healer's blue, aided by a student in brown, examined a particularly scabrous specimen. The air reeked of disease and of unwashed humanity.

Alf followed the other, picking his way among the waiting bodies. The eyes which watched him pass were bright and scornful or dull and hostile or, once, languidly wanton; hands plucked at his robe, feeling of its fine fabric, inching toward the purse at his belt.

The blue-clad physician did not pause as his Master approached, although the student looked up in apprehension. "Thomas," said Dionysios, "rest yourself. This young gentleman will finish for you."

It said much for Dionysios' discipline that the man stepped back at once, without protest, although he regarded Alf in open and cheerful curiosity. Alf took his place quietly, well aware of the eyes upon him. But he had stood so, been watched so, more often than he could remember; and the first time, when he was truly the boy he looked, Master Dionysios had been drowsing at his mother's breast. He drew a breath to steady himself, and bent to the task.

"Well?" Bardas asked as Alf settled in the litter.

Alf regarded him for a moment, hardly seeing him. "You weren't there?" His gaze cleared; he shook himself. "Of course. You had other things to do. Did I see you leave?"

"As I recall," said Bardas, "you were lancing a boil and arguing with Master Dionysios: Was it God's will for a healer to quiet pain with wine or poppy, rather than to let the patient bear it unaided?"

"We weren't arguing. We were considering possibilities." Alf lay back against the cushions. "I'm to come back tomorrow."

"So you satisfied him."

"Not really. My name, says he, will not do at all. Since the Greek of 'Alf' is 'Theo,' then Theo I shall be; half a Greek name is infinitely preferable to the whole of a Saxon one. Moreover, we disagree on several crucial points. Bleeding, for instance. It's useless, I think, and often dangerous. I'm an abomination, Master Dionysios has decided: a twofold heretic, religious and medical. But I know which end of a lancet is which, and I have light hands. He'll suffer me to keep you quiet."

Bardas folded his hands over his ample stomach and allowed himself a brief smile. "You'll do. I don't suppose he mentioned payment."

"Of course not. I'm to wear a blue gown. Do I have one?"

"You will. You'll also have a salary."

Alf's eyes widened in shock. "Money? For healing?"

"This is Constantinople, lad."

"But—"

Bardas' raised hand cut him off. "No, boy. No Western scruples. If Dionysios has taken you on, by law he has to pay you according to your rank. Master physician, I should think, since he wants you to wear blue. Students wear brown and pay him; assistants get servants' wages. In one stroke you've become a man of substance."

"I don't want to be—"

"Boy," said Bardas, "this isn't your monastery. You do your healing. I'll look after your money."

"You can keep it. I owe it to you for all you've done for me."

"I'll keep it. Until you need it."

Alf framed a further protest; paused; closed his mouth. They rode on in silence.

Anna and Nikki were at the gate with the air of people who had waited a very long while. Even before the litter had stopped, Nikki was in it, pummeling Alf with his fists, moaning in a strange strangled voice. His face was red and furious, wet with tears.

Alf let Nikki's anger run its course until he suffered Alf's touch and let himself be held, though struggling still, fierce in his wrath.

"He's been here all day," Anna was saying, "crying and yelling and hitting the gate. He hit Corinna when she tried to take him away. He hit me. He even hit Mother."

Nikki quieted slowly, enough to sit in Alf's lap, fists clenched on his knees. Alf took the small scarlet face in his hands, smoothing away the tears of rage. Very quietly he said, "I told you that I would come back. I will always come back. Always, Nikephoros."

Nikki's black eyes were angry still. He raised a fist as if to strike again.

Alf caught it and unfolded it. "I promise, Nikki."

For yet a while he clung to his outrage. But Alf smiled, and he plunged forward, burrowing into the limp and bloodstained robe.

There was a silence. Bardas cleared his throat. "Where's your mother, Anna?"

"In the garden," Anna replied, "with the lady who came a little while ago."

"A friend? Lady Phoebe? Aunt Theodora?"

"Oh, no. We've never met her before. She came to see Alf."

He froze in the act of rising; swayed under Nikki's weight; drew himself erect by force of will.

Anna babbled on. "Her name is Althea. She comes from Petreia. She's been to the West and to Jerusalem. Her tales are as good as Alf's. Better, because she puts him in them and doesn't try to make him look modest. Did you really save your Abbot's life, Alf? And kill a man with his own sword?"

All color had drained from his face. "Yes," he said in a harsher voice than they had ever heard from him, "I killed a man. In the chapel of my abbey. The Abbot died, but not before he'd sent me to Jerusalem."

"They call you a saint in Anglia, she said. Are you really—"

"Anna." Bardas spoke softly, but she stopped short. "Go and tell

the ladies that we'll be with them shortly. Alf will bathe and change
first."

Alf shook his head. "I'll go directly."

"Don't be a fool," Bardas said. "Put the boy down and let him
walk like a man, and go to your bath."

In the coolest corner of the garden where an almond tree shaded a
small stony waterfall, Bardas and the ladies had settled with sweets
and wine. Alf came to them scrubbed clean, wearing his best coat
over a tunic of fine linen no paler than his face.

Thea sat with her back to the tree trunk, demure in a plain gown,
her pilgrim's mantle laid aside in the heat; she had braided her hair
and coiled it about her head and covered it with a light veil. She
looked very young.

As he approached, she rose with her own inimitable grace, smiling as if there had been no quarrel between them at all. "Little
Brother! How well you look."

"And you." He took her hands like one in a dream. "I'm . . . very
glad to see you."

"No more so than I. You've been ill, my lady tells me; and Jehan
in the camp."

"You've seen him?"

"He told me where to find you. I'd meant to stay in Petreia, but
there was nothing there for me after all except a ghost or two. So I
came to the City. I met Jehan as he was coming back from here." *And
spent the night with him,* she added in her mind. *Everyone was fiercely jealous.
Such a lovely white hound, I was.*

Alf smiled without thinking, and remembered at last to let go her
hands. Both Bardas and Sophia were drawing alarming conclusions.
The blood rose to scald his cheeks; he sat down too quickly in the
chair she had left, refusing to meet her bright relentless stare. She
stood between him and the sun and said, "It's a fine haven you've
come to, little Brother. I'm delighted to see you so well looked after."

"It's generally agreed that I need a keeper." The fire had fled as
quickly as it came. He had her hand again, God help him, and her
mockery upon him like a lash of cold rain. "Have you unveiled all my
black past yet? Murder, sorcery, heresy, and plain lust—have I forgotten anything?"

"As a matter of fact you have. The worst of all: burying your
brilliance in a monastery for longer than I care to think, and hiding
it with humility forever after."

"A failing you certainly are free of."

She laughed. "Certainly! I know what you're worth. As does the heir of House Akestas. How is he now?"

Her concern was genuine, and it eased his tension. "He's asleep in my bed."

A good place to be. Mercifully she did not say it aloud. She sat at his feet; he looked down at the smooth bronze braids, knotted his hands in his lap and forced himself to be calm. This was her revenge, this utter ease with its implications that even Anna could read. But he would not make it any sweeter than he could help. He accepted the wine a servant offered, and sipped it, hardly tasting its spiced sweetness, listening to the flow of conversation and saying very little. It tormented him to have her here so close after what they both had said and done and thought. Yet when she glanced up at him, he found himself smiling like the veriest, most besotted of fools.

Far too soon she rose again, saying words that meant nothing but that she must go. "No, no," Sophia said, "there's no need. We have ample room, and a friend of Alfred's is more than welcome."

"Even when you know—" He had said that; he bit back the rest. They knew nothing that mattered. Yet they knew everything, down below reason where the great choices were made.

"Hospitality is sacred here," said Bardas. "You know that, Lady; you're one of us. Honor us by honoring it. Stay with us."

It would be best if they both went far away, from the Akestas and from each other. But when Thea nodded and bowed and acquiesced, his heart turned traitor and began to sing.

7

From the Latin shore Constantinople seemed vast beyond imagining, vast and marred.

"That's a good stretch of palace wall we've taken down," said Thibaut de Langliers, peering under his hand, "and a company of our men inside to keep an eye on the Emperors."

Jehan leaned back against the tent pole and sighed, replete with good solid fare after a Mass well sung. "I don't envy anyone who has to live in that wasps' nest."

Another of the young knights regarded him with surprise. "Why, they've been made very welcome. Fed well, too. Better than we, and we're faring like princes."

"Now we are. Wait till the crisis comes. Do you think we'll get what we've been promised? Supplies for the voyage to Jerusalem, and two hundred thousand marks in gold; ten thousand Greek troops for a year and five hundred more committed to the Holy Land for life, and the union of our churches besides. Will we get all that? Will the Devil turn Christian?"

"Provisions you will have," Alf said, "for a while. The rest is a fool's dream."

Even Jehan turned to stare at him. He had been all but voiceless throughout the Mass and the meal after, sitting in the shadow of the tent with Thea in hound-shape seeming to drowse at his feet. He met the stares with wide clear eyes, and toyed absently with Thea's ears. "A young pretender promised you the world to win back his empire. Now he has what he aimed for, and it's considerably less than he thought it was. He can feed you for a time, pay to keep your fleet, but no more. If I had taken the cross, and were wise enough, I'd take what he could give and leave before another week had passed."

"And what of honor?" demanded the youngest knight.

"Honor is not the same as wisdom."

The boy leaped to his feet. "Are you calling me a fool?"

Thea raised her head from her paws; Jehan braced himself for a battle. But Alf sat back unruffled. "Did I say anything of the sort? Come, Messire Aimery. Won't you concede that the wise course is not always the honorable one?"

"That's true enough," said Jehan a shade quickly. "Look at the Greeks. Any knight worth his spurs would settle his troubles the honorable way, in the lists; but a Greek will think and ponder and negotiate and intrigue, and get what he's after without a fight."

"Greeks and priests." Aimery had subsided into his seat again. "You excepted, of course."

"There are those who say I shouldn't exist: a priest who carries a sword. And uses it too."

"And what of Saint Michael?" Alf asked.

"Well. He's an archangel."

"He does provide a precedent."

"That's our usual argument. But when God and knight's honor demand different things, it presents a dilemma."

Alf nodded slowly. "What does one do when God seems to be on both sides of the battle? When Christian attacks Christian and each wears the cross of the Crusade—what then?"

"One loses all one's illusions," Jehan answered him grimly. "We took Zara; have you heard that?"

"I've heard."

"They were Christians; they'd taken the cross. But they'd rebelled against Saint Mark, and it was part of our price of passage that we defend the Republic's interests. The Pope was livid. And yet he didn't make more than a token protest. I was appalled. How could all that was high and holy be so besmirched? Christians slaughtered Christians; Crusaders killed Crusaders—for what? Money and provisions to take the Holy Sepulcher. Would Christ want it to be saved by such horrors as we are?"

"Perhaps it's not to be saved by anyone." Alf examined his laced fingers, seeing a pattern there, clear for his reading. "I've had strange thoughts of late. What arrogant creatures men are, to presume that they know God's will. And priests are more arrogant than any, for they not only purport to know but presume to execute the commands of divine Providence. Yet, is it Providence or their own desires? If God places the Holy Land in the Saracens' hands, perhaps after all He wants it to be so?"

"That's heresy," Aimery muttered.

"It is; and I was a priest once. I'm no fit company for God's knights."

"Is that why you're not a priest now?"

Jehan drew a sharp breath. Alf smiled and shook his head. "No. I was raised in an abbey and took vows there. But I found that I couldn't be the sort of priest I wanted to be. I asked that my vows be dissolved. It was easy enough in the end. There's a law, you see, that a man raised by monks must not take full vows before his twenty-fifth year. I was much younger than that. So, a stroke of the papal pen, and suddenly I was a layman. My mind marked the occasion by conceiving half a dozen heresies."

"That's not so," Jehan said hotly, "and you know it. Here, finish off the wine and stop trying to frighten these poor boys."

"Oh, no," said a new voice, "I find him fascinating."

They started to their feet. The newcomer stood with hands on hips: a pleasant-faced young man in clothes as rich as a prince's. Although they were of Greek cut and fabric, from round-cut head to spurred heel he was indisputably a Latin. He regarded Alf with a steady brown stare, head cocked slightly to one side, lips quirked. "In drove a Greek, in accent a Latin; in name, if I'm not mistaken, a Saxon. You're an interesting man, Master Alfred."

The young knights had gone pale. Even Jehan seemed nonplussed. But Alf returned the other's gaze with perfect calm. "It seems I'm known among the high ones, my lord."

"How not, when your priestly friend has described you so lovingly, and told us that you were to be honoring our camp with your presence? You have a clear eye for all our weaknesses."

"And for your strength."

"What may that be?"

"Courage," Alf answered, "to face so great a city with so few."

"Perhaps, after all, God is on our side."

"He may be. Who am I to say?"

The young lord smiled. "Who indeed? Who is anyone, when it comes to that? Come with me, wise master. There's a man I'd have you meet."

Alf bowed his head. As he followed the brown-eyed lord, Jehan fell in behind, a solid presence, and with him the quicksilver that was Thea. Her amusement danced in his brain. *Another conquest! And a lofty one too. There aren't many men who'd bandy words with Messire Henry of Flanders.*

I'm old in insolence, he responded coolly, without pausing in his stride.

In the center of the tent city stood a great pavilion, all imperial purple with the lion of Saint Mark worked upon it. Under its canopy in sweltering shade a number of men sat over wine. Yet Alf saw first not faces, but a cloud of clashing wills. Two men leaned toward one another, one young and one not so young; although they smiled, the tension between them was solid enough to touch.

"So, my lord Boniface," the younger man said, "you would ride away to Thrace with young Prince Popinjay and leave the City to its own devices."

The other's smile neither wavered nor softened. "Why not? Someone should be with him to pull his puppet-strings. Or are you unsure enough of our position here to be afraid to leave it?"

"I fear nothing at all. But I see an empire with its young emperor abroad doing battle with the usurper he cast down, and in the palace naught but an eyeless dodderer. A fruit ripe for our plucking."

"Might not the empire do the same with us?" asked the man who sat between them. He glowed darkly, dressed in the same imperial splendor as the pavilion; on his head was a crown, but it was fashioned of cloth and marked with a white cross. He was old, bent and shriveled with age, the skin deep-folded over the strong bones of his face. The eyes which burned under heavy brows burned upon nothingness, for he was blind. Yet when he spoke his voice was deep and firm, gathering all these proud rebellious lords into the palm of his hand.

Alf moved forward, caught by the brilliance of the soul which flamed behind the useless eyes. "A blind emperor," he said; "a blind Doge. But one is a dotard, and one is stronger than any paladin."

The black eyes flicked toward him; the crowned head cocked. "A stranger? Has a spy come to overhear our counsels?"

"A sage, Messer Enrico," Henry answered, "a pilgrim from Anglia who has settled among the Greeks. I found him corrupting our youth with the aid of my lord Cardinal's secretary."

The Doge beckoned. "Here, pilgrim. Come over where I can see you." His hard dry fingers explored Alf's face, swift and impersonal, a stranger's scrutiny. "A boy," the old man muttered, "and pretty as a girl. Yet, a sage, says milord Henry, who has a legion of faults, the worst of which is his inability to lie. Who can read me this riddle?"

Henry sat beside the young lord. So close, they were as like as brothers can be, though Count Baudouin frowned at this interruption and Henry smiled, saying, "What can be simpler? In Anglia, prophecies come from the mouths of babes, and fatherless boys foretell the fates of kingdoms. This pilgrim has seen all our future, and sat in judgment upon us."

"And the verdict?"

Alf drew a breath. They watched him narrowly, all of them, the greater and the lesser, skeptical, credulous, annoyed, afraid. That was Jehan's fear for him, that he had betrayed all his secret.

But he had never had any fear to spare for princes, nor even for commoner kings crowned with linen. Calmly he said, "If you intend to fulfill your vow and take the Holy Sepulcher, you had best do it now, or none of you will ever see Jerusalem."

"Is it our death you foretell?"

"Yours," Alf answered, "or this city's."

"How do you know all this?"

"I use my eyes and my wits, and I listen to all the wind brings. I'm not as young as I look and sound, Messer Enrico Dandolo."

Suddenly someone laughed. Marquis Boniface grinned at Alf like an aging wolf, and smote his thigh. "Ha! At last! A match for our old fox. Tell me, sir oracle. Which sly Greek serpent has sent you to confound us?"

"None, my lord. I speak on my own authority, and perhaps on God's."

"The least and the greatest. You cover all eventualities."

"But of course, my lord. After all, I'm a scholar trained."

Baudouin glared at him. "This camp is infested with priests and spies. Will no one rid us of this one?"

"No." Baudouin shut his mouth with a snap. The Doge went on unruffled, "No spy would come to us so openly, or led by your brother. A madman might; but a madman is seldom so logical. Sit down, sir pilgrim, and be wise for us. Wisdom is in short supply here."

Alf did not move to obey. "If it's wisdom you look for, my lord, I have little to offer. For you"—he bowed low to them all—"are lords of high degree, and I am but a commoner without name or lineage. Should I presume to counsel princes?"

The Doge's black eyes glittered. "Why not, if princes need good counsel? There's pride in your humility, pilgrim. Sit or stand, I hardly care which, but stay by me. I like the feel of you."

"And I detest it!" Baudouin burst out. "The rest of us can see what comes with it. If this isn't one of His Majesty's ball-less wonders, then I'm—"

"My lord," Alf said gently, "if you would be an emperor, you would learn well that no man holds a throne by setting all his allies at odds."

Baudouin sneered. "I suppose you know intimately how an emperor must act."

"I know what I see," Alf responded. A squire had set out a chair for him; he took it. Thea crouched at his feet. Jehan stood beside and a little behind him, as a guard will, his hands fisted at his belt close to the hilt of his sword.

The Doge smiled and raised a new-filled cup. "To wisdom," he said, "and to foresight." He drank deep.

After a moment Henry followed suit, and Boniface after him. But Baudouin glared and left his wine untouched, though Alf saluted him, smiling wholly without malice.

8

It was very late. The lamp burned low; Alf quenched the wavering flame and sat in the dark that for him was no more than a gray twilight. Beyond the rose-rimmed window the air was warm and close, windless, the stars half hidden in haze. A burning day, a steaming night, a white-hot day thereafter. That had been the pattern for days now.

He looked down at the book open in his lap, and up into the cat-flare of Thea's eyes. She eased the door shut behind her, smiling a little. "You couldn't sleep, either."

"Who can in this heat?"

"You, for instance, when you choose." She came closer. Life in House Akestas had taught her modesty of a sort; she wore a brief shift which left her arms and her long legs bare. Briefly he thought of Saint Ruan's far away in green Anglia, and of the monk who had lived long years there without ever thinking of a woman.

"You never had me to think of." She perched on the arm of his chair and peered at the book. "What are you reading, little Brother? Theology? Philosophy? Stern moral strictures?"

Without his willing it, his hands moved to close the book. She caught them; he struggled briefly and fiercely. All at once he surrendered. She brandished her prize. "See now! What secret are you hiding?" She opened at random. Witch-light welled through her fingers; she read a few words, stopped and looked up. "Why, this is beautiful."

He sat perfectly still, face turned away from her.

She shook her head, incredulous. "Who would have thought that a monk could have taste? And such taste at that.

> *'Once, when the world was young,*
> *Tantalus' daughter became a stone*
> *upon a hill in Phrygia;*
> *and the daughter of Pandion*

touched the sky, winged as a swallow.
O that I were a mirror,
that you would look at me;
a tunic, that you would wear me,
water to bathe your body,
myrrh for your anointing.
Gladly would I be a cincture
for your breasts, a pearl
to glimmer at your throat,
a sandal for your slender foot,
if only you would tread on me.' "

She touched his cheek. It burned under her hand. "Would you really, Alf?"

He tossed back his hair so suddenly that she started. "No!" he snapped, more startling still in one so gentle. "It's only a book. Irene lent it to me."

"Did she?"

Her eyes were dancing. He stood and sought the window. It was no cooler there, nor had he escaped her. Although she remained where he had left her, her voice pursued him, as relentless as it was beautiful. "Irene is in love with you, little Brother."

He breathed deep. The scent of roses filled his brain. "What is there in this world, that even on the edge of ruin no one has any thought but that?"

"It's the Law," she answered him. " 'Go forth; be fruitful, and multiply.' "

"Even our kind?"

"Especially our kind. If there were any god but the One, and we could choose our own, it would surely be Aphrodite."

"You are an utter pagan."

She laughed; he knew without looking that she tossed her free hair. " 'Immortal Aphrodite of the elaborate throne, wile-weaving daughter of Zeus, I beseech thee' . . . tame for me this lovely boy, who looks on me by day with priestly disapproval and cools these torrid nights with Anakreon and Sappho and others no less sweet."

"The patron of this city," he said deliberately, "is the Blessed Virgin."

"She protects you a great deal better than she's protecting her city."

He turned to Thea then. He had won, for the moment; her eyes yielded although her smile had only begun to fade. "You see it too," he said.

She shivered. All mockery had left her. "I don't have your sight. But I feel it. Something is going to break, and soon."

"Very soon. Alexios is in Thrace with many of the Latins. But Baudouin is here as he wished to be, and the old Emperor is as feeble in mind as in body."

"Old!" She tried to laugh. "He's younger than either of us."

"Do years matter? 'Boy,' you call me, though I've lived longer than most men ever hope to."

"And 'dotard' is what Isaac is. Hopeless, my friends tell me. Completely out of his mind."

"Your friends?"

She twined a lock of hair around her finger and watched him sidelong. "My friends," she repeated. "I have a few, you know. You're not the only one who goes out and about and explores the City."

"I never thought I was."

She smiled. Alf frowned. There was something suspicious in the way she looked at him, as if she treasured a secret she knew he would not approve of. The last time he had seen her so, she had been frequenting the harem of a Saracen emir.

"In Constantinople?" She laughed. "Hardly. My friends are good Christians. *Latin* Christians. Saxons."

"Saxons? Here?"

"In the palace, in the Varangian Guard."

For a long moment he stared at her, blank with shock. This was worse than the Emir's harem. Or the Lord Protector's kennel. Or the Prince's mews. Or— "How do they see you?" he demanded. "As a cat? As a hound? As a falcon?"

"Of course not. Beasts can't ask questions or make friends with guardsmen."

His breath hissed between his teeth. She was smiling, relaxed in his chair, leafing idly through Irene's book. No sheltered Eastern maiden, she, who had run off in youth with a Lombard prince and ridden to battle with the princes of Rhiyana and gone to the stake as a witch and a heretic. Yet—

"Guardsmen," he said. His voice sounded thin in his own ears, and cold. "Soldiers. If you have no care for your own honor, might you not at least consider that of your hosts? What would Bardas say, or Sophia, if they knew that their guest ran wild among the Varangians?"

Her eyes glittered, emeralds ringed with fire-gold. "Their *female* guest. Don't forget to add that. Their male guest, of course, is far too holy ever to exceed the bounds of sacred propriety."

"I am a fool and a coward, but I know what is fitting. Do you even put on armor and take up an axe? Or . . . is it . . ."

Anger flashed through her mockery. "Why not just say it, little Brother?"

It caught in his throat. But it was in his mind, clear to read.

She said it for him. "You think I've found a cure for my five years' sickness. A great tall Varangian with braids to his waist and arms I can hardly circle with my two hands, and a huge besom of a beard. Someone who'll tumble a yellow-eyed witch with no qualms at all, and laugh with her at the pallid little priest she's been breaking her heart over. A bull to make me forget my white cat from Anglia."

She was standing in front of him. Half of her was laughing; half of her trembled with anger. "You won't be rid of me so easily, Brother Alfred. Nor is my virtue as easy as that, whatever you may think. I can be a man's friend without leaping into his bed."

He flushed, but his voice by some miracle was steady. "You are beautiful. Any man would desire you. Even I, armored in my vows, have never been immune to you. Is it wise, Thea, to walk among men of war who can take by force whatever they wish for?"

She laughed aloud. "I should like to see them try!"

"And then they come to House Akestas and dispose of the witch's familiars."

She sobered abruptly. "No, Alf. That, they will never do. I'm wild and I'm wicked and maybe I'm a harlot, but I am not a traitor."

"Then you'll stop seeing the Varangians?"

"I never said that." She rose and tossed the book to him; he caught it without thinking. "You've done your duty, Father Confessor. I'll do as my conscience bids me. If that is to visit my friends and to look and listen and to catch what rumors I can, what right or power have you to prevent me?"

"I, none. Your conscience—"

"My conscience is my own, and I am my own woman. Whatever you may say."

"I never said otherwise."

"Didn't you?"

She had reached the door. It closed upon her before he could speak; her mind barriered against him with calm finality.

9

"Hell," said Jehan, "must be somewhat cooler than this."

Even in the depths of House Akestas, in high-ceiled dimness, the heat was like a living thing, bearing down with all its weight upon the gasping City, felling the old and the weak and rousing the minds of the strong to bitter rancor. Anna and Irene had already been sent away for quarreling; Nikki, forbidden to play with Jehan's sword, sulked in solitude.

Alf himself was pale and silent and alarmingly abstracted. He had held Jehan's surcoat for him after the other had shown off his panoply; he held it still, crumpled in his lap, entirely forgotten.

"Hell *is* cooler," Sophia said, watching as Jehan knelt on the tiles wrapping his mail-shirt carefully in oiled leather. It made a massive bundle with the chausses and the padded gambeson and the great flat-topped helm. "Especially," she went on, "since no one in Hades is condemned to wear armor. How do you stand it?"

He shrugged. "You get used to it. Though it's never pleasant, damnably heavy as it is, like to rust at a word." He sat on his heels, his task done. "Every time I set my squire to work cleaning any of it, he mutters about entering a cloister. Never mind, I tell him; a few more years and he can win his own spurs, and find some other poor victim to keep his hauberk clean."

"Is that why knighthood perpetuates itself?"

Jehan laughed. "Why else?"

Alf rose, trailing the surcoat, and wandered to the window. The others watched him in sudden stillness. He looked like a wild thing caged.

Sophia's glance crossed Jehan's. His lightness of mood had vanished; he frowned. "How long has he been like this?" he asked softly, though not too softly for Alf to hear if he chose.

She sighed a little. "He's been very quiet for a day or two. Since the rising in the Latin Quarter."

Jehan's frown deepened. "If you'll pardon my saying it, my lady, that was an ill thing."

"You need no pardon," she said. "It was worse than an ill thing. It was a mad thing. For our people to march on the merchants in their own places, burn their shops and houses to the ground, and kill any Latin they found . . . it was despicable."

"Could they help it, when it comes to that? It's hot; it's miserable; there's an invading army camped outside the walls. And no chance of relief from any of it."

"That doesn't excuse murder. Half the people killed were Pisans—Latins, to be sure, but they fought for us; if it hadn't been for them and for the Varangians, the City would have fallen long before it did."

"True," Jehan conceded. "But they were Latins, and they were a target when your people needed one. No; the ill I see is that all your loyal Latins have come over to us. You've lost one of the mainstays of your army."

"A fine strong empire this is," she said bitterly. "You must feel nothing but contempt for us."

"I?" Jehan shook his head. "I'm not that much of a fool. But I am afraid for you. There've been rumblings in the camp. People are talking about revenge and about making the City pay for what it did to the Pisans."

"And well we ought to," she said. But she had gone cold beneath her veneer of courage.

Alf turned back to the room. Before Jehan could frame a response, he said, "The wind is blowing from the north."

"Ah, good!" she said with more enthusiasm than she felt. "That will cool us splendidly, and blow away any chance of plague."

He shook his head. "No. It's the worst thing anyone could wish for."

Sophia glanced at Jehan. He watched Alf with peculiar fixity; in his eyes was something very close to fear. "What is it?" he demanded. "What do you see?"

Alf shivered convulsively. Jehan's surcoat slipped from his hands to the floor. He stared at it as if he had never seen it before, and bent, lifting it, folding it with exaggerated care. When it was arranged to his satisfaction he laid it gently down upon a table, tracing with his finger the lion rampant that was for Sevigny, and the Chi-Rho which Bishop Aylmer had placed in its claws for the young knight who was also a priest. His eyes were enormous, all pupil; by some trick of the light it seemed to Sophia that they flared red.

He spoke to her and not to Jehan, with quiet intensity. "My lady, if you love your family, keep the children and the servants in the house. Let none of them go out for anything. And send for Bardas. Tell him a lie if you need to. But get him here and keep him here."

"What—" she began.

He cut her off. "See that you have water. All the water you can draw, in every vessel you can find. And food enough for a week at least. Get it now. Get it quickly."

It was madness, surely. Yet it made Sophia tremble. Jehan had risen, death-white under his tan; his sword was naked in his hand.

"No," Alf said to him, "no weapons. Go back to the camp, Jehan. Stay there. Promise me."

"Why? What's going to happen?"

"What you foresaw. But worse. Far worse." Alf looked from one to the other. "Why are you wasting time? Go on!"

He himself was at the door, moving with speed which startled Sophia. Even before Jehan could spring after him, he was gone.

She caught the priest's arm as he passed her. "Wait! Where are you going?"

Jehan stared down at her, eyes wild. "After him. My lady," he added after a moment.

"Is he mad?"

Obviously Jehan was burning to be gone; equally obviously he could think of no courteous way to escape her. "Mad?" he echoed her. "Alf?" He laughed with an edge of hysteria. "I suppose he is. Have you ever seen his back?"

She nodded, wincing involuntarily as she remembered it.

"He was supposed to be burned for a witch. They flogged him instead, as a penance. Then the people canonized him. He has his legend now in the north of Anglia, and even his feast day."

"What does that have to do with—"

"Nothing. But if he's mad, then so are half the saints on the calendar. And all the prophets."

Sophia could find no words at all. Even as she hunted for a response, the door flew open. It was not Alf returning to sanity, but her maid, breathless, disheveled, and scarlet-faced with heat and exertion. "My lady!" she gasped. "My lady! The City's on fire!"

There was something inevitable in it, like the climax of a tragedy. It surprised Sophia that she could think so clearly. She set the woman in a chair, fanned her and refreshed her with a sip or two of wine, and extracted the news from her bit by bit.

It was as Jehan had said. The Latins, incensed by the injury done to their countrymen in the City, had roused to revenge. A troop of them had come armed from the camp, their target the quarter given over to the Arab scholars and merchants. They had sworn to kill Saracens; Saracens, then, they would kill.

The battle had its center in the mosque, the heart of the abomination, a colony of Infidels suffered to live and worship as they pleased within a Christian city. Someone, whether Latin or Moslem or Greek—for Greeks had come to aid their neighbors against the invaders—had brought fire into the battle. By then the breeze which had come to break the terrible heat had grown to a brisk north wind; it fanned the flames despite all efforts to quench them.

"You know how narrow the streets are, my lady," said Katya, almost calm now. "And all the houses are of wood and half of them are falling down. They're burning like logs on a hearth."

Suddenly Sophia was very tired. The servants would be in an uproar; the children would be terrified. And Bardas—if he was in his chamber in the Prefecture, she could lure him home; if not . . .

The hiss of metal on metal brought her eyes to Jehan. He had sheathed his sword; his brows were knit. His face, pleasant and rather foolish in repose, was suddenly hard and stern. "My lady," he said, "you'd best do as Alf told you, and soon. I'm going after him."

"He told you to go back to camp."

"He should have known better, and he should never have left like that before he'd packed me off."

"You know where he's gone?"

"To the fire." Jehan took up the hooded mantle with which he had concealed his foreignness, and threw it on. "I'll come back for my things. Leading Alf, or carrying him."

10

The City was deceptively quiet, basking in the respite from the relentless heat. But beneath the surface, terror had begun to stir. Jehan won passage through the midday crowds with his size and his determination, searching with desperate hope for a familiar white-fair head.

He had hoped for it, but he did not credit his eyes when he saw it under the arch of a portico. For an instant he feared some calamity, illness or violence or perhaps true madness. But Alf met Jehan with clear eyes and a forbidding frown. "Why are you following me?"

"Why are you waiting for me?" Jehan countered.

Alf's frown darkened. "You're an utter fool." He gripped Jehan's arm with that startling strength of his and drew him forward. "Stay with me and keep your head covered."

They heard and scented it before they saw it, screams and cries and an acrid tang of smoke that caught at the throat. As they rounded a corner, fierce heat struck them like a blow. Flames leaped to the sky, dimmed and thinned by the sun's brightness.

All the strong current of the crowd rushed away from the fire, carrying everything in its wake. Alf breasted it like a swimmer, battling it, borne backward one for every two steps he advanced. Once he stopped; Jehan braced himself, expecting them both to be hurled down and trampled. Yet, although the panic-scrambling was as wild as ever, Alf made his way forward again all but unimpeded.

The roaring in their ears, Jehan realized, was not simply the clamor of many voices raised in terror, but the fire itself as it devoured everything in its path. He saw it leap from roof to roof across the narrow street, take hold upon dry timbers and flare upward like a torch. Black demon-figures leaped and danced within it, casting themselves forth, shrieking as they fell.

Here and there amid the inferno were islands: lines of people struggling to hold back the flames, beating at them with cloaks and blankets and rugs, running from the cisterns with basins and buckets and jars; winning small victories, but losing ground steadily as wind and fire conspired to overrun them.

Alf passed them. The air shimmered in the fire-heat; as if by a miracle the crowd had thinned to nothing. Figures staggered about: a man bent under a heavy chest; a small child clutching at one still smaller and crying; a charred scarecrow with a terrible seared face, that wheeled about even as Jehan stared, and plunged into the flames.

Alf halted so suddenly that Jehan collided with him. "God in heaven," he said softly but distinctly in Latin. Jehan, peering at his face through eyes smarting with smoke, saw there neither fear nor pity but a white, terrible anger. He swept the children into his arms, murmuring words of comfort, and passed them to Jehan. "Take them to safety," he said.

The children were limp, passive, worn out with terror. Jehan settled them one on each arm, with the absent ease of one who had had numerous small siblings. "And you?"

"I'll come back to you," Alf answered.

Jehan hesitated. But the children whimpered, and Alf's eyes were terrible. He retreated slowly at first, then more swiftly.

Left alone, Alf stood for a moment, his face to the fire. It tore at him, buffeted him, strangled him with smoke. He reached inward to the heart of his strangeness, gathered the power that coiled there, hurled it with all his strength against the inferno. The flames quailed before it.

He laughed, the sound of steel on steel, with no mirth in it.

Yet the fire, having no mind, knew no master. It surged forward into the gap it had left, and reached with long fingers, enfolding the slim erect figure. Enfolding, but not touching. That much power he had still.

He laughed again briefly, but his laughter died and with it his anger. Pain tore at his sharpened senses, mingled with terror. There were people in the heart of that hell, alive and in agony or trapped and mad with panic. He set his mind upon a single thread of consciousness, and followed where it led.

Jehan, setting the children down within the safety of the fire lines, saw Alf cloaked in flames. He cried out and bolted forward; a stream of fire like a shooting star drove him back. He would have advanced again, but hands caught him and held him in spite of his struggles.

"Will you show some sense?"

The voice was sharp and familiar. He stared blankly at Thea, who glared back. She was dressed as a boy, her hair caught up under a cap.

"You kept him from being burned," he said. "Now he's gone and done it, and where were you?"

"Don't be an idiot." She let him go. "He's perfectly safe. The last thing he needs is to have you blundering after him and getting killed before he can stop you. Here, see if you can talk these people into getting upwind and staying upwind, and keeping the fire back."

Already she was drawing away from him. "Where are you going?" he called after her.

"To be an idiot." She vanished as Alf had, into a wall of fire.

The sun crawled across the sky. Beneath it, steadily, inexorably, the flames advanced. Not only wood but fired brick and even stone fell before them. With the sun's sinking, the City wore a girdle of fire from the Sea of Marmora to the Golden Horn.

Jehan lowered his burden to the ground and coughed. Pain lanced through his scorched throat. The woman he had carried from her smoldering house moaned and twisted, overcome more by hysteria than by the smoke. She could heal herself, he thought with callousness born of a long day's horrors. He coughed again, more weakly, and nerved himself for another foray.

A shape grew out of fire and darkness. Its face seemed vaguely familiar, but he saw only the cup it held out, brimming with blessed water. He snatched eagerly at it, caught himself with a wrenching effort, dropped stiffly to his knees. The woman gulped the water greedily and cursed him when he took the cup away half full to give the rest to the boy who lay beside her.

Gentle hands retrieved the cup, returned it filled. "That is for you," Alf said firmly.

He drank slowly in long sips. With each he felt his strength rise a little higher. When no more remained in the cup, he surrendered it. Alf hung it from his belt and set his hands on Jehan's shoulders. They were warm and strong, pouring strength into him, soothing his hurts.

"Where—" Jehan croaked. "Where—"

"We've opened Saint Basil's as a field hospital. Thea is there, and Bardas—Sophia had no luck in fetching him to safety."

"But you—the fire—"

"We've been bringing all the worst wounded to Saint Basil's. Come with us and help us." Carefully, without waiting for an answer, Alf raised the boy who had drunk the half of Jehan's first cup. The woman he ignored, though she tugged at him, whining.

Saint Basil's lay on the very edge of the inferno yet separated from it by a circle of garden. Streamers of fire, wind-driven, seemed to pass over it or else to fall short of it. The air felt cooler there, and cleaner; even amid the cries of agony and the bodies crowded into every space, there remained a sense of order and of peace.

After Alf had seen the wounded boy settled, he brought Jehan to a tall hard-faced man in blue who surveyed them with a grim eye. Jehan knew how unpromising he must seem to a master surgeon of Constantinople: filthy, stumbling with weariness, his mantle long lost, the rest of his garb charred, tattered, and all too obviously that of a Latin priest.

Alf laid an arm about his friend's shoulders and said, "I've found the man I spoke of, Master. He's trained as well as I am, if not better, and he speaks excellent Greek."

"Do you now?" said Master Dionysios. "Prove it."

"He flatters me, sir," Jehan answered, "but then, he did the training. I suppose he's entitled to brag a little."

The Master glanced from the soot-streaked young face to the one which was somewhat cleaner and seemed a good deal younger. Whatever his thoughts, he only growled, "I suppose you know what a bath is for. When that's done, you can find work enough to do."

Jehan bowed.

"And," Master Dionysios added grimly, "mind you, sir Frank. If anyone dies here, he won't be sent to Heaven or Hell by a heretic. We can use your hands, and your training if you have any. Leave the prayers to those who can say them properly."

Jehan's eyes smoldered, but he held his tongue and bowed again with frigid correctness.

Deep night brought no relief, no slackening in the flood of wounded and dying. With all the hospital's rooms and corridors filled, Master Dionysios sent the rest into the garden to be tended by the light of lamps and of the fire itself, a fierce red glow all about them.

Bathed and shaven and dressed in a fresh tunic that strained at every seam but was at least clean, Jehan labored in the garden. The scent of flowers was sweet and strong even over the stench of smoke and burning flesh; it refreshed him as the water had when he came out of the fire. Sometimes he saw Alf, marked by his luminous pallor, tending those whose hurts were greatest. Once he thought he recognized Bardas' heavyset figure, if truly it was His Majesty's Overseer of the Hospitals who held a man's head while a surgeon cut away the remnants of a hand.

Thea attached herself to Jehan soon after he began, still in her boy's clothes but without her cap. "I thought you'd be helping Alf," he said.

She handed him the knife he had been reaching for. "He doesn't need any help."

"And you think I do?"

"I have no talent at all for healing," she said, "but I'm good at holding heads and at talking sense into people."

"And at keeping fire away from hospitals?"

"Maybe."

"Well enough then," he said. "If anyone asks you, you're my apprentice." He had a glimpse of her swift smile before she bent to comfort the child who lay at their feet, his eyes fixed in terror upon Jehan's knife.

Alf saw the sunrise from the roof of Saint Basil's, whither Master Dionysios had driven him with orders that he not return until he had rested and eaten. Food, he could not face; his body, stronger than a man's, was not yet desperate for sleep. Others of the healers tossed and murmured under a canopy drenched with water to keep off the fire, with Jehan among them sleeping like the dead.

He sat on the roof's edge and clasped his knees. The dawn light seemed a feeble thing beside the fire which raged still in the City. It had retreated somewhat from the hospital, feeding now to the southward; flames had crept forth to lick the dome of Hagia Sophia. All between blazed or smoldered or crumbled in ruins; tenements, gardens, palaces, churches, and the arches and columns of the fora.

"People are saying that it's the wrath of God," Thea said, settling beside him.

"The wrath of man can be well-nigh as terrible."

She leaned against him and laid her head upon his shoulder. "If you're tired," she said, "I can shield us alone for a while."

He sighed. "I'm not as tired as that. House Akestas is safe; Saint Basil's will be now, I think."

"Unless the wind changes."

"Pray then. God ought to hear one of us."

She was silent. His arm had settled itself about her shoulders; he seemed unaware of it, staring out again over the ravaged City. His eyes were bleak. "All our power," he murmured, "great enough in old days to make us gods. But neither of us can do more here than keep the fire away from a pair of houses."

"Have you tried?"

"A little." He shivered. "Not enough to do any good at all."

"It's too big now for only two of us, and one all but untrained."

"I know that. It's only . . . I saw this, Thea. I *saw* it. And when it started, when I could have done something, I couldn't move. I could only stand and gape like a fool."

"When I was in Rhiyana," she said, "the King's sister fell ill. She was mortal, you see, and not young. Gwydion has great powers of healing, almost as great as yours, and his Queen has no less. They stayed with the Lady Alianora through every moment of her sickness and did everything they could do. But she died. We all mourned her, Gwydion most of all. She had been his favorite, his little sister who loved her changeling brother more than anyone else in the world. But . . . she died. Some things none of us can change."

"Death and fate and the destruction of cities. I can bear that because I must. What's unbearable is that I have to know it all before it happens."

"*Have* to, Alf?"

"I've always been able to see at will in that place inside of me where my power lies. It looks like a tapestry with its edges stretching away into infinity. But when fate is strong or disaster imminent and inevitable, I can hardly think or feel or see. I only know what must be, and what no effort of mine can change."

"It's been heavy on you ever since Jerusalem."

He nodded. "When Morwin died, he wanted me to find peace in the Holy City. For a little while I did find it. But I forgot what I should have known, that neither happiness nor peace can long endure. Not in this world."

"Of course not. We need to be miserable to know what it really is to be happy." She rose, drawing him with her. "We can't work as much of a miracle as this city needs. But we can do more than most. Especially when we've put a little food in our stomachs."

"I'm not—"

"Hungry," she finished for him. "You never are. But you're feeling very, very sorry for yourself. How much sorrier you'd feel if you'd lost your house and all you owned, and most of your family, and a good part of your skin besides."

He started as if she had slapped him; flushed, and paled. "I could learn to hate you," he said.

"You could. I'm too fond of telling the truth, aren't I, little Brother?"

"And I can't become a falcon to fly away from it."

That struck home, but she laughed. "See? You've caught it from me. Come down with me and be kind to your poor body for once, the better to fight the rest of this battle."

He hesitated. She turned her back on him and began to pick her way among the sleepers.

As he followed her, the sun climbed at last over the rim of the world, its great orb the color of blood or of fire.

11

The fire was dead. The last embers smoldered sullenly, while here and there among them figures moved, searching for the dead, beginning the long labor of clearing away the ruins and building anew where they had been. Even lamentation was muted, cursing subdued, numbed by the immensity of the destruction.

Alf lay in his own bed in House Akestas, its softness strange after so many nights of catching what rest he could wherever he might. To be clean, to breathe air which bore no taint of smoke, to have no pain about him but only the peace of a sleeping household—he could not yet believe that it was so. In a little while Master Dionysios would wake him, or a bolt of agony would pierce through all the levels of his sleep and thrust him back into the battle.

His mind slid away from remembrance. He had passed beyond weariness to a state like drunkenness, all his inner defenses weakened or cast down. His body seemed made of air, the hand he raised before his face a thing of mist and moonlight. It turned, flexed—wonderful creation, so to yield to his will. His eyes ran from it along his arm to his shoulder, down the long line of his body to his distant feet. He did not often stop to consider himself. Feet had to be shod or sandaled for walking; hands served one's needs; hair had to be washed and cut and kept out of one's face. Everything between, one kept clean and fed and covered as much as one might, and tried to forget.

It was not an ill body. Somewhat too thin perhaps, but strong, with few enough needs. Its curse it shared with his face: its moonwhite skin which could endure no sunlight without the shielding of power, and its beauty. He had seen its like along the Middle Way, in old gods and in the marble *kouroi* which smiled inscrutably upon the City, shameless in their nakedness.

He breathed deep. The air smelled of roses and of rain. Idly, without thought, he let his hand follow the lines of hip and thigh. There was a lazy pleasure in it, in tracing the planes and angles, the taut play of muscles beneath the skin, so different from a woman's smooth curves. From one woman's, from one body he had never had the courage to learn, nor the will to cast away.

He was on his feet. Supple and serene this body was, when the clamoring mind would let it be. It could glide, it could turn. It could dance, great sensuous sin, to the music that was in it. Heart and blood, lungs and brain, set the measure, ceaseless, complex, inescapable. He spun; his hair whipped his shoulders, scarred flesh oblivious, whole flesh struck with a lash of pleasure. His eyes blurred darkness into light, and light into nameless splendor, and nameless splendor into the sheen of bronze and gold.

He dropped exhausted. The glory died. He was mere mud, sweat and earth shaped in a form that men's eyes reckoned fair. Fair and foul, stained with sin and the will to sin, centered on flesh, who had vaunted his knowledge of God. He had never known more than his own vanity.

His fingers raked his hair. Thick as a woman's, fine as a child's, tear it, tear it out. The face, the beautiful beardless face, rend it, mar it—

"*Alfred!*"

All his body snapped taut, arched back from the vise that bound his wrists. It tightened into pain, into agony. Without warning it let him fall. His dream, formless light, had taken flesh; it glared down at him, bronze and gold and unbearably beautiful.

He swallowed. His throat ached. She was splendid in her anger, and surely she knew it; she was always angry. "You always give me reason to be." Thea dragged him up and shook him. "Idiot! How long since you slept? How long since you ate?"

"You made me," he said, "or Jehan. I forget." He willed her into focus. "You went away."

"I've come back." She was still holding him. He touched her

cheek. For all the fire of her temper, it was cool, and she did not shake him off. It was he who drew back, who gathered himself together, who found a blanket to cover his nakedness.

"I ate," he said with care, with a touch of bitterness. "Sophia saw to it. I drank honeyed milk with the rest of the children. No wine, milady nurse."

"No sleep either, and no sense at all."

He lay where she willed him, where his own will would have him. Her temper was shifting, changing. Her eyes were more gold than bronze. She was as bare as he, and he had not even seen. She bent over him.

He thrust her back, spinning her about, felling her with force that shook them both. He had forgotten how hideously strong he was.

He fell to his knees beside her, choking upon self-disgust. He had bruised her, hip, breast, cheekbone.

She sat up. He could not read her eyes within the tangle of her hair. He smoothed it away from her face. His fingertips brushed her cheek; the hip he had dashed against the floor; and, hesitantly, her tender breast. His hand might have lingered there; he forced it to fall. "I'm sorry," he said, meaning more than the simple words, the simple wounding. "I'm . . . most . . . sorry."

She shook her head. "Don't be." Her gentleness was worse than any scolding, her kiss more terrible than a blow, chaste upon his stiff cheek. "Sleep now," she said, "and forget. We all have our midnight madnesses."

"I—" His voice died. She began to walk away. The words fought free. "I love you, Thea."

She was gone. He sank down where she had left him, drawing into a knot, trembling deep within. So easily it had come out, so suddenly and so irredeemably. And she had not even stayed to hear.

In a moment he would laugh. In a moment more, he would weep.

12

Sophia closed her account book firmly and laid her pen aside. "No more today," she said to the house steward. He bowed with Arab formality and withdrew.

Once he was well gone, she indulged in a long delicious yawn and stretched until her bones cracked. Voices from outside came clearly to her ears as they had throughout the morning; she rose and sought the window. In the garden below, her guest and her children sat in a circle, three dark heads and Alf's fair one. They all had pens, even Nikki, and writing tablets; when Alf spoke they wrote. Greek now. It had been Latin earlier. The cadences were familiar. Homer?

Alf paused. The girls continued to write; he bent toward Nikki. From her vantage directly above them, she could see the tablet in her son's lap. The scribbles on it looked remarkably like letters.

Her fingers clenched upon the window frame. No, she thought. They had all told her, doctors, priests, astrologers: He would never speak or read or write. "Raise him as you may," the most learned of the doctors had told her in ill-concealed pity. "Train him as you would a puppy or a colt, else he will run wild. More than that, short of a miracle, none of us can do."

For a moment Alf's hand guided Nikki's. He drew back. Nikki paused, head cocked. Suddenly he nodded and bent over his tablet. If he had been any other child, and if any word had been spoken, she would have said that he had been instructed; had questioned and been answered; and had returned to his task with new understanding.

She drew a breath to calm herself. She hoped for too much; it made her see only what she wished to see. What could one young Latin do, however brilliant he might be, where all the wise men of Byzantium had failed?

In the garden Anna said, "There. All done. Now will you teach me a new song? You promised!"

Though Alf's voice was stern, Sophia could have sworn that there was a smile in it. "Patience is part of your lesson, demoiselle. Come, let me see if anything written in such haste can be perfect."

"It is," Anna insisted. "Alf, what's *dem—demi—*"

"That means 'young lady' in Frankish," Irene informed her virtuously, "and he's being much more polite than you deserve."

"Every man owes a lady courtesy," said Alf in a tone which so withered Irene's pretensions that Sophia stifled laughter. "Yes, Anna, it seems that you've done the impossible. There's not even an iota out of place. However—"

It was Irene who cut him short. "Then you'll sing for us? A new song, please."

"Ah," he said. His voice had deepened a full octave. "A conspiracy. For that I should give you ten more lines apiece to teach you how to treat your master." As they burst into loud protests, he added, "But since we've already had our full hour and more, just this once I will yield to your impudence."

Even Nikki laid aside his tablet, leaning forward eagerly. Alf's voice in song was at once deep and clear: like the rest of him, an uncanny mingling of potent maleness and almost feminine beauty. It caught Sophia and held her fast. She did not move when all too soon it fell silent, but stood by the window, gazing out with eyes which saw only sunlight.

Someone came to stand beside her. "There doesn't seem to be much he can't do," Bardas said.

The rough familiar voice called her back to herself. She smiled and took his arm and walked with him out of the workroom. "It's a bit of a scandal, you know. How can we allow a Latin—a boy—to teach our nubile young daughters? Are we positive that he's only teaching them Latin and tutoring them in Greek, with a little music on the side?"

"That sounds like my sister," Bardas muttered.

"Well, yes. Theodora was here yesterday. We visited the schoolroom." Sophia's eyes glinted. "Alfred, as usual, was infallibly polite. Theodora, as usual, completely failed to captivate him with those famous eyes of hers. And she suggested that maybe we weren't entirely wise to expose him to such temptation, with Irene growing so pretty, and he so young and evidently a man entire."

" 'Evidently,' " he said. "I like that."

They paused just past the door which led to the garden. Alf and the children were out of sight round a corner of the house, but they heard Anna's tuneless treble and Irene's sweet soprano rehearsing the song Alf had sung. "It's obvious enough to me," said Sophia, "but I think I'd trust him with any woman living. Except perhaps for one."

He raised an eyebrow.

She raised both. "Well? Have you ever seen anyone look at a woman the way he looks at Thea?"

"It seems to me," mused Bardas, "that I saw a boy or two mooning after you in your day. And you inveigled your father into marrying you off to an old man from Constantinople, purely and simply for his money."

She glared at him. "Money, forsooth! I had enough of my own. Good sense, that was what I admired in you. No fumbling, no foolishness. You knew what you wanted and that was that."

"Two of a kind, weren't we? Though as I recall, the first time I saw you you were flat on your behind in a dungheap, roundly cursing the half-broken colt who'd thrown you there. I admired your vocabulary. And," he added after some consideration, "your trim ankle."

"You saw more than that, that day." Sophia smiled, remembering. Bardas sat on a stone bench against the house wall where the sun was warm, drawing a breath, of contentment perhaps, that caught and broke into a spasm of coughing.

Sophia sprang toward him, but he waved her away. His breathing had steadied; he leaned back. "Something in my throat," he muttered.

He said that every time. Often lately, since the fire. She looked hard at him. He seemed as strong as ever. A little thinner, maybe. A little grayer. He would be sixty on Saint Stephen's Day.

"It's true," he said in almost his normal voice, "those two children seem unduly interested in each other. Has anyone caught them at it yet?"

She knew he was leading her away from himself, but she did not resist him. "I can't imagine Alfred doing anything of the sort. He's too . . . well . . . *young.*"

"Is he?" Bardas smoothed his beard. "How old would you say he was?"

"Seventeen, maybe. Eighteen. But that's not what I mean."

"I know. In some things he's a complete innocent. Blushes like a girl if he hears a coarse word. It's the other things that concern me. He can tell a rare tale when he has a mind. Ever stopped to wonder how he could have been a monk and a priest, taught that great clever ox from the camp, gone on pilgrimage to Jerusalem—the last of which, by his own account, took years, with a year at least in the holy places afterward—and all before he's even grown a beard?"

"Latins take vows almost blasphemously young, sometimes."

Bardas frowned. "There are times when I think he's about fifteen. Other times I'm sure he's as old as the Delphic Oracle. Those eyes of his—he's no boy, Sophia. Whatever else he is, he's no boy."

She shivered in the sunlight. "I know," she said very low. She remembered the doctor in Chalcedon and shivered again. "I don't think he means us harm. The children love him, and I think he returns it. The servants quarrel over the privilege of waiting on him."

"He's bewitched us all, hasn't he? You should hear the stories they tell in and around Saint Basil's. He's supposed to have walked unscathed through the fire, carried any number of people out of it, and worked authentic miracles of healing, aided by a golden-eyed angel in boy's clothes and another disguised as a Frankish priest."

"Jehan is no more uncanny than you are," Sophia said quickly.

"You think so?"

"Of course I think so. He's a good deal brighter than he looks, and he knows more about Alfred than he's telling, but he's no more than he seems to be."

"That still leaves the other two."

Bardas shifted slightly; Sophia sat beside him. "You aren't going to send them away, are you?" she asked him.

He regarded her in honest surprise. "Why would I do that?"

"The stories—"

"Are just stories until they're proven otherwise. I don't deny that I'm highly suspicious, and I'm not at all sure what we're harboring here. But I agree with you. Neither of them means us any harm. Whatever they are."

"Maybe, after all, they're only a pair of pilgrims."

Bardas snorted and stifled another cough. Before he could answer her, a procession rounded the corner: Anna running ahead with Nikki, Irene walking more sedately behind, and Alf in the rear most dignified of all.

Sophia could not quite suppress a guilty start. What if Alf had heard them?

He showed no sign of it. The younger children paused only briefly before vanishing in the direction of the stable; Irene excused herself to attend to her studies—"A love poem, *I* bet," Anna said, and was firmly ignored—and Bardas had business in the City.

Which left Alf, and Sophia sitting in the sun. There was an awkward pause. "I should see to the kitchen stores," Sophia said to fill it.

Alf sat where Dardas had been, with no show of self-conscious-
ness. Since he neither responded to her inanity nor looked at her
except to smile his quick luminous smile, she stole the chance to look
at him. His face was smooth, unlined, with no mark or blemish that
she could see; the last scar of the burning was gone wholly, without
a trace. It could have been a cold face, white and flawless as it was.
But the tilt of his brows warmed it, gave it a hint of the faun; and when
he smiled it could melt stone.

"Should you be in the sun?" she asked.

His eyes flicked to her. They seemed to change whenever she saw
him, sometimes gray, sometimes silver, sometimes colorless as water.
Now they were palest gold, with the same sunstruck sheen as his hair.
"I'll go in in a little while."

"Soon, then." He was silent; she added, "I liked your song. Was
it Latin?"

He nodded. "A hymn for Rachel bereft of her children. 'Why are
you weeping, maiden mother, lovely Rachel?' " he sang very softly in
that marvel of a voice: " '*Quid tu virgo mater ploras, Rachel formosa?*' "

He sang no more than that, although she waited, expectant. After
a moment she spoke. "Do you miss your monastery?"

She could hear his breath as he caught it, see his fists clench in
his lap. For an instant his face was truly cold. Yet he spoke quietly,
without either pain or anger. "Yes. Yes, sometimes I do miss it. The
peace; the long round of days from prayer to prayer and from task to
task, with now and then a feast or a guest or a villager who needed
healing or comfort. I miss that. The Brothers whose faces I'd known
all my life; my Abbot who was my friend . . . there are times when
I ache to take wing and fly back and never leave again."

"Why don't you?"

He startled her with a flicker of laughter. "For one thing," he
said, "I don't have wings. For another, I don't belong there anymore.
My Abbot is dead; the world has claimed me."

"Has it?"

"Do I look so much like a monk?"

"You look like a gentleman of the City."

"Who longs for his cloister." That had been her precise thought;
she stared at him, silenced. He smiled bitterly. "I suppose one can't
repudiate one's whole upbringing in a day or even a season. But I'm
going to have to do it."

"Why?"

He paused. His eyes had darkened almost to gray. "Many reasons," he answered, speaking as quietly as ever. "I killed a man, you know that."

"Against your will and in defense of your Abbot."

"No," he said. "It started that way. But when the stroke fell, I knew exactly what I was doing, and I wanted to do it. I took a human life; for that I was truly repentant and atoned in every way I knew how, even to Jerusalem. I shall never free myself from that guilt. Yet that I killed when I did, whom I did—he was mad, and he wanted to destroy three kingdoms, and he murdered my friend who had never raised a hand against any living thing. I rid the world of him. I've not been able to regret it."

She took his hand. It was the left, his writing hand, its fingers stained with ink. Black, not blood-scarlet. "You killed one man. How many have you healed?"

"That's what everyone says. I know about sin and repentance and absolution; who better? But I can't go back to Saint Ruan's. It's more than the act of murder long since atoned for. It's that I could do it and feel as I do about it. I've changed too much. They raised me to be a ringdove, Thea says; I grew into an eagle."

"Thea has a clear eye."

"Thea has a gift for irony. She also says that no one can turn a leopard into a lapcat. By that, I suppose, she means that I'm innately vicious."

"She means that you were stifling in your abbey. Maybe someday when you've had all the world has to offer, you'll be ready to go back and find peace."

The bitterness had left his smile. It was gentle and a little sad. "Maybe," he said without conviction. He rose. "Master Dionysios will be looking for me. Good day, my lady."

When she found her voice again, he was gone, and she had asked none of the questions she had meant to ask. She realized that she had crossed herself; cursed her own folly, and turned her back on the garden.

13

Though the sun shone almost with summer's brilliance, the wind which scoured the City was icy cold. Alf drew his hat down lower and huddled into his cloak.

"The worst thing about this city," his companion said, "is its climate. A furnace all summer; then before you can get your breath it's winter, with a wind howling right out of Scythia."

Alf smiled. The other's tone was as cheerful as his words were glum, his round cheeks bright red with the cold; he grinned up at Alf and clutched at the hat which threatened to take flight and leave his bald crown bare. "There's your turning. I suppose I'll see you tomorrow then?"

"Wait." On impulse Alf said, "Let me walk you home."

The smaller man's grin widened. "Are you being protective, then? Eh, brother? They aren't hunting doctors today, only Latins."

"I want to walk," Alf said, "and I'm not expected home quite yet."

"First time you've ever left Saint Basil's when you're supposed to, isn't it? Trust Master Dionysios to know when you're working too hard."

"I'm not—"

"Oh, no. Thin as a lath and white as a ghost, and you're not overworking. Of course not. And half the people who come in insist that no one but Master Theo tend them. If we weren't so fond of your pretty face, my friend, we'd all hate you with a passion."

"I can't understand why you don't."

"Didn't I just tell you? It's your face. Besides the fact that you're the best doctor we've got. And don't glower at me like that. Fat old Thomas is babbling on again as usual, but it's the truth and you know it. There are some who'd gladly see the last of you, but most of us are happy enough; you do all the work, and we get to watch and collect some credit." Thomas grinned and patted Alf's shoulder, which was as high as he could reach, for he was a very small man. "Look, I've talked us right up to my doorstep. Come in and warm up before you go back."

Somewhat later, Alf strode away from Thomas' house with a cup of wine warming his belly and a smile on his lips. Strange that in this half-burned and crumbling city he should have found more and better friends than he had in his own country.

What's strange about it? I've always known you're a Greek at heart.

He looked about. In the throngs about him he could not see Thea's face. Though perhaps the striped cat in the doorway, or the pigeon which took wing in front of him—

Close by him scarlet blazed, a pair of Varangians leaving an alehouse. They were big men and young; he had seen faces like theirs on many a villein in Anglia, long Saxon faces thatched with straw-fair hair. As he paused, one stared full at him and grinned. The eyes under the blond brows were startling, golden bronze.

He knew he was gaping like a fool. The Varangians parted almost within his reach; the one whose eyes and mind were Thea's stopped short in front of him and swept him into a muscular embrace. "By all the saints! Alfred! What are you doing abroad at this hour?"

Behind the strange male face, the deep voice, Thea laughed at his discomfiture. Her mockery steadied him. "I'm walking home from Saint Basil's," he answered her. He looked her over and laughed a little. "No wonder you were angry when I read you my lecture on mingling with guardsmen. What a pompous fool I was!"

"Weren't you?" Thea drew him into a passageway away from prying eyes. Almost at once she was herself again, stripping off her bright gear and bundling it together, dressing in the gown she had worn when he saw her that morning, drawn it seemed from air. The trappings of the Guard vanished as the gown had appeared; she turned about with dancing eyes. "How do I look?"

"Beautiful, of course," he said. "You'll have to show me how you do that."

She paused in adjusting cloak and veil. "What? Shape-change?"

"No. Make things vanish."

"It's easy enough." She took his arm and entered the throng again. "Tonight after everyone's abed, I'll show you."

He smiled.

"You're cheerful today," she said.

He shrugged slightly. "There's a man at Saint Basil's who seems to have decided that I'm worth troubling with."

"Don't tell me you honestly doubted it." He did not respond; she added, "He can make you smile. That's a power to equal any of mine."

"Am I always so morose then?"

"Not morose. Preoccupied, mostly. It's a game in House Akestas to get a smile out of you; the day someone tricks you into an honest-to-God grin, we'll have a festival."

He stared at her in dismay, until he caught the mirth behind her eyes. "On me," he said, "a grin would be a disgrace."

"You're vain."

"Surely." A vendor passed them, balancing a tray laden with hot and fragrant cakes. Alf tossed him a coin and gained a napkinful that warmed his hands and set his mouth to watering. "Here," he said to Thea, "aren't you hungry?"

They ate as they walked, Alf more than usual but still very little. The rest of his share he wrapped and secreted in his robe.

"Nikki will have a feast tonight," Thea said.

"And Anna, and Irene if her dignity will allow it."

"You should have had a dozen brothers and sisters and an army of cousins."

"I had hundreds. Fellow novices when I was a child, and pupils for years thereafter."

They paused upon the steps of Holy Apostles. Over the roar and reek of the City, they heard chanting and caught the sweet strong scent of incense. "Novices and pupils aren't the same," she said.

"Close enough."

"Did you ever know any girls? Or teach any?"

"A few," he said. "Enough to learn that girls need be no less intelligent than boys. Though most change when womanhood comes, forget logic and philosophy and think only on husbands and children."

"Or at least on young men and on what gets children." Thea stood a little apart from him with a cold space between. "I have been rebuked."

"I said *most*. Not *all*."

"There is Sophia," she agreed.

"And there is you."

"I don't know any philosophy. And as for logic, Aristotle would be appalled. All I know is the pleasure of the body."

A sigh escaped him. "You know a great deal more than that. But if you think you have any need at all for what I can teach, I'll be glad to be your master. If you will teach me—"

She leaned forward, breathless.

"If you will teach me the ways of power."

There was a silence in the midst of the City. Suddenly Thea laughed. "It's a bargain. Power for philosophy, and we'll see who makes the better student." She linked arms with him again and plunged into the crowd.

"Filthy Latins!"

With an effort of will Jehan kept his hand away from his sword. It was as much as any Frank's life was worth to walk unconcealed in the City, but both he and his companion were well cloaked and hooded. The cry of hatred had not been meant for them.

He stopped to get his bearings. Left here round the bulk of the church. The wind was cruel. He shivered and wrapped his cloak a little tighter; turned to speak to the man beside him, and caught too late at his hood.

"Barbarians! Murderers!"

Something whistled past his ear. He whipped about, sword half drawn. An iron grip stayed his hand. "No!" hissed the other.

Jehan fought free. The crowd had thickened about him, the murmur of their passing turned to a snarl. In the instant before he let go the hilt, they had seen naked steel.

He drew up the deep hood and made himself advance. Left past Holy Apostles. Left—

Alf stopped short as if he had struck a wall. Thea whirled, every muscle taut. Behind them the crowd eddied, drawing in those who paused upon its edges, rumbling ominously.

A shout won free. "Frankish bastards!"

Without a word, both sprang toward the uproar.

Two men filled its center. One lay in a pool of black and blood-red. The other stood astride him, holding off blows and missiles with the flat of his sword.

"Hold!" bellowed a deep voice. "What goes on here?"

A giant in scarlet shouldered through the mob, ignoring blows and curses, wrenching a stone from a man's hand, roaring for silence. His uniform and his rage and the axe which he carried lightly in his great hands cowed all but the boldest. Those he faced, bulking before the Frank with the sword; his beard bristled and his tawny eyes blazed.

A stone flew; he caught it with his axehead, shattering it. "One more," he growled. "Just one more. Who fancies a year or six with the Emperor's jailers?"

For a long moment the balance wavered. Teeth bared; hands drew back to throw. The Varangian shifted his grip on his axe and braced his feet.

Slowly the mob melted away.

A figure in healer's blue slipped round the Guardsman and dropped beside the fallen man. Blood stained the tonsured crown, pouring from a deep gash there.

Alf looked up into the eyes of the Lord Henry of Flanders. "Sheathe your sword," he said, "my lord."

As Henry obeyed, Alf explored Jehan's wound with light skilled fingers. The young priest stirred under his hands and groaned. His touch stilled both voice and movement; he probed the gash again. It was deep though not mortal, and bloody. He wiped the blood away with a corner of his mantle, drew up his outer robe and tore ruthlessly at the fine linen of his undertunic.

Without his willing it, his power gathered and focused. He could only slow it, turn it aside from full healing as he bound up the wound.

He slid one arm beneath Jehan's shoulders. "Help me," he said, breathing hard for Henry's benefit. Together they raised the great inert body, supporting it on either side, its arms about their necks. But Henry hesitated, glancing about. "The Guardsman. Where did he go?"

"Back to his barracks, I suppose, my lord." Alf bent his head and stepped forward. The young lord followed perforce.

Jehan swam up out of darkness to a raging headache and Alf's calm face hovering over him. "What did you keep me under for?" he demanded of it fretfully.

"Convenience," Alf answered.

Jehan glared and winced. "Did someone hit me over the head with a mace?"

"A stone with sharp edges." Alf laid a cool hand on his brow. The pain faded; his sight cleared. He could see other faces: Thea's, Sophia's, Henry's. He reached out to the last. "You're all right? You're not hurt?"

Henry smiled. "Scarcely a bruise," he said. "They tell me you'll live."

"Maybe," Jehan muttered. He sat up dizzily, saw that they had stripped him down to his shirt. His head was bandaged, his hair damp from a washing. "How long was I out?"

"About an hour," said Alf, propping him with pillows. This, he realized, was Alf's own bed.

They settled about him, Alf at his side, an arm about his shoulders. The support was somewhat more welcome than he had thought it would be. *You're all but healed,* Alf's soft voice said in his mind, *but the shock to your body was severe. You'll need to sleep, and sleep deep.*

Jehan yawned, thinking of it, and clenched his jaw. He would not sleep like a baby while the others talked. *And none of your sorcery!* he thought at Alf.

His friend smiled, perhaps at him, perhaps at Henry. "Well, my lord, how is it that we see you here of all places?"

One of the servants entered with wine. Henry accepted a cup with a murmured courtesy, all the Greek he knew. As he spoke Thea whispered in Sophia's ear, the Greek of his *langue d'oeil*. "I came back from Thrace a week and more ago with the rest of our forces and the young Emperor. Life in camp can be stifling after one's been on the march. When my priestly friend told me he was going to dare the City—which is more than anyone else will do—I invited myself."

Alf's smile faded. Henry met his level stare for a moment, then looked away. "I am no one's prophet," Alf said very softly.

"I do not ask," Henry responded more softly still.

"You," said Alf, "no." His voice changed; a hint of his smile returned, then flickered away. "You were foolhardy, both of you, to venture here in so poor a set of disguises. Next time you should have the sense to dress as Greeks, and you, Jehan, to wear a hat. If anything maddens the City more than a Latin knight, it's a Latin priest."

"It is bad," Henry agreed soberly. "I hadn't known precisely how bad. Out in Thrace we were victors; here we're monsters. Pierre de Bracieux and his men quit the palace this morning in terror of their lives, though milord is howling for revenge."

"He's too brave for his own good." Jehan caught Alf's eye and flushed. "I know what I am, damn it! and he's a fighting fool. He had plenty of tales to tell. People are strengthening the City's walls, do you know that? Quietly, without fanfare, and without asking anyone's leave."

"Neither Emperor seems to be objecting," Henry said. "Isaac's mind is at least half gone, and Alexios has immured himself in his palace where neither we nor his own people can come near him. If my lady will pardon my saying it, this city is not well ruled."

Sophia's eyes sparked. "I know it," she said through Thea, "and I deplore it. But not all of us are cowards. Some of the nobles are beginning to take matters into their own hands."

"You among them, my lady?"

Her lips met in a thin line. "I'm only a woman, and my husband is a bureaucrat, not a prince. I have no power. Only anger."

Henry bowed to her in sincere respect. "I regret that we've come to this, my lady. If I had my wish, we would be in Jerusalem and your city would stand intact."

"Regret!" she snapped. "You should have thought of regret when you sailed up the Horn. Admit it, sir Frank; your holy war has turned into a merchants' quarrel, and this is the richest city in the world. Now you've seen how rich it is, you'll not be bought off except with all we have."

He did not deny it. But he said, "We've done as we contracted to do. His Majesty has not. He owes his throne to us; and we need food and money, and winter is coming. What little he's given us is far from enough. Already many of us are urging that we put aside our patience and take what we need."

"And in the City," Thea said on her own account, "they say that enough is enough. They never chose the Emperor you've set over them, and the one of their own choosing is beneath contempt. They've endured for nigh a thousand years by discarding rulers who can't rule and setting up those who can. One morning, my lord, you'll wake and find that there's a new head under the crown."

"Will it be any better than the ones before it?"

"Who can tell?" She glanced at Alf, who listened without expression, offering nothing. "The walls aren't repairing themselves. There's a man commanding it, one of the Doukas; people call him Mourtzouphlos, Beetle-brows, an alarming man to meet in a dark corridor. He married a daughter of the Emperor you so valiantly cut down in Thrace, and he hasn't forgotten it; and he's far enough into the new Emperors' confidence that they've made him Protovestiarios. That, my lord, is more than a noble valet and esquire or even a steward; he controls the Private Treasury, and through it the imperial favor. You'd do well to watch him."

"So we do," Henry said. "Why do you think we took Alexios off to Thrace?"

"You're giving away state secrets," Sophia murmured.

"No, Lady. I'm saying what everyone knows. Before I left we were more allies than enemies. Now the balance has shifted. I'd like to see it change again."

Alf stirred beside Jehan. "It was the fire. Whichever side kindled it, no one has forgotten that the Latins struck first that day. No one will forget. The hate is too strong and runs too deep."

"On both sides," said Thea. Her face twisted in sudden fierce anger. "By God and all His angels! Can't a one of you think of anything but hating?"

Alf reached out to touch her clenched fist. Face to face, they looked startlingly alike. Gently he said, "The root of it isn't hate. It's fear. Every stranger is an enemy, and every friend could turn traitor. Yet each side shares the same thoughts, all unknowing."

Light dawned in her eyes. "If they could know—if their minds could be opened—"

He shook his head. "No, Thea. No. They're not made for it. It would drive them mad."

"They're sane now?"

"Perfectly sane. Only blind and afraid. Yet there are some who see." His eye caught Sophia, who had just begun to understand through Jehan's translation, and Henry, whose face displayed a mingling of confusion and fascination. "We can pray that they may rule."

"When has good sense ever had the upper hand?" She pulled away from him. "We women aren't pleasant to listen to, are we? A pity there isn't a lady or two of sense and breeding in the camp. We'd put an end to all this idiocy, and quickly too."

"What can a woman do that a man can't?" Alf demanded of her.

"Make a peace we can all live with. And we'd have done it long since, too. Held off the fleet, talked them round, and saved more lives and property than anyone can count. Unfortunately," she added bitterly, "there was neither woman nor wise man at the head of either side that day."

"There was Dandolo," said Henry, "who knows what he wants; and Marquis Boniface, who wants what he can get; and my brother, who won't settle for the leavings. And for the Greeks, a mindless mob and a coward. The usurper died of wounds taken in battle, and every one was in his back."

She faced him. "Why don't you rule?"

"I?" He seemed truly shocked. "My lady, I'm my brother's loyal vassal. Whatever he commands me to do, I do, for honor of my oath."

Regardless of the dishonor of the command?"

Jehan sighed heavily. "Yes, there's the rub. Thea, if you can persuade the people to elect you Emperor, I'll be your most avid supporter. But at the moment I have a splitting headache, and it must be past time for us to go back."

"Yes," she said tartly, "go back and try to open some eyes. If the sight of your bandages doesn't rouse the whole army."

"No fear of that. More likely they'll cheer the marksman who brought down the Pope's varlet."

"Go to the Doge," Alf said, cutting short her sharpness and Jehan's bitter levity. "Tell him what we've said here. Tell him too that he can win this war, but it will bring him no joy. And if he loses, his death will most cruelly hard."

Jehan paused with his cotte half on. Before he could speak, Henry said, "Those are perilous words to say to the Master of Saint Mark."

"He asked for them. Did he not?"

Henry was silent. Slowly, with Alf's help, Jehan finished dressing. His headache, feigned when he spoke of it, had begun to approach agony. "We'll tell him though it kills us."

Alf's fingers brushed his brow. They were warm and cool at once, drawing away the pain, lending him strength. "Dear friend," Alf said, "I'd never send you to your death. Nor do I ask you to come back here. It's too much danger for too little cause."

"I hardly saw you at all." Even to himself Jehan sounded faint and fretful, like a tired child.

"But you did see me." Alf eased something over Jehan's bandage, a hat, broad-brimmed and much worn.

Jehan's groping hand found the braided band and froze. "I can't take this away from you!"

"You can keep it till I come for it. Now, your cloak. You'd best be quick; it will be dark soon, and you won't be able to find a boat to take you across the Horn."

Jehan grasped at the little that mattered. "You'll come for it?"

"Or you'll bring it. When it's safe, and only when." Alf embraced him briefly, tightly. "Take care of yourself, Jehan."

14

Nikki pulled at Alf's hair. *White,* he wrote on his tablet. And at Alf's coat: *Blue.* And his own: *Red.*

Alf swallowed laughter, for Nikki's eyes were mischievous. *No,* he said in his mind; scored through the last and waited, pen poised.

Green! Nikki cried, snatching the pen and writing it in a jubilant scrawl.

Alf's mirth won free. *Yes, green,* he said, *and well you knew it. Now what is it?*

Coat, Nikki answered with his pen. *I wear—him?*

It, Alf corrected him. He nodded, brows knit, forcing himself to remember. Words were a wonder and a delight, but they were hard to keep hold of, shifting and changing as quickly and inexplicably as people's faces. He thought tiredness at Alf, and the other nodded. *Enough now. Go and rest.*

Not rest. The picture in his mind was of the stable and of the three kittens there. He clasped Alf's neck in a quick embrace and left him, skipping as Anna had taught him to do.

Alf tidied the nursery which did duty as a schoolroom, thinking of the one in Saint Ruan's with its gray walls and its hard benches and its rows of novices in their brown robes. Brother Osric, who had been master there when he left, was Abbot now; young Richard had taken the mastership. Though he would not be so young after all—thirty-five? forty? He had been a very hellion when he entered the abbey, fifth son of a poor baron, determined in his contempt for the monks with their pious mumblings. But under the contempt there had been a brain, and a reluctant fascination for the words which the monks had mumbled.

They had sent him a gift through Bishop Aylmer in Rome: his own *Gloria Dei,* copied and illuminated by the best hands in Saint Ruan's, with a commentary over which both Osric and Richard had labored for long years. It lay now in his clothes chest, its beauty hidden in the plain cover which Brother Edgar had made for it to turn aside thieves, nor had he opened it since it came to him.

His will reached, *so*, and it lay in his hands. He sat at the worktable and opened it. His fingers trembled a little. It was even more wonderful than he had remembered.

There folded within was the letter which had come with it, written in Osric's minute precise hand. News of the abbey, small things, this Brother ill and that Brother recovered, a splendid apple harvest and enough mead to make everyone tipsy on Saint Ruan's Day; Duke Robert had given a magnificent bequest, and Lord Morfan was maintaining that the southwest corner of the oak forest had belonged to his family since King William's day. And among all of this, the lines which with the release from his vows had sent Alf from Jerusalem: "Already the younger ones make a legend of what you did, and tell the tale of the Archangel Michael who came to be Our Lady's champion and slew the Abbot's slayer in her Chapel; and there is the sword hung over the altar as proof of it. You yourself we've let them forget, all of us old dodderers, because you asked it, nay demanded it, in the letter the King of Rhiyana sent to us; and because, the world being what it is, maybe it was wisest. We put it in the Necrology: *'Dead on the winter solstice in the tenth year of the reign of His Majesty, Richard, called Coeur-de-Lion: Alfred, foundling, novice, monk and priest of Saint Ruan's upon Ynys Witrin; master of the school, author of the* Gloria Dei, *Doctor misteriosus. May the peace of the Lord rest upon him.'* "

He smoothed the parchment, staring at it, not seeing it. The pain was piercing, as he had known it would be. But not as it had been before. This he could bear. It was pain, not agony. And half of it he had had to force with a flood of memory.

In spite of himself, he was healing. He looked at the book which he had written, and he saw not the cloister but the schoolroom of House Akestas. The words of the monk from Anglia seemed strangely distant. Someone else had written them long years ago, someone he no longer knew. Even the person who had wept when the letter came, only a year past, was not the one who read it now. This new Alfred had no tears to spare for a man five years dead, or for an abbey whose walls could only be a cage.

Carefully he closed the book. He could not read it. Not yet. That pain was real, and deep enough to make him gasp.

He turned. Sophia stood in the doorway, her face reflecting his own, white and shocked. For an instant she had seen in him the full count of his years.

"My lady," he said.

"I wish you wouldn't call me that," she said more sharply than she had meant. In a gentler voice she added, "Are you feeling well? You look ill."

"I'm well." He straightened, brushing his hair out of his eyes, and smiled as best he could.

"Corinna said you were in here at dawn."

That was when Nikki liked to be taught and he to teach, while everyone else slept. It was their secret, theirs and Thea's, for sometimes she came to sit with them, bringing them booty from the kitchen, most of which Nikki ate. Honey cakes this morning, and a bowl of raisins. "I'm well," he repeated.

"But won't you have any—" she began.

He was already gone, his book under his arm.

Alf woke to a timid shaking and a voice calling his name. Sophia's maid bent over him, her hair down, a nightrobe clutched to her ample bosom. Her grief and fear, mingled with embarrassment, shocked him into full consciousness.

"Master," she said, "Master, I'm sorry, but my lady wouldn't let me send Diogenes." She was very careful not to look at him save in quick glances. "It's Master Bardas. He's—"

Alf was up, pulling a tunic over his head, striding forward even before it was settled about him.

He heard Bardas' coughing in the passage, stilled as he opened the door. "Damn it, woman!" Bardas said hoarsely. "You didn't have to wake the whole household."

Sophia moved aside as Alf came to the bed. By lamplight her face was death-white. But Bardas' was gray, clay-colored, filmed with sweat. The hands which tried to thrust Alf away had no strength. "What did you get up for? You don't sleep enough as it is." His voice cracked into a cough; he groped for a cloth, snatched it from his wife's hand.

As the spasm passed, Alf reached for the napkin. Bardas gripped it tightly, but the strong slender fingers pried it away and smoothed it. The stains upon it were scarlet.

Alf met Sophia's eyes. They were brave and steady, but beneath lay terror. She had seen the death in her husband's face.

Alf folded the cloth and laid it beside Bardas' hand. "This isn't the first time," he said.

"It's a touch of lung fever, that's all. I'm getting better. No need to drag you out of your bed."

Alf knelt by Bardas' side. Fear was thick in the room, Katya's,

Sophia's; and Bardas', a deep well of it overlaid with anger. *Dying, I know it, damn this body; dying, and what will they all do? War's coming, Sophia's as good as a man but who'll believe it, little as she is, no bigger than a child. Sophia, the girls, poor half-made Nikephoros who was all the son I could manage; some bull of a Frank will trample them all and leave them for dead.*

Alf examined him with the light sure touch which so comforted the people who came to Saint Basil's. In spite of himself Bardas sighed under it. Pain stabbed his lungs; his eyes darkened as he fought back the spasm. But the hands were there, deft and gentle, and the face like a lamp in the gloom. There was nothing boyish in it, nothing even youthful. *No,* it seemed to say to him without moving its lips. *No one will harm you or yours. Nor will you die. Not yet. Sleep, my friend. Sleep deep.*

Bardas fought to hold to the light. But he had no strength against that gentle, implacable will. His eyes closed; his breathing eased and deepened.

"He'll sleep now," Alf said, "and be better when he wakes." He straightened, drawing a long breath. His face was drawn, his eyes staring blindly into the dark. But the gray pallor had left Bardas' skin; he slept easily, without that terrible rattling of breath which had frightened Sophia even before the coughing began.

Alf was turning away, wavering a little. She caught his cold hand, though once she had it she could think of nothing to say. He swayed visibly. She pushed him into a chair and held him there while Katya ran to fetch wine. A sip or two seemed to strengthen him; his eyes lost their blind look, and a ghost of color tinged his cheeks.

Relief made Sophia's voice sharp. "Don't you go too," she snapped at him.

"I can't," he said faintly, or perhaps she imagined it. A moment later he spoke in a different, stronger voice. "Bardas is very ill. I won't hide that from you. But if he rests and refrains from fretting, he can recover somewhat. Enough to see this war to its end."

She had known it, but the blow brought her to her knees. Alf reached for her; she shook him off. If her knees had given way, her mind had not. "You're not well yourself. Go to bed now and give me one less thing to worry about."

"It was only a passing faintness."

"Go to bed, I said!"

It was the same tone which she used with a recalcitrant child. She saw a spark of anger in his eyes—after all, she had sent for him and made use of him and thanked him not at all—and with it a glint that might have been amusement, but he obeyed her meekly enough.

He had left his wine almost untouched. She raised the cup, stared at it for a long moment, and drained it to the dregs.

But the strong vintage of Cos had no power tonight to dull her wits or to lull her body to sleep. After a wakeful while she left Bardas in Katya's care and went where her feet led her.

The garden had succumbed to frost some time since; the waxing moon lent a cold beauty to its ruins. Sophia walked through the brittle grass among flower beds covered thickly with leaves until spring. Although the air was cold, the wine warmed her.

A flicker of light, a murmur of voices, drew her to the far corner. The moon glinted on Alf's pale head as he sat crosslegged on the ground, a white dove nestling in his hands. Even as Sophia paused, shrinking back instinctively into the shadows, he said in a soft clear voice, "You know I can't do that."

The dove stirred, ruffling its feathers.

"I've tried," he said. "I can't. I do everything just as you've told me; and when the change begins, when nothing inside me is solid or stable, terror drives me back into myself."

The white bird spread its wings. His hands were empty; a hound stood before him, glowing white as if its coat had trapped the moon. Its ears were the color of blood.

Something moved in Alf's shadow. A small figure danced about the beast, and the beast leaped with it, licking its laughing face.

Alf's grave expression softened. "Yes; that's my favorite shape, too." His hands gathered light, fingers flying; he wrapped Nikephoros in shimmering strands like jewels, or like chains.

Sophia sprang forward in fear, in consuming anger. She snatched up her son, hardly aware that the cords of light had thinned and fallen away, or that the witch-hound had fallen back leaving her face to face with the creature she had begun to love as a kinsman.

"Sorcerer!" she hissed at him.

He flinched as if she had struck him, but said no word. He looked very young, and wounded to the heart.

He had ensnared them all and corrupted her son. Nikki struggled wildly in her arms, not knowing her at all, aware only that she had taken him away from his delight.

"You're hurting him," Alf said softly.

She tightened her grip. "Better I than you. How long have you had your spell on him? How long before you make him one of you?"

"Since we met," he answered, "and never. No human can become what I am."

Surely his candor was a trap. Nikki had quieted, chest heaving, each breath catching in a sob. She held him more lightly and turned him to face her. A sharp pain wrung from her a cry; he broke free.

His teeth had drawn blood. She pressed a corner of her shawl to the wound and stood still, watching without comprehension. Alf had not drawn the child in or otherwise sealed his victory. Nikki clung to him with frantic strength; gently but firmly he pried the clutching hands away and set Nikki on his feet. For a moment his hands rested on Nikki's shoulders. They stiffened, then sagged. Nikki turned slowly, drew his mother's arm down, kissed the place where he had bitten her. His face was wet with tears.

She kissed them away. His arms locked about her waist. But only for a moment. He stood back, head up, and turned his face from her to Alf and back again. His pleading was clear to read.

She hardened her heart. "Who is your master, witch-man? The Lord of Lies?"

"No," he said, the flat word, no more.

"Why? Why did you turn out to be like this? We took you in. We trusted you. We loved you. Why didn't you—oh God, why didn't you keep me from seeing this?"

He touched her hand. She recoiled. But he pursued, rising, towering over her. His fingers closed about her wrist; he turned her arm, uncovering the wound. It had bled very little, but it ached fiercely. He brushed her skin with a fingertip, rousing a deep shudder, yet the touch was warm. The pain ebbed away; the marks faded like smoke in the sun.

He let her go. She drew back step by step until she was well out of reach. "Why?" she cried to him.

"I wanted you to know from the first. You wouldn't listen. The doctor knew in Chalcedon. You wouldn't heed him. And I was weak enough to let you be. Tonight . . . Bardas is dying, Sophia. Within a year he will die, nor can any power of mine do more than slow his dying. And before he slept he wanted me to tend you as a grown son would when he should be gone. Could I let either of you depend upon a lie?"

Her voice caught in her throat. She forced it out. "Does—does he—"

"He knows."

"But when—"

"Before I made him sleep. He said he always knew I wasn't like anyone else. He didn't want you to know. You are a jewel among women, he said, but after all you are a woman."

"But he didn't *say* any of that!"

"He thought it."

There was a silence. Sophia gathered her scattered wits into what order she might. Alf stood unmoving. The moon had caught his eyes and kindled them.

She rubbed her arm where the pain had been, slowly, eyes fixed upon him. "What would happen," she asked in a steady voice, "if I called a priest?"

"He would be extremely annoyed to be roused so late."

She strangled laughter that was half hysteria. "And for nothing, too. I can't hate you, Alfred. I may be endangering everyone who's dear to me, but I simply can't."

"I'll go away," he said. "I should have done it at the first."

Sophia wanted to hit him. She seized his hand instead, too quickly for either of them to shrink away, and held it fast. "Don't be ridiculous. You have a place here. There's no point in running away from it."

"I'm corrupting your children."

"You're keeping my husband alive."

He bowed his head. His face was in shadow, the lids lowered over the strangeness of his eyes. He was a legend, a tale of wonder and of terror. Yet she realized that she felt no fear of him at all. His hand was warm in hers, made of flesh like her own; she had seen him ill and she had seen him well, healing where men had destroyed.

"No," he said, "don't judge me now. It's only the wine and your anxiety for Bardas, and guilt that you spoke to me as you did, though you had the right."

"I had no right!" she countered sharply. "I forgot everything I'd ever seen of you. I spoke to wound you who'd already worn yourself to a rag for Bardas and for me; and I thought things of you that no man would ever forgive. And you never moved to defend yourself. Whatever you are, Alfred of Saint Ruan's, you're far closer to Heaven than to Hell."

"You've seen what I can do."

"Would you harm me or any of us?"

"No." He answered at once, without doubt, though the rest was soft, almost hesitant. "I couldn't. It would hurt me too much."

She embraced him tightly. "You're safe now," she said. "No more fears and no more secrets. There's only one thing."

He tensed.

Sophia drew his head down, the better to see his face. "Do you always know what everyone's thinking?"

His eyes widened in dismay and in understanding. "Oh, no! Only when there's need, or when the other wishes it; or when there's no help for it."

She let him go, oddly comforted. "Of course," she said. "There would be laws and courtesies. And you are a philosopher."

"Of sorts."

"You're not as young as you look, are you?"

"No," he answered, "I am not."

"Sometimes it shows." She touched him again, a brief caress. "Thank you, Alfred."

"For what?"

"For everything. Even for telling me. I still trust you with my children."

He bowed low, unable for once to speak.

15
🦋

"Aristotle," said Thea, "was a mere maker of lists. Plato was a philosopher."

"Plato lacked a system." Alf closed his book, rose and stretched.

Thea watched him from her corner of the window niche. "A philosopher has to have a system?"

"If he wants to capture the fancy of the schoolmasters."

"And you?"

"I prefer Plato." He sat down again, close but not touching, and took up his book. "I'm illogical, old-fashioned, and very probably a heretic."

"Very probably," she agreed. "I'm tired of the *Categories*. Where's the book you found in Master Dionysios' library?"

"The Plato? In my room. Shall I fetch it?"

"Let me." She set it in his lap, snatched out of air. Their hands touched; his withdrew quickly. He opened the book more quickly still.

His eyes ran over the words, but his mind reflected Thea's face.

He stole a glance at her. She sat with knees drawn up, head cocked to one side, waiting. A difficult pupil, she; lethally quick-witted and well aware of it, acknowledging him her master but allowing him not an instant's rest upon his laurels.

She would catch him now if he did not bring his mind to order. But it would not shape itself as he willed it. He watched his hand stretch out to trace the curve of her cheek.

She smiled with the familiar touch of mockery. "Was that in your book?"

"Dreams," he said, "are shadows of the life we live, and life a shadow of the Reality."

"Have your dreams been strange of late?"

"My body is seventeen years old. My mind in sleep follows it and it alone. What are six decades of philosophy in the face of that?"

"What use is philosophy at all? Except to keep dry old men busy and to put young ones to sleep, where they dream of love and wake to foolish shame."

"My teaching bores you then? Do you want to end it?" He managed to sound both eager and regretful.

She laughed and weighed their two books in her hands, Plato and Aristotle. "Bored? I? How could I be? You're the best of teachers, and you know it. But I'm a poor philosopher. All those wordy old men with their heads in the clouds . . . even Socrates, who knew a thing or two of the world, what was he doing but escaping his termagant of a wife and finding excuses for his poverty?"

"There's more to the world than what we see."

"Who should know that better than I? And I like to give my mind a bit of exercise. But I can't look at all those sober speculations in the proper light. If you and I are only shadows, or faulty conglomerations of the four elements, or a dance of atoms in the void, why is life so sweet?"

"To you perhaps it is."

"And to you it isn't? Humans have trapped you, little Brother. They live a little while, bound in flesh that must decay; some do the world a bit of good, but most, like angry children, destroy as much of it as they can before they're snatched away. Or they make up stories about the foulness of flesh to convince themselves that they don't want to stay in it. They forget how to live, and say that God, or the gods, or the Demiurge, or whatever power you will, set them here to test them and prove them worthy of an afterlife. Or else, and worst of all, they deny that there is any meaning in anything and give themselves up to despair."

"Would you rather that no one thought on his fate at all?"

"Too much of anything is dangerous. Look at you. The monks made you in their own image and taught you to shrink from the world. Maybe they were made for Heaven, but you weren't."

"Then I must have been made for Hell."

She glared at him. "Don't talk like a fool. You were made for earth, which stands precisely between. And which means that you can reach for both. Heaven if you live as you were meant to live, in full realization of what you are. And Hell if you deny any part of yourself."

"If I turn my power loose, I can destroy the world."

"That's arrogance, and a denial of your conscience. We are gifted with one, you know. Or cursed if you prefer."

"*We*, you say. What are we? Changelings, say people in Anglia. But all the legends tell of human children stolen and monsters set in their places, troll-brats or mindless images which shrivel away with the dawn. Not elf-children of the true blood."

"Who's to say what real elf-children are like? Maybe we are monsters, too hideous or too incomplete to be endured, or else miserable hybrids whom none of our lofty kin would acknowledge. Though I've talked with beings of the otherworld, ghosts, and once a demon; and I've heard tell of one of us who met a Power under a hollow hill. None of them could or would tell us what we are. Maybe we really are changelings. Maybe we're God's joke on humankind. Maybe we don't exist at all. Who knows? There are only a few of us that I know of, and those few have all gone to Rhiyana or known its King."

"Gwydion, for all his wisdom, knows no more than you or I."

"Yet you asked me, woman that I am, and anything but royal. I'm flattered."

"I was shouting in the dark."

"And avoiding the main issue as usual. Your body isn't as easy to distract as your mind is. When are you going to listen to it?"

"When it stops bidding me to sin."

"Is love a sin?"

"Love, no. This is lust."

"Can you be so sure of that?"

That was her essence: to shake the foundations of his world. He unclenched his fists, took the books from her, rose. "I can't separate the two when I think of you, but I will do it. Then we shall see."

"Then you shall no longer have me to trouble you."

She spoke so quietly and so calmly that she frightened him. He moved by instinct, closer to her; standing over her, looking down into her face. The books weighed him down; he willed them away and set his hands upon her shoulders. So thin she was, all brittle bones like a bird. She had had no more sleep or food or peace of mind than he had.

Without conscious thought, he bent and kissed her. She responded with more warmth than he had looked for or dared to hope.

"Yes, damn you," she said angrily, "I love you, God help me. Love you, lust for you, and snatch with shameful eagerness at any crumb you deign to drop in front of me."

He stroked the smooth softness of her hair. She closed her eyes and shivered. "Damn you," she whispered. "Oh, damn you."

He knelt face to face with her and took her cold hands. "Marry me, Thea," he said.

Her eyes opened wide. He met them, baring his mind to her, all defenseless. *I mean it,* he said. *I want it. Marry me.*

Her eyes, then her hand, freed from his, explored his face. Her fingers tangled in his hair. "I love you," she said.

He waited, heart hammering, unable to breathe.

"I love you," she repeated, speaking carefully, "but I don't want to marry you."

His heart stopped. All the blood drained from his face.

She played with his hair, smoothing it, stroking it. "You want me almost as badly as I want you. But you're afraid of the sin. Marriage, you think, will take away both the sin and the fear. You don't see yet that words mean nothing; that love, not a priest's mumbling, is the sacrament."

"I do see it," he said in a voice he hardly recognized as his own.

"Only with your eyes. In your mind, Alfred of Saint Ruan's, you're still in your cloister, though the Pope has given you a writ that says the opposite. And I won't marry a monk."

For a long while he knelt there under her hand. Little by little his heart went cold. She saw it; he watched the dismay grow in her eyes. But she said, "I would be your lover if you were the Lord Pope. Your wife I cannot and will not be."

He rose slowly. He understood now why she had flown from him in Petreia. But her anger had been fiery hot. His was ice-cold. "I beg your pardon, my lady," he said. "I have offended you. I shall not repeat my error." He bowed with careful correctness and began to turn away.

"Alf!" she cried.

He turned back. She faced him, and he saw a stranger, a woman beautiful in her anger, who after all meant nothing to him.

Her own passion froze; her head came up, her chin set. "No," she said, "do not offend me again."

Once more he bowed. This time she did not try to prevent his leaving.

16

This was going to be a bad day, Sophia thought. The children had been quarreling since they woke; the cook was in bed with a fever and breakfast had been all but inedible; and Bardas had risen from a sleepless night, dressed, and announced that he was going out and be damned to them all. Even the sky wept, a gray cold rain that would turn to sleet by nightfall.

She paused in the passage between the kitchen and her workroom and rubbed her aching eyes. "God," she prayed under her breath, "give me patience, or at least a decent night's sleep."

Swift light footsteps brought her erect. Alf descended the stair from his room, fastening his cloak as he moved. He slowed when he saw her; his eyes warmed.

The world seemed a little lighter for his presence. Sophia put on a smile for him and said, "Good morning. I didn't see you at breakfast."

"I ate in the nursery with Nikki." He drew up his hood and settled a hat over it. All his face receded into shadow save for the uncanny ember-flare of his eyes. Yet even that comforted her, in its own fashion.

He touched her cheek, the merest brush of a fingertip. "Bardas won't harm himself," he said gently.

"In this weather?"

Alf smiled, a white flash in the depths of his hood. "He'll be well.

I've seen to that. And he's better off as he is, working and making himself useful, than fretting in his bed."

Her answering smile was faint but genuine. It faded as she sensed a change in him like a sudden, freezing wind. Thea stood at the end of the passage, stiff and still. Alf inclined his head to her politely, as to a stranger; bowed to Sophia, murmuring a word or two of farewell; and took his leave.

"A gray morning," Thea said. Now that Alf was gone, she seemed her usual self.

That cold moment had brought back Sophia's headache in full force. She could find no smile for Thea and barely a pleasant word. "Gray? Black, rather. Have you ever had days when the whole world seems out of sorts?"

"Too many." Thea's arm settled about Sophia's shoulders. She had not Alf's gift of heart's ease; she was fire and quicksilver, bracing rather than comforting.

Sophia sighed and let herself lean briefly against the other. "You two," she said. "What would I do without you?"

Although Thea's voice was light, Sophia felt the tension in her body. "Don't go thinking of us as angels of mercy! We're like cats; we look after our own comfort. If it adds to anybody else's, why then, how pleasant for him."

"You're too modest."

They walked toward Sophia's workroom. It was warm there, a warmth which crept up through their feet from the hypocaust below. Thea went to the window and stood gazing out at the rain which lashed the barren garden. Her face in profile was unwontedly still.

"Is something wrong?" Sophia asked her.

She did not turn. "No," she answered, "of course not. What makes you think that?"

"You and Alf. You've been avoiding one another for days now. Has something happened? Is there anything I can do?"

"No," Thea said again. "It's all right. It's nothing."

Sophia approached her and laid a hand on her arm. "If I'm prying, I beg your pardon. But it's *not* nothing when the whole family can feel a difference. All's not well between you. Is it?"

"You are prying," Thea said in a thin cold voice. She clasped herself tightly, tensely, dislodging Sophia's hand. But she did not move to go.

The other waited, silent.

Suddenly she spun about. "Stop thinking sympathy at me!"

"I can't help it."

"You aren't trying."

"I'm sorry."

"You aren't." Thea drew a shuddering breath, controlling her face and voice, mastering her temper. "I . . . sometimes we forget; humans have eyes too. Has it been so obvious?"

"Rather. It's Alf, isn't it?"

"How can you tell?"

"I have eyes," Sophia said without irony. "For all his sweetness, he has a temper. A terrible one, with staying power. You're much quicker to anger, and to forgive."

"Sometimes," Thea muttered. "Sometimes not. God, what fools men are!" She prowled the small room, restless as a cat. After a circuit or two she stopped. "He asked me to marry him."

"And you refused?"

"Of course I did! He doesn't want a wife any more than I want a husband."

"Then why did he ask?"

"Temporary insanity. Why else? But now he's got his pride to think of, and a wound in it that he won't let heal. Does he think I don't have any of my own? Marriage is bad enough for any woman without her having to contend with a husband who's still more than half a monk."

"You could cure him of that, if you would."

"Not by marrying him," Thea said. "He was a monk for longer than you'd ever believe, with no more thought for his body's needs than a marble saint. The first time he realized he was made of flesh, and warm flesh at that, he hardly knew what was happening. When he found out, he was terrified. Terrified and disgusted, as if God hadn't made that part of him too."

"Can you honestly blame him?"

"For being afraid, no. Not even for being ashamed; that's only his upbringing. But I won't marry him. He has to come to me without shame, with no more fear than anyone might expect of a man who's never taken a woman; as a lover, or not at all."

"You're proud too," Sophia said. "As proud as he is. One of you is going to have to yield."

"He won't. And I refuse to crawl at his feet."

Sophia shook her head. "Stubbornness never solved anything. God forgive me for encouraging a sin; but if I were you, I'd go to him tonight and stay there until I'd broken this deadlock."

"No," said Thea, immovable. "I'm done with begging. He'll come to me or he won't come at all."

Sophia sighed. Quarrels, she thought. What had they ever brought but grief? And this one shadowed the whole household.

She bit back angry words, tried to speak gently. "Whatever else God gave you beyond what He's given the rest of us, He didn't take away your capacity for foolishness."

"Probably not," Thea agreed willingly. "I have business in the City. Is there anything I can do for you there?"

You know well, Sophia thought, but she held her tongue.

Thea left pleasantly enough, even with a smile, leaving Sophia to her accounts and to her troubled thoughts.

Alf was late in coming to Saint Basil's. Even as he shed his sopping cloak, a throng of students, doctors, and walking wounded converged upon him. He had promised to teach a class in anatomy; Stephanos was much better but still in pain; he was not permitted to tend the women, but this one surely, he must advise, such symptoms, no one here had ever seen . . .

"Master Theo!" a voice called over the din. It was one of the students, her high voice pitched even higher with urgency. "Master Theo! You must come at once. Master Dionysios—"

The name freed Alf from the pressing crowd and sent him striding swiftly toward the Master's study.

Just within the door, he stopped. Dionysios sat in his accustomed chair, a book in front of him fallen open to a brilliantly painted page. But he was not alone. On either side of the door stood a guard in splendid livery, and across from the Master sat the most elegant creature Alf had ever seen.

"This is the man called Theo?" The voice was soft, cultured, and contralto, yet not a woman's. Nor, though the face was beardless and beautiful, was it a woman's face. It registered some little surprise, and perhaps amusement. "So; for once the tales were true."

"What did you expect?" Alf asked coolly, offering no more greeting or courtesy than he had received.

The eunuch smiled. "Less than what I see. Oh, much less. They said that you were tall; fair; angelic in face and humble of bearing, but at the same time royally proud. Well then, I looked for a light-haired man of middle height or a little more, with some claim to handsomeness, and an air of ill-concealed arrogance. Who would have thought that for once the rumors would be true?"

Alf glanced at Dionysios. "Sir," he said, "have you called me here for a purpose? Am I to amuse your noble guest?"

"He's noble certainly," said the Master without either awe or pleasure. "His name is Michael Doukas. He's come from the Emperor."

"Truly?" Alf's calmness did not waver. "Which one?"

"Need it matter?" asked Michael Doukas softly, toying with one of his many rings. "Yet if it concerns you, I shall be formal. His Sacred Majesty, Isaac Angelos, commands you to attend him in his palace at Blachernae."

Alf's eyes widened slightly. "I am of course greatly honored. But why?"

The Emperor's messenger looked him over slowly, dark eyes glinting. "You are a very famous man, Master Theo. Even our exalted Emperor, set aloft upon his throne, has heard your name and wondered at it. Wondered indeed which of the many tales is true. Did you will the fire of accursed memory, great master? Or did you will it away?"

Dionysios stood abruptly. "Emperor or no Emperor," he rapped, "I'll not have courtiers' games played in my presence. If you have to take my best man away from me on a day when I can ill spare him, do it, and let me get back to my work."

"Certainly His Majesty has no intention of keeping you away from your duties." Michael Doukas rose with languid grace. He was nearly as tall as Alf, and slender as a woman. "Come, Master Theo. You are expected."

Beneath Dionysios' annoyance Alf sensed fear. It was most irregular, this summons. The Emperor, Dionysios well knew, was not sane. And Michael Doukas was as deadly as he was elegant. Who knew what trap had been laid, or why?

Alf met the Master's gaze and smiled. Dionysios scowled in return. *Go on*, his eyes said, *get yourself killed. Should I care?*

"Come," said Michael Doukas.

17

The Emperor Isaac Angelos sat upon his throne with his crown upon his head and in his hand the orb of the world. Beside him on a second throne lay the source and center of his power, that which alone might rule the Lord of the Romans, the Heir of Constantine, the voice of God on earth: the book of the Gospels laid open to the image of Christ the King. All about the double throne stood the high ones of the court. Above them arched trees of gold bearing fruits of diamond and ruby and emerald, and on the branches jeweled birds; before them crouched a lion of brass.

The lion, Alf noticed, was tarnished, and tilted at a precarious angle; the birds neither moved nor sang. The living courtiers seemed splendid enough, yet most looked bored beyond words. He caught at least one ill-concealed yawn before he turned his eyes away from them to the man upon the throne.

By rite and by custom the Sacred Emperor was more than a man. His every moment was hedged about in ritual as ornate and as holy as the Mass itself. His every thought was shaped in and for his office. Or so the makers of the empire had ordained over the long years. Like the beasts and the birds, the office was failing, the man marred.

Isaac Angelos might have been handsome once. His features, though strongly drawn beneath the graying red-gold beard, were furrowed deep with pain and petulance. Over his ruined eyes he wore a band of silk, imperial purple, that gave him the look of the blinded king in a play.

Every step of Alf's approach from palace gate to the dais' foot had been a step in a solemn hieratic dance. It should have brought him into the sacred presence in a state of mindless awe; but he was only weary, fastidiously distasteful of the robes which he had been made to wear. Magnificent though they were, of priceless Byzantine silk embroidered with gems and gold, they had not seen a cleaning in all the reigns since they were made.

He bowed as his guide directed him, the last and deepest of many such obeisances, full upon his face as if before a god. Above him the

Emperor stirred. His voice rang out unexpectedly deep and rich. "Is he up yet? Eyes—where are my Eyes?"

Alf rose. A small figure had come to stand beside the Emperor. Despite its size, it was no child but a slim honey-brown youth with a proud wisp or two of beard. With his great dark eyes fixed upon Alf, he began to sing. He had a clear tenor voice and a relentless eye for detail, and the gift of painting a portrait in words. What he sang, the Emperor saw, even to the slight wry smile as Alf heard the inventory of his robe's smudges and stains.

The sweet voice stilled. The Emperor sat in all his majesty. Beneath the bandage his cheek twitched slightly, spasmodically. His fingers loosened upon the golden orb; it rolled from his lap, fell to the floor with a leaden thud, bounced like a child's ball upon the steps of the dais. It halted at Alf's feet.

No one dared to touch it, although several of the guards and eunuchs had started forward aghast. Nor did Alf move to pick it up. Among the courtiers, some had stirred, alive to the portent. Magicians, those: sorcerers; diviners and astrologers. They watched him avidly, some with knowledge and perhaps with fear.

"Sire," Alf said in the silence, clearly and directly as if this had been a Western king and not the sacred Emperor, "surely you did not summon me merely to look at me."

The Emperor started a little, his fingers opening and closing, finding only air. "To look? To look, you say? With what?"

"Why, Sire, with your Eyes."

"My eyes are gone. Right in my palace he did it, my brother, my little brother who always swore he loved me. Do you have eyes, child?"

"Yes," Alf answered. Off to the side a courtier drooped against his fellow, limp with ennui.

"Cherish your eyes, little one. So beautiful they are, so clever to take in the light." Isaac Angelos trailed off. For an instant he seemed to subside into a torpor; abruptly he drew himself up in his seat. His fists clenched upon the arms. "You," he said in a new voice, a strong one. "They call you Theo. What is the rest of it? Theophilos? Theodoros? Theophylaktos?"

"Only Theo, Sire."

Above the bandage the Emperor's brow clouded. "No man has but half a name."

One of the sorcerers made his way to the Emperor's side. He was a prince of his kind, a turbaned Moor with a smooth ageless face the color of ebony and a fixed, serpent's stare. "Your Sacred Majesty," he said softly in perfect Greek, "no man may have so little of a name. But is he a man?"

Michael Doukas stirred beside Alf, as languid as ever. "A boy then. A youth, in courtesy, and quite likely to become a man. Of that, learned master, I can assure you."

No one quite ventured to smile. Skeptical of the Moor's magics they might be, but they knew enough to fear his influence.

He did not deign to reveal anger. "I questioned not his gender but his species. Look, sacred Eyes. Is that the face of a mortal man?"

"He is very fair," sang the dwarf, "like to the old gods."

The sorcerer bent, speaking in the Emperor's ear. "Your Majesty, his name, his face, hint at great mysteries. The tales you have heard, the marvels of which your servants have told you—"

"Marvels," Isaac Angelos echoed him. "Magic. Mysteries. An angel in the fire. It burned, my City, like old Rome. But nobody sang its fall to the lyre. He was working miracles. A house fell down and he walked out of it, no scratch or burn, and in his arms a man of twice his bulk. He laid on his hands and men healed. He healed them. He heals them. Come here, child, and lay your hands on me."

Alf spoke gently, with compassion. "Sire, if I have a gift or a skill, it is of God's giving. But He has granted me no power to restore what is gone. I cannot give you back your eyes."

The Moor was a basilisk, the courtiers carrion birds, circling, waiting for their prey to fall. None yawned now or wished for release.

The Emperor turned his head from side to side as if to scan the audience. "No healing? No recompense? A throne—how easy after all to win it back. But I would rather have my eyes." He leaned forward. "They said there would be a miracle. They said one would come. It was in the stars, and in the crystal, and in the fires."

"Aye," intoned the Moor. "The time will come, beloved of God, when you will see again. You will have your eyes, your youth and strength, your empire in all its glory. You shall rule the world."

Alf stooped and lifted the orb. Its fall had dented it, shaken loose a jewel or two, bent askew the cross that crowned it.

The courtiers had taken up the sorcerer's proclamation, an interchange of verse and response, caught up short as Alf raised the sphere of gold. Suddenly he was weary of all this, the ritual, the tarnished splendor, the Emperor whose mind wandered on the paths of madness. They had made him so, these fawning servants, ruled by men who boasted of power and magic. Charlatans, all of them. Liars, sycophants, parasites.

The Moor, who had more knowledge than most if no wisdom, drew back a step. In his eyes Alf saw himself, a frail figure in a great weight of soiled silk, grown suddenly terrible.

"Sire," Alf said quietly in silence thick enough to touch, "your empire has fallen from your hand."

"Then," said Isaac Angelos, reasonably, "give it back to me."

"I cannot."

"I am the Emperor. I command you."

"I cannot," Alf repeated. "It has gone the way of your eyes. There is no healing for you, Lord of the Angeloi. Your eyes are gone. Your empire is gone. Your city will fall because you have not ruled it but have sat upon your throne dreaming of miracles, paying heed to these false prophets who gather like jackals about you."

"Lies!" thundered the Moor. "Who has sent you, O liar without power? The Doge? Marquis Boniface? Or," he added with a venomous glance at Alf's guide, "our own Doukas?"

Alf regarded the sorcerer calmly. "His Majesty summoned me, as you know well who brought my name to him. What was it that you wished for? That I add my voice to yours, echo your feigned foreseeings, strengthen your lies with mine? Or that I speak the truth as all my kind are bound to do, and perish for it, thus removing the threat of my presence? For true power must not endure if smooth words and conjurors' tricks are to prevail."

The Moor's lip curled. "A poisonous serpent, you are, bloated with lies and twisted prophecies."

With a sudden movement the Emperor smote the arm of his throne. "Prophesy, boy. Prophesy!"

"No one commands my power," Alf said softly, "not even His Sacred Majesty."

"Command it yourself then," snapped Isaac Angelos.

Alf did not quite smile. "Very well, Sire. What would you know?"

That took even the Emperor aback. "What? There are no incantations? No fires or crystals or arcane instruments?"

"I am not a sorcerer, Sire. My power comes from within. Ask and I will answer."

The Emperor paused for a long while, stroking his beard. At last he spoke. "Where is my gold sandal?"

In the breaking of tension, one or two of the courtiers laughed.

Alf betrayed neither scorn nor fear. "You asked me to prophesy, Sire, not to find what you have lost. Your sandal," he added coolly, "lies with its mate in the dragon chest which came from Chin, under your robe of crimson silk embroidered with pearls."

The Emperor's fingers knotted in his beard. "Prophesy," he said. "Prophesy!"

Alf looked up into the haggard blinded face, with the orb a dead weight in his hands. The crowd of courtiers waited, minds and faces set for mockery. He drew a long breath and loosed the bonds of his seeing.

18

This must be how one felt after love: this glorious release, this utter lassitude. Alf's power, sated, returned docilely to its cage; he turned from it to the outer world, sighing a little, suddenly aware of his body's weariness.

Rough hands seized him. Voices roared in his ears, shaping slowly into words. "Liar! Impostor! Latin spy!"

The hall was in an uproar. Even the Emperor was on his feet, howling like a beast. "Kill him! *Kill him!*"

The hands began to drag him away. They belonged to Varangians, he realized. Even yet he was too numb and spent to be afraid. The last thing he saw before a scarlet darkness enfolded him was the Emperor's mad rage, and beyond it the Moor's wide white smile.

As the tumult receded, Alf struggled free of the Guardsman's cloak which had wrapped him about. They half dragged, half carried him down a long glittering corridor, marble-cold and deserted.

Alf fought to walk; after a step or two they let him, keeping still a firm grip upon his arms. "Where are you taking me?" he asked them.

Neither replied. Nor did their faces tell him anything. The eyes of both were blue and hard.

The palace was a labyrinth, their passage through it tortuous and interminable. Once they passed from building to building under the sodden sky. Alf's feet ached; he might have laughed at himself, the tireless pilgrim, grown too soft from his months in the City to walk any proper distance.

Abruptly the Guards halted. A door opened; they thrust him through it and slammed it behind him.

He had fallen to one knee. He straightened slowly, shaking back his hair. This was no prison cell. A reception room, he thought, furnished with a chair or two, a wine table, a divan beside a glowing brazier. The walls shimmered with mosaics, beasts and birds in a garden, a golden fish leaping high out of a fountain spray.

His eyes returned from the wall to the divan. On it reclined a languid smiling figure. "Greetings," said Michael Doukas.

There was a chair nearby; Alf took it.

"No doubt of it," observed his host, "you have style. Courage, too, or should I call it folly? To prophesy so calmly, in such exquisite detail, and to his own face, the downfall of an emperor."

"He asked for it," Alf said.

"He asked for a web of soothing lies. It's well for you, sir prophet, that he never asked your true name or nation, and that his sorcerer knows you only as the healer of Saint Basil's."

Alf's entrails knotted. Michael Doukas smiled, arching a delicate brow. "So, Alfred of Saint Ruan's, is your courage not absolute? Or do you fear for your friends in House Akestas?"

Alf clamped his jaw, but the other read the question in his eyes.

"I have my spies. The Doge admires you, I understand, though you've never performed for him as you have for us. We're enormously flattered, if somewhat disconcerted. Has anyone ever called you Cassandra?"

"Yes."

"Indeed?" Michael Doukas was interested. "Someday you'll have to tell me the tale. I plan to survive this, you see. The others will tell themselves that you lied, that all your dooms were simply empty words. I shall build upon them."

"Can you be sure that I tell the truth?"

"How not? I've read a book and I've heard a tale or two. I know what you are, Master Alfred. Alf—Theo—who named you so wisely and so well?"

"A monk in Anglia and the Master of Saint Basil's." Alf raised his chin. "You aren't alone in your wisdom, sir. The Moor too knows what I am."

"What. Not precisely who. Or," added Michael Doukas, "where."

"So," Alf said. "What will you do with me?"

The dark eyes glinted upon him. "I have you in my power, don't I? It's not often I have to deal with one quite so good to look on. More than good, if truth be told. What is it like to look in the mirror and see what you see?"

He expected an answer. Alf gave it, shortly. "Maddening."

Michael Doukas laughed. "Indeed! You're behind it and can't enjoy it. There's a tragedy for old Euripides."

"Aristophanes," Alf muttered.

Again that sweet, sexless laughter. "Such wit! You have an alarming array of talents, master seer. And very little patience to spare for me. I play with you, you think, like a cat amusing itself before the kill. No doubt you expect me to keep you here until I tire of you, then hand you over to His Majesty's torturers."

"You don't serve the Angeloi," Alf said. "You only seem to. Are you going to make me prophesy for your black-browed cousin?"

"No," answered Michael Doukas, "of course not. My handsome kinsman has no use for a seer. I serve myself, Master Alfred, and perhaps the City. If what you foretell comes to pass, there will be great need of a man with wit and intelligence and a thorough knowledge of the empire's workings. Rulers may change with dismaying regularity, but a competent administrator is worth more than a hundred kings."

"And I, who know all of this, am in your hands. In all senses. The Emperor has decreed my death. You know all there is to know of me; most particularly that while I have no dread of my own death, I feel quite otherwise about the deaths of my friends. Again I ask you. What will you do with me?"

"I like you, Master Alfred. Yes," Michael Doukas said, "I like you very much indeed. Brave as only a Latin can be, clever—almost —as a Greek, and completely unafraid to tell the truth. Would you enter my service?"

"What would I be? Your prophet? Your bedmate? Your fool?"

"Fools are a Frankish affectation. A prophet you've already been. The other . . . you are heartbreakingly beautiful. But you are also quite obviously, and quite tiresomely, the sort of young man who cares only for women."

Alf's face was stony. Michael Doukas smiled. "No, I want you for other things. To look at, perhaps. To tell me the truth."

"Then you should find yourself a slave. Or an intelligent lap-dog."

"And not a Latin wanderer who tries to pass as a Greek? Rather successfully, I might add. Your accent could merely be provincial."

"I've refused to serve the Franks, who after all are my own people. Should I turn traitor?"

"Some might say you already have. You're here, are you not?"

"Not of my own accord."

"No one forced you to come to the City."

"I came as a pilgrim. I remain as a healer. To which occupation I would like very much to return."

"Well then, you shall be my physician."

Alf regarded him with a clear pale stare. "You are in excellent health and likely to live to a great age if your intrigues do not bring you to a sudden end. You have no need of my services, Michael Doukas."

"How proud you are! Lucifer before his fall." Michael Doukas rose and smoothed his robes. "You are adamant?"

"Yes."

"So." The eunuch raised his voice. "Guards!"

They came at once, filling the room with their presence, no longer the Emperor's Varangians but those who had accompanied the chamberlain to Saint Basil's. He indicated Alf with a languid hand. "If the Emperor should ask, this man is dead. He died in most exquisite agony, as befits a spy and a traitor. Upon his death, in the way of sorcerers, his body shriveled and fell to dust."

"And if the Moor asks?" Alf inquired.

"If the Moor asks, we cut you up and fed you to the menagerie." Michael Doukas paused, half smiling. "You had better not appear at Saint Basil's for a time."

"Until His Majesty is well distracted?"

"You know your own prophecy." He beckoned. "Take him away."

Alf stood in their hands, eyes upon the eunuch. "Why?" he asked.

Michael Doukas shrugged. "I like you. And," he said, "you might be of use to me later. Remember what I know, and what I have not done."

"Could I forget?" Alf smiled suddenly, startling that polished courtier into a brief, wide-eyed stare. "You are an utter villain. But for all that, a strangely likable man. Look for me at Armageddon."

19

The City was like a beast crouched to spring.

Across the Horn the Latins held to their camp, although the bitter wind clove through their tents and the sleet hissed in their watch-fires and their bellies knotted with hunger.

Within the walls, the Greeks nursed their hatred.

Alf could taste it, a vileness upon his tongue; could sense it as a throbbing in his brain. House Akestas offered no refuge, his shields no defense; even barricaded with all the power he could muster, his head ached with dull persistence.

"I said," Bardas' voice was slightly raised, "Master Dionysios has been inquiring after you."

With an effort Alf focused upon his surroundings. They were all staring at him: Anna and Irene with a book between them, Nikki playing on the floor with a kitten, Sophia in the midst of a letter; and Bardas on a couch, sitting upright in defiance of all his nurses but leaning more heavily on the cushions than he wished anyone to see. His eyes upon Alf were sharp in a face thinned and grayed with sickness. He raised a brow. "Well, sir? The Master wants to know, will you be coming back from the dead before winter ends?"

"Yes," Alf said. He willed his voice to be steady, even light. "Soon, in fact. A month in the tomb is quite long enough for any man."

"Is it safe?" Irene asked barely audibly. "After all, Master Dionysios knows the truth about you, but no one else does. Except us. And the Emperor—"

"His Majesty is mad beyond recall." Alf closed his eyes. It did nothing for the ache, but it kept him from seeing the others' concern. "I did that, you know. I told him what would be; and it thrust him over the edge. He's convinced now that he's God's deputy on earth; that when the sun comes round into the Lion he will slough off his skin like a snake in spring and emerge with his eyes and his youth restored, and proceed to rule the world."

"Could he do that?" Anna asked seriously.

"Of course not." Her father snorted and stifled a cough. "The young fool isn't thriving either, from what I've heard. He's tried to get back into favor by turning on the Latins, but it's too late for that. People are beginning to look round for a new emperor."

"Beginning?" Sophia shook her head. "It's gone past that. Isn't the Senate meeting in Hagia Sophia?"

"It is," Bardas answered. "Without a word from the palace."

"And not a man in all that assembly will accept the crown." Alf rose slowly. "Your pardon, but I think . . . I need to lie down."

They all would have sprung to his aid, but he waved them away. "Please, no. I'll be well enough. It's only a headache."

In the end he had to submit to Corinna's brusque and competent ministrations. She saw him undressed and laid in bed with a pungent herbal brew mixed with wine inside him and a cold compress on his brow. When she left him alone in the darkened room, he sighed with relief.

A small hand slipped into his; another touched his cheek. He opened his eyes to meet Nikki's wide worried stare. Through the shields which guarded his power, he loosed a dart of reassurance.

It had little effect. *Sick,* Nikki responded. *Father's sick. You're sick. The air feels bad. I'm afraid.*

Alf sat up, casting aside the compress, wincing as the movement set his temples throbbing.

Nikki's face twisted. *You hurt!* He held his own head in his hands. *You shut it in. That makes it worse. It hurts me.*

Carefully Alf knelt and smoothed Nikki's hair. His hands healed where they touched. *Better?* he asked.

After a moment Nikki nodded.

Alf smiled. *I have to go out. I'll come back as soon as I can. Will you wait for me?*

Nikki's brows knit. But he stepped back and watched Alf dress. Before the other was well done, he had fled.

Alf paused. He had seen no tears on Nikki's face, nor sensed aught but anxiety and a mind-picture of consolation in the form of a kitten. He shrugged slightly and reached for his cloak.

The Emperor Alexios prowled his privy chamber, gnawing his nails. His chamberlains watched him in white-faced silence. He was not an imposing man, this youngest of the Angeloi. Tall enough, handsome enough, with his father's strong features, but both his face and his movements lacked something. Resolution perhaps, or strength of will.

Suddenly he spun and smote his hands together. "Where *is* the man?" he cried.

The servants glanced at one another. After a moment one ventured forward, bowing to the ground. "Most sacred lord, His Excellency the Protovestiarios has gone as you requested to—"

"I know where I sent him!" Alexios resumed his pacing. "I sent him across the Horn. The Marquis must help me. The cursed mob will elect an emperor and kill me after, I know it. Marquis Boniface was my friend. He will stop them. He'll do anything if he's paid well enough, and I've offered him the richest bribe I can think of. For his priests, our Church—what's a word or two in the Mass if I survive this?—and for him the palace we're standing in. It's no loss. We can move to the Sacred Palace next to Hagia Sophia. It was good enough for Justinian and Basil and half a dozen Constantines. It's good enough for the Angeloi. Oh, sweet saints in heaven, let my lord win safe to the Marquis and bring him back with his knights!"

In the rear rank of chamberlains, eye met eye. One of the eunuchs, young and darkly elegant, nodded infinitesimally and slipped away.

Alf drank deep of the open air. He had not left House Akestas since he came back from the palace; his body, long inured to confinement as any monk's must be, nonetheless rejoiced in freedom. No matter that the sun was shrouded, the clouds heavy with rain. Even his pain had lessened, as if the walls of the house had gathered it all into too small a space.

While his feet bore him through a dim alleyway, his mind opened slowly, lowering each shield with care. The mood of the City washed over him, hate and fear and slowly hardening determination.

And something else. A very small thing, a pricking on the edge of consciousness. He probed, met nothing. A random thought then, nothing to fear. He dismissed it and bound mind again to body, making his way through the narrow crowded streets.

"Sire! By all that's holy, man, let me through to His Majesty!"

Alexios whipped about. The grating voice sawed through the sudden tumult at the door, harsh always, harsher now with emotion. Close upon it came its owner, a thickset man in rich garb now rumpled and soiled, with black eyes glittering under a single heavy bar of brow. He stopped short just within the door, breathing hard as if with exertion yet ghastly pale. As his eyes found the young Emperor, he plunged forward to fall at Alexius' feet. "Disaster, Your Majesty," he gasped. "Utter disaster!"

The Emperor stood with his mouth open, speechless.

The black-browed lord raised himself with visible effort. "Sire, it's worse than we ever dreamed. My embassy is discovered; the people are up in arms, howling for your blood. That an heir of Constantine should sell his Church and his empire to barbarians with his palace for a surety—"

At last Alexios found his voice, an octave higher than its wont, almost a shriek. "Blood? My blood? The Marquis—"

"He consented. But there's no time for him to move. Even now the mob converges on the palace. Sire, by your leave, all your guards and soldiers have fled. Only the Varangians remain loyal to you. Let me set them to defend the walls and to delay the attack."

Alexios clutched at his minister, half blind with terror. "It's all lost, I know it, I know it. They'll catch me, rend me. I'll die!"

The Protovestiarios seemed to have regained much of his composure if none of his color. "No, sacred lord. Not yet, if your loyal men have any power left. The mob will come—it must. But you need not be here. I know a place, a safe place where you may rest and restore yourself and work to regain all you have lost."

The young Emperor was close to collapse. But some remnant of strength stiffened his back and sharpened his voice. "There is no safe place for me, my lord Mourtzouphlos. I shall be recognized and cut down."

Something glittered in the other's eyes, anger perhaps, or contempt. "My lord knows how well I have always served him. Will he not trust me now? I have the Marquis' promise of sanctuary, and loyal men waiting to bring us both to him. Come, Sire, I beg you. Come."

Alexios wavered. Mourtzouphlos knelt. "Sire, I beseech you, before it's too late."

The Emperor stared at him. "Too late?" he repeated. All at once he crumpled. "Oh, anything, anything! Only get me out of here!"

Mourtzouphlos gestured sharply. Men came forward with a heavy cloth. "My lord will pardon this indignity. Only for his life's sake do we subject him to it."

He was limp in their hands, all strength gone out of him with his brief resistance. They wrapped him in the rug and lifted him as if he had been no more than that, bearing him away.

Mourtzouphlos followed. On his face was the beginning of a smile.

* * *

The palace loomed in the dusk like a rock out of a tide-race. Beyond its walls a triple line of Guardsmen held off a mob alit with torches. The axes of the Guard glittered, raised to defend but not yet to strike.

Alf paused for breath on the edge of the tumult. All the wide space between himself and the palace gate was a tossing sea of humanity, and over it the flicker of fire.

He had all but forgotten the small prickle in his mind until it came again, slightly stronger. This time his swift probe caught something and gripped, drawing it to him.

A figure stumbled out of the throng to fall against him. He stared down at it in astonishment and growing horror. "Nikephoros!"

Nikki drew himself erect, hand to head. *You hurt me,* he accused.

Alf's fear for him turned to wrath, swiftly throttled. Nikki felt it and paled, though he did not flinch.

You hurt me, he repeated.

You followed me. Alf's mind-voice was cold. *You hid your mind from me.*

Nikki paled even further. He was close to tears. *I wanted to see where you went,* he said. *People always go out, but I never do. I'm tired of being locked up. I want to go out like everybody else.*

"Sweet Jesu," Alf said aloud. Nikki watched him with eyes gone huge, bracing himself for dire punishment. When Alf raised a hand, he fell back a step.

Alf caught his shoulder in a light strong grip. *Of all times for you to turn rebel . . .* He held Nikki's eyes with a white-hot stare and spoke to him even beyond mind-words, a wave of pure will. As Nikki responded with acquiescence, he took the child in his arms under his cloak and plunged forward swiftly into the mob.

It was quiet in the palace, an eerie quiet like the deeps of the sea while a storm rages overhead. Alf passed as a shadow among shadows, unseen even by those few servants who, out of ignorance or courage, went about their accustomed duties.

In a hall all of gold with pillars of golden marble, Alf met one who had eyes to see him.

"Too late," said the Varangian with Thea's eyes burning in his Saxon face. "The young Emperor is taken. The old one—"

"Is safe enough. I know." Alf spoke coolly, as to a stranger. "I was looking for you. I would prefer that you not risk yourself in this madness."

"You would prefer?" The unfamiliar deep voice was rich with scorn. "You can have a preference? And stand here to tell me of it with the heir to House Akestas in your arms?"

"He followed me," Alf said shortly. "Come home, Thea. This is no place for any sane being."

Thea's jaw set. "Here, my name is Aelfric."

"Appropriate," he observed, unyielding. "Come. Or are you going to wait until the battle comes this far?"

"It won't," she said flatly. "But you had better go back where you came from. It's death for you to be seen here."

"All the more reason for us to be quick."

She made no move to obey him. In this form she was as tall as he, broader and probably stronger, and in power, for all his native strength, she had the greater skill. He met the eyes which remained hers for him whatever shape she took, and held them.

For a long moment they did not waver or fall. Then they slid away.

"Come," he said.

When he turned, she followed him.

Mourtzouphlos inspected himself in the glass a servant held up for him. He looked well in imperial purple; the purple shoes of an emperor were an excellent fit. Better, he thought with the hint of a smile, than the green ones of the office he was forsaking. He adjusted his girdle slightly and smoothed his beard. "That will do," he said.

His men ranged themselves about him, the vanguard of those who held the palace. Soon the Varangians would learn that they had a new emperor to defend. But the head did not matter to the Guard, nor the feet, nor the body between; only the crown and the buskins that marked the Emperor.

Torchbearers waited on the balcony, the mob below, in spreading silence. He stepped forth.

A roar went up, as sudden and as mindless as the cry of a beast. But the closest and the keenest-eyed marked the face of the man above them. His name ran through the crowd, a manifold mutter: Alexios Doukas, Mourtzouphlos. "Mourtzouphlos. *Mourtzouphlos!*"

He let them shout their fill. It was like wine, sweet and heady. He allowed himself a smile. The mob here, the young idiot safe in irons, the Senate bickering uselessly in Hagia Sophia; he had them all precisely where he wanted them.

The tumult had died to a mild uproar. Mourtzouphlos beckoned;

a torchbearer moved closer, raising his brand high. Its light flashed upon the regalia of an emperor. Save the crown. That, Mourtzouphlos held in his hands, raising it for all to see. Another shout rose, hushed when he lowered the crown and handed it to his elegant young chamberlain.

A thin wind ruffled his hair, struggling to lift his heavy mantle. He set his hands upon the cold stone of the balustrade and raised his voice. Though rasping-harsh, it had power; it carried easily. "People of the City," he said. "Romans. You know me."

He paused to let them bellow their assent, and continued. "You know me," he repeated. "I have served the empire for all the years of my manhood, and the emperors to the best of my ability. In this past grim year, I have done all that I may to protect the City from her enemies. I have fought in her battles; I have strengthened her walls. I have counseled her rulers and shown them the enemy where they looked for friends."

The mob began to seethe again. "The Latins! The filthy Latins!"

Mourtzouphlos raised his hands but not his voice. "Yes, the Latins. The wolves are at the gate, the fire in the field. I have shown Their Majesties what their allies are. I have beseeched them to cast the barbarians out; I have implored them to destroy this plague before it destroys us all. And yet—" His voice thickened with emotion; he fought to clear it. "And yet, while they pretended to listen—while they smiled and promised to take thought for their imperiled people—all the while, they were betraying us."

This was a lion's roar, deafening and deadly. Scarlet flared in torchlight, the ranks of the Guard swaying under a sudden assault. But it wavered and dissipated before the threat of the Varangians' axes.

"This very day," Mourtzouphlos said, "the Emperor Alexios sent a message to the Frankish camp." He had won silence, a multitude of ears straining to catch what he could tell. "He has struggled in recent days to make us forget who set him upon his throne. Yet the City has never forgotten. We, loyal to the City and the empire, have never let ourselves forget. And today, with our remembrance clear for him to see, he revealed his true allegiance. He sent to the Latins to ask their aid. Against the City and the empire he asked it. As surety"—Mourtzouphlos choked upon the words he had to say—"As surety, he offered two things: this palace, home of emperors since the great days of the Komnenoi; and our Church. Not only our city but our very souls would lie in thrall to—"

What more he would have said was drowned in the people's rage. It rose to a crescendo, so powerful and so prolonged that Mourtzouphlos began to be afraid. If this mob escaped his tenuous control—

He set his teeth. He held it. It raged, but it did not surge forward to overwhelm the Guard and the palace.

When at last he could be heard, he spoke again, hoarse with the effort of carrying his voice over that multitude. "I have served the emperors as best I can. But when service to the ruler becomes betrayal of the empire, then must that service end. You, people of the City, have seen this for long and long. I, blinded by my loyalty, have looked only now to the full truth. The Latins gave us their puppet and called him our Emperor. His father, once our rightful lord, has lost his wits with his eyes. And I have come at last to the end of my devotion. What have the Angeloi gained us? A hostile army outside of our walls, and half the City within destroyed by fire, and grief for all our people. It is time we remembered who we are. We are Romans, the sons of Augustus, of Constantine, of Justinian; rightful heirs to the empire of the world. Shall we permit a stinking rabble, a pack of unwashed barbarians, to trample us into the dust? Shall we bow to the Doge, whose eyes we took for his spying and his treason, and acknowledge him our master? Shall we surrender even our ancient faith to worship at the altar of the schismatic and the heretic, to yield our will to the Pope who tyrannizes over ruined Rome? Tell me, people of Constantinopolis! Must we do these things?"

"*No!*" they thundered back in one voice.

"No!" he echoed them. "No, and no, and no. The empire is firm, yet it needs a head. Those lords who are both loyal and wise have beseeched me to place mine beneath the crown. I know I am not worthy. But I am willing to take up the burden for the empire's sake and with your consent. And I vow to you, whatever you choose, whomever you set up as your Emperor, I shall labor ever and with all that is in me to rid us of the scourge across the Horn. The Latins shall fall; the City shall be free again, so help me God!"

He had them. Aye, he had them. "Mourtzouphlos!" they roared. And in counterpoint that slowly overwhelmed the rest, the acclamation of the Emperor: "Long life! Long life! Long life to His Sacred Majesty!"

Slowly, carefully, and with great satisfaction, Mourtzouphlos set the crown upon his head.

20

"It's done now."

Alf did not glance back at Thea, who walked behind him still along the lighted ridge of the Middle Way. She had spoken in her own voice; a long stride brought her level with him and revealed her as herself, glaring fiercely at him. "The City has a new Emperor," she said with more than a touch of sharpness.

"I know. The storm has broken; I can think again." Alf halted and set Nikki down. The child stood unmoving, great-eyed with the wonder and the terror of all he had seen that night; as a wagon rattled past he started, reaching instinctively for Alf's hand.

It shakes, he said in his mind. *It hits the bottoms of my feet.* Safe in Alf's grip, he surveyed this new and frightening world.

How ever did you manage to follow Alf so far?

He looked up at Thea. She frightened him no more than Alf did, for all her pretense of fierceness. *I was busy,* he answered her. *I was following. I had to keep him from feeling me. But the people got to be too many and too—too pushing.*

It's a miracle you didn't get trampled.

He shook his head. *Not that kind of pushing. That wasn't hard to get out of at all. But they were thinking so much. So many and so much and in so many places at once.*

Thinking? Alf dropped to his knees, heedless of any who passed, and searched Nikki's face with eyes gone slightly wild. *You heard them thinking?*

"That's not the worst of it," Thea broke in upon Nikki's assent. "Humans can do that easily enough if they have to. It's the least of our powers. But how did a human child manage to shield his mind from you for as long as he did?"

"I was preoccupied," Alf said.

Thea made a sound which was neither delicate nor feminine. "You're not a tenth as inept with your power as you want me to think, little Brother. He shielded from you. Which is something even I was far from skilled at when I was five years old."

Nikki watched their faces. He could follow the thoughts behind their words, but he could not understand what they meant. They were excited and angry and puzzled and perhaps a little afraid, staring at him with eyes that were like no one else's and looking up to glare at one another.

He reached for Thea's hand. It was cold and tense. Carefully, covering up his thought with not-thinking, he brought their two hands together. They had clasped before they knew it, the glares turned to frank amazement. "He did it again," Thea said. "But he's not one of us!"

"Are you sure of that?" demanded Alf.

"He's human," she said with certainty. "Do you realize what this means?"

Alf rose abruptly, letting go her hand as if it burned him. "I realize that we are in the middle of the main thoroughfare of Constantinople. And it's begun to rain. Come, Nikephoros."

Thea drew breath to snap at him. But Nikki shivered and sneezed. She took the hand Alf had not seized, and spread her cloak over the small cold body. Alf moved to do the same. They checked, eye flashing to meet eye, and relaxed all at once, advancing in step with Nikki warmly content between them.

Nikki accepted his punishment with new-won fortitude: abrupt separation from the two who had brought him home, a bath at Corinna's hands, a bite or two to eat, and confinement to bed under her grim eye.

His mother, whose eye had been grimmer still, sank into a chair when he was gone and covered her face for a moment with her hands. When she lowered them, she was calm but pale. "I thought we'd lost him," she said.

Alf paused in nibbling at the supper she had set before him, and touched her hand. "Before God, Sophia, I'm most sorry. If only I'd known sooner that he was following me—"

"How could you have known? It's not your fault. If it's anybody's it's mine, for not realizing that he'd do such a thing. He's not a baby anymore, to hide in my skirts. And he's not an idiot or a monster that I should keep him locked up out of sight."

"He is certainly not either of those."

She looked down at her hands. Without knowing it she had taken a bit of bread and reduced it to crumbs in her lap. Carefully, fighting to keep her fingers steady, she brushed the remnants into a napkin, folded it, and laid it on the table before her.

Alf stopped even pretending to eat. "Sophia," he said, "you have no cause to grieve for him. Or to blame yourself for anything he is or does."

"He's my son."

"And one to be proud of."

Her eyes blazed with sudden, uncontrollable anger. "Stop it, will you? Just stop it! I may be a weak and foolish woman, but I know the truth when it slaps me in the face. My son is a deafmute. A deafmute he was born, and a deafmute he will always be. And no amount of weaseling words can ever change it."

"Maybe not." His quiet voice shocked her into stillness. "But he is also a human being. I know it. I can talk to him; I can speak so that he can understand."

"But not so that *I* can—" She broke off. "No. You said . . . of course. Being what you are, how can you not? And—can he—"

"Yes."

That was hope, that frail battered creature which staggered to its feet and began feebly to crow. She had taught herself to forget hope. A morning of early autumn; three children with their teacher in the garden, and letters on a tablet. "All this time," she said slowly, "and you never told me. You never even hinted."

"It had to find its time."

"Now?"

Alf nodded.

She had to take it in little by little. It was too much, losing her son and then finding him again, and learning that he had walked unprotected through a raging mob, and now this. "You aren't telling me of a miracle. 'The eyes of the blind shall see, and the ears of the deaf shall hear'—that's not what you can offer. This is . . . plain . . . magic."

"Power, we call it. Mind-seeing. For Nikki it's speech."

"But it's not speech!" Her vehemence brought her to her feet. "It's *not* speech. He'll never talk as other people talk."

"Maybe not." Alf poured a cup of wine warmed with spices and set it in her hand. "He's learning to read and to write. He knows what words are, and why people's lips move so often and so strangely. He's not the young animal all your wise men proclaimed him to be. He's a boy who one day will be a man. A good man, if his promise fulfills itself. Can you ask for any more?"

"Can I—" She was perilously close to breaking. "Why can't you make him whole? Really whole?"

Alf's face was white and still. "I am neither a god nor a saint."

"Then what are you?"

"I don't know," he said wearily. "I really don't know."

His words calmed her as no proper answer could have done. With calm came awareness of what she had said, of what wounds she had dealt him. He watched her with pale tired eyes, and waited for her to strike again, making no move to defend himself.

Sophia sat with care and drank deep of the wine. Its warmth gave her strength to speak. "Whenever you bare your soul to me, I trample it under my feet. How do you keep from hating me?"

"Why would I want to?"

"Oh, you are a saint!" She drained the cup and set it down. "I have to think. Will you pardon me if I go away to do it?"

"You needn't. I can—"

"Don't be noble. You've been ill and you're still wobbling on your feet, and you have a supper to finish." Once more she stood. She tried to smile. "When all of this has sunk in, I expect to be deliriously happy. Or absolutely terrified."

"Of me?" he asked very low.

"Of this whole mad world. I used to think I understood it, you see. I was very young then." She leaned over the table and kissed his cheek. "Good night, Alfred."

He was still there when Thea found him, the wine cold in his hand and the food untouched. His face did not change as she took Sophia's chair and began to fill a plate, although he passed the bread to her before she could ask for it.

"Thank you," she said, biting into the loaf. "Ye gods, I'm hungry. I can't remember the last time I ate."

There was no stiffness in her voice or manner, no hint of coldness. He gathered himself to leave her, noting meanwhile that she had bathed and washed her hair, and that she had put on a robe which precisely matched her eyes. Bronze shot with gold, that in certain lights seemed all gold.

Strange how very beautiful she was to look on, and yet how utterly of earth she seemed when she spoke. Such beauty should never speak, or should give utterance only to the sweetest of words.

"How unspeakably dull." Thea filled a bowl with stew. "On the other hand," she added as she reached for a spoon, "it would suit you to perfection. Mystic stillness alternating with verses even more mystic in the fashion of the Delphic Oracle . . . in no time at all you'd have people pouring libations to you."

He rose somewhat more abruptly than he had meant to, lips tight. "It's late," he said. "I'm tired. Good night, Althea."

"You see?" She downed the stew with relish, helping it on its way with bread and cheese and sips of wine. "Sophia says you hold grudges and I don't. You can certainly sit on a grievance as long as anyone I've ever seen. Do you intend to detest me for the rest of your unnaturally long life?"

"I do not detest you," he said through clenched teeth.

"Wasn't I precise enough? Very well then: I irritate you, annoy you, and drive you to distraction. In that order. You're a frightful prig, do you know that? And a bit of a pedant besides."

"I'm very well aware of it."

Her eyes widened, miming astonishment. "Who'd have thought it? Brother Alfred can see his hand in front of his face. Shall we try for the arm? You're arrogant too, assuming I'd come to heel in the palace just because you ordered it."

"You did, didn't you?"

"What else was there to do? I wasn't about to let old Beetle-brows prove me a fool and have me holding off the mob while he stole the crown. On my way to tell the truth to my friends I found you slinking about, mildly suicidal as usual and fancying yourself clever. Naturally I humored you. Why not? My mission was a lost cause in any case, and I saved your precious skin."

His nostrils were pinched and white; his eyes glittered.

She clapped her hands. "Ah, joy! At last I see you in a temper. Go on, hit me if you like. I don't mind."

His fists clenched, but he did not raise them.

She reached for the roast fowl in front of her, dismembering it neatly, biting into the leg. Her teeth were white and sharp; she ate like a cat, at once delicate and fierce. "The trouble with you," she said, "is that you don't know how to handle your temper. Either you crush it all into a tiny box and sit on the lid, or you nurse it and pamper it and tend it like a baby till it grows into a monster and devours you. Why don't you just let yourself go?"

"The last time I did that," he said, low and controlled, "I killed a man."

"No." She finished stripping the bone and turned it in her fingers. "Even that, at the last, was coldly logical. An execution, not a murder. There's passion in you, no doubt of it, but every time it makes a move toward freedom, you either throttle it down or go out of your mind with fear of it, or escape it by telling yourself its object means nothing to you. Doesn't it go against all your priestly training to lie to yourself so much?"

Her light dispassionate voice struck Alf deeper than any torrent of abuse. She had done with her meal; she sat back, sipping wine and watching him over the rim of the cup.

"You don't care for me," she said. "Oh no. You would have come to the palace for any stranger, ignoring all your instincts, that, sir prophet, should have told you there was no danger at all for me. Can it be that after all you're blindly and hopelessly in love with me?"

He drew a sobbing breath. Without warning he struck her.

But she was not there. She stood just out of reach, not quite smiling. "So," she observed with a world of understanding in the single word. "I've flattened you twice for saying the same thing to me. Do you want to try again? Do you love me, little Brother?"

"Yes!" It was a cry of pain.

Thea drew closer to him and laid her hands on his shoulders. He trembled and would not look at her, staring fixedly at the air above her head. "There now. Old grudges die hard, don't they? And the truth can be agony. Will you believe me if I promise you that your pride will recover?"

He shook his head from side to side, tossing it. "It should die the death."

"That's not wise, either. Look at me, you lovely idiot. Do you know what you've been doing to me with all your cold-shouldering? The best friend I've ever had, for all your shortcomings, and you've cut me off as if I were your worst enemy. For nothing."

"You call it nothing?"

"Wasn't it? You asked me to marry you. I said no, and told you why. You stalked off in a rage. And stayed in that rage for well over a month. You're still in it. Are you always like this when you can't have what you want, precisely when you want it?"

That startled him into meeting her gaze. She regarded him steadily, neither yielding nor resisting. His throat constricted; he forced words through it, painfully. "You . . . said I had to be the one who ended this battle."

"You came to the palace for me."

"I didn't intend—" That was not exactly true, and he knew it as well as she. "You were going to alert the Guard. That would have precipitated a civil war with you in the very middle of it. Could I lie here safely out of the way and let you do that?"

"By then, of course, I'd come to the same conclusion. I understand oblique apologies, little Brother, though this one is more oblique than most. I accept it. Now kiss me, to put the seal on it."

He hesitated. Her eyes laughed; her hands linked behind his neck. Laughter bubbled up within him for all that he could do. With sudden resolution, he bent his head and did as she bade.

21

Cartwheels rattled on the road; cattle plodded behind and among the wagons, lowing their complaint, while sheep milled and bleated and herdsmen hemmed them in with cries and curses. Over all rang the clamor of iron on iron and iron on paving stone: the heavy destriers, each bearing an armed and armored knight.

Jehan looked back along the column. As far as he could see before trees and the road's curving concealed it, the army advanced ponderously but in good order, each knight or squire or sergeant in his place, mail-coif up and helm ready at his saddlebow. One or two caught his glance and grinned. Victory had lifted all their spirits, the town taken and plundered behind them, its booty safe here among them or sent ahead to the camp, food and drink enough to sustain the army for a full fortnight.

His red stallion fretted, sidling, threatening the bay beside it with flattened ears and bared teeth. He brought the beast sternly to order and grimaced at the bay's rider. "He hates to drag along at a walk."

"Don't we all?" Henry of Flanders eyed the trees which closed in upon the road. "I'll be glad to come out into open country again."

Jehan nodded. "I like to see where I'm going, and what's waiting for me. Though this road is better than anything I ever saw in a forest at home. Deer tracks, those were. This is a *road.*"

"We're spoiled. All this Eastern luxury: roads and baths and spices, and silk by the furlong. Do you know, I have it on good authority that the Greeks don't heat their houses with simple fires.

They put the fire in the walls or the floor and stay warm all round."

"That's the old Roman way. Furnaces and hypocausts. I saw it in House Akestas."

There was a small silence. Henry brushed dust from his helm, saying slowly, "I . . . heard something in one of our councils. A rumor only. Before the new Emperor seized the throne, old Isaac had his fortune told. It wasn't to his taste. The soothsayer—he was, they said, no more than a boy, but he wore the robe of a master surgeon. They . . . disposed of him."

"I know."

There was no expression in Jehan's voice. Nor could Henry read anything in his profile with its strong Norman arch of nose and its stubborn jaw.

After a little Jehan said, "It was Alf. Who else could stand up in front of an emperor and say what he said?"

Sudden anguish twisted Henry's face. "How could he let himself die like that? So horribly, and for so little."

"He didn't."

Jehan had spoken so quietly and so calmly that for a moment Henry did not trust his own ears. "He—"

"He's alive," Jehan said. Face and voice had come to life again; Henry saw a touch of mirth there and a touch of compassion. "Not that he isn't capable of running after his own death. But it would take a good deal more than a senile old fool to finish off the likes of him. You can lay wagers that he read the future for His Majesty and didn't soften the truth to the smallest degree, and that afterward he arranged to drop from sight for a while to keep his friends safe."

"He sent you a message." It was less a question than an accusation.

Jehan shrugged. "Not really a message. Just . . . I know he's alive and well. I'd know if he weren't. Don't ask me to explain, my lord. Alf's not precisely amenable to explanations."

Even to himself Henry could not admit the depth of his relief. He turned aside from it to consider the road ahead. Nothing moved on it, not even a shadow; above the laced branches of the wood the sun was shrouded in cloud. The trees were thinning; beyond them he could see the open sky and the long stretch of winter-bared hills rolling down to the camp.

Somewhere behind, a pair of sergeants argued. Their voices carried on the cold still air, both amiable and contentious.

"Well now," drawled one, a light voice with the liquid accent of

Provence, "surely one emperor is as good—or as bad—as another. By
the time anyone learns how to pronounce the name of this latest
eminence, we'll be princes in Jerusalem."

The other spoke in a rumbling basso, a solid Flemish peasant's
voice with a hard head behind it. "I can say it already. Mourtzouphlos—Mourtzouphlos. Mourtzouphlos the warmonger. He's no coward of an Angelos. You don't see him sitting on his behind listening
to soothsayers, or dithering about from Latin to Greek and back
again. Hasn't he opened war already? Shoring up the walls, bricking
up the gates, building those towers on top of the towers he already
has, to keep us out; and riding abroad whenever it suits him to harry
our foraging parties. He'll give us a good dose of cold steel before he's
done."

"Empty defiance," said the southerner, undismayed. "He'll
never go beyond a threat or two. These Greeks are lazy; effete;
effeminate. One show of genuine force and they'll topple."

The Fleming grunted. "Tell that to the Varangians. If you can
persuade them to lay down their axes long enough to listen to you."

"Ah, but those are mercenaries. The Greeks are made of lesser
stuff. Haven't we just overrun a whole town full of them?" The
southerner laughed. "Oh no, old friend. We've nothing to be afraid
of. Come spring, we'll twist the Greeks' arms to get our money and
sail down to Outremer."

Henry sighed a little. He had not thought that anyone clung still
to that dream.

The Fleming most certainly did not. "If we leave this place, it will
be by fighting our way out of it. Or conquering it, if it comes to that.
Never trust a Greek, boy, and never underestimate him."

The southerner's laughter rang clear and mocking above the
myriad noises of their passage.

Abruptly it stopped.

Before Henry's mind woke to alarm, his body had hauled his
horse about, his eye flashed to find the armored figure toppling slowly
from its saddle. One eye was wide, astonished. The other had
sprouted an ell of black arrow.

Someone thrust Henry's helm into his hand. Jehan's was already
on, the priest reaching across to aid his friend. One of the cattle
bellowed, struck by a dart; men cried out, screams and curses and
prayers to every saint in heaven.

The bay destrier wheeled upon its haunches. The wood swarmed

with Greeks, an army all about the Frankish column, and at its head
under the imperial banner, the Emperor himself, crowned, cloaked
with purple. His soldiers slipped beneath the lances of the knights to
strike at the horses with swords and daggers, or shot from the
branches of the trees where none could reach them, or plunged
a-horseback into the howling chaos of men and cattle and wagons.

Henry filled his lungs. "Drop lances!" he bellowed. "Out swords!
Form up round the wagons!"

Even as he spoke he let his lance fall, drew his great sword,
spurred the charger forward. A Greek plunged toward him, a wild-
eyed fool who wore no helmet, only a circlet of gold about his brows.
Henry's blade swept down; the man's face dissolved in a spray of
scarlet. The young lord laughed; for he realized suddenly that he was
himself without a helm. He had dropped it somewhere, he knew not
where, nor cared. "To the wagons!" he roared. "To the wagons!"

Jehan's world was a clamorous darkness lit by a thin line of light,
the eye-slit of his helm. He heard Henry's voice, his lance already
forsaken, his sword red with blood, and in his mind a bitter clarity.
What fools we were, it observed, watching his sword cleave its way
through the massed attackers, *riding like ladies on a holiday and never
looking for an ambush. If we survive this, we'll take no credit for it.* And: *It's an
honorable death, I suppose.* And: *By our Lady! What bold brave knights we are!*
He whirled his dripping blade about his head and whooped, and
drove his stallion into the midst of the enemy.

Shapes whirled past him, a blur of blood and steel. A banner
whipped in the wind, bright, strange, heavy with purple and gold. A
mailed knight matched blade to his blade; another crept up behind,
a crawling in his spine. He touched spur to his stallion's side. The
great horse gathered and leaped, lashing out with deadly heels even
as Jehan's blade clove the helmet of the man in front of him.

An image floated above the press, a shimmer of gold and jewels:
a gentle Lady whose great eyes stared serenely into nothingness,
whose lips smiled, impervious to the clamor of battle. Beneath her
rode a figure of splendor, a knight in gold-washed armor upon a
milk-white mare, his helm surmounted with a cross; for surcoat he
wore a garment of cloth of gold, across its breast a cross of gems and
gold.

Jehan grinned within his helm. A poor priest, he was, in his plain
steel with his surcoat all bloodied, and the Patriarch of Constantinople flashing and glittering under the icon of the Virgin.

Not all the Latins had gathered about Henry. A bold handful raged among the Greeks. Jehan called out to them. "To me, my lads! To me!"

They came as the cubs to the lion, a shield for his back and his sides. He raised his sword and sprang forward full upon the Patriarch.

The guard of Greek knights scattered. The Patriarch hauled at the reins, but his mare jibbed, shying. Jehan's blade swept down. In the last instant it flickered. The flat of it crashed upon the nasal of the Patriarch's helmet. The reins fell from nerveless fingers; the mare bolted, her rider clinging blindly to her neck.

The icon swayed dangerously upon its great ark of gold and jewels. One of its four strong bearers had fallen, trampled under a charger's hoofs. Another stumbled.

Jehan shouted something only half coherent and leaped from his saddle into the very midst of the Greeks. They scattered before his sword. The icon was falling. He thrust his shoulder under the ark and staggered, eye to staring eye with a Greek well-nigh as tall as himself. The Greek yawned and dropped. A burly man in tattered surcoat and dented helm filled his place; and another, heaving up the mighty weight, raising it again toward heaven. The Virgin smiled her secret smile; the gems glittered about her, set in pure gold.

Henry saw the icon fall and rise again upon Latin shoulders. The Franks lifted a shout; the Greeks faltered in dismay.

Now, Henry thought. And aloud: "Now!"

All his gathered men drew together with Henry at the head of the spear. The enemy held before the charge; weakened; broke. Mourtzouphlos himself, within a circle of chosen princes, saw all his guard felled or driven in flight; and Henry's sword smote past his shield to send him tumbling over his horse's neck, sprawling ignominiously upon the ground.

Sick, half stunned, he staggered to his feet. The charge had swept past him. His mount was gone; his army was an army no longer but a fleeing mob. Over the Latin helms swayed the icon that was the luck of his City, and the bright banner of his empire.

No one paid him any heed, not even the crows that had gathered to feast on the dead. His dead, save for the one reckless Provençal whose laughter had roused the ambush.

He cast off his shield and his crowned helmet. Pain stabbed his right arm, the mark of Henry's sword. He set his face toward the distant City and began to run.

22

Bardas slept as easily as he ever did now, freed for the moment from the torment of coughing which racked his whole body, granted the release from pain which was all the healing Alf could give. His face, though thinned to the bone, wore a semblance of peace.

Sophia combed out her black braids. Freed, they tumbled to her knees: her one beauty and her one vanity. This morning she had found a thread of gray. Well; it was time. She was thirty-four.

Across the bed, Alf straightened. In lamplight and intent on his task, he looked strangely old, an age which smoothed and fined rather than withered and shrank, like the patina of ancient ivory.

She was obsessed with time tonight. As he began to gather the packets and vials from which he had made Bardas' medicine, she asked, "How old are you, Alf?"

A bottle dropped from his fingers, mercifully falling only an inch or two, striking the table with a sound which made them both start. Very carefully Alf picked it up again and laid it in his box of medicines. His voice was equally careful, his face completely without color. "How old would you like me to be?"

"As old as you are."

He tightened the knot on a bundle of herbs, head bent. His hair hid his face, whiter in that light than Bardas' yet thick and youthful. "That," he said, "could be embarrassing. Or frightening."

"To you or to me?"

"Both." He looked up. It was a boy's face with the barest hint of white-fair downy beard. But a man's voice, well settled, and eyes too unbearably ancient to meet.

He laughed as a strong man will, in pain. "I'm not that old! If I were like anyone else, I could conceivably be still alive."

"Then—"

"I was seventeen when I took vows in Saint Ruan's. Bardas was a very young child. In too many ways, I'm still seventeen."

"I'm neither embarrassed nor frightened."

Wide-eyed, surprised, he looked younger than ever.

She smiled. "I'll tell you a secret. I'm still seventeen too. I just don't look it, and I try not to act it. At least not in public."

"It doesn't matter? That I—"

"Why should it? I only wanted to be sure. I hate mysteries." She finished her combing and began to bind up the gleaming mass again. "It's reassuring, in its way. All that wisdom and experience, and a body strong enough to last out any storm."

"But also, all too often, at the mercy of its own unnatural youth."

"Unnatural, Alf? Did you buy it? Or induce it?"

"Saints, no!"

"Well then," Sophia said, "for you it's natural. It certainly looks well on you."

Alf closed the lid of the box and fastened it. He was smiling wryly. "There are two kinds of people in the world. People who want desperately to burn me at the stake, and people who take me easily in their stride."

"Not easily. Just . . . inevitably. What must it have been like for you? Raised as you were, trained as you were, and being what you were. Even with the monks' acceptance, or tolerance at least, you still had to face the Church. My poor little prejudices are nothing to that."

"I'm trapped in this body. I have to endure it. You have no need."

"Don't I? You're so wise about the rest of the world, and such a fool with yourself."

He bowed his head. "I don't think I understand people very well."

"You do. Perfectly. Except when your own person comes into it. The monks triumphed with you, I think."

That brought his head up, and won reluctant but genuine laughter. "I begin to see what I missed in all that lifetime without women. A clear eye, an acid tongue, and a wonderfully illogical logic."

"Only a man would find it illogical. It makes perfect sense to me."

"Of course it does." He came round the bed, took her hand and kissed it. "You're good for me, Sophia."

"Like one of your medicines: bitter but bracing."

He laughed again. She watched him go, smiling even after he was gone. "Naturally," she said to Bardas who slept on unheeding, breathing almost easily, "I'm in love with him. Who isn't?"

* * *

Alf's laughter died beyond the door. He was grave and almost sad when he stood in his own room, setting the box of medicines with his blue mantle, running a fingertip over the fine wool. It was early still, hours yet to midnight; he felt no desire to sleep. A bath he had had. A book? He had a new one, given him by Master Dionysios when he returned to Saint Basil's. "Take it," the Master had growled, glaring at him as if he had committed some infraction. But behind the glare lurked the joy no one else had even tried to hide.

He set the book beside his chair and undressed slowly. He glimpsed himself in the silver mirror that lay upon the table. Diogenes had left it that morning when he cut Alf's hair. Alf turned it face down and reached for the loose warm robe he always wore for reading at night. Settling into the chair, he opened the book.

This was not Dionysios' volume of Arabic medicine.

> *The moon and the Pleiades have set.*
> *I lie in bed,*
> *alone.*

Irene's love poems. He moved to close the book, found himself turning the page instead.

> *Immortal Aphrodite of the elaborate throne,*
> *wile-weaving daughter of Zeus,*
> *I beseech thee,*
> *vanquish not my soul, O Lady,*
> *with love's sweet torments.*

Bardas was dying. The Emperor had lost not merely a skirmish but the fabled luck of the City. Jehan lay cold and sleepless in the camp, rolling on his tongue the bitter dregs of his victory. And Alf could think of nothing but the fire in his flesh. He set the book down with exaggerated care and rose. The house slept about him, even Sophia drowsing on the cot she had had the servants set up near Bardas' bed, with Corinna stretched out at her feet in mountainous repose.

Softly on bare feet he ventured into the corridor. Something stirred, startling him: Nikki's kitten, mewing and weaving about his ankles. He gathered it up, settled it purring in the curve of his arm.

Its thoughts were small feral cat-thoughts, warm now and comfortable.

The women's quarters, though called that still, had been given over to the children; beyond it at the top of House Akestas Thea had claimed a room of her own. Its door was unlocked. Alf opened it slowly, fighting every instinct that cried out to him to flee.

Dim light met his eyes. A lantern hung on a chain from the ceiling, shaped like a hawk in flight. It illumined a small room simply and plainly furnished, almost like a servant's. The only extravagance was the bed's coverlet, a blaze of flame-red silk embroidered with the phoenix rising from its pyre. Thea sat cross-legged upon it in a woollen robe, her hair free, mending a shield strap. That was so very like her that Alf smiled without thinking and was in the room before his terror could master him.

She returned his smile, not at all disturbed to see him there where he had never come before. "Welcome to my empire," she said. "Sit down and keep me company while I finish this."

There was nowhere to sit but on the bed. Alf sat stiffly at the very end of it. She had returned to her mending, frowning with concentration. Her hair had fallen forward; he wanted to stroke it back. But he did not move.

The kitten yawned hugely, stepped out of its nest, negotiated the descent to the bed. After some thought, it curled in a hollow beyond the crest of the phoenix and went complacently to sleep.

Thea took the last stitch and tugged at it. Satisfied, she laid the shield down beside the bed, tossing back her hair. The lamp caught the gold lights in it, deepened the shadows to black-bronze. "Inspection tomorrow," she explained. "His Majesty, having run home from battle with his tail between his legs, wants to assure himself that he still has enough power to make an army miserable."

"Isn't he claiming the victory? A few Greeks fell, to be sure, and he lost his horse. But he routed the Franks and brought the icon and the standard back to the treasury where they belong."

"So he says." She stretched like a cat; her loose robe clung to breast and thigh. "A few people believe him. The rest know he has to save his skin. Before he took the crown he promised his supporters that he'd rid the City of the Latins in a week. A month, he's saying now. Soon it will be a season. And he may not last that long."

He found that he had moved closer to her, close enough to touch. His hands were icy cold. His heart beat hard. *Coward,* it mocked him. *Coward, coward, coward.*

She stroked the kitten, rousing it to a drowsy purr. "Under Mourtzouphlos," she said, "for all that he's had his failures, the palace feels different. He may have lost a battle today, but he's won others; and he's willing to *act*. The Angeloi never even began to try."

Alf listened to her in growing despair. He had succeeded; he had convinced her that he could not give her more than he ever had. Love, but love of the mind only, that of the body twisted and made powerless by his lifetime in the cloister. Companionship, friendship, even kinship he could give, for after all he was the only being of her own kind in this part of the world. But nothing more.

She had fallen silent. He could have wept to see her so beautiful, and he too little of a man even to touch her except as a brother. He would have been better as a eunuch, like Michael Doukas, who had never known how to desire a woman and who could never know it.

No, said a voice deep in his mind. *Even this is worth the price.*

If he could live his life again, he would have her in it just as she was now. Watching him, saying no word; ready to be hurt, more than willing to be loved.

Even though I am no maid?

He stared blankly. He had never even thought of that. "For me," he said, "only one thing matters. That you are you. Thea. None other." He heard himself speak and realized that it was the truth. And that she too was afraid. Not of her body—that, she had mastered long ago—but of that which had been between them since they met in Anglia, and was like nothing she had ever known. Beside that, his own terror was a small thing, a child's whimpering in the dark.

It doesn't frighten me. He held her hands and met her wide eyes, and remembered as he so seldom did that she was younger than he.

"Do you know what it means?" she cried. "We're bound. One soul, the humans say. They don't know the half of it. Wherever you go, I must go; whatever you do, I must be with you. If you hurt, I hurt; your joy is my joy. We can never be free again."

"Free?" He kissed her palms and held them to his cheeks. "What is freedom?"

Her fingers tensed; he felt the prick of nails. But she did not try to pull away. "Bodies are simple. An hour's play, a moment's pleasure, and there's the end of it. But this is forever. Forever, Alf!"

"It's not an easy thing to face. And yet . . . many a time I've wished you far away, or regretted the day I met you; we've quarreled and I've come close to hating you. But if you left and never came back, I know that I could not live."

"It's a trap. A vicious, impenetrable, eternal trap."

"So," he said, "is all this wonder of a world. See what blessings we're given to make it easier. Beauty and agelessness and power, and the bond which has held us together from the moment of our meeting. Although I'm not much of a blessing for a woman, nor indeed much of a man at all."

"Who lets you think that?" Indignation put all her fears to flight. She pulled away from him, only to take his face in her hands and kiss him on the lips, shivering him to his foundations. "You're a man," she said with conviction.

"I'm afraid." And of that he was, folly though he knew it to be.

"Of course you are. So was I, my first time, and it's worse for a woman than for a man. I soon got over it."

"I—I don't think—I'm not ready—"

"No?" She looked down; he blushed. "Your body most certainly is."

"I can't," he said in sudden desperation. "It's useless. I was a monk for too long. I'm still a monk. I'll never be anything else. Let me go!"

She was not holding him. Nor did he take flight. Even as he begged for release, his fingers lost themselves in her hair; her arms circled his neck.

"The body knows," she whispered in his ear. "Trust it."

The body, yes, and the power. Gently, delicately, he wove himself into the web of her mind. All its threads were air and fire, eternally shifting and changing, yet at the center of them ever the same. Whatever shape she chose to bear, she remained herself.

Her awareness enfolded him. For an instant it turned upon itself; he saw through her mind a structure of perfect order, a temple of light, its center a sphere of white fire. Himself as she knew him, taking shape about the fire, a slender youth in the habit of a monk that bound him like chains. Yet as he watched, his bonds melted away; he lay beside her clothed only in his skin, drawing her into his arms.

She was warm even to burning, and supple, and slender-strong, slim almost as a boy yet curved where a boy would never be. What his eyes had known against his will yet unable entirely to escape, his hands now explored in wonder and delight. "Oh, you are beautiful!"

"And you." She kissed his brow and the high curve of his cheekbone, and after an instant his lips. She tasted of honey.

Before he had truly partaken of her sweetness she withdrew, turning, drawing him with her. He was above her now, her arms about him. Her hands ran down his back along the knots and ridges where the whip had gouged deep. "I love you," she whispered. "I have never loved anyone else as I love you. Nor ever shall."

She had forsaken all the armor with which she faced the world, all her sharpness and her mockery and the hard fierce glitter of her wit. Her eyes were meltingly tender; she tangled her fingers in his hair and brought him down to meet her kiss.

Deep within him a seed burst and sprouted and grew and put forth a blossom, a flower of fire.

She moved beneath him, opening to him. His blood thundered in his ears; his body throbbed. He was all one great song of love and terror and desire, and of sheerest, purest joy.

> *Behold, thou art fair, my love, behold, thou art fair!*
> *Thou art beautiful, O my love, as Tirzah, comely as*
>   *Jerusalem, terrible as an army with banners.*
> *I will get me to the mountain of myrrh, and to the hill*
>   *of frankincense. . . .*

To all his words and songs and fears she had but one, and that one lost in light. "Yes," she breathed, or thought, or willed. *"Yes!"*

23

Thea sighed with contentment and settled more comfortably in the circle of Alf's arm. His free hand, moving of its own accord, found her breast and rested there, as Nikki's kitten curled purring on the curve of her hip.

She traced an aimless wandering pattern on his chest and shoulder to make him quiver with pleasure, and let her hand come to rest over the slow strong pulse of his heart. "I love you," she said.

"Still?"

She laughed softly. "Still! I knew there was fire under it all. And such fire!" She kissed the point of his jaw, paused, nibbled his neck with sharp cat-teeth. "There are lovers and lovers. With some, once is enough. With others passion lasts for a little while, then fades. But a few—a precious few—are like the best wine in the world. The more one has, the more one craves, and one never grows weary of it. You, my little Brother, are one of the last."

"I know you are." His lips brushed her hair. "Now I know why the Church calls it a sin."

"Only the crabbed old men in their cloisters. Which you, my love, most certainly are not."

"Not anymore." For the first time he sounded almost glad. "So this is what all the poets mean. *Dulcis amor!*"

He sang the Latin so sweetly and so passionately that her heart stopped. Then she laughed. "Sweet indeed! Now I'm sure of it; you were born for this."

"To each living creature its own element."

She drew back a little to see his smile. Their eyes met and kindled; their bodies twined, to the kitten's utter and heartfelt disgust. Even in the midst of the fire they could laugh as it stalked to the bed's farthest corner and sulked there, lamenting its lost sleep.

Sophia woke abruptly. The lamp was guttering, the room silent save for Corinna's soft snores.

It began again. Bardas' coughing, deep rending spasms that shook the heavy bed. She half fell from the cot, stumbling over Corinna, groping blindly for the medicine Alf had left. But she could make no use of it while the storm lasted. It was long, agelong.

At last it ceased. Bardas lay gasping. His face was a skull, his eyes deep-sunken in black sockets. Open though they were, they saw nothing, but stared blankly into the dark. He swallowed the potion by instinct, without even his usual grimace at the taste.

Corinna loomed beside her with a bowl of water and a cloth. Silently the woman began to sponge the fever-sweat from Bardas' body. There was so little of him now, skin and bare bone and the horror that devoured his lungs.

Resolutely Sophia bit back tears. Bardas needed a level head and a steady hand, not a flood of weeping.

The new storm struck without warning, longer and even worse than the last. When it subsided, it was only a lull. Bright blood stained the sheet, a thin stream which did not cease.

She had lived with fear through all that black winter. But this was stark panic. "Alf," she whispered. "Alfred."

Corinna straightened. Her deep voice was calm and calming. "I'll fetch him, my lady."

"Please," Sophia said. "Please bring him."

Left alone, she took up the cloth Corinna had laid down and gently wiped away the blood from Bardas' lips and chin. But more flowed forth, a great gout of it as a spasm shook him. There was no awareness in his eyes. There was only his pain and the battle for his life.

Corinna was gone for an interminable while. Sophia did not, would not, count the crawling moments. Nor would she yield to her terror. Deep in her mind, a child shrieked and pummeled the walls.

The door opened. She spun toward it in an ecstasy of relief.

Corinna's chin was set, her scowl terrible. No tall pale figure stood behind her. "He's not in, my lady," she said in a flat voice.

Sophia drew a shuddering breath. "Of course he's in. He must be in. Did you look in the schoolroom? In Nikki's room? In the bath? Or maybe the garden. He might be in the garden. Go, look there. Go on!"

"I looked there. Also in the library, the kitchen, the stable, and the garderobe."

Sophia's hand went to her mouth. She would not scream. She would not. If only she could think. "I'll look myself. You stay here. Don't let Bardas—don't let him—" She broke off before her voice spiraled into hysteria. "I'll come back. Watch well."

Everyone lay in his bed where he belonged, save Alf. His lamp burned still; a book lay on the table, his clothes folded neatly on the stool but his bed untouched. Sophia stood upon the Persian carpet and forced her mind to work. Where had Corinna not looked? The servants' quarters—no. Her workroom. The larger dining room for guests, and the lesser one for the family alone. No, and no. He might have gone out for some reason of his own, duty or the compulsion of prophecy.

No. He could not have done that. Not tonight. Then where—?

Abruptly she knew. She sprang forward half running.

She flung open Thea's door, panting, hand pressed to her side. Three pairs of eyes met her own, wide and startled. One was the kitten's, differing from the others' only in size. Sophia released what little breath she had in a cry of relief. "Alf! Thank God!"

He was already on his feet, snatching at his robe. She reached for him as a drowning man reaches for a lifeline. "Bardas—blood, so much blood, it won't stop, it won't—"

He clasped her hand for the briefest of instants. Then he was gone and Thea holding her up, clad only in her tumbled hair. Sophia clung to her with desperate strength. "I couldn't find him anywhere. I thought I would go mad."

"But you did find him." Thea drew on her robe, dislodging Sophia's hands with some difficulty. Once clad, she half led, half carried the other down the passage. "Alf will do all he can. You can be sure of it."

At the head of the stair, Sophia stopped suddenly. "You—you were—and I—"

Thea smiled. "It doesn't matter."

"But—"

"Come," Thea said in a tone which suffered no resistance.

With Alf laboring over Bardas and Corinna lending aid where he asked, Sophia regained her self-control. Thea brought wine for her, warmed with spices; she drank it without tasting it, mechanically, intent upon Alf's face. It was grave, absorbed, yet otherwise unreadable. She struggled to decipher it.

The coughing eased. Alf knelt now very still, one hand on Bardas' chest, the other smoothing the sparse white hair with absent tenderness. His face froze into a mask, white as death but with burning eyes.

Thea moved softly to stand behind him, hands resting on his shoulders. Sophia waited hardly breathing for she knew not what. The only sound was the rattle of Bardas' breath and the creak of Corinna's aging bones as she lowered herself to her knees. She crossed herself and began to pray.

A priest, Sophia thought. *I have to send for a priest.* But she did not move or speak.

Alf's face tensed. Sweat beaded his brow; almost invisibly he began to tremble. Light shimmered about him, a faint sheen like stars on silver.

A sound brought her eyes about. The door opened barely enough to admit a child. Nikki crept into her lap, blinking sleepily but holding her hand in a warm firm clasp. She held him to her and rocked him, knowing full well that it was not for his comfort that she did it but for her own.

The long night wheeled into dawn. The lamp flickered and failed; cold gray light crept into the room.

Alf sank back upon his heels. The rumble of Corinna's prayer caught and died. Bardas lay still, gasping but no longer coughing.

Sophia had no voice to speak. Alf raised his face to her, the same white mask but with eyes bereft of all fire. "I cannot heal him," he said softly and clearly, with all the weariness in the world.

She rose, setting Nikki on his feet. Slowly she made her way to the bed. Bardas turned his head a fraction. His eyes were clear but a little remote, as if his soul had already begun to withdraw from his body. He smiled at her; his lips moved with only the breath of a whisper. "It doesn't hurt anymore. It's just . . . a little hard to breathe."

Alf slid an arm beneath his shoulders and raised him a little, propping him with a cushion.

"Better," he sighed. "Come here, Sophia." She came and took his hand. It returned her clasp with a faint pressure, soon let go. All his strength bent upon the battle for breath. Yet he was losing it, inch by inch. It was not only the corpse-light of the winter dawn that touched his face with death. Slowly it spread, robbing his limbs of their warmth, advancing inexorably toward his heart.

His breathing faltered, rallied, caught. She covered his lips with hers. His eyes smiled his old, private smile. As she straightened, the smile touched his mouth. Slowly she drew back.

His body convulsed. Even before the spasm had ended in a torrent of blood, she knew that he was dead.

24

Sophia had no use for the extravagance of Eastern grief. She would dress all in black as befit a widow; she would forsake her perfumes and her jewels and refrain from painting her face. But the servants had their orders. No wailing; no excesses of lamentation. The house was still and silent, even the children muted, stunned. Later, when she thought of the day which followed Bardas' death, her first memory would be of Anna's face when she heard that her father was dead: the huge shocked eyes and the cheeks draining slowly of color, leaving her as pale as the corpse upon its bier. Irene wept immediately and wildly. Anna did not. She looked long at Bardas; touched his cold hand, half in love, half in revulsion; and went away without a word.

                              *   *   *

Alf found her in the stable, currying her pony till the dust flew up in clouds. It was warm there from the bodies of the beasts in their stalls: the pony, and the mules that drew Sophia's carriage, and the old dun mare which Bardas had ridden on his travels outside of the City. She whickered as Alf passed; he paused to stroke her soft nose and to feed her a bit of bread.

Anna ignored him resolutely. She laid down the currycomb; he took it up and began to groom the mare. There was a moment's pause before she reached for the brush.

He kept his back to her, working diligently. As he bent to inspect the mare's hoof, Anna sneezed. He did not glance at her. She had stopped her brushing altogether; he felt her eyes upon him.

He released the hoof and straightened. "Are you going to ride?" he asked.

"It's raining," she said flatly.

"Not anymore."

"I don't feel like it." Yet she clambered onto the pony's back, tethered as he was, and sat there stroking his neck.

Alf left the mare and brought out a crust or two for the pony.

"All he cares about is food," Anna said almost angrily.

"He likes his ease too. And you, when you spoil him."

"When I feed him." Carefully she unraveled a knot in the thick mane. Her brows were knit; her mouth was tight. She looked very much like her mother.

"Alf," she said abruptly, "what happens when somebody dies?"

He sat on the grain bin while the pony nosed his hands, searching for another tidbit. "Many things," he answered. "The body doesn't work anymore. The heart stops; the flesh grows cold. The soul—the self—goes away."

"Where?"

Under her hard stare, he raised his shoulders in a shrug. "I don't know. I've never been allowed to follow the whole way. After a while, the light is too bright. I have to turn back."

"Is that a story?" she demanded.

"No. I don't tell stories."

"Except true ones." Her eyes narrowed. "Why do people die?"

"The world is made so. Man lives his life as he wills, and if he is good, as God wills too. When the time comes, God takes him. Life, you see, is both a gift and a test. A gift because it's sweet and there's only one of it for every man. A test because it can be very bitter, and a man's worth is judged by how well he faces the bitterness. At the end of it he gains Heaven, which is all sweet and no bitter and wholly free from death."

"Father died." She said it as if she were telling him a new thing. "He went to Heaven."

"Yes. He went to the light."

"Everyone dies. Everyone goes to Heaven if he's good. Mother will die. Irene will die, and Nikki, and Corinna. I'll die. When I get old, I'll die." She studied her hands. Small narrow child-hands, sorely in need of a washing. "I'm not old yet. Father was old. Mother's not quite old. I don't want her to die too. She won't die. Will she, Alf? Will she?"

Despite the stable's warmth, Alf was suddenly cold. He spoke with an effort, keeping his voice quiet. "That is in God's hands."

Anna slid from the pony's back and stood in front of him. She was very pale. "Father died and went away. That's not him back there on the bed. Mother will go away too. I'll be alone."

"No." He took her cold hands in his warm ones. "Your mother will take care of you. If ever she can't, I'll be there. I promised your father that. And I keep my promises."

She shook her head slowly. "Everybody dies. You'll die too."

His fingers tightened. He relaxed them carefully and drew a deep breath. "Anna, I'm not like other people."

"I know that," she snapped impatiently. "You and Thea. You can talk to Nikki. You can make sick people well. But not Father. *Why* not Father?"

"God wouldn't let me."

"Then God is bad."

She glared at him in defiance, heart thudding, half expecting to be struck dead for the blasphemy.

He regarded her with a quiet level stare. "God cannot be bad," he said, "but He can let bad things happen for His own reasons. Death is only evil for those who love the dead. For the dead themselves, it's a joy beyond our conceiving. Imagine, Anna. No more sorrow and no more pain. No more sickness and no more fear. Only joy."

"You were crying too. I saw you."

"Of course I was. I loved him, and I'll miss him sorely. It was myself I cried for. Not your father."

She freed her hands and buried them in the pockets of her gown. He was silent. She wanted to hit him, to make him angry, to rid him of that maddening calm.

"I'm not calm," he said. "I'm only pretending. What good would it do if I screamed and cried and upset the horses?"

"I'd feel better."

"Would you?"

"Yes!" she lied stubbornly. But she added, "You're always pretending?"

"Most of the time. Monks learn how to do that."

"Monks are horrid. You're horrid. I hate you!"

"Why?" he asked.

She stared openmouthed. He stared back with wide pale-gray eyes. She plunged toward him, hands fisted to strike him; but her fingers laced behind his waist and her face buried itself in his lap, and all the dammed-up tears burst forth. He gathered her up and rocked her, not speaking.

It was a long while before she stopped. She lay against him. He was warm and strong and more solid than he looked. "I've got your coat wet," she said in a muffled voice.

"It will dry." He set a handkerchief in her hand; she wiped her face with it, sniffing loudly.

Her hair was in a tangle. He smoothed it with a light hand. She blinked up at him, her eyes wet still, but her mouth set in its old firm line. "If you go away," she said, "or die, after what you promised Father, I really will hate you."

"I swear to you, I'll neither die nor leave you. Not while you need me."

"You had better not." She slid from his lap and stood a moment. The likeness to her mother was stronger than ever. "I think I'll ride after all. Will you come?"

He nodded. "For a little while." He reached for the mare's bridle and turned toward her stall as Anna began to saddle the pony.

Bardas lay in his tomb beyond the City's walls. The long rite of grief was ended, the funeral feast consumed; the guests and the mourners had gone back to their houses. There remained only the Akestas, family and servants, in a house gone strangely empty.

Alf was the last to go up to bed. He had spent a long evening with Sophia, most of it in silence. There had been no need of words.

He bathed slowly, weary to the bone. They crowded him, all these humans, clinging to him, barely letting him out of their sight. He had not even been able to sleep in peace; Nikki had shared his bed every night since Bardas died.

But it was not Nikki he found there tonight. Thea sat in his usual place, combing her long free hair. She looked up as Alf hesitated in the doorway, but did not smile.

His heart thudded against his ribs. He quelled an urge to turn and bolt. "Where is Nikephoros?"

"I sent him to keep his mother company. She needs him. You," said Thea, "have me."

He tried to swallow. His mouth was dry.

"I know," she said. "I've left you alone too long. You've had time to think."

Carefully he closed the door behind him.

She laughed a shade too shrilly. "Poor little Brother. Has guilt struck at last? Thou shalt not look on a woman with lust in thine eye; thou shalt not know her carnally; and most of all, thou shalt not enjoy it."

"Particularly," he said, "when thine host is dying in thine absence."

"He would have died no matter where you were. He should have died months ago. But you kept him alive. In the end, God lost patience and came to claim His own."

Alf left the door to stand near the bed, but not close enough to touch. Her eyes upon him were bright and bitter. "When I was most off guard," he agreed, "God struck. It was His right."

"And now, in atonement, you've vowed to cast me off."

He advanced a step. She tilted her head back, the better to see his face. He spoke with care. "The nights have been long and dark. I haven't slept much. Mostly, I've been thinking. I've pondered sin and guilt and repentance. I've considered all that I am and all that I've taught and all that I've been taught."

Her lip curled; her eyes mocked him.

He continued quietly, weighing each word. "Yes, it is a lot of thinking, even for a scholar. I can't help it; it's the way I'm made. Just as you were made with mind and body in balance, thought and action proceeding almost as one. But even I can come in time to a decision."

"This time," she said, "when I leave, I won't come back. Ever."

He looked long at her. She could not hold his gaze; she glared fiercely at her hands, turning the ivory comb in her lap. She was all defiance over a hurt and a fear which she would not let herself acknowledge. So well she fancied she knew him.

"Thea." She would not raise her eyes. His voice firmed. "Althea, look at me."

She obeyed, a flash of gold-rimmed green.

He met it with cool silver and ember-red. "You know me very well, Thea. Yet you don't know me at all. What makes you think, now I've had all of you, that I'll ever let you go?"

She drew her breath in sharply, a gasp, almost a sob.

"Beloved." His voice was gentle. "Oh, I had all the thoughts you blame me for, and others besides. After all, I was sworn to chastity for a man's whole lifetime. But I was also trained in logic. And logic told me that nothing so sweet, indeed so blessed, could truly be a sin. I found light in it, but no darkness. Not where there was love."

She searched his face and the mind behind it, open wide for her to see. Suddenly, almost painfully, she laughed. "See, even I can be a fool! I knew how you would be. I *knew.*"

"I was. I flogged myself with guilt. But I must have imbibed a drop or two of your good sense. In the end, early this past morning when you stood night watch with the Guard, it won. I was going to make Nikki sleep tonight and come to you." He kissed her lightly, with a touch of shyness, for he was a novice still. "It's been a long while."

"Too long." She laughed again, more freely, as he dropped his robe and lay beside her. "How could I have forgotten? You were not only a monk; you were a theologian."

"And the theologian, though late in emerging, always gains the victory. An agile mind in a willing body, and the fairest lady in all the world. So much has God blessed me." He loosed the lacing of her gown. "I love you, Thea."

Her answer had no words, and needed none.

25

At Candlemas, as you know, Your Holiness, our forces took two great and holy trophies: the standard of the Roman Empire and the blessed icon of the Virgin which bears with it the luck of Constantinople. Shortly thereafter we received word that the usurping Doukas had disposed of his rivals, the young Emperor strangled in his prison cell, his father slain soon after by age, sickness, and grief. No bond of honor or treaty now compels us to keep peace. As Lent draws to its end in fasting and abstinence no less devout for that our circumstances force it upon us, we advance inexorably toward the conclusion of this conflict. Count Baudouin has sworn to celebrate Easter in Hagia Sophia. That, he will do, by God's will and the will of our army.

Jehan set down his pen and flexed his fingers. A few sentences more, and that would be the end of His Excellency the Cardinal Legate's latest epistle to the Pope; and His Excellency's secretary would be free for an hour to do as he pleased. The sun was gloriously warm, as if the past bitter winter had never been; he gazed longingly at it from the stifling prison of the Cardinal's tent, and swallowed a sigh.

Soon, he promised himself. Grimly he took up the pen again. Its tip was beginning to splay already after only a line. He needed a new quill. And none in his writing case; he had been meaning to replenish his supply and had kept forgetting.

A shadow blocked the sunlight in the tent's opening. That would be Brother Willibrord returning most opportunely from one of his endless Benedictine Offices. He had little love to spare for a sword-bearing Jeromite priest with pretensions to scholarship, but he carried an exceedingly well-stocked writing case.

"Good day, Brother," Jehan said, squinting at the robed shadow against the sun. "Could you spare a new quill for God's charity, or at least for the Pope's letter?"

Brother Willibrord said nothing. That was one of his few virtues:

silence. Even as Jehan turned back to his letter, the monk set the pen in his hand, a fresh one, well and newly sharpened.

"Deo gratias," Jehan said sincerely but rather absently, eyes upon the parchment. Now, where was he? . . . *the will of our army.* Yes. *After much deliberation, the captains have determined to assault the City with all the forces they can muster. The attack will commence before—*

He stopped. Brother Willibrord stood over him still, a silent and hopeless distraction. He looked up, barely concealing his irritation. "Yes, Brother?"

Alf smiled down at him, a smile that turned to laughter as Jehan's jaw dropped. "Indeed, Brother! Has all your labor made you blind?"

"Alf," Jehan said. He leaped up, scattering pen and parchment. "Alf? What are you doing here?"

"Fetching my hat," Alf answered. "Didn't I say I would?"

"That was months ago. *Months!* With every rumor imaginable coming out of the City, and some of them declaring you dead."

"You knew I wasn't."

"I did," Jehan admitted grudgingly. He pulled Alf into a tight embrace. "By all the saints! Next time you commit imaginary suicide, mind that you do it where I can get at you."

"If I can," said Alf, "I will."

"That's no promise." Jehan held him at arm's length and inspected him critically. "You look magnificent. A little tired, maybe. But magnificent."

Alf returned his scrutiny with a keen eye, running a hand down his side. Under the brown habit there were ribs to count. "You, on the other hand, could use a month or two of good feeding."

"It's Lent. I'm fasting." Jehan dismissed himself with a shrug. "All's well in the City?"

"As well as it may be," Alf answered soberly. And after a pause: "Bardas died just after Candlemas."

Jehan's jaw tightened. "I . . . couldn't have known. He was a good man. His family—are they—"

"The Akestas refuse to be daunted by so feeble a power as death. I'm the weak one. Do you know what Bardas did, keeping it secret even from me? Adopted me as his son and made me the guardian of his estate, to hold it in trust for his lady and his children. Not," Alf added, "that Sophia needs my help. She has a better head for business than I'll ever have."

Jehan stared, and laughed amazed. "You're a rich man. You. If only the Brothers could see you now!"

"Thank God they can t. I'm written down in the City as Theophilos Akestas, Greek, doctor, and adopted heir of a minor noble house." Alf shook his head, torn between pain and mirth. "There's irony in heaven and high amusement here below. It serves me right, says Thea, for being such an insufferable saint."

"Bishop Aylmer will laugh till his sides ache."

"He always has been certain that I'm one of God's better jests."

"He thinks the world of you." Jehan looked down at the unfinished letter and grimaced. "If you'll give me a moment to finish this, we can talk for an hour after."

"Finish it then by all means," Alf said.

Jehan bent to his task. *The attack will commence before the Ides of April.* He paused to dip his pen in the inkpot. *With reference to the quarrel between Father Hincbald and the Abbot of Marmoutier . . .*

Slowly Alf walked round the tent. Before the Ides of April. And March already at its end.

He stopped in front of an ornate crucifix and crossed himself without thinking. The tent walls seemed to close about him. Too many men had dwelt in this place for too long with too little care for cleanliness. And war, war everywhere, a great surge of power and purpose bent upon destruction.

"Alf. Alf, are you all right?"

Jehan was shaking him, peering anxiously into his eyes. "I left the City to get away from this," he said irritably: "fates, prophecies, and the firm conviction that the walls are about to fall on me."

His friend said no word but led him out into the free air. He drank it in great gulps, turning his face to the sun that now seemed less an enemy than a long-sought refuge.

Little by little his mind steadied. He smiled at Jehan a little wanly. "Someday, my friend, I'll manage to get through a day without scaring you out of your wits."

"I'm not scared. I'm used to you."

"I hope I gave you time to finish your letter."

"It's done." Jehan held up a worn and shabby hat adorned with a palm of Jericho. "Here's what you came for."

Alf took it and set it on his head. Arm in arm they walked through the camp, down to the shore of the Horn.

Men swarmed there, repairing and refurbishing the fleet: Saint Mark's mariners, with scarcely a glance to spare for a Frankish priest and his companion. They found a place of quiet amid the tumult, a curve of sand round a pool but little larger than the basin Alf bathed in.

Jehan slipped off his sandal and tested the water. "God's feet! It's cold!"

"It's still winter in the sea." Alf lay on his cloak, hands laced behind his head, hat shading his eyes. "In the City the earth is waking to spring. The almond tree is blooming in our garden; the children are making me teach them spring songs."

"Love songs?"

Alf glanced at Jehan, half smiling. "Irene asks for them. Anna groans and endures them. They're pretty enough, she admits."

"Especially if you sing them."

Alf's only response was a smile. Jehan sat and watched him, asking no more of him than his presence. The Horn stretched beyond him, aglitter in the sunlight, dividing the Latin shore from the walled might of the City.

"You know," Jehan said slowly, "you're an Akestas now. A Greek. An enemy."

"No, Jehan," Alf said, "not an enemy."

"That's not what anyone here would say." Jehan leaned toward him, intent. "Alf. Don't go back there. You don't have to fight, just to be here with your own kind."

"And what of the Akestas?"

"They can leave the City. Don't they have kin in Nicaea?"

Alf shook his head. "They won't go. Nor will I."

"You're all mad. There's war coming, can't you see? *War!* If we win you'll be condemned as a traitor. If we lose the Greeks will turn on you, a Latin in Greek clothing. Either way, the Akestas will suffer for harboring you. Do you want that?"

"They won't leave their city. I won't abandon them. They're my family now, Jehan. I'm bound to protect them."

Jehan stared at him. He was Alf still, but he had changed. Jehan remembered how he had felt in Saint Ruan's when he learned that Alf was gone and that Thea had gone with him. Angry at first, and jealous, and stricken to the heart.

One did not keep a friend by clutching at him. King Richard had said that, without even Jehan's assurance that one day he would see Alf again.

And yet. "There's no safety for you in Constantinople. Won't you see sense just this once, and escape while you still can?"

"I can't," Alf said.

"You don't want to."

"Maybe not." Alf rose and began to walk aimlessly. The other scrambled to follow him. He did not pause or glance aside. "Jehan," he said after a time, "Brother Alfred is dead. He can't rise again. It's not fair even to ask him to."

"I'm not. I only want you to be safe."

Alf gripped his arm and shook him lightly. "I love you too, brother. But I don't need a keeper."

"You need a good whipping," Jehan muttered.

Alf passed him, mounting a low hill. From that vantage he could see all the ordered sprawl of the camp, seething within and without, arming itself for battle. Ten thousand men, swelled with the Latin allies whom the Greeks had driven out of Constantinople: they were a strong army in the reckoning of the West. Yet they faced the greatest city in the world.

He turned toward it. Burned and battered though he knew it to be, riddled with dissension and cowardice, it stood firm about the curve of the Horn, held up with the pride of a thousand years of empire.

"She is old," he said. "She wavers and begins to fall. But no power of the West will long prevail against her."

"You've fallen in love."

"I've fallen into prophecy." Alf shook himself. "This was the wrong place to come to escape from it."

"How did you come here?"

"Witchery, of course," Alf replied.

Jehan nodded, unperturbed. "I thought so. That's what's different about you. You're freer with it. Freer all over. Almost like . . . well . . . Thea."

"She's labored long and hard over me." Alf kept his eyes on the City. "The end was a battle royal. She tried to make a man; the monk fought to remain as he was. She won."

There was a small pause, a bare concession to Jehan's priestly vows. The young knight broke through with a whoop. *"Eia!* I've won my wager."

As Alf stared, Jehan laughed aloud. "I knew you'd come to it sooner or later. Henry swore you never would; you're too saintly. That shows how well Henry knows you. *He* never heard you when you were still a pious monk, coming out with 'Lovely Flora' in place of an *Ave Maria*. And he's never had a proper look at Thea. How ever did you manage to resist her for as long as you did?"

"Ironclad idiocy," Alf answered. "You're a wretched excuse for a priest. Not only condoning sorcery but aiding and abetting it, and now rejoicing in a confession of open and thoroughly shameless fornication."

"Why not? I've just won Henry's best sword. And you look as close to happy as I've ever seen you. Unwanted wealth, forebodings of doom, and all."

"Everything has its price."

"Are you asking me for absolution?" Jehan asked, suddenly grave.

"No," Alf said. "If you gave it I'd refuse it. The Church frowns on everything I am and do."

"Not everything, and not all of us. Maybe I'm lapsing into heresy, but I don't think there's any sin in you."

"Thea would laugh. A theologian, she declares, can reason his way out of anything."

"That's the beauty of our art. How else can the Pope both deplore this war and make the best of it?"

"The same way a renegade Latin monk can throw in his lot with a family of schismatic Greeks." Alf drew Jehan into a brief embrace. "Our paths won't cross again until the war is over. Promise me something, Jehan."

"If I can," Jehan said warily, fighting down an urge to clutch at him and never let him go.

"You can," said Alf. "Whatever happens, victory or defeat, promise me this, that you'll do all you may to protect the women and children. I know in my bones that it's going to go ill for them. Very, very ill."

"I promise." Jehan caught Alf's hand. Once he had it, he could not say what he had meant to say. Only, "God be with you."

"And you," Alf responded.

And he was gone. Vanished like a flame in a sudden wind, and in Jehan's hand only empty air.

26

Alf knew well how Jehan had felt when he refused to take sanctuary outside of the City. For the thousandth time and with patience outwardly undiminished, he said, "Master Dionysios has done all that he may to make Saint Basil's secure. He's repaired the walls and strengthened the gates and hired guards to watch over them all. He's dismissed most of the students, and those doctors and servants who've asked for it; he's sent away the malingerers and the walking wounded. All of us who remain can take refuge in the hospital, with such of our kin as wish to go."

Sophia nodded. "I know that. I understand it. I give you leave to go and to take the children with you."

"But you won't come."

She shook her head. Grief had not changed or weakened her; the certainty of war had roused in her no senseless panic. Yet something had gone out of her. Joy; the deep delight in life which had lain beneath all she did or thought or felt. "This is my house," she said. "I won't be driven out of it by anyone. Not even you."

Alf sighed. "Very well. I stay here. I can't protect two places at once."

"No!" Her tone was almost angry. "I want the children safe and under guard in Saint Basil's, and I want you with them."

"They've lost a father. Will you deprive them of their mother?"

"I intend to come out of this with my life and my fortune intact. My family I entrust to you. If harm comes to any of them, I'll see that you pay a due and proper price."

"No one will touch them while I live. But, Sophia—"

"I'm content." She rose from her chair. "I'll speak with Anna and Irene. Nikki I'll leave to you."

As she passed Alf, he held out a hand. "Sophia," he said, not quite pleading.

She chose not to understand him. "Yes, you'll be wanting a servant. Corinna, I think. She's as strong as most men, if it should come to a fight, and she's loyal to a fault."

Alf opened his mouth and closed it again. Sophia smiled a small smile with no mirth in it, and left him standing alone.

Jehan shifted, searching in vain for a comfortable resting place. Men snored on either side of him, one with an elbow wedged in the small of his back; he winced and eased away from it. Water hissed and slapped against the ship's hull; below, in the hold, the horses stirred, uneasy in their nightlong confinement.

Cautiously Jehan rose. The deck seemed sheathed in metal, shimmering in starlight: rank on rank of armored men, each clad in mail with his head pillowed on his helm. Jehan picked his way through them, rousing grunts and drowsy curses, to lean upon the rail. Shields hung there for ornament and for protection. A fine brave sight they would be, come morning, each with its vivid blazon.

He ran his hand along the rim of his own. Its blood-red lion glared at the City in defiance of the sigil it bore, the banner of the Prince of Peace.

All hope of peace had died long since. The fleet lay off the farther shore of the Horn, heavily laden with men and horses, grotesque with the shadows of the towers built wall-high upon their decks, awaiting the dawn and the assault upon the City.

Soon now. It was black dark, but the air tasted of morning. Far in the east over the forsaken camp, Jehan thought he could discern a faint glimmer.

Among the ships, men had begun to stir, a low muttering that grew slowly louder, mingled with the chink and clash of metal, the thudding of feet on the decks, and the neighing of the horses in the holds.

The glimmer in the east swelled to a glow that conquered all the horizon. One by one the stars faded.

"Can't you sleep either?"

Jehan glanced at Henry. His face was a pale blur in the dawn light. "I never sleep before a fight."

"Praying?" asked Henry.

Jehan laughed shortly. "I save that for afterward. Especially when I'm not at all sure which side God is on."

"Then why do you fight?"

"Why not?" Jehan flexed his shoulders within his mail, and stretched. "His Eminence would be happier if I didn't. But I don't want to sulk in my tent like some shavepate Achilles when my friends are out risking their necks. Besides, I swore an oath. I gave my word when I took the cross, that I'd follow wherever the Crusade and the Doge of Saint Mark led. Should I be forsworn?"

"You have higher vows."

"The Pope himself set me free to follow my conscience. I would in any case, he said; the least he could do was make it legal."

It was light enough now for Jehan to see Henry's smile. "You were wasted on the Church, I think."

"No," Jehan said. "When this is over, if God spares me, I'm going back to being a monk again. Cloisters, hourly Offices, all the study I could wish for . . . I'll be dreaming of it out there when the fighting gets hot."

"You make it sound almost pleasant."

Jehan laughed truly this time, and freely. "Of course it is, the morning before a battle when I'm too shaky to sleep."

Henry grinned and filled his lungs with the morning air. "Fight beside me today, brother."

"Would I be anywhere else?" Jehan turned side by side with him and went to gird himself for the battle.

Well before dawn, the soldiers of the empire had ranged themselves along the walls that faced the Golden Horn. The farther shore was a shadow only, a presence in the night, but a presence grown deadly.

Morning crawled over Asia. Slowly the shadow-ships took shape, and after a long while, color. Every ship bore on its sides the shields of its men; from every masthead flew a banner or a pennon. The new sun struck fire upon their blazons.

"They're moving," muttered a voice among the Varangians.

Slowly, weighing anchor, raising sail, striving with oars against the current of the Horn.

A young Guardsman glanced over his shoulder. His eyes were bronze-gold; two minds gazed out of them, Alf's enfolded in Thea's. Within the walls across the half-cleared ruins of the fire rose the Hill of Christ the All-seer. A monastery crowned its summit; upon the hill before the gates spread the vermilion tents of the Emperor.

Silver flashed beneath the imperial banner. Trumpets rang; timbrels sent their clamor up to heaven. The Emperor's cry went up, a deep roar: "Christ conquers!"

And from the ships thundered the reply: "Holy Sepulcher!"

The air thickened with stones and arrows. Near Thea, a man bellowed in pain; his fellow nocked arrow to string and let fly. She swept up a heavy stone and hurled it with all her inhuman strength, well-nigh as far and as true as a catapult; another followed it, and another, and another. Upon the ships, shields bent and shattered; men toppled to the decks.

But the fleet advanced, all the power of the West gathered together, half a league from end to end. The first prow ground to a halt upon the shingle. Armed figures swarmed from it. Ladders swung up against the wall.

A galley ran aground full in front of Thea. From the tower upon its broad deck a bridge unfolded, crashing down over the parapet, bending under the weight of a dozen men.

On either side of Thea, Varangians gripped their axes. With a roar they sprang forward. Half hewed flesh and steel; half struck at the bridge, battling the Franks who would have bound it to the wall.

Thea turned her axe against the bridge. As she smote, she laughed. "The wind fights with us!" she cried. "Ho! There it blows!"

Southward, driving against the ships, thrusting them back. Of them all, but five had reached the walls; and those wavered, losing their precarious grip.

A sword glittered before her eyes. She parried it with a vicious, curving blow that whirled the swordsman about. He staggered upon the bridge and fell. Thea's axe crashed down where he had been. The bridge rocked. Two more axes struck it; three; half a dozen. With a groan of parting timbers it collapsed.

For an instant no one moved. One Latin only had set foot upon the tower. He lay dead, sprawled over the parapet. With a swift contemptuous gesture a Guardsman thrust him off. His body plunged to earth in the midst of a company of his fellows, a missile more deadly than any stone.

The Guardsman turned back to the rest, a feral grin upon his face. "That for the cursed Normans," he said.

"But he was a Fleming."

"Eh?"

Alf stared blankly up at Thomas' round puzzled face. He looked down. His body seemed thin and frail after Thea's robust Varangian-shape. It lay on a pallet in a small bare room, the air sharp-scented with herbs, the air of Saint Basil's. Nikki slept beside him, Anna and Irene guarded by Corinna across the small space. From the angle of the sun, it was full morning.

He rose, careful not to wake Nikki, smoothing his rumpled tunic. Thomas managed a creditable smile. "Isn't that like a child? Up

all night, determined not to miss an instant of the adventure; and
sound asleep by sunup."

Alf followed him out and eased the door shut. "It's an adventure," he conceded, "but it frightens them too."

"Of course it does. That's half the pleasure." Thomas looked
hard at him. "Were you having a nightmare when I came in?"

"No," Alf said, "not precisely a nightmare. Why did you wake
me? Is something wrong?"

"That depends on what you call wrong." Thomas was as grave
as he could ever be. "The Franks have attacked."

"I know."

"Know everything, don't you?" Thomas shook his head. "You
and the Almighty. And of course, Master Dionysios. He wants you up
and working. Just because you have a bed here, I'm to tell you,
doesn't mean you're ill."

"Or privileged." Alf shook back his tangled hair. "May I have a
bath first?"

"I'll pretend you didn't ask." Thomas grinned up at him. "Don't
take too long about it."

From the walls, empty now of enemies, Thea could see the sweep of
the battle. Most of the fleet had retreated out of catapult range, driven
by the brisk south wind. The shore was thick still with Franks, most
afoot, a few mounted on horses that slipped and shied upon the
shingle. But she had marked the companies which struggled back to
their grounded ships, straining to thrust them out into the open water.
More now as the sun sank. Those who fought on, fought against a
solid wall of Greeks.

Up on his hill the Emperor sounded his trumpets. Below the wall,
the Greeks gathered and charged. The army above them hurled a
new volley into the sea, mingled with that horror of the East, the
dragon-blasts of Greek fire.

And the Latins crumpled. Some few strove to hold fast; but their
strength had broken. All at once and all as one they gave way. One
ship and then another clawed away from the deadly shore.

The enemy had fled. The City had held against them.

"Victory!" roared the Guard. They laughed and whooped and
threw their axes up flashing in the sun. "Victory! Victory!"

Jehan stood in the stern of the last ship, leaning on his sword, paying
no heed to the few missiles which fell spent about him. All along that

lofty and impregnable wall, the ranks of Greeks had turned their backs and bared their buttocks to the fleet.

Beside him Henry laughed, a tired, bitter sound. "Now we know what they really think of us."

"Didn't we always know it?" Jehan wiped his blade on his cloak and sheathed it. "I can't believe it's ending this way. After all that's been said and done and promised . . ."

"You put too much faith in soothsayers."

Henry was jesting. Perhaps. Jehan pushed back his mail-coif and let the wind cool his burning brow. "So," he said, "we lost. What now?"

"A council," Henry answered him.

They held it on the northern shore of the Horn beyond the camp, in the empty shell of a church; their table was the broken altar.

Count Baudouin struck it with his fist. "Are we knights or women? We've lost a battle, true enough. We won the last one. Who's to say we won't win the third?"

One of the Frankish lords swept his hand in the direction of the City. "Against that? There are a hundred thousand Greeks inside those walls, and an empire full of them all around us. We lost a hundred men today; they lost none that we know of. How can we hope to face them?"

"How not?" Baudouin's eyes flashed round the assembly. "It's more than our hides we're fighting for. It's our honor. Are we going to let a herd of traitorous Greeks boast that they had the better of us?"

A young lord nodded eagerly. "They tricked us into setting up an emperor. Then they murdered him and told us all our treaties were worthless. Now they want to trample on our prowess in war. No man will ever be able to say that Thibaut de Langliers was bested by any coward of a Greek."

The younger men murmured, assenting; their elders sat silent. Baudouin faced the latter. "My lords! Does honor mean nothing to you?"

"Not," said a grim graybeard, "when it's so obvious that God is punishing us for our sins. We've pursued this unholy war against Christians, under Christ's cross; we'll die for it in God's wrath."

From among the bishops and the abbots, a man in Benedictine black leaped to his feet. "Not so!" he cried in a voice honed and trained at the pulpit. "God tests us; God tries us to find us strong enough to fight His battle. Have not the Greeks rebelled against our Church? Have they not denied the Lord Pope and twisted the words ui our Creed and turned the Mass into a celebration of pagan magnificence? God cries out against them. Woe, woe to my people, that have become even as the Infidel!"

Jehan, seated behind the Cardinal Legate, bit back the words that crowded to his lips. His Eminence sat like a graven image, making no move to suppress such idiocy. They were all in it now, priests and knights, disgustingly eager to set the seal of divine approval upon their folly. A just war, a holy war, a Crusade—God willed it; they had only to obey.

It was a lie. But it gave them strength. Their cheeks lost the pallor of fear; their eyes glittered with newborn courage. Someone began to chant a hymn: " 'Vexilla Regis prodeunt'—'Forth advance the banners of Heaven's King.' "

He would not sing it. He would not.

"Another attack!" a baron called out as the *Amen* died away. "We failed on the Golden Horn. Why not try the other side? The Bosporus, maybe, or the Sea of Marmora. All the Greek defenses face us here. We can take them from the other side and be in the City before anyone can stop us."

The council had waked to life and to hope. The Doge cut into the excited babble with a quiet word. "No," he said. "We cannot venture upon the Bosporus. Well before we could mount an assault, wind and current together would sweep us away from the walls into the open sea."

"That," someone muttered, "might be all to the good, if only we can be away from here."

Dandolo glowered in the direction of the dissenter. "Our loss today is a disappointment, but far from the disaster it appears to be. We need only to rest, to restore ourselves and our ships, and to prepare a new and stronger assault. Two days, my lords. Only two, and we can return in force to take the City."

"Two days' rest," said Baudouin, "and a new plan of attack. Aye, my lords. I swore I'd hear Mass at Easter in Holy Wisdom; that, I swear anew by God and all His saints, I shall do."

"So shall we all." Thibaut de Langliers sprang up with a cry. *"Deus lo volt!* God wills it!"

They echoed him, all of them, even the grimly smiling Doge. But Jehan set his lips together and said not a word.

27

"It's *not* a just war!"

The Cardinal Legate regarded his secretary with lifted brow. He was, perhaps, amused. He was certainly not afraid, although Jehan's white fury would have given most men pause. "Certainly," he agreed, "it is far from just."

Jehan struggled to master himself. "Out there," he said in a voice that was almost steady, "priests are saying Mass. They're preaching sermons. They're telling the men that God is with them. The Greeks are traitors, oathbreakers, worse than Infidels."

"I know. I can hear them."

"And you sit here? You read your breviary, say a prayer, meditate on the Infinite? You're the ambassador of the Holy See!"

"So I am." Pietro di Capua brushed a speck of dust from his scarlet sleeve. He was always immaculate, this prince of the Church; his fine white hands had never known greater labor than the raising of the chalice in the Mass. But the eyes which he fixed on the other were clear and sharp. "I know my rank and my station."

"Then use it!" cried Jehan, unabashed by the open rebuke. "You know what His Holiness thinks of all this. He excommunicated the Doge and all his followers with full and formal ritual after they took Zara. But those madmen from Francia have called them back to the sacraments and told them they're forgiven. Is the Pope's will worth nothing at all?"

The Cardinal shook his head slightly. "Have you been preaching that gospel to the army?"

Jehan drew in his breath with a sharp hiss. "I'm outraged, but I'm not insane. One of the bishops tried to get me to preach his lies, flattering me with foolishness about my famous way with words. I escaped before I said anything we'd all regret."

"So," His Eminence said. "As you have so bluntly reminded me, I am the vicar of the Vicar of Christ. Unfortunately I dwell in the midst of Gehenna. The army can escape this trap only by fighting; the priests are in like case. Should they preach what you would have them preach, and die for it, and drive the army in turn to its death?"

"I fight because I swore an oath, and because I can't bear not to. That doesn't mean I have to proclaim a lie from the very altar." Jehan leaned across the Cardinal's worktable. "My lord! Are you going to allow it?"

"I have no choice."

Jehan spun on his heel and stood with his back to the Cardinal, fists clenched at his sides.

"The Pope has no choice," His Eminence continued quietly. "The Church has a head, but that head is far away. The members are here, and strong, and accept no guidance. They will do what they will do, whether His Holiness wills it or no."

"He could condemn them from every pulpit in Christendom."

"Could he? Would you, Father Jehan?"

The title stiffened his shoulders and brought his head up. He swallowed hard. Slowly he turned to face the Cardinal. "My lord, I . . . forgive me. I presumed far too much."

The other did not quite smile. He was a small man, dark and inclined to plumpness, but in that instant he made Jehan think of Alf. "My son, you are forgiven." He made a quick sign of the cross over the bent head. "Go now. I need to meditate." His eyes glinted. "Upon, of course, the Infinite."

Jehan prowled the camp, restless and ill-tempered. It did his mood no good to see the men, knight and common soldier alike, laboring with new and firm purpose, preparing for the morrow. There were no idlers; the few who were not at work gathered round the priests, deeply and devoutly absorbed in prayer.

A commotion drew him toward the shore. Women's voices, shrieks and sobs, and the occasional sharp cry of a child. Under the hard eyes of a troop of monks, all the whores and camp followers crowded aboard a waiting ship. The army would sail to battle with all stain of sin washed away, all temptation banished as far as wind and oar would carry it. Great temptation, some of it, languishing against the guards, pleading to be left behind. Not one man yielded.

The last buxom harlot flounced onto the deck. Mariners sprang to draw up the plank; others weighed anchor. The ship slid slowly out into the Horn.

He watched it go, scowling so terribly that no one ventured to approach him. Women he could face. They only tempted his body, a hard battle but one he could win; for though he was young and his blood was hot, both his will and his vocation were strong. But there were worse temptations.

He had his sword with him; he had been meaning to try a round or two at the pells to work off his temper. Slowly he drew the bright blade. It was Henry's best, the winnings of his wager, the edges honed to razor keenness, the steel polished until it shone like a mirror. It could cleave a hair or a body with ease, needing only a firm hand upon the hilt. Chanteuse, he had named it, for it sang when he wielded it.

He swung it about his head, rousing its sweet deadly voice. But it would drink no blood this day.

It flashed home to its scabbard and fell silent. He was on his knees, sword upright before him, fists clenched upon the guards. The carbuncle upon the pommel blazed at him like a great fiery eye. Alf's eye set in a rim of silver, piercing him to the soul.

"I swore an oath," he whispered. "I took the cross. I promised . . ."

To slaughter Christians? The voice was like Alf's, remote and clear and not quite human.

"Schismatics," Jehan said. "Heretics. They deny the procession of the Holy Spirit from the Father and the Son, and ignore the supremacy of the Chair of Peter, and—"

Quibbles, said the other.

Jehan's jaw tensed; his mouth set in a thin line. He was closer to handsome when he was smiling, a lady had told him once. When he was angry he was frankly ugly.

Vain youth. The voice sounded both amused and impatient. *Do you intend to join in this final spasm of the war? Swordplay in plenty, great deeds of daring, and a place in a song at the end of it.*

"Aye," muttered Jehan, "the *Requiem aeternam*. Not that I care. I like to fight. It's simple, and it keeps me from thinking."

Yes. One must never think. That one's best-loved friend is there among the enemy; that all one's conscience cries out against this murder of Christian by Christian; that—

"Enough!" Jehan's ears rang with the power of his own cry. He bent his head upon his fists. The swordhilt was cold against his brow. More softly he said, "I've fought till now. I'll see it through to the end. Whatever that end may be."

Valhalla, most likely. You've earned it. All those battles against your soul's protests: Zara, and the conquest of the City before Alf ever came there. You've fought well and valiantly and gained the admiration of even the staunchest priest-haters. There's not a man in the army who can call you a shaveling coward or mock your long skirts. Ah yes; you're a man among these mighty men, and well you've proved it.

Jehan bit his lip until he tasted blood. That was not Alf's firm and gentle guidance. It was more like Thea, who could prick a man into madness with the barbs of her wit.

O bold brave Norman, earl's son, knight of Anglia, the world will marvel that you challenged the power of Byzantium. And perhaps, by God's will, won.

He squeezed his eyes shut. Warm though the sun was, he shivered convulsively; cold sweat trickled down his sides. Fight—he would fight, though it damned him. He was not afraid to die.

Truly he was not. No more than he was afraid of the women on the ship now far down the Golden Horn, riding the current into the open sea.

His trembling stilled. He opened his eyes. It came all at once, as they always said it did. Light; revelation. For a moment he was back in the West with a long anguished day behind him, driving himself to distraction with some complex question of logic or of philosophy, and then, without warning or transition, he knew. So clear and so simple; so beautifully obvious.

He rose slowly, cradling Chantcuse in his arms as if it had been a child or a woman. He was smiling. If his coy lady had seen him then, she would have conceded that indeed he was not ugly at all.

On this last Lord's Day before Palm Sunday, the City kept festival. The enemy was driven back, the Emperor's words echoing from Blachernae to Hagia Sophia and from the Golden Gate to the Golden Horn: "Never have you had so splendid an Emperor. All your enemies shall bow before me, and I shall see them hanged upon the walls they would have taken."

As the day wore toward evening, Alf left his labors and went up to the roof. The air was soft, the garden coming into bloom; birds sang there, piercingly sweet above the manifold sounds of the City.

Nikki had followed him. After a little, Anna came to settle on his other side. He laid an arm about each and held them close. From his vantage he could see the imperial tents on their hill. Thea lay in one of them, stretched out at her ease, half asleep, half watching the dice game in front of the open flap.

That is no place for a woman, Alf said sternly.

She laughed and rolled onto her back. A man's back and a man's body, with no hint in it of the truth.

He shuddered inwardly, unable to help himself. Witchery he was learning to accept, even to take delight in. But this went against nature.

Thea stretched luxuriously. *One day, my saintly love, you must try the shape of a woman. It would teach you a few valuable lessons.*

Thank you, he said, *but no. Do you insist on pursuing this devil's work?*

I'm defending the City. Rather well, I might add. We'll drive the Latins off yet.

He drew a sharp breath. A sudden chill had struck him, like a cloud passing over the sun. But the sky was clear. *Thea, I command you. Come back to Saint Basil's and put an end to this game of yours before it kills you.*

Now you see why I won't marry you. "Wives," intones the great but misguided saint, *"obey your husbands."* Though, she mused, *I probably wouldn't pay him any heed even if I were decently and lawfully wedded. I never met a man yet who had sense enough to command himself, let alone anyone else. Now a* woman . . .

Eve, having been created in Paradise, can be regarded as infinitely more blessed than Adam who was shaped outside of it. Alf's mind-voice softened although his will did not. *Thea, for once will you listen to this poor lump of clay? It's driving me mad to have you out there so far from me, so perilously close to death.*

I can take care of myself, she snapped.

Then, he said, *I'm coming to join you.*

She sat up appalled. *You are not!*

I can fight. I have a gift for it. I only need gear and weapons. Surely you can arrange that?

No!

Well then, I'll do it myself.

She struck him with a lash of power that staggered him where he sat.

He shook his head to clear it, and confronted her, determined as ever. *I promise I won't shame you, in battle or out of it.*

You never have and you never will. It's not shame I'm thinking of. It's plain good sense. There are enough and to spare of us fighters. We don't need another, not even one whose skill is pure witchery. But true and talented healers are few and far between. You belong where you are. Stop your foolishness and stay there.

She had the right of it, as usual. But the shadow lingered. He cursed his power that granted no clear foreseeing when he needed it most.

You're seeing the general slaughter, she said without the slightest sign of doubt. *That's all. And I don't intend to be part of it. I'm too fond of this handsome hide to let anyone spoil it.*

She would not yield. Nor could he force her, short of entering the camp and carrying her off bodily, a feat which he suspected was somewhat beyond him.

And, she added with a touch of smugness, *being what I am, I'd simply witch myself back again. Be gracious, Alf. Grant me the victory.*

He never knew for certain what he would have done, for a student burst upon him crying, "Master Theo! It's one of the women, the one who's been so ill—she's birthing too soon with too much blood and the child too large, and Master Dionysios says the law be damned, with Mistress Maria gone we need you."

She pursued him with the last of it, finding herself entrusted with the care of the two children. Their rebellion gave her more than enough to think of; she gave up her effort to catch him and settled to the task he had left her.

Night had long since fallen when Alf straightened from his task. The woman was dead. Her daughter lay weak but alive in the arms of a wet-nurse. The woman surrendered her when he asked, with some surprise; he cradled the small body tenderly, looking down into her clouded eyes. "Ah, child," he murmured, "what a place and a time you chose to be born in, and no mother to ease your way for you."

They were staring at him, all the women there, most in wonder, a few in disapproval. He regarded the last with weary amusement. "Our Lord healed women, did he not? and he himself neither woman nor eunuch. Then why not I?"

He left them to ponder that, walking slowly, weary to the bone. And battle tomorrow, with such darkness in the thought of it that his mind shied away. He had to sleep, or he could not endure what must be.

But there was no mercy in Heaven tonight. Thomas met him at the door of the sleeping-room, his face for once utterly serious. Over his head Alf could see empty beds, and Nikki huddled with Anna. They looked both miserable and furious, their eyes red with crying. There was no sign of Irene or of Corinna.

"Gone," Thomas was saying. "Both of them gone. Irene first, and Corinna went after her."

Anna stood up, breathing hard. "They went home. Irene swore

she would. She said one of us should stay with Mother. It was going to be me. It was *supposed* to be me!"

"Corinna will bring her back," said Thomas with confidence he did not feel.

"Corinna *won't!* Corinna thought Irene was right. I could tell. Now they're home and I'm here, and I'll hit you if you try to keep me in."

Alf breathed deep to calm himself, to gather what strength he had left. "I'll go and get them. Anna, if you try to follow me I'll lock you up and set a guard over you."

As he turned, he swayed. Thomas caught him. "You're not going anywhere either, my young friend, except to bed."

He shook his head, resisting. "I have to go. It's deadly for them there."

"It will be worse for you if you fall over before you get there. Now, lad. In with you. In the morning you can fetch them, if the Lady Sophia hasn't already sent them packing."

"Not tomorrow. No time. I must—" Darkness swooped close; he struggled to banish it. It retreated; he was lying down and Thomas bending over him, undressing him with plump deft hands. He resisted, but his body would not heed him.

"Thea," he breathed. "Witch! Let me go. Let me . . ."

His voice faded. The darkness covered him.

28

Once again Jehan beheld the dawn from a crowded deck. Yet it was a new dawn, and he had slept well and deeply, without fear or foreboding.

He yawned and stretched. The wide sleeves of his habit slid back to reveal the glint of mail beneath. He turned from his post and picked his way to the cabin.

Henry emerged from the reeking gloom, rumpled with sleep, stifling a yawn. "How goes the morning?"

"Bright and clear and a good wind blowing," Jehan answered, bowing to Count Baudouin, who stepped past his brother to peer at the sky.

The Count turned his narrowed eyes on Jehan, taking him in in the pale light. "What, priest! You're in the wrong uniform this morning."

Jehan smiled. "No, my lord, it's my proper one."

"Mail under it," said Henry, gripping his arm and finding it steel-hard. "No sword, man? What foolishness is this?"

"Not foolishness. A vow."

"To die under the walls of Constantinople?"

Jehan shook his head, still smiling. "I'll be with you in the battle. I promised you that. I didn't promise to carry a weapon."

"You've gone mad." Henry looked a little wild himself, holding hard to Jehan's arm, glaring at his brown habit.

"I'm wearing mail," Jehan said. "I'll carry my shield. I won't burden any man with fear for my safety. But I'll carry no weapon against a Christian in battle."

Baudouin seized him and spun him about, tearing him from Henry's grasp. So like they were, those brothers, and so different. Baudouin was clever, Jehan decided, and ambitious, and reckless when it served his purposes. Henry was wise, which was a far rarer virtue.

The Count's eyes upon Jehan were both cold and burning. "Why?" he demanded. "Why now?"

"I'll help you take the City, my lord," Jehan said, "but I'll kill no Greek doing it."

Baudouin bared his teeth in a mirthless smile. "Ah," he said. "So. What did he say to you, that white-faced witch, when he crept like a thief into our camp?"

"Witch, my lord?" Jehan asked. "Thief? I've had no dealings with any such creature."

"Don't lie to me, priest. What did he say? How much did he give you to betray us?"

In spite of Jehan's control, his lips tightened and his eyes began to glitter. "My lord," he said, cold and still, "I never gave you cause to insult me. If by your words you mean that you saw me with Master Alfred a fortnight past, neither he nor I made any secret of his presence here."

"All the more clever of him to lull our suspicions while he spied on our army."

"If you believe that of Alfred, my lord, nothing I say will make any difference to you."

"My lord!" someone called. "My lord Baudouin!"

The Count paused for a long moment, eyes locked with Jehan's. The priest did not falter. Abruptly Baudouin turned on his heel. "Take him with you," he rapped over his shoulder to his brother, "and mind you watch him. At the first false move, kill him."

Jehan stood still, face to face with Henry. The young lord was pale—with anger, Jehan realized. Even in battle he had never seen Henry angry.

"Pay him no heed," Henry said after a moment, keeping his voice light with a visible effort. "He's never in his best humor before a fight."

Jehan shook his head. "No, my lord. He's right, as far as he goes. It does look suspicious, Alf being where he is and what he is, and now this sudden whim of mine. There'll be no duel of honor fought between us."

Henry's eyes upon him were dark with worry. "You aren't ill, are you?"

Jehan laughed aloud. "Ill? I? Never! Here, the sun's almost up and you're hardly out of bed. Well; they said of Alexander that he slept like a baby before a battle, and had to be shaken awake to get to the field on time. That's a reasonable precedent."

"You're well enough," Henry said, reassured. "But, Jehan, that vow of yours—"

"Is between myself and God, and you'll not trouble yourself with it. Now where's your lazy lout of a squire? You don't even have your surcoat, let alone your sword. Did you even remember to bring your helm?"

Henry laughed and let Jehan herd him into his squire's waiting arms. Even as he moved the trumpets rang, rousing the fleet to battle.

It was the same long line, each of the forty great rounders mounted with a tower. Yet in place of the singlefold assault which had failed so dismally, the Doge had bound the ships together in pairs, two towered ships for each tower of the City which defended the Golden Horn. Behind them on the freshening wind sailed the lesser vessels, bristling with armed men.

The city awaited them with its full might. Every inch of wall and tower seemed rimmed with steel, a wall of men above the walls of wood and stone.

A lone arrow traced its arching path over the water to fall spent upon the deck of the foremost ship. There was a breathless pause. The Latin archers fitted arrow to string and quarrel to crossbow.

As one, City and fleet let fly.

The City's barrage was terrible, not arrows alone but stones too great for a single man to lift. But Saint Mark's mariners had guarded against them with walls of timber woven with vines. The stones struck with unerring aim, bounded back from the limber shields, fell into the sea.

Steadily the ships advanced. Close under the walls, in a hail of stones and arrows and a searing rain of Greek fire, they dropped anchor. All the shore, like the walls above it, was black with men, that same unyielding army which had driven the Franks already into the sea. They sang and they shouted; their words would have made Jehan's ears burn if he had been a proper pious priest.

One after another the smaller ships beat toward the land. Greek hands and spears thrust them back. Men leaped from them, waist-deep in water. The Greeks surged to meet them.

Jehan kept to his ship. Henry had commanded it, holding his men back with hand and voice and sheer force of will. Yet, command or no command, and in spite of the vow he had sworn, Jehan yearned toward the struggle.

The Greeks fought like demons, yielding not an inch although the sun crawled up the sky and the water reddened with blood. Latin blood, most of it. The City was standing fast. Again, thought Jehan. They were brave after all, those scheming Byzantines.

The sun touched the zenith. Jehan squinted at it. A breeze fingered his hair, freshening as he paused, blowing from the north. The ship bucked underfoot and tugged at its anchor.

Shouts and cries drew his eyes to the wall. One of the great ships lunged against its cable, the bridge swinging loose from its tower. To the very end of it clung a small desperate figure.

It struck the edge of the wall. The single Latin clung for his life, hands locked upon the tower of the City, feet hooked through the bridge. Greek steel flashed down upon him.

Again wind and water surged, thrusting bridge and tower together. A second reckless warrior lunged across the narrowing space, over the hacked and bleeding body of his fellow into the Varangian axes. But he, well armored, sustained their blows and drew his sword. With a shrill yell he fell upon the defenders.

They fell back before him. Latins swarmed behind, binding bridge to tower, overwhelming the Emperor's forces. Full before his eyes they did it as he sat his white stallion on the Hill of the All-seer, raging at the craven weakness of his army.

The wind whipped attacker and defender alike and rocked the

great ships upon their moorings. The bridge, fast bound to the tower, groaned under the strain. The tower itself trembled; for it was Mourtzouphlos' second and lesser rampart, built of timber upon the solid stone of the wall.

Far below upon the deck the captain bellowed upward, "Cast off! Cast off, you fools! You'll pull the damned thing down on us!"

The last of the Latins whirled about, hacking at the ropes with their swords, while beneath their feet the tower swayed and groaned. With an audible snap the last line parted. The ship swung free.

But the tower was won. The last Varangian fell at its foot; upon its summit the Franks raised a roar, brandishing their swords. "Holy Sepulcher!" they cried. "Holy Sepulcher!" A banner caught the wind above them, the proud blazon of their lord, the Bishop of Soissons.

"Trust a priest to take the first honors," Henry said, standing beside Jehan.

"The laymen are following," Jehan said. "There! Another's fallen to us. Bracieux, that is, the old war hound. He never could bear to be outfought."

"Come to think of it," mused Henry, "neither can I." His grin flashed round the circle of his knights. "Well, sirs? Is it time?"

"Aye!" they shouted back.

"Then what are you waiting for? Over the side with you!"

The wall of Greeks had broken under the tide from the West; great gaps lay open within it. Through one such Henry plunged with his men close behind and Jehan at his right hand. The wall loomed above them, poised surely to fall upon them. They stumbled over dead and groaning wounded, advancing in close company.

Jehan thrust an elbow into Henry's mailed ribs and set his helm against the other's. "Look. There. A gate!"

A postern, walled up but plainly visible. The company bolted toward it, unlimbering bars and pickaxes. Quarrels rained down upon them, and stones as huge as hogsheads, and a torrent of pitch searing all it touched.

"Shields!" Jehan roared. "Shield wall!" He flung up his own; others jostled with it, overlapping, shielding the heads of the men who tore at the wall.

It was dim under the laced shields, as clamorous as any smithy Jehan had ever heard, reeking with sweat and pitch and the sulfur stink of Greek fire. His arm rocked under the force of a falling stone; but he grinned within his helm and braced his shield arm with the other to ease the strain.

Mortal flew under the blows of the pickaxes; stones loosened and fell, pried out with daggers and even swords. Light stabbed through a chink. The men pounced upon it, tearing at the stubborn stone, widening the gap.

A young knight tore off his helm and thrust his head into the opening, jerking it back with a cry. "Greeks! Bloody Greeks—thousands of them!"

Jehan laughed, short and sharp. "You laymen! Can't you go anywhere without a priest to lead you?" He tossed down helm and shield and shouldered through the press, bending to thrust himself into the gap.

Henry cried out behind him. "You fool! They'll kill you!"

A pickaxe lay close to his hand. Its haft was warm still from the hand of the man who had held it, a solid and satisfying weight. He crawled forward with it into a rough-hewn shallow tunnel with a mass of yelling faces beyond. A strong hand seized his ankle; he kicked violently, striking something that yielded and groaned in Henry's voice. The fingers snapped open. He scrambled forward, half falling into open air.

Stones hailed about him; Greeks closed in upon him. He roared like a cornered lion and charged, brandishing the pickaxe like a club. The Greeks shrieked and fled.

He stopped, breathing hard. No one menaced him. No one even dared to face him.

"It's clear!" he bellowed through the gap. "All clear!"

Henry was the first to pull himself through, with the others hard upon his heels, spreading along the wall in a wary line. One had brought Jehan's shield; he settled it on his arm, letting the pickaxe fall. Now, he thought, the enemy would come and sweep them all away. Now, truly; for as he looked up, he gazed full upon the Emperor's hill rising before him, a long open slope, new green with spring. Near the summit a great force gathered with the Emperor at its head. Trumpets rang the charge; timbrels set its swift pace.

"Stand fast," Henry said, low and clear. "For your honor, my friends, stand fast."

Each man set himself, feet braced, shield raised, sword at the ready.

The Emperor charged.

The thin line held firm.

The white stallion slowed. The Greeks faltered. Mourtzouphlos wheeled about; the trumpets sounded the retreat.

The Latins stared, stunned.

Henry struck his sword upon his shield, rousing them with a shock. "You—you—you. That gate yonder—open it. We're going to take the City!"

They tore apart the iron bars with swords and axes and flung the great gates wide. The wind blew fresh and strong upon their faces.

From the ships a shout went up. The sailors of Saint Mark drove their vessels to the land. Men and horses poured forth through the gate, into Constantinople.

The Greeks had fled from a handful of men on foot within their city. Knights in full panoply, mounted upon the great chargers of the West, sent them flying in panic. The Emperor himself was swept into the tide of terror and borne away.

The sun hung low over the walls and turrets of the City, casting long shadows upon the streets. In a great square under the cold eyes of old gods and emperors, the Latin army gathered. Weary though they were, spattered with blood, many limping with wounds, they counted scarce a handful of dead. All the blood was Greek blood.

Jehan sat on his stallion in grim silence. No Frank within his reach had slain any but the Emperor's soldiers, but his reach was no longer than one man's could be. He had done little good. By far the greatest number of slain were unarmed citizens, old men, women and children.

The Latins drew together now, as the heat of their blood cooled and it sank in upon them that they had dared in their small numbers to violate the greatest of all cities. All about them the labyrinth of streets and passages glittered with hostile eyes. Surely at any moment the enemy would surround them and hew them down.

Their lords gathered in the center of the square, dismounting stiffly, greeting one another with weary courtesy. The Doge stood in the very midst of them, erect and in full armor, with his sword in his hand.

Jehan nudged his stallion closer to halt beside Henry's bay, exchanging a glance of recognition with the squire who held the bridle.

"We have won," the Doge said in his strong old voice, "for the moment. All this quarter of the City is ours. But the rest holds still against us."

"God save us all," muttered one of the barons, crossing himself.

"We'll have to fight for every alley. It will take us a month at least of hard work before we can claim the victory."

Count Baudouin spoke clearly and sharply. "What use to count the hours? We hold what we hold. I for one will not let go one inch of it."

"Commendable," said Marquis Boniface, "and better certainly than despair. But we can fight no more tonight."

The Doge sheathed his sword with a firm practiced motion. "No; we cannot press the battle further before morning. Let us mount guards within the City to keep watch against attack. The bulk of the army shall camp by the sea walls to keep open the path of escape. And mark me well, my lords: Let no man of guard or army stray out of the sight of his fellows. Cowards the Greeks may be in open battle, but in the dark and upon their own ground, they are deadly."

"Born thieves and cutthroats." Baudouin turned toward the hill which the Emperor had abandoned, where the tents glowed crimson in the sunset, glinting with gold. "There," he said, "I shall mount my guard."

Marquis Boniface fixed him with a hard stare. "I shall make my camp on the Middle Way, as near to the Forum of the Bull as I may go. For," he said, "one man at least should guard against the greatest massing of the enemy."

Baudouin smiled. "My valiant lord. I'll think of you when I lie in the Emperor's bed."

"Which," said Boniface, "is also a coward's."

Henry stepped swiftly between them, catching Baudouin's hand as it fell to his sword hilt. "My lords! Haven't you exchanged blows enough with the enemy that you have to turn on each other?" Under his steady brown eye they subsided, glaring at one another but saying no word. Henry smiled and bowed to them, and again to the Doge. "I, for my part, am minded to keep watch over the servants and eunuchs barricaded in Blachernae. If my lords will agree to it?"

They all nodded assent. "Go," said the Doge, "do as you will. In the morning we shall renew the battle."

Henry took his charger's bridle from the squire's hand, flashing a smile to Jehan, and swung lightly astride. "Until morning, my lords, God be with you."

Anna had camped all day with Nikki atop the roof of Saint Basil's. She saw the towers taken; she saw the gates flung open and the

Emperor routed by the very sight of the knights in their bright armor; and she saw the army's gathering and its swift dispersal.

Alf was with her at the last of it, his day's labor over, his soiled robe laid aside for the only one he had to spare, his best one of pale gray silk embroidered with silver. He looked, Anna observed, as if he were going to a banquet.

They watched in silence as the sun sank and Latin fires kindled before the Emperor's tents. The invaders had pulled down the imperial standard and put up their own, bright and crude as it was, snapping proudly in the wind over the conquered camp.

Anna clenched her fists at her sides. "Why did my people run away? *Why?*"

"They were afraid," Alf answered gently.

She stamped her foot. "They were cowards! Everyone's a coward. Look at all those people down there like an anthill when you kick it, yelling and crying and trying to run in all the wrong directions. *I'm* not running. I'm staying here. And if any of those barbarians tries to break in on me, I'll kill him!"

"I'm one of them," he pointed out.

"You don't count," she said. "You're an adopted Greek. Though maybe you're ashamed to be one, now you've seen what cowards most of us are."

"Your people are civilized. Civilization has never been much good against a determined army of barbarians." Alf shivered slightly, for her benefit. "It's getting cold. Come down to supper and let the City fend for itself for a while."

Saint Basil's was quiet, but not calm. The eyes of healers and sick alike gleamed white, afraid; many prayed softly, a droning murmur.

If there was fear within those guarded walls, there was panic without. As the night deepened, a crimson furnace-glare stained the gathering clouds. For the third time Latins had set fire to the battered and beaten City. Flames raged through the streets along the Golden Horn, a burning wall between the Greeks and the invaders, licking against the foot of the All-seer's hill.

Alf walked slowly down the street which led from Saint Basil's to the Middle Way. In the darkness, lit by the sullen light of the fire, the great thoroughfare was like a road in Hell. People thronged upon it, fleeing the City's center, laden with their children and their belongings, shrieking and weeping and praying in loud voices.

The side ways were quieter, a quiet born of terror. Behind the barred gates men buried or concealed what treasures they had, while their women and children cowered, awaiting the end of the world.

Alf turned aside from the tumult to a street which curved past one of the City's thousand cisterns, a small lake set in a garden and surrounded by high narrow houses. As he passed from stone pavements to the grass of the garden, he paused. The street was full of fleeing figures, but among them advanced a torchlit company. The man at its head glowed in a rich cloak of crimson and gold; armor flashed beneath it and on his head blazed the jewels of a crown. His voice rasped over the cries of panic, harsh yet penetrating. "People of the City! Romans! Why do you flee? The barbarians are within our walls, caught like the fly in the spider's trap. We have but to fall on them and obliterate them." He seized a man who ran wildly past. "You—where are you running? Have you forgotten all the pride of our empire? We have them, I say! We have them where they cannot escape. Come with me and drive them out. Come with your Emperor!"

With an inarticulate cry, the man broke free and fled.

Mourtzouphlos' face was livid in the torchlight, suffused with fury. He pressed forward against the current, shouting, "Are you men or worms? All the world will mock us and call us cowards, who had the enemy within our grasp and let him conquer us."

No one heeded him.

Alf stood motionless upon the grass. His hood had slipped back, his cloak blown away from the silver robe.

Mourtzouphlos drew near to him, silent now, his face a mask of despair. The torch flared in a sudden gust.

The Emperor stopped, staring at the apparition on the hill above him. Slowly he moved closer, motioning to his torchbearer to raise the brand higher. Alf's form leaped out of the darkness, all white and utterly still.

"A statue," muttered the Emperor.

Torchlight struck Alf's eyes and kindled them.

Mourtzouphlos' breath hissed in the silence. The torch wavered as the bearer recoiled, crossing himself. "Stand, you fool!" the Emperor snarled. Mustering all of his courage, he advanced, stretching out a hand. Marble, it should be. Cold, solid marble. Naught else.

"Your Majesty," Alf said.

The Emperor froze.

"Sire," said the apparition, "I am no graven image."

Mourtzouphlos snatched his hand away, but not before he had

felt the warmth of flesh and the smoothness of silk. But he was in no way comforted. "You. Angel, demon—what are you?"

"Neither, Majesty, only one of God's lesser servants. How is it that you walk the City tonight?"

An angel, the Emperor thought. Or as close to one as made no matter. He was of a piece with this terrible night, this shattering of the world that had been Byzantium. It would not rise again. Its people were soft, weakened by centuries of luxury and power, rotted to the core.

Alf shook his head sharply. "Not so, my lord! There's strength in the City still."

"Where?" demanded Mourtzouphlos. "Not in any quarter which we still hold. I've worn my feet to the bone and my voice to a thread, and not one man will follow me. Not one! They flee, all of them, and curse me if I hinder them. Terror is their Emperor tonight, not Alexios Doukas."

"How can they follow you if you yourself despair? You speak brave words, but your heart does not believe them; and your people know it."

"My people are groveling cowards!" Mourtzouphlos tore his crown from his head and cast it on the ground. "Let the filthy Latins rule them. They deserve no better."

The crown lay upon the grass, a splendid glittering thing half hidden in Mourtzouphlos' shadow. "Your Majesty," Alf said quietly, gazing at it, "you know not what you say. You loved your city once. You fought for it when no other man would. Will you surrender now? Remember your own words! The Latins are trapped and cannot escape save past you, for they have set fire to their own path of retreat. If you fall upon them now, you can defeat them. If you do not . . ." Alf raised his eyes. They were terrible. "If you do not, my lord, then this city shall see such horror as she has not seen in all her thousand years of empire. The sack of Rome herself was nothing to what this shall be. For Rome was rich, but Constantinopolis is the richest city in all the world."

"Constantinopolis is dead. She died the day that thrice-damned fleet came within sight of her."

"The Franks have no knowledge of that. They wait in dread for you to smite them. Will you let them conquer out of senseless fear?"

"They have conquered." Mourtzouphlos' voice was flat.

Alf lifted his hands. "Then truly the City is dead, and you have killed her. May your fate be no better than that to which you have sentenced your people."

Mourtzouphlos drew himself up. His eyes glittered; his fingers worked. And yet he laughed, hoarse and wild. "God Himself has damned us all. Tell Him for Mourtzouphlos, angel of the bitter tongue; tell Him that I laughed at Him. He may doom and He may damn, and He may make my empire a sty for Latin pigs to wallow in; but my City was my City. There shall never be another like her." He stooped and snatched up the crown and turned, swirling the splendor of his cloak. That was the last Alf saw of him: a guttering torch and a flare of crimson, and the glitter of the jewels in his crown.

29

Jehan sat up abruptly. It was dark in the tent, but through the flap he could see the gray light of morning. Someone stood there. Henry, he saw, narrowing his sleep-blurred eyes; and another beyond him speaking rapidly in a low voice.

Beneath and about the muttered words, Jehan heard a deep roaring like the sound of the sea: voices shouting and cheering.

He groped for his sword, remembered with a start that he had left it on the other side of the Horn. The others were stirring now, knights and squires of Henry's household, and Jehan's own long-faced Odo, fumbling for their weapons as Jehan had. "An attack?" one mumbled. "Have the Greeks attacked?"

Henry turned quickly. "The Greeks?" He began to laugh softly, and caught himself. "No, sirs, the Greeks have not attacked. The Emperor fled in the night, and his army has surrendered to my lord brother on his hill. The City is ours. We rule in Constantinople!"

They all leaped up, shouting, questioning, fouling one another with their weapons. Jehan fought his way through them and confronted his friend. "My lord. It's true?"

Henry gestured to his companion, a sturdy man with a lined intelligent face. "Can I doubt the Marshal of Champagne? He rode through the City with a small escort, and no one molested him. We're masters of the City. We've won the war."

Jehan shook his head in disbelief. Then he raised it, cocking it. "Then those are our men."

The Marshal nodded. "The sack has begun."

"But," Jehan said, "it was decided there was to be no looting."

"Tell that to ten thousand victorious Franks," the Marshal said dryly. "My lords, I'm for the Count's camp again before the army goes quite mad with joy. Have you any messages for me to carry?"

"Only," said Henry, turning his eyes to the loom of the palace wall, "that henceforward he can send his dispatches to me within Blachernae."

The Marshal bowed and took his leave.

Jehan hardly saw either of them. "We've got to stop the sack."

Henry shook him lightly, recalling him to himself. "Breakfast first, and a council. After that, the palace. And then, my dear priest, you may save as many souls as you please."

Well before either meal or council was ended, the gates of the palace swung wide. Henry's troops, restive already with their lords' slowness, drew into rough formation.

But no army descended to sweep the Latins away. A single figure rode forth on a gray mare, escorted by tall guards, each with an empty scabbard and no spear in his hand. They advanced steadily until they met the leveled spears of the foremost rank. The rider dismounted and spoke for a moment, too far and soft to be heard from Henry's tent. At a bark from their sergeant, two Flemings lowered their spears and seized the Greek. He made no effort to resist, even when they searched him, stripping him of all but his silken undertunic.

Henry was on his feet. "Enough!" he called out. "Return the man's belongings to him and bring him to me."

He received his garments, but was given no time to don them; with them bundled in his arms and two stout Flemings flanking him, he came before the young lord.

A fine elegant creature he was, Jehan thought, even in this state; he bowed smoothly, with all courtesy, and said in passable Latin, "Greetings to my lord."

Henry frowned. "Please, sir, dress. And," he added with a swift cold glance at each of the Flemings, "please be certain to reclaim your jewels."

Those hardened faces moved not a muscle; but when the eunuch held out a slender hand, the Flemings emptied their pouches into it. He dressed then, quickly and without embarrassment, and faced

Henry with a smile and an inclination of the head. "Michael Doukas gives thanks to my lord."

"No thanks are necessary," Henry said. "You have a message?"

The eunuch sighed just visibly. Ah, his eyes said, these impetuous Latins. Aloud he murmured, "My lord is wise and courteous, after the fashion of his people. I, who was but the poorest of His Sacred Majesty's poor chamberlains, come now to you as a suppliant. His Serene Highness has departed, leaving his palace unguarded and his city in disarray. We of his followers know not where to turn. We have heard my lord's praises, even here where honest praise is rarer than the phoenix. Will my lord please to take us and our palace into his protection?"

Behind Henry, his barons muttered. A sword or two hissed from its sheath. "My lord!" cried a grizzled knight. "Will you trust these slippery Greeks?"

The rest echoed him, some of them in terms which would have sent a Latin flying for his sword. Michael Doukas merely smiled.

Jehan rose, towering over them all. The eunuch's eyes ran over him. "My," he said, "what a great deal of man that is."

"Enough," growled one of the knights, "for both of you."

Jehan schooled his face to stillness. "My lord, I think he can be trusted."

"Why?" demanded Henry.

"He's as treacherous a Byzantine as ever haunted an emperor's court. But now he's in a corner. We'll overrun his palace whether he surrenders or not. This way he has a chance of escaping with his skin intact."

"And perhaps with that of a friend or two into the bargain?"

Michael Doukas looked from lord to priest and smiled. "No, my lord, you think too well of me. The holy Father is quite accurate. And, perhaps, a shade more intelligent than he looks."

"A shade," Henry said dryly. "Very well, we accept your surrender. You'll come with us, of course. Close by me, if you value your life as much as you pretend."

"It is my most precious possession." Michael Doukas bowed low. "I am entirely at my lord's disposal."

"Come then," Henry said, striding toward his horse.

The calm of Saint Basil's broke soon after sunrise. The Latins' rampage had not yet reached that quarter save for a distant and terrifying tumult, but the wounded had begun to make their way there as best they could. Crawling, some of them, or staggering and carrying others worse hurt than they. The gates opened for them and shut again, with the strong company of Master Dionysios' guards at arms within.

"They're beasts," said a boy whose arm had been all but severed by a sword-stroke. "Animals. Demons. My—my mother—they—"

Alf laid a hand on his brow, stroking sleep into him. He was not the worst wounded in body or in mind, and he was only one of the first.

So many already, so sorely hurt, and so few to tend them. Still more of the healers had fled in the night, mastered at last by their fear; those who remained were white and trembling, ready to bolt at a word.

The boy was as comfortable as he might be. Alf left him, crossing over to the women's quarter. There were more women than men, for the pillagers were less eager to kill women this early in their madness. Only to rape them.

Only, Alf thought, bending over the nearest woman. A child truly, little older than Irene, in the tattered remnants of a gown. It was of silk, and rich.

She lay like a dead thing save for the sobbing of her breath. One eye was swollen shut, the other squeezed tight against the world. When he touched her she recoiled violently, gasping and retching.

"Hush," he said to her in his gentlest voice. "Hush, child. I bring you no hurt. Only healing."

She drew into a knot as far from him as she could go. Her mind knew nothing of him. She was in her house as the barbarians battered down the door, and one struck her father when he ran against them, no weapon in his hands; and his head burst open like a melon in the market, and his face still angry and his eyes surprised. One mailed monster came toward her, all steel, stinking the way the gardener stank after his holiday, and laughter rumbling out of him, and hands stretching out to her, bruising, tearing, hurling her down; and that, oh that, the *pain*—

She shrieked and lay rigid on the bed, her good eye wide, roving wildly. It caught on the white blur that was Alf's face. All her mind bent to the task of making clear those features, of drowning memory, of forcing him into focus.

For a long while she simply stared. At last she spoke, soft and childlike. "Are you an angel?"

He shook his head a little sadly.

"Ah." It was a sigh. "I hoped I was dead. I'm not, am I? I hurt. I hurt all over."

Even through his healing; for it was her mind and not her body which tormented her. He did not venture to touch her, but his voice caressed her. "You hurt. But the hurt will go away and you will be well. No one will harm you again."

She did not quite believe him. But she believed enough that she let him summon one of the women to undress and bathe her and cover her with a clean gown, when before she had let no one near her. Nor would she allow him to go until sleep took her; even at the very last she fought it, in terror of the dreams it would bring.

Alf rose from her bedside, gazing down the length of the room. It was not full, not yet, not with bodies. But it was filled to bursting with pain.

An uproar brought him away from a woman who had taken a dagger in the breast, to collide with Thomas in the passage. "Latins!" the small man panted. "They're beating down the door, I can tell by the sound."

Alf shook his head. "Not yet. It's something else. I think . . ." His eyes went strange; he leaped forward, nearly toppling the other.

The guards had braced themselves against the gate. Heavy fists hammered upon it; a deep voice roared, "Let us in, damn you! We're friends!"

"Let them in," Alf said.

One of the men whipped about. "Have you *seen* them? They're—"

"I know them." With that strength of his which seemed to come from no visible source, Alf set the men aside and shot the heavy bolts.

Half an army tumbled in. Later, when Alf counted, there were only nine, but they were massive, huge tawny men in scarlet, armed with axes. But he had eyes only for the foremost. The Varangian with Thea's eyes was blessedly unhurt, grinning as he stared, sweeping him into a vast embrace. "Little Brother! It took you long enough to open up."

Alf wanted to crush her close, even as she was. But there were eyes upon them. Her companions stood in a circle about them, eyeing him with interest and a touch of contempt.

It amused him, but it angered Thea. "This," she said in Saxon, "is Master Alfred. Any man who says an ill word of him will have my axe to face."

No one argued with her, although her fierce glare challenged them all to try. After a moment she named them for him: "Ulf, Grettir, Sigurd, Wulfmaer; Eirik, Haakon, and Halldor, and the downy-chick is Edmund Thurlafing. I, of course, am your own dear brother Aelfric. Can your guards"—her glance at them was scornful—"use reinforcements?"

Dionysios contemplated the invasion with a total lack of surprise. "Where you are," he said to Alf acidly, "all manner of prodigies follow. If they can feed themselves, you can keep them. They'll billet on the roof."

They had brought all their gear, and food with it, enough for several days. The roof suited them admirably, although young Edmund gnashed his teeth as the enemy rioted below. He would have plunged into the midst of them, even from that height, had not burly Grettir wrestled him down and sat on him. "We guard," the big man rumbled. "Not fight."

"Guard!" The boy spat. "That's all we've ever done. Guarding and no fighting. Look where it's got us."

"Edmund," Thea explained, "still has a few ideals intact."

"That seems to be true of all of you," said Alf.

Haakon shrugged. He was the eldest of them and the only one with a wound, a deep slash in his arm that Alf had bound up over his protests. "Our company has always been the odd one. Heming—that was our decurion—died in the fighting on the walls. We were called back to guard the Emperor. When he bolted, most of the Guard surrendered or bolted after him. We didn't. We swore an oath: We'll hold off the damned Normans or die trying."

"And I knew exactly the place to do it," Thea said.

"This one." Alf touched her arm, the most he could allow himself. "I have duties, and I can't shirk them any longer. You'll be well?"

"Perfectly, little Brother. Go on, work your miracles. When Edmund is ready to be human again, we'll see about coming to terms with the idiots at the gate."

As Alf left her, he heard Grettir's hoarse whisper. "So that's your famous brother." He laughed like a rumbling in the earth. "It's easy to see who's the beauty in your family."

Thea's reply was lower still, the words indistinguishable. But her flare of temper was bright as a beacon. Alf smiled wryly and descended the stair into Saint Basil's.

*   *   *

The Latins' madness abated not at all with the sun's sinking; rather, it worsened as they drained the City's vast store of liquors. Wine ran in the streets, mingled with beer and ale and Greek blood.

Somewhat after midnight Alf withdrew for a moment to one of the few quiet places in Saint Basil's, a room just beyond Master Dionysios' study, no more than a closet. Books lined its every wall, save where a slit of window looked down on the inner court; he leaned against the frame and closed his eyes.

Strong slender arms circled his waist; Thea kissed the nape of his neck and laid her cheek against his back, between his shoulders.

He turned in her embrace. She was in her own shape, clad in something dark and loose, with her hair free. She smiled up at him.

He kissed her hungrily. "God, how I've missed you!"

"It's only been a few days."

"Years." He kissed her again. She dropped her robe, but he withdrew a little, reaching for it. "Not here. Not like . . . like . . . a soldier and his doxy."

Her hand stopped his. "Certainly not. We're a soldier and her handsome lad."

His answer was a gasp. And, much later: "We're utterly depraved."

"Aren't we?" She raised herself on her elbow, looking down at him, her cat's-eyes flashing green. He lay on his back, knees drawn up in the small space, his robe spread beneath him like a pool of silver. Even as she gazed at him, he drew down his undertunic.

She caught his hand and kissed it. With a sudden movement he drew her to him, holding tightly. "Thea, beloved," he whispered, "don't ever—don't ever—"

She felt his tears hot and wet upon her breast. "There now," she crooned, stroking his hair. "There."

He pulled away sharply. His cheeks were wet, but his eyes glittered diamond-hard. "Promise me, Thea. You won't go out of Saint Basil's for anything."

"Why," she said startled, "you sound like an anxious nursemaid. What's got into you?"

"Promise me," he repeated.

"What for? I won't bind myself just to keep you quiet."

"You won't—" He broke off and rose, pulling on his robe. His eyes were unwontedly angry. "Not even if I tell you that your death is waiting for you?"

She blanched. But she laughed. "You worry too much. Don't you know how hard it is to kill one of us?"

"It's as easy as a dagger in the heart." He tossed his hair out of his face. "As God is my witness, woman, if you get yourself killed, I'll slaughter every Latin thereafter who comes within reach of my hands, and myself at the end of it."

Thea was silent. She knew his gentleness, which was clear to see, and his strength, which was not. She had thought she knew his temper, which could be terrible. But now he frightened her.

He knew it; he softened not at all.

Nor, fear or no fear, would she. "I can't promise," she said. "I can only try my best to do as you ask. Can you accept that?"

For a long moment he said nothing. He looked proud and cold and hard. His cheek, when Thea laid her palm against it, was rigid.

Little by little it softened into flesh. "Why," he asked softly and reasonably, "can you not be like any other woman?"

"If I were, would you want me?"

He regarded her long and steadily, weighing her words. "No," he said at last. "Unfortunately for my sanity, I would not."

"Love me then," she commanded him, "and leave the rest to God."

The hammering began in the early morning; hammering and shouting, with swordhilts and spearshafts and drunken Flemish voices.

Alf, lying flat on the roof beside Thea in her Varangian guise, peered cautiously down. A large company of men-at-arms massed in the narrow street, growing slowly as more of them staggered out of broken doorways. They were strange fantastic figures, burly and whiskered, wrapped in costly silks over their mail, with rings on their thick fingers and gold about their necks and wrists, and jewelled brooches fastened to caps and cloaks and boot-tops, swilling ale from glittering cups and singing in raucous voices.

The first rank endeavored to batter down the gate of Saint Basil's. It was of oak strengthened with iron, triply barred within; it yielded not at all to their blows.

On the other side of Thea, Edmund hissed. His mind was full of strategies, stones and arrows, boiling oil, even brimming chamber pots.

Thea dragged him back. Well before it was safe, he leaped to his feet. "Quick," he said, "while they're too fuddled to look up. If we can pick off a few—"

"We'll bring them swarming onto the roof," Thea finished for him. "The longer it takes them to think of that, the better we'll be. Go down now and lend a hand at the gate."

Edmund balked and glowered. "I came here to fight!"

"You'll have your chance," Alf said. "And soon."

Thea nodded. "You can believe him, too; he's Sighted." She took Edmund's arm. "Meanwhile you can exercise that outsize carcass of yours and help us build a barricade."

Come now, Alf said as she dragged Edmund away, *he's but a lad.*

Oh aye, she agreed with a touch of malice. *He looks almost as young as you.*

Alf laughed, undismayed.

Having failed to break down the door with brute force, most of the Latins wandered away in search of easier prey. But a tenacious few remained, one of whom wielded an axe. The heavy oak splintered under his blows but held.

Within, Master Dionysios had built a second gate all of iron, with narrow bars. Beyond this, several of the guards and Varangians heaped up a barricade of timber, breaking up whatever furnishings the Master would spare. Others meanwhile kept watch on the roof and prowled vigilantly along the garden wall.

The walls of Saint Basil's were thick, the rooms of the sick turned inward, so that the uproar was muted even to Alf's ears. With the gate beset, no more of the wounded ventured in; those who had come before tossed uneasily in dread of the enemy without. The air was thick with fear.

As the hours advanced, one of the healers broke. He left his binding up of a man's wounds and fled, weeping in terror.

Alf saw him go. Leaving his own labors, he followed swiftly.

The man made straight for the gate. The outer door was broken through, but the inner barrier of iron defeated the enemy's axes; the wooden barricade caught the arrows which pierced the bars. Alf's quarry tore at the heap of timber, beating off the guards with a makeshift club. Panic lent him strength; even as Alf halted, a blow hurled one of the guards to the ground. It was young Edmund, bolder than the rest but reluctant to draw weapon on one of his own. He crouched on the stones, shaking his head groggily, while the madman attacked the barricade.

"John!" Alf said. At the sound of his name, the man stiffened and paused. Alf leaped.

He spun, whirling his club. It whistled past Alf's ear as he writhed aside, swooping beneath it, catching John's wrist.

The man fought like a cornered beast. His free hand flailed at Alf's face; Alf caught it and held it in a grip no human could break. "John," he said quietly. "John, you have duties. Why are you neglecting them?"

John struggled and bit, and kicked, a foul, futile blow.

An arrow sang between their bodies to lodge quivering in a fragment of the broken barrier. John stared at it in horrified fascination, and suddenly collapsed.

Alf gathered him up as if he had been a child and not a tall, rather portly man. "You had better rebuild your wall," he said to the speechless guards, "and cushion it somehow. Carpets, I think. Or hangings. Ask the Master."

Edmund staggered up. "I'll ask," he said. "Where is he?"

Alf paused, the healer a dead weight in his arms. "In the men's quarters." His eyes took in the other's face. One cheek was swelling and blackening, and the cheekbone had split, sending a trickle of blood through the young beard. "Have someone see to you when you're done."

Edmund grinned, ignoring the pain. "What's a bruise? Here, let me carry the man for you."

Alf was already moving. "I have him. Hurry now, before the Franks bring up a crossbow."

Alf saw John settled in a quiet place, where he would be watched but not troubled. He had fallen from panic into a kind of stupor; his mind was dull, his thoughts lost in a gray fog of despair that neither voice nor power could dispel.

Alf drew back at last, defeated. Edmund was standing near him, watching him. The bruise on his cheek was in full flower; the cut had begun to close.

"Shouldn't you be on guard?" Alf asked.

The Varangian shrugged. "We made a wall of carpets. Your Master was none too pleased, but he came to lend us a hand. To make sure we did it properly, he said. Just when we were done, they started with crossbows. I saw that our wall was holding and left it to the others." His eyes upon Alf were bright and fascinated. "You aren't half the dainty lass you look, are you?"

Alf dipped a sponge in water and began to cleanse the blood from the other's cheek. Edmund tried to evade him, failed, submitted with a growl. Alf set him on a stool and continued, saying, "To each man his own skills."

"In the palace they'd have marked you out for the angels' choir."

"I sing well, they tell me." Alf set down the sponge and reached for a pot of ointment. "Next time you set out to stop a club with your head, put on your helmet first."

The ointment stung. Edmund's eyes watered, but he was too proud to flinch. "Why didn't you go for the Guard? You're fast enough. Strong enough too, though you don't look it."

"Of the two of us," Alf said, "Aelfric is the fighter. He makes wounds. I heal them."

"And keep lunatics from making them."

"That too." Alf straightened, wiping his hands. It struck him then. "Aelfric. I didn't see him with the others. I can't sense—" He caught himself. "Where did he go?"

"I don't know," Edmund said. "He was there till just before you came. Then he muttered something that sounded like a curse and bolted. I haven't seen him since."

He—she—was nowhere in Saint Basil's. Alf cast his mind wide, thrusting it into the roiling horror that was the City, hurling back fear with grim determination. She would not promise. She would not. And she had gone out into that, without a word to him.

"God in heaven!" he cried aloud. He hurtled past the stunned Varangian, making blindly for the rear of Saint Basil's, away from the beleaguered gate. The enemy had resorted to fire; the guards held it off with water and the same carpets which had foiled the arrows.

They could defend themselves. He came to the bolt-hole, a postern in the garden wall. Thea's presence was a beacon before him. He slid lithely round the startled and babbling guard and out into pandemonium.

He paid no heed to it. Later it would come back in snatches, like remnants of a nightmare.

All round the edge of a great square, men in mail struck at the marble gods with hammers, with axes, or with clubs of wood or iron, shattering the stone, grinding the shards underfoot.

A woman lay sprawled in the street, weeping silently, with her skirts above her waist and blood streaming down her thighs. A man-at-arms, running past, stopped and fell upon her like a beast in rut.

Within the broken doors of a church, a mule brayed, laden with spoil; beyond it, men hacked at the altar with their swords.

A sergeant rode down the street upon an ass, with a priest's

vestments over his armor and a jewelled crown on his head and in his
hand a chalice filled to the brim with ale. He was chanting, with
dolorous piety, the responses of the Drunkards' Mass.

Swift as Alf was, and strange, and wild-eyed, few ventured to
molest him. Someone snatched at his robe, half tearing it from his
body; he pulled free and ran on, circling a troop of Franks clustered
about a silent woman and a shrieking, struggling boy. One of those
on the edge, glimpsing Alf as he passed, flung out an arm, overbalanc-
ing him.

He had a brief and terrible vision of a bearded face over his, and
a breath that reeked of wine, and hard hands groping under his torn
tunic. The heel of Alf's hand drove into the man's jaw, snapping his
head back. He rolled away, convulsed, his soul shrieking into the
dark.

They had broken down the gate of House Akestas over the body of
the feeble old porter and swarmed into the courtyard, a company of
men who shouted and cursed in the accents of Champagne. All the
precious things in the house, all those which did not lie hidden in a
great chest under the almond tree in the garden, tottered in a great
untidy heap in the center of the court. Close by it like a broken doll
lay Irene. Her mother crouched beside her; and Sophia's face was
terrible.

Beyond them a battle raged. Thea, in full Varangian gear, stood
back to back with Corinna, who wielded a bloody sword. But there
were over a score of Franks and a rich prize to fight for; and Corinna,
for all her formidable strength, was no swordsman. A tall Frank struck
past her awkward guard to open a long gash in her forehead; blood
streamed from it into her eyes, blinding her. She stumbled; the Frankish blade bit deep. She fell like a tower falling into massive ruin.

No one watched the gate. Alf poised in it, all his world centered
on this that had brought him from Saint Basil's. His mind had room
only for wrath. He could not flay Thea with it for blinding his power
to her escape, for blocking him when he would have come direct to
her by witchery, for striving even to fuddle his mind as he ran until
he circled back to his starting place; but that, he had conquered. He
called to himself all the forces of his power and shaped them to his
bidding.

Thea cried out in her man's voice, a great roar of wonder and of
challenge. The Latins, looking back, saw all the far end of the courtyard filled with shining warriors, and at their head a figure of white

light. He advanced, raising his hands. He bore no weapon, yet such was the terror of him that the Franks shrieked and fled, running wildly, striking at one another in a blind passion of horror.

There was silence. The last man gasped out his life upon his comrade's sword. The warriors melted into the sunlight; Alf stood alone, half naked, pale and tired.

He sank to his knees beside Irene. She was dead, her neck broken, her eyes staring up at him in innocent surprise. Tenderly he closed them.

Sophia sagged against him. "They didn't touch her," she whispered. "They tried, but she fought; one of them struck too hard. That—that one came then." Her eyes found Thea, whom she did not know in that shape. "He fought well. So well, and for nothing. You . . . both of you. Oh, you were wonderful in your power!"

Alf's arm circled her shoulders. She felt thin and cold, trembling in spasms. His mind brushed hers; he gasped.

"Yes," she said, "I offered to trade myself for her. Perfidious, they call us Greeks. And what are they? They . . . accepted . . . and thought to have both of us. And Corinna after. It took three of them to hold her back, till the stranger came and she broke free. But she died. She . . . died. Who will nurse the children now?"

Alf moved as if to lift her. "You will," he answered her, "after I've healed you."

She shook her head. "No. It's too late even for a miracle. I'm all torn. I've lost too much blood already. And there's this." Her hands had been clasped tightly to her belly. She opened her fingers. Blood oozed between them. "One of them had a dagger in his hand. It won't be much longer now."

Alf covered her hands with his own, summoning the last of his power.

She smiled and shook her head, as a mother will whose child persists in some endearing folly. Her lips were white, but her will was indomitable. By it alone she clung to her body. "My beloved enchanter. Tend my children well for me."

He nodded mutely. Her smile softened. She laid her head upon his shoulder; closed her eyes and sighed.

Gently Alf laid her down. Her hands, loosening, bared what she had hidden. He swallowed bile. Behind him he heard Thea's catch of breath.

From the heap of plunder he freed an armful of richness, the carpet which had lain in his room. He spread it over them all, mother and daughter and the body of the servant who had died for them, and knelt for a long while, head bowed. At last he rose.

The courtyard was like a charnel house. All beyond was stripped bare, stained with the blood of its defenders. Even the stable lay open and plundered, the old mare slaughtered in her stall, the mules and the pony gone.

Yet one creature remained alive. Nikki's kitten wove among the bodies, mewing plaintively. Alf gathered it up. It clung to him with needle claws and cried, until he stroked it into calmness.

His eyes met Thea's. They were as bleak as his own, and as implacable. Minutely she nodded.

For a little while the street was quiet, littered with flotsam. In the center of it, Alf turned. House Akestas loomed before him, brooding over its dead.

He called the lightnings down upon it.

30

"They're gone."

The defenders of Saint Basil's stared dully at one another, blinking in the torchlight. The hospital stood intact, its defenses unbreached.

"They're gone," Edmund repeated. "They've given up. We're safe."

"For the night." Thea leaned on her axe and mopped her brow. "Why should they wear themselves out in the dark, and on our territory at that? We should follow their example. Short watches for all of us, and plenty of sleep."

One of Dionysios' men frowned. "There are a thousand easier prizes in the City. Maybe they won't come back."

"Don't lay wagers on it," she said. "Edmund, you look lively enough. Relieve the men in the garden and send them to bed. I'll take the first watch on the roof."

In the unwonted quiet, even Master Dionysios succumbed to sleep. Thea walked the dim ways on soft feet, her watch over, her man-shape laid aside.

Alf lay on his pallet with open eyes. Nikki clung to him even in sleep, cheeks damp, eyes swollen with weeping; the kitten crouched like a tiny lion in the curve of his arm, wide-eyed and watchful. In the far corner of her own bed Anna huddled awake, oblivious to all save her own terrible grief.

Softly Thea lay on Alf's free side, stroking his hair away from his face. He shivered under her hand; his wide eyes closed. *I can't weep,* he said silently. *I try and I try, but no tears come. Thea, if I don't weep I'll go mad.*

She kissed his eyelids, his lips, the hollow of his throat. *You grieve. I feel it in you.*

It goes too deep. Irene—I let her go. When I could have fetched her back again, I tarried to play avenging angel before the Emperor; and after, I let myself forget. I could have forced them both to my will, Irene and her mother. Her mother . . . oh, dear God, the agony I let her suffer!

You, Alf? Thea raised her head from his breast. *No. It was God. As well you know.*

Anna hates Him, he said.

But not you. You, she loves.

Alf's breath caught as he drew it in, almost a sob. *I'm all she has left. Her mother is dead. I burned down her house. It was dead and it was a horror, but it was hers. I never asked her what she wanted to do with it.*

You did the only thing you could have done.

He was silent, mind and voice. When at length she slept, he was still awake. Even she could not follow where his mind had gone.

Morning dawned damp and gray: the third day of the sack of Constantinople. As the light grew sluggishly, the guardians of Saint Basil's looked about them and swallowed cries of despair. All about the walls on all sides massed an army of Franks, knights and men-at-arms in full array. And each company bore a ladder cut to the height of the hospital.

A horn sounded, short and sharp. The ladders swung up.

Varangian axes met them. But there were only nine of the old Guard and a dozen ladders, and sixscore men swarming up them; and on the roof across the way, a company of bowmen rising from concealment behind a parapet.

Edmund thrust back a laden ladder with the haft of his axe, and laughed as it fell. "Ha! Here's a fight at last!" He wheeled, struck aside a Flemish sword, clove helm and head together with a single sweeping blow.

In the garden below, Dionysios' guards fought hand to hand with men who had scaled the wall and strove now to throw open the postern.

Edmund began to sing.

All the sick in Saint Basil's lay in the centermost of its great wards, the women set apart from the men by a curtain. Of the healers who had labored there when the City was whole, only Master Dionysios remained, and Thomas, and Alf; and two frightened but loyal students. All the rest had fled.

"This is ridiculous, you know," said the woman Alf was tending. She had been a tavernkeeper until a Frankish sergeant beat her senseless for refusing to serve him in the cup he proffered, a chalice from Holy Apostles. "The devils will set fire to us, and here we'll be like rats in a trap."

A man's voice called through the curtain, as calm as hers. "It won't happen. They must think we've got real treasure here, with the Emperor's axemen guarding us. We're a nut they'll crack before they try to light any fires."

"Maybe they'll take pity on us," said a boy's breaking voice.

"Them?" The man laughed until his breath caught and he choked.

"They don't pity anything," the woman said for him. "They're devils, I say. Devils straight out of Hell."

Another of the women stirred on her cot. "We should surrender. Why are we fighting them? We'll only make them angrier."

"Would you rather be alive now or dead two days since?" Master Dionysios examined the last speaker with a hard eye and gentle hands. "Well, mistress, you'll walk out of here if I have anything to do with it."

"They do admire courage," Alf said softly, as if to himself. He rose from the tavernkeeper's side and passed on to her neighbor.

Slowly the Varangians gave way before the enemy. There were but six now, Grettir fallen with Sigurd and Eirik before the Latin swords; and Halldor had dropped his axe to wield his sword awkwardly left-handed, with an arrow in his right shoulder. Edmund sang no longer. He had no breath to spare for it.

A bolt caught Ulf in the throat. He toppled, taking a Latin with him, gripped in a death embrace. Wulfmaer howled in grief and rage and flung himself forward.

Thea hauled Edmund back by the belt. The three who remained, with Edmund, held the door into Saint Basil's.

Halldor reeled and fell.

Thea's arm was leaden; she breathed in gasps. Her body ached and burned under the Varangian armor. Before her she saw not human forms but a thicket of blades.

Haakon loosed a gurgling cry; and her left side, her sword-side, was empty. On her right, young Edmund hacked and cursed and wept without knowing what he did.

In the garden, a shout went up. The enemy had broken through.

Thea kicked open the door she guarded and flung Edmund through it. He tumbled headlong down the steep stair. She whirled her axe and sent it flying, mowing down the startled Franks; slammed the door upon them and shot the bolt. It was a full second before the first body crashed against it.

She was already at the stair's foot, dragging Edmund to his feet. He swore and struck at her with his fist, bruised and winded but unharmed. She cuffed him into submission. "The hellhounds have got into the garden. Move, or they'll find the wards before we do!"

Without a word Edmund bolted down the passage. Thea ran fast upon his heels.

Behind them, the enemy hurtled through the door.

Both forces met in the wide passage outside of the inmost ward. No gate or door stood in their way there; but a pair of Varangians held the entry, one armed with his axe, the other with a sword. Beyond them the attackers could see what precious hoard they guarded: a roomful of the maimed and the dying, a child or two, and three weary men in blue.

The Latins gaped. For this, they had forsaken the rich plunder of Byzantium?

With a howl of frustrated rage, one of the captains charged. His pike pierced through Edmund's guard and clove his mail, striking him to the heart.

He fell against Thea, staggering her with his dead weight. Her eyes flared green in the Varangian face; her lips drew back from sharp witch-teeth.

Alf saw the crossbow raised, the finger tensing on its trigger. "Thea!" he cried sharply.

She turned startled. The quarrel, aimed for her heart, plunged deep into her side, piercing the mail, driving her back, sprawling, shifting and changing under the shock of the blow. It was Thea whose body Alf caught, the helm falling from her head, her hair tumbling over his hands to mingle with her blood.

Very gently he laid her down. No one had moved, save by instinct to shape the sign of the cross.

Deep within him something broke. He took up the sword that had fallen from Thea's hand.

In silence more terrible than any cry, he sprang upon the bowman. The man fell with his head half severed from his shoulders. Alf drove deep into the ranks, crowded as they were, hampered by the narrowness of the passage. They closed in about him. He backed to the wall, holding them off with a circle of steel.

Alf. Thea's mind-voice was feeble. *Alf, don't!*

He faltered. A pikestaff swung round and struck him hard on the side of the head. He staggered, but kept his feet and his sword. With a panther-snarl he slipped beneath the pike and hewed its wielder down.

Stop! Thea cried through the haze of her pain. *Stop, you fool! They'll kill you!*

"I want them to," he said aloud, fiercely.

A scarlet figure wavered in his vision, with a host of shadows before and behind it. Thea beat her way through the massed Franks, armed only with her fists and the dying flare of her power on which no weapon could bite, and threw herself upon him. The sword dropped from his numbed hand. He saw her face, white as death, and her wild eyes. The ring of steel drew in upon them both.

"That," said Master Dionysios, "will be quite enough."

The Latins could not understand his Greek, but his tone was clear. He made his way through them by the path Thea had opened and glared at them all impartially.

One or two men raised their weapons. But a helmed knight struck the blades down. "No. Enough. He can't fight; he hasn't even a knife."

Alf crouched at the knight's feet, holding Thea close, eyes burning with wrath thwarted but far from quenched. "Murderer," he hissed in the *langue d'oeil.*

The knight's blank helm betrayed no emotion at all. He seemed to be scrutinizing the upturned and hating face, pondering it. "You speak Frankish, do you? Tell the old man we're claiming this house in the name of the Crusade."

Alf bent over Thea's body, probing her side. Mail and the fading remnants of her power had slowed the quarrel, but it had gone deep, ncarly to her back. The black bolt stirred slightly with an indrawn breath; the point of it grazed the farther side of her lung.

A mailed foot drove into his hip. He surged upward.

Dionysios seized his arm and clung grimly. "Kill yourself if you like, you young lunatic, but don't drag us into it. Tell the beast he can have what he pleases if he leaves the sick and the medicines alone."

There was a long pause. Alf shuddered and looked about as if he could not remember where he was. Slowly he repeated the Master's words in Frankish.

The knight unfastened his helm and handed it to a man-at-arms, baring a lined ageless face, tired and sweating and somewhat pale. "You'll look after our wounded, then. These"—he indicated Alf, and Thea whom he had gathered into his arms—"we take."

"The woman is mortally hurt," the Master snapped.

"The boy is a doctor. Is he not?" The knight turned away as Alf choked on the Greek, beckoning to one of his men. "Bind them."

Dionysios stood his ground. "The woman will die. I will not have it. Get out of my hospital!"

"Bind them," repeated the knight implacably.

31

House Akestas was a smoking ruin, black and hideous in the rain. It stank of burning and of charred flesh.

Jehan stood in the half-burned garden, cowled against the drizzle. His face was as bleak as the sky. "Sometimes," he said to it, "it's perilously easy to hate my own people."

His escort of Flemings prowled through the rubble, pausing now and then to take up something of interest, skirting the occasional beds of coals. Even in the rain the embers smoldered unabated, as if they disdained to die.

A shout brought him about. Part of the stable stood intact, set apart from the house as it had been. His squire struggled with someone there, a scarecrow figure, very small and very black. Jehan strode toward them.

Odo's captive was a boy, ragged and covered with soot, who

struggled and bit and cursed in half a dozen languages. Even the squire's hard blow neither stilled nor silenced him; but when he saw Jehan he froze. To his wide eyes, the priest seemed a giant.

Odo shook him roughly, nursing a bitten hand. "The little beast was rooting in the straw."

"Wet, probably, and cold," Jehan said, speaking Greek—it would not hurt Odo to exercise his brain a little. "Look; his teeth are chattering. He's thin as a lath, too. He was on short commons well before we closed down the markets."

"Please," the child whined. "Please, noble sirs. You don't want me. I'm too thin, no meat on my bones, see. Just skin."

Jehan laughed without mirth. "So we eat little children, do we, lad? What else do we do?"

"Kill," the boy answered with sudden venom. His voice slid back into its whine; he cringed in Odo's hands. "Please, great lord, holy Patriarch, I'm worth nothing, I never was. Don't kill me."

"Why should I want to?"

That, the boy seemed to think, was unanswerable.

Jehan freed him from Odo's grasp and held him lightly but firmly. His arms were no bigger than sticks. "If you can tell me something, I'll let you go. I'll even give you money."

The black eyes narrowed. "Show me."

Jehan took a bit of silver from his pouch. The boy swallowed. It was more money than he had ever dreamed of. His fingers itched to snatch at it. But Jehan's grip was too strong. "Here. This for the truth." He held the coin up in front of the child's eyes. They fixed on it, fascinated. "Did you see what happened to this house?"

The urchin's eyes flickered. Fear, or the effort of inventing a lie?

Fear, Jehan decided. The emaciated body shook with it; the dark cheeks grayed. He tried in vain to break away.

Jehan turned the coin until it glittered. "Tell me."

It took a long while, for the boy was truly terrified, more of the memory than of the man who held him. But greed in the end was stronger than fear. With his gaze riveted on the coin, he said, "It was an angel." Pressed, he went on in fits and starts. "I was hiding. I peeped out. The dev— Your people were all over, killing and stealing and doing things to people. Some were in the house. Then there was nobody in the street, or nobody much. And he came out. He was an angel, like in church."

Have you ever been in one? Jehan wondered. But he said, "Go on. What was he like?"

"An angel. All white. He—I think he had people with him. I didn't notice them much. He came out of the house. He stood and he shone. And the fire came down."

Jehan gripped the boy till he yelled, then let go. The urchin snatched the coin and bolted. Jehan hardly noticed him. "Fire," he said slowly. "Fire came down."

"A patent lie," Odo declared. "The looters must have torched the place."

"What?" Jehan had forgotten the squire was there. "What? Set fire to it? No. Not they. There are bodies in those ruins. Several bodies, if my nose is any guide. And an . . . angel. He would look like that when his power was on him. He lives, then. Thank God. But why destroy House Akestas?"

"Divine vengeance?" Odo suggested, not quite flippantly.

"I hope not," Jehan said. "For his sake and for all our sakes, I hope not."

Jehan almost wept when he saw Saint Basil's. It was beautifully, blessedly intact, save for the splintered outer gate; although Latin guards stood there, the courtyard was whole, untouched.

They let him in readily, with proper respect for his priesthood. Wonder of wonders, he thought, they were both sober and sane. Nor had they plundered within. Part of the hospital was a barracks, but a well-disciplined barracks; the rest kept to its old function. And there bending over a wounded soldier was Master Dionysios, as brusque and grim-faced as ever, tyrannizing over the conquerors as he always had over his own people. Even the Frankish surgeons seemed content to bow to his rule.

As Jehan approached him, a shrill cry echoed through the room. Anna ran down an aisle among the beds, her braids flying, to fling herself into Jehan's arms. She was babbling like a mad thing, too swift and incoherent for him to follow.

He held her for a long while. They were all staring at him. Latins, he noticed, lay beside Greeks, all mingled and apparently amicable.

Anna had fallen silent, weeping; her whole body shook although she made no sound. He sat with her on the side of an empty bed.

She stiffened in his arms. He loosed his hold; she sat on his lap, looking into his face, letting the tears fall where they would. "Mother is dead," she said very calmly. "So is Irene. So is Corinna. The Latins killed them. Alf made our house a pyre for them."

Jehan had known how it must be. But it was the worst of all the past days' horrors to hear it from her in that quiet, child's voice ancient with suffering, all her world destroyed in a handful of days. And no hate; before God, no hate. She had gone past it.

She regarded him with grave concern. Her tears had stopped; his had only begun. She wiped his face with a small warm hand. "Don't cry, Father Jehan. You've won. You should be glad."

"*I* haven't won. No one has, except maybe the Devil. We found the greatest city in the world; we've made it an outpost of Hell."

Anna shook her head. "Hell isn't here. It's underneath us. You know that, Father Jehan."

"And belike I'm going there." He mastered himself with an effort. "You're safe, God be thanked. Is—is—Anna, is Nikki here?"

Her face twisted. "No. N—no."

"Dead?"

"No." She was crying again.

"For God's sake, you great lout, stop tormenting the child."

Jehan met Master Dionysios' cold eye. "I'm tormenting myself," he said levelly. And at last: "Where is Alfred?"

The Master glared. "What is that to you?"

Suddenly Jehan could not bear it. "Everything!" he shouted. "Everything, damn you!"

"We are not deaf." Dionysios' expression had not softened, but his eyes had, a very little. "Nor do we know where he is."

"They took him," Anna said. "He fought. Thea—Thea was somebody else, and then they shot her, and she was herself. He tried to kill everybody. They tied him up and took him away. Thea too. Nikki and his cat went after. Nobody could stop him. They were too busy holding me down."

Dionysios nodded shortly. "That in essence is the truth. The woman had a bolt in her lung below the heart. She could not have survived the hour under such handling as they gave her. But mercy is not a virtue you barbarians are guilty of. Your friend was taken with her; where, no one seems able to tell. Some vile prison, no doubt, reserved for those who had the temerity to defend their city."

If Jehan had not been sitting, he would have fallen. "Alf— wasn't—hurt?"

"Not that any of us could see, though he fought like a madman once the woman had fallen."

"It didn't matter," Anna said, "if he wasn't hurt, if Thea was."

No. It did not. And if Thea was dead—

Jehan rose unsteadily, setting Anna on her feet. She held to the cincture of his habit. "Take me with you," she said.

"Child, I can't. You're safe here. There's the Master, and Thomas, and—"

"Take me!"

"What would I do with you?"

"Take me," she persisted.

He hardened his will. She tightened her grip on his belt.

"It's death out there!" he cried in desperation.

"Not anymore," she said. "The riots are over. Everyone says so. All the Latins are sick and sorry and very, very rich. Besides," she added, "you're big enough to take care of six of me."

But not to withstand the pleadings of even one of her. He tarried, hoping that she would weary of waiting and abandon him. Vain hope. He questioned every Latin in Saint Basil's, of every rank, and she never took her eyes from him.

No one knew where Alf had been taken. Lord Bertrand had commanded it; Lord Bertrand was gone and his men with him. He could be anywhere in the City.

When Jehan left Saint Basil's, he had a small companion. A boy, it might have been, dressed as a healer's apprentice, with a cap on his head and a small, satisfied smile on his face.

Nikki huddled miserably in a corner with his kitten in his lap. It was dark where they were, and damp, and cold. Things scuttled in the darkness, fleeing when the cat sprang at them, creeping back boldly when it paused to make a meal of one of their kin. Once, when men brought food and water, the light of their torches caught the brown-furred bodies and the pink naked tails and the redly gleaming eyes.

Alf did not notice. Alf noticed nothing except Thea. His robe lay under her body, shielding her from the crawling dampness; for himself he had only his thin undertunic. The men had had things to say of that; Nikki had felt their minds when they came, and seen their faces. Not good faces, but not bad ones either. One had tried to touch Alf where a person was not supposed to touch, but the other had stopped him, angry and a little disgusted, thinking words Nikki was not sure he understood.

Alf had not even known they were there. Thea lay very still on his robe. He had eased the bolt out of her side with hands and power, and stopped the bleeding. Strange bleeding, bubbling like water out of a fountain. It frightened Alf, a fear that made Nikki cower in his corner. She was dying the way Father had died. She would die, and there would be no world left for Alf.

Hour after hour she lay there in the darkness and the cold and the pale glimmer of Alf's power. Close to death, hovering on the very edge of it, yet she held firm against his healing. Her will and her consciousness had no part in it; those were long gone. But her body clung grimly to life, and her power kept doggedly to its resistance: two instincts, each powerful, each implacable, each striving blindly to thwart the other.

Alf drove his power to the farthest limits of its strength and even beyond. His body, abandoned, sprawled beside hers; his mind cupped like a hand about the wound which drained her life away, but could not move to mend it. Her shield was like adamant.

He spun back into his body. For a long while he lay motionless. Her face was white and still and achingly beautiful. Already it had the marble pallor of death. Drop by drop, blood trickled into her lungs, crowding out the precious air. Her heart strained; her limbs grew cold as all her forces gathered at her center.

Slowly Nikki crept from his corner. Alf seemed as close to death as she, willing it, longing for it.

There was a small space between them. Nikki wriggled into it. Thea was hard and cold in her armor, Alf cold and rigid, no warmer or softer than the stones on which he lay. They were gone; they would never come back. They had left him alone. He began to cry, deep racking sobs without help or hope.

Alf's power, all but spent, sent forth a last feeble tendril.

Thea's barrier wavered and melted.

Nikki, between them, wept as if his heart would break. Through the perfection of his grief, Alf's healing flowed.

It was very little. He had no more left to give. Yet Thea's life, balancing upon the edge of dissolution, seized the thread and clung. Inch by tortured inch he drew her back. Cell by cell her body began to mend.

At last, exhausted by his weeping, Nikki slept.

Alf woke by degrees. His mind ached at least as much as his body. There was a grinding pain in his stomach; only after a long while did he recognize it as hunger.

His nose twitched. There was food somewhere within range. Blindly he groped for it. Something warm and furred moved against his hand, he started, half sitting up, to meet the bright eyes of Nikki's kitten.

Thea lay on her side, pale and ill to look on but sleeping peacefully. Nikki coiled in the hollow of her body. All around them was a room of stone, bare of furnishings, with a steep ladder of a stair leading up to a heavy door. Not a prison, Alf thought as his mind began to clear. It had not that aura which prisons have, of hate and fear and pain. This place spoke rather of ancient wine and of long-gone cheeses.

Close by him lay a plate and a bowl and a lidded jar. The plate held bread, dry and rather hard but of decent quality; a stew filled the bowl, now cold and congealed, and in the jar was thin sour wine.

He raised the jar with trembling hands. He was as weak as if he had roused from a fever. He drank a sip, two. The wine burned his parched throat, but it warmed his belly. Carefully he set the jar down and reached for the bread. A little only; a spoonful from the bowl. His stomach growled for more; his mind, trained to fasting, refrained.

With his body's needs attended, he sat clasping his knees, chin upon them, gazing at the two who continued to sleep. Perhaps he prayed. Perhaps he dozed. His mind was empty of thought, utterly serene.

He started awake. The kitten crouched at his feet, every hair erect.

Iron grated on iron. Bolts thudded back; the door swung open. Light stabbed Alf's dark-accustomed eyes. He threw up a hand to shield them.

The stair groaned under the weight of several men. They were armed, he saw from the shape of their shadows; mailed though not helmed, and cloaked over it. One carried the torch that still made Alf's eyes flinch. Two others stood with drawn swords.

The fourth stood over him. The little cat struck fiercely with distended claws; met mail; spat and yowled, defying the intruder to advance.

Alf rose unsteadily with the furious cat in his arms, and bowed as best he might. "My lord," he said, neither surprised nor afraid.

Count Baudouin looked him up and down; folded his arms and cocked his head a little to one side. "So, Master Alfred," he said, "even your familiar will fight for you. Have you anything to say for yourself?"

"You judged me when first you saw me," Alf responded coolly. "What could I say that would change it?"

Baudouin's jaw tensed. "My judgment has proven correct."

"In your eyes, perhaps."

"Four of my men died at your hands."

"How many innocent women and children died at theirs?"

"Greek women and children," said Baudouin. "You, sir, are not a Greek."

"No. I am merely a man who saw half his family cruelly murdered and his lady wounded unto death by men gone mad with wine and plundering."

"You took arms against your own people."

Alf's eyes glittered; his voice was deadly soft. "My people, my lord? The only one of my people in this city lies yonder with the wound of a Flemish quarrel in her side. She lives, and will live, but she owes her life to no act of your army."

Baudouin looked from him to Thea. She was little more than a shadow and a gleam, her slender body lost in the Varangian armor, her face hidden by the fall of her hair. He approached her slowly. Alf, with no appearance of haste, moved to stand in his path.

There was a pause. Baudouin glared; Alf met him with a cold and quiet stare. His eyes dropped.

"My lord," Alf said very gently, "with me you may do as you like. But I advise you not to touch my lady."

Baudouin laughed, high and strained. "That? Your lady? A fine lusty wench she must be, from the tales I've heard. But then," he added with a flash of malice, "you seem to be a man after all, now I see you without your silken skirts. Do you keep her satisfied?"

"What can it matter to you, my lord, whether I do or not?"

Baudouin's hand flashed up. Alf seemed hardly to move; but the heavy gauntlet never touched his skin, only ruffled his hair slightly with the wind of its passing.

The Count clenched his fists and spoke through clenched teeth. "Lord Bertrand would like to make an example of you."

"What sort of example, my lord?"

Baudouin bared his teeth. It was meant to be a smile. "We've hanged a number of our own for keeping back more than their fair share of the plunder. It's quieted the men down, to be sure. But it's time we gave them a genuine criminal or two. What could be better than a Latin witch who has thrown in his lot with the Greeks?"

"What indeed?" Alf asked as quietly as ever. "I ask only one concession."

"I grant you none," said Baudouin. "I gave you enough in

coming here at all and in letting you fray my temper with your insolence. Lord Bertrand may let you live; you can pray for that if either God or your black master will listen to you. Or he may rid the world of you."

"That is his right. But let him set my lady free. She is a Greek, and fought loyally for her Emperor; she does not deserve a traitor's fate."

"That's for Lord Bertrand to decide. I wash my hands of you."

"And Pilate spake, and having spoken, turned away."

Thea's voice spun them both about. She lay as she had lain for this long while, but open-eyed, weak yet alert; Nikki's great eyes stared up from the curve of her side.

Carefully, shakily, she raised herself on her elbow. She regarded Baudouin with a bright mocking stare, for he was gaping like a fool. He had not thought to find her beautiful.

"Yes, Count," she said, "you're wise to let someone else do your dirty work. You can't have brother Henry guess what you've done, now can you? He might even begin to suspect the truth, that most of your hatred of Alf is simple, sea-green jealousy."

"Jealousy?" cried Baudouin. "Of *that?*"

"Of a man for whom, on a few moments' acquaintance, your much beloved brother conceived a great and lasting friendship. A friendship which he was rash enough to declare in your presence, with considerable and glowing praise of its object."

"Henry is a trusting fool. He saw a handsome face, heard handsome words, and let himself believe in them."

"And you were like to die of envy. He never praises you, except on rare occasions when he thinks you might deserve it. If you want to be Emperor, lordling, you're going to have to learn to be more like your brother."

Baudouin had begun to recover from the shock of her beauty in the bitterness of her words. He opened his mouth to denounce her.

She laughed, sweet and maddening, with a catch at the end of it. "Oh, certainly! I'm at least as bad as my paramour. You'll have to hang us both, your lordship, or you'll never have peace."

"Thea," Alf began, setting the cat upon the floor, sinking to one knee beside her.

She kissed the finger he laid to her lips, and shook it away. "Go on, my brave lord, my Emperor-to-be. Condemn us both to death. Then you'll have no rival for your brother's affections, and no one to take vengeance on you for murdering her lover."

Baudouin's sword hissed from its sheath. She laughed at it. He gritted out a curse and whirled away, half running up the steep stair. His men scrambled after him.

32
☙

Jehan prowled the room Henry had given him in Blachernae. It was a chaplain's cell, with a chapel close by it; in comparison with the rest of the palace it was very small and sternly ascetic. But by the standards of a priest from Anglia, it was almost sinfully opulent.

Anna sat on the large and comfortable bed and watched him. Here in seclusion, she had taken off her cap; her braids hung down very black and thick on either side of her narrow pointed face. She tugged at one. "Won't you let me cut them off?" she begged.

"No!" he snapped. He stopped in front of the saint painted with jewelled tiles upon the wall, and glared into her huge soulful eyes. " 'Holy Saint Helena,' " he read, " 'finder of the True Cross, pray for us.' . . . If you could find a Cross buried for three hundred years, why in God's name can't you find a handful of prisoners lost for a day?"

"Maybe because you haven't asked her before," Anna said reasonably.

He growled and began to pace again.

Someone knocked softly at the door. Anna stuffed her braids into her cap. Jehan muttered something in Norman; and louder, in Greek: "Who is it?"

"You ordered food, my lord," said a light sexless voice.

Jehan shivered a little. These eunuchs made his skin creep, silent gliding creatures, neither male nor female, serving their new masters with obsequiousness which masked deep and utter contempt.

He found his voice. "Come in then."

The servant entered with bowed head and laid his burden on a table. Anna, with the perfect ease of the Greek aristocrat, stepped round him as if he had not been there and began to investigate the various plates and bowls.

The eunuch made no move to go. He was a young one, over-dressed as they all seemed to be, painted and perfumed like a woman;

there were jewels in his ears and on his fingers and everywhere between. As he lifted his face, with a shock Jehan knew him. Either the chief steward of the palace had suffered a great reduction in rank, or there was something afoot.

Without conscious thought, Jehan reached for his sword and drew it and set himself between the eunuch and the child.

Michael Doukas looked from the bright blade to the cold eyes behind it and smiled slightly. "I take it, holy Father, that we know one another."

"I think," said Jehan, "that we do. Are you in the habit of running errands for minor clerics when there's nothing of greater import for you to do?"

"On occasion," replied Michael Doukas, "I will stoop to it." He laid a delicate finger on the flat of Jehan's blade, just below the point, and moved it fastidiously aside. "Do you mind, my lord? It's quite vulgar to greet one's guests with steel."

"Barbaric too, of course." Jehan returned Chanteuse to its sheath and relaxed a little, though ready at a word to cut the eunuch down.

Michael Doukas sighed, relieved. "Ah. Now I can breathe again. Father, will you hear my confession?"

That caught Jehan completely off guard. "But you're a Greek!"

"So I am. Will you, Father?"

"You know I can't."

The eunuch shook his head sadly. "Such injustice. And all for a word or two in an ancient prayer. Where can I go with such a burden as my soul carries?"

"This place is swarming with priests of your persuasion." Jehan's eyes narrowed. "All right. Out with it. What did you come here to tell me?"

Michael Doukas inspected him in detail, turning then to examine Anna, who ate hungrily but watchfully. One of Jehan's daggers had found its way into her belt. "Your boy, Father? Or—no." He snatched, too quick even for Anna's quick hands, and brandished her cap, meeting her glare with laughter. He was, Jehan realized, much younger than he looked, hardly more than a boy himself. "Indeed, my lord, you take them up young! and out of hospitals too, it seems."

"Saint Basil's," she snapped. "Who are you?"

"My name is Michael Doukas. And yours, noble lady?"

She chose not to answer him. "Michael Doukas? Did you smuggle Alf out of the palace?"

"Indeed, lady," he replied, "and how do you know of that?"

"He's my brother. We're looking for him." Her eyes glittered with eagerness, her anger forgotten. "Do you know where he is?"

"Your brother?" mused Michael Doukas. "Ah, then you are an Akestas."

"Of course I'm an Akestas! They took him away with Thea, and Nikki too though they didn't know he was following till it was too late. Now we can't find him. Where is he?"

"How strange," Michael Doukas said. "I have a friend, you see. He has a friend who knows a man, who knows a woman who plies a very old trade near the All-seer's hill. She likes to talk while she works, and her clients, it seems, like to talk to her."

"Why?" asked Anna. "What does she do?"

"Never mind," Jehan said quickly, glowering at the eunuch. "Go on. What rumor did she hear?"

Michael Doukas sighed and shook his head sadly. "Business, she asserts, is better than ever before, but the clientele leaves something to be desired. But she has a little Frankish, learned in the trade; and, as I've said, she likes to use her tongue. Last night she had a client of somewhat higher rank than usual, a sergeant-at-arms who served one of the Flemish knights. A very handsome man he was, for a Frank, and very proud of it. Our good dame took due note of this. Ah so, quoth he, but he had a rival in beauty. Indeed? said she. Impossible! And he sighed, languishing, and averred that alas, it was so, but certainly she would never see this paragon, seeing that he lay in prison awaiting the hangman's pleasure."

Jehan's fingers locked about the eunuch's throat. "Where, damn you? *Where?*"

Michael Doukas swallowed painfully. "My lord—might you—?" Jehan relaxed his grip by a degree. "My lord, if I may continue, our keen-witted woman of affairs, having some liking for her trade and a certain desire to improve its quality, continued to question her client. He was pleased to tell her what he knew, for her persuasions were quite irresistible. Yes, he had seen the man he spoke of; yes, it was certain: he was destined for the gallows, for he, Latin-born, had fought as a Greek; and there was a whisper of darker things, witchery perhaps—certainly he had a familiar, a small fierce cat that had followed him into his prison. And truly he had enemies. Not the least of whom was my lord the Count of Flanders."

"Baudouin!" Jehan muttered. "I knew he had a hand in this." His fingers tightened till the eunuch gasped. "If you don't tell me now where Alfred is, I'll choke it out of you."

Michael Doukas licked his dry lips. He was not precisely afraid, but he was very much concerned for the safety of his skin. "Very well, my lord. He lies not in any proper prison but in a guarded chamber, very close indeed to Madame's place of business. She, it seems, knows the place well; it was a tavern once before the fires swept past it. Its cellars are intact, and well and strongly bolted."

Jehan loosed his grip but did not set the eunuch free. "Take me there," he said. But then, abruptly, "No. Not quite yet. Where is my lord Henry?"

The City was deathly quiet under the stars, lying stripped and torn upon her hills, her people cowering still in terror of the conquerors. Yet the Latins were quenched at last, exhausted with their three days' debauch; their lords moved now to rule the realm which they had taken, and to repair the ravages of war and plundering.

Along the shore of the Horn, Saint Mark's fleet rode at anchor. One galley glowed vermilion in the light of its many lamps; the lion banner of the Republic caught the light with a glimmer of gold.

Enrico Dandolo received his late guests in a cabin as rich as any emperor's. Weary though he surely was, no less weary than the young men who faced him, he betrayed no sign of it. He listened quietly to the tale Michael Doukas told, lids lowered over the fierce blind eyes, his face revealing no hint of the thoughts behind. The eunuch, for his part, seemed not at all alarmed to be here, face to face with the man who had ordered the conquest of his city.

"What," asked the Doge when he was done, "have I to do with this market tale?"

"An innocent man is like to die," Henry answered him. "I know better than to confront my brother in one of these moods of his. You on the other hand, my lord, he plainly respects. If you pleaded Master Alfred's case, he would be likely to listen."

"Is he innocent?" asked Dandolo.

Michael Doukas smiled. "As to that, my lord, I know he was no creature of ours. Indeed I would have wagered that he was yours, if anyone's."

Anna shook herself awake in Jehan's lap. "He wasn't anybody's! He worked in Saint Basil's and mended the hurts the fighters made. He only actually hurt anybody when they hurt one of the family. They—they killed Mother, and Irene, and Corinna. And then they shot Thea. He loves Thea better than anything else in the world. If he killed people after that, can you blame him?"

"Of blame," said the Doge, "I can say nothing. He is a Latin. He slew Latins."

"Hasn't there been enough killing?" She was close to tears. "He told you you'd win. I know—he said so."

"So he told the Emperor Isaac," said Michael Doukas.

Anna slid out of Jehan's lap and stood in front of the Doge. "You can save Alf's life if you want to. Why don't you?"

"Child," Dandolo said to her, "I am not all-powerful. Count Baudouin is a great prince, at least as great as I. If he chooses to dispose of a man for whom he has no love to spare, there is nothing I can do."

"You can try!"

It was a strange sight, the small girl in ill-fitting boy's clothes and the ancient and terrible Doge of Saint Mark. He, who could not see, yet felt it; a spark kindled deep in his eye. "Very well then. If I set your Alfred free, what will you give me?"

"My thanks," she answered.

The young men and the eunuch exchanged glances, half in alarm, half in laughter.

The Doge nodded gravely. "A fair price, when all is considered. I suppose you expect prompt service?"

"Immediate, sir."

"So." He raised his voice slightly. "Paolo! My cloak!"

With great care and with Nikki's help, Alf eased Thea out of her armor. The wound in her side seemed a small thing to have brought her so close to death, a circle of scarlet beneath her breast, no wider than her finger. Gently, with water from the jar and a strip torn from his tunic, he washed away the last of the blood.

She sighed a little under his hands. "So much metal," she said. "It weighed on my soul as much as on my body."

"You regret your bravery?"

"Of course not!" She had moved too quickly; she winced. "I regret that I didn't give Edmund a better escort into Hell. He was a fine lad. A fool, but . . . a fine one."

Alf touched her cheek. She blinked fiercely. "I'm *not* crying!" she snapped, although he had not spoken. "I'm giving the dead their due. That's all. It's over; we survive, as usual; life goes on. That, dear pilgrim, is the wisdom you came all this way to find."

He touched his lips to the center of her body's pain. *Let me heal you,* he said silently.

No Her fingers tangled in his hair. *I want to do my own mending.*
Why?

Because, she said, *I want to.*

Monk that he had been, he understood. But he was a monk no longer, and he loved her. *Let me!*

No, she repeated. Aloud she said, "I don't suppose there's anything to eat in here?"

It distracted him, as she had meant. Yet he paused. She thought hunger at him; he yielded at last, with reluctance in every movement.

Jehan's torch, raised as high as the ceiling would allow, illuminated very little. Other senses than sight told him that the space below was bare of furnishings though not of life.

A pool of scarlet caught the light. For an instant his heart stopped. He all but fell to the stone floor; the torch flared wildly as he fought to keep his feet. The toe of his sandal nudged dry softness.

A cloak the color of blood; and under it, curled together for warmth, three larger bodies and a much smaller one. They opened eyes blurred with sleep; Thea smiled and yawned. "Good—morning, is it?"

"It's just after midnight." Jehan was suddenly and blindingly angry. "Aren't you even surprised to see me?"

"Not surprised," Alf said. "Glad, yes. Very, very glad."

Very carefully Jehan unclenched his fists, then his teeth. "I should have known better. You being what you are, and Thea being what she is . . . you've made a fool of me, do you know that?"

"Of course we haven't," Thea said.

Alf was on his feet, hale and calm, embracing Jehan with a quiet joy which slew all his anger.

Light flooded the cell. Henry stepped away from the stair, and after him what seemed to be a great number of men. Some bore torches; others supported a bent figure in rich vermilion, easing his passage down the steep narrow way. Yet, once upon the level, he stood alone with but his sheathed sword for a prop.

Alf bowed low. He had barely straightened before a small whirlwind overtook him. "Alf! Is Thea all right? Why didn't you witch yourself out as soon as you got here? They said Jehan had to go down first, and not me—I don't know why. I'm angry. *Alf!*"

He gathered her up. She buried her face in his tunic and babbled into silence.

"Thea," said that lady, "is quite well. But not, yet, quite up to any greater magic than the healing of her own body. Jehan, help me up."

He approached her almost fearfully. She looked pale even for one of her kind, and thin, almost transparent; but her eyes were bright. Under the cloak she was all but naked; he draped it around her carefully and helped her to her feet.

She drew a cautious breath. "My lords will have to pardon me if I neither bow nor curtsey. I'm . . . slightly . . . indisposed."

"Please, my lady," the Doge said, "spare your courtesy and lie down again for your body's sake."

She made no objection. By that, Jehan knew truly how ill she was. But she insisted on sitting up and on speaking as clearly as ever. "My thanks for my lords' indulgence. To what do we owe the honor of your presence?"

Jehan eyed her suspiciously. She did not seem to be mocking them. But with Thea, one never knew. "It's just a little thing," he said. "A mere rescue. I don't suppose you either wanted or needed to be rescued?"

"Surely they wanted it," said Michael Doukas, moving out of the shadow by the stair. He met Alf's eyes with a smile and a slight bow. "Indeed, master seer, we meet again at Armageddon."

Alf smiled in response. "And now I owe you my life twice."

"Oh, no," said the eunuch, "you owe nothing. You permit us to flatter ourselves that we can aid you. But I owe you all that I am. Had you not foretold this war's ending, I might not have had the good fortune to serve my new and most noble lord." He bowed low to Henry. "Surely that was worth my telling a friend of yours where to find you."

"Just in time too," Jehan said. "I was going mad. When I found out that, with your usual talent for putting yourself in your enemies' power, you were in Count Baudouin's hands, I was somewhat less than delighted. I went straight to my lord Henry; he took me to the one man who could set you free. And that, Messer Enrico did."

"Easily," the Doge said. "Ridiculously so. My lord would not even see me; informed of my errand, he granted what I asked without a word of protest."

"Not quite, my lord," Jehan said. "We all heard him shouting. 'Take him and be damned! Take them all! Only let me never see or hear of them again!' "

Thea smiled. Jehan scowled. "If I'd known you were alive and conscious, I never would have bothered."

"You would have," she said calmly, "and we owe you thanks for it."

Anna snorted, a small defiant sound. "Thank him? What for? He just did the work. Saint Helena did all the rest of it."

"Then," said Alf, "when we've rendered all proper thanks to her earthly instruments, we'll sing a Mass of Thanksgiving in her honor. Meanwhile, demoiselle, shall we leave this place?"

"The sooner, the better," she said.

33

The altar stood in the garden of Saint Basil's, hung all with white and gold for the great festival of Easter. The Latin wounded had been brought out to hear the Mass; some few of the Greeks, Alf knew, listened but would not show their faces. Save for Thea, seated beside him, and the Akestas children. They had insisted upon being there, for it was Jehan who served upon the altar, moving smoothly and surely through the rite.

And Master Dionysios. The Master had made the best of a great evil, and he had prospered. Many of his people had crept out of hiding after the orgy of plundering and returned to their work; with the Latin surgeons, Saint Basil's boasted a full complement of healers. They would do well, whatever became of the City.

We'll always need doctors, Thea said, laying her hand lightly in his.

He laced his fingers with hers. A week's rest and tending, with her own witch-born strength, had done much to restore her to herself. Only a slight thinning of her cheeks, a hint of transparency under her skin, remained to tell the eye of her wounding; and to the mind a slight but persistent pain and a weakness which would not fade.

You'd be weak too if you'd been tied to your bed for a week. Without, she added with a sidelong glance, *any of the usual compensations.*

Such thoughts, he said, priestly-stern, *are not fitting in this place.* But she had caught the flicker of guilty laughter beneath.

Jehan left his acolytes to clear away the vessels of the Mass and sought the four who sat on one stone bench, basking in the sun.

Doctors and servants had taken most of the others away; they were all but alone.

Anna gave him her place on the end of the bench and climbed into his lap. "You sang beautifully, Father Jehan," she said.

"I tried my best." He frowned a very little. "Do you think your mother and Irene would have minded that I sang a Latin Mass for them?"

"Oh, no," she answered. "We had a proper priest sing their Requiem. They're buried with Father now. I'm sure they're happy to know that you remember them."

"How could I ever forget?" Jehan's blue eyes looked gravely into her black ones. "What are you going to do now?"

She shrugged. "We're still rich, you know. Mother put all our best things in a box and buried it; we dug it up yesterday. It's in our room now, with a witchery on it to keep anybody from touching it. Alf wants to take it and us to Grandmother and Uncle Philotas in Nicaea. A lot of our people went there; there's even a man who calls himself our new Emperor. Though everyone says it's Count Baudouin who's got the crown."

"The lords elected him, that's true enough."

"He didn't hang Alf. That proved his clem—clemency. And his troops like him. So they crowned him and gave the other man a palace and a kingdom and one of the old empresses. The most beautiful one, of course. I think the other man came out a lot better than he did."

Jehan laughed. "So do I! But His new Majesty doesn't think so. He's succeeded in hearing Mass today in Hagia Sophia, and from the throne besides, with everyone bowing and calling him Emperor. There's not much more he could wish for."

"Except," Alf murmured, "an empire worthy of the name."

"Prophecies again, little Brother?" asked Thea.

"No. Plain observation."

Anna ignored them. "So with the Count and the Marquis taken care of and the Count on the throne, Alf wants to take us to Nicaea."

And leave us.

Jehan blinked. The voice was silent, but it was not either Alf's or Thea's. It was softer, with an odd, blurred, toneless quality. He looked down at Nikki, who sat upon the ground playing with a handful of pebbles. The child returned his stare. *He wants to take us and leave us there and go away with Thea.*

Jehan swallowed. "He—is he—"

"No," Thea said, "he's as human as you are. Or was. That's a matter Alf is going to have to resolve for himself. For our monk that was, out of purest Christian charity, opened his mind to one doubly sealed by deafness and by humanity. The deafness hasn't changed. The other, it seems, has. Our Nikephoros, through constant proximity to power, has found it in his own mind."

Jehan shivered involuntarily. Alf, he saw, was pale and still, rebuking himself bitterly for what he had done.

Nikki's brows knit. With a shock Jehan realized that the child had read his thoughts. *If you want me to stop, I will. But you'll have to stop thinking so hard at me.*

"I—" Jehan struggled to speak normally. "I'll try."

Most people are worse than you, Nikki said comfortingly. And in a darker tone, *If Alf tries to go away and leave me, I'll follow him. I can do it. He'll never even know I'm there.*

"And I'll help you." Thea's eyes flashed upon Alf. This, it seemed, was an old argument. "You can't go away and leave him as he is now. What would the humans do to him? He needs guidance and teaching from someone who understands him. Not from people who would call him witch and changeling and cast him out."

"He needs his kin," Alf said. "They both do. Wanderer that I am, without home or family, what kind of life can I give them?"

"You can stop wandering," Anna said. "You're an Akestas. You can take our money and build a house, and we can all live in it together."

"No." Alf was on his feet. "Not in Baudouin's domain. Not anywhere in this sun-haunted East. My pilgrimage is over. I want—I need—to go to my own people. It will be a long journey through lands you call barbarian; it will be hard, and it may be dangerous. How can I take either of you with me? You're Greek; your faith is different, and your language, and all your way of living. And when you come to Rhiyana—if you come to Rhiyana—you'll find yourself among people twice alien. Don't you think you'll be happier in Nicaea with your kin, among properly civilized people?"

"Civilized!" Anna snorted. "I've had enough of civilization. I want to see new places. Different places."

"What would your mother say if she could hear you now?"

"She'd be coming with us," Anna said.

Besides, Nikki said, *you promised. You swore you'd always take care of us.*

Alf's breath hissed through his teeth. "You call it taking care of you? Dragging you off into the savage West, corrupting your pure souls with the heresies of Rome, turning you into rank barbarians?"

"You're clean," said Anna. "You speak Greek. I can learn to put up with the rest of it."

"Wait till you see the inside of a Frankish castle," Alf warned her. "And sleep in a Frankish bed. And contend with Frankish vermin."

I'll think them away, Nikki said serenely.

Thea laughed. "Acknowledge yourself conquered, little Brother! You've won yourself a family and a fortune; and neither of those, once gained, is at all easy to lose."

Alf tried to glare at them all. But none of them was deceived. Anna seized Nikki's hands and whirled him in a mad dance, singing at the top of her lungs.

He sighed deeply. "God will judge me for this," he said. A smile crept into the corner of his mouth. "Or else He already has."

Jehan grinned at him. "To be sure, He has! Who knows what He'll do with you next?" His grin faded; he ran the ends of his cincture through his fingers, suddenly tense. "Have you given any thought to how you'll travel back to Rhiyana?"

"On foot, I suppose, as I came," Alf said. "With a mule for the children."

"And the wealth of House Akestas in your wallet?" Jehan leaned toward him. "Tomorrow morning a ship sails for Saint Mark with news of the victory. I'm to be on it as my lord Cardinal's messenger to the Pope. Will you come with me?"

"On a *ship?*" Anna cried in rapture.

Alf opened his mouth. Jehan broke in quickly. "I've seen the ship. It's splendid, its accommodations are princely, and the Doge has offered passage to all of you for a fraction of the usual price. You'd pay more for a good sumpter mule—provided you could find one, with the City as it is. And," he added, having kept the most telling blow until the last, "Thea won't be up to long walking for some while yet. Why linger here under Baudouin's less than friendly eye, or tax her with too much traveling too soon? You can take your ease on shipboard, she can mend at her own pace—"

And we can have adventures! Nikki tugged peremptorily at Alf's robe. *Say you'll do it.* We *all want to.*

"We're minded to go on our own, whether you will or no," said Thea. "Well? Are you coming?"

Alf raised his hands in surrender. "Have I any choice?"

"None at all," Jehan said laughing, half in amusement and half in sheer, youthful delight.

As often before, Alf stood in Master Dionysios' study and faced the Master's grim unwelcoming stare. His own was as fearless as it had ever been, with even a touch of a smile. "You asked for me?" he asked.

"Yes." There was a box on the table beside Dionysios' hand, small, plain, of red-brown wood carved on the lid with an intricate curving design. As he spoke, his finger traced the lines of it. "Sit down."

Alf obeyed.

Dionysios' finger continued along its path. His brows were knit; his lips were thin and set. After a time he said, "You're abandoning us."

"Tomorrow, sir. It's much sooner than I'd thought or hoped. But—"

"But you let that outsize heretic talk you into it. He's not thinking of you, boy. He's thinking entirely of his own pleasure."

"Doesn't everyone?"

Dionysios' eyes flashed up. "Sometimes I'm moved to curse the fate that made you a barbarian. Then I remember the time before you inflicted yourself on me. I had peace of mind then."

"You'll have it again when I'm gone."

"No," said Dionysios. His gaze held Alf's and hardened. "If I asked you to tell me the truth, would you?"

Alf nodded slowly, but without hesitation.

"Don't," the Master said. "I had you while I had you. It cost me more than I'll ever be able to recover."

"Some of it I'll give you back. If you wish."

"I don't wish!" snapped Dionysios. "I hired you to work in my hospital. My own well-being wasn't part of the bargain. I don't want to know what you did, or what you are, or what that needle-tongued witch of yours was or is or did." Abruptly he thrust the box forward. "This is yours. Take it."

Alf drew it toward him. It was heavy for its size. He opened it and drew a sharp breath. It was full of gold. "Master! I can't—"

"Stop your nonsense. Every coin is yours. Your due and legal salary, with additions for work done above the normal requirements."

With a fingertip Alf touched a coin. The wealth of the Akestas he kept in trust for the children. But this was his own. He had earned it.

It was only yellow metal. His payment was the passing of pain. Slowly he lowered the lid and fastened it. "I . . . thank you," he said.

"Why? You worked for it." Dionysios opened an account book and reached for a pen. "Take it and go. Don't bother to come back and say good-bye. You'll get enough of weeping and wailing from Thomas and the rest of them. I won't be troubled with it. Now go!"

Alf paused. He glared. Mutely Alf bowed and left him.

For a long while after, he sat unmoving, staring unseeingly at the half-written page.

The ship's name was *Falcon;* and she was as swift as her name, her hull painted the steel-blue of the peregrine her namesake, her prow adorned with a stooping falcon. Alf, remembering the bird which had pointed his way from Saint Ruan's to Jerusalem, felt his heart uplifted by the omen.

The others had embarked already, Thea borne in a chair like a great lady, angry though it made her to be so helpless. He met her glare with a smile that spread to Anna. She looked splendid in a gown that had come to her as a parting gift from the Doge: "For a brave and noble lady," the messenger had said who brought it, "so that she need not face the savage West as she faced the wicked Doge."

She stood very straight under the weight of the honor and of the silk; but her eyes were shining and her body trembling with excitement. "Won't you hurry?" she called to Alf. "It's almost time!"

As he set his foot upon the gangway, a sudden tumult brought him about. A troop of horsemen thundered to a halt at the end of the pier, one already afoot and running. Alf left the gangway and advanced to meet him.

Henry of Flanders came panting to a stop. Somehow, even in his haste, he managed to preserve his dignity. "Master Alfred. God be thanked! I prayed I wouldn't be too late."

"For what, my lord?" Alf asked, although he knew.

"To say goodbye." Henry's eyes were bright with more than exertion. "I wish that you could have stayed."

"To be your prophet?"

Henry shook his head impatiently. "We've gained ourselves an empire," he said, "but we won't find it easy to hold. We need strong men who also have their share of wisdom—men who can speak to the Greeks as to their own countrymen, but who can speak as well for us of the West. There are all too few of them. And two are leaving on this ship."

Alf glanced back at Jehan, who stood motionless on the deck, listening. "My lord, we would stay if we could. And yet—"

"And yet." Henry smiled a hard-won smile. "I should know better than to ask for what I can't have. But it's more than your talents I'll be missing, Master Alfred. Will you say goodbye to me as a friend?"

"Gladly," Alf said, coming to his embrace.

He stepped back quickly. "Farewell, my friend, and a fair voyage."

The captain bellowed from the bridge, cursing the laggard. Alf retreated to the gangway. There for an instant he paused. "Farewell, my lord Henry," he said. He smiled his sudden smile. "It will be something to brag of in years to come, that I had the name and the love of a friend from the Emperor of the East."

"But," Henry said, "I'm not—"

"Yet," Alf said in the instant before he turned and sprang lightly into the ship.

They stood at the rail, all of them, even Thea defiantly erect. Alf took his place beside her; Anna's hand slipped into his right and Nikki's into his left, gripping hard. Smoothly *Falcon* slid from her berth and came about, her bright sails swelling with the westward wind.

Slowly, then more swiftly, Henry's figure dwindled behind them, and beyond and about him all the ruined splendors of Byzantium.

"There never was a greater city," Alf said, "nor ever one so beautiful."

"Even in her fall." Jehan shook himself and turned his face toward *Falcon*'s prow. "Well, we're done with her. God help her and everyone in her. I'm for the West and home, and glad I'll be to get there." He left the rail, staggering a little as he found his sea legs, holding out his hands to the children. "Who'll go exploring with me?"

Alf watched them go, smiling slightly as Nikki, running, snatched at his cat. The beast eluded his hands and dove beneath a coil of rope. He wavered, torn, and sprang forward with sudden decision in pursuit of his sister and his friend. Alf's smile widened almost into laughter.

Thea's arms slipped about his waist. "Well, little Brother? Has it been worth it?"

"Every moment of it."

"Even the pain?"

"Even that," he said. "Out of it, and in spite of it, I've gained more joy than I ever dreamed of: wealth and kin and friends, and," he added after a pause, "a lover."

"Last in your reckoning, I see. But I hope not least."

"No. Far from the least." He took her face in his hands. "Will you marry me, Thea?"

She pondered that with every appearance of care. "Maybe," she answered him at last. "Someday. If I'm properly persuaded. Meanwhile everyone is out and about, and we have a cabin fit for a prince, that's cost us no more than an earl's ransom. And in it . . ." Her gaze met his, bright and wicked.

He stared back, all innocence. "Yes, my lady?"

She tossed her bronze-gold braids and laughed. "Yes indeed, my lord!"

He swept her up and kissed her soundly, and bore her away.

Author's Note

The world of *The Golden Horn* is not precisely the world we know. Yet in that world as in this one, between spring and spring, 1203–1204, a Western army advanced upon and eventually conquered the city of Constantinople. Our historians have named this conflict, with its confusion of aims and motives and its devastating outcome, the Fourth Crusade.

I have taken few liberties with the framework of my history or with its major characters. Enrico Dandolo, Doge of Venice, may in fact have been a mere eighty years old at the time of the Crusade. He was certainly blind, and he was almost certainly the motivating force behind the diversion of the Crusade from Egypt and the Holy Land to Byzantium. The rivalry between Count Baudouin (Baldwin) of Flanders and Marquis Boniface of Montferrat simmered throughout the campaign, culminating some weeks after Easter, 1204, with the election of Baudouin as Latin Emperor of Byzantium. He was crowned in Hagia Sophia in May of that year. Boniface, for his part, married the great beauty, Margaret of Hungary, widow of the mad Emperor Isaac; and amid much bitter quarreling with Baudouin, established the vassal kingdom of Thessalonica. Though considerably older than Baudouin, he outlived his rival by two years.

The climactic battles of *The Golden Horn* are based solidly on fact. Henry of Flanders did indeed take the banner of the empire and the icon of the City from the Emperor Mourtzouphlos in a skirmish. It was not he, however, who pierced the walls of the City in the final battle and threw open the gates, but Peter of Amiens, among whose party was an impoverished Picard knight, Robert de Clari—the author in later days of an account of the Crusade and of his own part in it. Robert's brother, the warrior-priest Aleaumes, was first to climb through the gap in the wall, despite Robert's attempt to drag him back by the foot.

Once the Latin army had entered the City, the Greeks despaired, although the Emperor strode all but alone through the streets, striving to rouse them to battle. With his flight and the panic of his people, the enemy found themselves victorious. There followed an orgy of destruction: three days of unrestrained pillage and rapine. Constantinople was stripped bare. Her unparalleled store of sacred relics was scattered throughout the West; her works of art, both pagan and Christian, shattered or stolen (the Greek historian and eyewitness, Nicetas Choniates, bewails the wanton destruction of, for example, the Helen of Phidias; the four great bronze horses of San Marco in Venice stood once in the Hippodrome in Constantinople); her vast riches scattered among the Latins, never to be restored.

The Latin Empire of the East endured a mere sixty years. The Emperor Baudouin, captured in battle against rebel Greeks and their Bulgar allies at Adrianople in April, 1205—a year only since his taking of the City—died a prisoner. Enrico Dandolo, who came to the rescue of Baudouin's shattered army, died a month after, to be buried in Hagia Sophia. It was his great pride and his Republic's boast that he had ruled a quarter and a half of the Roman Empire; such is the inscription upon his portrait in the Doges' Palace in Venice. Certainly, whatever evil he wrought against the Greeks, he insured the hegemony of his city in the East for many years thereafter.

Henry of Flanders succeeded his brother as Emperor; he was, asserts the historian Donald E. Queller, "by far the ablest of the Latin Emperors, moderate, humane, and conciliatory." He died in 1216, still, at forty, a relatively young man, accepted not only by his own people but by the Greeks whom he had helped to conquer.

His successors could not equal his ability. At last, in 1261, Michael Palaeologus of Nicaea restored Greek dominion in Constantinople. He found the City in ruins and stripped of all its treasures. The empire he established would endure for two centuries until its final fall, in 1453, to the Ottoman Turks. But the greatest glory had long since departed. Byzantium would never again be the great power she had been before the coming of the Latin fleet to the shores of the Golden Horn.

My novel owes it background to many sources. I am particularly indebted, however, to the firsthand accounts of Geoffroi de Villehardouin and Robert de Clari; to Sigfús Blöndal's classic text, *The Varangians of Byzantium*, revised and translated by B. Z. Benedikz; and to that excellent, scholarly, vivid and detailed historical study, Donald E. Queller's *The Fourth Crusade: The Conquest of Constantinople, 1201–1204*.

The Hounds
of God

For Willie and Bonnie
For Brett

And for Jonika

He knew distinction in three abstractions of sound,
the women's cry under the thong of Lupercal,
the Pope's voice singing the Glory on Lateran,
the howl of a wolf in the coast of Broceliande.
　　　　　　　—Charles Williams,
　　　　　　　　Taliessin Through Logres

1

The fire had gone out some time since. For all its warmth of carpets and hangings and its chestful of books, the room was cold; icy.

Its occupant seemed not to notice. He sat in his plain dark robe that could have been anything, lord's cotte, scholar's gown, monk's habit, intent upon a closely written page. His only light was a stub of candle, the day having died somewhat before the fire, darkening one of the greater treasures of the Royal Chancery: the tall glass window that looked upon the sea. A second treasure lay on the desk near his hand, the heavy chain and the jeweled seal of the King's Chancellor, silver and sapphire, a shimmer in the unsteady light.

He shifted slightly on his tall scribe's stool. The candle, flaring, turned his hair to silver fire. He heeded the changing light no more than he had the cold.

Or the one who watched him, silent in the doorway, almost smiling. As he stirred, she stirred likewise. Her feet were soundless on the eastern carpet, her movements fluid, graceful. Her eyes glinted golden bronze. In a moment, perhaps, she would burst into laughter.

Directly behind the Chancellor, she paused. He did not move. She slid her arms about him and set her chin upon his shoulder.

He neither started nor recoiled. "Look at this," he said, as if she had been there reading with him for the past hour and more. "Every year for the past fifty, the Lord of St. Dol has taken a half-tariff from every boatload of fish brought into his demesne; taken it and sold it and turned a handsome profit. But here you see—the fishermen are wise. They take care to pause in certain havens and folds in the coast, and to dispose of goodly portions of their catches before submitting the rest to the lord's inspection, thus turning handsome profits on their own. So extortion requites extortion, and everyone knows and no one says a word, and each party grows gratifyingly rich."

"Very gratifyingly," she said, amused. It was not easy, shaped as she was now, to stand for long as she stood; she moved to his side. His arm settled itself round her swollen middle. She leaned comfortably against him. "And what will my lord Chancellor do to right this twofold wrong?"

Her mockery made him smile. "Wrong, Thea? The wrong is only this, that the King has no share in it. I'll give the lord His Majesty's justice: a half-tariff on his half-tariff. To increase accordingly if he tries to extort more from his people in order to keep up his profits."

She laughed. "That's royal justice! And the fishermen?"

"What of the fishermen? They pay their lord duly and properly. Their share is included in his."

She shook her head. "You'll spoil them, Alf. They'll begin to think they can wriggle out of their taxes elsewhere."

"They won't," he said, "unless it pleases them to have their less . . . public transactions recorded and taxed as well."

Her eyes went wide, mock-astounded. "Why, Alfred, my saintly love, you're devious!"

"It comes with the office." His free hand brushed the chain; paused; gathered it up. It was heavy. World-heavy. She knew; she had set it on his shoulders often enough.

He let it fall again with a cold clashing of silver. "I didn't want it," he said. "I didn't want anything except quiet and a book or two, and you. But Gwydion will never be denied."

"Maddening, isn't it? There's one man in the world who's more obstinate than you are. And being King, he can do proper battle against you."

"I'm not sure if I'd call it proper. He knighted me—that was bearable; I earned my spurs well enough, if not entirely gladly. But the spurs had titles attached. Lands; lordship. I had it all before I even knew it."

"Baron of the High Council of the Kingdom of Rhiyana," she said, savoring it. "Warden of the Wood of Broceliande. Kinsman of the King."

"And what of your own titles, my lady of Careol?"

"They're lovely. But not as lovely as your face the day Gwydion gave you yonder chain." Her eyes danced upon it. "What a splendid spectacle that was! Here was old Bishop Ogyrfan, raised up to join Saint Peter's Chancery, alleluia—where no doubt his talents would be in great demand. But who would take his place here below? Some elderly prelate, surely, as dry as his own ledgers, with an abacus for a brain. There were one or two very likely candidates. And Gwydion stood up in court and handed the chain to his dear kinsman beside him, and said, 'Labor well for me, my lord Chancellor.' "

"And his kinsman," said Alfred, "stood gawping like a villein at a fair."

"Actually," she said, "he looked like a monk whose abbot has ordered him to embrace a woman. Shocked; indignant; and—buried deep beneath the rest—delighted."

"That last, I certainly was not. I was appalled. Everyone knows what I am: a very reluctant nobleman, and in spite of all your teaching, still one of the world's innocents. Do you remember how shocked I was in Constantinopolis to learn that men are paid to be healers?"

"I remember. I also remember how you took what Gwydion gave you. Admit it now; you weren't taken completely by surprise. You'd wander into the Chancery, maybe to look up a record, maybe to argue law and Scripture with old Ogyrfan, and there'd be some small tangle somewhere. You'd look, lift that famous eyebrow of yours, and with a word or two you'd have it all unraveled."

"It was never that simple."

"Wasn't it?" Thea asked. His hand, forsaking the chain, had come to rest upon the generous swell of her belly. Her own settled over it. "You have a talent for ordering kingdoms. As for so much else."

Beneath their hands life woke, rolling and kicking, a prominence that might have been a heel, a tight coil of body. The sudden light in Alf's face made Thea's breath catch. Her laughter showed it, light, not entirely steady. "He wears armor, that son of yours. And spurs."

Alf's arms linked behind her; he smiled his swift brilliant smile. "You don't mind."

"Not much, I don't. Once he's born, I'll give as good as I get."

He laughed softly and laid his cheek where his hand had been. She looked down upon the top of his head with its thick, fine, white-fair hair; the pale lashes upon the pale cheeks, and the lingering curve of his smile. If she looked very closely in the candle's flicker, she could discern the thickening of down that might, in time, become a beard.

She shook her head wryly. She had never met a man less vain, or with more reason to be; but sometimes she caught him by her mirror, frowning at his reflection. It was always the same. Piercing-fair, luminous-pale, and very young. But the eyes as he stared into the polished silver, those were not a boy's at all.

Nor was his voice, that had the purity of a tenor bell. "Marry me, Thea," he said.

That ritual was years old. She completed it as she always had. "What! and ruin my reputation?"

"I'm thinking of our children." Which was the new litany, nearly ten months old.

"So am I," she said. "They'll be beautiful little bastards."

He stiffened a little at the word, relaxing with an effort. "They should not have to be—"

"It's somewhat too late for that. And what priest would marry us? I'm a Greek, a schismatic. I won't convert to Rome even for you, my love."

"Jehan wouldn't care. He should be here tomorrow—even today. He'd be more than glad to make us respectable."

"Jehan would go to Hell for you if you asked him. But you won't, nor will you ask him this. I won't agree to it."

He raised his head. He was neither hurt nor angry, only puzzled. "Why?"

"I love to be a scandal."

"In this place," he said, "that's not easy."

"Of course not. There's Prince Aidan—he wanted a full court wedding. And his bride a wild Saracen, an honest-to-Heaven Assassin. It took ten years and five Popes and all his mighty powers of persuasion, but he had his way. Then the Patriarch wouldn't say the words, and began a new battle royal. I have to work to keep up with that."

He sighed; rose and stretched. He was tall; he could seem frail, with his long limbs and his moonflower skin. Now and then a stranger would think him fair prey, a lovely boy as meek as a girl; would prick him and find the hunting leopard. It was not for his scholarship, or even for his feats in Chancery, that the King had dubbed him knight.

"I wish you would see reason," he said.

She smiled her most wicked smile. "I see it now. You want to keep me to yourself. Fie for shame, sir! I'm a free woman; I can do as I please."

His gaze rested upon her, clear as sunlit water and utterly undismayed. "There are two edges to that sword, my lady. Fidelity I gladly meet with fidelity. But if you, being free, decide to stray . . ."

"You wouldn't."

He smiled sweetly. "Gwydion's court is the fairest in the world. No lady in it surpasses you, but one or two could be your equal."

Her teeth bared; her eyes went narrow and vicious, cat-wild. "I'll claw her eyes out!"

Even in his amusement, he reached for her, afraid, for she shifted and blurred. For an instant the woman's form wavered behind that of a golden lioness tensed to spring. But the vision faded. Thea stood in her own form, glowing in amber silk, crackling with temper.

His hand retreated. He remembered to breathe again.

Her glare seared him. "And well you might tremble for provoking me so! Or do you want your son to be born a lion cub?"

He met her fierce witch-eyes. His own were milder but no more human; he smiled. "I want that for my son no more than you want it for your daughter."

"She might profit from it."

"Then so might he." Alf took her hands and kissed them. "My sweet lady, you have no rival and you know it. And it's only a little longer that you need suffer confinement to this single shape. When our children are born, when you're strong again, we'll run away for a while. An hour; a day. We'll run wolf-gray through Broceliande; we'll fly on falcon-wings. We'll be like young lovers again."

Her temper was cooling, but it smoldered still. "*We*, Alf? Are you going to forget your fears at last and venture the change?"

Slowly he nodded. "I'm ready," he said. "At long last. I think, with you to share it, I could let go."

"I'll hold you to that, Alfred."

His smile neither wavered nor weakened, although his fingers were cold. "I mean you to."

"Good, because you've left yourself no choice at all." She tilted her head slightly, looking up at him, making no secret of the pleasure she took in it. His hands were warming again to their wonted fire-heat, that made him impervious to winter's cold. He had willed his tension away, the old fear, the deep dread that struck in the midst of the change, when no part of his body was solid or stable and all his being threatened to scatter into the wind. But for all of that fear, he was a very great enchanter, equal to any of their people; save only, perhaps, the King.

"And you," he said softly, caught in her mind as she was caught in his.

"In some of the arts," she admitted, "maybe. In others you pass us all." Her laughter had come back all at once to ripple over him. "Then, sir prophet, how is it that you cannot see? Jehan is here. Has been here this past hour and more."

"You never——" He broke off. He knew her. Too well. "Witch! And you've let us dally here."

"He's had plenty to do. Gwydion gave him formal greeting first and a proper welcome after; all the Folk took it up. The last I saw, he had Anna on his knee and Nikki leaning on his shoulder, and he was telling tales to the whole court."

He took it from her mind, whole and wonderful; with mirth at the vision of Anna Chrysolora, woman grown and much upon her dignity, enthroned in the lap of her beloved Father Jehan.

Bishop Jehan it was now, though that was not immediately obvious. He wore as always the coarse brown habit of a monk of Saint Jerome; he seemed larger than ever, a great Norman tower of a man, with a strong-boned, broken-nosed, unabashedly homely face.

As it turned to Alf, it was suddenly, miraculously beautiful. "Alf!" Jehan laughed for sheer pleasure as he held his friend at arm's length, taking him in. "Alfred, you rogue, why didn't you tell me about Thea?"

They had all drawn back, the court, the King, even Thea, watching, smiling. Alf was hardly aware of them. "I knew you were coming for Christmas Court," he answered, "and that was more than time enough. You'll do the christening, of course."

"You'd be hard pressed to keep me from it." Jehan's grin kept escaping, stripping years from his face, bringing back the bright-eyed boy who had learned philosophy from a white elf-monk. But there was a ring on his finger, gold set with a great amethyst. Alf bent and kissed it.

"My homage to the Bishop of Sarum," he said.

Jehan bowed in return. "And mine to the Chancellor of Rhiyana. We've been busy lately, you and I, rising in the world."

"Every man receives his just deserts," said Alf.

The young Bishop looked at him—something in any case that he could never get enough of—and smiled. Alf looked splendid. Quiet; content. As if he were home and at ease, and completely at peace with himself and his world. No troubles, no torments. No yearning for the cloister he had forsaken.

"I can hardly go back to it now," he said, reading Jehan's thoughts with the ease of long friendship.

Jehan laughed and glanced at Thea. "Hardly indeed! She'd never allow it."

"Nor would I. We're having twins, you know. A son for me, she

says. A daughter for herself. It will only be the second birth among
the Kindred in Rhiyana, the second time two of us together have
made a child." Alf smiled. "Prince Alun is more excited than I am.
At last, while he's still young enough to enjoy it, he'll have cousins like
himself."

"He's what—eleven?"

"Twelve this past All Hallows. We all spoil him shamefully, but
somehow he manages to come out unscathed. That bodes well," Alf
added, "for the two who are coming."

"Love never spoiled anyone," Jehan said with pontifical surety.
He returned to the seat he had left, a bench set against the tapestried
wall. The court eddied beyond, returned to its own concerns, the
King on his throne with his Queen beside him, the high ones moving
in the ancient pattern of courts, fixed and formal as a dance. Music
had begun to play softly beneath the murmur of voices.

Alf settled beside Jehan. His eyes, changeful as water, had
warmed to pale gold; he rested his arm upon the wide shoulders.
They had sat just so at their last meeting—was it five years ago
already? And again, three before that; and three more. The same
bench that first time, the same rich hanging portraying David with his
harp and Jonathan at his feet, tall white-skinned black-headed youths,
each with the same eagle-proud face. Not that Jehan had noticed
them that time, or troubled to find the models in the King and his
princely brother—his nose had been new-broken then in celebration
of his emergence from two years' cloistered retreat, and though almost healed, it ached unbearably when the wind blew cold. Until Alf
touched him with that wondrous healer's touch and took the pain
away, and would have worked full healing if Jehan had allowed it.
"Let be," he had said, proud young priest-knight on the Pope's
errand. "It's not as if I had any beauty to lose; and I earned the stroke.
Entering a tournament with two months' practice behind me and two
years' softening in a library, and letting myself be matched with the
best man on the field. It's a wonder he left my head on my shoulders."

Alf had smiled and let be. But Jehan knew he knew. Helmless,
reeling, half strangling in his own blood, with God and fate and the
champion's arrogance to aid him, Jehan had struck his adversary to
the ground. The tale had run ahead of him, embroidered already into
a legend. Ladies sighed over him, whose face was all one hideous
bruise from chin to forehead, as if he had been as beautiful as the man
beside him.

The bruise was long gone, the face neither harmed nor helped by its broken arch. Soldier's weathering was proving stronger than the scholar's pallor, the lines setting firm, the hair beginning to retreat toward the tonsure. But he still had all his teeth, and good strong white ones they were; his strength had never been greater.

He drew a lungful of clean Rhiyanan air overlaid with wood-smoke and fresh rushes and a hint—a hint only—of humanity. The last of which, he knew certainly, did not come from his companion. Alf on shipboard, unbathed for a month save in sea water and toiling at the oars like any sailor, had no more scent than a child or a clean animal.

His eyes looked past Jehan, resting like a caress upon his lady, who held court near the fire. Lamplight and firelight leached all the humanity from his stare, turning the great irises to silvery gold, narrowing the pupils to slits. So even in the chrysalid child could one mark his kind, the people called by many names: changelings, elf-brood, Fair Folk; children of the Devil, of the old dead gods, of the Jann; but in Rhiyana, the Kindred of the King. Though that was not a kinship the law or the Church would recognize, of blood and of family, save for the two who were brothers, twinborn, king and royal prince: David and Jonathan of the tapestry, Gwydion the King and Aidan his brother. The rest had come as Alf had from far countries, brought to this kingdom by the presence of its King.

There were perhaps a score of them. They ran tall, although there were knights of the court who overtopped the tallest; they were paler of skin than most, although some were ivory. Man and woman, or rather youth and maid, for the eldest looked hardly to have passed his twentieth year, each with the same cast of feature, narrow, high-cheeked, great-eyed. And the same beauty—a beauty to launch fleets of ships, to whistle kingdoms down the wind, fierce and keen and splendid as the light upon a sword.

And as changeable, and as changeless. Just so had Alf been, monk and master scholar of an abbey in the west of Anglia, ordained priest long years before Coeur-de-Lion was born. Just so had he been in the debacle that was the Crusade against Byzantium, when the Great City fell and a Frankish emperor ruled over the ruins. Just so was he now with king and emperor long in their graves, and so would he always be. Blade or bolt might end his life. Age and sickness could not.

It should have been unbearable, Jehan supposed. He found it comforting. A deep, warm, pagan comfort that his priest's conscience chose not to acknowledge nor to condemn. Like the old Pope with his grimoires, who sang Mass with true devotion and called up his demons after, the scholar's mind knew its divisions. In one, God and the Church and all the canons. In the other, Alfred and his kin and his high white magic, and his perfect constancy. Whatever became of the world, he remained. Would always remain, a bright strong presence on the edge of Jehan's awareness.

His physical presence was a rare and precious thing, to be savored slowly, in silence. But this time the pleasure could not last. Memory flooded, cold and deadly. Jehan's muscles knotted.

Alf's grip tightened, though gentle still, a mere shadow of his strength. He did not speak. A warmth crept from his arm and hand, soothing, loosening, healing.

Jehan set his teeth against it. "You're perilous, you know," he said, trying to be light, "like lotus flowers, or poppy. Won't you let me suffer a bit? It's good for my soul."

"Is it?" Alf asked. "Not that I would know, who have none."

His glance was bright, full of mockery, but like Jehan's own it had a bitter core. Jehan flashed out against it. "You know that's not true! You of all people in the world, who wrote the book for all our theologians to build on."

"They build on Aristotle now," Alf said, "and on the Lombard's *Sentences*. Not on my *Gloria Dei*. Which may be almost as great as its flatterers make it, but it remains in its essence a testimony to one man's pride. If man you may call him—and when he wrote it, a beardless brilliant boy of thirty-three, he knew that he was not."

"You were scrupulous. You defined the soul according to Plato, Aristotle, Boethius, Martianus. You quoted Scripture and the Fathers and every recorded authority all the way to the Lombard himself. You corrected the philosophers' errors; you reconciled the canonists' contradictions. But nowhere," said Jehan, "did you exclude the possibility that you yourself, in your immortal body, might not possess an immortal soul."

"I still had hopes then of my own mortality. Hopes only, but they were tenacious. They dissolved long before my vows." Alf smiled with no appearance of strain. "It rather amuses me now. Arrogant innocent that I was, embodying all theology in a single book and sending my first copy direct to the Pope. As if all the vexed and vexing questions, answered, could encompass the reality of God—or even of a woman's smile."

"God and woman are great mysteries. But there's some comfort in answered questions, and more in your book, however you shrug it away."

"Not for me. And not for the busy scribblers in the schools or in the Papal Curia. They have no love for simple solutions, nor for my lamentable touch of mysticism. They'll lock all the world into their Categories; any who fails to fit them must be anathema."

Jehan shuddered deep and painfully. "You're prophesying. Do you know that?"

"For once," Alf answered, "yes. Tell me what you have to tell."

"What need of that? You know already."

"Tell me."

But Jehan, whose ready tongue was famous, could not bring himself to begin. "The King—does he—"

"He hears."

He was on his throne in a circle of nobles, deep in converse with a portly prelate, the Archbishop of Caer Gwent.

He was the Elvenking. He could hear what no mere man could.

Jehan drew a slow breath. *Foolish*, he upbraided himself. *It's nothing so terrible. Tell it and have done!*

His voice went at it cornerwise. "It's been a bitter year, this past one. John Lackland of Anglia dead and buried, and a child crowned in Winchester; though it's a strong regency we'll have, and I'll see my own country again. Pray God I can stay in it for more than a month at a time. I haven't done that since Coeur-de-Lion died, close on twenty years now. But I'm going back in fine fettle, with a bishopric to hammer into shape and a good number of friends at court and in the Church. I'll do well enough. I could only wish . . ."

"You wish," Alf said for him when he could not, "that Pope Innocent had not died hard upon the Anglian King, as if their long struggle for control of the See of Canterbury, once ended, left nothing for either to live for. And you wish that Innocent's death hadn't slipped the muzzles from his Hounds."

"The Hounds of God." It was a sour taste on Jehan's tongue. "The Order of Saint Paul of the Damascus Road. Hunters of the Church's enemies. Richard threw them out of Anglia for your sake; John at least had the sense to keep them out, and the Regents will see that they stay there. They're not faring so splendidly well elsewhere, either. When the Cathari in Languedoc murdered the Pope's legate, Innocent preached a Crusade against all heretics, and the Paulines swarmed in like flies to a carcass. But someone else had got there first:

that Spanish madman, Domingo, and his Preachers. That was Innocent's doing, who'd never had much use for his Hounds; he found them intractable.

"Now Innocent is dead and Honorius is Pope, and Domingo's irregulars have been signed, sealed, and chartered: the *Ordo Praedicatorum*, with a particular mission to preach the Gospel to the lost sheep of Rome. But Honorius is no fool. He knows he doesn't have Innocent's power, or the sheer gall, to kennel God's Hounds; and they're yapping in his ear day and night. Languedoc? What's Languedoc? A few villages full of Cathars, and a priest or two with a harem. There's a better target in the north. Small but fabulously rich, ruled not by mere mortal heretics but by children of the Devil himself."

"Rhiyana," Alf said calmly.

"Rhiyana," Jehan echoed him, without the placidity. "Or Rhiyanon, or Rhiannon. With such a name, how can it be anything but a lair of magic? And with such a king. Gwydion makes no secret of what he is, nor could he. The whole world knows how long he's held his throne. Fourscore years, of which he shows a mere score—and he was a grown man when he began. Even the Pauline Father General doesn't try to deny that the throne came to him from his safely mortal father. His mother was another matter. A woman of unearthly beauty, come out of Broceliande to love a young king, bearing his sons—and a daughter who died as mortal women die, though no one has much to say of that—and keeping her loveliness unaltered through long years; and when her lord died, vanishing away into the secret Wood, never to be seen again. It's fine fodder for a romance. It's meat and drink to God's Hounds."

Alf was silent, clear-eyed, unfrightened.

Jehan's hands fisted on his thighs. "Rome has always walked shy of Rhiyana. It's never submitted to invasion, but neither has it encroached on its neighbors, nor meddled—publicly—where it wasn't wanted. Its King is noted for his singularly harmonious relations with his clergy, is in fact a most perfectly Christian monarch, unstinting in either his gifts or his duties to Mother Church.

"True, he's banned the Hounds from his domains, and he's been strict in enforcing it. But it's not the Hounds themselves who make me tremble. It's not even the fabric of lies and twisted truths that they've woven around the Pope; they've been weaving it since their founding." At last he let it go. "They're preaching a Crusade."

"Ah," said Alf. "It's no longer a mutter in the Curia. It's a rumble in the mob."

"It's more than a rumble. It's a delegation sent to investigate the Church in the realm, and it's a gaggle of preachers mustering men in Normandy and Maine and Anjou. All your neighbors; not your great allies, but the little men who are their vassals, the barons with a taste for plunder, the mercenaries with a taste for blood. And the poor and the pious, who shrink from slaughtering their fellow man—however doctrinally misguided—but who would be more than glad to rid the world of a sorcerer king."

"The delegation we know of," Alf said. "It's to arrive by Twelfth Night. A legate from the new Pope with a train of holy monks. They will, His Holiness informs us, undertake to ascertain that all is well with the Church in Rhiyana; that the clergy are doing their duty and that the King harbors no Jews nor heretics."

"God's teeth!" cried Jehan. "How can you be so calm about it? Even without Gwydion's lineage blazoned on his face for a blind man to see—even if the Folk can bottle up their magic and the human folk resist the Pope's Inquisitors—they'll all burn for the rest of it. Rabbi Gamaliel in his synagogue near the schools, the Heresiarchs debating the divinity of Christ with the Masters of Theology, and Greeks and Saracens mingling freely with good Christians in the streets. This kingdom is a very den of iniquity."

"Monstrous," Alf agreed. "Like the madman—heretic surely, and lost to all good doctrine—who proclaimed: 'There is neither Jew nor Greek, there is neither bond nor free, there is neither male nor female: for ye are all one in Christ Jesus.' "

Jehan realized that his mouth was open, gaping. He closed it with a snap, and suddenly laughed. "Alf! You're dangerous."

"I can hope so. For so are our enemies. Deadly dangerous; and for all our power, we of Gwydion's Kin are very few. If I can hold off the attack by my wits and my tongue, mark you well, I will."

"But it will come. I'm a mere man and no prophet, but I know that. I feel it in my bones."

Alf said nothing. His eyes had returned to Thea. It was as clear as a cry: the love he bore her and the children she carried; the fear that he would not—could not—admit. And he was a seer. He knew what would come.

Jehan seized him with sudden fierce strength. "Alf. Go. Go soon. Go *now*. Go where nothing human can touch you." His heavy hands should have crushed those fine bones, but they were as supple as

Damascus steel. "You can," he pressed on in Alf's silence, easing his grip a little, but not the intensity of his voice. "You told me years ago, when Gwydion gave you Broceliande. It's only half in this world now—the Wood, the lands and the castles, even that part of the sea. You can close it off completely behind a wall of magic—"

"Power," Alf corrected very gently.

"Isn't it all the same?" Alf's face was unreadable, his eyes— slightly but clearly, damn him—amused. Jehan persisted doggedly. "Gwydion was born in the Wood. He's always meant to go back; to be King for as long as he's needed, to withdraw gracefully, to vanish into legend. It's all very pretty, very noble, and very much like Gwydion. But even he—he's wise, the wisest king in the world, but I think he's waited too long. If he goes now, before the delegation comes—if you all go—you'll be safe. And Rhiyana won't suffer."

"Will it not?"

"How can it? You'll all have vanished with perfectly diabolical cowardice. Rhiyana will be an unimpeachably human kingdom."

"And Rabbi Gamaliel? The Heresiarch Matthias? Hakim ibn Ali and Demetrios Kantakouzenos and Jusuf of Haifa? Not to mention my own dear brother and sister, the last of House Akestas—what of them? Shall we abandon them to the Church's tender mercies?"

Jehan's fear turned to sheer annoyance. "Don't tell me you haven't found a refuge for each and every one of them, and all their goods and chattels."

"If so," Alf said, unruffled, "it's not this way that we would go, like a flock of frightened geese."

"Not even for your children's sake?"

Alf went stark white. His eyes were truly uncanny, vague yet piercing, seeing what no other could see.

Abruptly they focused. Jehan saw himself mirrored in them, pale and shocked but set on his course. "Go," he said. "Take a day if you must, settle your gaggle of friends and infidels, and leave. Or do you want to see Rhiyana laid waste around you, and your people under Interdict, and a stake on a pyre in every marketplace?"

Alf smiled. But the color had not returned to his face. "Jehan, my dearest friend and brother, we know exactly what we do. Trust us. Trust Gwydion at least, who rules us all. He's known for long and long what must finally come to be, the payment for all his years of peace. He will not leave it to his poor people, who love him and trust him and look to him for protection. Only when they are truly and finally safe will he leave them."

"But he is their danger. You all are. Without you—"

"Without us and with all our infidels gone to haven, the Crusade loses it target. Or does it? This is a land of fabled wealth, soft and fat with long idleness. A splendid prize for an army of bandits, far more splendid than poor ravaged Languedoc. Where, I remind you, my lord Bishop, the Cathari have been the merest of pretexts." Gently, with no perceptible effort, Alf freed himself from Jehan's grasp. "I grant you, the Crusade is our fault, for existing, for tarrying so long in the mortal world. But Crusades have a way of outgrowing their makers, like the demons in the tales, destroying the sorcerers who invoked them."

Jehan knew that as well as Alf. He had been to Constantinople. He had helped to shatter that city in a war that had begun in order to free the Holy Sepulcher; had twisted and knotted and broken, turning from a Crusade against the Saracen into the gaining of a throne for an exiled Byzantine prince, and thence into an outright war of conquest.

"Yes," Alf said, following his thoughts. "But this will be no Byzantium. Not while Gwydion is King."

"Or while Alfred is Chancellor." Suddenly Jehan was very tired. He had ridden all the endless way from Rome into the teeth of winter, striving to outrace the Pope's men. He was not old, but neither was he so very young; and he had a long battle ahead of him in his own country, a bishopric to claim and defend, a kingdom to aid in ruling. And this was no land and no people of his—by his very vows he should have shunned them.

And yet, like the great, half-witted, ridiculously noble fool that he was, he loved them. Alf, Thea, the two young Greeks they had brought out of the fallen City; Gwydion and his Queen and his fiery brother and all his wild magical Kin; even the land itself, the prosperous towns, the green burgeoning farmsteads, the woods and the fields, the windy headlands and the standing stones. Certainly he was a bad priest and very probably he was damned, but he could not help it. He could not even wish to.

Alf's hands were warm and firm upon him, Alf's eyes as gentle as they were strange. "God knows," he said softly, "and God is merciful. Nor has He ever condemned love truly and freely given. To do that would be to deny Himself."

So wise, he, to look such a boy.

Alf laughed. Jehan flushed, for that was a thought he had not meant to be read. "Didn't you, brother?" The thin strong hands drew him up. "Come. It's a bed you need now, and a long sleep, and a day or two of Rhiyana's peace. That much at least is left to us all."

2

It was all silence and a splendor of light.

If Nikki chose, he could enclose it in words. High cold sun in a blue vault of sky; waves crashing, sea-blue and sea-white, and the White Keep glowing upon its headland. But closest, within the reach of his eyes, the city in festival. Bright as its houses always were, carved and painted and gilded, they shone now in the winter sun, hung with banners, looking down on a vivid spectacle. Lords and ladies with their trains, mounted or afoot or borne in litters, brilliant with jewels, gleaming in precious fabrics; knights in glittering panoply; burghers robed as splendidly as princes; free farmfolk in all their finery; whores dressed as ladies and ladies dressed well-nigh as shamelessly as whores, laughing at the cold. Jugglers and tumblers; dancing bears and dancing dogs and apes that danced for coins; a rope-dancer on high among the rooftops, actors mimicking him broadly below; jesters in motley and friars in rags, and now and then an eddy where a minstrel sang or a musician played or a storyteller spun his tales.

His nose struggled to match his eyes. Humanity, yes, from rank villein to rank-sweet noble. Incense—a procession had gone by with a holy relic, drawing much of the crowd after it until some new marvel caught their fancy. Perfume and spices, roasting meat, bread new baked and wine well aged, and manifold delights from the sweet-seller's stall a pace or three upwind.

A hand shook him as if to wake him from sleep. He looked into a laughing mischievous face, nearly on a level with his own although it was much younger: the face of a boy, a page, a tall slight gangle of a child with hair like ruddy gold. "Dreaming, Nikephoros?"

With the words came understanding, and with understanding, all in a flood, the clamor of the festival. Nikki reeled.

Alun held him up, still laughing, but chiding him through the mirth. "You shouldn't do that."

No, indeed he should not, but the silence made the rest so wonderful.

"Maybe," Alun said, speculating.

And Alun should not do it either. Nikki put on his best and sternest frown. It would have been more effective if he had been larger or his eyes smaller, or his mouth less tempted to laughter. At least he had the advantage of age—a good six years' span—and, just barely, of wisdom.

"Just barely." Alun was alight with mockery, but he was obedient enough. For the moment. He linked arms with Nikki and drew him forward. "Come, cousin! This is no day for dreaming. The sun's high and the city's wild, and Misrule is lord." He leaned close, laughing, gray eyes dancing. "Why, they say the King himself has put off his crown and turned commoner—or maybe that's he in cap and bells, dispensing judgments from Saint Brendan's altar."

Nikki laughed and ran with him, eeling through the crowd. To watch—that was wonderful. To be in it was sheer delight. They cheered the rope-dancer on his lofty thread. They devoured meat pies—paid for with kisses because the buxom seller would not take money from such handsome lads; and Alun blushed like a girl but paid up manfully, to Nikki's high amusement. They heard a minstrel sing mournfully of love and an orator declaim of war. They whirled into a street dance and whirled out of it again, breathless, warm as if they had stood by a fire.

Near the gate of the cathedral, a conjurer plied his trade. They watched him critically. *Brave man,* Alun said in Nikki's mind, *to bring his trickery here.*

He was very clever, but he had not gathered much of a crowd. A fool, Nikki decided, to think his cups and apples and scarves would earn him a living in the city of the Elvenking. But yes, brave, and good-natured too, although he looked as if he had not eaten well in a long while.

Nikki's eyes slid, to find Alun's sliding likewise. *Should we?*

Nikki set his lip between his teeth. Alf would be appalled.

So would Father.

They stood still. Those were names of power and terror. And neither would be so unsubtle as to deal out a whipping. Oh, no. The Chancellor and the King were much more deadly. They flayed not with the rod but with the mind and the tongue.

And yet.

It was the Feast of Fools. The one day in all the year when the world turned upside down.

Alun laughed aloud and Nikki in silence. *You first*, the Prince said, magnanimous.

Nikki bowed assent. The conjurer had not marked them. They were only a pair of boys amid the throng, and he was making a scarf vanish into the air. It was to come back as a sprig of holly. Nikki began to smile.

The scarf melted as it was meant to. The man's hands wove in intricate passes. At the height of them, Nikki loosed a flicker of power. There in the man's hand lay a newborn rose, pink as a maiden's blush.

Brave indeed, was that poor conjurer. He paused only an eye-blink and continued as if nothing had gone amiss.

Alun bit down on laughter. The holly—now a rose—should become a cup of water. A cup indeed it was, but it steamed, giving forth a wondrous fragrance of wine and spices. That attracted a passerby or three. Particularly when the wine, cooling, sprouted the leaves of a vine, growing and twining in the air, blossoming, setting into cascades of purple grapes.

The conjurer knew he had gone mad. Knew, and laughed with the wonder of it.

The vine faded dreamlike. But the cup was full of coins. Copper mostly; neither Nikki nor Alun had gold to spend. Still, it was more than the mountebank had earned in a month of traveling; and more had clinked into the bowl at his feet. People in Caer Gwent knew when they had seen real magic.

"Was that a sin?" Alun wondered as they drank hot ale in a tavern beyond the cathedral.

Nikki shrugged. It had not felt like one. And the man was happy, and would sleep warm tonight and eat well; maybe he would not drink away all his money at once.

"Someone will tell him what happened," said Alun. "Someone should have told him before he came here. But he had quick hands. I wonder if I could do what he did?"

It only took practice. Like swordplay, or writing.

Alun nodded. He was adept at both. "Or like power itself." He wrapped his hands around the mug, warming them, taking in the tavern with quicksilver eyes. Most of the people knew who he was, but out of courtesy they let him be. It pricked him a little, for he was proud, and yet it pleased him. He lounged on his stool like a man of the world, or at least like a squire on holiday.

"And soon I shall be one," he said.

In a year or two, maybe.

"That's not long."

Only half an eon.

Alun made as if to throw his mug at Nikki's head. "Will you never learn respect?"

Nikki grinned, thoroughly unrepentant.

"Insolent Greek." The Prince sighed with great feeling. "It's the women, surely. They spoil you, drooping after you and pleading for a glance from your black eyes. How many conquests now, Nikephoros?"

Nikki's grin began to hurt, but he kept it staunchly.

"Myriads," Alun answered himself. "More loves than stars in the sky; more kisses than—"

The inn-girl, hastening past with a fistful of emptied tankards, stumbled and fell full into Alun's lap. Without a thought, with the instinct of her calling, she kissed him soundly and rolled to her feet again as if she had never paused.

Nikki applauded, shaping words in his mind as he seldom troubled to do. *Bravo, cousin! At today's pace, you'll be passing me yet.*

"Heaven forbid!"

Nikki laughed his soundless laughter and drained his tankard. The ale sat well and comfortably in his stomach; the inn was clean and only a little crowded, no tax upon his senses. And the company . . .

The King's sole and much beloved son had gone back to his exploration of faces. Minds, no; that was the courtesy of the Kindred, strict as any written law. But they all loved to study their shortlived cousins, the other-folk who filled the world and boasted that they ruled it.

They, and *they*. Nikki inspected his own hand upon the table. Narrow wiry young man's hand, brown even in winter, with a white crisscross of scratches—he had had an argument with a cat a little while ago. The cat had repented almost at once. Quick in their tempers, cats were.

He was none so slow himself, although people called him gentle. That was his damnable calf-eyed face, and his silence. The former he could not help, short of acquiring some frightful and impressive scar. The latter was more troublesome.

His sister raged at him. Anna was visibly and publicly volatile, and voluble too. It did little good to shut eyes and mind against her. She would pummel him until he opened them, or pursue him until he yielded. "Idiot!" she cried. "Lazy slouching fool! Open your mouth and *talk!*"

The half of it that he could do, he would not, setting his lips together with stubbornness to match her own.

Her eyes snapped with fury. "You could if you would try. You know how. Alf taught you. Years he spent, while you sat like a block of wood, stubborn as a mule and twice as lazy. It's *work* to make words, even in your head. Make them aloud? Who needs them?" His glance echoed her speech. She struck out at him, almost shouting. *"You* need them, Nikephoros Akestas. Look at you! Grown already and playing kiss-in-corners with every girl in Caer Gwent, and mute as a fish. The Kindred don't need to talk, either, but they do. Every one of them. And they're not even human."

Am I? It was a gift of sorts although its tone was bitter, words spoken into her mind.

"You are!" She seized him. She was very small, a little brown bird, all bones and temper. "You are human, Nikephoros. Flesh and blood and bone—human. You eat and you sleep and you run after women. If you keep running, one of them will bring you up short with a bouncing black-eyed bastard as human as yourself. And when your time comes, you'll stop running altogether; you'll stiffen and you'll age and you'll die."

Does that make me human?

"You can't deny your blood."

He laughed without sound, with a twist that came close to pain. Blood was one thing. There was also the brain, and what lay in it. Fine handsome youth that he was, not an utter disgrace as a squire, making up somewhat in quickness for what he lacked in size and strength; not too ill a scholar though easily distracted by small things, a girl, a cat, a new bit of witchery. Who would believe the truth? Youth and pride and black eyes and all, he remained a pitiable thing, a half-made man, a cripple.

Anna slapped him hard. "You're no more crippled than I am. Less. I can only hear sounds. You hear minds. And sounds when it suits you, whatever your ears may lack."

He could never hit her back. It was not chivalry; it was plain cowardice. In his mind where it mattered, she was still the tall, terrible, omnipotent elder sister; and he was five years old, a roil of nameless feelings, a pair of eyes in a world that had no words—a silence that was a lack, but a lack he did not recognize.

Until that one came. Before names or words, he was only *he,* the stranger who came from the vast world outside the gate, hair more white than gold round a frightful sun-flayed face. But he beckoned; he fascinated. He was not like anything else. And when Nikki ventured near him, the world reeled and cracked and opened. And there were words and names, things, actions, ideas to smite him with their utter abstraction, a whole world focused upon an alien thing.

Sound. Alf gave him words, because it was Alf's nature to heal and to teach, to open minds and bodies to all that they could know. But he had not known the extent of his own power, until Nikki—human, mortal, utterly earthbound—waking to words, woke also to what had begotten them. Power; witchery. White magic. The healing, in striving to mend what could not be mended, had wrought a new sense in place of the lost one.

The small half-savage child had not even known what it was. For a little while, in his innocence, he had even been glad, thinking that now at last he was like everyone else.

The young man knew he was like no one at all.

He could not speak. He could not.

"You won't," Anna said. "It would spoil your game."

Sometimes, when he could bear it no longer, he would shout at her. He had a voice, oh yes. A hideous strangled animal-howl of a voice. It always drove her away—or himself, driven by her ears' revolt.

But she always flung the last of it at him, whether it was he who fled or she: "They'll go away, all the Kindred you cling so close to. And then where will you be?"

Alun was studying him steadily, without diffidence. Reading him with ease, head tilted, frowning a very little. "You're one of us," he said.

Nikki's fingers knotted. Suddenly he leaped up; grinned; pulled Alun after him. The innkeeper caught the coin he flung; bowed and beamed, for it was silver. He whirled back into the festival.

3

The moon was high and white and cold, the wind wild, shrilling upon the stones. Far below thundered the sea, casting up great gleaming gouts of spray.

Alf followed the long line of the battlements, circling round to that corner which jutted like the prow of a white ship. The wind whipped the breath from his lungs; he laughed into it, and stumbled a little. Surprised, he looked down. His foot had caught upon a small crumpled shadow: cloth, a softness of fur, a heap of garments abandoned by the parapet.

He smiled wryly and gathered them up, warming them under his cloak. High above the castle soared a seabird, abroad most unnaturally in this wind-wild midnight.

But then, in or about Caer Gwent, nothing was unnatural.

The bird spiraled downward. It flew well, strong upon the strong wind. Alf's ears, unhuman-keen, caught a high exultant cry. His smile warmed and widened.

Wings beat above his head. Gull's shape, young gull's plumage, dark in the moon.

Whiteness blossomed out of it. Toes touched stone where claws had been; Alun lowered his arms, breathless, tumble-haired, and naked as a newborn child.

He dived into the shelter of Alf's cloak, clasping him tightly, grinning up at him. "Did you see, Alf? Did you see what I did?"

"I could hardly avoid it," Alf said dryly. "So it's a shape-changer you are then. How long?"

"Ages." Alf's look was stern; Alun laughed. "Well then, *Magister*. Since just before my birthday. October the thirty-first: All Hallows' Eve."

"Of course."

"Of course! It's been a secret, though Mother knows. She's been teaching me. She was there when it happened, you see. We were playing with the wolf cubs, and I thought, *How wonderful to be one!* and I was. I was very awkward—and very surprised."

"I can imagine."

"I like to be a wolf. But a gull is more interesting. I think I fly rather well."

Alf helped him to dress, swiftly, for he was already blue with cold. When he was well wrapped in fur and linen and good thick wool, warming from the skin inward, he returned to Alf's cloak. "You're always warm," he said. "How do you do it?"

"How do you fly?"

Alun considered that and nodded. "I see. Only I can't . . . quite . . . *see.*"

"You only have to will it. Warmth like a fire always. No cold; no discomfort."

"Not even in summer?"

Alun's gaze was wide, innocent. Alf cuffed him lightly. "Imp! In summer you think coolness. Or you suffer like everyone else."

"*I* do. You never seem to suffer at all."

"It's known as discipline. Which leads me to ask, are you supposed to be out here at this hour?"

"Well . . ."

"Well?"

"No one told me not to." Alun tilted his head, eyes glinting. "Are you?"

Alf laughed. "In fact, no. I should be safe in bed. But I couldn't sleep, and for once Thea could."

"It's not easy to have a baby, is it? Especially toward the end."

"No. But she doesn't complain."

"She's very proud of herself," Alun said. "And happy—sometimes I look at her and all I see is light."

"I too," Alf said softly.

"Your children will be very beautiful and very strong and very wise. Like your lady—like you. Can you see, Alf? He looks like both of you together, but she has your face. She's laughing; she has flowers in her hair. I—" Alun laughed breathlessly. "I think I'm in love with her. And she isn't even born yet!"

Alf looked down at his rapt face, himself with wonder and a touch of awe. Another seer, with clearer sight in this than he had ever had. He smoothed the tousled hair, drawing his cloak tighter round the thin body. Alun was warm now, growing drowsy as a child will, all at once, eyes full still of prophecy.

It could be tantalizing, that gift they both had, drawing the mind inward, laying bare all that would be. All the beauty; all the terror.

Alf caught his breath. It was dark. Black dark and bone-cold. *Thank God,* sighed a small soundless voice, *that the beauty is his to see, and not—*

He could not see. Could only know as the blind know, in darkness, the slight boy-shape, all bones and thin skin, gripping him with sudden strength. "Alf. Alf, what's wrong?"

Light grew slowly. Moonlight; cold starlight; Alun's face, thin and white and very young, brave against the onslaught of fear. His cheeks were stiff with cold. "You're seeing again," he said. "All the bad things. But they'll pass—you'll see."

Alf shuddered from deep within. This was not like the rest of his visions; they were brutally vivid, as dreams can be, or true Seeing. When his inner eye went blind, then truly was it time for fear, for his mind would not face what his power foresaw.

Yet Alun saw beyond, into sunlight.

He drew a slow breath. Was it his own death then that he went to? He had never feared it; had longed for it, prayed for it, through all his long years in the cloister. How like Heaven to offer it now, when at last he had something to live for.

He smiled at Alun, and warmed the frozen face with his hands. "Yes," he said. "The bad things will pass. Then there'll be only sunlight, and flowers in a girl's hair." His smile went wicked. "I can guess who'll put them there."

Alun's cheeks flamed hotter even than Alf's palms. But his eyes were steady, bright with moonlight and mirth. "Will you object?"

"Only if she does."

"She won't," said Alun with certainty.

4

"Check," said Anna.

"Mate," said the Bishop of Sarum.

She looked from his endangered king to her own truly conquered one, and laughed aloud. "Father Jehan! I almost did it." Her mirth died; her brows met ominously. "Or did you—"

He spread his hands, the image of outraged innocence. "Anna Chrysolora! Would I stoop so low as to let you win?"

"You have before." But she did not credit it herself. Not this time. She had fought a battle to tell tales of, and he had—almost—fallen.

She let her grin have its way. "I'll have you yet," she promised him.

He laughed his deep infectious laugh and saluted her with her own ivory bishop. "Here's to courage! Another match, milady?"

As she paused, considering, lutestrings sang across the hall, a melody like the washing of waves, three notes rising and falling over and over, endlessly. A recorder wove into it, high and clear and lilting as birdsong.

The Queen herself played on the pipe. The lutenist—O rarity!—was the King's own Chancellor. He was ridiculously shy of playing and singing in company, but his skill was as precious-rare as his displaying of it.

They clustered round him, the court, all the Kindred: Thea banked in cushions at his feet, Alun drowsing against her; Nikki with lovely Tao-Lin in his lap; Gwydion stretched out like a boy in a bed of hounds and Fair Folk.

Alf's voice grew out of the music, soft, achingly pure.

> *"Chanson do·lh mot son plan e prim*
> *farai pois que boton oill vim;*
> *e l'auzor*
> *son de color*
> *de manta flor. . . .*

" 'A song I'll make of words both plain and fine, for the buds are on the bough, and the trees bear the colors of a mantle of flowers. . . .' "

They gave him their accolade, a full ten breaths of silence. Thea broke it with laughter both tender and teasing. "My lord, my lord, you torment us—such yearning for spring, here in the very heart of winter."

His eyes met hers and sparked. "There is fitness," he said, "and there is fitness. Take this to heart and mind, milady"—sudden and swift and fierce, all passion, all mockery:

> *"No vuoill de Roma l'emperi*
> *ni c'om m'en fassa apostoli,*
> *q'en lieis non aia revert*

per cui m'art lo cors e·m rima;
e si·l maltraich no·m restaura
ab un baisar anz d'annou
mi auci e si enferna!

" 'I would not wish to be the Emperor of Rome, nor make me its Pope, that I could not return to her for whom my heart both burns and breaks; if she will not restore me from this torment with a kiss before the new year—then me she slays, herself she sends to Hell!' "

"Bravo!" they all cried as the lute thundered to a halt.

"You heard him, Thea," Alun said. "And here it is, almost Twelfth Night. You'd better do it quickly before his prophecies come true."

But before she could struggle up, Alf had her, drawing her bulk easily into his lap. She glowered at him. "Coercion, this," she said darkly. "Compulsion by poetry. Cruel, unusual—"

He sighed, languishing. "Then I am slain, alas. Or shall I take refuge on Saint Peter's throne?"

"I yield, I yield!" And after a goodly while: "You wouldn't." His eyes were glinting. "Dear God! I believe you would."

"Imagine it," said Jehan. "Pope—what? Innocent? Boniface, with that bonny face of his? He wouldn't be the first enchanter in the Holy See, and he's closer to a saint than most who've sat there."

Anna's brows went up. "Some would say there's no 'close' about it. Thea for one. Though to my mind, the distance is just exactly the breadth of her body."

That, coming from a woman and one of breeding besides, disconcerted the Bishop not at all. In fact it delighted him. "Anna my love, we should loose you on the schools."

"Don't," she said. "They'd never survive it."

"Oh, but what a wonder to watch them fall, laid low by one woman's wit."

"Poor proud creatures." She took the ivory bishop from his hand, returning it to its home on the board. "I rather pity them. Masters and scholars, clerics all, professing a celibacy few care to observe—and they fulminate at length on the frailty of the female. Should I be the one to disabuse them?"

"It might do them good."

She shook her head. "No. Let them play. I've enough to do here with all these wild witch-children."

"Children!" He laughed. "Some of them are ancient."

"Do years matter to them?"

He looked hard at her. He had a sharp eye, and a mind sharper still behind the battered soldier's face. "Anna. Is everything well with you?"

"Of course." She said it clearly, without wavering, even with a smile and a glint of mischief. "Let me guess. You worry. Little Anna's not so little anymore. And here she is where she's been for the past dozen years, living in Caer Gwent, studying what and when it suits her, traveling when the urge strikes her, lacking for nothing. Except that any self-respecting woman of her age ought to be safely married, whether to a suitable man or to God."

"Do you want that?" he asked.

"I never have. I'd like to go on and on as I am. Except . . ."

"Except?"

She shook her head. "Nothing. This is an odd place to live in, don't you know? All the magic. All the Folk—the wonders; the strangenesses. You'd think after more than half my life here I'd be used to it. But I'm not. I can remember when I was little, living in the City. Mother, Father, Irene; Corinna—do you remember her? Franks killed her. They killed my whole City. But Alf and Thea took me away, took me in and brought me up, taught me and tended me and loved me. They gave me so much; still give it, unstinting. I don't think anyone has been as fortunate as I am.

"But you see, it can't last. Sooner or later they'll go away. Probably sooner. Then where will I be?"

"Where people have always been when they grow up."

"Alone."

"Alone, maybe. But luckier than most. You have wealth, you have learning; you can live as you please."

"I can, can't I?" She took his large hand in her own very small one. "In that case, I know whom I want for my knight."

"What! Not one of the handsome fellows here?"

"None of them is also a bishop."

"You *are* clever, taking in heaven and earth in one fell swoop."

"Why not, when it's so convenient?"

He laughed and bowed extravagantly and kissed her hand. "At your service then, fair lady, and gladly too." He rose. "Shall we abandon the chessboard for a turn of the dance?"

They were dancing indeed, steps and music new from Paris, with variations that were all Rhiyana. Even the humans here had an air, a grace that was not quite of their kind, a hint of magic. It made their court the fairest in the world; it made their dancing wonderful.

Nikki whirled out of a wild *estampie,* dropping to the floor beside Thea, lying for a moment in a simple ecstasy of stillness. He grinned at her; she smiled back and patted his cheek. "Handsome boy," she said. "When I finish atoning for my last sin, will you help me commit another?"

He laughed. His breath was coming back. He sat up, appropriating a share of her cushions, settling with the ease and completeness of a cat. The dance spun on; would spin the night away with hardly a pause, beating down the old year, pressing out the new.

Thea, bound to earth by the weight of her body, could only watch. She played with Nikki's hair, smoothing it, trying to tame it. It curled, which was fashionable; it curled riotously, which was not. Women always yearned to stroke it. But only Thea could do that when and as she pleased.

He looked at her and stifled a sigh. She was so very beautiful. They worried a little, Alf, the King; she was not well made for childbearing, too slight, too narrow. But she was strong; she had carried well, with both grace and pride. She had been riding and dancing right up to Yuletide.

His teeth clicked together. He examined her more closely. She was unwontedly sedentary tonight, content to recline like an eastern queen, gravid, serene. But Thea was never, ever serene.

Was she a little paler than she should be?

Her mind seemed to hold nothing but pleasure in his presence and intentness on the dance. The swift drumming of the *estampie* had given way to a subtler rhythm. Strange, complex: a clatter of nakers, a beating of drums, a high thin wailing of pipes. Gwydion had left throne and crown to tread the new measure; his image whirled beyond him, gold and scarlet to his white and silver, dizzying to watch: man and mirror, twin and twin, king and royal prince caught up in the rhythm of the dance.

"They dance for the life of the kingdom," said Thea.

Nikki nodded slowly. He could feel the swift pulse of it, strong as the beating of the drums, frail as the wailing of the pipes. They were all in it now save only she. Even Alf, tall sword-slim youth with hair flying silver-fair, reticence and scholarship forgotten, unleashing for this moment his lithe panther's grace. With each movement he drew closer to the center, to the King. The pattern shaped and firmed about him. Wheels wove within wheels. Human bodies, human wills, human minds babbled oblivious; but at the heart of them swelled a mighty magic. Here in the White Keep at the turning of the year, under the rule of the Elvenking, his Kindred had raised their power. Power beyond each single flame of witchery, power to shake the earth or to hold it on its course; power to sustain their kingdom against all the forces of the dark.

Thea tapped Nikki between the shoulders, a slight, imperative push. "Go on. Help them."

He hesitated. He—he was not—

"For me," she said, fierce-eyed.

There was a space, a gap, a weakness in the pattern. He let it take him.

A much larger presence took Nikki's place at Thea's side. Jehan had left Anna with a crowd of young scholars, all wild and some brilliant, concealing their awe of the royal court behind an air of great ennui. The presence of a bishop, a friend of the Pope himself, had been rather too much for them.

Thea could remember him as a novice with a pocketful of stolen figs, reading the *Almagest* in a hayloft. She grinned at him; he grinned back. "There's magic in the air tonight," he said.

"Ah, shame! You've been here a scarce week and already you're corrupted. You'll be singing spells next."

"The Mass is quite sufficient for me."

"And what is that but the very greatest of enchantments?" She shifted a little, carefully. With no apparent haste he was there, supporting her, easing her awkward weight. His eyes were very, very keen.

Irritably she pushed him away. "I am *not* delicate!" she snapped.

He was not at all perturbed, although she could blast him with a thought. Calmly, boldly, he laid his hands upon her belly. "Not delicate," he said cheerfully, "but none too comfortable either. When did it start?"

A hot denial flared, died. He was human; he had no power; but he had never been a fool. She lowered her eyes. "It's nothing yet. Just a pang here and there."

"How long?"

"Since before dinner."

His fingers probed gently, unobtrusively, and with alarming skill. He did not say what she knew as well as he: that one small body was as it should be, but the other was not, the daughter as willful-contrary as her mother.

"You've been shielding," he said.

"For my own peace of mind. The longer it takes Alf to start shaking, the better we'll all be."

He shook his head. The humans had fallen one by one out of the dance. It was all of the Kindred, and Nikephoros among them, small and dark and solid but utterly a part of them. The King had left their center; one spun there alone, all the pattern in his long white fingers, all the power singing through him, about him, out of him. If he let go—if he even slipped—all would shatter, pattern and power and the minds of those who shaped both.

Jehan loosed his breath in a long hiss. "But it's Gwydion who should be—"

"The King is King of Rhiyana, mortal and otherwise. That," said Thea, "is the Master of Broceliande."

Jehan understood. "God's strong right arm!" he muttered. "Our Brother Alf, the master sorcerer of them all."

"Exactly. And tonight of all nights, he needs his full power. No troubles; no distractions."

"But—" Wisely Jehan set his lips together and began again. "He's arming the last of your defenses. But I thought they were all in the Wood."

"Gwydion won't neglect the whole of his kingdom. Nor," she added, "will Alfred. Those two are a perfect pair."

He did not smile at her mockery. He was still absorbing what she had told him. "I always knew he was strong. But as strong as that . . . How did you ever get him to admit it?"

"We didn't. He hasn't. He's simply doing what he has to do."

In fire, in splendor; leaping, whirling, soaring like a falcon, swooping down to strike the earth itself, strike it and hold it and guard it, and drive back all who dared to ride against it.

Thea's teeth set. Jehan saw. There was no shielding from those eyes or those hands. She gripped him with strength enough to make him wince. "Don't—*don't*—"

It was a gasp, but it was loud, startling. The music had stopped. The dancers stood poised, their pattern complete.

It frayed and shredded. Its center flashed through a rent, like light, like white fire. Jehan fell back before him.

Thea regarded him without fear, even with amusement. "Dearest fool," she said, "it's only childbirth. It happens every day."

"Not to you." He lifted her. He was breathless, his hair wild, his face both flushed and pale; he looked hardly old enough to have fathered a child, let alone to be the prop and center of all Rhiyana's magic. But his eyes were still too bright to meet. "What I should do to you for your deceit—"

"It served its purpose, didn't it?" She let her head rest upon his shoulder. "Well, my love, are we going to make a spectacle of ourselves here, or would you prefer a little privacy?"

For a moment the flush conquered the pallor. He held her close, kissed the smooth parting of her hair, and strode swiftly toward the door.

5

"It's taking a very long time," Alun said.

They had converged upon Jehan's small chamber: Alun, Nikki, Anna. That it was very close to Thea's childbed, being the chaplain's cell of the Chancellor's Tower, had something to do with their presence there, but they seemed to take comfort in the occupant himself.

None of them had slept much. Alun was owl-eyed but almost fiercely alert, perched at the end of the hard narrow bed. "All night it's been," he said. "I don't like it."

Anna looked up from the book which she was trying to read by candlelight. "It often does take a while, especially with first babies. Your mother was two days with you."

"Yes, and it almost killed her!" Nikki drew him into a quieting embrace; he pulled free. "We're not like you. We're strong in everything except this. It's so frighteningly hard even to get children, and then we can't bear properly. As if . . . we weren't meant . . ."

Jehan grasped his shoulders and held him firmly. "Stop that now. Alf is there, and your mother, and your father. They won't let anything happen."

Alun drew together. Too thin, too pale, too sharp of feature, he had not come yet to the beauty of his kind; he was all eyes and spidery limbs, quivering with tension. "Alf is afraid," he said.

To his indignation, Jehan laughed. "Of course Alf's afraid! I've never met a new father who wasn't. And the more he knows of midwifery, the more terrified he's apt to be, because he knows every little thing that can go wrong." The Bishop held out his hands. "Here, children. Let's sing a Mass for them—and for us, of course, to keep us from gnawing our nails."

Alun looked rebellious. Anna frowned. Nikki tilted his head to one side, and after a moment, smiled. *Why*, he said clearly in all their minds, *it's Epiphany. Twelfth Night. We can ask the Three Kings to help Thea.*

"And the Christ Child." Alun leaped up. "They'll listen to us, I know it. Come, be quick! We've no time to waste."

The chapel was small but very beautiful, consecrated to Saint John, the Evangelist, the prophet, and incidentally, Jehan's own name-saint. Long ago, when this had been the Queen's Tower, this chapel had been hers. Alf had kept the century-old fittings, adding only new vestments and a new altar cloth of his own weaving. For that skill too he had, a rare and wonderful magic, to weave what he saw into a tangible shape. Snow and moonlight for the altar, sunlit gold for the chasuble, both on a weft of silk.

The children sat close together near the altar, two dark heads and one red-gold; two wide pairs of black eyes, the third fully as wide but gray as rain. Alun, in the middle, held a hand of each of his friends.

Only he sang the responses; Anna never would and Nikki could not. His voice was almost frightening, high and achingly pure, soaring up and up and up, plunging with no warning at all and with perfect control into a deep contralto. Even in his trouble, or perhaps because of it, he took a quiet delight in that skill, smiling at the man on the altar.

Of course, Jehan thought; the boy was Alf's pupil. Small wonder that he could sing like an angel—or like a Jeromite novice. The others were devout enough, but he was rapt. As if there were more to the rite than words and gestures, a depth and a meaning, a center that was all light.

What priest he would make!

Jehan sighed a little even in the Mass. What a priest Alf had made, and he had had to leave it or go mad. And this was a royal prince, heir by right to a throne, even without the fact of his strangeness. His damnation, the Church would decree. Absolute and irrevocable by his very nature, because he was witchborn; he would not age, he would not die.

The Church is a very blind thing.

Nikephoros' voice, distinct and rather cold.

While Alun made a rippling beauty of the *Agnus Dei*, Jehan met the steady black stare. He did not try to answer. Nikki had heard it

all, attack and defense, a thousand times over. And being Greek,
tolerant of Rome but never bound to it, he could judge more calmly
than most.

*Nor am I . . . quite . . . human. I was certainly born with a soul; it's a moot
point whether I've lost it since.*

Another of Alf's clever pupils.

And Thea's. Nikki's head bowed; his eyes lowered. His whole body
spoke a prayer.

Pain was scarlet and jagged and edged with fire. Pain was something
one watched from a very great distance, and even admired for its
perfect hideousness. But one did not mock it. Not after so long in its
company.

A most unroyal crew, they were. A slender child in a smock like
a serving maid's, ivory hair escaping from its plait, lovely flower-face
drawn thin with weariness. A tall young man with his black brows
knit, his shirt of fine linen much rumpled with long labor. And closest
of all to heart and body, a youth as tall as the other, still in his cotte
of cloth of silver, bending over the focus of the pain: a body naked and
swollen, gone to war with itself.

"It was just so with me," said the girl, who was no girl at all but
a queen. "A battle, Alun's power against my own. And here are two,
stronger still in their minds' bonding, struggling to keep to the
womb."

No. Thea had no breath to say it aloud, but her mind had a little
strength left. *It's not only that. I'm too small. Fighting myself, too. Alf, if you
need to cut—*

He shook his head, stroking her sweat-sodden hair out of her
face.

Anger flared with the pain. *Damn you, Alfred! I'm* tired.

"Not too tired to rage at me."

And he was taking the pain, setting her apart from it. But she was
past repentance. *Out!* she cried to the center of the struggle. *Out with
you!*

It had power, and it was stark with fear, all instinct, all resistance.

Alf's hands were on her, startlingly cool. "Push," he commanded.
He reached with his mind, drawing in the others, aiming, loosing.

A cry tore itself out of her.

He was relentless. *"Again."*

Oh, she hated him, she hated his will, she hated the agony he had
set in her. She gathered all her hate and thrust it downward.

Maura was there beside Alf. "Almost, Thea. Once more. Only once."

Liar. There were two of the little horrors.

She pushed.

Something howled.

Something else tore, battling.

Little witch-bitch. Kill her mother, would she?

"Turn her." Gwydion, but strange, breathless. Excited? Afraid? "Alf, turn—"

Like a blocked calf.

That was Alf's shock and his utterly unwilling amusement. And his power, stretching and curving, turning—slipping.

Strong little witch.

Holding. Calming. Easing, inch by inch. Down, round.

Ah, *God!*

Out.

The world had stopped.

No; only the pain.

Gwydion was grinning, impossible, wonderful vision. Alf was far beyond that. He laid a twofold burden on her emptied body, red and writhing, hideous, beautiful, and suddenly, blissfully silent. She met a cloud-blue stare. That was the little witch. And the little sorcerer without armor or spurs, only his strong young heels, with dark down drying on his skull; but his sister had none at all, poor baby.

With great care and no little effort, Thea touched the damp soft skin. Real, alive, breathing, and strong. Strong enough to put up a magnificent fight and almost win it. Tired as she was, she laughed a little. "Alf, look. See what we made!"

If he had shone with joy before when the children moved within her, now he blazed. His hand brushed them, found their mother, returned to the small wriggling bodies. They moved aimlessly, lips working, seeking. He laughed in his throat, soft and wonderfully deep, and eased them round, holding them without effort as each found a brimming breast.

This too was pain, but sweet, swelling into pleasure. She curved an arm about each and realized that she was smiling. Grinning rather, like a very idiot.

Gwydion bent and kissed her brow; bent again to her lips. She tasted the fire that slept in him. "Now," he said imperiously, "name them for their King."

She met Alf's gaze. Her arm tightened about her daughter. "Liahan, this is."

"And Cynan," Alf said, cradling his son more carefully.

"Good Rhiyanan names," said the Elvenking.

"They're Rhiyanan children." Alf's eyes glinted. "Whatever their parents may be."

"A Greek witch and a renegade Saxon monk. A splendid pedigree." Thea yawned in spite of herself. Liahan began to fret; Alf gathered her up deftly, one-handed. Her mother smiled.

Within Thea, something shifted like a dam breaking.

Her arms were empty. "The babies—where—"

"Maura has them." Gwydion was death-white, calm again. Too calm. Alf she could not see. She had lost her body again.

"I want my children. Why did you take them away? I want my children!"

Alf came back to her mind first, then to her eyes. His hands—

A gust of laughter shook her—hysteria. "Alf! You've murdered somebody. You're all blood." She could not see properly. Could not think. Horror struck deep. "You killed them! You killed—"

Strong hands held her down. She fought.

Alf's voice lashed out. "Stop it!"

Gentle Alf, who never shouted, who would never even quarrel. She lay still, straining to see him. "Alfred—"

He spoke quietly again. Very quietly, very levelly. "Thea. The blood is yours, and only yours. If you love me—if you love life—you will let me heal you. Will you, Thea? Can you?"

Fear had gone far away. Alf was a white blur, a babble of words echoing in her brain. Her power throbbed like an ache. He was holding back the flood. Holding, but no more. Her barriers held too firmly against him.

He could live in her mind. He could set his seed in her. He could—not—invade her thus. Reaching deep into her body, shaping, changing, outsider, alien, forbidden—

"Thea!"

His anguish pierced where reason could not, stabbing deep and deep. Relief like pain; the swelling of that most miraculous of his powers. Slowly she yielded before him.

Thea slept. Alf wavered on his feet. Even for one of his kind, he was far too pale.

Gwydion braced him. He allowed it for a moment only, drawing himself up, firming his stance. "She'll live now," he said, little more than a sigh. "My lord, if you would, I should bathe her; and the bed—the servants—what Dame Agace will say—"

"We'll see to it."

He stiffened. "I can't rest now. The embassy from Rome—"

"Your place," said Maura, "is here." She extricated him from Gwydion's hands, drawing him with her. "Here, sit. Water is coming; you can bathe, too. And eat, and then sleep."

He would take the bath and the food; he could even let his King and his Queen together clear away the bloodied sheets and spread fresh ones sweet-scented with rose petals. But he would not sleep, nor would he sit by while they tended the unconscious body of his lady, washed it and clothed it in a shift and laid it in the clean bed. "If I need rest," he said rebelliously, "then what of you?"

"We'll snatch an hour," Gwydion answered, "but only if you rest now."

Alf's eyes flashed with rare ill temper. "Blackmail!"

The Queen laughed. "Assuredly. Lie down, brother. I'll watch over you all and keep the throngs from the door."

"And your husband in his bed."

"That too," she agreed willingly, and laughed again, for the King's brows had met, his rebellion risen to match his Chancellor's. But he knew better than to voice it. Proudly yet obediently he retreated.

The Queen circled the room. Alf slept twined with his lady in the curtained privacy of their bed. Their children breathed gently in the cradle that had been Alun's and bore still in its carvings the crowned seabird of the King; but the coverlet was new, embroidered with the falcon of Broceliande and the white gazehound of Careol. Maura smoothed it, moving softly, smiling to herself. Already the children's faces were losing the angry flush of birth, taking on the pallor of the Kindred.

By the bed's head stood a table laden with books. There were always books where Alf was; he and Gwydion between them had made the library of the castle a scholars' paradise, filling it with the rare and the wonderful.

She took up a volume of Ovid. It was intricately and extensively written in, in Alf's clear monkish hand, and now and then Thea's impatient scribble: glosses, commentary, and acerbic observations.

Maura sat by the cradle, rocking it with her foot, and began to read.

The door eased open. She looked up. A head appeared, eyes widening as they met hers. Alun hesitated, drew back, slid round the door looking guilty but determined.

His mother held out her hand and allowed her smile to bloom. "You're somewhat late," she said.

As he came into her embrace, the room seemed to fill behind him—Anna, Nikki, Jehan looming over them all. Their expressions mingled joy, anxiety, and a modicum of respect for the Queen's majesty.

Alun voiced it all in a breathless rush. "Mother! Are they well?"

"All very well," she answered him. "See."

The young ones crowded round the cradle, silent, staring. Jehan waited patiently, but his glance strayed most often to the bed. "Thea?" he asked very quietly.

"Weak, but well." His worry was a tangible thing; she smiled to ease it.

He blinked, dazzled, and smiled back. "I understand . . . it was a battle."

Alun turned quickly. "And when I wanted to go and help, you pulled me down and sat on me."

"So," said Jehan, "I committed a crime. *Lèse-majesté.*"

"That's only for kings." Carefully, almost timidly, Anna set the cradle to rocking. "They're beautiful children, these."

Alun turned back beside her. "They're all red."

Nikki grinned. So had Alun been when he was born, shading to crimson when he howled.

He glared but did not deign to respond. Nikki only grinned the wider.

Alf's head appeared from amid the bed curtains, peering out at the gathering. If it surprised him to see them all there after Maura's promise, he gave no sign of it.

Even so little sleep had brought back his sheen. He emerged with care lest Thea wake, drawing everyone at once into his joyous embrace. Even Jehan—especially Jehan, who had never been one to stand upon his dignity. "The old Abbot should see you now," the Bishop said grinning. "He'd be cackling with glee."

"Wouldn't he?" Alf laughed for the simple pleasure of it and stooped to the cradle, raising his son, setting the blanket-wrapped bundle in Jehan's arms. But his daughter he gave to Alun with a little bow. "My lord, your bride."

Alun held her stiffly, staring at her face within the blankets. She was awake and a trifle uncomfortable. He shifted his grip, easing it, relaxing little by little. She blinked and stirred, but in comfort, learning this body in this new world, in the cold and the open and the sudden awesome light.

"I remember," Alun said slowly. "A long, long time ago . . . everything was so strange. All new. As if it had never been before, but now it was and would always be." He blinked—had he known it, exactly as Liahan had done—and shook his head. Alf was smiling at him. "I *do* remember!"

"I believe you. My memory goes back not quite so far, but far enough."

"Oh, but you're old!"

Alf laughed. No one had ever heard him laugh so much. "Old as Methuselah, and happy enough to sing."

"Do that!" cried Anna.

"Yes." Thea's voice brought them all about. It was somewhat faint and she was very pale, but she was sitting up, smiling. "Do that, Alf."

His mirth faded. Turned indeed to a frown as she stood swaying, as white as her shift. Swifter than sight he was beside her, sweeping her up. "You, my lady, are not to leave your bed for a day at least."

"Indeed, my lord?" She linked her hands about his neck. "Am I such a weakling then?"

"You almost died."

"Only almost." She sighed deeply. His stare was implacable. "Well then. I suppose I can humor you. *If*—"

"No *ifs*, Thea."

"If," she continued undaunted, "you forbear from fretting over me. Aren't you supposed to be receiving an embassy?"

"You'd send me away now?"

He looked almost stricken. Her eyes danced. "Not just now. You can hover over the cradle for a bit. You can sing for us all. But first and foremost," she said, drawing his head down, "you can kiss me."

6

Alf paused just outside the King's solar. Nikki, in the gray surcoat and falcon blazon of his squire, straightened the Chancellor's chain of office and smoothed his cloak of fine wool and vair. He was oblivious to the service, ears and mind intent upon what passed beyond the door.

Nikki smiled wryly. *There's one advantage in being late,* he said. *You don't have to stand through the usual round of ceremonies.*

Alf turned wide pale eyes upon him. Slowly they came into focus. "Gwydion is alone in there."

Alone with half his court.

"Servants and secretaries."

And the Bishop of Sarum.

But none of his Kin. He had commanded it. The Pope's men could have seen them in the hall, tall fair people mingling freely with the human folk, but there would be no closer meetings. Not while the kingdom's safety rested upon the goodwill of the embassy.

Abruptly Alf strode forward. Nikki stretched to keep pace. The guard bowed them through the door.

The Pope had chosen his men with great care. The Legate himself was slightly startling, a young man for a cardinal, surely no more than forty, lean and dark and haughty, with a black and penetrating eye. But he was no fanatic. No; he was something much more deadly. A true and faithful man of God, deeply learned in both law and theology, and gifted with a rare intelligence. It took in the arrivals; absorbed but did not yet presume to judge, although the kind of the tall young-faced nobleman was clear to see.

His attendants were less controlled. Ordinary men, most of them, uneasy already in the presence of one of the witch-people. They crossed themselves as Alf passed, struggling not to stare, fascinated, frightened, but not openly hostile. But one or two among them struck Nikki's brain with hate as strong as the blow of a mace. He staggered under it.

They never saw. He was only a servant, human, young and rather small, invisible.

He firmed his back and raised his chin. He could see who hated. They looked no different from the rest, Cistercians by their habits, eyes and faces carefully matched to their companions'. Only their sudden hate betrayed them, a hate thickened with fear.

Gwydion seemed undismayed by it, sitting as he sat when he would be both easy and formal, his cloak of ermine and velvet cast over his tall chair but his crown upon his head. He rose to greet his Chancellor, gesturing the others to remain seated, holding out his hand. "My lord! How fares your lady?"

Alf bowed over the King's hand, as graceful a player as he, and no less calm. "She is well, Sire, I thank you for your courtesy."

The King turned to the Legate. "Here is joy, my lord Cardinal. His grace the Chancellor is new come to fatherhood: a fine pair of strong children, born on this very day of Epiphany."

Had Nikki been free, he would have laughed. The poor monks were appalled. The Hounds in shepherds' habits were outraged. Benedetto Cardinal Torrino was wryly and visibly amused. "My felicitations, my lord," he said, smooth and sweet and impeccably courteous.

Alf bowed. The Cardinal regarded him under long lids, considered, offered his ring. Devoutly Alf kissed it.

Nikki's mind applauded. The devotion was real enough, but the drama was splendid. One good simple monk, chosen for his faith more than for his erudition, looked to see the Devil's spawn expire in a storm of brimstone.

He did not even flinch. The Cardinal smiled. "So, sir, you are the White Chancellor. Even in Rome we have heard of your accomplishments."

More even than he knew, Nikki thought.

"Your Eminence is kind," Alf said with becoming humility.

"I am truthful. You are, so they say, a man of exceptional talents."

The fair young face was serene, the voice unshaken. "I am no more than God has made me. And," he added, "no less."

"The Devil, they say, may quote Scripture." That was meant to be heard, the speaker one of those who hated. He stood close behind the Legate, a man whose face one could forget, whose mind blurred into a black-red mist.

Nikki's shields sprang up and locked. He stood walled in sudden silence. Alf moved to sit beside the King, not, it seemed, taking notice. But that mind was *wrong*. Nothing human should be all hate. Nothing sane; nothing natural.

His throat burned with bile. He laid his hand on Alf's shoulder, opening the merest chink of his power. Through it shone Alf's reassurance: *He can't touch us here.*

He had no need to. There was something in him. Something strong. Something with power, but not the power Alf had, the white wizardry of the Kindred. This was black and blood-red.

You needn't stay, Alf said.

Nikki thought refusal, with a touch of temper.

Alf shrugged invisibly against his hand. That choice was his to make. But let him listen and be firm and not be afraid.

This time the flare of anger made Alf start. Nikki muted it in sudden shame, but he could not entirely quell his satisfaction. He was alarmed, not craven; certainly he was no weakling.

Alun shook himself hard. His long sleepless night was creeping up on him. Anna sat where the Queen had been before, reading the book Maura had left behind. Thea drowsed in the bed with Cynan curled against her side. In his own arms, Liahan hovered on the edge of sleep. By witch-sight she glowed softly, power as newborn as herself, flickering a little as he brushed it with his own bright strength.

Sometime very soon, she was going to be hungry. He could feel it in his own stomach, which in truth was newly and comfortably filled. He smiled and touched a finger to the small round belly with its knot of birth-cord.

She stirred. She was startlingly strong, adept already at kicking off her blankets, as at objecting when the cold air struck her skin. Her lungs were even stronger than her legs.

"Here," Thea said, rousing and holding out her arms, "let me feed her."

Alun surrendered her with great reluctance, to Thea's amusement. Which deepened as he backed away, blushing furiously, looking anywhere but at the swell of bare breast, white as its own milk.

He clenched his fists. She was laughing. Of course she would, who had made an ardent lover of an Anglian saint. He pushed himself toward her, even to the bed at her side, where Cynan was waking to his own sudden hunger.

"This could get inconvenient," Thea observed as Alun settled her son into the curve of her free arm. He banked her with pillows.

Twofold mother though she was, her smile was as wicked as ever. "Greedy little beasts. No wonder sensible ladies put their babies out to nurse."

He perched on the bed's edge and tucked up his feet. His blush was fading. "I think you're sensible. As long as you're . . . able . . . I mean, *two* of them—"

"I mean to be able." Her expression was pure Thea, both tender and fierce. "I went to a great deal of trouble to have these two little witches. I'm not about to hand them over to someone else to raise."

"You did it for Alf, didn't you?"

"I did it for myself." She softened a little. "Well. For him too. Rather much for him."

"I remember when he first knew." Alun grinned. "That was something. The whole castle shook with it. Drums and trumpets and choruses of alleluias; you could have lit a chapel with his smile."

She laughed. "Only a chapel? No; a whole cathedral."

"He's still as happy as he was then," Alun said. "Happier."

"Sometimes I think we're all too happy." But Anna smiled as she said it, exchanging her book for a milkily sated Cynan. "Though I remind myself that bliss is never unalloyed where there are children. Especially witch-children."

"When have there ever been—" Alun stopped and swung at her, mock-enraged.

Thea deposited her daughter in his outstretched arms. "Oh, yes, sir, we all suffered with you. Now you can pay back the debt. Put her to your shoulder. Yes, so. And have at her—thus." She clapped her hands. "Bravo! You'll make a mother yet."

Alun rose, wobbling a little. Cynan lay already in the cradle and already asleep. Carefully the Prince laid Liahan beside him. Her eyes were shut, her mouth folded into a bud. But her hand, wandering, found his finger and gripped hard.

He looked up into the women's wide smiles, and down again, smiling himself, a little rueful, much more than a little smitten. Nor could all their mockery change a bit of it.

The Cardinal sipped slowly, appreciatively. The King's wine was excellent. He looked over the cup into Gwydion's face and sidewise to that of the Chancellor. The Bishop of Sarum had managed to station himself behind the latter, a formidable bulk with a face set in granite.

He set down his cup and folded his hands. They were the image of amity, all of them, seated round a table of ebony inlaid with lapis and silver, flanked each by his loyal servants. Though to the Cardinal's lowly monks the witch-lords boasted a bishop apiece—and for the King besides, the Archbishop of Caer Gwent, Primate of all Rhiyana. Who said in the way he had, slow and deliberate, pondering every word, "My lord Cardinal, you say you come merely to offer the greetings of the Pope to the King of Rhiyana. You deny any knowledge of troops gathering against us, let alone troops who march under the Cross. And yet, Your Eminence, my priests in the Marches bring me word of this very thing. Are my clergy to be accused of falsehood?"

The Legate allowed himself a very small smile. "Certainly not, my lord Archbishop. Some anxiety would be understandable, what with the deplorable events in Languedoc; when one's neighbors arm for war, one naturally fears first for oneself. Even when that fear is without cause."

"Is it?" The Archbishop leaned forward. "Would Your Eminence swear to that on holy relics?"

"Guilt speaks loudly in its own defense," said the monk on the Cardinal's right hand. "Do you fear because you have reason to fear?"

Alf had been silent throughout that long slow hour, intent on the faces round the table, on the voices speaking at length of lesser matters, on the pattern of wood and stone and silver under his fingertip. Now he raised his eyes. They were quiet, a little abstracted. "Suppose," he said, "that we declare the preliminaries ended and come to the point. There is a Crusade arming against Rhiyana. Its purpose sits here before you. Your task is to offer the Church's clemency, to present conditions under which the armies may be disbanded and the kingdom preserved." He lowered his gaze and traced the curve of a silver vine. "You come, in short, to the first cause of the conflict. Rhiyana's King."

"There is no conflict," the Cardinal began.

Again Alf looked up. The Cardinal inhaled sharply. Great eyes, pale gray as they had seemed to be—they were not gray at all, but the color of moonlit gold. And they were no more human than a cat's.

Alf smiled very faintly. "No conflict, Eminence. No mortal reason to preach a Crusade. Rhiyana is a peaceful kingdom, as orthodox as any Pope's heart could desire; its churches and abbeys are full, its people devout, its clergy zealous in pursuit of their duties. And yet, my lord Cardinal. And yet. If there is no mortal reason, there remains the other. Again, my King."

"Not he alone," said the monk who had spoken before.

Alf raised a brow.

"He has kin," the monk said, "creatures of his own kind, marked as he is marked. Some even more clearly than he."

"Yes, Brother? How so?"

"Only take up a mirror and see."

The Chancellor sat back as if at ease. "Oh, I'm a most egregious monster, I admit it freely. But he? He is the very image of his father, or so they tell me; certainly he bears a close resemblance to his nephews and cousins."

"Somewhat distant cousins, and great-nephews thrice over."

"Ah well, Brother. It's not as if he were unique in the world. 'Adam was one hundred and thirty years old when he begot a son in his likeness, after his image; and he named him Seth. Adam lived eight hundred years after Seth, and he had other sons and daughters.' "

" 'The whole lifetime of Adam was nine hundred and thirty years; then,' " said the monk, " 'then he died.' "

"So he did," Alf said. "And by that reckoning, my King has a while yet to live before he is proven immortal."

"You mock the word of God."

"No," Alf said softly. "That, I do not. Nor am I mad or possessed or begotten of demons. No more than is my lord. If he has ruled long, has he not also ruled well? Has any son suffered? Has any woman wept or child died because Gwydion wears Rhiyana's crown?"

"The flesh is dust and ashes, its comfort a lie. Only the soul can live."

"As no doubt it lives in Languedoc, its housing ravaged with war and starvation."

The monk drew himself up. His face was white, his cheekbones blotched with scarlet. "Your very existence is a corruption of all it touches."

Alf contemplated him, head tilted a little to one side. "You do not think," he said. "You only hate. You, who profess to serve the God of love. Enemy though you be, I find I pity you."

The flare of hate struck Nikki blind. Sightless, walled in soundlessness, he clutched at air, wood, firm flesh sheathed in vair. He could not see, could not hear, could not—

* * *

Alun tensed. The air wavered; the children's faces blurred. Something reached. Darkness visible. Hate that groped, seeking, black and crimson, wolf-jaws wide to seize, to rend, to devour.

Liahan!

She lay still. Her eyes were open, fixed.

He called on all his power. Somewhere, faint and far, voices cried out to him. *No, Alun. This is too strong for you. Alun!*

It had Liahan. His lovely laughing lady with flowers in her hair. It had her; it gripped her.

He struck with every ounce of his strength.

The wolf-darkness wavered, startled, turning at bay. He laughed, for he had marked it, a long searing-bright wound. Again he struck.

The enemy sprang.

Anna saw Alun leap erect over the cradle. His shape blurred and darkened. And yet he laughed, light and strong and free. The darkness swelled like smoke; coiled about him; hurled him down.

Behind Anna, Thea cried out, a harsh inhuman sound, raw with rage. Anna wheeled. The lady stood by the bed, swaying. Anna caught her. "Thea, don't, Alf said not—"

Anna gripped fur round a slash of teeth, white hound, mad eyes, no Thea left at all. Grimly she clung. The darkness swooped, wolf-jawed, hell-eyed. The light whirled away.

7

Nikki could see. He must.

They were all staring. Alf, closest, whose cloak Nikki clutched—Alf sat bolt upright, white as death. "No," he whispered. "Oh, no."

Fiercely Nikki shook him. He could not turn prophet now. The monk's eyes were avid. The Legate watched with deadly fascination.

With infinite slowness Alf rose. He was lost utterly in horror only he could see. "Sweet merciful God—

"Alun!"

Not he alone cried out. Gwydion aloud, Nikephoros in silence: a great howl of anguish.

Nikki's hands were full of fur, the cloak empty, people gaping. He saw none of it. He saw only darkness and light, and Gwydion's face. It wore no expression at all.

And the King was gone, the solar erupting in a babble of voices. Nikki's mind was one great bruise, all the patterns torn and scattered. He made the babble stop—willed it, commanded it. So many eyes. And he could not vanish into air. He did not know how.

With a last wild glance, he spun about and bolted.

Someone pounded after. Father Jehan, miter tucked under his arm, stiff robes hauled up to his knees. Behind Nikki's eyes, a small mad creature was snickering. That great frame had never been made for racing, least of all in full pontificals.

Nikki whipped round a corner. His lungs had begun to ache. His feet beat out a grim refrain. *Too late—too late—too late.*

Alun was gone. Anna was gone. Thea was gone. The children were gone. *Dead, gone, dead, gone, dead—*

A sob ripped itself from him. He flung himself forward.

It was very quiet in the Chancellor's bedchamber. The bed was tumbled, empty. The cradle rocked untenanted, the coverlet rent and torn as if with claws.

Alf stood over it like a shape of stone. At his feet crouched Gwydion with a limp and lifeless body in his arms, his eyes flat, fixed on nothing, dead.

The Queen wept, huddled by him, stroking Alun's hair. The same gesture over and over. Gwydion had no tears. He had nothing at all.

Nikki tasted blood. Then pain, his own hand caught in his teeth. It throbbed as he let it fall, stumbling into the room. The air stung his nostrils as after lightning, the memory of great power unleashed and now withdrawn.

With infinite slowness Alf sank to one knee. His lips moved, and his hand with them, signing the Cross. *"Kyrie eleison. Christe eleison."*

Gwydion turned his head. Nikki, out of range of his stare, still flinched. Alf met it fully. The King's voice was as terrible as his eyes, flat and stark and cold, emptied of all humanity. "God has no mercy."

"Kyrie," said Alf, *"eleison. Pater noster, qui es in coelis—"*

"We have no God. We have no souls. Only flesh and the black earth."

"—sanctificetur nomen tuum; adveniat regnum tuum—"

"God-damned devil-begotten renegade priest." In the flint-gray eyes, a spark had kindled. Rising, swelling, raging, lashing in his voice. "What is your God that He should take my son?"

The Queen reached for him. Lightning cracked; she recoiled, hands pressed to her face. One of them was red, angry, blistering.

Alf reached in his turn to the wounded lady. She shook him off. Her eyes bled tears, but they were hard and fearless. "This is not God's work. This bears the stench of His Adversary."

"They are the same." Gwydion rose, the bright head rolling loosely upon his shoulder. "They must be the same. Else it would be I who lie here in all my pride and guilt, and not—"

"You in all your folly." She stood to face him. She was very tall; she had only to raise her eyes by a little. Yet it was not to him that she spoke but to the air. "Aidan. Do what must be done."

Fire flashed from Gwydion's eyes, sudden as the lightning. "I have not yet lost my wits!"

"No," she said. "Only your son."

He stood very, very still. His face had gained not a line, yet it showed every moment of his hundred years. "Only my son," he said slowly. "Only—" He drew a ragged breath. "Let me pass."

She moved aside. He trod forward. Jehan retreated, leaving him a clear path. He followed it pace by pace, and the Queen after. Her back was straight, her head high. Only with power could one know that, even yet, she wept.

Nikki ventured cautiously into the room. The crackle of power was fading, a mingling as distinct to his senses as scents to the nose of a hound. Maura, Gwydion—grief and hot iron. Aidan startlingly, unwontedly cool. Alf walled in stone. And dimmer memories: Alun, Thea, the faint sweet newness of the children.

Alf had risen by the cradle. All the anguish was locked in his mind behind his frozen face. "They're gone," he said. "Gone utterly, as if they were dead—but if Thea had died, so too would I. Ah, God! How can I live with half my mind torn away?"

Jehan thrust past Nikki, dropping cope and miter, seizing Alf's shoulders. Alf froze. His eyes were wide and wild, glaring without recognition. He was as still as a stalking panther, and fully as danger-ous. "I will kill him," he said without inflection. "Whoever has done this—I will kill him. Death for death, maiming for maiming—"

Jehan struck him a ringing blow. With a beast-snarl, he lunged. Jehan fell before the force of him, defending only, with neither hope nor intention of subduing him. There was nothing of reason in him, only rage and bitter loss.

Nikki's head tossed from side to side. It was all beating on him. Madness, death; loss and hate and numbing terror; Alf's mind that, stripped of all its barriers, was an open wound. Were they so weak? Could they not see? They had played full into their enemies' hands.

They rolled on the floor, Bishop and Chancellor, like hounds quarreling in their kennel. Fools; children.

Nikki made his mind a whip and lashed them with all the force he had. *Be still!*

They fell apart. He was hardly aware of it. The one scent, the vital one, was well-nigh gone. But he could follow, must follow, down the long winding ways of the mind. It was strong, and arrogant in its strength; it had not shielded itself fully although it overwhelmed the minds of all its prey together.

He was close—closer. Walls and sanctity. Walls, and sanctity.

Snake-swift, it struck.

Nikki swam up out of night. Alf stooped over him. The world reeled into focus. Alf was corpse-pale; a bruise purpled his jaw. But his eyes were sane.

Nikki seized him. *I know,* he said. *I know where they are.*

The sanity staggered, steadied. The voice was soft, but the mind was a great swelling cry. "Where?"

In Rome. With a power—

Alf's face shimmered. Nikki snatched with mind and hand. *No!* He must not go, not knowing, not seeing—

Alf was strong. Before that Hell-strong stroke of power, he kept his consciousness, if little else.

Nikki glared at the face beside his own. *With a power,* he continued grimly, *greater than any I've ever known. It's on guard now; we won't get closer to it than we have. Not from here, and not with the strength that's in us.*

Alf sat up with care and pushed his hair out of his face, holding it there, drawing a shuddering breath. "In Rome," he muttered. "From Rome, he—she—whoever, whatever it is—did this." His eyes closed. "Dear God."

"Dear God indeed." Jehan knelt stiffly beside them. For Alf's lone bruise, he had a dozen; already one eye was swelling shut. "A force that can reach through all Rhiyana's walls, kill Alun, take Anna and Thea and the twins, drive you back—it must be the Devil himself."

"Or one of his minions. Or," Alf said, "one of us."

Nikki's body knotted with denial, but his mind spun free of it.

Yes. Horrible as that was, it could well be. It was power he had scented, and power that had felled him.

But the Kindred were gentle people. They did not, they could not hate as that one hated, without measure or mercy.

"No?" Alf smiled with all the sadness in the world. "Nikephoros my child, you saw me only a moment ago. And I am one of the gentlest of us all."

Nikki groped for his hand and clung with convulsive strength. As if that one weak mortal grip could hold him; could unmake it all and bring back the brightness that had been the world. *Thea will be strong. I know she will. We'll get her back, or she'll come back herself, hale and whole and spitting green fire. Why, she could make trembling cowards out of the very devils in Hell!*

Alf smiled faintly but truly. "And Heaven help any mere black sorcerer." He rose, wavering, steadying. "As for us, for now, we're needed here."

That was all Alf and all sanity. Yet they stared, taken aback. That he could be so calm, so easy; that he could abandon his sister and his lady and his children, abruptly and completely, with no visible qualm.

His eyes flickered. Like Gwydion's: deep water above and fires raging below. Their gazes dropped.

"Come," he said. "We have much to do."

8

One could forget, for a little while. One could drive oneself, body and mind, until thought was lost and all one's being focused on the duty at hand.

Until one was weary beyond telling, and one reached for the strong bright other, steeled against her mockery, bolstered already by the prospect of it—and met nothingness. She was gone; she was not. There was only the void, bereft even of pain.

Alf could not sleep. His bed, his whole tower, was full of her absence. The cradle tormented him with its emptiness.

He should dispose of that at least; he could not bear to. As if the act would make it real and irrevocable. They were gone; they would never come back.

No. He would find them. He must. Somehow. If there was a God. If there was such a thing as hope.

The chapel was dark and cold. Neither too dark nor too cold for the Brother Alfred who had been, but he was dead. Rhiyana's Chancellor found the stone floor hard, the crucified Christ impassive.

In shock, in the suddenness of Alun's death, the priest had stirred in his deep grave. He had spoken the words for the dead; he had faced unflinching the terrible grief of the King.

He was gone again, as he must be. Alf sank back upon his heels, eyes fixed upon the crucifix but focused within. Seeing Gwydion in the hall, Alun in his arms still, a blur of people; voices raised in startlement, in confusion, in piercing lamentation. The men from Rome, at a loss as were they all, although some rejoiced in secret; the Cardinal excusing himself with graceful words, half-heard and half-heeded—but his sorrow, even to the touch of power, was real. The Archbishop of Caer Gwent with a following of loyal monks, weeping unashamedly, begging and cajoling and finally commanding the King to give his son over for tending. Prince Aidan as white and still and terrible as his brother, saying with searing cruelty, "Hold him then. Hold him till he rots." And in every mind with power, the brutal vision, swelling and stench, flesh dropping from bones, worms—

Gwydion had surged forward, mad-enraged, poised to kill.

Gently Aidan eased the body from his brother's arms and laid it in the hands of the monks. Gwydion stood motionless, as if power and strength had deserted him in that one wild rush. His eyes could not even follow the Brothers as they bore their burden away. He was empty; broken.

The Prince touched his shoulder. His own hand came up in turn. It was uncanny, like a vision of mirrors. But one image, the one in well-worn hunting garb, had let the tears come. The other would not.

Still would not, as Alf would not sleep. The castle thrummed with it, a tension that would not break, a grief beyond all bearing. Not for friends or brother or Kin would Gwydion give way, not even for the Queen herself.

He had shut them all away. Maura tossed in Aidan's bed while the Prince and his Saracen strove between them to comfort her. She was not cruel enough to resist, but there was no easing that suffering, even by the magic of the Flame-bearer's voice.

Alf's head drooped; he shivered. Half a day and half a night of this had poisoned the whole castle. Worse yet, a storm had come up out of the sea, fierce and bitter cold as the King's own heart. The winds wailed more heartrendingly than all the women in the city; the clouds were as black as grief.

Not a few folk suspected that the storm was the King's own, called up out of his madness. Was he not the greatest mage in the world?

"It cannot go on."

Alf started at the sound of his own voice. His fists had clenched upon his thighs. He regarded them as if they belonged to a stranger. "It has to stop," he said to them.

Granted; and everyone admitted it. But no one had been able to do a thing about it.

"Someone has to."

Aidan himself had tried and failed, and he could rule his brother where even the Queen could not.

Alf shook his head. His hair swung, heavy, half blinding him. It needed cutting. Thea had meant to do it—before—

His teeth set. He was as mad as the King, he knew it. But he had learned a greater skill in concealing it.

Maybe that was what Gwydion needed. A skill. A mask. Enough to hold his kingdom together before it shattered.

Alf was erect, walking. He let his feet lead him where they would.

Like the Chancellor, the King had his own tower, set close to the prow of the castle. Light glimmered in its lofty windows, all but lost in the murk of the storm.

Alf climbed the long winding stair. It was black dark; he walked by the shimmer of power about his feet. Solid though the stones were, they trembled faintly in the wind's fury; its shrieking filled his ears.

The door of the topmost chamber was shut but not bolted. For a moment Alf hesitated. He was not afraid; but one did not pass this door lightly. Common folk whispered that there was the heart of Gwydion's magic, that it was a place of great enchantment, full of marvels.

In truth it was plain enough. A circular room with tall narrow windows all about it, and when the sun was high, a splendid prospect of land and sea. It held a table, a chair or two, a worn carpet; a chest of books—but not a grimoire among them—and a writing case, and a trinket or two. A lamp of bronze, very old; a silver pitcher in the shape of a lion, its open mouth the spout; and the only possible instrument of wizardry, a ball of crystal on a stand of ebony.

The windows glistened blackly in the lamp's light. Gwydion stood framed in that which by day looked upon the sea. Tonight, even for witch-eyes, there was nothing to see; yet he gazed upon the darkness, erect and very still.

Alf eased the door shut behind him. Gwydion spoke, soft and even. "Not a good night for riding, this."

"Would you try?" Alf asked with equal calm.

One shoulder lifted. "I did at least once, if you remember."

It was the first Alf had ever seen of Rhiyana's King. A storm out of Hell, a weary mare, a rider all blood and filth, beaten, broken, and yet indomitable.

The wounds had healed long ago, the bones knit, even the shattered sword-hand learned again its skill, although to a keen eye it bore a memory of maiming, a slight twisting, a stiffness when it flexed. He had never let Alf heal it properly. Like Jehan, he needed the reminder.

"And I heed it," he said. He turned. His face was still; his eyes burned. "I rule myself. I do not pull down these walls about my head."

"No. You merely pull down your whole kingdom."

The King said nothing. Alf sat near the table and closed his eyes. Now that he needed most to be alert—now, by nature's irony, he knew he could sleep.

When his eyes opened, Gwydion stood over him. He let his head rest against the chair's high back. "You can't go on like this," he said. "Mourn, yes; storm Heaven and Hell; swear eternal vengeance. But not while Rhiyana needs you."

Still no response. He sighed. "Yes. Alun is dead. Your only son. As if he were all you could ever beget in all the eons before you; as if he could have been King after you and not the mortal cousin to whom the throne should rightly pass. As if no other man in all the black and bloody world had ever looked upon the murdered body of his child—as if God Himself had not known the pain that you know now, that you thrust upon us all without a thought for our own grief."

"If it troubles you," Gwydion said just above a whisper, "get out of my mind."

"I can't. You won't let me. You want me to suffer as you suffer, drop by bitter drop, down to the very dregs." Alf spread his hands wide. "All Rhiyana must howl with your agony, though it be destroyed. The Crusade will enter; the Church will rule in blood and fire; all you built through your long kingship will vanish, burned or stolen or slain. Was one child, however beloved, however brilliant his promise—was one half-grown boy worth so much?"

"He was my son."

"He would hate you for this."

There was a silence full of ice and fire.

Alf let his heavy eyelids fall. "I loved him too," he said, "and not because he was any prince of mine, or because he was the son of two whom I love, friends who are more to me than blood kin. I loved him because he was himself. And he is dead, foully murdered, my sister taken, my lady torn from me, my children slain perhaps as yours was slain. Must I bear all your burdens besides?"

"You do not know that they are dead."

"I do not know that they live!" Alf drew himself into a knot, trembling a little with exhaustion and with grief. "If you do not school yourself to endurance," he said carefully lest his voice break, "then I give you fair warning, I will do all I can to compel you."

"You would not dare—"

Alf looked at him. Simply looked. "You see, Gwydion. Rhiyana, its people, even my kin—in the end, they matter less than this plain truth. Your self-indulgence is driving me mad."

Gwydion stood motionless. They were evenly matched in body and in mind. But Alf huddled in the tall chair, and Gwydion poised above him, tensed as if to spring.

The King's hands rose. Alf did not flinch. They caught his face between them; the gray eyes searched it, searing-cold. Yet colder and more burning was the voice in his mind. *You were always the perfect cleric. All crawling humility, but beneath it the pride of Lucifer.*

Which, said Alf, *I have always and freely admitted.*

"Bastard." It was a hiss. "Lowborn, fatherless, whelped in a byre—I gave you honor. I gave you lordship. I even gave you the teaching of my son. And for what? That he should lie dead in defense of your ill-gotten offspring, and that you should threaten my majesty with force."

"No majesty now," murmured Alf with banked heat. He rose, eye to kindled eye. "Have you had enough? Or do you need to flog me further? You've yet to castigate all my charlatan's tricks." His power gathered, coiled. But he spoke as softly as ever in a tone of quiet scorn, the master weary at last of his pupil's insolence. "Control yourself or be controlled. I care little which, so long as I have peace."

It was the plain truth. Plain enough for a human to read, even for the Elvenking in his shell of madness. He drew a sharp and hurting breath. No one, not even his brother, had ever faced him so, addressed him so, looked upon him with such utter disregard for his royalty. "I curse the day I called you my kinsman."

Alf's lips thinned, setting into open contempt. Gwydion struck them. They bruised and split and bled. The eyes above them raked him with scorn. No king, he. Not even a man, who could not bear a grief any mortal villein could overcome. He wallowed in it; he let it master him.

Weakling. Coward. Fool.

He whirled away. He was strong. He was King. He would command—he would compel—

Alf touched his shoulder. A light touch, almost tentative, almost like a woman's. Aye; he was as beautiful as one, with that bruised and beardless face. Body and brain armed against him.

Gently, persistently, he drew Gwydion about. "Brother," he said, close to tears. "Oh, brother, I would give my imagined soul to have him alive again."

Gwydion's power reared like a startled colt. Braced for the whip, it had fallen prey to the silken halter: that gentle hand, that breaking voice, that flood of sorrow.

His body stood rooted. Light hands upon his shoulders; tears streaming down pale cheeks; great grieving eyes.

They blurred. A spear stabbed; a dam broke. Somewhere very far away, a voice cried aloud.

Gwydion looked once more into Alf's face. It was as quiet as his own, emptied, serene. "Bastard," he said to it calmly.

Alf smiled, not easily, for it hurt. Gwydion ran a finger along his lip, granting ease of the small pain. "Behold, your beauty saved. It's a great deal more than you deserve."

"You're sane enough," Alf said, "though you're talking like your brother."

"And why not? I feel like my brother. Angry."

"Glad." Alf's knees gave way; he sank down surprised. "Did you fight as hard as that?"

Gwydion dropped beside the other. As abruptly as he had wept, he began to laugh. It was laughter full of pain, but genuine for all that. "Someday, my friend, you'll meet a man you can't witch to your will."

"There is one woman—" Alf bit his mended lip and struggled up. "My lord—"

"*Now* it is 'my lord.' " Gwydion caught him and held him. He resisted; the King tightened his grip. "No, Alfred. Here, one does not heal with love and hot iron, and walk away with one's own wounds still bleeding."

"They are cauterized," Alf said. "Maura's are not."

"You are always armed, my knight of Broceliande." Gwydion let him go and paused. A gust of grief struck him, shook him, passed. He swallowed bruising-hard. His voice when it came seemed hardly his own. "Yes. She needs me more. At this moment. Later . . ."

"Later will come when it comes."

"And then we will speak," said the King, still with that edge of iron, but with eyes cleansed of all his madness.

Nikki had cried himself to sleep and cried himself awake again. His eyes burned; his thoat ached. He felt bruised, mind and body.

He drew into a knot in the center of the bed. His companion stirred and edged closer, curling warmly against him. She recked nothing of loss or of sorrow; she knew only that he had need of her presence. In a little while, when he lay still, empty, she began to purr.

He stroked the sleek fur. He got on well with cats; people liked to call this one his familiar, because she never seemed to be far from him. Sometimes Thea, playing her witch-tricks, had taken on that sleek black form with its emerald eyes, and nestled in the curve of his belly as the true cat did now, and waited till he wavered on the brink of sleep; and flowed laughing into her own, bare, supple shape.

It was only a cat tonight. Thea was gone, Anna was gone, Cynan and Liahan were lost, Alun was dead. The world had broken in a single stroke of power, nor could it ever wholly be mended.

A light weight settled on his bed's edge. He opened his eyes to Alf's face. It was the same as always, though tired and drawn, shadow-eyed. It even smiled a little, in greeting, in comfort.

Nikki sat up, suddenly ashamed. It was not as if he had never known his world to break. It had shattered utterly when he was very young, sweeping away his house and his family and all his city; beside that, this was a small thing.

"But this is now, and that was long ago." Alf lay down as if he could not help himself, resting his head in the crook of his arm. The cat, enchanted, found a new resting place against his side. Her body shook with the force of her purring.

He stroked her idly, his face quiet. Nikki watched him. He would sleep soon. It was his own bed he could not bear.

"No," he said though he did not move to rise. "I don't mean to—"

I don't mind, said Nikki.

Alf flushed faintly. "It's true I'd rather not—I haven't slept alone since—"

Since he came to Thea's bed. Nikki schooled his face to stillness.

"It becomes a habit," Alf said after a little. "A necessity of sorts. Even—especially—to one like me. I was a priest so long . . . Do you know, I never knew what it was to desire a woman until I saw her? She was the first woman of my own kind that I had ever seen. The only one who—ever—"

Nikki held him while he wept. It was not hard weeping. Most of it was exhaustion, and power stretched to its limit.

Yet it seemed a long while before he quieted. When Nikki let him go, he lay back open-eyed. *You'll sleep now,* Nikki said.

He stiffened. "I can't. I mustn't. If anything—if Thea—"

We're all on guard. Sleep, Nikki willed him. *Sleep and be strong.*

Little by little his resistance weakened. His eyelids drooped; his breathing eased. At last, all unwilling though he was, he slept.

9

Benedetto Torrino hesitated. The chamber was tidy, swept and tended and strangely empty. A fire was laid but not lit, the air cold. Something—someone—had lived and loved here. Lives had begun; at least one had ended. But they were all gone.

He shook himself. It was the endless, damnable storm; the errand he was coming to hate; and the pall of grief that lay on the whole kingdom. This was only a room in a tower, rich enough though not opulent, with a faint scent of flowers. Roses. On the table beside a heap of books lay a bowl full of petals, dry and dusty-sweet, a ghost of summer in this bleak northern winter.

His hands were stiff with cold. He found flint and steel upon the mantel. The fire smoldered, flickered, flared. He crouched before it, hands spread, drinking up the heat.

After a moment he straightened. He had not kindled his own fire in—how long? Years. That was servants' work, and he was a prince of the Church. Kinsman to half a dozen Popes, likely to be Pope himself one day if he played the game of courts and kings, outlasted and outwitted the seething factions of the Curia.

If he survived this embassy.

He considered Rhiyana as he had seen it, riding through it. Not a large kingdom, but a pleasant one even in winter. Its roads were excellent, and safe to ride upon. Its people knew how to smile. Had he been in any other realm in the world or on any other errand, he might have fancied that he had come to a country of the blessed, without war or famine, fire or flood or grim pestilence; a peaceable kingdom.

Under a sorcerer king. Gwydion was that, there was no doubt of it. He breathed magic. One could glance at him, see a tall young man, a light, proud, royal carriage, a pale eagle-face. But the eyes were ages old and ages deep.

He was strange; he could be frightening. But he woke no horror. None of them did. They were hiding, Torrino knew, as he could guess why; yet he had seen them here and there at a distance, tall, pale-skinned, heart-stoppingly fair. They had mingled with the throng in the guardroom not an hour past, some close enough to touch, cheering on the two who locked in fierce mock combat. Anonymous though the combatants were in mail and helms, they were well enough known for all that, the Chancellor and the Prince. They were of a height, of a weight, and nearly of a skill; light, blindingly swift, with a coiled-steel strength. Together they were wonderful to see.

"Imagine it," he said aloud to the fire. "A champion born—he learns his skill, he hones and perfects it, he ages and he loses it and he dies. But if he should not age, what limit then to the perfection of his art?"

"Why, none at all."

He turned with commendable coolness. The Chancellor was still in his heavy glittering hauberk although his helm was gone, his coif thrust back upon his shoulders. His cheeks were flushed, his hair damp upon his forehead. He looked like a tall child, a squire new-come from arms practice. Even the true squire looked older, the dark boy Torrino had seen before, moving past Alf with the sheathed greatsword and the helm, shooting the Cardinal a black and burning glance.

Torrino settled into the single chair. It was not precisely an insolence. The Chancellor's brow arched, but his words were light and cool. "Good day, Eminence. If you will pardon me . . ."

He could not have seen the Legate's gracious gesture, bent from the waist as he was in the comic-helpless posture of the knight shedding his mail, with the squire tugging and himself wriggling, easing out of his shell of leather and steel. When he straightened in the padded gambeson, he was breathing quickly; the gambeson too fell into the dark boy's hands. He was less slight in his shirt than he had seemed in his state robes, less massive than in his mail, wide in the shoulders and lean in the hips, with very little flesh to spare.

A pair of servants brought in a large wooden tub; pages followed them bearing steaming pails. It all had the look of a ritual. Torrino could read the faces: skepticism toward this odd unhealthy habit; deep respect for its practitioner, shading into worship in the youngest page. For him Alf had a smile and a word or two, nothing of consequence, but enough to send the child skipping joyfully out the door. The others followed, save the squire, who had put away all Alf's panoply and set his hand to the shirt beneath. The Chancellor let him take it.

Torrino caught his breath. Someone, somewhere, had taken a whip to that back. Taken it and all but flayed him from nape to buttocks, leaving a trail of white and knotted scars. It was shocking, appalling—the worse for that, even so marred, it was still as fair a body as the Legate had ever seen.

He forced his eyes away from it. He was not like many in the Curia, or outside of it either. He had kept his vows; he had refrained from women and disdained that other expedient, so easy if one were a cleric, so simple to explain away.

The squire's brown hands moved over the white skin. Alf stood still, head bent as if in weariness, letting the water wash away the battle.

"I see," Torrino said slowly. "I begin to see."

Alf did not move. The squire looked hard at the Cardinal, who found himself staring back and shivering. This was a boy in truth, human if strikingly foreign, dark, slight, quick. Italian, Greek, Levantine—he had never been born in this cold and windy country. And yet he had a look, as if he saw more, or more clearly, than any mortal man should see.

Torrino found himself nodding. "*There* is all the fear. Not evil, not even witchery. But by your very existence you make the world waver. There is no place for you in our philosophy."

Alf stepped out of the tub and let himself be rubbed dry. He was indeed too thin. One could count his ribs, follow the tracery of veins beneath the translucent skin. But there was strength in him, more visible now than when he wore armor.

"Only regard yourself," said Torrino. "You have it all, youth, beauty, great magic. Anything mere men can do, you can do better. And you never age or die." He sighed. "Angels we can bear—they are pure spirits, invisible and intangible. Saints we love best if, born to all human imperfections, they come through struggle to their victory. Heroes are best and most conveniently dead. You . . . you are here and solid, and hence triply bitter to endure."

"Envy is a deadly sin."

"Deadly," the Legate said, "yes."

Alf was clad, white shirt, black cotte and hose, black hood, somber as a monk, his face the paler for the starkness of his garb. "Will you call your Hounds upon us then?"

Torrino inspected his hands. They were clean, well kept, without mark or scar. On one finger burned the ruby of his rank. "Several of my monks have been . . . escorted elsewhere. At, I understand, the King's command."

"It is contrary to every monastic rule for a monk to claim a habit other than his own. And," Alf added coolly, "the King has forbidden his realm to the Order of Saint Paul."

"The temporal authorities may not interfere with the sons of the Church."

"But the Church may contend with its own, and invite the secular arm to assist."

"Or be compelled to do so."

Alf sat on the hearthstone. His eyes, catching the fire, burned ember-red. "The Archbishop of Caer Gwent needed no compulsion. Indeed he had to be persuaded to leave his captives both alive and unmaimed."

"And unensorceled?"

Beneath the terrible eyes a smile flickered. "Our arts leave no trace on the body or on the soul."

"You found nothing." Torrino's voice was flat, taking no joy in the knowledge.

"By then," Alf said, "there was nothing to find."

"Nor ever had been."

"No?"

Torrino leaned forward. "I regret deeply the death of the Prince.

He was cut down most cruelly and most untimely. But, my lord, it is no secret that he died by sorcery. And Rome has naught to do with such arts."

Alf was silent, his gaze steady. A shiver traced Torrino's spine, a sensation like a touch yet without flesh, brushing him, moth-soft. The ember-eyes lidded. "It is from Rome that Prince Alun's death came."

"From Rome, it may be. But not from the Lateran. The Pope does not oppose sorcery with sorcery."

"The Pope, perhaps. Elsewhere . . . if the end were good, would not some care little for the means?"

Carefully Torrino sat back. "It is possible. I cannot say that it is so."

Alf turned his face toward the fire, and after a moment, his hands. The flames bent toward his fingers, licking round them, harmless as sunlight. Gathering a handful, he plaited it idly, reflectively, drawing in a skein of shadow, a shiver of coolness.

Torrino watched, sitting very still. "Your King has bidden your people to conceal themselves and by extension their witcheries. Yet you work open magic. Were I merely clever, I might think that you were the murderer, intent on Rhiyana's destruction."

"And on the destruction of my lady, of my sister, and of my newborn children."

"Concealment merely, to lend verisimilitude to the deception."

Alf laughed, startling him. "Oh, clever indeed, Your Eminence! But all your speculations shatter on a single rock. You do not know my lady Althea. She could never vanish even in seeming, and leave me to effect a knightly rescue."

"Nor," said the Cardinal, "would you do vile and secret murder."

With a sudden movement Alf rose and flung his plaited cord into the fire's heart. "Your false Cistercians knew nothing. Not one thing. They were blank, innocent, scoured clean. And yet, when Alun died, I knew the power had used them as its focus. Listened, spied, and chosen its target, and struck with deadly force. Leaving its instruments as it had found them, mere frightened men, taught to hate what they could not understand."

"*Were? Could?* Are they dead?"

"No," Alf said. "We sent them away where they can do no more harm."

"You will pardon me if I ask you where."

"You will pardon me if I do not tell you. They were used and discarded. So too might you be; and what you do not know, you cannot betray."

Pride stiffened the Cardinal's back. "No one would dare——"

"That one has dared to murder a royal prince."

"A witch and the son of a witch."

Alf bowed with graceful irony. "Well and swiftly countered, Eminence. Yet if the enemy is of our blood as I fear he must be, then he is certainly mad, a madness that cries death on all witches yet despises your kind as mere and mortal beasts. As easily as he would destroy me, he would use your eyes and your brain, nor ever ask your leave."

Torrino sat erect and haughty. But horror darkened his mind. Used, wielded like a club, dropped when the moment passed——

Hands gripped him, bracing him, as the clear eyes met his and the clear voice shored him up. "We will do battle as we can, and not only for ourselves. Believe that, Lord Cardinal. We are not of mortal kind; we are true and potent witches; but we do not traffic with Hell. No man or woman or child in this kingdom shall suffer for what we are."

Torrino looked at him with great and growing sadness. "By your own mouth are you betrayed." He shifted; Alf let him go. He stood. "When I was sent here, I had hoped that the tales would be false or unduly exaggerated, or that you would conceal what must be concealed for the sake of the peace. But you have been truthful; you have let me see what you are. You have left me no choice."

"Have I?"

This was the Chancellor's place, his squire at the door, barring it, hands on the hilt of the sheathed greatsword. Torrino looked up into Alf's face. "You do have a path or two of escape. All your folk may give themselves into our hands to be judged without harm to the human people of the kingdom; or you may take flight."

"And if we stand and fight?"

"Interdict. With, inevitably, the loosing of the Crusade."

Alf nodded once. "I understand. You must be bound by the Canons and by His Holiness' command. Poverty, chastity, those fade and are lost. But obedience holds fast still."

"What God commands, man must perform."

"God!" Alf's voice cracked with sudden bitter anger. "You obey the Pope, who obeys the whisperings of fools, men twisted with hate and with lust for power. There is no God in any of it—unless, as with Job, He has left His Enemy to work His will."

"You are not evil," Torrino said steadily, "but law—Scripture— It may well be that the evil lies not in you but in what you are and in what you do to us. The wolf in himself is an innocent creature, faithful to his nature, which is to hunt and to kill. Yet when he kills the sheep, so in turn must he die, lest all the sheep be lost."

The anger was gone, leaving Alf cold and quiet. "How are Rhiyana's sheep lost? They are all faithful children of the Church. They confess their sins; they hear Mass; they are born and they marry and they die as Christians should. What harm has it done their souls that their King is the Elvenking?"

"They suffer a witch to live."

"They also eat of unclean beasts, travel on the Sabbath, and forgo the rite of circumcision. Are we all then to go back to that old and vanished Law?" Alf laughed without mirth. "But my back remembers—some laws are more convenient than others. I was to be burned once, until a certain bishop recalled that I had a king's favor. So I was suffered to live, though not with a whole skin."

Torrino struggled to breathe quietly, to be calm. This—man— had endured much. He must endure more, because he was what he was. And there was no way . . .

"If you could swear," the Legate said, "if you could lay down all your magic arts to remove yourselves utterly from humanity, to live apart and in penitence, I would let you live. With no Interdict; no Crusade."

Alf's smile was gentle, and as terrible in its way as the fire in his eyes. "You have a wise and compassionate spirit. Unfortunately . . . We do intend to withdraw. Utterly, as you say; finally. Men are no better for our peace than we are for theirs. But our power, our pride, those we will not forsake. Our King will not depart a penitent with ashes in his hair, atoning for what to him is no sin."

"Not even for his kingdom's sake?"

"That," said Alf, "is why we will fight."

"As must we. The Church will not be mocked."

"She too is proud. We are all proud; intransigent." Alf closed his eyes for a moment. "Your pardon, Eminence. My wisdom is all scattered; I have neither the will nor the wit to treat with you as your office demands. If this can be settled at all, perhaps . . . You will not immediately pronounce your sentence?"

"I must follow the proper procedure," the Legate answered. "I will not delay it, but neither will I hasten it."

Alf nodded. "We can ask no more. Only, for my King's sake I beg you, allow his son a Christian burial."

"Can I prevent it?" Torrino asked.

Their eyes met. Alf bowed slightly. "For that, Eminence, my thanks."

There was, thought Torrino, very little else that he could be thanked for. He bowed with respect, with regret, and turned. The door was open, the squire gone. With back stiff and head up, he took his leave.

10

Prince Alun lay in state before the high altar of Saint Brendan's Cathedral. The light of many candles caught the broidered silver of his pall, winked in the jewels of his coronet, turned his hair to fire-gold.

Jehan's eyes blurred. He blinked irritably. There had been tears enough here, a whole kingdom's worth. He needed to see.

A boy asleep. Not handsome, not sturdy; always too pale, blue-white now, the bones standing stark beneath the thin skin. With his quicksilver stilled he was haughty indeed, his nose like his father's, arched high; his lips thin and finely molded, closed upon the greatest of all secrets.

Slowly Jehan crossed himself and knelt by the bier. The air was full of chanting, the slow deep voices of monks, ceaseless as the sea. He let them shape his prayer for him.

By day and by night Rhiyana's people kept vigil over their prince. Women veiled in black, men in dark hoods, had come to look, to pray, to weep or to turn quickly away. Fewer came as the night advanced; of those few, some took refuge in side chapels, praying as Jehan prayed, silently, while the monks sang.

Perhaps he drowsed, arms folded on the bier's side, head bowed upon them. Stiffly he straightened his neck.

Others had come in silence to stand about him, a circle of hooded shadows, tall and black and shapeless on the light's edge. The chanting had paused. The only sound was his own breath, loud and quick.

One by one the hoods slipped back. Alf was a sudden luminous pallor across the bier; Prince Aidan came to kneel at his side as Nikephoros knelt at Jehan's. And at Alun's feet stood the King; at his head the Queen.

The monks' voices rolled forth anew.

> *"Dirige, Domine, in conspectu tuo viam meam.*
> *Introibo in domum tuam:*
> *adorabo ad templum sanctum tuum in timore tuo.*
> *Domine, deduc me in iustitia tua;*
> *propter inimicos meos dirige in conspectu tuo viam meam. . . ."*

" 'Because of mine enemies . . .' " Alf spoke softly yet very clearly. "They are many, and they are one alone who can slay with power."

"Perhaps he did not mean to kill," murmured the Queen.

Aidan's eyes flashed green. "Ah, no; he meant only to taunt us, to set all our power at naught, to escape unscathed and unconquered. Who but a fool would venture so little when there was so much more to gain?"

"Whatever his intent," Alf said, "this he did. From Rome, all at once, with deadly ease. I'm proud enough, cousins, but I tell you freely, I'm afraid."

"So are we all." Maura's hand rested on Alun's cheek, lightly, tenderly. But her eyes on Alf were level. "God alone knows when he will strike again, or where, or how."

"We're ready for him now," Aidan said. "He struck once through all our ramparts, all unlooked for. But never again."

"Can we be sure of that?" Alf sounded ineffably weary. "I've met our enemy. Only from afar and only for a brief moment, but I tell you, strong as you all insist that I am, trained and honed in my power, he is as much stronger than I as the sun is stronger than the moon. All the careful weavings of our magic are to him as spider threads, to be snapped at his pleasure."

He hates us, Nikki said. *I felt that when I found him.* Abomination, *he called us.*

Aidan shook his head, sharp with impatience. "One stroke and you've let him conquer you. He may be the greatest of all mages, or even Prince Lucifer himself, but he is one, alone. There are a full score of us. Surely we can band together against him."

"How and when," Alf asked, "and for how long? A score is a very small number when half of them are untrained or relatively weak, and one of the very strongest lost already to that same enemy."

And if we—you—band together as you say, what happens to Rhiyana? It needs our bodies now, preferably in armor, and as much of our minds as we can spare.

The prince leaped up and began to prowl, oblivious to the altar and the holy things save as obstacles to his passing. They all watched with a measure of indulgence. He was as changeful as the fire he was named for, volatile always, in small calamities as in great ones. Maura even smiled, as if she took comfort in his restlessness.

He halted in a swirl of cloak. "As to Rhiyana, some of the Folk are useless in physical combat: most of the women; Akiva the scholar; our handsome jongleur. But of these, many are strong in power. Let them wall themselves in Broceliande. The rest of us, who fight as well with the body as with the mind, can stand to Rhiyana's defense." His white teeth bared in a grin. "We'll see how a rabble of hedge-knights and hired soldiers will contend with my lady of the *Hashishayun.*"

"Not to mention the Flame-bearer himself." Maura's smile died. "I know how we intend to face the threat of the Church and its Crusade; that was settled long ago. But this new danger may be worse than either. Our armies can drive back invaders; our clergy can treat with the Pope's embassy. How must we face the sorcerer? His body lies in Rome, long leagues away. His power can strike us down one by one. In the end, if we are gone, can all Rhiyana's priests and men-at-arms stand fast?"

"Not under Interdict." Alf bowed his head under all their stares, and raised it again almost defiantly. "Why do you stretch your eyes at me? Of course the Church will use that most persuasive of its weapons. No Mass, no sacraments. No offices of the Church anywhere while the Pope sustains his ban."

"Without us," Aidan said with a touch of bitterness, "there would be no such ban."

"There might," murmured the Queen, "if rebellion persisted—for pride, for honor. Remember, brother. Always remember Languedoc."

"So," the Prince said, "the sorcerer threatens us all—then let us do battle with him. Go to Rome, challenge him, cast him down. Then we can get to the work of defending our kingdom."

"It's a month's ride to Rome," Jehan muttered.

Aidan laughed like a whip-crack. "For us, dear Bishop, a moment's journey at the speed of a thought."

That supposes you can find him instantly. Nikki flushed a little under
the Prince's glare, his own quick temper rising to match it. *He scorns
us; he let me see the shape of his city. But not precisely where he was, and he doesn't
mean us to find out. And Rome is a big and complicated place.*

"I could find him," Aidan said.

Could you destroy him?

"Peace," the King said. Only that, but in each the lightnings
retreated; Jehan's hackles settled, caught in the middle as he was, with
fire on either side.

They looked at Gwydion. Almost they had forgotten his presence
as he had seemed oblivious to theirs, walled in his private grief. His
face was waxen pale, yet his eyes were clear and quiet. They rested
on each in turn, and lifted to the altar, to the golden glitter of its cross.
"Those of the Folk who cannot wield a sword will go to Broceliande.
The rest remain here in the world as we had decided, some to ride
with the army to the Marches, some to guard Caer Gwent under the
Queen's regency." No one spoke, to approve or to protest. With
startling suddenness his glance seized Alf. "You go to Rome, you and
Nikephoros. I charge you to find your lady and your sister and your
children; to track our enemy to his lair and to dispose of him however
you see fit; and finally to confront His Holiness the Pope. He let this
war begin. Let him treat with us directly, with no intermediaries, and
let him make an end."

"But," Alf said in the stunned silence, "you need me here. My
power, my sword—"

The King's gaze was compassionate although his words were as
harsh as stone. "You are of no use to us as you are. Your sword is
skilled enough, to be sure, your power likewise. A human might
almost be deceived.

"But you are not what you were. Your temper is uncertain; you
struggle to keep your mind clear and your body strong. You are
perilously close to breaking."

Alf shook his head, mute.

Gwydion's eyes bound him. "Behind your shields, half your mind
is torn away. Struggling, enduring, but bleeding to death slowly and
surely. I command you to seek the only possible healing. Find Althea
and the children she bore you. Avenge them and your sister and my
son. And speak for Rhiyana before the Chair of Peter."

Or die in the trying. That was in all their minds, clear as a shout.

Slowly Alf shrank, drawing together, covering his face with his
hands. Jehan noticed as if for the first time how thin those hands were,

thinned to the bone. He was terribly, frighteningly fragile; he was beginning to break.

Aidan's every muscle was taut with protest. Maura was white and silent. Nikki alone seemed glad. He had been chosen; he could go, he could act, he could conquer or die. He was very and truly young, as not one of the others could be.

Alf straightened. His hands lowered; his head came up. He seemed perceptibly to gain in breadth and strength—a wonder, a marvel. He met the King's stare directly and smiled, bright and splendidly fierce. "Yes," he said in a strong sure voice. "Yes, Gwydion. In Rome it began, and in Rome it will end. Alun will have his blood-price, I my kin. That I promise you, by my Lord and all His hallows."

Jehan wanted to hit him. "I know you have to go. I know you'll be in constant and arcane danger. I *know* you'll probably get killed! And I'm. Going. With you."

Alf's burst of strength had passed. He lay on Nikki's bed; Nikki lay beside him, face to the wall, ears and mind closed, deeply and blissfully asleep. He himself would have sought the same blessed oblivion but for Jehan's persistence. "Jehan," he said with weariness that came close to desperation, "I love you dearly. You've been a brother to me; a son. I know you'd happily go to your death for me, as would I for you. But. This is no errand for any mortal man, let alone an anointed bishop. Even if you manage to escape with your body and your sanity intact, what will become of your life? You'll be worse than discredited. You'll be unfrocked; excommunicated. In a word, destroyed."

Jehan's jaw set. "I won't be a drag on you. I know Rome. I lived there off and on for a good twenty years, remember? I know people, places—"

"We can't use them." Alf sat up and caught Jehan's wrists. His fingers were fever-hot. "We have to find the enemy first and in complete secrecy, or he can simply reach out and shatter us. If we have you with us, well known as you are in the city and the Curia, and without power besides, we'll be doubly pressed to defend our concealment."

"And what's more invisible in the Eternal City than a Jeromite monk with a pair of pilgrims in tow?"

"Anything at all, when that monk is the very large, very famous, and very distinguished young Bishop of Sarum."

"My size," growled Jehan, "I can't help. But in a well-worn habit, with a well-worn beard—"

Alf's glance was eloquent. Jehan grimaced. "Well. I've got almost a day's start. With a little help from you . . ."

With great reluctance Alf laughed. "You ask me to bebristle your chin when I can't even manage a beginning on my own?"

Jehan's wrists were still imprisoned, else he would have given Alf a good shaking. "You could if you would, and you know it. Stop your nonsense now and think. Who will look after you when you're in one of your trances?"

"Nikki—"

"Nikephoros is a charming boy, an excellent squire, and a passable scholar. But can he stand in the market and haggle over the price of a turnip?"

"He would never need to—"

Jehan snorted. "Maybe he wouldn't. Those eyes of his are lethal to anything female. But he can't talk, and very likely he'll be in a trance himself. You need someone without power, to keep your bodies together while your souls do battle."

"You." Alf released him and sighed. "We're all going to regret this."

A grin welled to the surface. Jehan throttled it. "We never have before."

"Thanks to God and Dame Fortune."

"So we'll say our prayers and do our best to keep our balance on the Wheel. When do we leave?"

Alf shook his head and smiled. "Patience, patience, my lord Bishop. When Alun is in his tomb and I have settled my affairs, then we go."

"Two days," Jehan mused. "Three at most. Good. I'll be ready. And Heaven help you if you try to leave without me!"

11

The light came back slowly. Infinitely slowly. Its focus was dim, more suggestion than shape: vaulted arch, loop of chain, clustered shadow outlined in flamelight. A lamp—lamps, set in a wheel of iron. But only one was lit, the one directly overhead.

Anna blinked. She did not know that lamp. There was nothing like it in any room she could have been sleeping in. But then she seldom woke with hurts in so many places, with a throbbing in her head to match the throbbing in her hands.

She raised one. It was stiff, swathed, bandaged. The sleeve was indubitably her own, the tightness of her white linen camise, the embroidered edging of her third-best cotte, gold on russet.

Her hand fell again to a clean rough sheet, a blanket she did not recognize, heavy and well woven though not rich. There was a pallet under her, a bare floor, a wall beside her of smooth pale stone. Four walls, a heavy door—she did not know any of it.

Something stirred against her foot. She recoiled, knotting against the angle of the wall.

It was only a hound. A white alaunt with ears more red than brown, crouched at the foot of the pallet as Anna crouched at its head. A heavy collar circled its neck, with a chain welded to it and welded again to a ring in the wall. Even had the beast tried, it could not have reached Anna; the chain was too short.

Anna's heart slowed its pounding. She was not afraid of a hound. This one was very beautiful. It—she. A bitch, her teats swollen with milk, her belly distended as if she were newly delivered of pups. Beneath the sheltering body something moved, a tail, the pink tip of a nose. Two half-blind half-formless creatures, seeking each the sustenance of a nipple. One was male, red-eared like its dam. The other, female, was all silver-white. Or, no; pale, pale gold. The exact color of—

Anna snapped from her crouch. Bright witch-eyes gleamed strangely in the beast-faces, Thea's, Cynan's, Liahan's; Thea's temper snarled in the collared throat. Those fangs were deadly sharp; Anna's fingers remembered beneath the bandages.

Yet she dropped to her knees well within striking range and gripped the collar. It was massive, all iron, and welded shut; though not precisely choking-tight, it gave not an inch to Anna's tugging. Her fingers found evidence of Thea's own futile efforts, fur worn and roughened, the beginnings of a gall.

Anna could not breathe properly. She found herself at the door, beating on it, gaining no response. It was bolted as solidly as a castle gate; the grille above the level of her eyes looked out upon darkness. For a long moment she dangled, clinging to the bars, biting back a howl. Then she dropped and turned.

Thea had not moved. Her eyes held a glint of mockery.

Anna faced her again. "This is a joke," she said. "The Folk are playing pranks again. Morgiana—the things an Assassin will laugh at, even a tame Assassin—"

Thea's muzzle wrinkled. Anger, scorn, or both. "It is a joke," Anna persisted. "It can't be what it seems to be. We were in the tower, and Alun was falling hopelessly in love with his own prophecy, and—"

A stab of pain brought her up short. This time Thea had not broken flesh, only nipped it scathingly. Anna hit her.

Tried to. One could not hit air and fire. Even air and fire in an iron collar, with ears pressed flat and fangs bared.

Very slowly Anna sank down, huddling into her skirts. She was cold, and not only with the damp chill of stone untapestried and uncarpeted, with neither hearth nor fire to warm her. Anger was no help. She had been in the White Keep, warm and glad, and now she was elsewhere. And Thea—Thea was a shape-changer, that was her nature, the white gazehound her most beloved disguise; but not collared and chained and in visible discomfort, perhaps even in pain, her children transformed as was she, not after she had labored so long against her very nature to bear them in their proper forms.

"Thea," Anna said as steadily as she could, "Thea, if this isn't a joke or a game, you had better put an end to it. Your babies are too young yet for shape-shifting."

If Thea's eyes had blazed before, now they blinded; her snarl had risen to a roar. Anna caught her before she could lunge—stupid, stupid; but her hands were tightly bound, protected.

At length Thea quieted. She crouched panting, trembling, her

short fur bristling. Shakily Anna smoothed it. "You can't," she translated. She felt weak and dizzy. The Kindred were powerful, invinci-
ble. Nothing could bind them, nothing compel them. Not prayers, not
cold iron, not any mortal prison. There was *nothing* they could not do.

Thea made a small bitter sound, half whine, half growl.

"But what? Who? *Why?*"

Thea could not answer. She could not even set her voice in
Anna's mind; and that was worse than all the rest of it together.

Anna had never been a very womanly woman. In extremity, she
did not weep or storm or otherwise conduct herself as befit her sex.
No; she became very still, and she thought. Brooded, some might say,
except that she did not let revenge overwhelm her reason. She returned to the relative comfort of the pallet, spread the blanket over
herself and her companions, and concentrated on staying warm, still,
and sane.

It was cruelly hard. She kept seeing Alun falling and Thea changing, melting and dwindling into a maddened beast. Then darkness,
and this. Whatever this might be.

At first she thought she had imagined it. A glimmer. A humming.
A tensing of the air.

She had no weapon, not even the little knife she used for trim-
ming pens. Thea's head was up, ears pricked, a silent growl stirring
her throat.

Shadows shifted and took substance. Anna stared. They remained: a bowl, two jars, a plate. The bowl held meat, blood-raw; the
plate a hard gray loaf and a lump of cheese, an onion and a handful
of olives. One jar sloshed with liquid; the other was empty, but in
shape and size eloquent enough.

Anna's body knotted from throat to thigh. She had not known
she could have so many needs all at once, amid such a nightmare.

The air, having yielded up its burdens, was still. Anna fought to
quell her thudding heart. "What is this? Who plays these games with
us?" Silence. "Where are we? Who are you who taunt us with your
power?"

Nothing changed. No voice responded. No figure appeared
before her. She had been speaking Rhiyanan; she shifted to the *langue
d'oeil*. Nothing. "*Who?*" she demanded in Provençal, in Saxon, in
Latin, and last of all, with fading hope, in Greek.

The closed door mocked her despair. She leaped toward the
grille and clung. Without lay only darkness, and silence, and empty

air. "Damn you!" Anna screamed at it, still in her own native Greek. *"Who are you?"*

She could as easily have shouted at the stones, or at Thea, who at least would acknowledge that she spoke.

Her hands cried pain; she unclamped them, dropping the hand-span to the floor. There was wine in the smaller jar, sour and much watered but drinkable. She gulped down a mouthful, two, three, before she choked.

Thea wavered in front of her. She had a terrible head for wine; she was dizzy already. She blinked hard. The hound was on her feet, and the wavering was not entirely in Anna's vision.

Anna picked up the bowl. It was surprisingly good meat. She set it where Thea could reach it.

The witch-hound sniffed it, shuddered, turned her head away.

"You have to eat," Anna said.

Thea's eye was as yellow as a cat's, pupiled like a cat's, more alien even in that face than in her own.

"Eat," Anna commanded her. "You were never so fastidious before, when you didn't need your strength except to play. Eat!"

Thea did not precisely obey. Rather, she chose to taste the offering.

Anna had less restraint. She had to struggle not to bolt it all down at once. Like the wine, like the meat, the food was inelegant but adequate, far better than any prison fare she had ever heard of. And it gave her strength; it brought her to her senses, and woke her to a quiver of hope. Whatever was to become of them all, certainly they would not starve.

Having eaten and drunk and put the chamberpot to good use, Anna lay on the pallet. Thea had finished the bowl after all and licked it until it gleamed dully; she returned to her whimpering offspring and began to wash them and herself. And that, reflected Anna, was a tremendous advantage; she might be condemned to speechlessness, but she would be clean.

She could also sleep, abruptly and thoroughly, as Anna could not. Anna stroked her flank, and after a pause, the small bodies nestled against it. They were warm and soft and supple, a little damp still from their cleansing, breathing gently. Very carefully Anna lifted one, the silver-gilt creature who was Liahan, cradling her. She fit easily into two joined hands, who in other shape had made an ample armful. Anna swallowed hard. The small things were always the worst to bear. "We'll get out of here," she whispered into the twitching ear. "Somehow. We'll get out. I promise you."

12

Prior Giacomo was in no very good mood.

Never mind that the day was glorious, bright as a new coin and touched with a fragile, fugitive, springlike warmth. Never mind that he was free to enjoy it within certain easy limits: the Abbot's dispensation to walk abroad, good company in young Brother Oddone, and an errand smoothly and swiftly completed, the collection of an annual and strictly symbolic rent from a house of minor princes. Crumbling old Rome looked almost fresh although its green was winter-muted; the Tiber's reek was only a twitch in the nostrils; the pilgrims were crowding thickly and some were singing, one or two even on key:

> *"O Roma nobilis, orbis et domina,*
> *cunctarum urbium excellentissima. . . ."*

Prior Giacomo snarled and hid his head in his cowl.

Insult to injury—Brother Oddone raised his own voice in an echo as willing as its pitch was uncertain.

> *". . . Roseo martyrum sanguine rubea,*
> *albis et virginum liliis candida—"*

"One would think," Giacomo said acidly, "that after seven years in a monastery, even a cat would learn to sing on key."

Oddone shut his mouth in mid-note and wilted visibly. But nothing could quell Brother Oddone for long. After a judicious moment he said, "Brother Prior, you really shouldn't take it so hard."

Giacomo's scowl, with the brows black and beetling over a nose as nobly Roman as his pedigree, would have put the Abbot himself to flight. Oddone met it bravely and with the best will in the world. His Prior was sorely tempted to strike him.

But Giacomo had learned discipline. Not easily, but by now quite thoroughly. He restricted himself to a growl and a slight speeding of his pace. No, he should not take it so hard. It was not as if the world had ended or the barbarians invaded, or his family lost the last of its sadly eroded property. So his sister had taken the veil. He should be rejoicing that another of his blood had found a vocation—and his favorite sister besides, his pet, pretty Fioretta.

The veil he could have faced, if she had not gone mad with it. He would have seen her into any convent in Rome and made certain that she was well treated there. He could even have borne her departing elsewhere, if any Continelli would dream of forsaking her city, if only she was content.

But this. Not for Fioretta Saint Benedict's learned nuns or Saint Anastasia's holy nurses or the cloistered solitude of Saint Anthony. No; nothing so simple or so reassuring. Fioretta had gone with the new madwomen, Clara and her barefoot sisters, camp followers of the Friars Minor. Her veil was a rag and her feet unshod, and when she was not begging on the highroad she was ministering to those who were. And she was not content at all. She was gauntly, luminously, maniacally happy.

"Plague take the girl!" he burst out. "Why couldn't she have settled on something less drastic?"

"But if she had," said Oddone with sweet reason, "she wouldn't be your sister."

Giacomo had stalked forward another half-dozen strides before the barb sank in. Oddone's face was all innocence; his eyes were guileless.

His Prior stopped short. The crowd of passersby eddied and swirled. Already Oddone was almost swallowed in it, a weedy brown-cowled figure, a sallow circle of tonsure. With a bark of sudden laughter, Giacomo pushed in his wake.

Giacomo, though not tall, was solid, a respectable weight even against a market-day mob. Oddone had neither height nor girth, and no muscle at all. Once the current caught him, it swept him along like flotsam. Giacomo snatched once, caught the wrong hood, stared into startled eyes. Female eyes—and male ones beside them, promising murder.

It took him some little time to extricate himself; when he looked again, Oddone was gone. Half a dozen tonsures bobbed within reach, and half of those above Jeromite habits, but none was Brother Oddone.

Who, besides his body's frailty, had been known to faint for no reason at all, once even in the street. But that street had not been so busy or so full of jostling humanity. Nor had it been so far from his monastery; and he had a fine mind and the hand of an artist, but no head at all for directions.

There was nothing for it but to go forward as Oddone must have gone, and strain eyes and neck in searching for him. Pilgrims, monks, matrons, pilgrims, idlers and marketers and beggars, servants, pilgrims. No Oddone. A princeling and his bravos; a lady in a litter; a cardinal in state. Of Oddone, not a sign. And all Rome to be lost in and a piazza before the seeker, with great ways and small radiating from it like the spokes of a wheel.

The people were not so crowded here. The street had confined them; they had space now to scatter. Pilgrims clustered round the statue on one edge, an image out of old Rome: Dionysus in his robe of fawnskin, crowned with vine leaves, with a leopard fawning at his feet. Guides always swore that it was a saint in the arena, taming the beast that would have slain him. One was swearing it now, loudly, in bad Norman. Giacomo could understand enough to be sure of that.

No Oddone here. These were all hulking towheaded northerners, with a scatter of stragglers on their fringes, hawkers of relics and tokens, beggars, the odd pilgrim. Giacomo skirted them, mounting above them, for they overflowed the space about the image and poured up the steps of the little church called, of course, Saint Bacchus. From the top he might be able to see his way.

Intent, peering over heads, he collided with an unexpected obstacle. It grunted and said in a familiar tuneless voice, "Prior Giacomo, look. Just look!"

Giacomo seized him as if to shake him, half for relief, half for white rage. All his anxiety, all his desperation, and Oddone was not even surprised to be found again. He could only gape at an old statue like half a thousand other statues in this city of marble and memories, beautiful maybe, but a beauty grown lusterless with surfeit. His narrow face was rapt; his sallow cheeks were flushed. He looked feverish. "Sweet saints," he breathed. "I have to paint that face."

Giacomo sighed gustily. "So paint it. Or any one of its thousand twins."

That managed to startle Oddone, but not enough to free his eyes from their bondage. "*Twins?* Brother Prior, there can be none like it in the world. Only look at it." Oddone caught Giacomo's arm with amazing force and turned him bodily. "*Look!*"

There was Saint Bacchus with his ringlets tumbling down his marble back, no face to be seen. There was the leopard with its fanged grin. There were the pilgrims, row on row. Not all after all were Norman. One stood among them like a child in a field of tall corn, his black curly head bare to the sun, his black eyes sparkling with mockery as the guide rambled on. His face was dark and young and wild, a deal more handsome than not, and as utterly un-Norman as any face could be. Levantine, Giacomo would have said, or Greek.

Oddone shook his Prior lightly. "Do you see him now? Have you ever seen his like?" And losing patience at last, he pointed. "By all the angels, Brother Prior, are you blind?"

His finger pointed directly to the right of the dark boy, to one of the tall figures that hemmed him in. That one, Giacomo saw, stood slightly apart, an inch perhaps, or a world's width. From the steps he seemed to stand almost face to face with the statue, a pilgrim clothed like any other, hat and hood, gown, cloak and scrip and staff. But the face he lifted as if to exchange stares with the marble god . . .

Giacomo swallowed. No one should have a face like that. White like marble, but living, breathing, tilting over the boy's head toward one of the brawnier Normans, smiling a very little and murmuring something far too faint to be heard.

"I have to paint him," Oddone said. "For my archangel." He stopped and sucked in his breath. "Brother Prior! Could he—could he really be—"

"The age of miracles is over." As soon as he had said it, Giacomo wished that he had not. Not that he had wounded Oddone—the lad was well past it—but that he might after all have lied.

Oddone looked fair to lose himself again, though this time at least he had a visible destination. Giacomo got a grip on the back of his cincture. He hardly seemed to notice the weight he towed behind him.

Yet once he had reached his quarry he hung back. Shy, Giacomo thought, then saw his face. It wore the same look as when he stood with brush in hand and model before him, and page or panel waiting for the first stroke.

The guide had ended his tale and gathered his flock, herding them churchward, hangers-on and all. Only three were not to be moved, the dark youth, the big Norman with his rough sandy beard, and Oddone's archangel. The boy wandered up to the statue, exploring its base with quick light fingers. The Norman, who alone had no hat but only a hood, let it fall back from a tonsured head and said in excellent Latin, "Well, brothers, what now?"

Neither of his companions responded. The boy ignored him utterly. The other turned his head from side to side as if questing. His eyes were enormous, colorless as water. He should have had a bleached look, all white as he was; he should have seemed browless and lashless, naked and unfinished. But his brows were fine and distinct and set on a definite tilt, just touched with gold; his lashes were thick and long; and all his pallor had a sheen like light caught in alabaster. Beside him the marble Dionysus was a dull and lifeless thing.

The Norman sighed. "I for one," he said with elaborate patience, "would like to know where my head will rest tonight. And how we're going to occupy ourselves until we get there."

Oddone had found his opening, a sending straight from heaven. "Why, good pilgrims, if that's your worry, I know just the place."

The big man looked down in startlement to the voice that chirped by his elbow. He had a battered soldier's face, but his eyes were blue as flax flowers. They took in Oddone from crown to toe and back again, not a long journey at all. Surprise and suspicion had turned his face to flint; now it softened and his stare turned quizzical. "Do you, Brother? Where may that be?"

"Why," said Oddone quickly, "in our own San Girolamo. We don't keep a regular hostel, but we have a guesthouse, small but very comfortable, with its own garden. And to a brother of our own Order and to his companions, we can offer a warm welcome."

Giacomo gaped in astonishment. Shy Brother Oddone, diffident well-nigh to tears, not only stood up to a man thrice his size; he offered lodgings on behalf of his whole monastery.

The Norman monk was interested, even a little amused. "Is that San Girolamo near the Palatine? The one with the lovely campanile?"

"Yes!" cried Oddone, delighted. "Brother, you must come, you and the others. Must they not, Brother Prior?"

Now at last he was mindful of his own low rank—now all his sins were committed. Giacomo made no effort to smooth his face, although he knew he looked formidable. "Prior Giacomo," he named himself with the formality of suspicion, "of San Girolamo."

"Brother Jehan," the foreigner responded, "from Anglia." If Giacomo's manner daunted him, he gave no sign of it. "For myself,

I'd be glad enough to take your Brother's offer, provided you approve. My companions I can't speak for."

Slowly the strange one turned. His expression was remote, even cold, but his gaze was clear enough. As it flickered over Giacomo, the Prior shivered. It seemed to have substance, a touch like wind, both burning and cool. "I would be content," he said. His Latin was flawless, his voice as uncanny as his face. "With the Prior's consent."

Giacomo's scowl deepened. Oddone was quivering like a pup before its master, uncertain whether he had earned a reward or a whipping. The two tall men waited, the boy coming between them, bright-eyed with curiosity but offering no word.

At last Giacomo spoke. "Of course I consent. It's in the Rule. Hospitality to all who come, out of Christ's charity. Our Abbot won't argue with that."

Oddone clapped his hands. "Come on then! We're taking an easy way back; we're at liberty, you see, and needn't hurry. Are you hungry? Thirsty? Is there anything you'd like to see?"

A grin transformed Jehan's face, stripping away a full score of years. "You choose, Brother. We're even freer than you—at loose ends, for a fact; we'll follow wherever you lead."

And lead them Oddone did with skill as amazing as everything he had done since he came to Saint Bacchus, chattering happily with the Norman monk, harkened to with silent interest by the young Greek, and quite undismayed by his strange one's abstraction.

Giacomo trailed after the oddly assorted company. After some little time he discovered that he was matching his pace to that of the white stranger. The others had drawn somewhat ahead up the remnant of an old paved way, a road like a green tunnel through one of Rome's many wildernesses. The sun was shut out here; the awareness of humanity, of the city, was dim and distant. Yet Oddone was leading them through the city itself, from the mighty fortress bulk of the Colosseum toward the Palatine Hill and, past that, San Girolamo in the hollow of the hill. This was not true wasteland as Rome knew it, vast expanses of open field and tangled copse and malarial marsh strewn as thickly with ruins as a battlefield with bones, but rather a garden gone wild. Through the knotted canes peered a pale blurred face, old god or old Roman set on guard here and long forgotten.

Within reach of the image, Giacomo's companion slowed. He took off his hat as if it irked him, and let his hood fall back, shaking out a remarkable quantity of winter-gold hair. The gesture struck something in Giacomo, made him conscious that he had been seeing no living man at all, but only an ageless abstract beauty. The beauty had grown no less, yet something, maybe the green solitude, had thawed the ice; the marble angel had become a man, and a very young one at that, a princely youth who looked about him with newborn awareness. His eyes had darkened although they were light still, clear silvery gray, alive and alert and very, very keen.

They found the crumbling statue, examined it, let it pass in favor of the living face. Bright though they were, the terrible brilliance was gone; they saw no more than any eyes had a right to see.

Giacomo began to bristle. He was not a marble Roman, to be stared at for so long a count of heartbeats down so elegant a length of nose. Yet for all its pride, it was not an arrogant stare; it had a strange clarity, an innocence that asked no pardon and never dreamed it needed any.

"Well, sir," said the Prior as the silence stretched, "do you find my face ugly enough to be fascinating?"

The pilgrim lowered his eyes. "Your pardon, Brother Prior. I meant no discourtesy."

"I suppose I can forgive you. You're a nobleman at home, aren't you?"

He looked almost dismayed. "Is it so obvious?"

"Rather," Giacomo said.

"How strange," murmured the pilgrim. He walked more slowly still, pondering. Giacomo might have thought him mad, or slow in the wits; the former all but certainly, if only instinct had not rebelled. There was something eminently sane about this young man, although it was not the sanity of the common run of mankind. It was in fact very like Oddone's. Brilliant, narrowly focused, and generally preoccupied.

His focus shifted abruptly to Giacomo; just as abruptly he said, "I'm called Alfred, or Alf if you like. Like my friend, I come from Anglia."

"So," said Giacomo, "Oddone was almost right. Not an angel after all, but an Angle."

Alf smiled a little ruefully. "I earned that, didn't I?" And after a moment: "Your face is not ugly at all, and yet I do find it fascinating."

"All Rome in a nose," Giacomo said, half annoyed, half amused. "You wouldn't happen to be an artist too, would you?"

Alf shook his head with a touch of regret. "I'm but a poor student of the world and its faces. Sometimes, as you've discovered, to the point of rudeness."

"It's forgiven," Giacomo said.

As they hastened to catch the others, now lost to sight, he realized that all his ill humor had evaporated. Nor could even Oddone's tuneless singing bring it back.

> *"O Roma nobilis, orbis et domina,*
> *cunctarum urbium excellentissima. . . ."*

There was only one reasonable defense. With a better will than he had ever expected to have, he added his own rich basso:

> *"Roseo martyrum sanguine rubea,*
> *albis et virginum liliis candida. . . ."*

New voices joined them, strong trained Norman-accented baritone and sudden, piercingly sweet tenor.

> *"Salutem dicimus tibi per omnia,*
> *te benedicimus—salve per saecula!"*

They made quite a passable choir, Oddone notwithstanding. Even as their singing faded into the clamor of Rome and died, Giacomo discovered that he was smiling.

13

As prisons went, Anna supposed, this one was quite luxurious. It was clean; if not warm, it was certainly not too cold to bear, and she had the blanket; the food was edible though somewhat monotonous. Her hands were healing well; she had taken off the bandages some little time since, reckoned in visits of their unseen jailer. Food appeared at regular intervals; the chamberpot was never full, the lamp never empty. It was like a tale out of Anna's eastern childhood, save that her nurse had never told her how very frightening it was to be waited on by unseen hands, watched over by a guard whom she could not perceive. At first it nearly drove her mad, not to know who watched, or where, or why. But with time she calmed. Let him watch, whatever he was, wizard or demon or renegade of the Kindred. Let him know all she did, thought, said. She had nothing to be ashamed of.

She huddled at her end of the pallet, or prowled the cell, or played with the children. *Pups* she refused to call them, and she was adamant. Yet pups they were. Rather dull at first like all newborn creatures, all their beings focused on food and sleep. But as time crawled on, they grew and changed with the swiftness of beast-kind. Their eyes learned to see; they learned to walk, an awkward big-bellied waddle that transformed itself into a lolloping run. They found their voices, and they discovered play in all its myriad avatars. Only their eyes betrayed their kind, cat-pupiled blue paling slowly to white-gold, marked now and then with a sudden uncanny clarity.

Thea, chained, was nurse and refuge, her temper held at bay for their sakes. Anna was friend, playmate, even teacher. For she talked to them. She talked constantly, and the invisible one be damned. She told them of their father and their kin and their inheritance of power; of Rhiyana and Broceliande and the great world; of magic and the Church, orthodoxy and heresy, philosophy and theology and all the high learning her imprisonment denied her.

"Boredom," she would say while Liahan dueled with a wickedly snarling Cynan for possession of her lap. "That is the curse of the prisoner. Stale air, stale light, unremitting confinement—what are they to the mind that has work to do? Nothing at all! But put it in a cell without book or pen or parchment; without conversation, without games, with nothing to do but count cracks in the stone, pull straws out of the pallet, dispute with imaginary philosophers, and invent progressively less inventive fantasies; and directly it rots away. If I didn't have you imps to chase after, I believe I'd barter my soul for one glimpse of a book. Or," she added with deep feeling, "a bath." For that was worst of all, worse even than the long bookless hours, to be so dismayingly unkempt, cleaned sketchily and stickily with wine and the edge of her camise, gaining nothing for her efforts but a steadily more draggled hem. At least her courses had not begun, which belied the eternity she seemed to have been here; she refused to consider what would happen when they did.

She was still dreaming of rescues. All the Fair Folk in a storm of fire. Father Jehan in white armor with a cross on his breast. Alf walking calmly in and bidding them be free. She shut her eyes tight, the better to see his face. He was smiling. His body gleamed softly as sometimes it did at night, as if his skin had caught and held the moon. His eyes were red like coals, like rubies, rimmed with silver fire; about his head shone a white nimbus of power.

She sighed and shifted, and groaned a little. Her neck was stiff. Unwillingly she opened her eyes.

He was *there*. Living, breathing, shining pale, all in white and gray silver, looking down. Her whole being gathered to leap into his arms.

Knotted. Cramped. Recoiled.

It was Alf. It was *not*. Tall, pale, yes. Beautiful, ah yes, more beautiful than anyone had a right to be and still be unmistakably a man. But not Alf. The face was the merest shade broader. The hair was merely gilt, with no glimmer of silver. The eyes were a hard clear gray like flint. And on the lean young cheek was a distinct shadow of beard.

She tried to swallow. Her mouth was burning dry. This not-Alf, this creature as like to him as a brother, was Brother indeed, severely tonsured, habited—impossibly, terribly—in gray over white. A Pauline monk, looking not at her at all but at the hound who lay silent at her feet. Thea was awake, frozen, every hair erect.

From beneath her burst her son, hurtling upon the stranger with an infant roar. The monk's eyes flickered. Anne's own hackles rose as at the passing of lightning. Cynan ran full into a wall no one could see, tumbling end over end yet snarling still with irrepressible fury. His mother's forefoot pinned him; he struggled wildly beneath it.

Thea's voice rang in Anna's mind. *Demon. Coward. Judas. Bind me, beat me, compass me in the mind of a hound—whatever betrayal you hunt for, you'll never get it from me.*

He looked at her, a flat gray stare, revealing nothing. From behind him came a second Pauline monk. Quite an ordinary monk beside that other, a heavy florid man, unmistakably human. Yet, Anna saw with bitter clarity, he was no fool. For all their heavy-lidded languor, his eyes were sharp, gleaming with amusement. "Spirit," he said in the *langue d'oeil*, "is always to be admired, even in your kind. But spirit can be broken."

Or killed outright. Thea's quiet was deadly. *You have us, I grant you that, and it's no mean feat. But for how long?*

"For as long as we please." The monk folded his arms and smiled. "Do you care to test us?"

Although Thea's eyes burned, her silent voice was cool. *I'm not an*

utter idiot. Can I say the same of you? It's clear enough what you holy Hounds
*are up to, casting nets to trap witches in, with your own tame witch to lay the bait.
You caught us in a moment of weakness. You'll catch no more.*

"We caught three." The pale monk even sounded like Alf, damn
him: clear, light, melodious. "We killed another. The world sings to
be free of him."

Anna tasted blood. She had bitten her tongue. She felt no pain,
yet.

Alun. Thea mourned, but in wrath. *You murdered him.*

"Executed a witch," said the worldly cleric.

Murder, Thea repeated fiercely, her eyes fixed upon the other, the
fair one. *He was your own kin!*

"He was an abomination," said that travesty of Alf's voice, if not
his accent at least; this was strange yet familiar, a softening of the
vowels, a quickening of the words' flow. "A spawn of the Pit, a child
of—"

Then so are you.

His eyes focused and began to burn. "He was foul. He stank to
Heaven. I stretched out my hand; I called on my God; He came and
smote him down."

You killed him. You killed with power.

His hand came up as if to strike. Thea crouched over her children, snarling on a low and deadly note. "God smote him," he
repeated. "God shall smite you also, who take refuge from righteousness in the body of a beast."

"Better that, perhaps, than a glittering travesty of humankind."
The worldly man did not sound as if he believed it; rather as if it were
an idea he toyed with, testing its weight. He regarded the witch-
hound with a touch of regret and more than a touch of satisfaction.
"You are an attractive creature as hound bitches go, although your
eyes are more than a little disconcerting. But that, Brother Simon tells
me, should change with time. The mind within that elegant head is
clear enough now, and quite witch enough, if held most strongly in
check. How long before the change begins? Already I see it in your
whelps, who have forgotten that they ever wore any shape but this.
Soon you shall follow them. Your mind shall begin to darken, the
edges to blur, the higher thoughts to slow; the will turn toward the
belly; the yellow demon-eyes grow soft and brown and bestial, matching at last the inner to the outer being. Witch no longer, woman-fetch
no more, but hound in truth, with neither memory nor sorcery to free

your O1," he said after a calculated moment, "your offspring. Unless, as may well be, it is already too late for them."

The hound's head shook with an odd gracelessness, human gesture fitted ill to inhuman body. But Thea's eyes were still her own, and they were eloquent. *Never,* they flared. *Never!*

The monk smiled. "You may defy us as much as you like. It changes nothing. Rage; threaten; taunt. Watch your children fall ever deeper into the darkness of the beast. But"—he leaned forward almost within reach of her spring—"*but.* That need not be so. They can be free in their proper forms, and you with them. Free and at peace."

Dead, Thea said.

"Not dead. Alive and sane."

At what price? Murder and mayhem? Mere treason?

"No price. Only acceptance of God's will. Thus far we have been gentle; we have simply confined you to the shape you yourself chose, giving you ample time for reflection. Now you must decide. You may rise a woman, or you may remain as now you are."

And if I yield? What am I yielding to? What happens to my children?

"Ah," said the monk, drawing it out. "Your children. You defend them very bravely and, I gather, with somewhat more strength than Brother Simon would have expected. In vain, in the end. He has no desire to harm them, but so he will do if you compel him."

She stood over them, Cynan restrained but uncowed, Liahan watching with eyes too wide and too clear for either the infant she was or the pup she seemed. *Touch them,* her mother said, *even cast a thought at them, and you will see exactly how strong I am.*

"We will have them," Brother Simon said, light and cool and dispassionate. "Satan's grip on them is feeble yet. We will bring them to salvation."

The other nodded with approval more fulsome than flattering. "Salvation, yes. The light of the true God. They will live and grow and be as strong as ever you could wish. Nor need they be torn from you. While they have need, they may remain with you, provided only that we have your promise to teach them no black sorceries. You will be nurse and mother as God has made you. Others will have their teaching."

You, said Thea. *Simon. Simon Magus, Simon-pure, Simon the simple. Don't you think I can guess what you want with us? You have one tame warlock. Here are two more, firm in your hand, young enough to mold as you would have them, powerful enough to make you lord of the world. After, of course, you've disposed of this minor inconvenience.* She grinned a wide fanged grin. *Not so minor after all, am I? He can't get at my babies while I'm determined to ward him off, and I'm not such an idiot as to give way to your persuasion. It's an impasse.*

"No," said Brother Simon. "I will break you if you compel me." He moved swifter than sight, swifter even than Thea's jaws, snatching up the still and staring Liahan. He held her with gentle competence, stroking her leaf-thin ears, evading her sudden snap as easily as he had her mother's. "You can wall her mind in all your defiance. But can you defend her body? A chain confines you—"

Thea leaped, twisted, dropped to a bristling crouch. The chain hung limp. Her eyes flared green; the collar dropped with an iron clang. Her muscles knotted, tensing to spring.

His calm voice went on with scarcely a pause. "Attack and I strike. This neck is delicate; how easy to break it. And I am swifter than you."

Thea sank down, ears flat, eyes slitted. *Give me back my daughter.*

"Give me your choice. Your children now and under your care, or later and in despite of you."

Anna could endure it no longer. "No!" she cried. "There's no later. There's only now."

They stared at her, both the brothers of Saint Paul, as if she had burst upon them from the empty air. Maybe to them she had. She was only human, and they had three witches to burn.

She was past caring. She plunged on recklessly, relegating the fat one to nonexistence, fixing the whole force of her rage upon the other. "Simon Magus, Simon traitor, even I can see the truth, lowly mortal female that I am. You need these children, and you need them now; and you can't get at them any more than you can get at Rhiyana. And time's pressing. Any moment the Pope could call off the Crusade, or the Fair Folk could find a way to overcome you and set us free."

"God is with His Holiness. Your fair demons, the dark king, the white one who may be more than a king—" Simon's face stiffened; his eyes narrowed. But he laughed, a light terrible sound out of that face of ice and flint. "That one had his own splendor of folly. I think I chastened him a little. All his fire and wrath merely pricked me. Have your mighty Kindred no more to send?"

When Anna was afraid, she was also most angry. "He scared you, didn't he? He wasn't expecting to clash with real power; he didn't have all his strength ready. You routed him, but it cost you. Closed out of Rhiyana, with Thea holding you at bay here—what's left but a round of pleas disguised as threats?"

"I am not held at bay." That was not anger, certainly. It was more like amusement. Simon set Liahan at her mother's feet, where she remained, watching him. "Your kin, little one, have fled within their walls. Wise creatures. So too would I, if it were myself I faced."

"You'd be gibbering under your bed behind a barricade of blankets."

"You are a fierce little shrew," observed the florid monk. Anna smiled sweetly; he returned the smile with one fully as lethal. "You are of no account. Flotsam merely, drawn up in the net. And things of no account are swiftly cast away."

Thea moved with suppleness more of the cat than of the hound, setting herself between the monks and the woman. *Touch her,* she said very gently, *and though I have neither power nor speed to match with yonder magus, I assure you I am perfectly capable of tearing out your fat throat.*

"Only," said the nameless monk, "if yonder magus permits."

She flowed toward him. Her eyes held his, burning bright. She blurred. He cried out sharply. She sat at her ease, licking her lips. From one small prick, a droplet of blood swelled and burst and broke, runneling down the thick neck to vanish beneath the cowl.

You taste vile, she said to him.

But Anna, and perhaps Thea herself, had misjudged him. The color drained from his face, leaving it utterly calm. Deep in Anna's mind, a small separate self observed that he must have been a strikingly handsome boy. The bones were fine under the thickened flesh, the forehead broad and clear, the profile cleanly carved still although it blurred into the heavy jowled throat.

He looked down at Thea with no expression at all; and that was less a mask than his joviality had been. "You did not do as you threatened. I doubt very much that you can."

Thea could not be disconcerted. She settled once more on guard, but easy in it, almost lounging with her children close against her. *To return to the point, monk, I'm fair enough prey when all's considered, and we have the matter of the young ones still to settle. My sister is no part of this. You would do very well to let her go.*

The monk smiled. "I think not, milady witch."

"Why?" demanded Anna. "Because you think I'm the closest thing you'll find to a weakness in her?"

Of course, Thea said, *and he can't threaten you or his own neck is in jeopardy. On the other hand, the possibility's always there. One never discards even a potential weapon unless one has to.* She tilted her head, considering him. *Weapons, you know, can be used by either side in a battle. Take care you don't find yourself on the wrong end of this one.*

"I do not intend to." He examined her again, deliberately, as if he could make her writhe. She only arched her back and stretched like a cat. His jaw clenched. "One way or another, we will have it all: you, your cublings, Rhiyana itself. You may choose the way of it, whether salvation for your children and a swift and merciful end for your kind, or a long slow deadly war fought with the mind as well as with the body. Brother Simon is a mightier power than any you can muster, and God is with him; he cannot but conquer. With your aid he will do so quickly and cleanly. Without it, I can promise only anguish. For you, for your kind, and for your children."

So that's my choice. Swift death or slow death. What's the difference, in the end?

"Pain," said Brother Simon, sudden as a stone speaking.

All the more reason to give my people time to arm against you.

"They cannot. They cannot even find me. But I find them with perfect ease. Shall I test my power on them?"

Thea was on her feet, but the nameless monk stood in her way. "Not yet, witch-lady. You still have a choice to make. Swiftly now, before we make it for you."

She stood erect, at gaze, trembling just visibly. *It is made,* said the voice in all their minds, *made thrice over. No, and no, and no. Better death in this shape than slavery to the likes of you.*

"We shall see," he said, "how long this pretty show of defiance can last." He drew up his cowl with a ceremonious gesture. "Examine well your heart, milady witch. If heart indeed you have."

14

At first Thea seemed only glad to be free of her chain. She whirled round the cell, mocking the bolted door with every line of her body.

Yet at length she quieted, dropping panting to the floor beside the bed. She grinned at Anna, who stared levelly back and said, "It's no good, is it? You can't get us out."

Not yet, Thea said, inspecting each child with care, washing Lia-han all over until the memory of Simon's touch was scoured away. *But he's cocky. He's leaving me free enough inside this place, though every wall is also a wall of power. He'll learn to regret that.*

"He could be listening to you now."

I know he is. Thea leaped up again, as if her long captivity in alien shape had left her sated with stillness. She prowled the cell, coming to a halt under the lamp-cluster. Her eyes sparked. The lamps burst into a blaze of sudden light. She stood beneath them, watching them, while Cynan stalked her manifold shadow.

The light died. Thea's eyes closed; she seemed to dwindle, to shrink into herself. *He's strong,* she said. She sank down slowly.

There was a little water left. Anna wheedled it into her. It seemed to strengthen her; she raised her head, drawing a long breath. *I'm not in the best of condition for this.*

"Is anyone?"

I plan to be. I won't give in to those cursed Hounds, and I don't intend to die for it.

"Maybe someone will come," Anna said.

Thea rounded on her. *Pray for it if it suits you, but don't lie back and wait for it. We're hidden completely. We're not even in Rhiyana.*

Anna had guessed that much. But to hear it spoken made it real, a knot of pain where her stomach should be. "Then where——"

Rome, Thea answered. *Old Rome itself, that's more than big enough to hide us even if anyone can track us here. He knows it, that captor of ours. He's very pleased with his own cleverness.*

"He's a horror. To call himself Simon after the notorious wizard, the first heretic——"

Or after the Prince of Apostles, for the matter of that. No; he's not our captor, he's merely our jailer. I meant the other. The mastermind in the guise of a fat fool. Brother Paul as his mind was trumpeting to me, loudly enough to make it certain that that's not the name he was christened with. He's the one to look to. He's the evil genius in this.

"But he's only human."

Thea laughed with a bitter edge. *Poor Anna! We've ruined you. All our visible power, our disgustingly pretty faces, our stubborn refusal to let time touch us; we've let you think we're perfection, or as close to it as earth allows. We've failed completely to teach you something much truer. No one's only human, Anna. He might be as ugly as Satan himself; he'll certainly be dead in a hundred years; he hasn't a glimmer of our magic. But he has something more powerful than all the rest. He has a brain. A thinking brain. Whether by chance or his own black brilliance, he's caught one of us, trained him to jesses and a lure, and hunted him with all too much success. You can be sure he's not resting on it.*

Anna shook her head obstinately. "The fat one might be giving the orders, but the other is only letting him. If he really has that much power—"

He has more. Do you remember how Alf held down the dance the night— Thea's mind-voice caught for the merest shadow of an instant—*the night the babies were born? Do you remember how he was? Ruler in the circle, master of enchanters—as Brother Simon himself has said, greater than a king. Now remember your worst and falsest image of yourself. That's how much weaker Alf is than this second Simon Magus.*

"Then how can anyone control him, let alone that fat lecher of a monk?"

I don't know, Thea said, *but this Paul can. And does.*

Now came Anna's time to pace with Cynan for escort, and Thea's to watch in silence. Except that Thea gave it up after a turn or two and turned her attention upon Liahan. The little witch had not moved since Simon set her down, not even to protest her rough and thorough cleansing. Her eyes were wide still, bright and fixed. And yet when Thea nosed her, they blinked; her tail wagged very slightly in recognition.

Anna stopped, alarmed. "What has he done to her? Has he hurt her?"

Thea's response was slow in coming. *No, I don't think . . . he wouldn't dare . . .* Her lip wrinkled. *He wouldn't dare!*

Anna knelt beside them. Liahan did not flinch or snap when Anna lifted her. She felt as she always did, warm and silken-furred, wriggling a little against Anna's shoulder. "Her mind," Anna said. "Her wits. Has he—"

He can't, Thea snapped. Cynan, jealous, scrabbled at Anna's knee; his mother caught him by the scruff of the neck, roughly enough to startle him, and all but drove him to nurse. Her head whipped back toward Anna. *I'm nothing to that tower of strength, but I bore these children in my body. While I have any power at all, he can't touch them.*

"The other one—Paul—he said—"

I'm a long way yet from losing my mind. Liahan— Thea tossed her head, a very human gesture, yet also very canine. *I can't touch her mind. It's walled and guarded. But there's no stench of Simon Magus about it; and yet she's too young. She can't know how to shield. Not like that. Not from me.*

Anna caressed the hound-child, stroking her favorite places, behind the ears, along the spine. She squirmed with pleasure, climbing higher, burying her cool wet nose in Anna's neck. "Liahan," Anna said, for what good it could do, "he's gone. You can open your mind now."

Thea made a small disgusted sound. *Talk. As if she could understand.*

Anna ignored her. "Witch-baby, shields are splendidly useful things and you are a wonder for having made one so young, but it's making your mother angry. Open a chink at least and let her in."

Liahan stiffened a fraction. Anna cradled her, holding her face to face. Her eyes were all gold. Winter-gold like Alf's, shining as his shone when he wielded his power. "Oh, you are your father's child. Your mother's too, stubborn as you are and laughing in it. Won't you lower your shield? Just for the practice?"

The little witch blinked. Anna reeled with sudden dizziness. Those eyes—

Liahan! Thea's will cut like a sword, severing the spell. Yes, Liahan was laughing even now, though chastened, reaching to lick Anna's cheek, begging to be set down. Once freed, she set to nursing as if she had never been more than she seemed, a very small and very hungry gazehound pup.

Witch, Thea said, half in exasperation, half in pride. *Born and bred contrary, and determined to stay that way. I almost pity our poor enemy.*

"Pity *that?*" cried Anna.

That, Thea agreed. She began to bathe her son, who, sated, lay on the verge of sleep. Anna watched in silence that stretched into peace.

The air's singing shattered it. Anna watched the bowls and cups appear. It was no less uncanny for that now she knew how they had come, and by whose will.

One would think . . . Thea mused. She shook herself. *No.*

"What?" Anna snapped the word viciously.

Thea lowered her head to her paws, reflecting. *Simon the Magus is a coincidence. Of course a man of the Folk, if he were tall and light-eyed and flaxen-fair, would look uncannily like Alfred. It's the cast of the face—it's the same in all of us. But that he should be so very like, and be so bitterly our enemy . . . that must be God's black humor.*

"He's not quite . . . right, is he?"

One could not deceive Thea with an air of indifference. Not that it mattered. Thea had never weakened anyone's will with a show of compassion. *He's utterly mad. He's a travesty; a caricature. A nightmare of a might-have-been.*

"He makes me think of Nikki too. Somehow. In the way he's

twisted; in the way he seems to be missing something. I remember how my mother used to talk, once in a great while, when she didn't know I could hear. Before Alf came and changed everything. She'd been told to raise my brother like a colt or a puppy, because that was as close to a man as he'd ever get; she could train him, maybe, and she did housebreak him and teach him to eat decently. But he'd never be properly human."

He would never have been like yonder creature.

"How do you know?" Anna flared at her. "How can you imagine what he would have grown into? You know what a brain he has. Alf set it free. What if Alf had never come? Maybe we all would have died when the City fell. That would have been a mercy. But if we hadn't, if Nikki had grown up, trapped, treated the way people never could help but treat him—all that wit and all that wildness with no way out of his head and no way in . . ."

I can imagine it.

Thea's inner voice was so flat that Anna stopped short. Remembered, and felt the heat rise to burn her cheeks. Her tongue had run away again. Would she never learn?

Thea was choosing not to take offense. *Nikephoros would not have let himself sink into a madman. No more than Alf did. He'd have raged; he'd have fought. He would have tried to make something of himself.*

"Sometimes I think, if you ever got tired of Alf, you'd have Nikki in your bed before the hour was out." No. Anna would never learn.

An hour? Thea laughed. *That long? Anna Chrysolora, you credit me with altogether too much restraint.*

"So that's why you won't marry my elder brother. You've got your eye on the younger."

Of course. Would I be myself if I didn't?

In spite of all her troubles and her festering temper, Anna began to laugh. Thea had the eye and the tongue of a notorious harlot, but for all of that, her heart was as fixed and immovable as the roots of Broceliande. She could look, she could laugh, she could tease; she could no more turn from her dozen years' lover than she could make herself a mortal woman.

Not, she agreed, *at the moment. There's a significant lack of opportunity here. As for Brother Magus . . . Have you ever suspected how very little I like smooth-skinned fair-haired boys? I'm one for a fine black eye and a warm brown skin and plenty of curly beard to play with.*

"Nikki doesn't have enough to—"

He will when he's a little older. No, Anna; I despise a pale man. You can imagine how shocked I was when I discovered that I'd fallen in love with the palest of all pale men. All he had to commend him was a good breadth of shoulder—which he was always managing to hide—and a certain indefinable air. This fetch of his obviously has neither.

"How can you tell under the habit?"

Thea's eyes sparkled wickedly. *How could I tell under Alf's? Sometimes I forget you never knew him when he was Brother Alfred. He was the loveliest boy who ever put on a cowl, the meekest white lamb who ever lay down before an altar. A more perfect monk never graced an abbey. But now and then when he was most off guard, I could catch it. A look, a word, a hint of something else. And there were always those shoulders; not to mention another attribute or two, once I got the habit off him.*

If Brother Simon was listening indeed, this was surely driving him wild. Anna inspected the food which Simon's power had left, found it much the same as ever. She brought the meat to Thea, settling herself with the rest. Between bites she said sagely, "Oh, yes. Those attributes."

Thea nibbled the edge of her portion, her eyes bright, amused. *I admit, though I was expecting more than a weedy boy, that first good look . . . I was a hound at the time; he was bathing, and he didn't even know I was there. Saints and angels! What a lovely moment that was! Then he saw me, or more likely heard me panting, and he didn't do anything I'd expected, except blush in the most fascinating places. He just kept on washing, ignoring me steadfastly and not saying a word. Not hurrying to hide anything, either. That was when I knew I had to have him. White skin, white hair, and all.* She sighed, letting the meat fall back into its bowl. *My poor love. Left all alone, and Alun gone who might as well have been another son . . .* Damn *these devils of monks!*

15

It was very quiet in San Girolamo. Strangely, when Alf stopped to think; Jeromite monks kept no constant vows of silence, and Rome lay outside with its bells and its clamor. But the walls were high and thick, the monastery itself set somewhat apart in the hollow of the hill. From its tower one could see the loom of the Palatine with its white ruins;

the city sprawling and crowding down to the river; the bulk of the fallen Circus and the green waste within, and at its far curved end the battlements of a castle. But within the abbey's walls one might have been in a separate country, a kingdom of quiet. In a round of days marked off by the ringing of bells, the monks went about their business, soft on sandaled feet.

Not that they shuffled and whispered. They spoke and laughed freely enough; the novices had their moments of boisterousness, and the Offices were well and heartily sung. Yet no amount of human uproar seemed able to shake the calm of the ancient stones.

It was sinking into his bones. He had entered it with deep misgivings, even with fear; castigating himself for a fool—he had grown up in just such a place and guested in many since, both as a pilgrim and as a lord of Rhiyana—but trembling still, because he had left Saint Ruan's far behind but never quite lost the yearning for it. Yet how easy, after all, to walk through the gate, to exchange courtesies with the gentle aging Abbot, to settle into the guesthouse which was all Oddone had promised and more. How simple after attending Mass as courtesy demanded, also to take part in the Offices, even those of midnight and of dawn, for the bells were insistent and sleep had become a stranger. And if he was there, he could not but join in the prayers and the singing, stumbling a little at first but waking soon to memory. Within a day or two, he never knew exactly how, he found that he was no longer relegated to the outer reaches of the chapel with the guests and the pilgrims and the Roman matrons in their black veils; he had a place in the choir between Jehan and Brother Oddone, with Prior Giacomo in his stall behind.

With the same invisible ease, he found himself in the refectory with the Brothers, partaking of the common fare. Jehan, bishop though he was, was claiming to be but a lowly monk; he could not in good conscience dine thrice daily at the Abbot's table. Nor would his companions partake of fine meats and wine while he dined on black bread and refectory ale; they joined him among the monks, taking their frugal meals in silence to the sound of the reader's voice.

"You fit with us well," said Prior Giacomo.

After days of rain, the sun had returned at last. In celebration, Oddone had haled Alf off to a corner of the cloister, set him down, and begun to sketch him under the Prior's interested eye. "Just a short time you've been here," Giacomo went on, "and you've made yourself one of us."

At Oddone's bidding, Alf raised his chin a little. A vagrant breeze played with his hair. Although he had gone to Brother Tonsore to have it cut, commanded the man to have no mercy, he had lost a scarce inch. It was too handsome, the barber had told him with fine Italian logic, and he was no monk to have to go about looking like one.

With that in his memory and a faint wry smile touching his lips, he said, "I try to be a good guest."

"By now," said Giacomo, "you're hardly one at all. Brother Marco tells me you've been putting in a good day's work in the scriptorium."

"He seemed to have need of another hand." And it made the days easier. Nikki did his hunting in body as well as in mind, roaming the ways of the city with Jehan at heel like a watchful mastiff. Alf could not search so. He stumbled; he groped like a blind man; he forgot to move at all. But in the scriptorium, in the scents of ink and dust and parchment, where the only sound was the scratching of pens and the occasional turning of a page, his body could look after itself. The words flowed from eye to hand to parchment; the lines stretched out behind, letter after swift meticulous letter; and his mind ran free, hunting the coverts of its own strange world.

Prior Giacomo sat on a stone bench, taking care not to intrude on Oddone's light. For all his brusque air, he was a pleasant presence, a gleam of friendship. Alf let it ease him. His mind was still a raw wound; the sun though winter-pale was strong, his shields against it unsteady. Once long ago, when after a bitter quarrel Thea had left him and closed her mind to him, he had let the sun work its will. It had burned him terribly for his foolishness. And he had not even been her lover then, only her friend and her fellow pilgrim.

Although this was not the awful glare of August on the shores of the Bosporus, yet it was potent enough to touch such a creature as he. It pressed down upon his head, deceptively gentle. Shielded, he could meet its glare, his eyes—night-eyes, cat-eyes—unwinking. Unshielded—

Light stabbed him to the soul. His shields leaped up and locked, a reflex as sure as his eyes' flinching. Even so brief an instant had nearly destroyed them; he could feel the tightness of his skin, the beginnings of pain.

To the monk and the Prior it was only sunlight, cool and frail. So must he be to his enemy, feeble, powerless, unworthy of notice.

The Prior was watching him; he saw himself reflected in the dark eyes. Other faces, however flawed, at least were honest, the parade of emotions all open and clear to see. His own was like a mask, white, perfect, serene. For a fiery instant he hated it.

Giacomo was speaking again. He forced himself to make sense of the words. This was not Caer Gwent, where the strange moods of the Kindred were known and accepted. But the man was speaking in the Roman dialect, the old Latin tongue blurred and softened into foreignness, and Alf could not make his wandering brain remember its ways. He could barely even remember the pure and ordered Latin of the schools.

He must have risen. He did not know if he spoke. The sun and the cloister were gone; the cool shade had him, the old, old refuge, the chapel walls. These were strange and gaudy with their glittering mosaics, but the altar was still the altar, the Christ dying still upon his familiar cross. A man dying for men; what cared he for the anguish of the one who knelt before him? Anguish born of mortal sin: sorcery, fornication, abandonment of the vows that had made him a priest forever.

Yes. Mortal, in all its senses. All his being howled in pain, but not the smallest speck of it knew any repentance. He was not human, to subject himself to human doctrines of sin and salvation. Sorcery he was born to; it was his nature, as much a part of him as his eyes or his hands. Fornication he might atone for if he had ever found any foulness in it, if it had ever brought him aught but joy. For his vows' forsaking he had the Pope's own dispensation, signed and sealed and laid away in a coffer in the House of the Falcon.

So facilely did a scholar dispose of his sins. He sank back upon his heels and lowered his face into his hands. Darkness was no refuge. It deepened, broadened, gaped to swallow him. Not his own death but Alun's. Not his body's destruction but the shattering of his mind.

He could not find Thea or his son or his daughter. For all his power knew of them, they might never have existed at all. He could not even sense their nearness—not even the nearness of the power that had taken them.

His fingers tensed, clawing. He could not see. He could not *see*. All prophecy was gone from him. There was only the cavernous dark. He thrust against it, striking it, striving to tear it; raging, half mad and knowing it and caring not at all.

He flailed at air and shadow. It yielded, ungraspable yet deadly as the mists of Rome with their burden of fever. His mind reeled, toppled, fell.

Voices babbled. Light flickered. He shrank away.

Meaning crept through his barriers. "Signore. Signor' Alfred. Please, are you sick? Signore!"

Another voice, deeper and rougher, cut across the first. "He's taken a fit, I think. Go fetch Brother Rafaele. I'll look after him."

Alf struggled, snatching at a retreating shadow, pulling it up short. The shadow gained substance. Brother Oddone gaped down at him, for once far taller; he was lying on the stone, its cold creeping through his heavy robe, and in his hand in a death grip, the hem of the boy's habit. "No," he tried to say. "I'm not—" Oddone's incomprehension stopped him. His eyes began to blur again. He willed them to be clear, and his brain with them. He had been speaking no tongue a Roman would understand, the Saxon of his childhood.

He dared not trust his wits with Italian. He groped for Latin words, found them at last. "Please, Brother. Don't trouble Brother Rafaele."

The hands on him were Prior Giacomo's, holding him down although when he tried to sit up they shifted to aid him. "We'll trouble the good Brother, sir, and no arguments. Whatever it is that knocked you down, it hasn't let you go yet."

Alf pulled free, not gently, staggering to his feet. For no reason at all, he was whitely angry. "Have you no ears? I do not wish to be carried off to your infirmary!"

"So carry yourself," Giacomo said sharply, meeting glare with glare and temper with temper. "If you're not sick, Rafaele will say so. If you are, he'll know what to do about it."

"Leeches. Purges. Ignorant nonsense."

"If you know so much better, what were you doing in convulsions on the chapel floor?"

Alf's body snapped painfully erect. Rage tore through it. Blind babbler, mortal fool; how dared he—

Convulsions?

Giacomo had him by the arm. That was ignorance in the man, to be so utterly fearless. Yet he was walking obediently, strength and power and skill in combat forgotten, lost like all the rest of his proper self.

He willed his feet to be still, his frame to stiffen in resistance, his voice to speak levelly. "There is nothing any physician can do for me. I know. I have been one."

The Prior scowled.

For the second time Alf freed himself, but smoothly now, his temper mastered. "Your concern does you credit, Brother Prior, but my illness can have no earthly remedy. It's past for the moment; let it be."

Giacomo might have burst out in bitter words. But Oddone, thrust aside and all but forgotten, leaped eagerly into the gap. "Is it so, signore? Is that why you came here? For a miracle, to cure it?"

Alf turned, mildly startled. As always, Oddone's thin nondescript face warmed something in him; almost he smiled. "Yes. Yes, that's why I came to Rome."

"I'll pray," Oddone said. "I'll pray as hard as I can. God will listen."

The smile won free. Alf touched the narrow shoulder lightly.

Darkness howled.

He staggered. Giacomo caught fire with vindication; Alf fled his hands. For a moment, he had *seen*, his power whole and keen and terrible, potent enough to set him reeling. But there was no joy in that sudden glorious release. Even for a man, born only to die, Oddone was frail. Death sat like a black bird on his shoulder. Its servants prowled his body, haunting the lungs, the laboring heart, the innocent brilliant brain. They had had a long lodging in him, from weak and struggling infant to sickly child to fragile dauntless man. In a little while they would conquer him.

Alf shook his head, tossing it. His face was fixed, frightening, but Oddone did not know how to be afraid. The brown eyes were wide and trusting, troubled for him, thinking he was perhaps in pain.

Death would abandon no mortal creature, not even at the command of elvenkind. Death's servants had no such strength. Alf called on all the singing splendor of his power. And it came. Limping a little, wounded, yet it came.

Oddone blinked. Alf unclamped his hand from the monk's shoulder. "Good day, Brother," he said. "Pray for me." He bowed to the Prior, genuflected to the altar, and left them all.

"How strange," Oddone murmured. "How very strange."

Giacomo would have liked to spit. He satisfied himself with a snarl. "Strange? The man's an utter lunatic!"

The other had not even heard him. "I feel warm. Especially where he touched me. He's amazingly strong; did you notice?" He shook himself slightly. "I have to get back to my drawing. The look he had when he touched me—if I can manage—a line or two, I think; a touch of light, color—"

And he too was gone, still muttering to himself, leaving Giacomo alone with the altar and the crucifix and the glittering angels. "Is it the world that's mad," he demanded of them, "or is it simply I?"

They offered no answer. He stiffened his back and throttled his bafflement and spun on his heel, setting off after the others. However far behind they had left his wits, his body at least could follow where they led.

16
🌿

"This is getting us nowhere."

Jehan stalked from end to end of the room they all shared in the guesthouse. They had it to themselves; it was spacious, the walls painted with faded vistas, a brazier set in the center of it to ward off winter's chill. Nikki sat crosslegged on the bed Jehan shared with Alf, mending a rent in his mantle. Alf sat on a stool near the brazier, turning the pages of a book he had found in the library. Both had glanced up as Jehan spoke, a flash of black and one of silver.

He stopped just short of a peeling pomegranate tree and spun about. "A full month we've been here. In a little while it will be Lent. And what do we have to show for it? One copy of Silvestris' *Cosmographia*. Two pairs of blistered feet."

"Fifteen pages of the Gospels in a slightly antiquated hand." Alf's irony was not clearly perceptible. He closed the book and let it lie in his lap, regarding Jehan with a cool and steady stare.

The Bishop of Sarum raked his fingers through his beard. Since its sudden, uncanny, and fiercely itching birth, it had done well enough by itself, although he doubted that after all it was much of a disguise. That he had seen few familiar faces in all his daily travels, and that none of those had hailed him by name, was probably due more to Heaven's good grace than to any deception of his own. "I know you're doing all you can," he said to both the waiting gazes, "or at least, all you can think of. But it's not working."

Nikki nodded. It was not. His mind was as sore as his feet, and he had not found a trace of the enemy, let alone of the ones he searched for. He had not even come across a memory of any of them, a hint in a human brain that their quarry existed. Rome was large and sprawling, full of ruins and of churches, with people crowded together round the foci of the river, the Pope's palace in the Lateran, the Leonine City beyond Sant' Angelo. But no Anna, no Thea, no children; no mad and mighty power.

"And Rhiyana isn't holding still for us," Jehan said. "The Cardinal's investigation grinds as inexorably as the mills of God, but a great deal faster. The King's gone to the Marches; the raiding's begun, and men have been seen wearing the Cross and crying death to the Witch-king."

Nikki took up the litany. *The Heresiarch in Caer Gwent has been taken by the priests. The Greeks and the Saracens are finding urgent business at home. A Jewish child has been found dead outside of one of the churches in the city.* His eyes glittered; he flung down his mended cloak. *There must be something else we can do!*

"We can go to the Pope," said Jehan. "I know how to reach him. We were friends before his elevation; he consecrated me himself. He won't keep us waiting for an audience."

I should like to see the Pope, Nikki said.

"We should have gone to him as soon as we came. This is an excellent monastery, and by a miracle there's no one in it who knows me, but we're not finding anything by staying here."

Alf's eyes had followed the debate but had lost none of their coolness. His voice was cooler still, almost cold. "We've barely begun to hunt. Would you start the deer before you've even taken the bow out of its case? That's what you'll do if you go to the Pope now. Friend or no, he's in the Hounds' power; he'll certainly be watched by our enemy. If he learns of us and our troubles, even if he's disposed to be lenient, we'll lose our kin in truth; for the enemy will never relax his vigilance."

Where I go, Nikki pointed out, *no one with power can follow. What if he is on guard every instant? He'll never know I'm there to guard against.*

"Nikki can shield His Holiness," Jehan said, "just as he's shielding us now. The enemy need never know—and the Pope may well know where the Hounds have their kennels."

Alf shook his head once. "He won't know of this one. And if the enemy is on guard, invisibility is no use; a wall is impenetrable whether or not the invader can be seen. He has to be at ease, to think us all shut behind our own safe walls in Rhiyana. Then maybe he'll let slip the bolts on the postern gate."

"He hasn't done it yet."

"He hasn't had time."

"God's bones! It's been a month. Wars have been won and lost in far less time than that."

"This war is still in its infancy."

Jehan's hands knotted into fists; he loomed over Alf, who merely looked up at him, unmoved. "Thirty days ago—even seven days ago I'd have said you were keeping up your courage by seeming not to care. But there's a limit to that kind of courage. I think you've passed it." Alf stirred by not a hair's breadth. "Oh, you still care whether your family lives or dies. That's a torment in the heart of you. You don't care to hunt anymore. You've given up. You've surrendered. You've let the enemy have his victory."

"You have not been listening," Alf said with icy precision. "For the third time, we have only begun to—"

"We haven't! We've failed in the first sally. We have no new tactics. And you won't exert that famous brain of yours to find any."

"We need none. We have only to hunt; to keep our minds open and invisible; and to wait."

"Nikki hunts. Nikki keeps us invisible. You do nothing but wait."

Alf rose. He had never had much flesh to spare, and that was very nearly gone. Yet to Jehan's eyes he seemed not more frail, but less, like a blade of steel. "That," he said, "is known as wisdom."

I call it passivity. I don't mind your cloistering yourself here; you've never been skilled at walking in a trance. But you can't lie back and trust to fate. Time doesn't wait. War won't hold off till your opening presents itself to you. And, Nikki added grimly, *while we stumble about in the dark, God alone knows what that madman is doing to his captives.*

"They're alive," Alf said in a flat voice.

"You hope." Jehan struggled to master his temper, to speak reasonably. "Alf, we can't continue the way we've been going, following our noses and hoping we catch wind of something useful. We need to try another tack. Not the Pope, if you insist, but there must be some other way to bring this quarry to earth. Can't you help us find it?"

"There is no need."

"Alf—"

And the silent voice: *Alf, for the love of Heaven—*

He cut them both off. "If you are tired of this seeming futility, you need not pursue it. I can hunt alone. My lord Bishop, you have but to say the word and I can transport you wherever you will, even to your own see of Sarum. Nikephoros, the King will be glad of your aid in the war; or you may serve the Queen or defend the Wood. No compulsion holds you here."

They stared at him, speechless. He sounded like a stranger; he looked like one.

Yes, Nikki thought. Ever since Thea vanished with the children she had borne him, he had been changing. His body had passed from thin to gaunt; his mind had retreated, turning inward upon itself. Above the hollowed cheeks his eyes were pale, remote; not hostile, indeed not unfriendly, but not at all the eyes of the one who had loved them both as brothers. "You may go," he said to them, "without guilt. I'll be well enough here."

They glanced at one another. Jehan's eyes were a little wild. Nikki supposed his own were the same. He knew he wanted to hit something, but Alf was not a wise target. Even in this new mood of his, he was still one of the Kindred, with strength and swiftness far more of the beast than of the human.

Nikki watched Jehan's mind turn over alternatives. It was a very pleasant mind to watch, quick and clear, honest yet subtle, able at will to relinquish control to the trained fighter's body. That body urged him to knock Alf unconscious, to hope that such a blow would return him to his proper senses. But the mind, wiser, held it back. Considered logic, persuasion, pleading, anger.

Settled at last. Unclenched the heavy fists; drew a deep sigh. "Don't be an idiot," Jehan said with weary annoyance. "I got myself into this; I'll see it through to its end. With your help or without it."

Alf did not say what he could have said of Jehan's efficacy as a hunter of shadows. That was mercy enough for the moment. He returned to his seat and opened the book again. Jehan drew back, stood briefly silent, turned away.

Without him the room seemed much larger yet somehow more confining. Alf was losing himself, quite deliberately one might have thought, in the mysteries of the world's creation. In his drab pilgrim's robe he seemed much more a monk than the man he had just put to flight.

Nikki could stand it no better than Jehan had. He sought the same refuge with somewhat more haste.

The sun was still high. He blinked in the light of it, faintly shocked. He had half expected the sky to be as grim as his mood, not blue as the Middle Sea with here and there a fleece of cloud. The air was as warm as Rhiyanan spring; grass grew green round the gray walls, sprinkled with small white flowers like a new fall of snow.

For an instant his yearning for Rhiyana was as strong as pain. But that passed; he drew a careful breath, finding to his surprise that his eyes had blurred. Was he as tired as that?

He shook himself. It was not only the endless futility of the search, and not even the bitterness of the quarrel. He was not made to shut himself up in the walls of an abbey. Father Jehan had a talent: wherever he found himself, there for the moment was his element. Alf was abbey-bred, more visibly so with each day he spent in San Girolamo. But Nikephoros Akestas was completely a creature of the world. Bells and candles and chanting and incense forged each the links of a chain; they dragged at him, they sapped his strength.

He found that he was walking very fast, almost running. It was not fear; it was the swiftness of the hawk cut loose from its jesses. No one was pursuing him. No one was setting him to hunt or to do squire service or to pretend to pray. He was free. He laughed and danced, stalked a cloud shadow down the empty street, put to flight a flock of sparrows. But then, contrite, he called them all back again, making amends with a bit of bread he found in his scrip.

When the Via di San Girolamo had given way to the broader, brighter, and far busier stretch of the Corso, Nikki had relegated all his ill humor to oblivion. He let his feet carry him where they would, and let his eyes for once take in the wonders of this strange half-ruined half-thriving city. Some of it was new, and raw with it, a bristle of armed towers, a crowding of churches and houses and palaces. Most of it was ancient, much of that built anew with the brick and marble of old Rome, some even built into the ancient monuments, people nesting like birds in the caverns of giants.

Yet just such people, Alf said, had raised those very monuments. Small dark keen-faced men and women who reeked of olive oil and garlic, who chattered incessantly and burst into song at will, and seemed to live and love and fight and even die in the streets outside of their patchwork houses. Nikki, wandering among them, felt as always a little odd. In Rhiyana he had been branded a foreigner from the first for his small stature, his dark skin, his big-eyed Byzantine face. In Rome he was completely unremarkable. Why, he thought with a shiver of amazement, he was not even particularly small. In fact, judging from the people he passed and the ones he knew in San Girolamo, he was somewhat above the middle height. It was distinctly pleasant to find himself looking over the heads of grown men.

He bought a hot and savory pie from a vendor and sat on a step to eat it. The stair was attached to a very Roman house, a sprawling affair with a façade of ancient columns, no two alike, and under and behind them an odd mixture of shops. The one nearest appeared to be a purveyor of ink and parchment and a book or two; the next was patently a wineshop.

The pie was wonderful, eel well spiced with onion and precious pepper. As he nibbled at it, he gained a companion, a handsome particolored cat that wove about his ankles, beseeching him with feline politeness to share his pleasure. In return she offered him her own sleek presence, curling in his lap and purring thunderously.

That was a fair bargain, he agreed, dividing the remains of the pasty. If it surprised his new companion to be addressed so clearly by a mortal man, she was far too much a cat to show it; she merely accepted her purchase and consumed it with dispatch. And having done so, washed with care while he licked his own fingers clean.

What made him look up, he never knew. His senses were drawn in upon himself and his contented belly and his sudden friend; his only further thought had been for a cup of wine to wash down the eel pie. As he raised his eyes, even that small bit of sense fled him utterly.

He was used to beauty. Sated with it, maybe. He had grown up with the Fair Folk; nor were the mortal women of Rhiyana far behind when all was considered. He had seen nothing in Rome to compare with either.

The girl on the step below him was not outstandingly beautiful. She had lovely hair, even in a braid and under a veil. Her face was pleasing, fine-featured, with eyes the deep and dreaming blue of the sky at evening. She was very pretty; she was nothing beside Thea or the Queen, or almond-eyed Tao-Lin with her flawless gold-white skin.

And yet she stunned him where he sat. It was not the quantity of her beauty; it was the quality. The way she stood, the way she tilted her chin, the way she looked at him under her strong dark brows, all struck with him with their exact and perfect rightness. Not too bold, not too demure; clear and level and keenly intelligent.

He rose with the cat in his arms. It seemed eminently natural to set the beast down with a courteous pat, to straighten, to relieve the girl of several of her awkward bundles and packages. She did not resist him, although she frowned slightly. He was, after all, a complete stranger. But he smiled and bowed with a flourish, burdens and all; she melted. "You're very kind, sir," she said.

He shook his head a little, but smiling still, stepping back to let her pass. She paused to greet the cat, which in its feline fashion was pleased to see her; her eyes danced aside to meet Nikki's. Well, and he was a stranger, but already a friend to Arlecchina; a man could have a worse patron.

She led him up the stair. Her back was straight, the braid of her hair swinging thick and long and lovely below the edge of her veil, just where he would have liked to set his hand.

He stopped almost gratefully as she set her hand to an ironbound door. It was latched but not bolted; it opened with ease upon a small ill-lit passage redolent of garlic, age, and cats. She turned there, meaning to thank him kindly and send him away. This time he did not smile. He knew what everyone said about his eyes; he wielded them shamelessly.

She stiffened against them. Her thoughts were transparent. For all her unchaperoned solitude, she was neither a whore nor a serving girl, to play the coquette with a stranger, a pilgrim from who knew where. No doubt with that face he had encountered many such, charmed them and taken them and left them; and she all alone, with the neighbors at their work and her uncle at his, and old Bianca deaf as a post and bedbound with the ague, which was why she had gone to market alone to begin with. Which, in purest honesty, was why she had gone at all. She had wanted to go out by herself, to do as she pleased with no eyes to watch and disapprove.

The consequence tightened his grip on her purchases and raised his brows. *Madonna,* he said in his clearest mind-voice, *I know what you're thinking. I assure you by any saint you care to name that I have no designs on your virtue. If you will let me bear your burdens the rest of the way, I promise that I won't even assault you with a longing look.*

His eyes held her; she did not see that his lips never moved. To her ears his voice was a perfectly ordinary young man's voice, speaking in the Roman dialect. She smiled at the words, hardly knowing that she did, or that her eyes had begun to sparkle. Her voice made a valiant effort to be stern. "Sir, you are kind, but I can manage. It's only a little way, and the servant is waiting for me."

Nikki smiled. *My name is Nikephoros. I'm a pilgrim, as you can see; I lodge with the monks in San Girolamo down in the Velabro. I've never yet seduced a virgin, let alone raped one; I doubt I'll begin today. My looks are against me, I know, but can't you find it in your heart to trust me? Even a little?*

The sparkle was very clear now to see and even to hear. "You talk exactly the way I was told a young man would before he began his seduction. As for your looks . . ." Her cheeks flushed; she bit her lip and went on a little too quickly, "My name is Stefania. Yours is rather unusual. Are you Greek?"

He nodded.

"Then why," she demanded with sudden steel, "are you a pilgrim to Rome of all unlikely places?"

May not even a schismatic Byzantine look on the City of Peter? However regrettable, he added dryly, *may be the delusions of its Bishop.*

The blade was not so easily returned to its sheath. "Your accent is not Greek."

I grew up in Rhiyana. My teacher was, and is, an Anglian.

"Now that," she said, "is preposterous enough to be true. Say something to me in Norman."

Nikki choked. Even he could not tell whether it was laughter or horror. He knew Norman, bastard dialect of the *langue d'oeil* that it was; he could read it and write it. He also knew a little Saxon. He did not know if he had an accent in either, since he had never spoken a word in any mortal tongue.

She was frowning again. He swallowed and tried his best. *Fair lady without mercy, is it thus you try all who come to your door?*

"Only strangers who chase me through it." She softened just visibly, though not with repentance. "Have pity on me, sir. Here you are, a young man, which is danger enough; born a Greek, schismatic and noted for craftiness—which I should know, being half a Greek myself; raised by one of a race of conquerors in a country of enchanters. Can you wonder that I test you?"

If you put it that way, he admitted, and once more she heard him in Italian, *no.* He sank to one knee, bundles and all. *Beautiful lady, may I please come in? My solemn vow on it: I'll preach no heresies, play no tricks, and make no—unwilling—conquests.*

"And cast no spells?"

No spells, he agreed.

She nodded, gracious as a queen. "Very well. You may come in."

Unappealing though the passage had been, the house proper was very pleasant. There were two stories to it above the scrivener's shop. "Uncle Gregorios doesn't sell parchment," she explained. "He sells what's written on it. He's a public scribe, a notary; he works here when he can, but elsewhere most often, writing letters and witnessing deeds and the like."

She did not show her guest into the upper story, where were the bedchambers and a storeroom. Not merely for the danger of letting a man see where she slept; Bianca was there, mercifully oblivious to what passed in the room below. That was a large one with windows on a courtyard, the shutters flung wide in the warmth. Behind it lay the kitchen in which, at Stefania's command, Nikki had deposited most of his burdens. In it stood a table and a chair or two, a bench, a chest and a cabinet, and a high slanted table such as he had seen in the scriptorium of San Girolamo. A stool was drawn up to the table; a book lay open on it and a heap of parchment beside that, folded and ruled and ready to write on. Nikki craned to see. The book to be copied was Greek. He moved closer. Greek indeed, marked as verse, and a fine ringing sound to the line or two that met his eye.

"Pindar," Stefania said. "A pagan poet, very great my uncle says, and very difficult."

He's copying the book for a client?

"No," she answered almost sharply. "I am."

Nikki smiled his warmest smile. She looked defiant, and surprised. He should have been dismayed, if not appalled, to have encountered a woman who could write. More, a woman who could write Greek.

So can I, he pointed out, *which makes me a strange animal, too.*

"You're a man. You can do as you like. A learned woman, however," said Stefania with more than a hint of bitterness, "is an affront to the vast majority of learned manhood."

Of course she is. She's usually so much better at it. Nikki perched on the window ledge between Arlecchina and a great fragrant bowl of herbs, green and growing in the sunlight; he folded his arms and considered Stefania with distinct pleasure. *I'm inured to such blows. My sister is no mere scholar; she's a philosopher.*

"No," Stefania said.

Yes, he shot back. *She'd be a theologian, too, except that there's not much call for the Greek variety on this side of the world. Besides which, she likes to add, there's always room for another natural philosopher; and the world is all too full of bickering theologians.*

Stefania laughed. "There's a woman after my own heart!"

She had put aside her veil and hung up her cloak. Her dress was plain to severity, but it was the same deep blue as her eyes; her body in it was lissome and yet richly curved. She was very much smaller than himself. When they had stood face to face, her head came just above his chin. Even little Anna was taller than that.

Yet how tall she stood in the plain comfortable room, her feet firm on the woven mat, her dress glowing against the whitewashed wall. There was no doubt of it, she was perfectly to his taste.

In the silence under his steady stare, her assurance wavered. She moved a little too quickly, spoke in a rush. "Would you like a cup of wine? It's very good. One of Uncle's clients trades in it; we get a cask every year for wages. It's Falernian, as in the poets."

It was strong and red and heavenly fine, served in a glass cup which must have been the best one because Stefania herself had one of plain wood. She only pretended to drink from it. After a sip or two of his own, Nikki cradled the goblet in his hands and said, *I'm keeping you from your work.*

She did not try to deny it. "I have a page to copy, and the housekeeping—"

I know how to sweep, he ventured. *I could learn to scrub.*

She stared and laughed, amazed. "You are a natural wonder. And generous too, though for nothing. I swept and scrubbed this morning; it's our supper I have to think of, and there's all my plunder to put away, and if I don't pay my respects to Bianca soon, she'll know I've been waylaid in the street."

He nodded slowly. *May I come again? Tomorrow, maybe? You shouldn't go to market alone; and you know how handy I am at carrying things.*

The sparkle had come back to her eyes. "You are persistent, Messer Nikephoros."

Do you mind?

She thought about it. "No," she decided, "I suppose I don't."

He gave her the full court salutation as if she had been the Queen of Rhiyana, yet his eyes danced. She accepted his obeisance in the same mirthful earnest. "Why, sir! Have I overstepped myself? Are you after all a prince in disguise?"

Alas, no. Only a very minor nobleman and a very callow squire.

She was not at all dismayed to find him even as close to royalty as that. "Tomorrow," she said, light and brisk, both promise and dismissal.

His answer was a smile, swift, joyous, and deadly to her hard-won composure.

17

They were torturing Thea. Herself Anna never thought of; she was fed, she was reasonably warm, she was ignored. Thea was the one who suffered, bound in alien shape, battling for her will and her sanity, holding high the shields between her enemy and her children.

That was evil enough. But as the slow hours passed, Simon began to haunt his prisoners. The more Anna saw of his face, the less like Alf's it seemed. It was heavier; it was coarser; now it was shaven smooth, now it was stubbled with beard. Every time she woke, it seemed that he was there, at first only peering through the grille, but advancing after a time or two into the room. He was always alone, always habited in white and gray. He always stood still, staring at Thea or at the children, flat-eyed, expressionless.

Sometimes he left her to her mind's freedom. Often he looked and raised his hand, and she sat or stood or lay mute in mind as in body, able only to curse him with her eyes. After a moment or an hour, he would turn his back on her and leave her. She could move then, speak from mind to mind, join in the children's playing. She seemed undaunted, but Anna was afraid for her. Her eyes burned with a fierce dry heat; her ribs sharpened under the taut hide. When she was silent, Anna knew she fought the power that held her prisoner. When she spoke, it was only a new battle in the war, each word calculated to cut her jailer to the quick. When she slept, which was seldom, she slept like the dead.

During one such sleep, while Anna sat by her, watching over her, the air in the room changed. Simon stood over them both. For an instant Anna knew the absolute purity of hate. "Sathanas!" she hissed. "Get thee behind us."

He did not move. For him she did not exist. Only Thea was real, Thea and the children who stared from the shelter of her side. Slowly he sank to one knee. Anna tensed to leap at him. But she could not stir. Could barely even breathe for the mighty and unseen hand that held her fast.

With one tentative finger he touched Thea's flank. She flowed;

she melted and changed; she lay a woman, unconscious, cradling twin alaunts. His eyes were flat no longer, but flint and steel. "Evil," he murmured. "Daughter of evil, Lilith, beautiful and damned." The same finger traced her cheek, almost stroking it. In her sleep she stirred, turning toward the touch as to her lover's caress.

His fist knotted on his thigh. "Beautiful, oh, God in heaven, you are beautiful, and cursed in your beauty. Dreaming of abominations, the creatures you bore, begotten in foulness, brought forth in black sorcery by that one, the son of Hell, the white demon. Monk he was, he, priest of God, mocker, blasphemer—" The mask had fallen; his eyes had caught fire. His face was contorted with hate. "A *priest* he dared to be, standing before the very altar of the Lord, mouthing the holy words. Oh, horror, horror . . ." He tossed his head, tearing at it with clawed fingers, raking it, opening long weals. Yet as each opened, it closed again, miraculous, terrible.

Suddenly he was still. His hands lowered, clasped. His face calmed. Anna knew then that he was truly and irredeemably mad. "I am not a priest," he said. "God's servant, I; God's slave. In His mercy He suffers me. I do not tempt Him by laying hands on the body of His son."

"No. Only by slaughtering innocents." Thea was awake with all her wits about her, and a fire in her eyes to match that which smoldered behind his.

"I work God's will," he said.

"No doubt King Herod thought he did the same."

His face tightened. Thea's body blurred, yet it did not melt. She was white with strain.

He shook his head as if to clear it. With a sharp cry Thea crumpled, shifting, struggling, woman to hound to white wolf to golden lioness. Out of the fading gold battled a great gyrfalcon, stretching gull's wings, blooming into such a white beauty as the world had never known outside of a dream. But the beauty raged, and the horn was edged bronze, lunging toward the enemy.

Simon smote his hands together. Thea fell without grace as if to grovel at his feet, all naked save for the cloud of her hair.

He regarded her with cold contempt. "Why do you persist in opposing me? I cannot be overcome. No power on earth is greater than mine."

She levered herself up on her stiffened arms. "So you admit it. You *are* the Lord of the World. Mere mortals are encouraged to do battle against you; should I do any less?"

"Your tongue," he said, "would not shame a viper. Be one, then; match your seeming to the truth of you."

Thea laughed in his face, a little loudly perhaps, ending it as a hound's bark. She crouched thus, braced for combat. But he only looked at her without expression. At length he said, "So would Brother Paul have you be. Remember that you chose it of your own free will."

He went away for a merciful while. But he came back as if he could not help himself, standing and staring, his fists clenching and unclenching at his sides. Anna was telling a tale to the children; none of them would give him the satisfaction of acknowledging his presence, although Anna's voice faltered now and then. She was in the midst of the tale of the pagan wanderer Odysseus, in its own age-old Greek, which no doubt outraged his fanatical soul.

The beautiful ancient words rolled on and on. Anna's mouth had gone dry. Simon stood like a shadow of death.

Her throat closed in mid-word, nor would it open for all her striving. Rage swelled, too great by far to let in fear. How dared he thrust his power upon her as if she had been no more than a buzzing insect? He did not even look at her as he did it. She doubted that he thought of her, except as an annoyance, like a crow cawing.

She could stand. She could, she discovered, raise her hand and make a fist. The absurdity of it flashed through her mind, a small brown mouse raging and striking at the Devil himself. She struck as hard as she could, as high as she could. Not very hard and not very high, but it did its work. He looked down amazed. It was well past time for her to be afraid. While he ignored her she had been safe from the direct lash of his power. She had sacrificed that. He saw her now; she watched him take her into account: wrath, impotence, and all. She braced herself for the lightning's fall.

His brows knit in puzzlement, in a little pain. "Why, child," he said in a voice so gentle it froze her where she stood, "what's the trouble? Has someone hurt you?"

She blinked. Her mouth gaped open; she forced it shut. She had to remember that he was mad. Yet he looked so sane, so kind and so kindly, lowering himself to one knee to gaze into her face. "What is your name?" he asked her.

He had killed Alun, tried to enslave Liahan and Cynan. He was tormenting Thea. Anna hated him with an enduring and deadly hate.

Tried to. This too was a spell. A spell of gentleness worthy of Alf himself. She stiffened her spine. "You know what my name is, you devil. Just pick it out of my mind."

Pain tautened the lines of his face. "You hate me. You too. They all hate me, all of them. Why? I never want to hurt anyone. But they hurt me so much. They tear at me. Why? God loves. God commands that we love not only Him, but each other too. Why do you hate me?"

He had seized her hand. Her skin crawled at the touch, but she had no strength to pull free. She barely had the strength to answer him. "Because you hurt. Because you destroy. Because you kill."

His head tossed in denial. "It's not I," he cried. *"Not* I! It's the other, the one who lives in me, behind my eyes. The rioting fire. It has its own will, and strength—dear Lord God, strength to rend worlds. But no soul; no intelligence to rule it. Mine is not enough, has never been enough. I try—I fight it. Sometimes it yields. Sometimes it rages without me, working its will as it chooses. Making. More often destroying. *It* is the one who kills. I am left to suffer for it."

He spoke as if it were the truth. Maybe for him, in that instant, it was. "There is only one of you," Anna said, cold now and quiet. "You can't separate power and conscience. Obviously you've never learned to control either, and that is more than a tragedy. It's a deadly danger."

The gray eyes were like a child's, wide and luminous with tears. "I know. Sweet saints, I know. All my life I've fought, I fight, but whenever I think I've gained the mastery, the power swells and grows and escapes. It's a monster in me, like the hideous thing, the affliction the doctors call the crab, that devours all it touches. O child with the beautiful eyes, if you have any wisdom at all, tell me what I can do to conquer it!"

Anna had gone beyond astonishment as beyond fear. She regarded him. Kneeling, he was not quite as tall as she, his fair face drawn with anguish. His grip was like a vise, just short of pain; his whole body beseeched her. He was so like Alf, not the splendid joyous Lord of Broceliande nor even the beloved guest of Byzantium, but the Alf Anna knew only in stories, the monk of Anglia with all his doubts and torments.

Once more she stiffened her back. This was not Alf, unless it were an Alf lacking some vital part. A strength, a resilience. A core of steel. This one had only stone, flint that could chip and shatter, with a heart of deadly and uncontrollable fire. "I can't master your power for you," she said. "Only you can do that."

"I'm not strong enough."

She glared. "Of course you aren't, if you keep saying so. Whining so, I should say. You're not human that you can afford either laziness or cowardice. Get rid of them and you'll have what you're begging me for."

"No," he said. "Maybe once—before— No. It's grown too great. I haven't grown with it. It's my master now, and I its slave."

"Because you let yourself be."

His eyes darkened as if a veil had fallen across them. He let go her hand. "Perhaps. Perhaps it is God Who is master. He speaks to me like thunder, like the whisper of wind in the grass. He commands me: 'Go forth, be strong, conquer in My name. Let no man stand against Me.'" He rose in the mantle of his madness. "No man, no woman, no creature of night's creation. I have been shaped in the forge. I am the hammer of God."

"You are a madman."

"Yes," he agreed willingly. "It's God, you see. He's too strong for flesh to endure. The old heathens knew. They said it, and I know it for truth. Whom the gods would take, they first drive mad." His hand rested lightly, briefly, on her shoulder. "I would regret it if I could. I don't like to cause pain, even in God's name."

Anna shook her head. She could not—would not—debate with lunacy.

He smiled the first smile she had ever seen on his face. It was sad and very sweet. She turned her back on it. Well before she moved again, he had gone.

To her surprise and much to her dismay, she found that she was crying. For anger. For weariness. For simple pity.

18

"Anna. Anna Chrysolora."

She opened her eyes, squinting in the changeless light. Almost she groaned aloud. Simon sat by her, saying her name with a soft and almost witless pleasure.

She snapped at him, cross with sleep and with the compassion he forced upon her. Hate was so much simpler, so much more satisfying. "Don't you have anything better to do with yourself?"

"No," he answered unruffled.

"No Masses? No Offices to sing? No other prisoners to torture?"

"It's after Prime. You know there are no other prisoners here. Only you and yonder whelps and that other who crouches in a corner and tries to find a chink in my power. She won't find one."

"You are arrogant."

"I tell the plain truth."

Anna sat up, knuckling the last grains of sleep from her eyes. She felt filthy; she ached. Her courses were on her at last, God's own curse in this place, in front of this monster.

He clasped his knees. It was a most unmonstrous posture, boylike indeed with his clear young face atop it. "Brother Paul is coming," he said. "He grows impatient. We gain nothing while yon witch defies me."

"I should think you'd hold us for ransom. Then you'd have a chance of gaining something."

"We have asked. The price, it seems, is too high."

Anna swallowed. Suddenly her throat was dust-dry.

He heard the silent question. "We ask no mere treasure of mint or mine. We will have the witches, all of them, subject to the justice of the Church, and Rhiyana ours to lay under the rule of God."

"And, no doubt, power in the Papal Curia above the upstart Preachers."

"You are a wise child," he said. "Our Order is older than Domingo's, its mission more clearly from God; it has been slighted most often and most unjustly. See now, we have it in our power to lay a whole kingdom before Peter's Throne, to destroy a whole people created by the Devil's hands."

"That's heresy," Anna pointed out.

His eyes glittered. "It is truth. They are evil. They wield the powers of darkness; they enslave men to their will."

"You're one of them."

He surged to his feet. "I am the servant of God. He made me to cleanse the world of that inhuman brood."

"Witch yourself a mirror. Look at your face; remember Thea's. Think of the power she has, and of your own. Different in degree, maybe, but clearly of the same kind."

"I am not. I belong to God. He set me among men little better than beasts; He tried me and He tempered me, strengthening me in the fire of their hate. *Witch*, they called me. *Monster. Cat-eyes, warlock, devil-brat.* They would stone me in the street; they would creep to me in the dark, begging me to wield my power for them. To heal or to harm; to mend a broken pot, to foretell a child's fate, to lay a curse on an enemy. God moved in me. I did as He commanded and often as they begged. Till the priest, moved by God's Adversary, thought to come against me. He was a dour old man, a drunkard, a begetter of bastards. He brought his bell and his book and his candle and all his black burden of sin. He had no mercy upon a child whose mother was dead, whose father none had ever known. He would have reft my power from me. He would have burned me." Simon shuddered with the memory, yet his gaze was fixed, fearless, terrible. "I burned him. He called me witch and devil; God flamed in me and through me, and I was exalted, and the false priest was consumed."

His eyes shifted, blurred. A small sigh escaped him. "I had not known what I could do. Not all of it. Not this. I think I was mad before—certainly there had always been two of me, the weak child who yearned to be human and the self who was all a fire of power. The priest in his dying made the power master. The child had no hope of victory thereafter.

"The power drove me away from the place where I was born, the small vile town on a rock in Tuscany. It sent me wandering through the world, a careless bedlam creature singing the glory of God. I shunned the Church then, for all I had known of it was that one bad priest. I lived on the fruits of power, save now and again when charity came unasked for or the fire in me saw need of earthly strength. I healed a leper in the City of Flowers. I danced on light above the hills of Lombardy. I grew, and I grew strong, and at last, when I looked into mortal eyes, I knew amazed that I had grown fair.

"There was a woman. A girl; she was hardly older than I. She labored in the fields as I walked past. Somewhere I had lost my garment; I had made one out of sunlight. She saw and she marveled, and I paused, and she was beautiful, all dark and small and lovely to the lean pallid length of me. It was a great magic, the meeting of our eyes.

"It was a great sin. We did not know; we were not spared for that. In the night as we damned ourselves with delight, God struck. He wielded my power as He wields the lightning; He struck her down with me beside her. Though I woke in awful agony, she never stirred again.

"I raged. I cried to Heaven and Hell. I flung myself against the stars; I smote the earth till it shuddered beneath me. And there I lay while the sun wheeled above me with the moon in its train; the stars stared their millionfold stare, unmoved by all my fury. A black dream took me.

"I wandered in it. Where I went, how long I traveled, I never knew. I know it was both long and far. When I woke I was a stranger to myself, tall, deep-voiced, hard-bodied, with a beard downy-thick upon my face. The place wherein I lay had a flavor of nothing I knew, stone and sweetness and a music of many voices.

"There God spoke to me. I knew that it was He although He spoke with the tongue and the lips of a man. 'Wake, my son,' He commanded me. 'Wake and be strong. I have a task for you.'

"I could not speak. I could only stare.

"God smiled at me through His instrument. 'Heaven's own miracle has set you here among Saint Paul's disciples, child of power that you are. Rise up and give thanks; here at last have you found your destiny. No force of Hell shall prevail against you.'

"Still I was silent. All words had forsaken me. I knew without comprehension that I had fallen into the arms of the Church; what so long I had evaded had reached out to embrace me. I was too numb to be afraid. But I could move, and I rose from my bed and bowed low.

"God raised me. Raised me up, exalted me, taught me my purpose. To serve Him; to wield my power in His name."

"Not God," Anna said harshly. "Some venal monk who saw a weapon he could use. Did you kill him too?"

He shook his head, neither grieved nor angered. "He is venal, yes, and he uses me, but God has chosen him. His commands arise from the will of the One Who rules him. And," he added quite calmly, "he has always been too pleased with his own cleverness to be afraid of me."

"I'm not afraid, either."

"I know." He smiled his rare smile, unbearably sweet. "She was much like you, the girl from the field. Not so prickly; not so wise. But she was younger, and she didn't know what I was, except that I was unique in all her world. She thought I was a wonder and a marvel. She never had time to learn to hate me."

"I don't . . . exactly . . . hate you." It was true, Anna realized. She did not like it, but she could not avoid it. "I can't hate someone I know. Just abstractions. War, injustice, corruption. The force that murdered a child simply because he existed."

Simon's face shifted with familiar swiftness. His smile was long dead. His hands tore at flesh that could not be wounded, at cloth that at least stayed torn. Heavy though it was, wool woven thick and strong, it shredded like age-rotted silk. Rough darkness gaped beneath. Of course he would wear a hairshirt, that mad servant of a mad God. "Hate!" he cried. "I—hate—I am a horror. With a touch, with a thought, I kill. The priest was not the first, never the first. My mother never wanted me, never wanted to love me, struck me when I cried till I learned not to cry, fed me and cared for me because duty forced her to. She hit me. I would be there where she could see me, and she would take a stick to me. And then it swelled in me, that thing, the other, and it uncoiled and at last it struck. It killed. I only wanted the stick to go away. *It* would have more. I hate it. I hate—"

Anna clapped her hands over her ears.

He was kneeling in front of her. Calm again, gentle again. Her hands were no barrier to his soft voice. "You understand. I have no power over that other. I can only do as I am commanded."

"By it or by your Hounds of masters?"

"By God." He sat back on his heels, hands resting lightly on his thighs.

Anna's own hands fell to her sides. She was very tired. Bored, even, in spite of all his dramatics. It was only the same thing over and over. God and madness and a deep, rankling hatred of himself. Her pity was losing its strength; very soon she would be irritated. Did he think that he alone had ever suffered? Some of the Folk had endured far worse, had come out of it singing. Even she knew anguish; she had not shattered under it. What right had he to rend worlds for his little pain?

He turned slightly, oblivious it seemed to her anger. After a long moment Anna heard the scraping of bolts. Her glance, passing him, caught and held. His face was stiff, set, yet blazing from within with such a mingling of hate and scorn, fear and surrender and something very close to worship, as Anna had never dreamed of. In a moment it had vanished behind the marble mask; Brother Paul filled the doorway.

Anna had seen him but once, and then only dimly in the reflection of his companion. She had not known that he was so large. He was as tall as Simon, as tall as Alf, and nigh as broad as Father Jehan. But he had not the Bishop's muscular solidity; his flesh swelled into softness. His eyes were as lazy as ever in the full ruddy face, taking in the tableau, Thea curled with the children in a far corner, Anna upright on the pallet, Simon at his ease nearby. "Brother?" he inquired of the last.

Simon straightened. "The woman does not yield." His voice once more was flat.

Brother Paul advanced a step or two, folded his arms, looked down at Thea. She did not dignify his presence with a snarl. "Your King and his wild brother have been fighting. They haven't fought well, I understand. Maybe it troubles them that their sorceries are held in check; that they have to live and fight as simple mortal men. One has even been wounded, I can't be certain which. They're so much alike, people say; now and again they exchange blazons. The man who fell fought under the sign of the seabird crowned."

Anna's breath rasped in her throat. Thea seemed unmoved, staring steadily up at the monk.

He shook his head with feigned sadness. "It would be a grim thing if your King should die. He's not dead yet, Brother Simon says; he can't work his magic to heal himself. He hangs between life and death. Now suppose," he said, "that you were to surrender. Brother Simon works miracles of healing; he could be persuaded to pray for yet another."

Thea yawned and said coolly, *You're lying. Even if Simon Magus can pierce Rhiyana's defenses—and I grant you, he's strong enough for that—even he can't overwhelm both Gwydion and Aidan at once. They're twinborn; they're far stronger together than the plain sum of their power.*

"So they may be, together. They had no time to prove it. Pain is a great destroyer of the mind's defenses."

If it's so childishly easy to overcome us, Thea said coolly still, *why do you need my submission? Why not just cut us all down at once?*

"It is not easy," Simon answered tightly. "Your King was open to me, fighting on the edge of his realm, struck with a sudden dart. God guided it and me. In a hunt amid pain like fire and flood, I found the part of him that heals; I sealed it with my seal. Only I can loose the bonds."

You are unspeakable. Thea said it without inflection, which was worse in its way than a storm of outrage.

"I do what I must. No one near your King has any powers of healing, nor can any such come to him unless I will it. He cannot age, but he can die. Would you save him? Surrender now."

Thea was perfectly steady. *What would be the use of that? If you have your way, he'll die anyway. This at least is a little quicker.*

"A witch's heart," said Brother Paul, "is ice and iron. Never a wife, hardly a mother, now you show yourself a poor vassal besides."

What if I do surrender? she flared with sudden heat. *What then? I'm dear enough to my lord King, I don't deny it, but he won't sacrifice all his people on my say-so. I doubt he'd do that even for his Queen. And you killed his son.*

Simon spoke softly, more to himself than to her. "Our people have tried and condemned a number of heretics in your royal city. Some are guilty of no more than believing their King and his Kin to be children of Heaven rather than of Hell. It's evil, but it's rather enviable how loyal your Rhiyanans are. They're to be burned tomorrow. The Queen has no power to stop it."

Nor, it seems, does the Pope's Legate. You can't tell me he approves such lunacy.

"He has power only against your kind. This I tell of is done by command of our Order under His Holiness' mandate. We winnow your fields, witch; we hunt out mortal prey. Soon they'll be crying for your blood rather than suffer more on your behalf. Then the Legate will be compelled to perform his duty. He's already seen enough to condemn you all thrice over—and it was your own lover who betrayed you." Simon's eyes glittered with contempt. "Oh, yes; he worked magic before the Cardinal's eyes, and told all your people's secrets, babbling like a child or a black traitor. Though I would be charitable; I would declare it plain folly and assurance of the power of his own beauty, even over a man who takes enormous pride in his chastity. Such men in the end are easily laid low. He knew. He was one.

"But the Cardinal has held against him. I've seen to it. In a week or a fortnight, the Interdict will fall and the people will rise up."

With your aid, I presume. Her mind-voice was rough. *Your course is set. You can't delude me into thinking I can change it, even if I grovel at your feet. I grieve for my King and my kin; I mourn for my country. I won't submit to you. Nor will any of the rest, however you torment them.*

"They will fall before me. God has said so."

She laughed, cold and clear. *When you sit your throne over the wasteland you've made, look about you and think, and then put a name to the voice that speaks in you. God; or Satan.*

"You are evil."

Take care, Brother Magus. It may not be I who break under the weight of truth. It may well be you.

Simon looked long at her, his eyes almost black, his face corpse-white. "You," he said at last, "would drive an angel to murder. Yet it is all bravado. I see you now; I see how you tremble deep within, weep for your King and your people, long for your white-eyed paramour. It does not even irk you to be helpless, not in the heart of you.

There, you have always been as other women, soft and frail, sorely in need of a man's strength to rule your waywardness."

She laughed again, but freely, with honest mirth. *Brother, you have a certain talent, but you'll never make a torturer. I have a weakness here and there, I know it perfectly well, and the worst of them is my love whom you hate so much and for so little visible cause. But as for the rest of it . . . Simon Magus, I'm a woman and I'm proud of it, and I've worn a man's body often enough to know I much prefer the one I was born in. It's infinitely stronger.*

"You pray for a rescue. You dream of a man's strong hands."

Yes, and in such places, doing such things . . . Why, lad! You're blushing. Have I shocked you, poor tender creature? Are you wishing someone would sweep you away from all my wickedness?

Simon bent close to her, even with his flaming cheeks. "Words, words, words. Your strength is all in your tongue. I hear you in the nights. I hear you weeping and crying your lover's name."

I hear you, she shot back, *mewling for your mother. But she's dead. You murdered her. I at least have a living man to yearn for.*

His fist caught her. Flesh thudded sickly on furred flesh; something cracked like bones breaking. She fell limp.

Anna sprang through a white fog of terror. Thea lay deathly still. No breath stirred her body; no pulse beat for all of Anna's frantic searching.

Her mind was extraordinarily calm. It could only think of Alf, how grief would drive him mad. As mad as Simon, at the very least. Then would come such a vengeance as the world had never seen. *Let it come soon,* she thought as she watched her hands. Foolish things; they tried to smooth Thea's coat, to settle her limbs more comfortably, as if it could matter.

Simon's shadow darkened the world. He was staring at his hand. It looked odd, swollen, a little misshapen. "Ice," he muttered. "Iron."

Thea stirred, tossing. She whimpered softly as with pain. Her eyes blinked open. Anna's cry died unborn. The voice in her mind was most like a fierce whisper, yet with the force of a shout. *Now, while he's lost in his pain—move!*

Simon rocked with it. Paul seemed dazed, unfocused. The door was open behind him. Had it been so from the beginning, all unnoticed?

Move! Thea willed her.

She jerked into motion. She could not—Thea must not—

A force like a hand thrust her sidewise round the two monks, toward the path Thea had opened for her. Suddenly, like a startled rabbit, she leaped for it.

The passage was long and bleak, a stretch of stone and closed doors, cold as death. She had no thought but flight, yet somewhere in the depths of her raged a fire of protest. Where could she go, what could she do, what would they do to Thea?

Walls of air closed about her. She struck the foremost with stunning force, reeled and fell, too shocked for despair. Simon spoke above her, cool and quiet. "A valiant effort. But not wise." She heard him step back. "Get up."

She would not. Part of it was plain collapse; a goodly part was defiance.

He lifted her easily and in spite of her struggles. A glance at his face stilled her utterly. It was expressionless, as often, but something in it made her blood run cold.

He set her in the cell. The door was shut. Thea crouched trembling, eyes clouded. A thin keening whine escaped her.

Simon's hands on Anna's arms were as cruel as shackles. "I am not to be mocked," he said. He flung her down; she gasped as her knees, then her hands, smote stone. But that pain seemed but a light slap, as all her being burst into a white agony. Nor would it end with the mercy of bodily anguish. It went on and on, stretching into eternity.

And all for so little.

19

Between the rain and the advancing evening, Rome seemed dim, half-real. Nikki picked his way through a waste of ruins and past the dark plumes of cypress, his feet uneasy upon the sodden earth. The mist that rose about him held a faint charnel reek, a warning of the fevers that lurked in it.

If this hunt ever ended, no doubt his mind would still continue it, set in a firm mold of habit. Sometimes he saw himself as a hound weaving through coverts; sometimes he was a cat stalking a prey it could almost see. Tonight he was a hawk on the winds of the mind-world, riding them in slow spirals, letting them carry him where they would. Yet he was also, and always, aware of his body, of the cold kiss of fog on his face, of the dampness that worked through his cloak and of the growing wetness of his feet. They would be glad to rest by the brazier in Stefania's house; she would insist that he linger, and old Bianca, recovered now and utterly smitten with his black eyes, would press food and drink upon him, and Uncle Gregorios keep him there with the plain joy of the Greek in exile who had found a countryman.

How easily they had taken him in, though not, to be sure, without suspicion. Even in his hunting he smiled to remember his first encounter with Bianca: returning from the market that second day with Stefania and finding the servant not only up but about, ancient, gnarled, tiny as old Tithonus who in the extremity of immortal age shriveled into a grasshopper. But she had the voice and the will of a giantess, and for all her ears' lack, her eyes were piercingly keen. She could see a handsome young man well enough, and roar at him for a rake and a corrupter of maidens, and purr when he smiled his best and whitest smile. Although she trusted nothing that was both young and male, nor ever would, she had been heard to admit that that particular specimen seemed less dangerous than most. Especially under her watchful eye.

He stumbled. His power plummeted in a flurry of feathers; battled for control; strained upward. A gust caught it, bore it up, and as it settled once more into an easy glide, hurled it madly skyward.

Vast wings opened above him. A monstrous creature filled the sky: an eagle, a roc, a dragon. Its talons were hooked lightning; its cry shattered stars.

It could not see him. That was his single greatest gift, the one that was his alone, to pass unperceived by any power. Next to the reading of thoughts, it had been his first skill; he had never had to learn it, nor had he ever been able to teach it. While he wielded it he was safe even from that immeasurable might which loomed over him, its wings stretching from pole to pole.

And yet he made himself as small as he might, small as a merlin, as a sparrow, as a hummingbird. His body shuddered with terror; his brain reeled. If he could only cling close, could follow, could—

An eye like the moon bent upon him. Widened and fixed; *saw*. Impossible, impossible. He was invisible. No one could see him unless he willed it.

The cruel beak opened. Laughter shrilled, high and cold and cruel. The talons struck.

Full between them Nikki flew, seared by the heat of their nearness, racked with the pain of it. But free and fleeing to sanctuary, the high-walled refuge of his mind.

It was deathly quiet. The world was like an image in a glass, clear and present yet remote, even the rain and the cold touching him only distantly. He floated through it with little care for where he went; he could not make his thoughts come clear. When he tried, he found only the memory of alien laughter.

Stefania was determined not to fret. She was a woman of both wit and wisdom; she had every intention of becoming a philosopher, whatever the world and the Church had to say. And a true philosopher should not care whether, or when, a pretty lad chose to favor her with his presence. Even when he had promised to come before dark, and the hourglass had emptied once already since the last gray light failed. Even though he had never before failed to appear precisely when he said he would. What did she know of him, after all? Maybe he had found another and prettier girl to call on.

Bianca had cursed him, exonerated him, and fretted over him. Now at last she had vanished into the kitchen to raise a mighty clatter. Uncle Gregorios was gone, called away on some urgent business. Stefania had only herself, half a page of Pindar, and a blot on the vellum that she could only stare at helplessly.

He was only a boy. A friend, maybe. Amusing; pleasant to look at; useful for carrying packages and scraping parchment and arguing theology. He listened wonderfully and never showed the least sign of shock at anything she said, although she shocked herself sometimes with how much she told him. Even her dream, outrageous and lunatic as it was and probably heretical, to have a house that was all her own with no man the lord of it, and a company of women like herself, women who had a little learning and wanted more. Like nuns, maybe, but neither cloistered nor under vows, brides not of Christ but of philosophy, each prepared to teach the others what she knew.

Nikephoros had not even smiled at that wild fancy. Of course, he had said; it would be like any other school, except that both masters and students were women. Nor had he been mocking her as far as she could see. And that was rather far; he was marvelously easy to read.

She thrust book and copy aside and stood. He was not coming.

He was a guest in a monastery; he had companions who might have kept him with them. His brother was ill, she seemed to remember; maybe there had been a crisis.

He could have sent a message.

She shook herself. This was disgraceful. An hour's wait for a stranger she had known a scarce fortnight, and she was good for nothing but to pace the floor.

Her cloak found its way about her shoulders. She snatched up her hood and strode for the door.

She had not so far to go after all. Arlecchina cried on the stair above the street, her coat dappled with the flicker of the wineshop's torches. Something dark moved beyond her, swaying, turning. Stefania tensed. A drunkard or a footpad, and she unarmed and the door open behind her.

The shadow flung out a hand. In the near-dark she knew it as much by its movement as by its shape. Nikki's face followed it, his hood and hat fallen back, his eyes enormous. His weight bore her backward.

Somehow she got both of them up the steps and through the door. He was conscious, breathing loud and harsh, stumbling drunkenly. Yet she caught no reek of wine.

Warmth and lamplight seemed to revive him a little. He pulled free and half sat, half fell into Uncle Gregorios' chair. He was wet through, shivering in spasms, his face green-pallid.

Stefania wrestled with the clasp of his mantle. He did nothing to help her. His hands were slack; his eyes stared blankly, drained of intelligence.

The clasp sprang free. The cloak dropped. She coaxed and pulled him out of his gown, his sodden boots, and after three breaths' hesitation, his shirt. He was well made, she could not help but notice, with the merest pleasant hint of boyish awkwardness.

Quickly she wrapped her own mantle about him and heaped coals on the brazier, reckless with fear for him. There was no mark on him, she had seen more than enough to be sure; he had not been attacked or beaten, not by any of Rome's bravos. He was sick, then. He had taken a fever.

Except . . .

"What is this?" shrilled Bianca. "What is this? Where's the boy been? Sweeping up the plague, I can see with my own eyes. Don't cry on him, child, he's wet enough without. You make sure he's dry; I'll make him a posset. Fools of pilgrims, they should know the air's got demons in it, thick as flies around the Curia."

Stefania was not crying. Not that she was far from it. Bianca renewed her clatter in the kitchen, to good purpose now and with suspicious relish. "Old ghoul," muttered Stefania.

Nikki huddled in her cloak. His trembling had stopped. "Nikephoros," she said, "you should never have come here with a fever."

He did not respond.

She frowned. "I know. You thought it was nothing. Just a touch of the winter chill. So you came out and you went all light-headed and maybe you got lost. It's God's good fortune you wandered in the right direction." She touched his hair, which had begun to dry. He started violently to his feet, nearly oversetting her. His eyes were wide and wild, and they knew her; he reached almost blindly.

She must have done the same. Hand met hand and gripped hard. His fingers were warm but not fever-warm. The green tinge had faded from his face. He looked almost like his proper self; he even tried to smile.

He had let the cloak fall. She looked; she was no saint to resist such a temptation. Yes, he was comely all over, slim and olive-smooth, his only blemish a red-brown stain on the point of his shoulder. It looked like a star, or like a small splayed hand. It begged her to set her lips to it. His skin was silken, but firm beneath, with nothing in it of the woman or the child. She rested her cheek against it. "You frightened me," she said. "In a little while I think I'll be angry. If you don't fall down in a fit first."

She stepped back a little too quickly. He did not try to stop her. She reached for the cloak, shook her head, took Uncle Gregorios' housegown from its peg. It was warm and soft and only a little too short. She did not know whether she was glad or sorry to see him covered, seated again and submitting meekly to Bianca's fussing, even forbearing to grimace at the taste of the posset. His hair, drying, was a riot of curls; she wanted to stroke them.

Bianca babbled interminably, hobbling about, bringing food and drink, poking at the coals. Nikki ate willingly enough, even hungrily, to the old woman's open satisfaction. "There now, nothing wrong with you but rain and cold and monastery food—pah! Food they call it, no better than offal, fit to starve any healthy young lad. No wonder you fainted on our doorstep."

Stefania swallowed a thoroughly unphilosophical giggle. It was that or scream. A fortnight's acquaintance and a night's anxiety, and it seemed that she was lost. Just like the wise Heloise away in Francia, all her learning set at naught by a fine black eye.

She glanced at him, pretending to sip Bianca's fragrant spiced wine. He was a little drawn still, a little grim as he gazed into his own cup. Concern touched her. "Tell me what's wrong," she said.

He was not listening. She reined in her temper, reached for the jar, filled his cup. He looked up then. "Tell me," she said again.

She watched the spasm cross his face. Pain; frustration; a sudden and rending despair. He shook his head hard, harder, and pulled himself up. His lips moved clumsily, without sound. "I—I must—"

"You'll wait till your clothes dry. All night if need be."

He shook his head again. His shirt was in his hand, the borrowed gown cast off. He dressed swiftly, fumbling with haste, but he did not precisely run away. In the moment before he left, he paused. He regarded Stefania; he bent, taking her hands. In each trembling palm he set a kiss. Promising nothing. Promising everything.

Fools, they were. Both of them.

20
❧

In the depths of Broceliande even the sunlight was strange, enchanted, more mist than light. It lay soft on Alf's bare skin, with but a shadow of its true and searing power; warmth but no heat, sinking deep into his winter-wearied bones. He stretched like a cat, long and lazy and sinuous, inhaling the crushed sweetness of grass and fern.

A light hand ran down his body. He turned to meet Thea's laughing eyes. His joy leaped sun-high; fear crippled it. His hand shook as he touched her. She was real, solid. His fingers remembered every supple line of her; his lips traced the swoop of cheek and neck and shoulder, lingered upon the rich curve of her breasts, savored their brimming sweetness. Slowly, tenderly, he left them, seeking out the arch of her ribs, the subtle curve of her hips, the hills and hollows of her belly, coming to rest at last in the meeting of her thighs.

He raised his head, drunk with fire and sweetness. She slid down to match her body to his. Her fingers roved over the webwork of scars that was his back, traced the patterns time and love had found there, waked the shiver of pleasure that dwelt along his spine. His every nerve and sinew sang.

> *Thou hast ravished my heart, my sister, my spouse;*
> *thou hast ravished my heart with one of thine eyes,*
> *with one chain of thy neck.*
> *How fair is my love, my sister, my spouse!*
> *how much better is thy love than wine! and the smell of*
> *thine ointments than all spices!*

Musk and silk, sun and salt and the sweet sharpness of fern. Her eyes were burning gold yet soft, as always—and only—for his loving. Heart and body opened to enfold him.

Love and light shattered together. He lay in darkness, shuddering with the last spasms of his passion. No sun shone down; no leaves whispered; no warm woman-shape filled his arms. There was only dark and stone and a memory of incense.

San Girolamo. The name brought back all the rest, with a remnant of sight, enough to see the shape of the room and the huddle of shadow that was Nikki on his pallet. The ample warmth at his back was Jehan, deep asleep and snoring gently.

Alf sat up. He had fouled himself like any callow boy dreaming fruitlessly of desire. He rose, sick and sickened, powerless to stop his shaking. Never in his life—never—

First there had been his vows, and his body never yet wakened to passion. Then there had been Thea. First innocence, then sweet and constant knowledge. Never this crawling shame. Mingled most horribly with grief for her loss, and anger at his weakness, and the languor that came always after love.

Thea would have braced him with mockery. The words of the great Song lilted incongruously in his brain: *Stay me with flagons, comfort me with apples: for I am sick of love.*

"Solomon," he said, "Solomon, if you could have known what manner of creature your words would drive mad . . ." His voice rang loud in the gloom. Neither of his companions stirred. Jehan, alone in the bed, had sprawled across the whole of it. A splendid figure of a man, maned and pelted like a lion; his dreams were like a child's, blameless, sunlit.

Alf backed away from them. With water from the basin he washed himself, scouring brutally as if that small pain could punish his body's betrayal. Now indeed he could see why so many saints had mortified their flesh. Hated it; beaten and starved it until its bestial instincts should be slain.

He had been a bit of an ascetic. Was still, for the matter of that. But not for any great sanctity; it was only carelessness and a body that bore easily the burdens of fasting and sleeplessness, cold and rough garments and long enforced silences. He had never had to wage true war with it, nor ever yet let it fall into proper saintly squalor.

His head came up sharply. And should he now? No vows bound him. He was a man of the world, a lord of wealth and power, with no fear of death to drive him into penitence. No Heaven to strive for, no Hell but this earth in the wreck of all his joy. If she was dead and both hope and hunt no more than a mourner's madness, then he would know there was no God for his kind; it was as the Hounds clamored, that they were the Devil's own.

No. He could not believe that his people belonged to the Evil One. Not Thea. Not gentle childlike Maura with her core of tempered steel. Not Gwydion—Gwydion who lay wounded beyond anyone's power to heal, forbidding Alf's coming with indomitable will, commanding the army from his bed and from the mouth of his brother. Aidan would have given more, would have dwelt in the broken body and surrendered his own full strength for Gwydion's sake, a selflessness as pure as any mortal saint's.

Still wet from his washing, Alf wandered into the courtyard. The air was raw and cold, he knew as one knows beneath a heavy swathing of garments. Soon now the bell would ring for the Night Office. The monks would stumble blinking and yawning from their beds; some would sleep upright through the rite, trusting for concealment to the dimness and to their superior's own drowsiness. Alf had never had that most useful of monastic arts. He had never needed it.

He was shivering. *Why,* he thought surprised, *I'm cold.* he reached for a handful of shadow, paused, stretched out his mind for an honest mortal garment. Without shirt or trews the rough wool of the pilgrim's robe galled almost like a hairshirt, as well he knew who had worn thus the habit of a Jeromite monk.

He was sliding back into it. Jehan noticed and worried. Nikki liked it not at all. "They don't understand," he said. "I am God's paradox. Child of the world's children, raised for Heaven; given the world and all its delights, only to see them reft away in a night and myself cast back into the cloister in which I began. My body was never meant for that, meekly though it submitted. My spirit . . . Dear Lord

God, but for a single earthly love I have never been aught but Yours.
And she, for all her mockery, is part of You; the love between us is
Your own although the Church would call it heresy. Yours even—
what sent me from my bed. Even that."

And if she was dead, what then? Himself, alone. Without her,
without Liahan and Cynan, with the whole of an immortal lifetime
before him, vast and empty, more bitter than any torments of the
mortal Hell. Yet if they lived—if he had them back again—nothing
could be as it was before. With Thea's aid he had schooled himself to
forget what he was. No longer. Her lover, the father of her children.
And a priest forever.

The truth racked him with its force, sent him reeling to the
ground. God's truth; God's hand. God's bitter jest, a laughter even his
ears could hear. Priest of what? A Church that had been raised up for
humankind and never for his own; a rite and a dogma that had no
place in it for those whose bodies would not die, and that condemned
all his gifts as blackest sorcery.

Blackest ignorance.

"Paul," he said, "whose monks have hounded us so far and so
fiercely, is called the Apostle of the Gentiles. What then am I? I'm
neither saint nor evangelist. Only a reed in the wind of God." And
such a reed. Barefoot, beltless and hatless, wandering down an empty
street with no memory of his passage from San Girolamo's courtyard
to this unfamiliar place. The sun was coming. He could feel it, a tingle
in his blood, a shrinking of his skin.

Prophets were mad. It was their nature. He was a seer although
the sight had been lost to him since before his kin were taken—since
he stood with Alun atop the White Keep. Blinded, he remained a
madman and a mystic.

The narrow street stretched wide. A piazza, the Romans would
say: a square with its inevitable church. No marble Bacchus here, no
throngs of pilgrims in this black hour before dawn, no Brother Oddone seeing in mere fleshly beauty the image of divinity. If he thought
he had it, would he worship it so ardently? He could not see his own
soul; he could not know what a singing splendor was in it.

The church was still and silent. It was very old, very plain. Its
distinction was the glory of gold and crystal beneath the altar, encas-
ing a strange relic, the coldness of iron, the harshness of chains. Once
they had bound Peter himself, the fisherman who became Prince of
Apostles. Another paradox; another who had lived in torment, be-
trayer and chief defender of his Christ.

"The world is a paradox," Alf said, "and men are lost in it. What is philosophy but a struggle to make order of chaos? What is theology but a child's groping in the dark? Jesu, Maria, God in high Heaven, what are you to me or to my kin?"

The echoes died slowly. He expected no answer. Perhaps there was none.

He sank to his knees on the stone. "My Lord," he said reasonably, as to any man, "the world is Yours in its fullest measure. I see You in it, albeit dimly, with eyes never made for such vision. I know I come from You; You shine in my people. And yet, my Lord, and yet, if I am to serve You before them, how can I do it? The Church staggers under the weight of its humanity. Its heretics offer only a stricter law, a harsher road to Heaven. Moses, Mohammed, Gautama, all the gods and prophets, have no help for us. For me. I stand alone." The word shuddered in his throat. "Alone. Shall we all die, then? Have You looked upon us and found us evil, and set Your Hounds to sweep us away? We are poor things, neither men nor angels, neither spirit nor true earthly flesh. And yet we live; we serve You as best we can. Must we pay for it with our destruction?"

He shook his head. "No. That's despair. We're being tested. Winnowed; shown our proper path. But ah, dear God, the testing is bitter and the winnowing relentless, and the path . . . I can see but little of that, and that darkly, and I am afraid."

Out of the shadows a voice spoke. It was quiet, a little diffident; it seemed honestly concerned. "But, brother, you're supposed to be afraid."

Alf whipped about. He knew he moved like an animal, startling to human eyes, but these showed neither fear nor recoil. Their owner was a man neither tall nor short, frail and sallow and gaunt to starvation, his eyes dark and gently humorous between neglected beard and much neglected tonsure. A beggar surely, a mendicant friar, ragged and long unwashed but extraordinarily clear of gaze and wit.

He took in Alf's face and form, and smiled with a wondrous sweetness. "Brother, you are a joy to see, even in your sorrow. Can you pardon me for having listened to it? I was saying my prayers in the chapel yonder when your voice came to me like a cry from Heaven."

"Or to it," Alf said. This man was no great delight to the eye or to the nose, and yet he lightened even Alf's spirit with his simple presence. He had a power; a gift of joy.

"To Heaven, yes," he responded. "Would any good man cry to Hell?"

"He might if he were desperate."

"I think," said the stranger, "that in such a case, God would hear. You agree, surely, or it's Hell you would have been calling to."

Alf's mouth twisted wryly. "I'm desperate, but I remain a creature of reason. It's one of my curses."

"You have more than one?"

"What earthly being does not?"

"None. But one should never keep count. Blessings, now; those I love to number. Brother sun and sister moon; mother earth and all her seasons, her fruits and her creatures, even her human folk. Especially they. So much in them is hideous, but how much more is beautiful, if only one knows how to see."

Alf nodded once, twice. "I'll never dispute that. Nor do I take pleasure in reckoning up my ill fortune, but it has to be done, else I'll suffer all the more for my heedlessness. God does not permit any creature to be too constantly happy."

"Of course not. Happiness needs sadness to set it off. Would you want to live solely on honey?"

"No more than I'd prefer a diet of gall. I've gorged on sweetness, you see; now I'm deluged with bitterness."

The stranger squatted beside him. "Are you that? I'm sorry for it. I suppose it's no great comfort that the gladness will come back."

"It's not." Alf's head bent; he sat upon his heels, weary beyond telling. "If I could see it, if I could *know*, I'd be stronger."

"No man may know what will come. He can only hope, and trust in God."

"Once," Alf said, "I knew. The gift has left me. Time was when I would have sung my joy to be free of it; but flesh is never content. I don't want it back, you understand. Not the strokes of vision that fell me in my tracks; not the forewarnings of wars and plagues and calamities. Not even the few glimpses of light, paid for as they are in such cruel coin. I could only wish for a single image. Sunlight, warmth, a child's laughter. Only that. Then I would have the will to go on."

"That will be as God wills," said the stranger. "He's very strong in you, did you know that? You shine like the moon."

Alf flung up his head. "It is not God."

"Why, of course it is," said the mild musical voice. "I'm sure you're one of His dearer children. He wouldn't test you so fiercely if He didn't love you exceedingly."

"That is not the orthodox position, Brother."

"It's the truth."

Alf laughed sharply. "What is truth? By Church law I was damned from my conception."

"No, brother. Someone has taught you wrongly. No man can be——"

"But I am not a man."

The beggar-friar blinked at him.

"I am not a man," Alf repeated. "I am neither human nor mortal. The doctrine holds that I have neither soul nor hope of salvation. Not a pleasant thought at the best of times, to the most irreligious of us. Which this is not, and which I am most certainly not. And I think—I know that I am called. A daimon with a vocation; an elvenlord who was born to be a priest. Can't you sense God's high amusement?"

"God's laughter is never cruel," the other said. Alf could find in him no sign of either surprise or disbelief. "I knew you were from Rhiyana; your face is unmistakable. So it's true what's being said of your people."

"Most of it. All, maybe, if you would make us the Devil's brood."

The dark eyes measured him. "I would not. Mother Church isn't remarkably fond of me either, you know; she finds me difficult to manage. I tell the truth as I can see it, and it's not always her truth, and I think too much of the Lord Jesus and too little of the Canons. She does what she can to keep me in order, and I try to obey her. But when truth stands on one side and the Church on the other, it's hard indeed to know what I should do."

"It's worse than hard. It's well-nigh impossible. One can only shut one's eyes and pray for guidance, and do as one's heart dictates."

"My heart tells me that I see you truly. Your trouble is the Crusade, isn't it? War is no way to spread the Faith. Very much the opposite."

"My people have no need of conversion. Our enemies know that. They intend to destroy us. For the greater glory of God."

"I would go," said the friar. "I would teach the Faith to those who have never professed it. The Saracens, the people afar in the silk countries—a whole world has no knowledge of truth. I would go to it and leave you in God's peace."

"But you are not permitted."

I have been. I shall be again, though perhaps not soon. His Holiness is most kind, but the world besets him; the Church grows too great, and she grows haughty in her greatness. Sometimes—this is not charitable, brother, but sometimes I think we need the Lord Jesus to come again and scourge this temple reared up in his name."

"Is that not what you are doing?"

The friar sighed. "I have no skill in scourging temples. Even when forced to it, I do it badly. I would much rather be doing God's gentler works. Healing, teaching, ministering to the poor." He sighed again, and coughed hard enough to rattle his fragile bones. "But one does what one must. Sometimes one escapes and tries to heal oneself in solitude."

"I too," Alf said. He realized that he was smiling faintly, a little painfully. "You've healed me a little. You've taught me something."

"Have I?" asked the other, surprised. "I wasn't trying to. I've done little but chatter about myself."

Alf's smile deepened. "That's one excellent way to teach."

The friar looked at him, smiling himself with such warm delight that Alf felt it like an open fire. "And doesn't misery love company?" He sobered suddenly. "I only fear . . . I never wanted it to go this far. It was only myself and God. Then my brothers came to share God with me and to help me with His work; only a few at first, but the word got out, and to keep them all in order I needed some sort of rule, and everyone said the Pope himself should sanction it. And suddenly we were an Order like the Benedictines or the Jeromites, and we had to be sealed with the tonsure and the threefold vows. To keep us safe, His Holiness said. To mark us for what we were, servants of the Church. And all I wanted was to live in peace in our Lord's poverty, carrying out his commands as best I knew how. What is there in the world that destroys all simplicity?"

"Human nature," Alf answered gently. "But there's much good your brothers can do as they are, they and their sisters. The temple will be scourged. The Church will cleanse itself. Though it will be long, long . . ."

He had the man's hands in his own. They were stick-thin, wrapped in bandages that though bloody were somewhat cleaner than the rest of him. Alf caught his breath at the festering pain as at the rush of sight. "Giovanni Bernardone, when you stand by the throne of God, will you spare a word for my people?"

"I don't think," said the friar, "that you need even my poor intercession. But for your sake, if I get so far, I'll do as you ask." He looked down at his hands, at Alf's cradling them like marble round clay. "Your touch is peace."

The pain was terrible. Nails piercing his hands, transfixing his feet. And his side beneath his heart—like a spear, like a sword. How could the man walk, talk, smile, even laugh, when every movement crucified his body?

For this there could be no earthly healing. Alf bowed low and low. "*Sanctissime.* Most holy father."

Fra Giovanni pulled him up, dismayed. "Please don't. No one's supposed to know about it. I can't have them all bowing and treating me like a saint. Least of all you, who truly are one."

Alf's incredulity struck him mute. There was holiness, to be so utterly oblivious to itself, even with the great seal it bore. Five wounds. Five stigmata. And he had thought that he knew pain.

He brought his head up and mustered all his calmness. "God brought us together here to mend and to be mended. For what they are worth, I give you my thanks and my blessing."

"They are worth more than kingdoms." The impossibly sweet smile returned although the dark eyes were sad. "Go with God, brother. May He shelter all your people and preserve them from harm, and bring them to Himself at last."

21

Anna could move, if she was very careful. She did not know that she wanted to. Even her eyelids throbbed and burned; she could see only through a blood-red mist.

Simon's voice spoke. It seemed to come from everywhere at once, soft as a whisper yet echoing deep in her brain. "See, woman. See what your folly has brought you."

It was like a dream, and it was not. It was too clear, too distinct, too grimly relentless. It seemed that she stood under the open sky, immeasurably vast after the walls which had enclosed her for so long, and the sun was shining and the gulls were crying. Beneath them like a carpet spread the kingdom of Rhiyana. Dun and gray and brown, white with snow and green with pine and fir, hatched with roads that seemed all to run toward the white pearl of Caer Gwent and the blue glitter of the sea. That seemed safe, serene, overlaid with a faint golden shimmer, but the borders seethed and smoldered. The shimmer there was dark and shot through with flame, and yet something in it put her in mind of Simon's eyes.

The land swelled and stretched and grew clear before her. She could have been a gull or a falcon hovering over the untidy circle of a town. Ants swarmed in it, men shrunken with distance and height, brandishing weapons surely too tiny to be deadly. Swords, spears— no. Staves and cudgels, rakes, scythes, here and there a rusted pike. Something fled before them, a small ragged scrambling figure, white hair thin and wild, weak eyes staring out of the tangle, blood-scarlet and mad with terror. The mob bayed at it. "Witch! Witch! Demon's get, sorcerer, God's curse—"

Anna struggled to cry out. But as in a dream, she was voiceless, powerless. The poor pallid creature stumbled and fell. The mob sprang upon it. A thin shriek mounted to Heaven.

Hoofs thundered. A strong clear voice lashed above the growls of men turned beasts. A company of knights and sergeants clove through the mob, and at their head a flame of scarlet. Anna could have sung for joy. He rode armored, the Prince Aidan, but for haste or for recklessness he had disdained both helm and mail-coif. His raven head was bare, his face stark white with wrath; he laid about him with the flat of his sword.

At the eye of the storm was stillness. The wretched albino lay twisted impossibly, his colorless hair stained crimson. The Prince sprang down beside him, knelt, brushed the broken body with a gentle hand. His steel-gray glance swept the gathered faces. "That," he said with deadly softness, "was no more a witch than any of you." He rose. Although one or two came near his height, he towered over them; they flinched and cowered. "Yes," he purred, "be afraid. Such return you give your King for all his years of care for you; such a gift do you give him, this roil of fear and hate."

Anna felt it. He could not. Not all his pallor was anger; he was sustaining himself by sheer force of will, and no power. He could not sense the gathering, the focusing, the sudden bitter loosing. Stone and hate struck him together. His eyes went wide, astonished. He reeled.

He did not fall. Blood streamed down his face, blinding him. He paid it no heed. His hand stretched out. His mind reached, clawing, slipping, failing. The mob closed in for the kill.

* * *

Anna's throat was raw with outrage. She flung herself at Simon; he held her away with contemptuous ease. "Two," he said, "are mastered. A third comes to my hand. *So.*"

She struggled; she fought; she willed her eyes to be blind. No use. Rhiyana unfurled before her, sweeping closer and closer, until Caer Gwent itself grew about her. The streets were crowded though it was the fallow time of Lent, as if lords and commons alike had chosen to take refuge far from the Crusade. Merchants did a brisk trade in dainties as in necessities. Singers sang; players plied their trade in front of the cathedral. But the clamor of the schools was muted, the gate of the synagogue barricaded shut, the austere houses of the Heresiarch's flock empty and silent. Only one man dared preach from the porch of one of the lesser churches, and he was a friar, a Minorite in tattered gray who proclaimed the poverty of Christ.

There were white habits and gray cowls everywhere. How had so many come so deep into Rhiyana in defiance of the ban? How dared they? They walked like lords, secure in their power. People gave way before them.

Anna plunged past them with stomach-churning speed and swooped toward the castle. Abruptly she was within it. Its familiarity tore at her heart. There was the Chancellor's Tower where she had lived whenever she was in Caer Gwent. There was the stable where champed her fiery little gelding, Alf's gift to her only this past nameday. And there was the Queen's garden, so wrought that it seemed far larger within than without, touched with her magic. Roses bloomed; small bright birds sang spring songs without care for the beasts which lazed on the ground below. Some were gifts from far countries, such of them as chose to sacrifice freedom and homeland for love of the Queen. Some had come of their own accord, a white hind and her red fawn, a sow and her piglets, badgers and coneys and sleek red foxes.

And the wolves. Not gray wolves of the wood but white wolves of the Wood, great as mastiffs, he and she, and their boisterous half-grown cubs. The Queen sat on the grass with the she-wolf's head in her lap. They were wonderfully alike, the lady in her white gown with her ivory skin and her ivory hair and her eyes the color of amber, the wolf all white and golden-eyed. "Sister," said the light childlike voice of the lady, "you are not being wise. The rest of the wildfolk will go back to their proper places with the next sunrise. You must not linger, not you of them all, whom humans call my kin and my familiars. They will destroy you as gladly as they destroy me, and no whit less cruelly."

Anna heard the response as a voice, husky like a man's yet somehow distinctly feminine. *We came when you came. We go when you go.*

"Then your children at least—"

They stay.

Maura's fingers buried themselves in the thick ruff. Her eyes had the hard glitter of one who refuses to weep. "Do you remember," she murmured, "when Alun was playing just where your cubs play now? And when we looked, the three young wolves were four and my son nowhere to be seen, but the largest and most awkward cub looked at us with startled gray eyes. He had that gift from me, the wolf-shape, yet his talent was greater. Like Thea's, limited only by his knowledge." She shook her head and mustered a smile. "Such mischief it led him into. When he walked as a cat and he met a she-cat in heat . . . his wounds were nothing, but his shock was all-encompassing. Cats, after all, are creatures of Venus, and when one takes a shape one takes on its nature as well."

The wolf's gaze was wise and strangely compassionate. *He hunted well. We mourn him under the moon.*

"I mourn him always. Always. But I must be strong. I must hold up my head under the crown. It is so heavy, sister. So monstrously heavy." She drooped even in speaking of it, but stiffened with a visible effort of will, rising to her feet. Her heavy braid uncoiled to her heels, rich as cream; she took up the somber pelisson she had discarded, the wimple and veil suited to a matron and a queen. Slowly she put on the dark overgown with its lining of marten fur. As she began to fold the wimple, a disturbance brought her about.

The animals were agitated, the more timid already hidden, the hunters alert, growling softly. Yet even without them she would have known that human feet had trodden in her garden. The Pope's Legate walked among the roses, vivid in the scarlet of his rank. He moved slowly, breathing deep of the cool clear air, but under the joyous peace of the garden his face was grim.

As he saw the Queen, both joy and grimness deepened. He bowed low before her. She bent her head to him, all queenly. "Eminence," she acknowledged him.

"Your Majesty," he responded. He looked about him as if he could not help it, his eyes coming to rest where they had begun, upon her. The grimness filled his face, yet he spoke gently. "Majesty, I beg you to pardon my intrusion."

"It is pardoned." She sounded cool and remote, unmoved by any trouble.

Silence stretched. The beasts had settled; the wolves sat or lay in a broad circle about the Cardinal and the Queen, even the cubs still, watchful.

Benedetto Torrino sighed faintly. "I know how few are your moments of peace," he said. "The crown is heavy even for one well fit to bear it; and what we have brought into this kingdom . . . Lady, I regret that we have caused you suffering and must cause you more."

"*Must*, Lord Cardinal? Is it the law of God that the Church must hound us to death and our realm to ruin?"

"It is the law of the world that a will to good must often turn all to evil. His Holiness wishes only that the world be cleansed of stain and brought back to its God. His servants labor to work his will, and His will, as best they may."

She laughed, cold and clear. "You believe that? Then you are an innocent. We suffer and we die so that one small circle of venal men may hold more power in the Curia than any of their rivals."

"Not entirely, Lady. Not entirely."

"Enough." The wimple was crushed in her hand; she let it fall. "I am weary, Lord Cardinal, and it seems I am to have no rest even here where none but my dearest kin may come. Why have you braved the wards and the ban?"

"I had no choice." From his sleeve Torrino took a folded parchment. "This has come to me. I think you should know of it."

She held it, looking at it. Her fingers tightened. She opened the missive, read slowly. Nothing changed in her face or her bearing, yet the air darkened and stilled as before thunder.

She looked up. Her eyes were the color of sulfur. "Your embassy is ended forthwith. You are to return to Rome. A man of firmer will and greater devotion to God and to Mother Church will fill your place. He will, of course, be a monk of Saint Paul."

"That is not the . . . precise . . . wording of the letter."

"That is its import." She turned it in her hands. "Pope Honorius never saw this."

"He signed it. There is the seal."

"And its secret mark, the exact number of points in Saint Peter's beard." She shook her head slightly, almost amused. "My lord, there is an old, old trick. A heap of documents, a high lord in haste, the crucial and betraying writ so concealed that only its margin is visible, ready to be signed. Men have been done to death in that fashion, as we may well be. For I have little doubt that with this His Holiness signed another addressed to the new Legate, granting God's Hounds full power and full discretion in the harrowing of Rhiyana."

"I cannot believe——" Torrino broke off. More slowly, more softly, he said, "I can. God help me; God help us all."

"You move too slowly to sate the bloodthirst of a Hound. You have not even lowered the Interdict; not by your command have innocent folk been burned in the markets and before the churches. The Hounds and the Crusade have advanced without you."

"I have made no effort to stop them." Torrino's voice was harsh.

"You have been powerless. So too have I. Did I enforce the ban when the gray cowls appeared all at once and with brazen boldness in every hamlet, even in my own city?"

"But not in your hall or before your court."

"They will not defile their sanctity with my presence. Not until they come triumphant to demand my life."

"Lady," he said. "Lady, believe. I came armed with righteousness to search out a tribe of devils. I found order and peace, a just king, a people no more evil than any other in this world. I do not believe that you have deceived me, or that I have deceived myself. Your sorceries, the infidels among you . . . they have not earned death or even Interdict, least of all without proper trial. I would have your people tried, given time to speak in their own defense, dealt with thereafter singly and with justice, without peril to your kingdom."

"What one would have and what one will have do not often meet. Will you obey your false orders, my lord?"

He took them from her hand. With a sudden fierce movement he tore the sheet asunder. The shards rattled like leaves as they fell. But he said calmly, "I may have no choice, although I shall fight with what skill I have. Letters can be delayed or mislaid; the kingdom is in chaos, the roads beset with mud and brigands."

"As they have not been since my King was young." Her fierceness like his was a flash of blade from the sheath, but she held it so, drawn and glittering. "Benedetto Cardinal Torrino, you know that your very presence here is a betrayal of your office."

"My office is that of judge and emissary; my calling is that of a priest of Christ. I will not surrender it all for a lie."

"The lie may be in us."

He regarded her. She stood as tall as he, but slender as a child, with the face of a young maiden. Her eyes, unveiled, were utterly inhuman. "And yet," he whispered, "not evil. Never so."

"They will say I have ensorceled you."

"Perhaps you have. You are all beautiful, you Kindred of the Elvenking, but you most of all, Lady and Queen. I have never seen a woman fairer than you."

"The White Chancellor surpasses me, Lord Cardinal, and well I know it."

He smiled with surprising warmth. "But, Lady, he is a man; and even at that I would not set him above you. I grieve that we meet only now and amid such havoc, but I cannot regret that we have met."

"Nor," she mused, "after all, can I." Her smile nearly felled him. He reeled; she caught him in great dismay. "My lord, pardon, I took no thought—"

The Queen had gone. In her place stood the maid who had loved two princes, but who had chosen the one for his gentleness—not knowing then that he would be King. But the Queen knew what the maiden had never suspected, that her face itself was an enchantment and her smile laden with power. She looked on this newest victim in visible distress, holding him by his two hands as if the body's strength alone could undo what she had done.

He steadied quickly enough. He was a strong-willed man; his vows protected him after a fashion. But he remained a man. He swallowed hard. "Your Majesty, I must go."

"Yes," she said, "you must."

They both looked down. Their hands were locked together. Neither could find the power to let go.

"Your King—" It was a gasp. "Your husband. He is mending, I have heard; one of your Kindred—she told me where you were—I thank God that he will not die."

"It is not yet certain that he will live. But we pray. He will allow no more. Even I—he will not let me come to him, and I cannot go as our people go. And there is the throne to hold for him. Ah, God, I hate these shackles of queenship!"

"You love him."

"Most sinfully, with body and soul." At last she could loose one hand, only to touch his pectoral cross. "I have never felt it as a sin. I gave him the only child I could give; I would joyfully give him another, a pair, a dozen. As he would give me—but wounded, walled against me—I fear that he is hiding—that he may be—"

His arms closed about her, inevitable as the tides of the sea. "He took an arrow in the thigh, but not so high and not so dreadful as you fear. I have it from witnesses; I know it for truth. He may come back lame, but he will come back a man."

"Or dead." Her head drooped upon his shoulder; he clasped her close. His face was rapt, brilliant, a little mad. He buried it in the silken masses of her hair.

"Three," Simon said, "or more likely, four. Who would have dreamed that a prince of the Church would fall so easily? I hardly needed to bait the trap."

Anna did not know how she could hate him, pity him, fear him, scorn him, all utterly, all at once. It choked the breath from her; it left her blank and staring, shaking her head slowly, unable to stop.

He had no eyes for her. Thea lay flattened at his feet, hackles abristle, lips wrinkled in a snarl. "The world shall be clean of all your kind," he said. "One by one they shall fall. Even those you deem safe in your forest—I have counted them; my power has marked each one. It grows, you see. With use, with mastery, its strength waxes ever greater. No wall may hold it away, no magic stand against it, no power overcome it." He reached as for something he could touch, smiling with terrible gentleness. "How beautiful, like a tower of light. How fragile; how easy to cast down."

Thea tensed as if to spring. He raised his hand. She froze. Her snarl died. The blaze of her eyes died into ashes. She shrank down and down.

"Your demon lover," he said, "is dead. He dared advance against me; I struck, and cast him down. He lingered for a little while; he struggled; he betrayed your people to the Pope's Legate. But at last he fell into the darkness that waits for those who have no souls."

"No," Anna whispered. "No."

Simon turned to her. "Yes. Great prince of devils that he was, masked in piety, he was no match for me. The world is free of him."

"No," she repeated. "He can't be dead. He promised me. A long time ago in Constantine's city, he promised. As long as I needed him, he wouldn't—" She could not finish. Not for grief, not yet; for rage. She faced her jailer in a white fire of it. "How dared he die? How dared you murder him?"

He fell back. She did not deign to be astonished. "Damn you. *Damn* you, Simon Magus. What right have you to make us suffer? Who gave you the power to ordain life and death? How dared you kill my brother?"

"God," he gasped. "God—"

"God damns you, you hound of Hell. Murderer, your power is so mighty—raise our dead. Do yourself to death in their places."

"It is forbidden. God forbids—"

"He who lives by the sword shall die by the sword. Who slays with power must die of it. That is the law of your kind."

"No law binds me but God's."

"Just so." Anna raised her clenched fists. "I curse you, Simon Magus. I curse you by your own power."

He backed away. "No. No, I beg, I command—"

"Monster. Coward. You dread death. You know what waits for you. Hellmouth. The Lord Satan. The fires unending. If," she said, "*if* you have a soul."

He struck at her feebly, white with terror, all the glory gone and only the craven madness left to rule him. Until he paused; his hands froze, warding. His eyes blazed with sudden lightnings. Again he struck, a great sweeping blow that hurled her from her feet.

22

The fall was endless, eternal. Thea flashed past; Anna snatched at her, caught her. Eye met eye. Thea's were dull, quenched, dim brown beast-eyes. Yet for the briefest of instants they flared green. Her body was gone, twin small bodies in its place, filling Anna's arms. One slipped free, or was torn free. The other she clasped strangling-close, falling down and down, whirling into nothingness.

She struck stone. It was wet; it was cold. Something whined and pushed against her. With a small gasp she thrust herself up on her arms.

She nearly fell again. Cynan huddled beneath her, bedraggled and shivering, but it was not the cold that shook his every bone. There were no walls. No *walls*. A green tangle, a worn pale pavement, a blazing-bright arch of sky.

It wavered. She tried to fight the tears, but they only came the harder.

Needle-sharp teeth closed, but gently, gently, on her hand.

Cynan released it, wobbling on his feet, meeting her stare. Stronger than terror was his determination. Something nudged her, but not upon her flesh; within, like a memory struggling to the surface. A word or a wish. *Up.* And, *Go.*

He too had his father's eyes, silvered gold. His father—

A howl welled up from the bottom of her soul. She locked her jaw against it. She struggled to an ungainly crouch, aware as one is amid a nightmare, of her filthy clothes, her rank body, her hair straggling over her face and shoulders and down her back. "Your father," her mouth said, "is dead. Alun is dead, and we—"

Cynan caught the trailing edge of her sleeve and tugged. *Go,* he willed her. *Go!*

Her body was beyond her mind's control. "I loved him. I *loved* him. And he promised—he promised—"

Pain shocked her into sanity. Cynan crouched flat, snarling, within easy reach of her torn hand. She staggered up. He did not rejoice, not yet. He nipped her hem. She tottered forward; he rose and followed.

Slowly her steps steadied, her mind cleared. Though valiant, Cynan was very young still; she scooped him up before he could tire. His weight was like a shield, a ward against panic. It was real, this road, this air, this sky. She was free. She had driven Simon to the edge, and he had not slain her; he had flung her away. Liahan, Thea—

With all her strength she mastered herself. She had Cynan, and he was thoroughly hale. Where they were, that must come next. Surely, despite its wildness, this was no wilderness; the road was clear of greenery, the greenery itself held just short of conquest amid a scattering of flowers. Something white glimmered through them. She let her breath out slowly. The face was marble, crumbling and streaked with moss, the body beneath it draped modestly enough in a mantle of laurel. She made her way past it, stretching into a freer stride. Her heart slowed its pounding. No walls sprang up about her, no Simon came to bar her way.

The road turned sharply. The trees opened. A whole world stretched before her. A city of hills and marshes and a broad arch of river, walled and towered among the works of giants.

Her knees loosened. She fought to stiffen them. After all her dread and her refusal to think of the choices, she had not been sent far at all. She was still in Rome.

A month's journey from Rhiyana on horseback with ample provision. Knowing not a soul here, looking like a beggar, with neither money nor food to sustain her. And for company an unweaned pup.

Cynan objected to that with body and mind. He had been trying himself at his mother's ration of meat. And he was a witch born; he had power. He could help her.

A smile felt strange upon her face. "You can," she said. "Unless—" She shut her mouth. One did not name the Devil. If she was to go on at all, she must go on as if she were truly free. She had her wits and her companion, and no one had taken her small wealth, the rings of gold in her ears. Surely those would buy her food, shelter, and maybe—she trembled at the mere prospect of it—a bath.

The sun had been middling low when she began; as she walked, it rose. Its arc was much higher than she remembered, the arc of winter turning toward spring, the air wonderfully warm. Even so, she was grateful for the furred lining of her cotte. Her soft shoes, never made for much walking, were wet through from the puddled road; she would not think of the growing soreness of her feet.

How huge Rome was. How terrifying with its crush of people, and yet how frightening in the wastes where people were not. She felt as glaringly conspicuous as a goosegirl in a king's hall, clad as she was for a Rhiyanan castle but draggled like a gutter rat, with a very young alaunt in her arms. He was stiff with fear, yet he stared in wide-eyed fascination, taking it all in, who had never known aught but the quiet of a prison cell.

She dared not let him walk lest she lose him. He did not ask more than once. There were too many feet, and too many dogs, whip-thin vicious creatures who looked starved for just such a tender morsel as he. But the one that ventured too close nearly lost a portion of its nose; the rest, beasts and men alike, kept their distance.

Anna knew she should try to find a place to walk to. A goldsmith or a pawnbroker who might give fair return for her earrings; a hostel where she might rest, gather her wits, find a way home. But the thought of closing herself within walls again, even walls with an open gate, made her shudder.

The sun, having won the zenith, began to fall toward evening. Cynan's weight dragged at Anna's arms. And he was growing hungry. She could fast if she must, however unpleasant it might be, but he was far too young for that.

She paused at last by a small oddity of a fountain set into a wall. From the mouth of an age-smoothed lion-face poured a thin stream,

gathering into a long narrow basin. The water was cold and sweet.
She plunged her face into it, briefly oblivious to aught but her senses'
delight.

Cynan, set on the basin's edge, lapped thirstily. When Anna
emerged, gasping and spluttering, he was gone. She looked about at
first without undue concern. The street was relatively uncrowded; she
had been lost to the world for no more than a moment or two. It
should not be difficult to catch sight of a white alaunt pup.

It should not; it was. He had vanished.

She stood, still dripping, warmed by an uprush of sheer fury.
"Damn all witches," she gritted. "Damn them, damn them, *damn*
them!"

A flash of white caught her eye. She spun toward it. Under a cart
redolent of fish, a small shape stirred. A cat.

Anna walked because she could think of nothing else to do,
calling Cynan's name without much hope, cursing him in Greek and
with some invention. People stared at her. She looked like a lunatic,
and she felt like one.

Her hem caught. She tugged at it. It tugged back. She whipped
about. Cynan grinned, tongue lolling, tail a blur. She shook her fist
at him. "You *imp!* Where were you?"

He ran ahead a pace or two, ran back again. *Come,* he commanded. *See.*

Anna groaned aloud. "See what? Aren't you hungry? Don't you
want to eat? Sleep? Be clean?"

He gripped her gown again. *See!*

With a deep sigh she let him lead her. He was, after all, a
witchling. She hoped it was his power that guided him.

They passed the fountain. They passed the fish-peddler. They
passed a goldsmith's shop, but Cynan would not let her stop.

The narrow street opened upon another somewhat wider and
somewhat more crowded. People milled about a long double row of
stalls which seemed to offer anything one could ask for. The scent of
grilling fish, of spices, of bread just baked, knotted Anna's stomach
with sudden pain.

Cynan drew her onward. He must have been tiring, although he
showed no sign of it.

At last he stopped. They stood between the baker's stall and one
heaped high with books. That for Anna was another sort of pain, an
urge to snatch the first dusty binding and plunge into an ecstasy of

words. Cynan seemed bent on doing just that, in a completely literal sense. He bounded into the open shop, Anna following perforce, her temper held on a tight leash.

It was dim within after the brilliance of sunlight. Anna discerned the shadows of books, a scribe's table, a man bent over it intent on his work. The bookseller, he would be, vouchsafing Anna one measuring glance before he returned to his page. His only patron was mildly startling, a girl younger than Anna and exceedingly pretty, dressed becomingly but very plainly. A basket lay forgotten at her feet, overflowing with the fruits of a day's marketing, while she leafed through a closely written codex.

Cynan arrowed straight toward her, gamboling about her, tugging the cloth covering from her basket and tangling himself in it until he could do no more than wriggle and grin.

The girl left her book before his antics had well begun. When she laughed, the whole crowded space seemed to sparkle. She swept up the bundle Cynan had made of himself and kissed his pointed muzzle, not entirely to his delight. "Ah, little monster," she teased him, "back to torment me again, are you? Or is it the fish in my basket?"

He struggled. She unwound him and set him down. He returned to Anna, looking extremely pleased with himself. *See,* he said. *Food and a friend. Love me, Anna?*

She shook him. She hugged him. She met the girl's gaze with one as bold as she could manage, but with a judicious touch of apology. "Your pardon," she said in Latin, "if this imp has been troubling you."

"He's yours then?" The stranger took her in without visible distaste, even smiling a little.

"He's mine," answered Anna, "to look after, God help me."

The girl laughed. "He's a terror, isn't he? He's beautiful." She fondled his ears, her eyes on Anna's face. "Your Latin is marvelous. Can it be that you're a marvel yourself? An educated woman?"

"I'm reckoned so," Anne said slowly.

"Would you know dialectics? Have you ever read the philosophers? Do you know Aristotle? Plato? Epicurus?" She caught herself, giggling like any featherhead of a girl. "I'm getting above myself! It's just, hearing you speak Latin, and so well—my wishes ran away with me."

Cynan was radiating satisfaction. *Witch-brat,* Anna thought at him, to no perceptible effect. She discovered that she was smiling. "Anna Chrysolora," she named herself.

"Stefania da Ravenna." Her own smile was radiant. "Would you be Greek? My mother was. My uncle is. If you asked him, he'd call me Stefania Makaria."

"I was born in Constantinopolis."

"And I in Ravenna. Are you here as a pilgrim? Or do you live here?"

"A Byzantine pilgrim in Rome?"

For a moment Stefania's face darkened. "I know one. I knew—" She shook herself firmly. "Of course not. But if you live here . . ."

Anna looked down at her own disarray and up into the clear eyes. They were as blue as evening, as the field of Gwydion's banner, as the sapphire in his crown. "I don't live here." The walls were closing in. Or was it only her sight's failing? "I have nowhere to rest my head. The world was walled and barred, and he cast me out because I dared to tell the truth. He said—he said my brother was—"

The rest was a blur. Anna walked, she knew that. Stefania had the basket. Cynan rode on top of it. Wizard-imp; he had plotted this.

He could not be two months old. He could not be very much more than one.

Precocious. Maybe she called him that. She was in the street; she was on a stair, struggling not to fall; she was in a warm bright room, facing wrath in the shape of an ancient crone. "Filthy!" it shrilled. "*Stinking!* Water, Stefania. Soap. Towels. Out of the way, puppy!"

A bath. Bliss unalloyed. Clean hair, clean body, clean shift somewhat too short, a bed and a blanket, Cynan's warm full-fed presence, sleep and peace at last. She embraced them all with joyous fervor.

23

Nikki paced from end to end of San Girolamo's cloister. The monks were singing the Office of Nones, Alf and Father Jehan among them. He had the cloister to himself with its ornate columns and its carefully tended grass, starred with windflowers about the grave of some forgotten abbot.

Somewhere in the night, his power had come back. He could hear again, if he wished to. At the moment he did not. He was born to silence, to the prison of his mind. His eyes were windows only, granting vision but no understanding.

Stefania did not know. She could not even guess. Oh, to be sure, he had been clever, keeping her eyes anywhere but on his motionless lips, speaking always and with care in words, never in his private language of face and body and will. She thought he was a man like any other. She thought she loved him.

She loved a lie. The truth would stun her, with disbelief at first, then with fear. Then, and worst of all, with pity. For without the armor of his power he was a poor creature, mute and walled in silence.

He could read, he could write. He was not without hope.

He was not a proper man.

Well? Need she ever know? He had been a fool to seek her out after the enemy's attack; he had been half out of his wits, he had not known what he did until it was done. He had never wanted any woman as he wanted her. She was made for him; she was perfection. Maybe . . . it could very well be that he loved her.

She had by far the keener mind. Not that he had ever pretended to be even a scholar, let alone a philosopher. He learned easily enough, and with Alf for a teacher he could not help but pass for an educated man, but his wits had neither depth nor brilliance. Where she led, he could only follow at a distance.

She knew that; she did not care. She loved his face and what wit he had and, quite frankly, his body: the totality of him as she knew it.

She must know. He could not keep up this deception. If he lost her—

His strides lengthened and quickened. His fingers worked, knotting, unknotting. He was supposed to be hunting for Anna, Thea, the twins. Not sighing after a lovely half-Greek philosopher.

He stopped short. He would tell her. Now. Today. Maybe it would not matter to her.

Maybe, by the same miracle, he would learn to speak.

He turned, and leaped back startled. Prior Giacomo was standing not a yard away, wearing his customary formidable scowl. His lips moved; with a wrenching effort Nikki made himself hear. ". . . troubled. Is there any help I can give you?"

Nikki stared. He almost laughed. Help? What mortal man could help any of them? A born witch and a made witch and a man mad enough to love them both; this excellent monk could not conceive of the troubles that beset them.

Prior Giacomo bridled a little. He did not know that he understood Nikki's wordless speech; he thought he was reading the boy's face, finding there the despair that was real and the scorn that was his own misunderstanding. "I know I presume," he said stiffly, "but I can't help my concern for the welfare of a guest."

Nikki shook his head from side to side. His lips were set, locked in silence. He could not tell the whole of it for Giacomo's soul's sake. His own small part meant nothing. He was in love, he should not be, he must not be. What was that to the enormities that had brought him here?

He watched awareness dawn in the Prior's eyes. "I've never heard you speak," Giacomo muttered. He looked hard at Nikki. "You can't, can you? And I was demanding answers. I deserve a whipping."

Nikki's power sharpened almost into pain, casting him headlong into Giacomo's mind. A flood of annoyance and of self-recrimination; of interest, and of guilt for it; of compassion. Nothing as ghastly as pity. "I don't suppose you can tell me why."

Nikki touched his ear. Giacomo glared. "You aren't." He paused. "Maybe. I knew a woman once, a cousin of my mother's. She went deaf as a child; she taught herself to read lips and faces. It was uncanny, sometimes, how much she could see."

He was not comfortable with his discovery, however much he berated himself for a fool. *Now they all make me uneasy,* he thought just short of speech. He detested uneasiness; it infected his whole spirit. But there was something distinctly odd about these pilgrims who had stayed so long in Rome nor shown any sign of departing.

His jaw tightened. No use to interrogate the boy. The other lad, the one whose face was taking luminous shape on Oddone's panels, would be no better, dreamer and mystic that he was, and more than half mad. Which left the monk; and that one, beside those others, was too perfectly sane for belief.

Nikki edged away. Giacomo took no notice. He was well if not auspiciously distracted.

Brother Jehan was not difficult to find. He was, however, engaged, and not pleasantly from the look of it. One of the Curia's innumerable functionaries had taken it into his head to call on his uncle the Abbot; having heard the Office with visible impatience and a widely roving eye, he had attached himself to the Norman. They were still in the nave of the chapel, the lion and the tomcat; Archdeacon Giambattista was in full and indignant voice. "But, Brother, I could swear you're the very image of—"

Jehan's courtesy had worn threadbare. "To be sure, sir, all of us Normans look alike."

"As like as this? Brother, your very voices are the same." Giambattista caught sight of Giacomo. "Brother Prior, would you believe it, I know this face as well as I know my own. But the last time I saw it, it belonged to a bishop."

"The poor man," Jehan said with clenched-teeth lightness. "Has he found a cure for it?"

Giambattista seemed not to have heard. "The voice, the bulk, the nose. The nose is incontestable. Why, I remember the very day it happened, that godless tournament in Milano—"

"The Abbot will see you now," Giacomo said abruptly, in a tone that brought the babbler up short and drove him into rapid retreat. It seemed to be Giacomo's day for putting young pups to flight.

There was a moment of blessed silence. "I confess," Jehan said at length, "to an appalling lapse in Christian charity."

"If I were your confessor, I'd give you prompt absolution. That boy was a pestilence in the cradle."

"From which, no doubt, he observed the tournament in Milan."

"He's not that young." After a moment Giacomo added, "If you're thinking of the same tournament I am. It can't have been more than ten years ago."

"Eleven. You were there?"

"I've heard about it. From Giambattista. At interminable length. The victor was his first living, breathing hero."

Jehan rubbed his battered nose. Catching Giacomo's eye, he lowered his hand.

"The victor," said Giacomo, "was a young giant, a Norman. He won against all hope, and after a blow that shattered a nose almost as imposing as mine. Or so Giambattista has always declared. The knight was also a priest, one of Pope Innocent's prodigies, guard and friend and messenger and privy secretary all in one. He's prospered since, I understand. The last I heard, he'd been named bishop of some unpronounceable see on the edge of the world."

"Even the edge of the world may have a thing or two to commend it," Jehan said.

"It's not Rome." Giacomo clasped his hands within his sleeves, looking up at the expressionless face. Its eyes gazed down, ice-blue. Simple monk or anointed bishop, this was not a man to trifle with.

They walked side by side, Giacomo stretching his strides, Jehan shortening his to an endurable mean. Bright daylight washed them; they turned toward the guesthouse. "Amazing," mused the Prior, "how you knew exactly what the archdeacon meant. I don't suppose you'd care to speculate further. Imagine a bishop who wants to be looked on as a simple Brother of Saint Jerome. It's much easier to get about; no one stands in awe of rank or holiness, no one tries to encompass every hour with ceremony. And with luck, no one even guesses the truth."

"Interesting," Jehan conceded, "but why would he want so much not to be recognized?"

"Who knows? Maybe he has an errand he'd prefer no one knew of. Maybe he has companions who might need a bit of explaining. Maybe he's simply trying to escape the attention of Giambattista and his ilk."

Jehan laughed without effort. "If so, he certainly settled on the wrong place to hide. The story will be all over the Curia in an hour."

The door of the guesthouse was ajar, the house empty; at the moment, apart from its most puzzling guests, it sheltered no one. Giacomo accepted a seat by the brazier, glancing about at the room the pilgrims shared. It was scrupulously tidy, uncluttered by any personal possessions except the staffs propped together in a corner and the cloak folded at the foot of the bed, a single small bundle atop it. They had traveled light, these oddly assorted companions.

Giacomo warmed his hands over the coals. "This time of year I'm always cold."

"It's Lent. Penance is a chilly occupation."

"How not, when we're forced to eat nothing but fish?" Giacomo's humor was a flicker, swiftly gone. He fixed Jehan with a cool and steady stare. "Mind you," he said, "I don't make a practice of invading my guests' privacy. But sometimes the circumstances would seem to demand it."

The Norman loomed like a tower, but with a face of polite attention. His hands were invisible behind him. Perhaps they were fists.

The Prior went on doggedly. "Your conduct here has been exemplary. I can say truthfully that San Girolamo has been the better—thus far—for your presence in it. As to what may happen later, I admit to some concern. Not that you may be a rather famous and rather exalted lord of the Church; I can believe it, and I can't censure an honest act of humility. But your friends are beginning to alarm me."

"How so?"

That was not the tone of a humble monk. Giacomo allowed himself a small tight smile. "I can't prove anything. I can only say that I'm uneasy. A Byzantine and a—Saxon? Boys of an age, it seems, a frail monkish scholar and a bright-eyed worldling, poles apart but as close as brothers. The Saxon is prone to a sort of falling sickness. The Greek is mute and deaf, though he doesn't seem much the worse for it. Neither has shown the least sign of haunting shrines in search of a miracle."

"Because," said a low clear voice, "the miracle is not to be found among the dusty relics and the sepulchers of saints. I doubt the Church would sanction it at all."

Alf came to Jehan's side, standing shoulder to shoulder. The contrast was not as striking as Giacomo might have expected. The white boy was a shade the shorter with scarce a third the girth, attenuated as a painted angel, and yet he stood like a sword beside a great iron club. Less massive, more subtly lethal.

"Good day, signore," Giacomo said calmly.

Alf bowed his head a precise degree. "Good day, Brother Prior. I regret that our presence troubles you. If you wish, we can find lodgings elsewhere."

Giacomo's head flew up, nostrils flared. "We go to war for insults here, sir pilgrim."

"Even before God?" demanded Jehan.

"Before God we stand on our honor. There'll be no more talk of leaving."

Alf raised a fine brow. "Are we prisoners?"

"You know you're not. All I ask is a simple assurance. If you're seeking sanctuary, or if you expect to need it, you'll tell us truthfully. We can give you God's protection, but only if we're asked."

"Against the very Devil himself?" Alf did not wait for an answer. He seemed to gather himself, to make a sudden painful choice. "Brother Prior, we need no more than we've been given, which itself is far more than we ever looked for. Our crime is our plain existence; for that there is no refuge. Our miracle is preeminently earthly and much out of the sphere of your abbey: We have an enemy who hates us with the bitterest of hates. By his strength and our negligence he seized our kin. My sister, my lady; my newborn children."

Giacomo was full of words, but not one could fit itself to his tongue.

"My children," Alf repeated levelly. "He has taken them; we've pursued him as far as this city. He is here, we're certain of that, but he has hidden himself and his captives beyond our skill to find them. That is the miracle we pray for. That is the cause of my sickness."

"Then," said Giacomo, "it may be I can help. What is this enemy? If he's a lord or a prince, my family may know him. If he's a churchman, I think I can find him."

Alf shook his head. "No. Thank you, no. The man is mad. If he knows we hunt him, he will certainly destroy his prisoners. He's already cut down one who tried to stop him, an unarmed child; he'll have no mercy on women and babes."

"They may already be dead. Even if they aren't, he has to be found and punished."

Alf's eyes burned white-hot. "They live. But not for long if he catches our scent. You're generous, Brother Prior, and braver than you know, but I beg you to say no more of this. We will find him. We will see that he pays the full and proper price."

"Three of you?"

"Three will be enough, or far too many. Does not one God suffice for all vengeance?"

"That's a trifle blasphemous."

"No doubt. My existence itself, for that matter, could be reckoned a blasphemy." Alf moved toward the warmth of the brazier, stirring the coals to new life, adding a fresh handful. The ruddy light limned his face, deepening the hollows beneath eye and cheekbone, turning the smooth youthful features to an ageless mask. "You may still ask us to leave, and we'll go without complaint. We never meant to presume so long on your hospitality."

"I told you not to talk about it. Besides, if you left, Brother Oddone would be prostrated. He wants to do a statue next, I think. Saint Raphael the Healer."

Alf smiled almost invisibly. "Maybe I'll be its first miracle."

"Not likely. Oddone is claiming that honor for himself. He swears he hasn't had a cough or a shiver since Saint Benedict's Day."

"I'm glad of that. You should cherish him, Brother Prior; he has a rare and wonderful talent. Nor will he live long, even with Saint Raphael's help. God's hand is on him."

"I call it consumption," Giacomo said harshly, "and I'm anything but blind to it. The truth is that Oddone says *you* cured him. He's convinced that you're an archangel in disguise."

Alf laughed with genuine mirth. For an instant he looked a boy again, the shadows held at bay in the deep places of his eyes. "Brother, you ease me, you and your beloved artist." From the bed he took what apparently had brought him there, the folded cloak. He bowed to Giacomo, smiled at Jehan, and turned to go.

The Prior held up a hand. Alf paused, brow lifted. With a scowl of frustration Giacomo waved him away.

24

Now he would do it. Now he would tell her. Now she would know what he was.

Nikki made a litany of it, striding blindly through streets grown familiar, as oblivious to both marvels and commonplaces as any Roman born. His nose and his feet between them took him past the tavern to the scrivener's shop. There his feet would go no farther. He could not mount the stair. He could only stare into the shop, realizing very slowly that the pale gleam within was a candle on Uncle Gregorios' bald head. The scribe was at work over a heap of documents.

"Behind again," he said by way of greeting, "thanks to all the uproar with the marriage contracts. Did you hear? No? Herminia Capelli was to marry Pietro Brentano, which was much to the advantage of both families, and which was very much to the taste of the bridal couple. But she was a widow with a young son, and there were properties settled on her on the boy's behalf; and someone somewhere had found an irregularity in the contract of that first marriage, which affected the inheritance and possibly the legitimacy of the union itself. Now if the marriage was improperly sealed and the boy improperly conceived . . ."

Gregorios' words washed over Nikki, sharp yet soothing, demanding nothing but a nod now and then. Nikki moved about the cramped confines of the shop, attacked a sheet of parchment with pumice until it took on the sheen of raw silk, trimmed the pens laid in a box for the purpose, scraped smooth the wax tablets Gregorios used for jottings and for teaching the pupils who came to him in the mornings to learn a little Greek. One tablet bore nothing but row on row of staggering alphas; in spite of himself Nikki smiled. New pupil, surely. He almost regretted the stroke that smoothed the tablet into waxy anonymity.

The voice had stopped. Gregorios, with his usual finesse, had ended tale and document together; he held a stick of wax to the candle's flame, gathering each scarlet droplet upon the bottom of the parchment. Nikki set in his hand the heavy notary's seal; he nodded his thanks. There was little in his face to suggest his kinship with Stefania. He was a little shorter than Nikki, neither fat nor thin, with a square-cut face and a strong blunt nose. As if to make up for the bareness of his head, his brows were thick and black and long enough to curl, beetling over the sudden blue gleam of his eyes; and his beard, though sheared short, sprang forth with a will and a vigor all its own. He looked mildly alarming, yet somehow, like Stefania, he struck Nikki with his perfect rightness. He could not be other than he was.

For a witch's fosterling, Nikki was dismayingly forgetful of the power of names. Even as he named her in his mind she was there, holding back the curtain that concealed the inner stair, regarding them with a total lack of surprise. But her relief was an undertaste as sweet as honey, a deep swelling joy to see Nikephoros there, healthy, holding her uncle's seal. Where he belonged, she almost thought. But not quite.

He could have cried aloud. He should have fled.

Gregorios muttered something about supper, and was it that late already? He squeezed past Stefania, trudging up the steep narrow steps.

She poised, alert, ready to bolt. A blush came and went in her cheeks. Her voice was more trustworthy; she kept it light and easy. "You look well, Nikephoros. You'll stay for supper, of course; even if Uncle could forgive you for refusing, Bianca never would."

He stepped toward her. She held her ground. He set his hands on her shoulders. Did she tremble? He was frightening her; she thought he might, after all, be ill.

No, he said. *No, Stefania.*

She was staring directly at him. She did not see. He kissed the lid of each beautiful blind eye. Very gently he set his lips to her forehead. *Milady philosopher, I fear, I very much fear—*

"Love is natural and inevitable." She said it a little quickly, a little breathlessly.

On whose great authority do you make that pronouncement?

"My own." Her fingers tangled themselves in his hair. She envied what she saw as his wry calm. "No doubt you've often found it so. Natural; inescapable."

He shook his head slowly, not denying anything, struggling to do what he must do and say what he must say. It was all framed and ready. *Stefania Makaria, you can't love me. You don't know what I am. I'm a liar; I've deceived you. These very words are false, not words at all but purest witchery. I'm a witch, an enchanter, a shaper of spells. I was born a cripple, deaf and mute, and so in spite of my sorceries do I remain. I'm never the lover you deserve.*

He got only as far as her name. *Stefania—*

She pulled free from him, but far more from a swelling desire. To kiss him there, where one black curl fell just athwart his forehead. To kiss him there, where hair mingled with young downy beard, curling against the arch of his ear. And to kiss him *there* on the fine modeling of his mouth, just where he would be warmest, except for—

Where did a maiden ever learn such things? Surely not in Aristotle!

She thought she had spoken unawares, he in response. Her cheeks were scarlet. "Come up to supper," she said, "before it gets cold."

He reached again. His hand fell short. Wait, yes, and tell them all, test them all, take all the pain at once and have it over. He snuffed the candle and followed her out of the shop.

Bianca was full of senile nonsense. Stefania was chattering incessantly and to no perceptible purpose. Gregorios overrode them both at intervals with words that meant nothing. Nikki must have nodded, smiled, responded properly; no one seemed concerned. His body fed itself hungrily enough to satisfy Bianca. He tasted nothing. Maybe he grew a little drunk. They had brought out the Falernian for him, and his cup was always full.

The pup appeared somewhere between the serving of the fish and the consumption of its last morsel. For that final bit was cooling in Nikki's fingers and the needle-teeth were disposing of it with a good will, their owner curled comfortably in Nikki's lap. He seemed to have been there for a goodly while. A handsome pup; a thoroughbred, or Nikki had never learned his way round a kennel. Except for the eyes. There was something wrong with them. They could see very well indeed, no doubt of that. They were bright with intelligence, alert to every movement.

They were silver. They were gold. They were pupiled like a cat's. Like a *cat's*.

Nikki gripped the wriggling shape. *Where did you get this pup?* he demanded across the currents of conversation. *Where did it come from?*

His tone brought them all round upon him, amazed. "Why," Stefania said, "he came to us. Haven't you been listening? He found me, or more properly my basket, in the market. He introduced me to his companion. Poor woman, she looked as if she'd been locked in someone's dungeon and then turned loose to beg, but she spoke to me in Latin, and it turned out that she was a philosopher too. She came home with me, she and the imp; she's very ill or she'd be down here to—"

Nikki never heard the rest. He was already gone.

The bed was Stefania's, demure in its blue coverlet. Anna lay in it in the deep sleep of exhaustion. She was a little thinner than he remembered, maybe; not that she had ever had any more flesh than a bird. Her skin had the sallow tinge it always had when she stayed too long out of the sun. Even in sleep her mouth was set tight.

The pup scrambled out of his slackened grip and onto the bed. Unlike any other young creature Nikki had ever known of, he did not pummel Anna into wakefulness; he met Nikki's stare and said very clearly, *You are my uncle. Mother told me. I saw you in her thoughts—the one with the basket and the fish. She's full of you.*

You, said Nikki, *could never be anything but Alf's son and Thea's. What are you doing in that body?*

He inspected each paw, his belly, his back and the white whip of his tail. *It's my body.*

You don't remember— Nikki broke off. Cynan's puzzlement was transparent. Nikki's throat swelled shut. His cool curiosity had shattered over the roil of his emotions. *Alf*, he said faintly. *Alf. For God's love, Alf!* His cry echoed in the void, unheard, unanswered.

The room flooded with unbearable brightness. Nikki flung up his hand against it. "What are you doing, standing here in the dark?" demanded Stefania. She set the lamp on the table by the bed, gathering Cynan to her and scratching his ears until he groaned with pleasure. "Do you know this woman?"

Yes. Nikki was curt, lest he break and scream aloud. *This is my sister. The one I told you of.*

She blinked. "Are you sure?"

I know my own kin! He snatched Cynan and set him down with force enough to stagger him. *Where were they when you found them?*

"I was over by Sant' Angelo in Pescheria when the pup started following me and begging me to notice him. Then he ran away and I went to Rocco's to see if he'd found any new books, and the imp came back with Anna. I've told you the rest."

I found her, said Cynan. *Stop thinking I'm too young. I've got power.*

Then tell me how, where, when— Nikki shook with eagerness, with fear. This could be a trap. Or an illusion; or a dream on the verge of becoming nightmare.

Cynan crouched on the coverlet near Anna's hand, ears flat to his head. *I can't tell,* he said in a very small voice. *He won't let me.*

Who?

I can't tell. Mother told me to, but he's too strong. He laughed when he let me go. Cynan snapped viciously at air. *I hate him!*

That was all he would say, for all Nikki's pressing. He bristled and cowered; he warded himself with both strength and skill, fierce in his terror.

Nikki could not torment him so. He cradled the small beast-body with its great fire of power, thinking calm and ease and freedom from fear. But behind it echoed a constant cry: *Alf! Why won't you come?*

I have. It rang in the room, strong and sweet as the note of a bell. The door was too low for Alf's height; he stooped to pass it. Stefania's eyes went wide as she looked up and up. Her breath caught once for the height of him; once again, sharply, for his face. He did not even see her.

Anna sat up with a high sharp cry. Cynan lunged savagely, slashing at the hand that stretched to him. Nikki swayed toward the witch-child, swayed back toward his sister, seizing her, shaking her as hard as he could bear to. She would not stop babbling. "I won't go back. I won't, I won't!"

Anna, Nikki willed her. *Anna, it's Nikki. You're free. Alf is here, see, he won't let you go away.*

"Not Alf. Simon, Simon Magus, I can't bear—"

Alf shook her far harder than Nikki had, ruthless in his strength. "Look at me, Anna. Look at me!"

She had no choice but to obey. Her eyes glittered in the lamplight. Her face worked. "You—you aren't—you can't be. You're *dead!*"

"Only half," he said without humor. "Anna, is Thea—"

"Alive."

"Alive," he repeated, soft as a prayer. He drew a long breath. "Thank God. When Nikki called me, when I knew—I thought it was ended. She was dead. My son, my daughter—"

"Cynan is here." Rigid on the floor, staring as if he could not stop, beginning to tremble.

Alf approached him slowly. He flattened. But he let Alf gather him up, the thin hands not quite steady themselves, the face and the voice carefully quiet. "Ah, child, are you afraid of me?"

Cynan moved within the curve of Alf's arm, still staring. *I remember,* he said. *I remember. He tried to make me forget.* Quickly, with utterly unwonted timidity, he thrust his nose into Alf's hand. *You were there when the world was born.*

Alf had had almost all he could bear. Nikki moved before he could break, too intent to be afraid, reaching to shake the steel-hard shoulder. *You've got him back,* he said forcefully. *And Anna. The others are alive. We'll find them soon. I know it.*

"You'd better," Anna said. Bold though her words were, her hands faltered, reaching for Alf as if her touch would dissolve him into air. "It's you. It *is* you. What are you doing in Rome?"

"Looking for you."

She surged up outraged. "You left Rhiyana? You abandoned it when it needed you so much? Gwydion could be dead by now. Aidan is dead. And you've been—"

Aidan is dead? Nikki seized her again, this time with real force, and no compassion at all for her bruised shoulders. *How do you know?*

"She doesn't," Alf said. He sounded weary but calm, in full control of himself. He would pay for that later, but for now Nikki was glad. "Your captor mistook my vanishing under Nikki's shields for my death. Perhaps Aidan found a way to deceive him likewise."

"I saw it. I saw him fall. Why weren't you there?"

"I was commanded. I was given no choice."

She turned her back on him.

Nikki could have hit her. She could be unreasonable—she had been in prison, she had suffered, she did not know truly what she did. But this was cruel.

He settled for harsh words, driving each through the stony hardness of her mind. *Gwydion sent him here. Now there's no going back. The walls are too high and too hard, and that one waits between.*

She whirled to face him. "What do you know of that horror?" *I've fought him.*

That surprised her. "You?"

I. His temper seethed in his eyes, about the edges of his words. *I know what his power is like. What of the man?*

Anna began to shake. She could not stop herself. "I—I can't—" She smote her hands together in a passion of frustration. As if a spell had broken, the words flooded forth. "His name is Simon. He's a monk of Saint Paul. He could be Alf's brother, the two are so like; but his power is beyond anyone's measuring, and it's mastered him. Is it true—did he kill Alun?"

Alf nodded once.

"I haven't wept for him yet," she said. "I wouldn't give our jailers the satisfaction. There was another, a fat one, all complacent and cruel. Thea said he was the mind; Simon was only the hand."

Alf sat on the bed, settled Cynan in his lap, reached for her hands. They came of their own accord, clasping hard, defying the set courage of her face. "Will you let me see?" he asked her.

She hesitated. It was Alf who asked. Alf. And yet . . .

"Yes," she gasped. "Quick. While I can still bear it."

He took her face in his hands. His touch was light, his gaze steady, clear as water. She leaned toward it; it closed over her head. Fear vanished. Grief swelled, broke, faded. Anger shrank to an ember.

Too late she remembered. She did not want him to see—

His face filled the world. She had forgotten how young it was. She had never seen it so thin. Gaunt. Frightening, now that she had the wits to see. Her finger traced his hollowed cheek; she pursed her lips. "Thea will be furious when she sees you like this."

"As furious as you?"

He was mocking her, but gently, to make her smile. She caught a lock of his hair and tugged until he winced. "You're too pretty, you know. Even with nothing on your bones but skin. Much prettier," she added, "than Simon Magus." All at once, with no warning at all, she burst into tears.

He gathered her into his lap, ousting Cynan, rocking her as if she were still a child. As to him, she knew in the perfection of despair, she would always be. He had not seen what was there in her mind to see; he had no eyes for anything so ridiculous as unrequited passion. He looked on her with deep and purely fraternal concern, soothed her and healed her as he would any creature in need of his care. Cynan offered no less, licking her hand and willing her to be comforted.

She pulled the witch-child into her own lap, dividing her tears between his flank and Alf's shoulder. Her despair was seeping away.

It was almost pleasant to let her body have its will, to let the tears fall where they pleased, with no care for her pride.

Nikki came to close the circle, walling out the world. *He* was brotherly indeed, a mingling of annoyance and compassion; he braced her, he strengthened her. She straightened shakily. Both her brothers eased their grips. Cynan's tail slapped her thigh. Still streaming tears, she laughed and hugged the damp wriggle of him. "You men; don't you know enough to let a woman cry herself out?"

It's wet, Cynan observed.

"So it is, imp. And so are you." Anna freed herself from all the hands and rose with Cynan, reaching for a corner of the sheet to dry him.

Stefania had not understood a word of it. It was almost as if— somehow—there were four people talking. But it was only the three and the pup. And what they spoke of made no sense at all. Something to do with Rhiyana, with the Church, with prisons and madness and death; yet they could smile, laugh, jest through tears. There was nothing like them in her philosophy.

The fair one, the one they called Alf, had taken the pup from Anna and commanded her to lie down again. After a moment's rebellion she obeyed. He was absorbed already in the young alaunt, regarding it as if he himself would have liked to weep, speaking to it not in Greek as he had since he appeared in the doorway but in some other, stranger tongue, both harsh and melodious. She recognized only the name, Cynan, and the tone, gentle yet stern.

Nikephoros blocked her vision, mere familiar humanity beside that shining wonder. For an instant she could only wish him gone.

Her mind cleared. He had seen; his brows were knit, his jaw set. She flung her arms about him.

For a long moment she feared that he would pull away. His rigidity eased; he completed the embrace. His sigh was loud in her ears, his voice soft. *I think we had better go.*

She drew back to see his face. For once she could not read it at all. "Why? Is there something I'm not supposed to see?"

She had come close, she could tell by the flicker of his eyes, the quickness of his response. *I can't explain now. Can you trust me, Stefania? For a while?*

Her brows drew together. He did not seem to be mocking her. "You know how I treat mysteries," she said. "I solve them."

I'll tell you, I promise. But not now. He drew her with him away from the others.

She considered escape. She did stiffen and refuse to move. "Who is that man? Can you tell me that much?"

He's my brother.

That silenced her completely. She was on the stair before she knew it, walking without thinking, struggling to imagine those two in the same family. Even without the beauty, that other was no more a Greek than he was an Ethiop. She stopped in mid-step, bringing Nikki up short behind her. "He's not," she said.

It was too dark for her to see Nikki's expression, but his voice had a smile in it, a hint of wickedness. *My father said he was, and I wasn't in a position to argue. It was a perfectly legal adoption.*

Stefania hit him. He laughed. She hit him again, but somehow she had his head in her hands and her lips upon his. It stopped the laughter at least.

She pushed him away, not hard. "You're insufferable, do you know that? Is he real?"

I've always thought so.

He was not as lighthearted as he pretended. Jealous? She decided not. It was something deeper. Something to do with Anna, and with the conversation she had not understood.

And with you. She could barely hear him. And how could he have said anything? She certainly had not.

She had imagined it. She turned and made her way down the stair, surefooted in the dark.

25
❧

"I can't do it," Alf said.

Jehan thought they had settled it, and with no help from himself. Anna was still with the people who had taken her in, who by God's own fortune were well known to Nikephoros; though that lad was no more a toy of chance than any of Gwydion's true Kindred, particularly where a woman was concerned. Cynan was here in San Girolamo, sound asleep in his father's lap, curled nose to tail and most comfortable. He had been there since Alf brought him in, wide awake at first, greeting Jehan with admirable courtesy and an even more admirable vocabulary.

But of course, he had said when Jehan was amazed. *Mother taught me. It was a secret.* He *was to think us witless.* He knew how to laugh as Nikki did, in his mind; it emerged as a broad fanged grin. *He did, too. So did Anna. She was surprised when I started to talk.*

Not much, Nikki observed, rather uncannily when Jehan stopped to think. Neither of them could or would utter a spoken word. *She knows Thea.*

It was Nikki who had told it all, with a little help from Cynan until sleep claimed him. Alf had been silent, remote as he often was in council or in company, stroking the beast who was his son.

He spoke at last when Nikki was done, breaking into a brief stillness. Nikki was feeding the brazier; he paused in mid-movement. Jehan, who had begun to ponder the whole strange tale, looked up sharply. "I can't do it," Alf repeated. "Cynan won't change. His mind is safe enough thanks to my lady's power, but his body remembers no shape but this. It won't return to the one it was born to." He laughed shortly, painfully. "He's certainly my child. I won't shape-change either, even to save my life. Though I promised her—when she was strong again—"

He was closer to breaking even than he had been before Alun's bier, when Gwydion laid this labor on him. Jehan tried to ease him. "Does it matter so much? You've got him back, and he looks sound enough except for this. When you find Thea, she can certainly—"

Alf raised his head. His eyes were wide, flaring blood-red. "Thea had no part in this. It was the enemy; then he had no need. Cynan holds to the form he considers his own, nor will he alter it even for force. If he keeps to it, however keen his wits or great his power, he'll end as the enemy desires, a mere beast. A mere, mortal beast."

"But—"

"The longer we wait, the harder the change will be. This is not a six-weeks' infant. This is a weanling pup. In a year he'll be grown and in a decade he'll die. But he'll have lost his power long before then. He'll have lost it before he's even grown. Time moves so fast for you, who a moment ago were a novice befriending a certain ill-made monk, and now are an anointed bishop. How much faster must it pass for a hound?"

Jehan spoke with care, considering each word before he spoke it. "You're saying that there's no time to lose. That Cynan has to change back now or not at all. But if that's true, then Liahan, even Thea—" He broke off. "Alf, what have you tried?"

"Persuasion. Pleading. Compulsion. He'll let me into his mind willingly, gladly. He'll give his very soul into my keeping. But his body will not yield."

Maybe, said Nikki, *it's your own fear that gets in the way. If you would change, it would convince him to do the same.*

Alf moved not a muscle, but Cynan started awake, snarling. With utmost gentleness his father stroked him into silence. But he did not go back to sleep. He watched them all, eyes gleaming as Alf's gleamed, fire and silver.

He let Jehan touch him. More surprisingly by far, Alf let Jehan take him and hold him. Over his head the Bishop said, "Nikki may be right. Not that I know much about it, but Thea's always insisted that you've got her gift if you'd only use it. Of course you can speed up the hunt and find her before it's too late for everyone, and she can change both children back again."

"I'm going to find her. I must. But she has the skill to keep the mind whole in the altered body. I don't. Already I can feel the hound-brain closing, the beast-thoughts gathering. I don't know how to stop them."

"You must!" Jehan burst out. "You're the strongest power in Rhiyana, bar none. Thea told me that herself. And she's not given to blind worship of her beloved."

Nikki's amused agreement was meant to ease the tension. It wavered and vanished in the blaze of Alf's denial. "Brute power means nothing. It's not a wall I have to batter down; it's a single thread in a weaving of utmost delicacy, that must be spun and colored and woven in one way and no other, or all the fabric frays and scatters."

"So learn how," said Jehan.

Alf rose. Jehan braced himself. Small comfort that he had Cynan for a shield; that was all too easily remedied, even if the little warlock did not choose to fight for his father.

Neither blows nor lightnings fell. Alf circled the room slowly, looking at none of them. Strange how seldom one noticed, how very feline his movements were. The grace, yes, that was inescapable, but it was the grace of the stalking panther.

It was his face. He always looked so young and so gentle. Meek as a maid, people said. He was not meek now. His jaw had set, his nostrils flared, his eyes widened and fixed. He stopped and wheeled. "If I fail in forcing the change, I'll destroy him."

You won't, Nikki said. *You'll have destroyed yourself first.*

Terribly, in a mindless, shapeless horror. Jehan did not know whose image that was; he cried out against it.

Alf was smiling. His smile had the exact curve of a scimitar. "So I will, Nikephoros. My thanks; I had forgotten. And you'll remain, who've hunted to so much better purpose than I. Maybe, after all, there's nothing to lose."

"There certainly is," Jehan grated, "if you go into it with suicide in mind."

Alf's smile warmed and softened, became his own again. But his eyes were diamond-hard. "Jehan my dearest friend, there is no other way to begin. Not for me. My power will only grow on the cutting edge of death."

"Now I know for certain. You revel in it."

"How not? I cut my teeth on the lives of the martyrs."

Cynan yawned noisily. *My teeth would cut meat if I had any.*

Alf swept him up. "You'll have some soon enough, if you're still in condition to want it."

"You're going to do it now?" Jehan cried.

"Shall I wait for my courage to fail?" Alf's glance allowed no answer. He set Cynan on the bed and paused, drawing a long breath. "Nikephoros, you had better stand guard. Jehan, you need not watch. Not that there will be much to see, until the end. One way or another. If you wish, I can set a sleep on you."

"I'll watch," Jehan said almost angrily.

Alf opened his mouth, closed it, shrugged slightly. "Stay well apart then. And whatever happens, don't touch me. Promise me."

"By my vows," Jehan said, crossing himself.

Alf nodded. Abruptly he embraced his friend; just as abruptly he let go, thrusting Jehan away beyond the glow of the brazier. "Remember," he said.

Cynan was waiting, expectant, firm and unafraid. But under the boldness, just within Alf's ken, hovered the faintest of apprehensions. *Will it hurt?*

"Not while I have power to prevent it," Alf said, his own fear walled in adamant. He dropped his robe, aware of Nikki's studied nonchalance, Jehan's sharply drawn breath; glancing down and then up again quickly. He had not realized that he was as thin as that.

He felt well enough. He lay beside Cynan, composing himself as if for sleep, not quite touching the sleek furred body. He allowed himself one brief brush of the hand over his son's ears; no more. Resolutely he closed his eyes.

With the sight of the body shut away, the sight of the mind took on a fierce clarity. Jehan was a banked fire, a glow of will and love and intelligence shot through with anxiety. Nikki was a white flame of power, man-shaped yet with wide wings enfolding them all, closing out the powers of the dark. Alf paused to wonder at him. This was born human, mortal, blind to his own great strength.

His mind touched Alf's briefly; his power reached as Alf had reached to Cynan, for reassurance, for love. As he withdrew, his fire brightened to blinding, deepened and widened and vanished. The shields were complete. While they stood firm, no enemy could come near.

Alf lay englobed in crystal. His body was far away, that thing of flesh and blood and bone laid naked upon a bed, warm in winter's cold. It breathed; it would have been hungry if he had allowed it. He drew a deep, illusory, swimmer's breath, and dived into it. Its lungs roared with the winds of worlds; its heart beat with a mighty and ceaseless rhythm; its blood surged like the sea. He plunged down and down, straight as a stone, down through the wind, through the tide, through the levin-fires of the brain into a region of stillness.

Here was the core of his self. Here was the eye of his power. From here came all his arts and his magics, the healing, the seeing, the weaving and the mind-speaking and the myriad lesser witcheries. And here was a ragged center of darkness. Once Thea had filled it, Thea and the growing presence of his children. Cynan's return, his presence so close, was but a waver on the edges.

The darkness was more than absence. It was fear. Behind it, or within it, glimmered a single spark. The art of shape-shifting, which was Thea's great art, in him was but a might-have-been.

The flicker that was Cynan began to dim and shrink, falling toward the heart of the blackness. He snatched wildly, uselessly. He had no hands. No fingers to grasp, no feet to bear him where his son had gone. Nothing. He had not the power. It was lost, wasted, abandoned to terror.

Mortal. Mortal sin. Witch, demon, were-creature, child of the night.

The darkness spun. He saw light. Dim and distant yet utterly distinct, an image in a glass: gray walls and gray mist, the hunched shadow of a thorn tree, the loom of a tor. Names rang through them all. Saint Ruan's Abbey upon Ynys Witrin in the kingdom of Anglia.

He had lived there for the whole of a mortal lifetime, cloistered and holy, going quietly, imperceptibly mad.

The sun was young, the mist like gray glass, thinning and melting to reveal a green undulation of fen and copse. Men were brown-robed giants, kind or stern or indifferent to the youngest of the abbey's orphans, the one who was all limbs and eyes and questions. Too old now for a wetnurse, too young for the schoolmaster, he had no certain place in the scheme of things; he was as free as he had ever been, as free perhaps as he would ever be. Free and strange, but he was not truly aware of either. He knew only that some people shrank from him, their thoughts darkening and twisting when he was near. But others saw him simply as a young creature, a potential noise, an irrelevance; and a precious few were like warmth and music and green silences, and those set all the rest at naught.

He was watching Brother Radbod. Brother Radbod was one of the warm ones, a dark pockmarked man whose eyes were always sore, but who was the finest illuminator in the abbey. He was setting gold leaf upon an intricately decorated page, fleck by precious fleck, creating a wonder of gold upon the painted wonders of blue and green and scarlet, white and yellow and royal purple. He was aware of his audience but not distracted by it, even though it was almost in his lap, watching and playing. The game was a new one, better even than calling clouds and making it rain, or walking up ladders of moonlight, or talking to the cows. Alf would look at one of the twining creatures on the page, or at one of the manifold shapes of leaves and vines, and his thoughts would turn and stretch and flex, *so,* and the hand on his knee would be a claw or a paw or a curling tendril. The tendril was strangest; it had its own will, and that was to reach for the light.

With some small regret, he turned the flexing upon itself. The tendril shrank and broadened and divided into a hand. It was odd to feel skin and bone again, the coolness of air, the warmth of blood.

He watched Brother Radbod's swift sure fingers. They were setting spots in a leopard's flank, while Brother Radbod filled his mind with leopards. He had seen one once, somewhere warm and far away, a splendid dappled creature, somnolent on a chain yet alive with power and menace.

It was far easier to change completely than to change a mere hand. The image set, *so;* the will flexed; the world shifted. Everything was larger. Sight was dim, all grays and blacks; sensation came muffled through thick fur. But sounds and scents burst in a flood, more intoxicating even than when, having played inside Brother Aimery's mind, he returned to his own; all his senses then had been dizzyingly keen, though Brother Aimery was young and strong and reckoned uncommonly sharp of ear and nose and eye. Yet even Alf's ears and nose could not compare with those of a young leopard.

He flexed his fingers. Claws arched forth from the velvet paw. His ears could move, cupping sound; he flicked his tail and stretched every fierce singing muscle. His murmur of pleasure came forth as a purring growl.

Brother Radbod turned. To leopard-eyes he was a shadow and a rustle, a quickening of heartbeat, a sudden sharp scent. Alf coughed at its pungency. His back prickled; his body begged to spring. His throat craved warm thirst-stanching blood, welling thick and sweet from a torn throat.

Brother Radbod was standing, hugely tall. Alf *flexed* and the world was itself again, except that he had lost his tunic somewhere. Brother Radbod's face was yellow-green; he crossed himself and backed away. Even Alf's dulled nose caught his rankness. Alf's mind, reaching in bafflement, found no warmth at all. No love, no indulgence, no quiet pleasure in his presence. Only a winter blast of horror.

Mortal. Mortal sin. Witch, demon, were-beast, child of darkness.

Alf tried to embrace him, to make him stop. He recoiled with searing violence. "Abomination! Hell-spawn, get thee hence, *in nomine Patris, in nomine Filii, in nomine Spiritus Sancti* . . . Angels and saints, Saint Michael Defender, Saint Martin, Saint George, O blessed Christ, if ever I have loved you—"

Mortal, mortal sin. Hate it, drive it away, wall it and bar it and ban it forever. But Brother Radbod would hear neither pleas nor promises. He would never be warm again.

"I remember," Alf cried, or gasped. "I *remember.*"

The window was dark, the vision gone. But the memory was there. The image, the precise turning of power about its center. It struggled, slipped, began to fade. He was letting it go. Yes; let it. It held only pain, a rejection as deep as Hell. He was monster enough. He need not be more.

Cynan. The name stabbed like a needle. *Cynan—for Cynan.*

He had it. It was briefly quiescent, like a page from a grimoire clutched in his hand. He could read it even thus. He could not will it to be. Even the thought was a tearing agony.

Cynan.

Thea. Thea in a blur of shapes: wolf, alaunt, lioness, lapcat;

falcon and dove, mare and dolphin and Varangian of Byzantium. Always, regardless of outer semblance, she remained herself, without either sin or guilt, nor ever a hint of fear.

He had promised her. They would be wolves in Broceliande, falcons above the House of the Falcon.

He could not.

Cynan.

He could—*so.*

He opened his eyes. The world was gray, all its colors poured into scent and sound. His body pulsed with a hotter and fiercer life than ever it was born to. When he stretched an arm it moved strangely, flexing claws.

He blinked. Knowledge woke from he knew not where. A half-turn of thought, a flexing of his will; he saw as he had always seen, but from the same unfamiliar angle. His arm, become a foreleg, was white yet dappled with shadow and silver. He raised his head.

They were staring, all three, in wonder and a touch of awe. He gathered his new body and flowed from the bed, testing his skill. He glimpsed himself in Jehan's open mind, a great leopard as pale as the moon, with the eyes of an enchanter.

As knowledge had swelled, so now swelled joy. So simple, so wonderful, to be his own soul's creature. The other, his blazon—

He laughed, and it was a hawk's cry, his wings stretching wide, exultant. A flick of power; his voice was his own again. He lowered his arms and turned. "See," he said to his son. "As easy as that. Come; will you not play the game with me?"

Brave child; he laughed behind the hound's face and plunged inward. Alf rode with him, steadying him, though he needed little of that. He was as strong as he was valiant. Together they found the center. The wall had gained a gate, and the gate was opening slowly. Cynan hesitated the briefest of instants. Then he loosed what lay within.

Alf looked down. A stranger looked up, a manchild of two summers or perhaps a little less. His hair was long and straight and fine, the color of chestnuts; his eyes were silvered gold. Even so young, he had Thea's pointed face and her wicked smile. *Do you like me better now, Father?*

"I could never like you better than I do," Alf answered as steadily as he could, "but I'm more than glad to see your proper face again."

I feel odd, Cynan said. He moved, exploring the ways of this new shape. It was clumsy; it was vaguely repulsive, smooth and all but hairless as it was. But its hands were purest fascination. He persuaded one to reach up, to touch his father's face. His lips stretched again into that strangeness called a smile, his tongue pausing to explore the broad blunt teeth. His other hand followed its mate to clasp Alf's neck; he rose dizzily to Alf-height, secure within the circling arms.

Alf wept, and yet he laughed. "Oh, yes, I like you very much this way. But even as a hound pup you can hardly be as old as this."

I don't want to be too little. Cynan wriggled, for the feel of it. *May I eat now?*

Hungry though he was, he could not help but play with the cheese and the bread soaked in milk, that Jehan brought and Alf fed him. Food was different to this body, richer and more savory, and his hands could grasp it in so many fascinating ways. Hands, he thought, made all the rest worth bearing.

He fell asleep with a crust clutched in his fist. He did not heed the closing of the shields about his mind, nor see them all gathered to stare, even, hesitantly, to touch. But even in sleep he heard his father's soft voice murmuring words of guard and comfort. He smiled and held the crust tighter, and lost himself in his dream.

26
❧

Stefania knew that she was dreaming. She was lying in her own familiar bed, bare as always under the coverlet her mother had made for her, with Anna breathing gently beside her and Bianca snoring beyond. The candle was lit, although she remembered distinctly that she had snuffed it as soon as she said her prayers. But surest proof of the dream was Nikephoros, who bent over her. Quite apart from the impossibility of his presence, he did not wear the pilgrim's mantle she had always seen him in, but the full finery of a northern nobleman. He looked splendid in scarlet.

She stretched out her hand to feel its richness. He bent lower still. His black curls, falling forward, brushed her cheeks. She pulled him down the last crucial inch. Since this was a dream, she could be as bold as ever she had yearned to be. She could—why, she could be frankly wanton.

How real this was. The coverlet was down round her waist, her skin reveling in the caress of silk with the young man's body behind it. His cheek pricked a little where it was shaven, tasting of salt and cleanness. His lips burned as she found them again.

At last she let him go. He hung above her, braced on his hands. The candle, flaring, made his eyes glitter. She blinked and peered. His brilliant cotte had vanished. He was a pilgrim again, and she was cold, but she was fiery hot. Her breasts had forgotten silk; they remembered the harsh pricking of wool.

She snatched wildly, clutching blankets, recoiling as far as she and the bed's head would allow. She was very wide awake and he was very solidly present, and it was abundantly clear that she had not dreamed the rest of it. Except the cotte. Small comfort that was; would she ever survive the shame?

Her mouth opened. His hand covered it. He glanced warningly at her companions, who had not moved through all of it; his free hand held up the dark limpness of her nightrobe. She snatched it and pulled it on, rising to finish, framing a scolding. His fingers, closing over her wrist, held it back once again.

By the time he had led her down to the lower room, lit a lamp, and stirred up the brazier, she had cooled considerably. It was not he, after all, who had played the wanton. In fact, as she remembered it, his eyes had widened when first she touched him. He had not been reluctant in the least, but he had certainly been surprised.

Well then, it was done, and there was no calling it back again. She called her thoughts to order and faced this welcome but utterly improper guest. "Has anyone ever told you, Messer Nikephoros, that a young man has no business rousing a respectable maiden from her bed?"

He smiled slightly, hardly more than a flicker. He had that look again, fey, a little wild. *I had to see you,* he said. *I couldn't stand it.*

"Restraint is the first virtue of the philosopher."

He tossed his head like a restless colt. *Don't throw words at me, Stefania. Stop thinking I'm just another rutting male. I want you and I'll always want you, but I can't bear—*

"There now," she said. He trembled under her hands, as only that evening she had trembled under his. Had he felt so powerful then, so piercingly tender? *Sweet saints,* she thought, and she was never sure that it was not a prayer, *I love this silly beauty of a boy.* Aloud she said again, "There now, *caro mio,* what's not to be borne? You've loved women before, I know, which sets you well in advance of me; and don't tell me it's never been like this."

It hasn't! he cried. He pulled back. *They knew—they didn't think I was—* They *knew the truth.*

"What truth is that? That you're younger than I? I know it; you told me. That you're higher born that you pretend? I guessed that long since."

He seized her. *Look at me, Stefania. Look at me!*

That was never difficult to do. She brushed the errant lock from his forehead. His eyes blazed. *Look,* he repeated. *See. See how I speak to you. Open your eyes; stop denying it. See.*

She went very still. No. Oh, surely, no. His lips had moved, of course they had. What mountebank's trick was this that he played on her?

He forced her hands up, one to the motionless mouth, one to the still throat. *I don't speak as men speak. I can't. I was born half-formed, good enough to look on but without ears to hear.*

"But you are—"

I told you I grew up in Rhiyana. Don't you know what that means? I'm one of them. A witch, a sorcerer. I'm reckoned quite skillful. I can make you think I'm a man like any other. I can walk in your mind. I can set myself in your dreams.

She shook her head. "No. It's not possible. Reason, logic—"

Reason and logic have no place among my kind. Haven't you been wondering why neither Bianca nor your uncle said a word about my brother?

"He came in and out through the back, by the courtyard."

He came in and out by magic. The little hound that he grieved over, that was his son. He's a very great enchanter, Stefania. He taught me; he made me what I am. I'm not of the true blood, you see. Mine is as human as yours; or was, before he changed me. Without him I'd have been nothing, a deafmute like those poor creatures who beg in the market, an animal in the shape of a man.

Strange how one could grow accustomed to things. A minute or two of the impossible and it was no longer impossible; it became a fact, like the existence of God. She had found logical arguments for the nonexistence of witches, had based a whole and yet unwritten treatise on them, contending that observation revealed the world *thus,* and *thus,* and *thus.* No doubt in due time she would have argued that God Himself was a creature of man's overly fertile mind, and then she would have gone to the fire for heresy. Rightfully; for if a witch could be, then so could God.

No, she rebuked herself. That was all folly. She had played with such arguments for the sake of playing with them, but never given them credit. In strict truth, she did not want to believe that this particular witch existed. This witch *per rem, per speciem;* this boy who had appeared on her doorstep and stolen her heart. Witched it away beyond any hope of recovery.

That was the impossibility. That he was one of the Devil's children, lost and damned, fair prey for any faithful son of the Church. He could not be a black sorcerer. Not Nikephoros.

She felt his pain as if it had been her own, touched with a faint, bitter amusement. *There at least you see clearly, my poor love. I'm not that kind of witch. I'm of the other faction, a white enchanter. Not that the Church cares. I'm still anathema.*

"Damn the Church!"

He shook his head, tossing it, his black brows meeting over his black eyes. He did not look—he seemed—

He had let go her hands. She caught his cheeks between them. She trembled; but not with fear, not precisely. It was far too late for that, or far too early. Especially when, caught off guard by her sudden swooping kiss, he responded with undisguised passion.

Only for a moment. He tore free. *It's not only that, Stefania. I lied. I let you think I was a whole man.*

Her eyes ran over him, halting midway. "Aren't you?"

He actually blushed. But his mouth was grim. *I pretended that I belonged to your world. I don't. I can't. The stroke of God that flawed me, the stroke of witchery that mended me, between them have set me apart. I'll never be human as you are human. I can't even—truly—wish to be.* She had neither need nor time to voice her denial; he plunged over it. *You saw how I was that night when I frightened you so much. I'd lost my power then. I was going mad in the silence. I couldn't endure to live so, always, even for love of you.*

"Do you think I'd ever force that on you?"

Do you think you could live out your life in the knowledge of what I am? My children could be like me. Could you bear that?

"I have no trouble enduring you."

What of your uncle? Of Bianca? Of your kin, your friends, the people you meet and speak to on the street? What would they say if they knew?

"Need they ever know?"

You're not thinking. You're just loving me.

"Of course. It's the only reasonable thing to do."

He grasped her, shook her. *Stefania Makaria, do you mean that?*

"Absolutely."

Then, he said, *come with me. One of my friends is a bishop. He'll marry us tonight. We only have to go to him and ask.*

She backed away a step or two. She gathered her robe about her, shivering, realizing that she was barefoot and the floor was cold. That cold part of her mind which he was trying to wake, the clever thinker, the philosopher, was saying exactly what he wanted it to say. He tested her; rightly. He was not what she had thought him. If he could walk through her mind, seeing God knew what secrets, it stood to reason that he could do much more, some of it even less appealing. And the natural man, if man she could call him, was sadly flawed.

On the other hand, if he had meant her ill, he could have overcome her long since and without this harrowing confession. He could have seized her, subdued her mind with her body, taken her, discarded her. Such, in tales, had always been the conduct of wizards.

But then perhaps this was a subtler torment, a more necromantically satisfying conquest.

However—

She hurled down her damnable logic and set her foot on it. "You know full well, Nikephoros, that if either of us is ready to marry, it's not likely to be tonight. For one thing, we have families, and these would prefer to be consulted. For another, we are in no condition of mind or body to be making a decision as serious as that."

Say it! he cried. *Say that you won't have such a horror as I am.*

Her chin came up. She knew her eyes were snapping; she felt the heat in them. "Nikephoros Akestas, what do you take me for?"

An eminently sensible woman. Damn it, Stefania, I'm an honest-to-heaven, utterly unrepentant, practicing sorcerer.

"You certainly look like one, with yesterday's razor-cut on your chin. And your hem is torn again. What do you do with it? Take it for walks through thornbrakes?"

Ah no; she had misjudged. He was too far gone to soften into laughter. Or was it that he persisted in seeing in her what—perhaps— she was adamantly refusing to see? He smote his hands together, and she heard it as thunder. Lightning leaped from his lifted palms. It coiled about him, hissing, spawning snakelets of fire, while he stood whole and fearless in its center. Surely it was only a seeming; just as surely, illusion or not, it raised every hair on her body.

It's not, Stefania, he said, and the voice was his but it was not, soft and inward, distant yet intimately close. He tucked his legs beneath him; he sat in comfort, cushioned on air. The lightning faded. Or perhaps it had entered him. He glowed softly like a lamp sheathed in parchment, light that shone through his heavy robe, leaving little to be imagined.

"What happens when you get angry?" she asked him.

I'm trained not to lose control. Even now he seemed proud of that. *We're not like the sorcerers in the stories. In many ways we're stronger. We're also more restrained. More ethical, you would say.* He tossed back his unruly hair; his brows met in a single black line. *You're not supposed to be so cool about this!*

"Very well, I'm not. Shall I have hysterics? Would it do any good?"

It would save you from me.

"It seems to me," she said, "that if you really wanted to do anything of the sort, you'd have left me on my doorstep that very first day. Or told me the truth then and there, before I formed an unshakable opinion of you."

What—

"I think you're a perfectly ethical witch, who also happens to be a very young and rather foolish boy. It doesn't *matter,* Nikephoros. Won't you accept that?"

He moved swifter than sight. Caught her. Held her prisoner. And she shrank; she shuddered, soul-deep. He felt no different. And yet—

As swiftly as he had come, he was gone. His eyes tore at her soul. Wide, clear, unspeakably bitter. *It doesn't matter,* he said in his voice that was no voice at all. *Of course not. You can force yourself to touch me, for proof. But if I touch you . . .*

"You startled me," she said sharply.

He could laugh. Only the sound of it was illusion, the roughness that was pain.

She hit him hard. And as he rocked with the blow, she seized him, but gently, running her hands along his knotted shoulders. Her mind was a roil. She wanted him; she hated him for his long deception. She shrank from his strangeness; she wanted him fiercely enough to weaken her knees. He was warm under her hands, solid, human, no lingering crackle of lightning. But it was there. She saw it in his eyes. Quiescent though he was, he was not harmless, no more than a young wolf trained to hand.

And that in itself was fascination. To know that power dwelt in him, power tamed to an arcane law; to know it would not wound her.

Yes. She *knew.* "Are you telling me," she asked him slowly, "that I can trust you?"

The flash of his eyes made her breath catch. Perilous, beautiful. Ineffably tender. She could trust him. Implicitly. But always with that spice, the knowledge of what he could do.

Well; that was true of any man. It was true of her own body.

Which, if she did not soon call it to order, would be taking matters into its own hands. She was naked under her gown, and she knew what lay under his, and they were all alone. His witchery could make sure they stayed so.

He moved before she did, standing away from her, although he spoiled it by taking her hands. *Stefania.* His lips followed the syllables, not too badly. *What do we do now?*

"I can't take it in all at once. I have to think. It's all changed. What I thought you were; what I thought the world was. I only know . . . I think . . . I still love you." She looked at him, drinking him in. "But for now, we should sleep. I in my bed, you in yours."

Yes. Yes, I should go. But he stood still. *Stefania . . .*

She waited. He shook his head, all words lost to him; he bent and kissed her, gently, but with fire in it. She wanted to cling; she wanted to hurl herself away in a madness of revulsion. She moved not at all, but stood like a woman of stone, marble veined with ice and fire. With infinite reluctance he let her go, turned, began to draw away. Her hand rose then, but whether to beckon or repel, even she did not know.

Alf knew when Nikki rose, dressed, and slipped away. The boy's trouble was as distinct as a bruise. There was little Alf could do for it, and Nikki would not have welcomed that little. The Akestas were most damnably independent.

Alf stopped trying either to force or to feign sleep. He felt strange to himself, his new power shifting within him, begging to be freed again. Just for a moment; just for its pleasure. He almost smiled. That was the first danger any of his kind learned to face, the first bright wonder of a new art, when any small pretext seemed enough for its use. Late as he had come to his people, strong as he had been even then, and wise as the long years had made him, he was no more immune than any child to this elation of newborn magic. But a child had inborn defenses lost to the man grown: he tired swiftly, and he slept as now Cynan slept, all his fires banked and guarded.

Alf raised himself on one elbow. Jehan was snoring gently. Cynan curled like the pup he had been, back to the warmth. His thumb had worked its way into his mouth.

Love indeed could pierce like a sword, and its other edge was loss. The winning of his son only made the keener the absence of his lady and his daughter. It shore away the armor he had forged so carefully of hope and patience; it thrust deep into the soft heart beneath.

Hope and patience had gained him something. He had Anna; he had Cynan. The madman's caprice had cast them out as easily as it snatched them away. And Simon Magus did not know that his strongest enemy lived. He thought he had no opponent now, no one who could thwart him, only toys to be tormented as a cat torments a mouse.

But Thea had been able to hold him off. She had failed to trick him into discarding both her children. What now would he do to her? More: What would he do to Liahan?

Alf was on his feet. Four feet. The power, in the moment of its master's preoccupation, had had its way. The leopard's muscles drove him round the room in a restless prowl; the leopard's instincts cried to him to begin the hunt in earnest. But where? demanded the enchanter's brain. Neither Anna nor Cynan knew where they had been held prisoner. There could be no scent to follow, no spoor to lead him to his prey. Or could there?

He returned to the bed, setting his chin on its edge, measuring its occupants with his eyes. Cynan greeted the touch of his power with the faintest quiver of gladness, welcoming him into a dream of warmth and peace; his fetch filled it already, a towering shape armed and armored with light. Very gently he freed himself from the dream and advanced beyond it. The path he had taken before was blazed for him, but only for him. Once he sensed an intruder, a stab of something alien, repulsed too quickly for recognition. It might have been Simon Magus. It might have been merely a fugitive human thought loosed unwittingly in sleep.

Deeper and deeper. There waited the young alaunt, shifting as he approached, blurring into a multitude of forms. Carefully he skirted it. It tried to follow, but could not keep pace with his smooth leopard's stalk. With visible regret it turned back.

He had not far to go now. Deeper than this and he would be trapped, bound forever within Cynan's brain, or else repulsed with force enough to destroy them both. He must hold to the line, narrow as a sword's edge, tracing it with utmost care. Somewhere, if knowledge and instinct guided him truly, was a thread. A link like a birth-cord, tenuous as woven moonlight but strong as steel. Alun had had it. Gwydion, Aidan—they had it although time had thinned and faded it, the bond of a child borne in the body of an elf-woman, conceived and carried in power. Thea would have made it stronger in defending her children against the enemy, and perhaps Simon would not have known of it. It lay too deep and stretched too thin for easy finding.

There. Moonlight and steel, yes; a glint of bronze. An essence that was Thea, maddeningly faint.

He wavered on the sword's edge, rocked with longing for her. Grimly he willed himself to be still. One foot slipped. He clawed for safety. Caught the thread itself; clung. It began to bend. With all his inner strength, he flung himself back and out, but never letting go the bond. It was finer than thread, finer than hair, finer than spidersilk. One slip and it was lost, irrecoverable.

He had it. The alaunt's form flashed past. The levels of Cynan's mind flickered, higher and higher, growing brighter and shallower as he ascended. On the edge of Cynan's dream he forced a halt. Carefully, delicately, he wound the strand about his body. Then at last he flowed from spirit into altered flesh.

Exhaustion bowed him down. Urgency raised him, drove him toward the door. It was not latched; he nosed it open.

Man-scent filled his nostrils. His hackles rose; his lips wrinkled. Dimly he knew he should retreat, take his own shape. But the leopard's body had already borne him into the courtyard, oozing from shadow to shadow. His will sufficed only to drive it into a deeper shadow, the postern of the chapel. Someone had left the door propped ajar, whether for laziness or for some tryst. Warily he peered round the panel.

The whole world stank of man and of incense. He saw no one, heard nothing. Inch by inch he insinuated himself into a niche, an angle of wall between the foremost stall and the first step of the altar dais. Instinct as deep as the beast's caution bade him stop here, pray, seek Heaven's sanction for his hunt. None but God need ever know in what form he did it.

He moved into the light of the vigil lamp. The beast's mind screamed danger; the monk that was grew all the stronger for it, all the more determined to sanctify the hunt with holy words. He bowed as best he could, crouching with his head between his forepaws, lifting his eyes to the crucifix. It glimmered like the thread he must follow. *Let me find her,* he beseeched it. *Help me.*

* * *

Oddone woke too early for the Night Office, but with no desire to lie abed. He rose and put on his habit, and went to the chapel to meditate until the rest of the Brothers should come.

One, it seemed, was there already, a pale blur in front of the altar. But the Jeromite habit was brown. And this was not quite—He narrowed his weak eyes; he drew closer to it. No, it did not look like a man. Not at all. It looked like—

His breath hissed loud in the silence. The creature whipped about all of a piece, as a cat would. A cat as big as a mastiff, dappled white and silver like the moon.

Oddone was much too astounded to be afraid. One heard of saints who found creatures of the wood worshipping at their altars, particularly on Christmas night. But not in Lent and not in Rome, and certainly not any creature as uncanny as this. It must have been a leopard, if any leopard could be so huge and so very pale.

He crossed himself slowly, in large part to see what would happen. The beast did not burst in a shower of sparks. Not that he had honestly expected it to. He was sure it had been praying.

It did not attack. It watched him, in fact, if not with benevolence—those eyes were far too fierce for that—at least without hostility. He knelt with considerable care, as close as he dared, and crossed himself again. Bowing his head, he gathered his wits. He had come after all to pray, not to stare at a prodigy.

His wits, gathered, kept scattering. The leopard bulked huge in the middle of them. His throat knew exactly where its fangs would close, if it decided rather to be a good leopard than a good Christian. He was not the stuff of which saints were made, secure in the knowledge of God's protection; his reason knew it, to be sure, but his instincts could not so easily be persuaded. His eyes opened of themselves and shot a glance sidewise.

No leopard. No—

A man. He sat on his heels as if exhausted, head and shoulders bowed, long pale hair hiding his face. Not that Oddone needed to see it, or knew surprise when it lifted to reveal itself. "Signor' Alfred," he said quite calmly.

"Brother," was the calm response. Alf crossed himself, bowed low to the altar, flowed and melted. His eyes, Oddone noticed, were the same in the beast as in the man. They lidded; the great strange creature turned and lost itself in darkness. Oddone sent a prayer after it, for charity.

27

❦

The earth quaked. Towers fell; mountains split and belched forth fire. "Jehan!" they roared. "Father Jehan, for God's sake!"

He tumbled into wakefulness, heart thudding with urgency, body half erect. The world was quite solidly still; the bed had stopped its rocking. Anna looked ready to begin again, with ample help from a wild-eyed Nikki; he saw someone else behind them, a girl he did not know, who looked a little weary and more than a little troubled, but considerably saner than the rest. He addressed her with all the politeness he could muster this close to sleep. "Your pardon, demoiselle, but what exactly is the trouble?"

She understood his *langue d'oeil*, but she answered in Latin. "I'm not sure I know, Father. We were in my house talking, and Nikephoros went all wild; he pulled Anna out of bed and ran here."

Nikki's impatience was as fierce as a slap. *It's Alf. He's gone. Vanished. Lost. I can't find him in my mind at all.*

Jehan looked about somewhat stupidly. "He's not here. Where—" His brain caught up with his tongue at last. He shook his sleep-sodden head and yawned until his jaw cracked. "Gone, you say? What do you mean?"

He's always in my mind, Nikki said, *on the edges, like a wall. But suddenly, a little while ago, he dropped away. Just like that. Completely.*

"He was here." Jehan started to rise, paused. Mutely Anna handed him his shirt. He pulled it over his head, and stood to put on his habit. The stranger, who must have been Nikki's Stefania, regarded his bulk with a great deal of respect, but she answered his smile with one both fine and fearless. "Maybe he's just gone to the chapel. It's almost time for Night Office; and you know how absolutely he can concentrate on his prayers."

"We looked," Anna said flatly. "He's not there."

And when he prays, he's more there than ever. Nikki's mind-voice snapped out with sudden force. *Cynan! Where is your father?*

Bright eyes peered from amid a nest of blankets. There was no sleep in them, nor any alarm. *Gone,* Cynan answered. *He's looking for Mother.*

Jehan caught Nikki before he could bolt, and held him fast. The boy was as quick as a cat, but he was no match for sheer Norman muscle. "Calm down, lad. You're not going to get him back with your temper."

When Nikki had held still for a long count of breaths, Jehan set him down. The look he shot from beneath his lowered brows promised dire vengeance. But not quite yet. Deliberately, carefully, he said, *My brother has gone stark raving mad. Even if he can find Thea, even if the trail is no delusion, the enemy will surely know he hunts. He doesn't have me, and he doesn't have my art. He can't make himself invisible.*

"He seems to have done just that," Jehan pointed out.

"Then Simon Magus has him." Anna sank down to the tumbled bed, rubbing her temples as if they ached. "I was afraid of this. We were let go too easily. We were bait, I think. Or Cynan was."

He appeared beside her on all fours and climbed into her lap. Clumsily he patted her cheek. *Don't cry, Anna. He's strong. He won't let the other one win.*

He won't have any choice, Nikki said bitterly. Stefania went to him in silence. He hid his face in her hair.

A new voice broke the tableau, a faint tuneless voice, trembling with shyness. "Please," it said. "Brother Jehan, please, I—"

Oddone looked like a frightened rabbit, shocked into immobility by the sight of two strangers. Two *women,* here, staring at him until he could hardly think. But he had his own kind of courage. He repeated Jehan's name, albeit in a dying fall.

"Brother Oddone." Jehan spoke gently as to an animal, careful to betray neither surprise nor dismay. God alone knew what the man had heard, and God knew what he thought of it. "Come in, Brother, don't be afraid. This is Nikephoros' sister, and this is his good friend, a lady of your own city. They've brought news that couldn't wait for morning."

As if Jehan's words had been beckoning hands, Oddone ventured into the room. A step, two, three. A deep breath; he plunged the full distance, all the way to the brazier with the women on the other side of it. The color came and went in his face. He kept his eyes fixed on Jehan, who was solid, male, and blessedly familiar. "Brother, I heard what you were saying. About—about the Lord Alfred. How he hunts. I saw him when he went."

Nikki started forward. Stefania caught him. He stood stock-still.

The monk blinked. His weak eyes looked dazzled; he smiled, remembering. "He was a wonder to see. He prayed, and I know God heard him. I saw him change. Is his the sort of quarry that were better hunted by a leopard?"

"A *what?*" Jehan burst out before he thought.

"A leopard," Oddone repeated patiently. "I saw a leopard praying in the chapel. Then it was Signor' Alfred, then it was a leopard again. He looked deeply troubled, but I think God comforted him a little."

"But Alf can't—" Anna began.

He can now. Nikki chewed his lip. He seemed a little calmer. *It might have worked. It just might.*

"What?" Jehan spoke for all of them.

Nikki shook his head, clearing it. *If a person—if a witch changes shape, sometimes, with care, he can seem a beast to the mind as to the eye. It's not invisibility, but it's close enough.* His face tightened again. *But it can't work. A leopard prowling Rome—why couldn't he have had the sense to be an ordinary cat?*

A cat is too small, said Cynan.

A leopard is too damnably big. Especially that one. All but albino in the middle of the night, terrorizing the city . . . Damn him for a lovestruck fool.

"The city isn't terrorized yet, is it?" Jehan had to be reasonable. Otherwise he would lie down and howl.

Nikki sat beside his sister. Dropped, in truth, as if he could no longer muster the strength to stand. *Is that the way we'll all go? One by one, without hope or help? Maybe I should simply turn myself in. Simon won't touch the rest of you, I don't think. It's witches he wants.*

Jehan scowled, pulling at his beard. Even Cynan seemed to have caught Nikki's despair, drooping in Anna's lap, shivering slightly. She gathered her cloak about him with absentminded competence.

"This," Stefania said clearly, "has gone far enough. Not that I understand precisely what's happening, but it seems to me that you aren't trying very hard to fight back."

We can't, Nikki muttered.

"Have you tried?" She rounded on Jehan. "Father, will you tell me what all of this is supposed to mean?"

Jehan hesitated only briefly. She knew too much as it was; the rest could not hurt. It might even help. She looked like an extraordinarily intelligent woman. Swiftly and succinctly he told the tale; when he had gone as far as he could, Anna took his place. None of it seemed to shock her, but then she had heard the worst of it already.

She had sat down while they spoke, taking Alf's customary chair by the brazier. She remained there after they finished. Her eyes when she pondered were the deepest of blues, almost black; she would have looked forbidding if she had not nibbled, childlike, on the end of her braid. "This Simon," she said slowly. "Anna, did you ever see anyone else but him and his master? No one ever looked in, or seemed to be outside when the others were with you?"

"No," Anna answered. "No." The second time she was less firm. "I never saw anyone else."

Stefania frowned. "That's very odd, you know. They held you prisoner for so long even before they let you see them, and then Simon at least was there almost constantly. But you weren't held in a hut somewhere apart from the world. You say the passage was long and full of doors."

"And with a door at the end."

"Open?"

"Open." That struck Anna; she sat up straighter, her brow wrinkling as she called back the memory. "I saw light beyond. It looked like daylight, though it was dim. We couldn't have been in a deep dungeon. But I don't see how——"

"The other doors. What were they like?"

"Doors. All on one side, the same side as ours. Only ours had a bolt. The rest were simply latched. They didn't look as if anyone ever used them."

"You were on the edge of—something. Where no one else seemed to go."

"A fortress," Jehan said.

"Or a ruin." Anna frowned. "It did look old. But not decrepit. You'll bear in mind that the one time I escaped, I wasn't noticing much, and the light was bad. And Rome is full of well-preserved relics."

Stefania nodded. "So it is. But no relic in that state of repair can be unclaimed. If we can learn where the Paulines have their houses——"

"It need not be a Pauline possession," Jehan pointed out. "The Order has a number of powerful friends. But we've been exploring every possible avenue for weeks now. If any human being knew where our people are, if any prince or prelate had given our enemies leave to keep prisoners in his domain, we'd have known it long since."

Unless Simon prevented it. Nikki straightened. *Isn't any of you taking time to wonder what sent Alf out so suddenly, without even calling me to help? He wouldn't have gone blindly. He must have known where he was going.*

"Simon let him catch a glimpse of Thea," Anna suggested. "Simon hates him, you know. Maybe because they're so much alike. Could they be brothers, Father Jehan? Alf's never known either of his parents, and Simon never knew his father."

Jehan shuddered. Somehow he could not face the prospect of a renegade enchanter roaming the world and begetting sons, and never tarrying to see what became of them. Even if one had grown into Alf. It was too heedless. Too inhuman.

Nikki's eye caught him. Inhuman? How many mortal lords did just that? Not to mention legions of soldiers and wanderers and clerics.

God's bones, Jehan thought. A wandering wizard-monk without morals or scruples—now there was a vision to make a strong man quake. "And it's useless," he said roughly. "Wherever they came from, we've got the grown men to contend with, and I think we can assume that they're about to come face to face if they haven't already. So what's to be done? How did Alf know where to go?"

He's in me, Cynan said. As they all turned upon him, he flinched, baring his teeth like the hound he had been. *He follows the birth-bond. The thread that ties me to my mother. You're not to go after him, and you can't find the bond. It's down too deep and it's much too thin. He says you have to wait here and be patient, and if he needs you, you'll know.*

He says? He commands? Nikki's own lips had drawn back. *What does he think we are?*

Human. Cynan said it without scorn, but without gentleness. It was a plain fact. *Don't think things at me. It won't help.*

Won't it?

Jehan came between them, bulking large. "Leave the boy alone, Nikephoros. He's only obeying his father. As, it seems, the rest of us will have to do. While we wait, I suppose we can pray."

We can always pray, Nikki growled, but he let Cynan be. *We've talked straight through your damned Night Office. Are you going to drag us all to Matins?*

"Only those who want or need it," Jehan responded, unperturbed. "Brother Oddone, I'm sorry we've kept you here."

The monk's eyes were shrinking at last to their normal dimensions; he even smiled. "Oh, no, Brother, it's my fault. I heard the bell, but it was all so fascinating . . . Do you mind if I stay a little longer? I'd like to see what happens, if I can."

"Stay and welcome," Jehan said. He meant it, which surprised him a little. The man was frail, and mortal, and probably in great peril of his vows if not of his immortal soul. But there was an obscure comfort in the presence of another habit among these Greeks and witches. It was a talisman of sorts. A shield against the uncanny.

Or at the very least, someone to talk to while Nikki brooded and Cynan drowsed and the women whispered and giggled about—of all things—Pliny the Elder. Not that Jehan was either averse to or ignorant of natural philosophy, but not in the dark before dawn, with Alf gone and no present hope of getting him back again. Oddone's gentle chatter was a rest and a relief, and in this black hour, more blessed than sleep.

28

Alf, hot on the scent, was aware of little else. As in the scriptorium, he let his body do as it willed, which was to hunt in the manner of a great cat, flowing from shadow to shadow, silent itself as a shadow. If anyone saw him, his observer thought him a dream, or else fled in superstitious terror. The leopard would have delighted in a kill, if not of a man then of the donkey that brayed and fought and overturned its cart, or of one of the dogs that ran yelping from his path; but the enchanter promised sweeter prey at the end of the hunt.

The thread had grown till it was as wide as a road, as blindingly brilliant as a bolt of lightning. Even had he wished to, he could not turn away from it. *Thea.* Her name sang in his bones. *Thea Damaskena.* Soon he would have her. Soon his power would be whole again. He would be healed, strong, made anew. Then let the Magus do what he would.

His body was running easily, exulting in its smooth swiftness. He was close now. The scent was strong enough to taste, almost unbearably sweet. *Thea, Thea Damaskena.*

Leopard's caution brought him up short. Leopard's instinct

made him one with deep shadow. Mind and body met with a bruising shock; he crouched flat, every sense forcing itself to the alert. He realized dimly that not only his eyes were his own; he had taken his proper shape. Sometime very soon, he was going to have to take this new power in hand.

He lay in a tangle of thicket. About him was wasteland, dark under a hard glitter of stars. Before him bulked a great shape of blackness. He sharpened his eyes. There was the loom of a castle, rough and raw and new yet backed and guarded by Roman walls. Part of those lay in ruins, but much was solid still, transcribing a shape he knew.

He swallowed bitter laughter. Many a day from San Girolamo's campanile he had looked straight into this open grassy vale with its long oval of walls. Once it had been the Great Circus of the city, his thicket its center, the spine of stone that had brought so many hurtling chariots to grief. And there in its curving end was the castle whose tower had seemed to stare at him, awkward bastard child of old Rome. Somewhere in or about it, in full sight of the long vigil, lay his lady and his daughter.

They slept within their strong walls, the Frangipani princes. None seemed to know what prisoners they held. Nor what approached them, a man moving as a leopard would move, his white skin dappled with mud and starlight. The scent led him round the castle itself, past the frown of the gate toward the older walls. The ranks of seats were gone, fallen or taken, but the skeleton remained; and it was thicker than it had seemed. Of course; there would have been a webwork of passages and chambers, stables, storage places for fodder and harness. Not the mighty labyrinth of the Colosseum, maybe, that had brought Nikki back one night in a fever of excited discovery, but space enough and more to hide two women and two children. And who need ever know? Not the Frangipani, secure in their fortress. Not the few folk who dwelt on this the edge of the populous places. Not ever the hunters quartered so close and never suspecting that their quarry lay in plain sight.

He paused in the lee of the wall. From here it seemed immensely long and high, impossibly complex. The scent that had been so strong was fading fast. The thread was thread again, thin as a spider's. He sped along it, abandoning both caution and concealment. Beast-shape would be faster, but flight was faster still. He spurned the earth, flung himself upon air, wingless yet swifter than any bird.

He nearly overshot the mark: an arch far down the wall, across the field from the place where he had begun. Of all the many arches, this one alone cried out to him; it gaped blackly, his height and more above the ground. He hovered before it, shaping light to see within.

A door shut. An axe fell. A great force severed thread and power together. He fell like a stone and lay stunned, blind and deaf.

With infinite slowness his sight restored itself. He could move. Nothing had broken, although every bone felt as if it had been stretched upon the rack. He dragged himself to hands and knees, to knees alone, to his feet. The arch yawned above him. The wall beneath, cracked and crannied, offered hand- and footholds. Grimly he attacked it.

This dark was no natural lightlessness. Starlight should have been enough even for cat-eyes, more than enough for witch-sight. But he was as blind as any human, groping his way down a stone passage with no power to guide him. Was this what it was to be human? Blind, deaf, wrapped in numbness.

The floor dropped away. Once more he fell, once more he lay on the edge of oblivion until pain dragged him back. This rising was harder by far; when he walked, he walked lame. But again his bones were intact, his steps steadying as the pain faded to a dull and endurable ache. He moved more slowly now, with greater care. Another fall might break him indeed; and being what he was, he would not die easily. He could lie long ages in agony before his enemy came to add to his torment, or until death claimed him at last.

Light.

His eyes mocked him with hope. No; it was growing. It flickered. Torchlight. Dimly at first, then more clearly, he saw what lay about him. A long passage a little wider than his arms' stretch, a little higher than he could reach. It was not Anna's passage; no doors broke the featureless walls. What it had been, what it was meant for, he had no wits left to guess.

He stumbled toward the light. It illumined a stair, a short downward flight. The torch was old, ready to gutter out, but he wrenched it from the crack into which it had been thrust. With it in his grip, he felt slightly stronger. He could move more quickly, indeed he must, before the light died.

Another stair. Upward. At last, a door, bolted. With ruthless, furious strength, he tore bolt and bars from their housings. Satisfaction warmed him, stronger than regret; his muscles at least had not lost their power, whatever had become of his mind and his senses. He strode through the broken door.

He was close now. This must once have been an entryway into the arena, a wider space bordered with arches. One was blocked with rubble and rough brickwork. The other, though barred below, offered a thin half-circle of open sky. Alf paused, drawing clean air into his lungs, drinking in strength. He advanced more steadily than before into a passage which, oddly, seemed less dark. In a little while he was certain. His power was returning. Even before his torch sputtered and died, he had no need of it; he saw clearly enough.

Yet another stair descended below the level of the ground, but its ceiling was a sloping shaft roofed with stars. The passage at its foot ended in a second door. This bolt he slid back almost gently, knowing what he would find.

This was Anna's corridor. The blank wall would face the outer world, the rim of the Circus. The doors would open upon chambers and new passages. There were not as many doors as she had remembered, perhaps at Simon's connivance—three or four at most, and the one, the one that mattered, set with a grille that scattered golden light against the wall.

Alf's heart hammered. His palms were cold, his head light. If this was all a grim deception, if they were gone, or if they had never been there at all—

The cell, the vaulted ceiling, the cluster of lamps, he had seen them through Anna's eyes. The pallet lay as she had recalled. On it . . .

He never remembered the door's opening. Perhaps he had simply willed himself through it. She was asleep or unconscious in her own beautiful shape, her white skin glimmering, her hair a tangle of silk, bronze and gold. Slowly he drew near. His mind uncurled a tendril, poised for any sorcerous assault, meeting none. With infinite delicacy it touched her.

Her eyes opened, all gold. "So early?" she murmured, still half in sleep, reaching drowsily to draw him down. As their lips touched, all sleep fled. Her grip tightened to steel; her warmth turned to fire. She clutched him with fierce strength, yet no stronger or fiercer than he, as if one madly joyous embrace could wipe away all the days apart.

Neither knew who cooled first to sanity, he or she. They were body to body still, flesh to burning flesh, but eye met eye with passion laid aside. He was above her, stroking her hair out of her face. She traced his cheek; frowned; followed the long beloved line down neck and shoulder and breast to count each jutting rib. "Alfred of Saint Ruan's," she demanded sharply, "what have you done to yourself?" She did not wait for an answer, if answer he could have given. She thrust him from her, rising in her turn above him, glaring down. "Look at you. A skeleton. And here. You idiot. You utter, hopeless idiot."

For all her wrath, and it was wrath indeed, her eyes had filled and overflowed. He kissed the tears away. She slapped at him; he kissed her palms. "You *fool!* This is exactly where he wants you."

"And where I want you." Not all the tears were hers. He laughed through them. "Thea. Thea Damaskena. I was dying, and now I live again."

"Not for long," she snapped. "He laid the bait, and you took it, royally. And all you can think of is the fire between your legs."

"Of course. It maddens him." Alf cupped her breasts in his hands. They were fuller than ever he remembered, infinitely sweet. "He'll be here soon. Shall we give him something to watch?"

"You're mad."

"I'm challenging him."

"You're suicidal." He laughed; she struck him again, not lightly. "He has Liahan. He came, freed me from the hound's body, took her away."

That killed his laughter, if not his ardor. "When?"

"After he flung Anna out and Cynan with her. Baited his hook, I should say. Liahan is his hostage. He'll kill her if you threaten him."

"Maybe not." He caught her hips, eased her down upon him. She gasped, half in resistance, half in desire. Resistance died as desire mounted. In the joining of their bodies she saw what he saw, weaving into his mind, filling all his emptiness as he filled hers, body and soul. They were whole again, both, in high and singing joy, nor could even his power of prophecy, reborn, cast it down to earth.

Joined, they held Simon at bay; their loving repelled him more completely than any shield of power. But even witch-strength could not suffice to prolong their union much beyond the mortal span. They lay entwined, the aftermath made sweeter for that there might never be another, and smiled at the one who had come to destroy them.

"Whore." Simon's voice did not sound in Alf's ears as his own did, but that proved nothing. It was certainly light for a man's, and it was purer than a human's would have been, even raw with outrage. And yes, the face was like the one he met when compelled to face a mirror, yet older, stronger, less girlish-fair. This one had grown to full manhood, had not frozen just on the verge of it, caught forever between boy and man.

In body, perhaps. In mind . . .

Alf rose, setting himself eye to eye. Simon's nostrils thinned and whitened. He flung something in Alf's face, a tangle that sorted into twin robes of unbleached wool. They were considerably finer than pilgrim's garb. Alf donned the larger, which fit well, and waited as Thea slipped into the smaller. "The last of God's Hounds who jailed me," he observed, "would not besmirch his habit by clothing me in it."

"The rules have relaxed," said Thea coolly, "since one of our kind found his way more or less legitimately into the Order." She circled Alf's waist with her arm, leaning against him with easy intimacy, stroking the soft wool that clung to his thigh. "Delicate skins, the Paulines must have. This makes the Jeromite habit feel like sackcloth."

"Saint Jerome's Brothers tend to be a shade austere." Alf regarded Simon with the suggestion of a smile. "Saint Paul, however, was the champion of moderation. In all things."

"You are abominable." Simon looked as if he were fending off violent sickness. "How could you do—*that*—"

The smile grew clearer. "Quite easily after such a parting; and for a long while before it, my lady was too great with the children to—" Alf stopped; he flushed faintly. "Ah, Brother, your pardon. I've been in the world so long, I've forgotten proper priestly discretion."

"You have forgotten nothing."

"Maybe, after all, I have not." The smile was gone. Alf's eyes were cool, his voice level. "I forget very little. Forgiveness is another matter."

"Do you think you can challenge me?"

"I do. I am. I challenge you, Brother Simon of the Order of Saint Paul. I bid you release my lady and my daughter. I command you to cease your harrying of my people."

" 'Canst thou bind the sweet influences of the Pleiades, or loose the bonds of Orion? Knowest thou the ordinances of Heaven? canst thou set the dominion thereof in the earth?' "

Alf's eyes glittered; he laughed. "Are you so mighty then, kinsman? 'Hast thou an arm like God? or canst thou thunder with a voice like him?' "

"I am the voice of God."

"Pride, my brother, has cast down greater powers than yours."

"I shall cast you down, demon, mock me though you will."

Simon stepped away from the open door. In it stood Brother Paul, languid as ever, and in his arms the still form of Liahan. Her eyes were open but dull. Her alaunt's body was limp. The monk stroked her steadily, a smile growing as Alf stared. "Good morning, my lord Chancellor," he said.

Alf stood taut, seeing him hardly at all, only his habit and his intent and the creature he cradled with such deceptive care. "If you have harmed my daughter—"

"Yes," Brother Paul cut him off lightly. "If we have. What then, my lord? What can you do? It won't be as it was before, I can assure you. No mere mortal men hold you captive; no king will ride to your rescue. This time, at last, the Order will have its revenge."

"You have a most un-Christian memory for slights."

"Slights, sir? Is it so you reckon it? By your doing we are banned from the whole isle of Britain; with your aid we were forbidden to enter Rhiyana. You've had no small part in the quashing of our Order, Alfred of Saint Ruan's."

"I'd lie if I professed remorse." Alf focused above the habit upon the florid face. Anna had been unduly prejudiced; it was a handsome face, if not at all in the mold of the Kindred. The accent, he noticed, was Anglian, but as for the man: "Surely you're not old enough to have been one of my inquisitors."

"I admit, I never had the honor. But I was there." Brother Paul's smile was rich with malice. "Brother Reynaud gave a good account of himself with the whip. He's still alive, you know. Still laughing, save now and then when he howls like a beast. When our postulants need to know what would become of humanity under your people's sway, they're taken to see him. It's very effective. The weak flee our walls in dread of a like fate. The strong grow all the more determined to destroy your kind."

"If you were there, you know that that was none of my doing."

"No? I ventured a test once. I drove a man to attack Simon. He went mad likewise. He died; but after all, Simon is stronger than you. Also, I think, more honestly merciful. I certainly would prefer death to the life Reynaud has lived since he ran afoul of you."

Alf's eyes had narrowed as the monk spoke. Memory was stirring, stripping away years. Evading the horror of a truth he had never known or wanted to know, that in return for the scars on his back he had broken a man's mind.

It was a trap, that truth, meant to break his will. He made himself see, made himself find the name this monk had had. He had been a youth then, dark and slender, languid-eyed, all sweet malevolence. "Joscelin. Joscelin de Beaumarchais." He shook his head, not incredulous, not precisely, but much bemused. "You had chosen the Benedictines, I thought. For the wine and the women and the boys when you wanted them. Whatever made you turn to Saint Paul?"

Brother Paul, who had once been a squire of the Lionheart, smiled the smile Alf remembered. The years had done nothing to abate its malice. "The wine and the women turned out not to be so forthcoming, and I lost my taste for boys. Your fault too, sir sorcerer. A beautiful boy was never quite so beautiful after I saw your face, and no man could ever come up to the king you robbed me of. At last I had to conceive a new lust. I went in search of power. What Saint Benedict had, seemed to me to lack spice. Saint Paul, on the other hand, offered power of a very peculiar kind, power to judge men's souls; and he didn't ask me to be a barefoot fanatic."

"And he led you to another beautiful boy," Thea said.

The monk laughed softly. "He led me to a power I hardly dared dream of. Imagine my thoughts when a vagabond stumbled into the abbey where I lodged, hardly a fortnight past my acceptance into my new Order; and that wandering madman was obviously, unmistakably an enchanter. A young one with no will at all of his own. He thought I was God. He thinks so still, nor can he be shaken."

"You were a contemptible boy. You've become an evil man."

He regarded her as she stood there with defiance on her face, holding to Alf as if she would be both protector and protected. "You could argue that I'm the instrument of God's will. Simon does so incessantly. I'm content to do as I please. In the end, who knows? Saint Peter's throne may be beyond me, but the generalship of Saint Paul's brethren is not."

"Unless," Alf said gently, "yon beast of burden flings you from his back."

"Was I ever averse to a good gamble?"

"Your luck, as I recall, was never remarkably good. The meek little monk you caught for your sport turned vicious and brought about your downfall."

"But now I have him again, and I don't intend to let him go. You made my fortune before, in your crooked way. You'll do so again." Brother Paul raised the hand with which he had been petting Liahan. "Simon. Take him."

On guard though Alf had been, the force of Simon's power smote him to the ground. For all the strength of his resistance, he might have been a child's doll made of sticks and sent to battle against the sea. His shields were useless, his defenses vain. He was utterly, hopelessly outmatched.

Somewhere far away, Thea was speaking. Spitting words: defiance, maledictions. As easily as a man separates two newborn kittens, Simon held her apart from her lover.

Alf rolled onto his back. Simon gazed down, expressionless. "Get up," he said.

Alf obeyed by no will of his own. It was all he could do to keep his head up, to speak without a tremor. "Is it thus you treat your brother?"

"We are no kin," Simon said. Did his voice break a very little?

"We are brothers, if not in blood, then in kind. Look at me, Simon. See that it is so."

"I see that you cannot overcome me. You can only plead with me."

Alf spread his hands. "Destroy me then. Am I not entirely in your power?"

"Entirely." Simon's face contorted; he shuddered. "You are so much—like—"

"So much like you. Slay me, my brother. Has not God commanded it? Cast me into the everlasting fire."

"Silence him," Paul commanded swiftly. His voice seemed to come from very far away. "He is ancient, my son, ancient in his evil. Silence his serpent's tongue lest it turn you from the very face of God."

Alf felt the closing of his throat, the freezing of his tongue. But he could smile. He could set his hands on the other's shoulders. They were narrower than his own, although the man seemed sturdy enough, lean rather than slender. *Brother,* his will said. *Brother.*

Simon struck the hands away, struck Alf to his knees. "Like," he whispered. "So like." He bent, searching the lifted face. His fist caught it. It rocked, steadied, blinked away tears of pain. Fair though the skin was, the bruise did not rise swiftly enough. His power uncoiled. It reached, at once delicate and brutal. It clenched; it twisted.

Alf gasped, more in surprise than in pain. He could not feel—he felt—

His face itched. Small annoyance; it baffled him. Simon was

watching with terrible fascination. He raised a trembling hand. The skin had roughened. No. Had grown—was growing—

He laughed for pure mirth. After all these long years, after all the taunts and all the doubts and all his hard-won acceptance, he was sprouting a beard. A soft one as beards went, but thick and growing as sturdily as Jehan's had that night in Caer Gwent.

Simon did not take kindly to his merriment. For that alone he kept it up. His voice was deeper. His skin felt harsher. Were his bones heavier? His hands were slender still, but not as slender as they had been. They were becoming a man's hands. Pale hair thickened on the backs of them. He itched elsewhere, his belly, his deepening chest. He was a little taller; a little broader. His beard was growing, curling, white-gold as the hair of his head.

His laughter faded. His knees ached. His back twinged, not scarred skin alone but the bones within. The skin on his hands coarsened. The joints knotted. Veins and tendons rose into relief. A tooth began to throb. His tongue, probing, found it loose. He was aging. Like a mortal man, but faster, far faster, a whole lifetime in a moment. Eyes and ears were dulling. His head was too heavy for his neck. Having grown, now he shrank and shriveled, trembling with the palsy of age.

His vision spun, staggered, sharpened to a bitter clarity. Simon had lent his own eyes. On the floor huddled an old, old man, a man who had lived every one of Alfred's many years.

And yet he was not pitiable. He was—yes, he was still comely, and the eyes in the age-ravaged face, though faded, kept much of their old brightness. There was no fear in them.

Again he dwelt behind them in the wreck of his body. Not an ill body even yet, and not an utter ruin. He could stand, with great effort. He could smile. He could wield a voice not thinned overmuch, not indeed much higher than it had ever been. "Alas, Brother Simon, you'll never slay my vanity until you slay me."

Simon's rage roared over him in blood-red fire. He tumbled over and over, helpless, but not, by God, not ever afraid.

The hand that held him from the floor was his own again, smooth and long-fingered. His cheeks bore only the merest downy suggestion of a beard. His teeth lay quiescent in their places; his voice, though well broken, was a clear young tenor. "My thanks, brother. In spite of its disadvantages, I do prefer this semblance. And now," he said, raising himself, hardening his tone, "and now I think there has been enough of this entertainment. Simon of Montefalco, monk of

Guillt Paul, kinsman of Rhiyana's King, I call you to the reckoning."

He had taken Simon by surprise. "You have no power—"

"I have the right. The Church does not deny fair trial to any, even to such as I. Let that trial, by my choice, be trial by combat."

"You cannot help but lose."

"If so," Alf said, "then so be it. I would far rather die in battle than at the stake."

Thea flung herself to her knees beside him. No one hindered her. Simon was motionless, unreadable; Paul frowned, searching transparently for a trick, finding none. She gripped Alf's shoulders with fierce strength. Although she knew that Simon would hear, she spoke in Alf's ear, just above a hiss. "Have you forgotten the children? Have you forgotten me?"

"Never," he answered, equally low. "Thea, we're all dead, one way or another. But I won't sell our lives cheaply. I'm going to try at the very least to mark him, to give him a wound that he will not forget."

Her breath hissed between her teeth. She glared into his eyes, her own as fiery dark as old bronze. He tried to speak to her below thought, to the place in his soul that was hers and hers alone. A hut of mud and wattle beset by a battering ram; a woman's hand upon a tapestry, embroidering the petals of a flower. And, as clearly as he dared, a small furred creature gnawing away the roots of an oak.

Despair shook him. She did not see. Her eyes and her mind held only anger, outrage, frustration. "I'm fighting beside you," she said, biting off the words. "You can't stop me."

He lifted one shoulder. His finger brushed the stiff set of her lips. They would not soften. "Whatever comes of this, know you well, Thea Damaskena, I regret not one moment of all our years together."

"Not one, Alfred of Saint Ruan's?"

"After all," he said, considering each word, "not one." He kissed her lightly, and then more deeply. When he rose she remained upon her knees, her face rigid, white as bone. He turned to Simon. "I am ready."

For an eternal while, Simon simply stood. Perhaps he prayed. Perhaps he hoped to lure Alf into attack. Alf was not to be lured. His formal praying was long past, the rest left to God. Fear had died to a steady roaring beneath the surface of his brain. He simply waited as he had waited for so long, with watchful patience. His shields were up, but lightly. His power gathered hard and bright and pulsing behind them.

He shifted his sight. The flawed hemisphere of his eyes' vision grew and rounded. But he saw no more and no better. Simon filled the world like the sun unbound, raging from pole to pole. It had consumed its own center, the mastering will. It was consuming the body that bore it. Unchecked, it could consume all that was. Could, although in the doing it would destroy itself.

Alf's fear howled within its chains, swelling into terror. He had never stood so close to death. Had never dreamed, even when he faced the stake, that dissolution could come so close.

He had never met a power greater than his own. He let wonder rise above the fear, riding on it, arming himself with it. If that mighty strength could be tamed, what a marvel it would be; what splendors it would engender. He shaped the wonder and the vision. He made them into a spear hafted and tipped with light. He cast them forth with all the strength of his compassion.

Simon struck as a man strikes at an insect, with casualness close to contempt. Alf's shields locked; he staggered but kept his feet. His dart had pierced its target. The sun-flare dimmed. A flicker only, scarcely to be seen.

The power lashed out in sudden rage. Alf dropped shields and fled. Wherever he turned, the power waited. He flung himself at it. Not as a spear, not as a sword, but as a rush of gentleness: a soft wind, a fall of water. He whispered through the walls. He flowed round the striking hand. He took shape in a zone of stillness within walls of fire.

Simon waited there as he waited in the world that men called real. "Wherever you go," he said, "I am."

Alf stepped forward. Simon drew no closer. Alf's body, illusion that it was, shaped and firmed by his will, had begun to fray. Just so had it been when he had lost the key to the change, when his form stretched and quivered and all his being wavered, poised on the border of formlessness. The same dread; the same black panic rising to master him, to fling him back, to set both body and soul in immutable stone.

Stone itself flowed like water, water dissolved into air, air sublimed into fire. He was trapped, caught in the center of Simon's power. There was no anchor, nothing solid or stable, no shape or focus or center. Death—not the death the Church foretold, the soul freed whole and glorious from the encumbering body. This was the death of the soulless. Decay; dissolution. Ashes to ashes, dust to dust, and a wind of fire sweeping away the last feeble fragments. But not into oblivion, nothing so simple or so merciful. He was aware. Lost, scattered, milliontold, he knew that he was, he knew that he suffered, he knew that he knew.

Of the myriad motes that had been the self called Alfred, one lone speck clung to light and will. It was no more than a thought, a wordless awareness. Not for his kind could there be any hope of Heaven, but Hell, it seemed, waited for them as for mortal men. If the wordless could have encompassed itself in words, it would have protested like a child. *It's not fair!*

A second mote drifted toward the first. *Fair,* it keened, *not.* A third. A fourth. *Not.* A fifth. Ten, twenty, a hundred. *Just.* Half a thousand. *Unjust.* A thousand. *Why for us only Hell? Why are we granted no entry into Heaven?*

Thought spawned thought. Raw protest transmuted into logic. Logic begot reason, and reason remembrance. Remembrance, and pain renewed. He had found form, and that form was a scream.

Pain was real. Pain was a center. Dissolution, dissolved, wrought stability. He clung, and clinging, grew; and the pain grew, waking into agony, and from agony into piercing pleasure.

He must endure. He knew not why. He knew only *must.* Though it wracked his newborn self, though it tore with claws of iron, though it cried to him to let go, he only clasped it closer.

He was mind amid pain. He was body. He was flesh flayed raw; and a hand closed about it, waking agony beyond even pleasure— ineffable, unendurable. And he could not lose consciousness; he had none to lose. He could not even go mad.

The hand tightened. Caught writhing on the very pinnacle of torment, he did the simplest of things. He wished himself gone.

Absence of pain was more terrible by far than its eternal presence. He had a body; it lay gasping. It opened aching eyes.

The hands upon him eased but did not let go. Thea's. He was englobed in power still, and she with him, and even as their eyes met they mingled. Yet without fear, with full and joyous will, mind to mind and body to body, he and she, they, one mind and one power. One body likewise, he and she, shifting, steadying, *she.* But the eyes were his; the hand also, for a moment, exploring the strange-familiar shape, familiar from his long loving, strange for that now he dwelt in it. He felt his lips—her lips—curve in a smile. Her smile. They called forth their power.

29

The hour of Matins had come and gone. Jehan had not gone to sing the Office, nor had Oddone. Anna and Stefania had quieted at last, Anna drowsing, Stefania seeming to drowse by the cooling brazier. Nikki knew that it was only a seeming; that she watched him, oblivious as he feigned to be, and brooded. Considered what she had fallen into; wrestled with flat incredulity. It could not be as she imagined. There was Anna asleep, the monk and the priest all but asleep, Nikephoros pretending to sleep.

But there was Cynan wide awake, playing on the floor with a shadow and a bit of string. The shadow in his hands had substance, although when he let it go it was merely shadow. And when he turned toward the lamp, his eyes caught its light and flamed.

Nikki left the bed without thinking, went to her, sat at her feet. She could not muster a smile, but she touched his cheek with a fingertip. He laid his head in her lap. So simply he did it; so simply she accepted it. But she did not cease her brooding, nor did her touch linger.

Nikki snapped erect. Cynan too had heard it, that cry of unspeakable anguish. The child's form flickered. Nikki flung himself at it. Dimly, distantly, he knew the shock of a great weight falling upon him. Then weight and world were gone, swept away.

Cynan struggled, protesting. *Why do people always fall on top of me?* Nikki, crushed, had neither breath nor wits to answer.

The tangle sorted itself. The weight was Father Jehan, staggering up and shaking his head groggily. The world was strange, but familiarly strange, Anna's old prison. Between the newcomers and those who were there before them, it was full almost to bursting. Alf and Thea, clad alike in voluminous white, lay side by side with a stranger who bore Alf's face. Over them all and regarding the arrivals with surprise stood Brother Paul, with Liahan struggling in his grip.

She won free, scrambling round the still bodies. Cynan met her in mid-flight. Their bodies twisted and blurred and mingled. An alaunt, a manchild; a womanchild, an alaunt; twin alaunts, twin children side by side, her hand upon her mother's brow, his upon his father's. The scent of power was chokingly strong.

Jehan, never one to reflect when action was wiser, launched himself at Brother Paul. Nikki had not long to watch the battle royal. Power, the power he had met twice before and to his sorrow, had risen against him. The fourfold will of witch and witchling offered no such tempting target as one lone, bemused human creature, given power himself but never born to it, marked and sealed with mortality.

It was immeasurably strong and immeasurably cruel. *Human,* it mocked him. *Mortal man.* It showed him himself as in a mirror, but realer than any image cast upon glass: a shape of earth and clay, ill-made, incomplete, brother to the mute beast. But even a beast had five full senses.

His image cowered. It was rank with filth. A strangled moan escaped it, an unlovely sound bereft even of human music; and he himself less lovely still, a scrap of bone and hair, a lingering stink, a hint of the death that waited to claim him.

Far down in the hollow that had been his soul, something stirred. It looked like himself, yet not the sorry creature the mirror had shown him; the Nikephoros Stefania had dreamed of. It lifted its head; shook it slowly, then more firmly. Its jaw set, stubborn. Little by little, with effort that drew the lips back from the white teeth, it stood erect. Raised its arms. *Refused.*

The power over him, vast ebon hand, paused in its descent. He was conquered. How dared he resist?

He was human. He could not help but resist. Poor impotent half-cripple that he was, he hurled himself upon the hand, upon the mirror it held, upon the lying image.

The mirror shattered. The image hung in the mocking air, but it withered and shrank, melting away.

Wrath rose in a blood-red tide. He flung back his tangled hair; he turned half-crouched, searching, nurturing his fury. Father Jehan had his knee in the back of the stranger-monk, the man choking out a plea for mercy. The rest had not moved at all.

He was forgotten. His victory had been no true victory; he had been discarded in favor of a stronger opponent. In the moment of distraction the fourfold mind of his kin had drawn Simon in, had beset him with power even he could not despise.

Nikki did not try his own bruised power. His anger was growing, honing itself into perfection. Human, was he? Crippled, was he? But he had hands. And he had a weapon. No named blade, no sword of heroes, only the little silver-hafted knife he used at meat, but it was Damascus steel, slim and deadly sharp. Alf had given it to him when he grew from page into squire; it had a falcon graven on its blade. He drew it, seeking neither silence nor concealment, advancing upon Simon. No lightnings drove him back. No mighty force of power struck him down. He knelt beside the still body. It might have been asleep. So Alun had seemed to be upon his bier, but Alun's breast had not risen with a slow intake of breath. Alun had died by this man's will, for no more reason than that he was there to be slain.

Nikki raised the knife. Lamplight flamed upon the polished blade. He narrowed his eyes, shifted his grip upon the hilt. This was a just execution. This was Rhiyana's salvation. With all his strength he struck.

Steel fingers snapped shut about his wrist. Simon regarded him coolly, eyes focused full upon him. The power waged its war upon Rhiyana; shielded itself from Rhiyanan retribution; toyed with the little creatures who had bearded it in its lair. But it was losing patience. Its prey had learned not to confront it; teased it, eluded it, made itself four and two and one and greater-than-one. Strength mattered little in such a battle. Subtlety it had never studied. It had never needed to.

Nikki, caught, struggling vainly, saw Simon's focus sharpen; felt the power shake off a score of trivialities—a dozen forays against Rhiyana's walls, a handful of spies in Caer Gwent, a thought maturing in a cardinal's mind. Here was an anomaly. A human with power. A living being who dared to bring steel against the hand of God. Dared, and had not died.

He would die. Slowly. With effortless, ruthless strength, Simon snapped the boy's wrist.

And screamed. Nikki's mind, white with agony, had opened wide; and the eye of Simon's power was fixed upon him. The dart of pain plunged deep and deep and deep. Simon fell writhing, all his myriad magics crumbling, no room for aught in mind or body but the reverberation of pain.

Nikki won the mercy of unconsciousness. Not so Brother Simon. The pain had caught him and bound him in its ceaseless circle. He could not escape. He could not heal it. The body was not his own; Nikki's will, unconscious, still repelled him with blind persistence.

Alf fought free of the nightmare. They were all in a heap, he and his lady and his children. Gently but firmly he pried Liahan's arms from his neck. Witch-children were never beautiful; that came with blossoming into man or woman. Yet she was a lovely child, great-eyed, with a cloud of spun-silver hair about a solemn face. Poor infant, she had never learned to smile. He kissed her and set her with her brother in her mother's lap.

They were all in his mind, interwoven, as he knelt above Simon. *Now we can take him,* Thea said, and Cynan who was fully as fierce as she. Liahan was a wordless reluctance. Alf looked down at the body of the one who had wrought so much havoc, and considered justice. Considered vengeance. Remembered compassion.

He can't live! Thea cried. *Can't you feel it? He's working loose. The earth is trembling. The stars are beginning to wobble in their courses. When he's free, our deaths will be the very least of it.*

He knew. He was a seer again; he saw clearly what she could only guess. Simon's wrath, maddened beyond all hope of healing, would make do with no small revenge. It would reach. It would strike. What it had done to Alun, it would do to the sun itself. And then, in a storm of fire, world's end.

He shook his head. He did not know what he denied. It was too much—it was too horrible. He was not strong enough to do what he must do. Even the simplest way . . . Nikki's dagger lay abandoned on the floor. He could not take it up.

Thea's will lashed him. Fool that he was; he had done justice before, long ago in Saint Ruan's, for the murder of a single man. Why was he so slow now, when the crimes were so much blacker?

That other criminal had been pure enemy, and human. This . . . this could have been himself. If he had grown up as Simon had; if he had not known the mystical peace of Ynys Witrin, that could sanctify even elf-blood, defending it from human hatred. He had been stoned in the streets of the village, he had faced more than one Brother Radbod, but he had always had that rock, the surety that he was loved. His nurse had loved him in her fashion; after her a Brother or two, a teacher, a very wise abbot; and a red-haired fellow novice who became fellow monk and fellow priest, who rose above him as abbot and died at the hands of a madman, and that madman had died in his own turn by Alf's hand. But Alf had not gone away desolate; he had had Jehan, he had had King Richard, and Gwydion, and Thea. He had always been rich in friendship; in love.

Simon had nothing. Terrible as that was for a mortal man, for his kind it was beyond endurance. No wonder he was mad. No wonder he had tried to destroy his own people.

"But," Alf whispered as the long body convulsed, *"I* love you." Somewhat to his surprise, he knew it for the truth. He stretched out his hands. He knew quite clearly that when he touched Simon, he would raise the power; he would die, they would both die, but the war would be ended.

Thea stood aghast within his mind. With all gentleness he nudged his children's awareness toward hers and shut them out. How lonely it was without them; how empty. The power was a warm tingling in his fingers. He laid them on Simon's breast.

Jehan saw him kneel, saw him gaze down as if in thought; saw him reach, and knew surely what that must mean. As hands touched white-habited heart, Alf's body arched like a bow. His flesh kindled blindingly bright; shadows of bone stood stark within.

Thea was already moving, beating against potent barriers. But Jehan had no power to hinder him. He braced his body, aimed it, and let it go. It lunged toward the dagger, snatched it up, took an eternal moment to measure its target. Swift as a serpent's tongue, neat as a viper's fang, the thin blade sank itself into Simon's throat.

The world rocked. The stars reeled. The moon was born and slain and born again.

Silence fell, the silence that comes after a whirlwind. Jehan was flat on his back, but unbroken, only bruised and winded. He sat up dizzily. He was all over blood; he wiped it from his eyes. More dripped down—his own. He had cut his forehead.

He could have howled. The monster was still alive. Alf likewise, glory be to God. They locked in a struggle as intimate as love, as frozen-fluid as a marble frieze. Waves of levin-power surged between them, and that was all that moved; all that mattered.

Someone, perhaps God, perhaps Thea, gave Jehan eyes to see. It was life for which and with which they battled. Simon's ebbed low with the pulsing of blood from his throat, too low for any miracle of healing. But Alf's flickered ember-feeble, all the rest burned to ash in the flare of his enemy's power. What remained between them sufficed, just barely, for one alone.

And they, mad saints, fought each to die that the other might live. Alf's hands that seemed to strangle strove to heal; Simon's, fisted, drove life and strength into a failing body. Drove relentlessly, drove inexorably, against a resistance that hardened as the life burned higher. Smote at last, low and brutal, with the faces of two children against a ruined land. With a wordless cry Alf tore free, only to catch the falling body of his brother. By blood indeed or simply by face and spirit, it did not matter now. Gray eyes looked up into silver, death into life. For one last, utterly illogical time, Alf reached out with healing in his hands.

Too late now, Simon said in his mind with the last of his power. *Which is well for you and most well for me. The power has fled, but not as far as death. I must go while I can help myself.*

"Brother—"

A smile touched the white lips, half gentle, half bitter. *What a good priest you are. You love your enemy as yourself.*

"Because he is myself."

Simon shook his head just perceptibly. *You are too wise, my brother. See—I admit it. We are kin. I would have destroyed you, and you foremost, but when the time came, I too was powerless. It took a pair of mortal men to break the deadlock.*

Alf spoke swiftly, urgently. "Simon, you can live. We can heal you. You can be one of us. The past doesn't matter; only the present, and the power."

The power, Simon repeated, *yes. For that I must die. Believe me, brother in blood, there is no other choice. Close the eyes of hope; unbind your prophecy. Let me go before I shatter the world.*

Alf bowed his head. But he said stubbornly, "I can heal you."

Proud, proud saint. Bless me, brother. I shall need it. I go murderer, suicide, very probably soulless.

"You go forgiven." Alf signed him with the cross: eyes, ears, nostrils, lips and cold hands, each gate of the senses sealed and sanctified. Simon's eyes closed as Alf blessed them; he sighed. As easily as that, as hardly as if he would indeed rend worlds, he let his spirit go.

Such a death for a mortal man was a journey into singing glory. Simon went into soft darkness. But at its edge glimmered light, and all of it wrapped not in oblivion, not in the agonies of Hell, but in spreading peace.

"I think," Alf said in deep, wondering joy, "I think—dear God in Heaven, I think that even we are granted souls."

"You're the only one who ever doubted it." Thea rose stiffly, catching Alf as he crumpled to the floor. Even unconscious, his face was too bright for human eyes to bear. She, who was not human, looked long at it. Her eyes when she raised them were brighter still, blinding. Her voice was cool and quiet. "It is over," she said. "For a little while."

Jehan turned slowly. It was like a battlefield. The living and the dead lay tangled together, conscious and unconscious and far beyond either; and Thea swayed above them, and for all her courage she was perilously close to breaking. Jehan sighed deeply. "How on God's good earth am I going to get us all out of this place?"

"My power will take us."

"All of us?"

"Not Simon Magus." She bent over him, her face unreadable. With hands almost gentle, she straightened his limbs, folding his hands upon his still breast, smoothing his ruffled hair. "This will be his tomb."

For a long count of breaths Jehan was silent. "It's fitting," he conceded at last. He paused. After a moment, in a clear and steady voice, he spoke the words that came to him. "Lamb of God who takes away the sins of the world, grant him rest. Grant him rest; grant him eternal rest."

30

Oddone cried out in wonder as they appeared all about him; and cried out again as he saw them clearly. Without another word he turned and bolted.

Stefania would have liked to follow, but one of the two slack bodies was Nikephoros'. His face was gray-green; one hand hung at an unnatural angle.

She dropped beside him with a strangled cry. He was alive, blessedly alive, breathing raggedly as if in a nightmare. His good hand clenched and unclenched, his head tossed, his mouth opened, gulping air. But he made no sound. That, more than anything he had shown her or told her, made it real. He was a sorcerer. They were all sorcerers.

They were like warriors after Armageddon, scarred and staggering, white with shock. And yet, even now, the slender woman's gold-bronze beauty cut like a sword. She raised Alf's body as if it had been a child's and laid it on the bed, settling it, pausing with head bowed as if she searched for strength. Jehan touched her arm to comfort her, his own face stark, frozen. She shook him off. "I can take care of myself and my beloved idiot. Go see to Nikki."

He wavered between them. "Go!" she snapped at him. Numbly he went.

But he was self-possessed enough when he knelt beside Nikki, a grim self-possession that cracked briefly but terribly when, stretching forth his hand, he saw that it was gauntleted with blood. Drying blood, crusting in cracks and hollows.

Jehan dragged his eyes away, back to Nikephoros. Stefania had his head in her lap. The black eyes were open, shadowed with pain. They seized Jehan with a fierce intensity; Nikki struggled to sit up. He must know—he must—

"Simon is dead," Jehan said without inflection. "I finished what you started."

It was all Nikki could do to hold himself erect, even with Stefania to brace him. *Alf.* The word came with great effort. *Alf—I can't— power—*

"Alf is alive. You're the only casualty. Lie down again, lad, before you fall down, and I'll see about robbing the infirmary."

"No need for that," said Prior Giacomo from the door. Brother Rafaele advanced with his gangling, stork-legged gait, Oddone trailing behind with an armful of bottles and bandages. Silently the infirmarian set to work on Nikki's arm.

The boy was well looked after, and well enough but for the pain that had saved all of them. Jehan wandered back to Alf. Prior Giacomo was there already, arms folded, scowling. Thea had laid her body beside her lover's, head pillowed on his breast, their children burrowed into his side. Jehan started forward in alarm, and stopped short. They were breathing. They looked as if they slept. But by the pricking in his nape he knew that they worked witchery.

"So," Giacomo said, "you found them."

Jehan nodded. He still had not washed his hand. Giacomo was staring at it, at him. His face was stiff. He had forgotten the blood there. He forced himself to speak. "It was . . . a bit of a struggle."

"So I see," Giacomo said. He extended his hand.

"Don't!" cried Jehan.

A spark leaped from Alf's brow to the lifted palm. Giacomo recoiled instinctively. His jaw set; his brows met. He tried again. A hand's breadth from flesh, the lightning crackled. It shocked but did not burn. He recovered his hand; folded his arms again, tightly; drew a breath.

"Don't touch them," Jehan said softly.

Giacomo shivered. In the silence, Anna came with bowl and cloth and chair. Mounting the last, she began to wash the blood from Jehan's face and hand. It was a mildly comical spectacle; Giacomo's lips could not help but twitch. Jehan smiled openly, with relief close to hysteria. He was in shock, he had come out of enough battles to know that, but at the moment he could not care. They were all alive, the enemy was dead—at his hand—at—

He let the storm of shaking run its course. Anna finished and rested her head briefly on his shoulder; she hugged him, rare concession. "Everything will be well now," she said.

Jehan swung her down from the chair. "It's not over yet." His eye caught the last of them, the one who might have been a bundle cast upon the floor. Brother Paul's eyes were shut, his face blotched livid and pallid, but the tension in his shoulders gave proof enough that he was conscious and far from vanquished. Joscelin de Beaumarchais, like a cat, had a habit of landing on his feet.

Maybe he already had. Giacomo, bending to examine him, looked up at Jehan. "May I ask what you've been up to, casting down and binding a secretary of the Pauline Father General?"

"An old enemy of ours. He'll be dealt with when, and as, we see fit."

Giacomo's brows went up. "Will he now?"

"A bishop," Anna said clearly and coldly, "may in certain circumstances exert full authority over a humble monk. Even though this monk is not in fact under His Excellency's jurisdiction, he has subjected himself to it by his actions. To wit, ordering the abduction and imprisonment of a noblewoman and her children; causing, albeit indirectly, the murder of a royal prince; attempting to cause the murder of a high lord."

"A sorcerer." Paul had flung off his pretense of unconsciousness. Sit up he could not, let alone stand, but he had a voice that carried well. "Sorcerers all, good Brother: elvenfolk of Rhiyana, condemned by papal decree."

"Not yet, I think," Anna said.

"Not yet," Jehan agreed, "and maybe not ever. Certainly not without a fair trial. Which I intend to get."

"You and your tame witches. Sarum may never see its Bishop, even if Rhiyana gets back its Lord Chancellor." Paul shifted. No one moved to make him more comfortable. "Meanwhile, Brother, it seems to me that you've been keeping guests under false pretenses.

Did you know what august personages had taken shelter under your roof? Sinful too, alas: a whore and her keeper and their tender little bastards."

Jehan's fist hammered him into silence. But the Bishop's voice was mild; lethally so. "Can you govern your tongue, Brother, or shall I govern it for you?"

The man's eyes glittered, but he did not speak again. Nor did Giacomo give voice to his thoughts. Brother Rafaele, having finished splinting and binding Nikki's arm and dosed him with strong herbs mixed in wine, wavered transparently between duty and curiosity. At last, with some regret, he yielded to his duty. "The boy should do well now, Brother Prior. The rest, I fear, are somewhat out of reach of my competence."

"I suspected they might be," Giacomo said dryly. "Many thanks, Brother; if we need you later, we'll send for you."

"*We*, is it?" Anna asked as the door closed with Rafaele on the other side of it.

Giacomo faced her. "*We*, Madonna. I'm afraid I've learned too much for my good, though I hope not for yours. And I brought your kindred here; I feel responsible. I want to be sure that they've come to no harm."

"Or that San Girolamo has taken no harm from their presence," she said.

"That too," he agreed unruffled.

Dawn, considered for itself, is a very great miracle. But it is quiet. No trumpets herald it; no lightnings accompany it. It simply comes, subtle and unstoppable. So they woke, all four sleepers, as if this were a morning like a thousand others. Cynan was vocally and Liahan quietly ravenous. Thea sat up yawning and stretching and shaking out the silken tangle of her hair. Alf simply opened his eyes and lay, feeling out the borders of mind and body. For the first time in an age beyond reckoning, he was whole. It was pleasure close to pain, hollows filled that that had gaped like wounds, powers lost and found again, ready to his hand. He reached with flesh and spirit, and she was there, their children no longer within her but close against her, nursing each at a breast. She smiled over their heads. "Great man and woman that they've made themselves, they should get the back of my hand and a bowl apiece of gruel."

He laughed, knowing as well as she that she would do no such thing. His mirth caught for an instant upon memory—Simon's face, the ruin he had wrought before he died, the mighty atonement he had made—and shook free, fixing upon this blessed moment. With some care he sat up. Dizziness swelled, passed. He realized that he was at least as ravenous as the little witches. He could not remember when he had ever been so hungry.

But first, pain cried out for healing. He passed faces glad, troubled, carefully expressionless. He set his hands on Jehan's shoulders.

Jehan wrenched away. "Stop it," he said roughly. "Stop it!"

"You hurt," Alf said, simple as a child. But he lowered his hands to his sides.

"Nikki hurts. I have a matter to settle with my confessor. Leave it at that."

Alf was not disposed to. There might have been a battle, for Jehan was adamant, had not Nikki come between them. Even lightheaded with Rafaele's potion, he was well able to shield his own pain, what the drug had left of it. *Brother,* he said to Alf, *go and eat. Oddone's raided the Abbot's kitchen for you. You too, Father Jehan. You can have your fight later.*

They glared with equal hauteur, equal intransigence. Nikki laughed at the likeness. Which brought their anger upon his head, but he only laughed the harder. Collapsed, in truth, giggling helplessly, until Stefania shook him to make him stop.

Bishop and Chancellor bent over him. He grinned, unrepentant. Alf sighed. Jehan's lips twitched. Alf said, "You too, infant. Don't you know it's deadly to balk power?"

We humans can take care of ourselves. Nikki said it with newborn pride. *Go and quiet your stomach, Alfred. It's growling like a starving wolf.*

It was a starving wolf, and it needed firm restraint lest it gorge itself into sickness. Alf took some small comfort in seeing that no one else went hungry, Nikki in particular, who would have settled for a cup of wine. Even Paul had his fill; Alf fed him calmly as one feeds a young child, although his glare was baleful.

Nikki ate as little as his brother's tyranny would allow, and outdrank them all. His temper had taken a turn for the worse. When Stefania stoppered the wine bottle and set it out of his reach, he scowled, flung his cup down, flashed his eyes over the gathering. *Simon Magus is dead. Rhiyana is free of his power. What now?*

"Rhiyana is free of little." Though fed and rested, Alf looked weary still. He had reclaimed his chair by the brazier, and Liahan was with him, half asleep. Her profile against his robe was his own, blurred and fined by her youth and her sex. He laid his cheek upon the kitten-softness of her hair. His voice, though quiet, was stern. "The Crusade rages. The Interdict has fallen. The King may be past any hope of healing.

"And yet," he said. "And yet I refuse to despair. Listen now, and hear what we shall do."

Nikki drew his hood closer about his face, and wished that Thea would. Or at least that she would bow her head in proper humble fashion. If she insisted on walking into the Mother House of Saint Paul rather than willing herself into it, for no other reason than a love for the dramatic and an hour to spare, she could at least forbear to invite curiosity. Particularly since she had done nothing to disguise herself save to swathe her body in mantle and hood, dark enough but to his eyes not particularly deceptive. She was still a graceful witch-woman with the bearing of a queen.

Stop fretting, child, she chided him silently. *Nothing human can see anything when it's as dark as this.*

I can, he muttered. But he eased a little, enough to raise his head and walk more steadily. They were close now to the place they sought, a fortress crowned with a cross, standing just out of the shadow of Castel Sant' Angelo. No shadow now, to be sure, with the sun long since set and Compline rung, and neither moon nor stars to lighten the sky. Thea walked coolly to the barred gate and set hand and power upon it; it opened in silence upon darkness and a scent of cold stone. Cold hearts, Nikki thought as Thea led him beneath the arch. As soundlessly as it had opened, the gate closed behind them.

For an instant his lungs labored, crying that there was no air. He gasped, struggling for quiet. Thea was already a horse-length away. He stretched to catch her.

If San Girolamo had made Nikki desperate for freedom, San Paolo Apostolo won from him a heartfelt vow. Never again, not even as a guest, would he shut himself up within the walls of a monastery. He would find his God under the sky, or if he must, in churches where the doors were never shut. Not in these prisons of the body that closed all too often into prisons of the soul.

Thea seemed unmoved, walking without stealth through cold halls and cold courts, up lamplit stairs, past the darkened cells of monks and the dormitories crowded with novices, to that arm of the stronghold from which the Father General commanded his Order. All was quiet there as elsewhere, even the clerks and secretaries sleeping, and no guards to challenge the invaders. Such arrogance, to trust in high walls and in the Pope's favor. Nikki's scorn almost made him forget his panic-hatred of the place.

The Pope's favor is no small thing. Thea opened a door like a dozen others along the passage, upon a cell as bare as a penitent's. It had not even a bed, only a crucifix upon the wall, and under it, stretched out like one crucified, a man of no great height or girth, remarkable for neither his beauty nor his ugliness. His face bore the ravages of pox, ill hidden by a sparse brown beard; his body was thin in the white habit, his feet bare and gnarled and not overly clean. Yet upon his face and in his mind blazed a white light.

Nikki's head shook from side to side. This man prayed exactly as Alf prayed, with a purity of concentration, in an ecstasy of communion. But what he prayed for and what he stood for, those were inimical to all Alf was.

"Father Alberich," Thea said. Her voice tolled like a bell. "Father Alberich von Hildesheim, you are summoned."

The outstretched arms folded inward. The still features woke to life; the eyes opened, gray-green, kindling as they fell upon her face. Their brilliance was like a blow. Yet far worse was their awful gentleness. Even Thea dimmed a little in the face of it. She raised her chin; she put aside mantle and hood. Beneath them she was arrayed in splendid simplicity, gown and overgown of deep green, her hair bound with a fillet of gold. "One of your Brothers is dead," she said, "and one is a prisoner. You are summoned to defend them."

Father Alberich rose. "Who summons me?"

"Justice."

"And if I cannot come?"

"You will come."

He smiled. He knew no fear that Nikki could see, and if any hatred touched him, it was lost amid his wonder at her beauty. "Ah, Lady," he said sighing, "it is a very great pity that you are of the Devil's children. Such loveliness should be consecrated to God."

"How so? My hair cut off, my body sheathed in sacking and ravaged with penitence?"

"Of course not, for then you would not be so beautiful. Though it could be argued that your soul's beauty would more than make up for your body's lack."

"Except," she said, "that in your philosophy I have no soul to beautify. But that may be as ridiculously wrong as all the rest of it. Your sorcerer monk is dead. I'm no authority, but one was there who can testify that he went to something other than oblivion."

"Cursed monk, Lady? We of all Orders can have had none such."

Nikki snorted. Thea laughed short and fierce. "Don't lie to yourself, Father General. You know what Brother Simon was. You always knew, however you chose to disguise it. Saint and worker of miracles, mystic, child of God—he was of my own kin."

With perfect serenity Father Alberich conceded, "Perhaps he was. I grieve that he is dead. He was a great warrior of God."

"He was mad and he was tormented. Your fault, Father General, as much as that of the low creature who ruled him. You did nothing to break that bond; you kept it strong, you left them free to work what harm they could. We owe you a debt, we of Rhiyana. Now we will pay it."

"If I die, our work will continue. Rhiyana is ours; it has returned to the hand of God. No sorcery can rob us of it."

"Rhiyana indeed is yours, if yours are war and hatred, death and destruction and the spreading of wasteland where once was peace and plenty."

His eyes were sad, his voice soft with sorrow. "War is always terrible, and the war for souls is worst of all. But a desert can grow green again, if men's souls are freed from darkness."

"And if there never was darkness? What then, priest of God?"

"Night is Satan's day and darkness his light. You tempt me, beautiful demon, and I may yet succumb, but the Order has won this battle in its long war. Nothing that you do can alter it."

"Can it not?" She held out her hand as to a wayward child. "Come to judgment, Father Alberich."

For one who had seen Constantinople before its fall, walked the length of the Middle Way and looked on the splendor of the imperial palaces, the dwelling of the Pope seemed an echo and a defiance of that royal glory. Its guardians were the images of old Rome, that some said carried still an antique magic: the she-wolf of the empire; the head and the hand of some forgotten giant, whether Samson or Apollo or the Emperor Constantine, his fingers clasping the orb of the world; and mounted on a stallion of bronze, right hand upraised in warning or in command, the image that pilgrims called Marcus or Theodoric and the Romans Constantine, who could have been any or none, but whose pride was the pride of the Pope of Rome. Behind the haughty back rose a tower of bronze like the Chalkê of Constantinopolis, the great gate and tower that had stood between the sacred

Emperors and the world; and beyond the tower, the palace of the
Lateran.

It stood in a city within and apart from the city of Rome, built
on the slopes and summit of the Caelian Hill near the eastern walls.
East of it lay fields and farms and the walls themselves; empty lands
stretched westward to come at length to the Colosseum and the
borders of the living city. There Romans and pilgrims preferred to
stay, the former by the banks of the Tiber among their own kind, the
latter gathered about the basilica of Saint Peter in the Leonine City.

"Pope Innocent had sense," Jehan had said to Alf once when
they had leisure to talk of trifles. "He built a castle up on the Vatican
Hill in the Borgo San Pietro, ample enough for a palace and strong
enough for a siege. More will come of that, I think. It was never a wise
choice to try to build a new city of God so far away from what was
left of Rome and its Romans, not with Saint Peter staking his own
claim out past Sant' Angelo."

But Saint John of the Lateran clung to his honors, and where the
Pope was and had been for nigh a thousand years, there was the
Curia and the heart of the Church. A heart of minted silver, many
would say, but the truth remained. Saint Peter's could call itself
foremost of all churches, *omnium ecclesiarum caput*. Saint John's was *caput
mundi*, foremost of all the world.

Jehan stood with Alf well within the gates of the Lateran, a
shadow among the many shadows of the Pope's bedchamber. Unseen
and unheard, they could hear with ease what passed in the workroom
without.

Cencio Savelli, Pope Honorius, was little like the vigorous young
man who had ruled before him. He was old, his hair thin and gray
round the tonsure; he had been tall for a Roman, but years and care
had bowed him. He looked too frail by far for the burden of his rank,
holy paradox that it was, prince of the princes of the Church, servant
of the servants of God. And yet he had outlived all Innocent's youth
and brilliance; when that had burned to ash in its own splendor, he
had risen in his turn to the Chair of Peter. Neither young nor brilliant,
one no longer, one never, in his quiet careful way he continued as
Innocent had begun.

"No," he said, gentle but immovable. "No, Brother, you may
not. We need you here."

The other was equally gentle, equally obstinate. "God needs me
among His poor." He was kneeling at the Pope's feet; he raised

bandaged hands, the bandages rather cleaner than the rest of him. "Holiness, I have dreamed. I have had sendings. I know what I must do, and that is not to be a hanger-on, however honored, of your Curia."

"Cencio's tame saint." Honorius smiled a little sadly. "Fra Giovanni, I too have my dreams and my duties, however much they may be clouded by this eminence. Not all destitution of spirit dwells in hovels; much of it has settled among the princes of the Church."

"Have I no Brothers to teach them by word and by example? May I not at least return to my own Assisi and minister to God's poor there, if only for a little while?"

"That," the Pope said slowly, "I may consider." Hope had leaped in the wide brown eyes; he laid his hands on the ill-barbered head. "My son, my son, we all have such need of you, and yet your remedy for our hurts is much too strong to be taken all at once. All the world at peace in the faith and the poverty of the Apostles—a vision worthy of our Lord, but not so simple to accomplish."

"It will come," Giovanni whispered. "God has promised. It will come."

"But not too soon," said Honorius, half in foresight, half in warning.

There was a silence. The Pope pondered. Giovanni, undismissed, bent his head in prayer. Suddenly he lifted it. He looked toward the inner door with clear and seeing eyes. "Holy Father, do you believe in angels?"

Honorius started out of his reverie. "Angels, Fra Giovanni? Of course." He said it as if to quiet a very young child. "They are in Scripture. But what—"

"One has come to speak with you. How generous of Heaven's messenger to wait upon another and much lesser petitioner."

"No creature of Heaven, I," Alf said. He had entered as no mortal might, through the closed door, bearing his own faint silver light. He was all in gray, rather like a Minorite, but no poor brother of Christ would have worn wool so soft, or belted and brooched it with silver. He went down in obeisance before the silent staring Pope, and remained kneeling as still Fra Giovanni knelt. "Earth bore me and earth keeps me; I have never been a messenger of God."

"No, brother?" murmured Giovanni.

He neither expected nor received a reply. The Pope looked from Alf's lifted face to that of the man who, recovered at last from the shock of Alf's vanishing, entered in more human fashion. Recognition sparked; bewilderment lessened. "Jehan de Sevigny, did I never give you leave to claim your see of Sarum?"

Jehan, prevented by the Pope's impatient gesture from kneeling with the others, stood straight and found his voice. "You gave it, Holiness. I've been detained."

"So it seems." Honorius' eyes returned to Alf. The wonder in them was untainted by either fear or hate, although he knew well what knelt so meekly at his feet. "It would also seem that both these men know you. May I share the honor?"

"Alfred of Saint Ruan's," Jehan said before Alf could speak, "Lord Chancellor of Rhiyana and emissary of its King."

Honorius rose from his chair. His gaze never left the fair strange face. "The White Chancellor. We have heard of you, great lord. We have heard it said that you were once one of ours. Impossible if you were a mortal man; disturbing if you are the being of the tales."

"If the Devil may quote Scripture," Alf said, "it follows that the Devil's minion may become a master of theology. Particularly if he be very young and rather too proud of his erudition."

"Yet orthodox," mused the Pope. "Most orthodox. My predecessor knew the truth of you, I think. He loved to read the *Gloria Dei*, so perfect it was, so succinct, so divinely inspired. But he would always smile when he spoke of its author."

"And you, Holy Father? Do you smile? Or do you gnash your teeth?"

"I have not Innocent's love for paradoxes. He was a great man; I am merely a man. I can do no more than guide myself by the Church's teachings."

"Even if they stem not from God but from human fear?"

"So speaks heresy, Lord Chancellor."

"Or so speaks wisdom," Fra Giovanni said with rare force. "Holy Father, hear the tale he has to tell. Any living thing deserves that much of you."

Pope Honorius paused, caught between wrath and strict justice. He had been invaded by what could be nothing but witchery, with boldness mitigated not at all by the enchanter's evident humility. And now the first of the Friars Minor, that gentle thorn in the Church's side, had arrayed himself with the enemy.

Honorius lowered himself again into his chair, making no effort to conceal his weariness. "Tell your tale, sir," he said, "but tell it swiftly."

Alf bowed his head in assent. As he raised it, the air shifted and shimmered. Thea walked out of it with Nikephoros, leading the Father General of Saint Paul. That brave man wasted no time in either astonishment or panic; he went down on his knees before the Pope.

Now three knelt and three stood, a tableau almost menacing in its symmetry. Father Alberich's presence lent no comfort. He had the look of a martyr at the stake, white and exalted. Honorius wondered briefly what his own face betrayed. Alf's eye caught his; he shivered. It was not a human eye, yet it was very, very calm. Serene. As well it might be. Saint Peter's throne offered little protection against such power as this creature wielded.

Alf shook his head slowly. "While my kind dwells in this world, it must admit the power of your office. Consider how very few we are, how very many the people over whose souls you rule."

The Pope shivered. Not even his thoughts were his own tonight. "If you chose, you would rule them all."

"We do not choose. We do not even dream of it. The one of us who did is dead; and he was our enemy, the power behind the Crusade, a monk of the Order of Saint Paul."

That brought Honorius erect. He had not known it. He did not believe it. God and the Church were not so mocked.

"His name," Alf said gently and inexorably, "was Simon. He had power the like of which even we have never seen, nor ever wish to see again. It drove him mad; it devoured him. Hear now what he wrought, he and those who made use of him."

Told all together in that soft calm voice, it was terrible; it was pitiable; it was most horribly credible. "Without Brother Simon," Alf said, "no doubt the Crusade would have mounted on the wave that shattered Languedoc. But Rhiyana could have withstood it, turned it back without bloodshed. Its people would suffer no war and no Interdict." He drew a slow breath. "What is done is done. Simon died repentant; God has taken him, he is at peace. Not so those who wielded him. Sworn to destroy all works of sorcery, they loosed a sorcerer mightier than any in the world; in their zeal to raise their Order above all others, they resorted to that very power against which they thundered. In God's name, God's Hounds turned to the ways and the arts of the Adversary."

"Or so they would say." Thea stood at Alf's back, hands on his shoulders, eyes on the old man in the tall chair. "As they would say that any means is just if the end is holy. Perilous doctrine. It permits murder and rapine and black sorcery in the name of an Order's furtherance, but it grants no mercy to those of us who try to live as the Church prescribes. The first of us who died was a child. He believed devoutly in God and the Gospels. He heard Mass every day. I never heard him speak ill of anyone, nor knew him to do harm to man or beast. And he died. If he had not been killed, if all had gone as our enemies intended, he would have been burned alive."

Honorius tore his gaze from her. She was not gentle; she was not quiet. She was afire with rage. And justly, said the cold judge within, if all was as he had heard. "What proof can you give?" he demanded of her. "How may I know that you tell the truth?"

"Look yonder," she answered.

Another white habit, another gray cowl. Brother Paul stood dazed, torn from a black doze under the eyes of two monks and two mortal women and two witchborn children. "Brother Paul," Thea said, "was the mind to Simon's hand. His was the genius that found the mad boy and knew him for what he was, and made him the chief of God's hunting Hounds."

"Not entirely." Even she stared at Father Alberich. He had listened in silence, motionless but for the flicker of his eyes; he spoke as coolly as Alf had. "Brother Paul was given the power of finding, but not that of making. Such was my part. Like him I saw God's hand in Simon's coming among us; I saw the working of God's will. Here was the sword we had prayed for, a keen weapon against the powers of the dark; here also was our shield and our fortress."

"You knew what he was. You accepted him; you used him. Are you any less culpable than the King of Rhiyana?"

"It was God's will." Alberich's words were like a gate shutting. "Your Holiness, if Brother Paul is to be punished, I beg leave to remind you that I am given full and sole jurisdiction over my wayward brethren."

Jehan stepped forward. "I claim episcopal exemption. This monk has committed grave crimes against a whole kingdom."

"Not yours, Bishop of Sarum," drawled Brother Paul.

"Mine for the duration of this embassy," Jehan shot back, "under the forty-third capitulum of the Synod of Poictesme, which states—"

Honorius smote his hands together. "Sirs, sirs! By no will of mine this has become a papal tribunal. It appears that we are trying the guilt of the Order of Saint Paul on a charge of murder and sorcery. Or is it that of Rhiyana's King and certain of his nobility on a charge of sorcery alone? Or shall it be both?"

"We do not deny either our possession or our use of power," Alf said, "which men call magecraft and sorcery. We do deny that that power either stems from or serves the purposes of God's Adversary. And we charge that our kingdom has been assaulted without reason or justice; that the guilt lies not with us but with the preachers of the Crusade. We have lived as best we could between the laws of the Church and the laws of our nature. In return we have been set upon with arms and with power; our children murdered or taken; our human folk condemned to suffer for us, for no better reason than that we live."

"You live," Brother Paul echoed him. "There is the heart of it. You live. You do not die."

"Save by violence."

"Exactly."

Thea tossed her head. "There's a dilemma for you, Lord Pope. God has made us, certainly, unless you subscribe to the doctrine that the Devil could have done so, and that is heresy; He made us immune to death by age or sickness. So if we are to die, we have only two choices. Murder or suicide. The latter is forbidden by the Church. So is the former, unless, of course, one calls it war. Or Crusade. Or destruction of a pestilence."

"You cannot live," said Father Alberich dispassionately. "You are against nature. All things on earth fade and die. Only spirit is undying."

"Such fine ecclesiastical logic. It exists; it should not; deny it and destroy it. Are you absolutely certain, Father General, that your vision is clear? That you see what we are without an intervening cloud of envy?"

"I see what you are. Beautiful; seductive. Deadly."

"Ah, but to what? To your sense of superiority?"

"You are superior to no man."

She clapped her hands. "Bravo, Father! Truly, we are not. But neither are we inferior. We are another face of God's creation, no more good or evil than our human cousins. Consider what sets us apart: our beauty, our power, our deathlessness. Have you nothing to counter these? Think, Father Alberich. Have you?"

He crossed himself deliberately, eyes averted from her shining face. To him she was doubly terrible, witch and woman both, and far too intelligent for a female creature. Demonically intelligent.

"Demonically accurate," she said. "Tell me what you have that we have not. Tell me why a good Christian faces worse punishment in long life than in early death. You have threescore years and ten, maybe more, very likely less. We have years uncounted, bound to earth apart from the face of God."

A soft cry escaped from Fra Giovanni. "I see. Oh, I see! He gives you the rest, the gifts men envy so bitterly, in recompense for that one great grief. Lady . . . Lady, how do you bear it?"

"With ease." Brother Paul's hand swept out, taking her in, close as she was to her lover, one hand unconsciously stroking his hair. "Can you believe that they suffer? Look at them! No expectation of Heaven, maybe, but none of Hell either. He can abandon priestly vows, sire bastards, sin with happy impunity. She can do exactly as her devils prompt her. And believe this, Holy Father. That lovely form is far from her favored one. Her nature and her instincts, whatever her likeness, are the nature and the instincts of a bitch in heat."

Alf surged up, breaking her strong grip with the ease of wrath. In spite of his courage—and he had a great deal of that, whatever his flaws—Brother Paul blanched. He was one of a rare few who had seen Alf enraged; and then as now, he had provoked it, and paid dearly after.

Alf smiled with sweetness all the more deadly for the white fury in his eyes. "Brother, Brother," he chided, "your language is most unsuitable in that habit and in this company. Will you make amends? Tell His Holiness a truth or two. Tell him why you made use of my poor brother who is dead."

"Whom you killed."

"He willed himself to death rather than wreak further destruction. Tell him, Joscelin."

The monk gripped Honorius' knees. "I cry foul, Holiness! He compels me with sorcery."

Alf's face set. He would not say it; he would not permit Thea to say it for him. It was Jehan who strode forward and lifted the man bodily, shaking him like a recalcitrant pup. "He does not. Do as he says, monk. A word will do it. Two. Power; jealousy. You had a weapon against the world, and a long-awaited chance to get revenge on the one who made your lover forget you. Worse—you thought him fair prey, and he had the temerity to best you."

Honorius startled them all; he startled himself. He smiled. As sternly as he might, he said, "Put him down, Jehan." The Bishop obeyed. Paul's glare promised murder—later, when there was no one to interfere.

The Pope steepled his fingers and closed his eyes. Not for weariness, not any longer, but to think in peace without the distraction of those crowding faces; the two in particular that were so heartrendingly fair, so young and yet so anciently wise. In ignorance of them, with Father Alberich and his monks hammering out their denunciations, it had been grimly simple. A race of sorcerers had established itself in the outlands of Francia; one had dared to crown himself King over Christian folk, and dared then to hold his throne for years beyond the mortal span. However well he ruled, he could not alter the truth. He was a creature of darkness, a child of demon Lilith or of the beings of Scripture, the sons of God who came down unto mortal women and begot halflings upon them. For far too long had the Church suffered his presence. The Canons and the safety of men's souls left no space for doubt. He and all his kin must be driven from the earth.

Now his kin had come to plead his case. And they were fully as perilous as Saint Paul's disciples had warned; but not, exactly, in the way he had been led to expect. The woman was a fierce creature with a tongue like a razor's edge, but she had a most disconcerting habit of speaking the truth. The man was worse yet. He was subtle. He was gentle; he was brilliant; he was so obviously a creature of God that it hurt to look at him, just as it hurt to look on Fra Giovanni. If he had been mortal, people would have said that he was not long for this world; God could not bear to leave his like among sinful men.

He was not mortal. He was not human. He was steeped in sins of the flesh, that he had confessed without shame or repentance; nor, all too clearly, had he any intention of putting an end to them. And yet he belonged surely and utterly to his God.

The Pope opened his eyes. They were looking at one another, Fra Giovanni and the enchanter; they were smiling the same faint unearthly smile. A mere man, even a man who was the Vicar of Christ, could only begin to guess what passed between them. If it was sorcery, it was divine sorcery: a communion of saints.

Saint Paul's brethren watched them. Honorius thought of Paul the Apostle while he was Saul the persecutor, watching the stoning of the martyr while the cloaks of the Jews lay heaped about his feet. He had had the law and the prophets behind him. So too did they. One proclaimed with malice, one with regret, both with honest conviction: The Church must not suffer these witches to live. Scripture, canon law, plain human expedience, all forbade it.

Innocent, Honorius thought, *I would give this tiara that was yours and is now mine, to pass this cup and this dilemma to you.*

If they had only been less beautiful. He could have thought more clearly then. Beauty seduced, yet it also repelled. One wanted to trust it; one dared not; then one distrusted one's own distrust, because yes, no man with eyes could help but envy that perfection of form and feature. And what if all his doubts were in truth the warring of his will against their enchantments?

He shook himself hard. More of this circling and he would go mad. No wonder Brother Simon had; between what he was and what he believed, his whole existence had been a contradiction.

The Pope's eyes opened upon Alf's face. There was one who had not taken leave of his sanity, a miracle as surely as any in the Gospels. What had been in the water's mind when it realized it was wine?

"Surprise," Alf answered softly. "Denial. Fear. Revulsion. But at last, at great price, acceptance."

Honorius shook his head in reproof. "My son, can you not grant me the privacy of my own thoughts?"

"Holy Father, you persist in invading mine. I have none of your inborn defenses; I must labor to shield against you."

The Pope could see the words as Alf spoke them. Men armored and immune like knights in battle; enchanters naked to every darting thought. "But not defenseless," Honorius said swiftly. "Far from that. Our weapons are few and feeble against the bitter keenness of yours."

The Paulines approved his words, if not in great comfort. They could see that the Pope was wavering; they dared not speak lest they cast him into the enemy's camp. So always had it been with the sorcerers. With their beauty they seduced; with their magic they bound men's souls. Not even the successor of Peter could be proof against them.

Behind Brother Paul's eyes, Joscelin de Beaumarchais stood up and cried revolt. He had lost this battle once. He would not lose it again. The witches were intent on the Pope and on one another. He was all but forgotten. He would have only one chance. He launched himself, joined hands a club with all his weight behind them, his target the back of Alf's neck.

The damned sorcerer sensed something. He half turned, his throat a better target still. So had Simon died. *So.*

Fanged horror lunged between them, bore Paul down, closed its jaws upon his throat.

Gently, gently. The beast's breath was searingly hot, its jaws a vise held just short of closing. He could not even struggle.

Of all the faces that had reeled past as he fell, he saw only Father Alberich's. The reproach in it was worse even than his failure. He had unmasked the were-bitch, but he had convinced the Pope. God's Hounds knew no reason nor justice. Their hate was blind, and in extremity, murderous. They were proven to be as the witches had proclaimed.

How he hated that beautiful voice, half boy, half man, all Christianly compassionate. "Let him go, my lady. He'll do no harm now."

Small comfort that his sweetness cloyed on her too. She reared up into woman-form, with the decency at least to witch herself into her dress as she did it; her response was blistering, and ingenious. Even Saint Alfred flinched a little, although his angelic perfection restored itself in an eyeblink. "Thea Damaskena," he rebuked her, "this is no place for—"

"You could have been killed!" she shouted at him.

The silence was thunderous. No one had the will or the wits to break it. Paul dared at last to sit up, to glares from the witch and the bishop and the deafmute boy, but none prevented him. Maybe, just maybe, there was a little hope left. Canon law was canon law, and it was most strict regarding sorcery. With which both witches had been blatantly free.

Honorius looked old and worn, beaten down by the weight of law and truth and the grim need to judge both fairly and in accordance with his office. His curse; he could not yield to plain expedience, nor force himself into Alberich's simple and immovable conviction.

"Holy Father." Fra Giovanni's voice was faint but not timid; excitement, not fear, had taken his breath away. "Holy Father, there is a way out of this tangle. My lord named it himself. When their kingdom is safe, he said, they will all go away. They've made a place for themselves; they'll take it out of the world. Isn't that what everyone wants? They can't bear us any more easily than we can bear them; this way they're gone and safe, and we're free of the stain of their murder."

Father Alberich nodded. "There is wisdom in what you say, Brother. Yet gone is not dead. And what if they choose to put it off? When their kingdom is safe, the sorcerer promises, they will depart. How do they reckon safety? Their King was King for fourscore years, and very many of those were years of stainless peace, yet he clung to his throne. Now that war and Interdict have wrought their havoc, must we wait another fourscore years for the land to be healed? How long can they prolong their presence in the world of men?"

"Not one more year." Alf measured each word with equal, leaden force. The face he turned to them all was as white as bleached bone, and old; so old that only deathless youth could embody it. He raised his hands. They were empty; they were laden with power. "I said that I must labor to hold up my shields against mortal thoughts. I have labored thus for every day of my life, every day of every year of fourscore and ten. And I am weary. Were I a man I would find rest in death. Since I am not a man, I can only dream of a place apart, among my own people, where all have power and none can die, and no fear or hate or human pity can come to torment me." He flexed his fingers; he closed them; he caught the Pope's eyes and held them. "Holiness, when I was young, before I knew I would not die, I used to dream sometimes of a text I loved. 'Come to me, all ye that labour and are laden, and I will give you rest.' Can you know—can you imagine—what it did to me to grow into the knowledge that my dream was a lie? For men, yes, there was an end. For me there was none."

The Father General spoke almost sharply, cutting across the Pope's response. "If the tale you have told is true, this new tale is a lie. You cannot die, but you can be killed, and on the other side of death is peace. Were you in truth so desperate for it, you would not fight this battle for your life."

"What will content you?" Alf demanded. "Would my death suffice to gain the lives of my kin? If I give myself to you and your fire, will you consent to see my people depart behind the walls of Broceliande?"

"If I knew you could be trusted not to wriggle away—"

"Enough!" thundered the Pope. They all gaped. None would have dreamed that he had such power in him. Much more quietly he said, "There will be no bargains struck except as I strike them. You, Lord Chancellor, have the disposition of a martyr, self-sacrificing to the point of parody. You on the other hand, Father General, would serve admirably in the part of the unregenerate Saul of Tarsus. Beware lest your road to Damascus become the road to Broceliande."

He left his chair, which suddenly was a throne; he drew himself to his full height. "You promise to depart, Lord Alfred, but in this much Father Alberich speaks the truth. You do not bind yourself. Your weariness may pass when you see what is to be done in Rhiyana;

and I forbid you to linger. It is Lent now. If by Pentecost you are not gone, you and all your people, I will hand you over to my Hounds. Then indeed, and justly, shall you burn."

Alf paused. Thea was silent, walled in stillness. Jehan had started forward, then stopped, face set and gray. Only Nikki who had been but a pair of eyes through all of this, who had kept silence of mind as well as body, ventured to raise a hand, to widen his eyes. Protest, assent, part and part.

Alf sank to one knee. His head bowed. His voice came slow yet strong. "Let it be done according to your will."

Honorius said nothing, did nothing. Paul's thwarted rage, Alberich's reluctant acceptance, rang like shouts in Alf's mind. From the Pope came only blankness. Alf looked up under his brows. Honorius gazed down in deep and somewhat painful thought; but Alf could not read it. Sometimes humans could do that. They could think sidewise, and evade easy reading. Nikki, with power behind him, had perfected the art; unless he wished it, he could not be read at all, or even sensed.

When at length the Pope spoke, it was to the Paulines. "Father Alberich, Brother Paul, what you have done is beyond forgiving. You have deceived me with lies and half-truths, you have abused your vows and your offices, you have proven yourselves not merely false witnesses but hypocrites. Your weapon is broken and your plot unveiled; your Order should be scoured from the earth. But I have some wisdom left. The great mass of your Brothers are innocent of your wrongdoing; many possess a true and laudable zeal for their calling, which is to preserve the Church's orthodoxy against the attacks of heretics. For their sakes, and indeed for your own—for however blind and misguided, you remain my spiritual sons—I shall be merciful. You are not suspended from your vows. You are not removed from your Order. But you are bidden to leave the world for a time. Brief or long, I do not know, nor do I prescribe; only that you wake to full knowledge of what you have done." He waited; after a moment they bowed, both, and kissed the hand he held to them. "Go now. Hold yourselves to your cloister. I will see that you are sent where I judge best."

As Paul passed Alf, he hesitated as if he would have spoken, or struck, or spat. Thea advanced warningly; Honorius raised his hand. With a last long look—a glare, yet tinged just perceptibly with something very like admiration, the acknowledgment of enemy and strong enemy—Paul spun away.

Alberich too paused. He did not threaten; he only searched Alf's face, carefully, as if he could find there some thing of value that he had lost. His faith, perhaps. His certainty that he had chosen the path of God.

With his going, the air lightened visibly. But indeed, beyond the walls it was dawn. Far away on the edge of human hearing, a cock crowed.

Honorius started a little, foolishly. None of his guests, the one invited or the four not, melted away into nothingness. If anything, they seemed the more solid for the day's coming.

Again he looked down into Alf's eyes. He would not see them again, and he was not grieved to know it, although the knowledge grew out of no hate nor even any dislike. They were too alien for mortal comfort, too much like a cat's and too much like a man's and too little like either. But worse, infinitely worse, was the truth he saw there. " 'A priest forever,' " the Pope whispered, " 'in the order—of—' "

"No," Alf said more softly still, in something very close to desperation. "I cannot. I must not. You must not even think of it."

"I, never. You threaten the roots of my faith; you menace the very foundations of my Church. I pray God that I have not erred beyond human forgiveness in granting you only exile, and not the finality of death."

The fair inhuman face was still. It did not stoop to beg or to plead. It had heard the will of Cencio Savelli. It waited upon the will of the Vicar of Christ.

Honorius laid his hands upon the bowed head. He felt the tremors that racked the body beneath. He willed his voice to be steady. "When you have passed the borders of your secret country, you will pass beyond the reach of man, and of the Church of this mortal world. But not, not ever, of God."

Alf sank down and down, prostrate at the Pope's feet. So must he have lain on the day he was made a priest. Had he trembled so? Had he so frightened that long-dead bishop as he did this aging Bishop of Rome?

"I leave you to God," Honorius said. "Remember Him. Serve Him. And may He and His Son and His Spirit of truth shine upon you, and guide you, and lead you into His wisdom. Whatever that may be." The Pope signed him with the cross; and hesitated, and signed them all.

Then at last they had mercy. They left him. But glad though he won to be free of their presence, he knew he would never be free of their memory. They had taken with them the surety of his faith, and his heart's peace.

31

They walked back to San Girolamo, by common consent, for time to think. The morning that swelled about them was like the first morning of the world: splendid with the victory of light against darkness; muted with the promise of the darkness' return. Alf passed through it in silence, and yet it was not the silence of grief. He walked lightly, easily, as if a bitter burden had fallen from his shoulders. He even smiled, remembering Fra Giovanni's farewell. The Minorite had kissed him and asked his blessing, and persisted until he consented to give it, and said then with quiet conviction, "Now I know beyond doubting that God walks in the world. *All* the world." Simple words enough, and truth that was self-evident. But the friar's face when he said it, the joy with which he spoke, had warmed Alf to the marrow.

It matters that much to you, doesn't it? Nikki was beside him, trotting to keep pace, lips a little tight with what the jarring was doing to his arm.

Alf slowed in compunction and settled his arm about the boy's shoulders. "What's the trouble, Nikephoros? Do I puzzle you?"

Nikki shrugged. *No more than you ever do. It was all very interesting to watch.*

"Greek to the last," said Thea on his other side, arm slipping round his waist. When he frowned at her, she laughed and kissed his cheek. "It's over, Nikki. We've won. Don't you want to sing?"

I can't. He pulled away from them both, half running toward the loom of the Colosseum.

They exchanged glances. His back was straight and unyielding, his mind walled and barred. "Akestas," Thea said.

Alf shook his head slightly. But he did not stretch his pace. His mind was clear, intent, looking ahead now, seeing what it had still to face. They had won in Rome, perhaps; but not yet in Rhiyana.

* * *

Nikki did not come back with the others. Not that anyone seemed to care. Jehan and Thea were full of victory, vying to tell the whole of it; Alf absorbed himself in his children. Liahan had learned to smile, and Cynan had discovered speech. "Father," he cried insatiably. "Father, Father, Father!"

Stefania retreated from the clamor. She understood as much of it as she needed to. They had got what they wanted, the witch-folk. Brother Oddone ventured so far as to favor Thea with a quick shy smile. Prior Giacomo was grimly amused, but glad too, as if all this proved that he had not erred in taking them into his abbey. None of them asked where Nikephoros was, or why he had vanished.

She found her cloak and slipped toward the door. She did not know precisely where she was going. First she had to find her way out of San Girolamo, not the easiest of tasks; the monks stared, which was disconcerting, or sternly refused to stare, which was worse. It was all she could do to walk calmly, not to run like a wild thing trapped in a maze.

The gate was blessed relief. She ran through it down the road into the city.

Nikephoros was nowhere between the abbey and the scrivener's shop, nor was he in the rooms above. As a last resort she peered into the tavern. It was very early yet, but a few devoted winebibbers bent over their cups. Just as she turned away, she saw him. He had found the darkest corner, and he was drinking with the dedication of a man who means to drown his sorrows.

"It doesn't work, you know," she said.

He had closed himself off again. She caught his face in her hands and made him look at her. His eyes were awash with the wine, but his mouth was bitter. He offered her his cup; she shook her head. He drained it with a flourish that would have made her smile, if he had not been so desperate.

Have you seen the deafmute begging in the piazza? he asked much too calmly, setting the cup on the table in front of him. *An appalling creature. Malodorous. Ill-favored. First cousin to the Barbary ape.*

She drew up a stool and sat, eyes never leaving his face. "I find him pitiable."

He hurled the cup at the wall. It shattered; the shards dropped heavily, scattering on the ill-swept floor. People turned to stare; the wine-seller lumbered forward scowling. Nikki flung him a handful of coins and staggered up, dragging Stefania with him into the merciless sunlight.

She dug in her heels. Abruptly he let her go; she fell backward. He caught her. For a long moment they poised, stretched at arm's length like partners in a spinning dance. She firmed her feet beneath her. His hand opened, dropped. All at once he looked very ill.

The wine left him in a flood. She held him, helpless to do more than wipe his streaming face with the end of her veil. When the storm had passed, he crouched on hand and knees and shook; but his mind-voice was uncannily clear and steady, with an edge of ice. *I am an utter disgrace as a drunkard.*

"You'd be a disgrace if you were one."

What do you call me now?

"Nikephoros." She took his hand and kissed it. "Come to the house with me. You need to fill your stomach with something more trustworthy than wine."

His fist clenched. But he let her pull him up and lead him toward the stair. At the foot of it he stopped. *No, Stefania. I can't face—*

"I'll get rid of Bianca."

He laughed, choking on it. *And persuade her to leave you alone with a man?*

"I don't call myself a philosopher for nothing."

She got rid of Bianca. Masterfully. The old woman was even pleased to scour the market for Messer Nikephoros' favorite sweets.

He shook his head in wonder. *Stefania Makaria, you are a deceitful woman.*

"I'm a dialectician." He was sitting in Uncle Gregorios' chair, nibbling a bit of cheese. She knelt in front of him and touched his splinted arm. "Does this hurt still?"

His good shoulder lifted. *Not much, unless he thought about it.* He abandoned the cheese for an olive.

Stefania's eyes widened. "How do you do that?"

What?

"You don't even need to—"

Resort to words. She had never known that one could make so many bites out of an olive. Or that one could say so much with a supple body and a mobile face and a splendid pair of black eyes.

Looking at them as they darkened, she knew. It was the Pope's command. It was the battle won yet lost, the Kindred saved but ordered into exile. It was the beggar, poor ill-made creature, who but for the grace of God and the power of a white enchanter, was Nikephoros.

She shook her head fiercely. "Your back is straight and your mind is clear and you are beautiful."

So was he! Words again at last, all the stronger for that he did not need them. *He was born as I was born. Beatings and starvation twisted him. The rest—the rest twisted and clouded because he never learned what words were. He never can now. He's too old. Even Alf can't work that great a miracle.*

"He did with you. For which I thank God."

He was not listening. *He showed me—the madman I helped to kill. He showed me what I truly am.*

"*No*, Nikephoros. He showed you a nightmare, and tricked you into believing it was true."

He laughed, cold and clear in her mind. *Oh no, I'm no cripple, I'm a great wizard, I'm utterly to be envied. Can't you see, Stefania? I'm not the mute beast I should have been, but neither am I human. Alf's miracle made sure of both.*

"You were born human. You have a man's eyes. You won't live forever."

It doesn't matter. I'm an enchanter. The Pope's decree binds me too.

"It does not!" she burst out. "Nikephoros, that command was framed for the Fair Folk. You are none of their kind. You have no need to leave the world; no one can call you alien."

No?

"No! Your beauty is a human beauty. It's warm; it's familiar; it makes people smile. Not so the one you call your brother. *He* looks like a marble god. He makes people stare and gasp and cross themselves in awe. That's what the Holy Father is sending out of the world."

That and the power. I have the power, Stefania. I am an enchanter. Just as easily as the Church can burn Alf, it can burn me.

"It won't. We'll find a way. I'm much too clever for anyone's good but my own; I'll convince the world that you're no more and no less than a mortal man."

For a whole lifetime, Stefania? We would have to live a lie.

"Not a lie. A careful skirting round the truth."

He shook his head. *I can't—* His eyes widened; he paled. *God in Heaven.*

"What? What, Nikephoros?"

It's preposterous. But what if . . . what if my power needs Alf and his people to sustain it? What if, once the Folk go away and the walls close about them, all my magics vanish? I'll be like the beggar.

"Preposterous."

He lowered his face into his hand. *I don't know what to do. They're my people. They're like me. They know me as no human being ever can. But I'm not of their blood. And I love you, and I can't ask you to go with me into such an exile as that, and I can't endure a world without them. I want to stay in Rome and browbeat you into marrying me; I want to go with my soul's kin into Broceliande.*

"I would go," she said very low. "I would go with you."

You're stiff with terror at the thought of it. They're all so beautiful; they're all so strange. After a very little while you'd come to hate them for being what they are, and me for binding you to an exile beyond the world's end.

She was silent. She wanted to protest; she could not. He was telling the truth. She was of the mortal world, utterly and irrevocably; she could not leave it.

She could give him up. She had lived a respectable while before he came to trouble her peace. She had never intended to bind herself to any man, let alone a pretty lad without the least aptitude for philosophy, four years younger than she.

Three.

"Three and a half." She frowned. "Did I give you leave to trespass in my mind?"

His eyes dropped. She fancied that she felt his power's withdrawal. Looking at him, unable to turn away, she realized that he had changed. These two days and nights had aged him years. His desperate stroke had begun the dance that ended in an enchanter's death; and he had paid for it in more than a broken wrist. His prettiness was gone. He was handsome still but rather stern, with a deep line graven between his brows, the signature of power and pain.

She buried her face in his lap. "I love you," she said. She was crying. She did not want to; she could not help it. "I love you so much."

Very gently he touched her hair, stroking it, loosening the tightly woven braid. He was crying too; she felt it.

Somewhere at the bottom of self-pity she found the remains of her good sense. She raised her head. He wept like a stone image, stiff-faced, with the tears running down unheeded. She levered herself to her feet, sniffing loudly, but dignified for all of that. "I don't suppose you have a handkerchief," she said.

He held up a napkin. She dried his face with it, and then her own. Tears pricked again; she willed them back. "I'm doing you no good at all. Why don't you curse me for a foolish female and leave me to my fate?"

Because he loved her.

"Foolish boy." The last binding gave; her braid uncoiled, tumbling over her shoulder. "Now look what you've done."

Yes; and he would finish it. His sorrow had shifted in a dismaying direction. He reached for her. Before she could stop to think, she was in his lap and he was freeing her hair, one-handedly awkward but very persistent. Her hands found themselves behind his neck. Her body had begun to sing its deep irresistible song. Only once. Only once, before she lost him.

They never knew who led whom. She mounted the steps in front, but he was as close as her shadow. They kept stopping. When they came to her bed, her veil was long gone, her gown unlaced. She had to do most of the rest of it, for both of them. Even with the sling tossed aside, his splinted arm got in the way. He did what he could with all his aristocratic lacings, thinking curses at them; of course his luck would bring him to this when he was dressed for an audience with the Pope. She laughed breathlessly. "Oh, to be sure, a pilgrim is much better attired for an afternoon's seduction."

Sacrilegious, he chided her, tugging at her gown.

She blushed furiously. Which was utterly absurd. He was as bare as the day he was born, as calm as if he were swathed in silks. Cobbling up all her courage, and helping by turning half away, she slid out of gown and camise and stood shivering on the cold floor. His smile gleamed in the corner of her eye. She was all a prickle of gooseflesh, but her face was afire. She made herself face him. "What odd animals we are," she said. "So ugly. So ridiculous."

But so beautiful.

Stefania raised herself on one elbow. He was almost asleep, his eyes dark with it, but he smiled and brushed his finger across her lips. She was shaky, excited, happy, sad, languid and tender, all at once, in a hopeless tangle. She wanted to tease him awake again. She wanted to lie down and rest in the drowsy warmth of him.

"I'm sorry," she said.

He roused a little, puzzled.

She bit her lip. "I know I didn't—I know you weren't—you did everything to please me, and I didn't even know what to—"

He was awake, but not the way she had wanted. *You pleased me very much.* He drew her head down and kissed her slowly, savoring it. *That's one of the great wonders of being a sorcerer. What delights a lover is double delight.*

"You know all about it, don't you?"

Woman, he said sternly, *are you asking me to count over old lovers? Shall I give you a ranking for each, as if we were allotting places in a tournament?*

"I don't know what I'm asking!" She laid her head on his good shoulder, muttering into it, "I'm sorry again. I'm trying to start a fight. To make it easier to let you go. Now—now I know what all the singing is about."

He laughed gently, caressing her back and her tumbled hair. *Do you really? I was afraid I hurt you.*

"Only at first." She lifted her head. "Now who's wallowing in apologies? Nikephoros, we both talk too much. But before I take a vow of silence—what did you do to Bianca?"

His eyes were wide and innocent. *I? Do anything to Bianca? Is it my fault that she's met a friend in the market and is gossiping the day away? And I'll remind you, ladylove, that it wasn't I who sent her there.*

"We're well matched, aren't we?" She tried something she had thought of a little while since, something deliciously wanton. His gasp of surprise gave way to one of piercing pleasure. "First payment," she said. And second, and third, and fourth. It kept her from remembering what he had omitted to say. He had not denied that he would go.

Too soon; but it was she who named the moment. He was asleep at last; she hated to wake him. But the day was racing toward evening. Bianca must come back before night, and Uncle Gregorios would be wanting his supper, and they would rage if they knew what she had done while they were gone.

She dressed slowly, combed and braided her hair. Her reflection in the old bronze mirror was no different than it had been the last time she saw it, ages ago; she was still Stefania. And he was still Nikephoros, but now that bare name meant more than worlds.

She was going to cry again, and she must not. When she had mastered her face, she bent over him and kissed him awake. His eyes opened; he peered without recognition. She kissed him again. Awareness grew; he smiled. She played a little with the tousle of his hair. "Wake up, love; it's getting on for evening."

He stretched and sighed. He would be happy to stay just where he was.

"You won't be when Bianca finds you. Up now, and tell me how all this goes on."

Termagant. He smiled ruefully and sorted out the tangle of his clothes, directing while she tugged and laced and—inevitably—tarried to play. Had she been even a shade less sensible, they would have ended as they began, with garments scattered and bodies twined.

She tore herself away, smoothing her gown and her ruffled hair. He was all lordly splendid, and growing lordly stern as passion faded and knowledge woke. *Come to San Girolamo with me,* he said. *Come that far at least.*

She hesitated. After a moment she nodded.

The lower room was bright with sunlight. Arlecchina blinked in it, purring loudly, enthroned in Anna's lap. Anna's face was stiff and pale, as if she had emptied herself of everything but patience.

Stefania felt the blood rush to her cheeks. "Anna!" she cried too brightly. "How long have you been here?"

"Not very long." Anna glanced from her to Nikki, seeing much too much, and understanding all of it. Her mouth took on an ironic twist. "They've been waiting for you, little brother."

Something in her tone brought him across the room. *Anna, what's happened?*

"Nothing." She smiled to prove it. "Alf is desperate to be gone. Poor Brother Oddone; he's too devastated even to cry, but the Prior at least is glad to see the last of us. His theology hasn't been very comfortable lately."

No good; he of all people could see through a cloud of words. *You aren't going.*

"I've decided not to," she said. "Stefania, do you still want to be a philosopher? I do, very much. And I have the means. Prior Giacomo knows of a house or two that might suit us, and that's a miracle in its own right; after what he's seen, he says, he finds a pack of female scholars frankly reassuring. Alf has given me gifts, not just my share of the family treasure, but *books.* You wouldn't believe—he has an Albumazar he insists he doesn't need, a half-dozen volumes of Aristotle, a Macrobius with his own commentary . . ."

"Do I want all that?" Stefania cried. "I dream about it." She stilled. "You're not joking, are you?"

Anna crossed herself Greek fashion. "By the bones of Chrysostomos, every bit of it is true. I came to ask you if you'd share it with me. Unless . . ." She glanced at Nikki. "Unless there've been changes."

"No," Stefania answered steadily, "there've been no changes. We were only saying good-bye."

You aren't going, Nikki said again.

"Of course I'm not." Anna glared. "What made you think I could? I've always known that when the Folk went into Broceliande, I'd have to stay behind. I can't face Rhiyana without them. Rome is a pleasant enough place, and I've found friends here just in the few days I've been free. Father Jehan's promised to come when he can; a bishop can always find excuses to call on the Curia. Or I can call on him, if it comes to that. I might find I want to do a little goliarding in a year or three, when Rome begins to pall on me."

She made it all so simple. But she was human. She had no need to choose.

"I have no choice." She drew a long breath. "May I stay here, Stefania? Just for a little while?"

"As long as you need to," Stefania said, embracing Anna quickly, tightly. "Are you coming with us to San Girolamo?"

Anna shook her head. "No. No, it was hard enough to do once. I'll be a coward and stay here."

And do her crying in privacy. Stefania hugged her again. "I'll come back as soon as I can. Tell Bianca where I've gone." She grimaced. "Don't be surprised if she puts you to work."

Anna smiled. "Go on now. Alf's been threatening to leave without Nikki; you'd better hurry before he actually does it."

Even yet Nikki hung back, looking hard at his sister's face, seeing all her sacrifices. At least he had had his love requited, if only for a day. She had had a deeply loving embrace, a fraternal kiss with a tear behind it, and a trove of treasures, none of it worth a single touch of Stefania's hand.

But what could he give her? An embrace, a kiss and a tear, his own share of the wealth of House Akestas since in Broceliande he would have no need of it. He held her for a long while between his strong arm and his splinted one, pouring into her mind all the comfort he could muster. She was going to thrive. She was going to be happy, one woman wedded to all the philosophers, with sisters to bear her company and riches to ease her way.

"And Father Jehan when I need him, and a whole life to make what I like of." She held her brother's face in her hands. "Good-bye, Nikki. Be good. You can if you work at it, you know."

I should want to?

She slapped him lightly and let him go. "Brat. Take care of Alf for me. Now stop dawdling; can't you hear him yelling for you?"

He looked back once. She was turned away from him, bent over the cat in her lap, steadfastly ignoring everything but the silken harlequin fur.

They were waiting, the strange ones and their massive brown-cowled Bishop, and although they were all courtesy, their impatience was strong enough to taste. Nikki made Stefania come all the way with him, gripping her hand, so that she stood face to face with the witch-woman. The gold-brown eyes passed quickly over her; she shuddered deep within. They were so close to human, and so very far from it. Their interest was warm enough, their assessment rather more approving than not, but they were not the eyes of anyone with whom she could share anything that mattered.

Nikki let her go. He was shaking, and trying not to, and surely he hated himself for it. She saw him again as she had once before, small and dark and flawed, human, mortal, no kin at all to the high beauty about him. And then he moved, or his magic moved, and he was inextricably a part of them. The light in his eyes had its reflection in the eyes of his brother. Or was Nikephoros the reflection? The moon to the white enchanter's sun, with no power but what his master chose to bestow upon him. And without it—

Eye met cat-flaring eye. The witch-folk drew together, drawing Nikki with them. On the very edge of hearing, the air began to sing.

"Nikephoros!" she cried.

The note died abruptly. The tall ones stood still. Nikki looked at her, and the pain in his eyes made her want to weep aloud.

"Stay," she begged him, with all her heart in it. "Stay and love me."

His hand rose, reached. *Come with me.*

"You know I can't."

The hand began to fall. All at once Stefania hated him, hated him with a passion only love could engender. "You *know* I can't! This is my world. This one, and no other. Just as it is yours. What will you do among the immortals? Trail behind them. Ape their mighty magics with your little borrowed power. Go slowly mad, and die gibbering, too far gone even to wish you had had the sense to escape while you could."

His head shook from side to side. This world promised only the dulled existence of a cripple. The other promised all the splendor of power, free and fearless, far from human terrors. *You can come. You can share it. Perhaps—even—*

"If I could ever have become a witch, that time is long past." She spoke quietly, almost calmly, but for the tremor she could not quell. "You are a coward, Nikephoros Akestas. You seduced me, knowing what you would do to me, knowing that I could never follow you. You wanted me, and when it was safe, you made sure you had me. This little pain that pays for it, that will go away. You have all your Fair Folk, and the glory and the lightnings, and the memory of a little mortal fool to reassure you when you wonder if you've made the wrong choice. What more could you ask for?"

Stefania, he whispered.

But he did not whisper. He had no voice that he would use. "No, child, you may not have me, and Broceliande too. It's one or the other. Choose."

For a little while she knew that she had won. He came toward her. One more step and his arm would come to circle her. Her body felt it already, yearned for it.

He stopped. He looked back. His kin did nothing, said nothing, only stood and waited and *were*. More beautiful than any mortal creature, more splendid, more powerful, mantled in magic.

She watched them conquer him. They did not mean to do it. No more did the candle mean to draw the foolish fluttering moth. He looked on their faces and fell headlong into their eyes, and when again he faced Stefania, it was from between the witch and the enchanter. His whole body cried pain, begged for forgiveness. It even dared, even yet, to beseech her to follow him.

She would not move. Even when his kiss touched her lips, an air-soft invisible ghost-kiss, lingering, burning. Trying to have it all, refusing to acknowledge the truth. With an effort that made her gasp, she willed him away. "Go," she said through set and aching teeth. "Go where you think you must." And more slowly, as the pain began to master her: "God—oh, damn you, God go with you."

They were there, all of them, close together. Then they were not. There was only a shimmer, fading fast, and a memory of Nikephoros' black eyes bright with tears.

32

The churches of Rhiyana were dark, their gates bolted and sealed, the vigil lamps lightless above the silent altars. The dying passed unshriven; the dead lay cold in unconsecrated ground. The living knew no consolation of holy Church, neither Mass nor sacraments; not even in the abbeys might monks sing the Offices, on pain of flogging and expulsion.

They dared it, Benedetto Torrino knew surely, as priests in the villages dared administer the sacraments in secret, even under the watchful eyes of God's Hounds. But the grimness of the Interdict, coupled with war and winter, beat down even the most valiant.

He had nothing to do with it. The Paulines had circumvented him; on the authority of their new Papal Legate, still on the road from Rome, they had lowered the ban. Having no authority more recent or more potent, and no army to defend it, he was powerless.

What little he could do, he did. Every morning since the Interdict began, he had sung Mass in the castle. He made no great secret of it. Even yet the Hounds did not dare to pass the gates, and they learned not to keep the people of the city from passing them. As they were learning that one winter's preaching and one week's Interdict could not turn Rhiyana's folk against their King of fourscore years. It only taught them to hate the men whose coming had wrought all their suffering.

Tonight again the Queen had sent her page. The Lord Cardinal was bidden to dine with her, as he had been bidden every night since that day in the garden. Tonight again he sent a gracious refusal. The words came no more easily this seventh time than they had the first. He saw her at Mass, and that was already as much as he could bear; he dared not sit beside her, even among her ladies and her courtiers, and try to conduct himself as if she were no more to him than any highborn matron. Not with such thoughts as he had, that not only she among her court could read. Nor with such dreams as he had been having, sweet torment that they were, impervious to prayer and fasting.

He dined on prayer and water, alone, his few loyal monks sent unwillingly away. His head was light with abstinence, the pangs of hunger vanquished. But not the pangs he longed to be rid of. This storm-ridden night they took flesh and stood before him all in white, ivory hair loose to ivory ankles, golden eyes shining.

"Lady," he prayed from his aching knees, "must you haunt me in the flesh as in the spirit?"

She knelt to face him. "There is war in Heaven," she said. "Do your bones not feel it? Does the wind not bring you its clamor?"

It was she. He caught the faint rose-sweet scent of her. By Heaven's bitter irony, her presence so close eased his torment. He could bow over her hand, he could rise and raise her with him, setting her in the chair which faced the fire. He could even venture to rebuke her. "Lady, you know you should not be here."

"Where else should I be? My lord is barred to me, and my own people have no comfort for me, and the world is ending."

"It is only a storm of sleet."

She laughed as clearly and as sweetly as a child. "O mortal man! May the world not end in sleet as easily as in fire?" She sobered; she spread her hands to the blaze, that turned their pallor to rose-gold. "I cry your pardon, my lord. I am a little mad, I think, and truly it is not all with grief. Our great enemy is dead by his own will, dead these two days. Our Chancellor has spoken with the Pope and gained pardon for us all. But still I cannot touch the mind of my King."

He forgot himself utterly; he seized her hands. "The Pope? They have gone to the Pope?"

"To Saint Peter's own successor. The Hounds are chastised and sent to their kennels. The Interdict is lifted—I have proclaimed it, which is presumptuous of me, mere temporal regent that I am, but it is too mighty a secret to keep from my people. We . . . we are forgiven, within limits. You need not fret now, Lord Cardinal; you are not obliged to send us to the fire."

"*Hosanna in excelsis!*" He was so glad that he sang it in full voice. "Lady, Lady, I do believe in God's mercy again. And you said"—his joy died—"the King is . . . dead?"

"No!" she cried. "He lives, but now truly he is dying, and his power struggles to preserve him against invasion. All invasion, even the touch of my mind. Even—even healing. It is our nature. In extremity, it turns against us."

"So your kingdom is saved, but your King—"

Her chin lifted; her eyes glittered. "He has not died yet, and my lord Alfred is coming. We shall see whether the King of Rhiyana can stand against the Master of Broceliande."

"If there is aught I can do, if I may ride or pray, storm a castle or storm Heaven itself, you need only command me."

She was careful of her smile. She kept it within mortal limits. Yet he was lost long since; he could only fall deeper into the enchantment. No matter that his mind was clear enough to mock him. Great prince of priests that he was, and no boy either, he flung himself at her feet like any callow simpleton of a squire.

"Alas, my lord," she said, "I have bewitched you. And alas for me, the spell also strikes the one who casts it. Perhaps we should both storm Heaven."

"But first, let us muzzle God's Hounds." Her witchery too; with her hands in his, he saw all that needed doing, and all that he could do. "My lady, if you will lend me a company of your guards and the aid of one or two of your Kin, I shall be pleased to cleanse this city of its pestilence. And," he added, "to free its Archbishop from the prison into which yon madmen have flung him."

He was on his feet, vivid with eagerness, but she gripped his hands. "Lord Cardinal, is it wise? Have you forgotten in whose name you are here?"

"Indeed not. Pope Honorius has spoken for you; and I am more than glad to take his part against the destroyers of your kingdom."

"Brave man!"

Torrino wheeled toward the strong clear voice with its touch of laughter. Maura started and cried out in gladness, drawing Thea into a swift embrace, and Jehan after her, and the children who faced all this strangeness with wide eyes and firm courage. As the Queen took them up gently and kissed their fears away, Thea said, "The others have gone to beat some sense into Gwydion. In the meantime, Eminence, if you're minded to hunt Hounds, here's an arrow for your bow."

He took the parchment with its pendant seals, running his eye over it. Here was proof positive of the Queen's tidings, confirmation of his embassy and full power to settle matters in Rhiyana as he saw fit. "So shall I do," he said, "with deep pleasure. My lord Bishop, would it please you to aid me? If it comes to a fight, whether the weapons be words or blades, there are few men I would rather have at my back."

Jehan grinned. "Do you think you can keep me from it? Lead on, Eminence; I'll be behind you."

"And we," said Maura, "will be beside you." As the Cardinal struggled between courtesy and flat refusal, she laughed. "You asked for a witch or two; so shall you receive. Cynan, Liahan, you must hold the castle for us. Tao-Lin will keep you company."

She came in the disconcerting fashion of the Kindred, all at once, out of air, settling herself with eastern serenity. When Torrino passed the door, she was enchanting her charges, quite literally, with a dance of crimson fire.

The King lay as he had lain for many days, in his castle of Carmennos half a league from the March of Anjou. His power in its throes had wrought wonders and terrors within those walls; dreamworld and solid world lay side by side, and the air shifted and shimmered with the flux of his pain. When his mind was clearer he had sent the human folk away, all but those whose love overmastered their fear. They guarded him; they gave him what care he would permit, and manned the walls against enemies who did not come. That much his power did for them. It drove back any who willed harm to castle or people.

And any who willed help. Alf, barred from Gwydion's presence as completely as any Angevin bandit, stood outside in the dark and the storm and gathered his own power. Already he was cloaked in it, shining with it. Wind and sleet had no strength to touch him.

Nikki could, though not easily; it cost him an instant of burning-cold pain. *Alf,* he said, a mental gasp. *Alf, don't waste power. Let me do it.*

Before Alf could frame a protest, Nikki had raised his own shields. Alf knew a moment of vertigo, disconcerting yet familiar, mark of the boy's strange power. They thrust forward against a wind that was suddenly bitter, into the lash of sleet, up the precipitous path to the gate. Shielded and invisible, they passed through oak and iron into a dark courtyard. And again, bold now, through nothingness into the eye of the storm.

It was flawlessly still. A room like a death chamber, lit by no earthly light. The King lay on the bed as on a bier, covered with a great pall of blue and silver, with a white sheen upon him and a hooded shape beside him. That one rose as the two entered, hood slipping back from Gwydion's own face.

Nikki ran to clasp Prince Aidan tightly, spinning him about with the force of the onslaught, nearly oversetting him. His grin put the shadows to flight; his cry would have waked the dead. "God be thanked! How did you get in?"

How did you? Nikki stood back, looking hard at him. *Anna said she saw you die. You don't look as if you're far from it.*

"I am now," Prince Aidan said, "though two days ago I was lying beside my brother. When you paladins broke the power that was killing us, Morgiana dragged me up and beat life into me. But Gwydion was already past that." His eyes glittered. "Damn you, Alfred. Damn your soft heart. How dared you reward that monster with an easy death?"

Alf raised a brow. "Would it matter to Gwydion if Simon Magus had died in agony?"

"It would matter to me." Aidan's eyes closed; he shook his head. He looked very old and very weary, and sick nigh to death. "Enough, brother. If there is aught that you can do, for God's love do it."

"For God's love," Alf said, "and yours." He held the Prince for a moment, catching his breath at the contact. Aidan had barely strength to stand, let alone to rage at him. "Nikephoros, take this valiant fool to the hall and feed him. And see that he sleeps after. Preferably with his Princess beside him."

Once gone, Nikki dragging the tall lord with inescapable persistence, they could not come back. Gwydion's shields were too strong; and Alf's own had risen, weaving a web even Nikephoros could not pierce.

Alf stood by the bed. Gwydion's state had one mercy: it preserved his body from decay. He looked much as he had when Alf left him, even to his stillness, which had the likeness of serenity. Alf folded back the pall. He was naked under it, his only wound that one which drained his life away. Deep but clean, all but bloodless, fresh as if the arrow had pierced it that morning. It had not even begun to heal.

"Thank all the saints," Alf said aloud, softly, "that the dart did not pierce the bone. And that it was not a handspan higher." His hands passed over the wound, not touching it. No healing woke in them. He ventured a brush of power. Nothing. The King might have been armored in glass and steel.

Without, beyond the center of quiet, the castle trembled. A creature of horror and shadow paced the halls. Men felt their bodies thin and fade, shriveling into mist.

Alf raised his head. Death was close now. As if Gwydion had only waited upon Alf's coming, clinging to life until the Master returned to Broceliande, and now he let the dark wings spread for him. He went without regret. He had lived long, he had ruled well, he had seen to the preservation of his kingdom and of his Kin. Kings dreamed of such an end; few indeed were given the grace to receive it.

"No," Alf said. His anger was rising. Ah, he was growing fiery, two fits of wrath in scarce three days. But he had had enough. Simon, Jehan, Nikki, Gwydion, every one stood fast against him. Every one had demanded to suffer; every one had balked the flow of healing. But healing, balked, ripened into rage. A white rage, blinding and relentless, edged with adamant. Alf drove it into the King's armor, implacably, mercilessly, with all the force of his thwarted pride. He clove shield and wall, he pierced flesh and bone, he thrust at the very roots of power, that were the roots of life. What Simon had refused, what Jehan had denied, what Nikephoros had turned away, all those he called together, and he beset the door that Simon had closed and Gwydion's will had barred. The wonted warmth was a cleansing fire, the wonted numbness an exquisite agony. It beckoned. It seduced. It lured him down the path that was the King's death.

He wrenched himself from the trap. He made a ram of his body. He drove it with wrath. The door trembled, bulged, swelled into a shape that was no shape, that had no name but blind resistance.

The wrath mounted to white heat and transmuted into ice. Alf made it a mirror. He shaped on it an image. Maura's face when she saw the body of her son. But it was Gwydion she looked on, shrunken in death, hands like claws on the still breast. And she must gaze, and suffer, and know that she could not follow. Her power would not allow it. Mindless shapeless obstinate animal, it knew only that it must live, and to live it must defend itself, and to defend itself it must yield to no will but its own. And for it, and for Gwydion's own folly, she must endure all her deathless life alone.

The mirror began to waver. The face for all its beauty was old beyond bearing, scored with grief that would never again know joy. Alf raised face and mirror together, each within each, and flung them toward the door that had risen once more to bar his way. The mirror smote it and shattered. The shards pierced the barrier, flecks of ice and silver that budded and blossomed into swords. The door trembled, buckled, fell. He plunged within, into a storm of heatless fire. It caught him, whirled him. He raised the last vestiges of his will and his wrath and his healing. He spoke to the heart of the madness. "Peace," he said with awful gentleness. "Be still."

Alf opened his eyes upon quiet. The light of power glimmered low. The wind had fallen; the sleet yielded before the softness of snow.

Gwydion's breast rose and fell, drawing deep shuddering breaths. Deep for life's returning, shuddering in fear of the fiery pain that but a moment before had filled all his body. But the pain had gone. The wound had closed. Even as Alf watched, it paled from scarlet to livid to watered-wine to white. The King's hand trembled upon it.

Alf met the clouded gray stare. Gwydion's brows drew together in a struggle to remember; he turned his head from side to side, testing its obedience. His hand traveled up to search his face. His beard, that had been close cut, felt strange; was long enough to curl. He fought to shape words. "How long—"

Alf answered beyond words, mind to mind, all that the dimmed awareness could bear. Like a newborn child forced at first to the breast, Gwydion learned hunger; he reached, he clung, he drew greedily upon the other's memory.

His grip eased. He lay still. After a long while, measured in his slow heartbeats, he said, "The war will end now." He spoke without either joy or anger, in that tone which even the strongest of his Kin had learned not to gainsay.

Alf was a poor scholar of such prudence. "So it will, but not by your riding from end to end of Rhiyana in a blaze of power."

"Would I be so flamboyant a fool?"

Alf simply looked at him, with the merest hint of a smile.

Gwydion sat up unsteadily. "I would." His voice was rueful. "I shall yield to your tyranny. My brother will go. And—"

"Your brother is in no better straits than you. Be wise, my lord. Remember the walls and the wards."

The King's eyes narrowed. His power sang softly, testing its limits and the limits of the web they had woven about Rhiyana, all of them, with Alf at their center, in the dance of the year's turning. Simon Magus had torn great rents in the fabric; his passing had not healed them, for marauding armies filled them, and human folk driven to madness and riot, and Hounds of God in Caer Gwent itself.

Gwydion touched the great blooming flame that was his Chancellor; the rioting fire of his brother; Nikephoros' deceptively quiet brilliance, and the manifold powers of his people. And at last, with deep joy, the moon-bright splendor of his Queen. As easily, as effortlessly as a lady chooses a thread for her tapestry, slips it through the eye of her needle and begins the veining of a leaf, Gwydion gathered them all into the shaping of his pattern.

The snow fell softly. The cold was almost gentle. Fires in cot and castle, banked until morning, swelled into sudden warmth. Hearts eased; dreams turned all to peace. But in the camps of wandering companies, in captured villages and in fortresses seized by assault or treachery, flames kindled for comfort gave birth to demons. Shadows woke to a life of fang and claw. Wolves howled; things of horror abandoned dreams for flesh. Men woke screaming to a nightmare worse than any in sleep, a land that had roused at last and turned against them. *Out!* roared the very stones. *Begone!* The shadows' claws were cruelly sharp, dragging laggards and cowards from their beds. Wolves and worse nipped at the heels of horses that knew only one desire, to bear their riders across the borders of this terrible country. But the horseless moved no more slowly. Some rode helpless on the back of the wind; others ran like driven deer, swift, blind, tireless. And those who had advanced farthest, the lords and captains whose forces had eluded Rhiyana's defenses to strike at the kingdom's heart, knew darkness and whirlwind and terror beyond mortal endurance, and some woke mad and some woke blind or maimed or aged long years in that single night, but all woke to morning far beyond the Marches of Rhiyana.

The Hounds of God rested complacent. Without Simon's power they could not know what had passed in Rome, save as mortal men know, at a full fortnight's remove by the swiftest of couriers. Their own chosen Legate was coming, lay indeed in an abbey two days from Rhiyana's marches. They had heard some nonsense of a royal proclamation, a denial of the Interdict and a confirmation of the Cardinal Torrino's authority, but they credited none of it.

"The King is dead," said the Father General's deputy in Rhiyana, taking his ease in his study with one or two of his brethren. "We can be sure of that. The Queen keeps up her pretense that he lives; this new folly is an act of desperation, a struggle to win the Church and the people to her dying cause. Little good it can do her, with God Himself binding her magics."

"And the Pope's own Legate disporting himself in her bed." The monk's lips were tight with outrage, the words bitten off sharply, but the glitter in his eyes spoke more of envy than of priestly indignation.

His superior regarded him with disapproval. "Brother, that is not charitable, nor is it proven. We cleave to the truth here. Never to mere speculation."

"And if it is proven, Father?"

"We have no need of that," the third man said with a flicker of impatience. "Whether she be an angel of chastity or the very Whore of Babylon, she rides now to her fall. We have won Rhiyana. Tomorrow, I say—tomorrow and no later, let us summon her to our tribunal."

The monk's lips curled. "A trial? Would you trouble yourself with such mummery? Hale her forth and burn her, and have done."

"Brother," they began, almost in unison.

The door burst open; a very young lay brother flung himself at the Superior's feet. "Attack!" he gasped. "Army—Queen—sorcery—"

"Impossible." The Superior was on his feet. "Cease this babbling and explain yourself."

The boy had his breath back, and some of his wits. Enough for coherence. "Father, I am not raving. We are beset by a company in the livery of the Queen. The Cardinal rides before them with the Queen and another witch, with an army of wolf-familiars and a man in the armor of a Jeromite warrior bishop. And . . . and with the Archbishop of Caer Gwent, who is in no forgiving temper."

"An army indeed," the Superior said, cool and quiet. "I hear no cries of battle."

"There is no battle yet, Father." Between youth and terror and the sheer unwontedness of it all, he was almost weeping. "They command that we open the gates and deliver ourselves up. They—they say they have a mandate from the Pope's own hand."

"It looks," the third man observed with an ironic twist, "as if Her Majesty has anticipated us. She would hale us forth; I wonder, will she burn us?"

The boy crossed himself. "Sweet Mother Mary defend us! Father, Brothers, they are terrible. They are mantled in sorcery. The bishop—the bishop who spoke for them, he bade me tell you that you will hasten, or they will fling down the gate and seize us all."

"They already have." He was immense; he was smiling the sweet guileless smile of a child, frightening on that Norman reiver's face. He stepped aside to admit the Cardinal Torrino and a grimly smiling archbishop and a fierce-eyed bronze-gold witch, and the ivory delicacy of the Queen. A delicacy that smote the heart even when one knew that she wore mail and surcoat like a man, and stood nigh as tall as the armored Bishop, and matched her pace to that of a wolf as great as a moor-pony. She took the Superior's seat as her right, the wolf settling molten-eyed at her feet.

Her own eyes were fiery gold yet strangely gentle, resting lightly upon these men who struggled not to shrink from her. For all their bitter enmity, none had yet stood face to face with any of her kind. "You will pardon the intrusion," she said, "but we have tidings which could not wait upon your pleasure. My lord Archbishop?"

With grim relish, he set the Pope's parchment in the Superior's hand. The Pauline priest read it slowly, with great care, without expression. When he was done he returned the writ to its bearer, calm still. But the witches knew and the men guessed what raged behind the mask. Raged and could not burst forth. It was all in order. Perfectly. It was all decided in the Devil's favor. They gloated, those women who were not women, those daughters of Lilith with their demons' eyes.

One man found voice to speak, he who had spoken of the Queen's adultery. "You have not triumphed," he said low and harsh. "We are not ordered out of this kingdom."

"You are." Benedetto Torrino had to fight to keep the satisfaction out of face and voice. "I so command it; and I am Pope Honorius' voice in Rhiyana."

"That can be argued."

"That will be obeyed. I have sent messages to your false Legate. If he would not be brought to trial as an usurper and an impostor, he had best refrain from completing his journey." The Cardinal examined each in turn. His fine Roman nostrils flared; his fine brows met. "You and all your ilk will join him as soon as may be. You have until sunrise to depart from this city, you and all your cattle; if by the fifth day hence this realm is not clean of your presence, I will loose its folk upon you."

"We fear no witches."

Torrino's voice was silken. "I was not speaking of the King's Kindred." Almost he smiled. Almost he was kind. "You had best be quick, Brothers. Morning may be closer than you think."

Deliberately, meticulously, the Superior made obeisance to him, to Bishop and Archbishop, to the Queen and her familiars. "We are vowed to obedience," he said. But he paused, face to face with Maura. "We go as we are bidden, without treachery, for we are men of honor as well as men of God. But you will have small occasion to rejoice. Our exile may endure no longer than the life of one aging Pope, and then we may return to greater victory. Your exile must endure for all of time."

"Perhaps not," said the bronze witch. "The world changes. Men change. One day we may come forth again."

"Not in this age of the world," said the vicar of Saint Paul in

Rhiyana. "No, lady witch; your triumph rings hollow. God and His Hounds and His mortal children have won this kingdom. Not all your spells and sorceries can gain it back again." He signed himself with the cross and beckoned to his companions. "Come, Brothers; we are cast forth, for a time. Let us go in what dignity we may."

33

"Tomorrow," Alf said, "we go."

Jehan forgot what he had come to the Chancery for. He forgot twenty years of hard lessoning in the world and in the church and, most brutally, in the papal Curia. He burst out like a raw boy, with a boy's sudden terrible hurt. *"Tomorrow!* It's still the dead of winter. Rhiyana's still in an uproar over the war. Gwydion's heir doesn't even know he's—"

"Duke Rhodri knows he will be King. Gwydion told him a long while ago, when he was a boy. Now he knows the day and the hour. Much to his credit, he's less elated than frightened that it has come at last; and he grieves for the loss of his dear lord."

Words, empty rattling words. Jehan shook them out of his head. "You weren't to go till Pentecost."

"We were to go no later." Alf caught the tail of Cynan's gown before it vanished over the threshold, and swung the child into his lap. "No, imp. No forays among my poor clerks." He laughed at his son's deep displeasure, and said still laughing, "Little terror; he drove Mabon the under-chancellor into hysterics by falling out of air into my lap. With his gown coming separately and somewhat later, and falling full on Mabon's head. He's not quite the master of his power yet."

"I am too," snapped Cynan, sounding remarkably like his mother. "I hate clothes."

"They keep you warm," his father said.

"I keep myself warm." He shut his eyes in concentration, opened them again. The gown vanished. He grinned at them both with wicked innocence.

Alf sighed deeply. "You are a trial to your father's soul."

"Your father is a trial to mine." Jehan's pain had lost its edge, Alf's doing, damn him. "You are a conniver, do you know that? A heartless manipulator. A damned, ice-blooded, eternally scheming witch. Why won't you let me do my hurting in peace? I'll tell you. Because it hurts *you*."

"It does," Alf agreed, calm as he always was when the target was only himself. "Jehan, we must go. The Pope has commanded it. For the kingdom's welfare, for our own good, we can't linger. Nor can we spread abroad that we go, or all Rhiyana will rise, some few to cast us forth, most to bar our way. Even yet Gwydion is well loved." He paused for breath, for compassion. "Tomorrow the King goes hunting with his Kin on the borders of Broceliande. We will not come back."

This was worse than death. In a score or two of years, Jehan himself would die; if the doctrine he preached was true, he would live again with those he loved about him. But not Alfred. Not any of these people whom he had come to love as his own blood kin.

"Except one," he said. "The one I hated. God help me! I slit the wrong throat."

"Jehan—"

He spun away.

"Jehan de Sevigny, what did you say to Anna about growing up?"

He spun back. "Is there anything you don't know?"

Alf went on quietly, almost absently, as if Jehan had not spoken. "I was never very good for you. I demanded so much of you. So much looking after; so much thankless pain."

"As if I didn't give back every bit of it ten times over." Jehan sat down slowly. Suddenly he was very tired. "I'm a disgrace," he muttered. "Anna, that stubborn little snip of a girl—she grew up. She let you go. But I who was preaching that doctrine to her, I've been bellowing like a weanling calf."

Alf said nothing. Jehan laughed painfully. "Don't fret, Alfred. I'll wean myself. When you're gone I'll do what they do in an abbey when a sainted Brother dies, and declare a three-days' festival."

Still silence. Cynan was utterly subdued, even when his father set him on the carpet by the fire and walked to the window. The cold snowlight leached the gold from Alf's hair, the youth from his face. He had never looked less human. Jehan had never loved him more.

His voice came soft and slow. "Jehan, there is one thing. I would—if you would—Thea and I, we would like our children to belong properly and formally to God, however we all may end. I know it is Lent, I know you should not, but since there will be no chance hereafter . . . will you perform the rite for them?"

Jehan's throat closed. He wrestled it open. "Of course I will. If you can still want anything to do with the Church that cast you out into the cold."

Alf turned swiftly, all his ice turned to fire. "But it did not!" He reached Jehan in a stride, grasped the wide shoulders, shook them lightly. "Jehan, Jehan, didn't you understand? Didn't you see? His Holiness exiled us all, and in a very strict sense we are excommunicate—cast out as no humans ever have been, set apart from every office of the Church. That was his duty, his obligation under canon law. But when he spoke to me, behind and among his words he told me another thing. He left me to God and to my own wisdom. He set me free."

Jehan shook his head, denying nothing, trying only to clear his fogged brain.

"Listen," said the eager beautiful voice. "See. He struck away the chains I forged of a lifetime in the cloister. He said, *Go, find your God where He waits for you, where He has always waited for His strangest children.* I was a priest, I am one still, I shall be forever, but of what faith or rite or order, only God may tell me. For what is a priest after all, but a servant of God?"

The mingling of exaltation and sorrow that had lain on Alf since they left the palace of the Lateran, that had seemed the simple bitter-sweetness of a victory won hard and at great cost, lay now all bare to Jehan's wondering eyes. Honorius, the devious old courtier, had shown Alf the way out of his long dilemma, and done it without a single uncanonical word. And Jehan had thought that the Pope was only casting all his troubles into the lap of a higher Authority.

"What more did he need to do?" asked Alf. "He has sense, does Cencio Savelli: the one thing I've never had. Thea would be angry, if she weren't so highly amused. It took the Pope of Rome to convince me of what she's always known, that I'm flesh and spirit both, and I can't deny one at the expense of the other. I can't go about as half a man, even the half that seemed so happy with its lordship and its lady and its worldly riches. I have to make myself whole." His hands left Jehan's shoulders; he shivered, and for a moment the light went out of him. "It's hard. I don't need prophecy to tell me it will never be easy."

"If it were, would you want to bother with it?"

"No," Alf admitted wryly, "I wouldn't. Sometimes I could sing for joy that the burden is gone. Then I sink down under a world's weight of terror and pain and loss. You're not alone in hating to grow up."

"You've already grown far beyond me." Jehan straightened, found a smile. "And if I know you, you'll get a treatise out of it all."

Alf laughed. "Yes; and I'll set it against that great arrogant folly of my youth, the *Gloria Dei:* a *Gloria magici*, a *Tractatus de rebus obscuris et tremendis*. And no doubt when I'm as old for my kind as now I am for a man, I'll smile at all these childish fancies."

"As long as you don't forget how to smile," Jehan said.

Alf smiled at that with every appearance of ease. Jehan turned away too quickly, eyes and ears and mind closed against any calling back.

It was meant to be a quiet celebration, a Mass and a christening at dawn in Saint John's chapel, with such of the Folk as would come, and no great fanfare. But even before the first glimmer of light had touched the sky, the small space was thronged to bursting. They had all come, all the King's Kin who were still outside the Wood, and the Archbishop in plain Benedictine black, and the Cardinal Torrino, and Duke Rhodri who would be King by sunset, and a number of lesser folk: courtiers, servants, clerks and officers of the Chancery. Everyone who knew that this day's hunting party would not return. Alf had not realized there were so many.

And yet no pall of grief hung over them. They were sad, yes; Rhodri above all looked worn and ill; but they could take a quiet joy in this gathering and this rite.

King and Queen held each a wide-eyed child, Liahan and Cynan both swathed in white silk, but the mere weight of fabric had no power to subdue them. Their minds wove and unwove and rewove with one another, restless, curious, taxing even Gwydion's legendary patience with a barrage of questions. Thea did not stoop to theology, and Alf was not answering: Jehan had coaxed and cajoled and bullied him into the sacristy, and all but forced him into alb and dalmatic. "Just once," the Bishop said. "Just one last time. For me."

But for Alf's own sake too, and Jehan was not fool enough to think that thought would go unread. Pope Honorius had set Alf outside the Canons, freed him from them, but spoken no word that forbade him to serve upon the altar. "And if he had," Jehan growled, "I'd give you a dispensation, and fight it out with him myself."

Alf laughed, but he was shaking uncontrollably. Absurdly, need-lessly; and how many times had he done just this, for Jehan, for Bishop Ogyrfan who was dead, even once for the Archbishop of Caer Gwent? He had not been free then. He had served out of a goodly measure of defiance, to prove to himself that he had escaped all the chains of the cloister.

He had never been as close to panic then as he was now, with the chains a glittering dust about his feet, and his exile full before him. Exile more isolate than any abbey, whiter than the whitest of the white martyrdoms of the island saints, and more complete, set apart within the walls of Broceliande. Once the last gate closed, no mortal man could enter, nor would any immortal depart, perhaps beyond the end of this world.

The altar waited, gleaming softly in its cloth of moonlight and snow. There would be none such where he was going, and no one to raise the Host before it, or to speak the ancient holy words. The chapel in the House of the Falcon was an empty tower open to the stars, with no emblem of any mortal worship. No cross, no crescent, no star or idol or sacred fire. No mask before the face of God.

Yet this altar and this cross, how familiar, how much beloved. This big man with his lived-in, ugly-beautiful face, and his clear eyes, and his heart that was even greater than his body, vesting slowly and trying not to resist Alf's ministrations—how hard, how cruelly hard to know that they would never stand so again. To stay, to cling, to refuse the burden . . .

So then. He could stay. He could defy the Pope, who after all was but a mortal man. And in a little while he would go mad, and there would be a new Simon Magus to torment the world. Even now his power surged against the walls of his control, urging him, tempting him to heal every hurt that came close to him, to open himself wide to all his visions of what would be. It was growing stronger. The duel with Simon, the battle with Gwydion, had swelled it from a constant and endurable ache to a desperate need.

No; it was as well that he was going away. His battered shields were falling one by one. In too brief a while he would be naked, and then he would shatter.

Jehan was vested, waiting, a line of worry between his brows. Alf took up the censer. With a small, childish, rebellious flare of power, he kindled the coal within it. A smile touched his lips, skittered away. Some of the fear fled with it. In the chapel without, Liahan was asking

Gwydion why she had to be presented to God, if He had made her. Was He so forgetful that He needed to be reminded?

The smile crept back, settled, grew a little. The fear slunk into shadow and pretended to sleep.

It was a Mass like any other, and yet it was not. Benedetto Torrino approved the devotion and the sheer physical presence of the man who wore the chasuble, but his eyes lingered most often upon the acolyte. The boy, as it seemed, who performed the duties of a servant, quiet, self-effacing, and bathed in a light that owed nothing at all to lamp or candle or rising morning. It flared to a white fire when King and Queen brought their charges forward. The words and the water flowed over the dark head and the fair one, but the Kindred were not looking at the mortal priest. Alf had emptied his hands of cloth and vessels, and his mind, it seemed, of human rituals. Even as the words of baptism rolled into silence, he raised his hands, and they were filled with light. It brimmed and spilled and flowed as the water had, and the words he sang were the same, and yet how utterly different, for he sang them not with throat and tongue and lips but with the purity of his power.

The light faded as water will, vanishing into air. Liahan shook her damp head and laughed, sudden and sweet in the silence. Alf kissed her brow and that of her brother, smiling the most luminous of all his smiles, and withdrew again into the meekness of the servant. The Bishop of Sarum blinked like a man roused from a dream, shook himself, continued the Mass.

"There walks wonder and splendor," said the Cardinal to the Queen, whom chance and perhaps design had placed beside him in the exodus from the chapel. Gwydion was well ahead with his brother and his somber successor; the lesser ones had scattered, the children been entrusted to their mother, the Folk gone to ready themselves for the riding. So were they alone, they two, if well within sight of the celebrants in the sacristy. From where he stood, Torrino could see the blur of white and gold that was Alfred divesting the Bishop of his chasuble.

"His Holiness saw with truly miraculous clarity," Torrino went on, "to do as he did with your kinsman. But did he know that there could be such glory in our own rite? The Mass of the white enchanter . . . There, surely, is one who has seen the light before the throne of God."

"So he has," she said, "and he has shown us its dim reflection. Which is fortunate for us, whether we be mortal or immortal; we have not his gift, to face the full Glory and live." Her face was still, her eyes downcast. "That is his task. To be the bridge; one might say, to be our saint. I find, now my queenship is over and my exile begins, that I am very glad of him. He at least is going to fulfill his nature."

"And you are not?"

She shrugged simply, as a child will. "I have never known, truly and indubitably, what I am. I was a village witch. I became a queen. I was never wholly content with either. Now I shall be . . . I know not what. Do you know that we will be alone? No servants. No attendants. Only ourselves and our power. It is going to be very strange." Her eyes lifted; they were clear gold. "It is a whole new world."

He looked at her and his own eyes dimmed. Already she had severed herself from humankind, had turned mind and heart upon that world no mortal would enter.

She and her wedded lord. She had greeted Gwydion's return with courtly propriety, but Torrino had seen the spark that leaped between them, and the sheen that had lain upon them since. He had made himself see it. He had made it his atonement.

He made himself bow, although a smile was beyond him. "Whatever you become, you can never be less than royal."

Her laughter both angered and soothed him. "But, Eminence, that is only habit and the weight of a crown. I shall be glad to see the last of both."

He was silent. Her eyes softened; her voice grew gentle. "I shall always remember you."

"That," he said with control that amazed them both, "is a very great gift."

"I must go." She kissed him lightly, yet that lone brief touch would burn him lifelong. "Fare you well, my lord."

They rode out in the cold clear morning, all the Fair Folk together, with hawks and hounds and the Queen's wolves and one small green-eyed black cat that rode in the fold of Nikephoros' sling, and a company of mortal men who would witness the passing of the Kindred. The King's aging seneschal led them, somewhat grimmer-faced even than his wont, and Jehan had attached himself to them. No one stopped him. Not that he had any delusions of anonymity; the beard he still wore, and the Jeromite habit kilted over high soft boots, were even less disguise here than they had been in Rome. He established himself beside Alf, and there he stayed, saying little, doing his best to think of nothing beyond the moment.

Nikephoros rode far back, somewhat apart from the rest. He had glanced back only once at Caer Gwent; at the tower from which the King's banner still flew, proud merciful deception; at the people lining the road between. They would not know until he was long gone that they had seen the last of their Elvenking. That even now the twice-great grandson of his sister, a mortal man, not young, sat in the King's chamber with his Duchess who had become his Queen, and contemplated the crown which Gwydion had laid in his hands. They were Rhodri's people now, who cried Gwydion's name, who even paused here and there and muttered against a king who could ride a-hunting so close upon so grim a war.

Nikki barred his mind to them. They had never been his own folk. He was born a Greek; he had become an enchanter. His adopted kin rode ahead of him, some silent and somber, some singing. More than once Tao-Lin looked over her shoulder, almond eyes at once bright and soft. He willed himself to smile in response. *Tonight,* she promised, a thought like a caress.

He shivered and cast up all his shields. The silence was blessed; appalling. His hands and feet, unguarded, throbbed with cold. He turned his face to the brilliant warmthless sun. The same sun that shone on Broceliande, yet not the same at all. The walls of power made it strange. Softened it, turned its glare to a wash of gold.

His traitor mind cast him back to the sun of Rome, potent even in winter. Showed him his own face that could not even blanch to white, only to sallow gray, so long had the eastern sun burned upon his ancestors. And raised up an image he had schooled himself never to see again.

On the night of the King's return, Tao-Lin had come to Nikki's bed. It was nothing new or shocking; she had come many a time before, as he had come to hers. The two of them had always reckoned that they were lovers, though not, to be sure, in the pure and single-minded fashion of those other scandalous sinners, his brother and the Lady Althea.

That night when the war ended, Nikki had welcomed Tao-Lin. Had made her laugh and exclaim that he was eating her alive. Had taken her with something very like brutality. And through every moment, seen not those bright black eyes, but eyes the color of evening. Stroked skin like perfect ivory, and remembered soft dark down on human flesh. Clasped her who had been a famous courtesan, and could think of nothing but a sweetly awkward, very mortal woman.

He shook his head, eyes clenched shut. Their choices were all made. She had returned to the course she had long since chosen, and he was riding to the fate that had been his since an Anglian enchanter fell sunstruck upon the road to Byzantium. What had been between them had been diversion only. Lust; infatuation. A few days' glorious folly. She had learned swiftly to hate him, and by now she would have learned to forget him. In Broceliande, where power ruled and human fear could not come, he would forget her. This was only pain; it would pass.

But ah, before it passed, how terribly it hurt.

It did no good to open his eyes. The sun smote them; the wind whipped them to tears. The earth was harsh and winter-gray and bitterly beautiful, stretching wide before him all unexplored.

He would explore the world within, the realm of power that was vaster than the earth and all upon it. And some of the Folk spoke already of wandering beyond; it was only the world of men that was barred to them. To rise beyond the circle of the moon, to walk among the spheres of the planets, to seek the stars in their courses—what was mere dull earth to that?

"What indeed?"

Nikki started a little. Alf was beside him, and his mind had fallen open by no will of his own, to gape like a wound. Fiercely he forced it shut.

But Alf had got inside it and would not be driven out. There was no defense against that voice. Soft, gentle, relentless. The face had nothing soft in it, and very little that was human. "Frankly, Nikephoros, I had thought better of you."

Nikki sat stiff and cold in the saddle. He would not ask.

He did not need to. "You know well what I'm getting at. Are you set on committing yourself to this madness?"

Are you?

"For me," Alf said, "it's the only sane choice. But I'm not speaking of myself or of my kin."

I am one of you.

Alf shook his head. "You are not. You never were."

Nikki abandoned words for his speech of the body, wild, cold, edged with iron. He was of the Folk. He was made to be like them. Alfred himself had done it.

"I gave you the words you longed for. I took away none of your essential humanity. Broceliande won't change that. You'll grow old there as you would here, and you'll die. And you'll die mad. She saw it, your lovely lady to whom you were so cruel. She saw it as clearly as I in all my prophecy."

Nikki's fingers tightened on the reins until his mare jibbed to a halt, protesting this utterly unwonted pain. Alf's gray stood as if she had never been aught but stone, and Alf's face was stone, but his eyes—

Nikki could not meet those eyes. Would not. Must not.

"Go back to her," said the quiet voice. "Go now. She weeps for you; she curses you, and she loves you. She will make a world for you."

She hated him who had loved her and left her.

"Of course she hates you. She loves you to distraction."

That, snapped Nikki, driven back to words, *is absolutely illogical.*

Alf laughed, merry and sad at once, and bitter to endure. "It's lovers' logic, and perfect of its kind."

Nikki rounded upon him. Rage was white, white as snow, white as steel in the forge, white as the sun before it struck the eye blind. *Why? Why now, when it's too late? I could have stayed; would have. But you stood. You said no word, but you had no need. You lured, you beckoned. You needed me. I was your only way to get at Gwydion. Now . . . I'm no use to you, am I? I'm an embarrassment. An old mistake you'd rather forget. A stink of mortality in the perfect air of your Broceliande.*

If Nikki's words dealt wounds, Alf did not betray them. He only bowed his head and said utterly without anger, "I needed you, yes. I thought you would see sense on your own, once the need was past. I thought you would stop clinging to me like a child and walk as a man."

That was manhood? To run straight to a woman's skirts?

A smile touched Alf's eyes. "And she into your arms, and soon a young one between you. That is the way of the world."

Nikki clutched at saddle, reins, mane. No—no, that he had not done, please God, he had not got her with child.

"No?"

The rage flooded back. *You can't force me that way. Not with lies, not with threats. I go where I must go.*

"Go then," said Alf, cool and dispassionate. It was not contempt that paled those eyes to silver. The Master of Broceliande, great heretic saint, did not stoop to contempt. "Only remember. Once the gates close upon you, there will be no returning."

A shudder racked Nikki to the core. He looked at Alf, and he saw a face as familiar as his own and more beloved, the face of a master, of a friend, of a brother. Its eyes were inexpressibly tender, and utterly alien. They saw no walls before them, but gates opening upon a myriad of worlds.

Nikki saw walls. He named them gates, he told himself of the worlds. But they were only walls.

The others were far ahead now, human and unhuman together. Tao-Lin was a flame in her saffron silks. Her thought of him had faded; she had retreated into one of her pagan reveries. Walking the steps of the Way, she called it. When Alf did it, he called it prayer.

When Stefania did it, it was philosophy. But it was not the same. It was warmer, less perfect in its focus, more perfect in its intensity. Humans were like that; all too easily distracted, but also more conscious of measure, of restraint. There was something almost frightening in the Folk, an absoluteness of concentration, poised forever on the edge between power and madness.

Alf sat his mare, all silver and fallow gold, and watched Nikki's mind in its flounderings. He was not cool, after all. He was not dispassionate. He was tearing himself by the roots from this earth which he so loved and so hated.

Nikki gathered the reins, touched leg to his mare's side, turned her slowly upon her haunches. Gray earth, gray sky. Gray cold winter-scented air.

But it was not gray. The sun was palest gold. The earth was russet, brown, wine-red and wine-gold, umber and charcoal and faintest, shyest green, spring enkerneled in winter's bitter shell.

The mare scented it. She flared her great Arab nostrils and snorted, pawing the road; it rang with each impatient stroke. In the depths of Nikki's cloak, the cat began to purr.

They would not dislike one another, she and Arlecchina.

No. No, he could not go back. Not now. Creeping, blushing, begging forgiveness for what could never be forgiven.

"Why not?"

Nikki opened his mouth, closed it.

"Yes," Alf said, "it's time you taught yourself to talk. To be a man in all senses."

Never. Never, while he had no ears, while he had power.

"You have Stefania."

No.

Alf was silent.

Stefania. Sunlight. Laughter and pain, quarreling, loving, growing and breeding and birthing and dying. Beauty flawed; squalor
flawed, because there was beauty in it. He of all men, he had eyes to
see. That fear, like the rest, had been purest folly. He would always
have them.

If he stayed to use them.

Stefania.

It burst out of him. Laughter, tears. Alf was laughing, weeping.
They did not touch, hand or body. Their minds met, embraced,
clung. Tore free, bleeding a little, pain as sweet as it was bitter.

Lovers' logic. Brothers'. Nikki's will gathered, though it trembled, though it yearned to turn coward and run. *Now,* it bade Alf. *Now!*

They were gone, cat and mare and boy who would learn now to
be a man. Alf's power returned to itself, with yet a vision of a rider
upon a hill and all Rome below; and a woman in it, and a sister, and
a world that he would make his own.

But it was Alf's no longer. He let the wind scour the tears away.
He would not weep again upon this earth.

The company had ridden out of sight if never out of mind. Alf
turned his mount back toward the road they had taken, and gave her
her head.

Broceliande grew slowly before them. A shadow at first over the stony
hills, no more substantial than a tower of cloud. Little by little the
shadow swelled. On the third morning even human eyes could see
that the darkness was the massing of trees, a mighty wall of bole and
branch that had stood since the shaping of the world.

Jehan knew what lay within. Trees and winding tracks, glades
that were glorious in spring and summer and autumn, a veining of
streams that gathered into a small swift river; open meadows rich for
tilling; and a lake like a jewel, and on its shore a mound and on the
mound a castle, the House of the Falcon. And beyond that, deep
wood and gray moor and the pounding of the sea. It was a wider
realm than one might think, more varied and more beautiful.

Yet riding toward it under a gray sky, in a bleak raw wind, he saw
only the looming shadow. Once the last exile had passed within, the
barriers would close. Mortal men would shrink from them in source-
less horror, or if for daring or folly they ventured in, would wander
the maze until it cast them out again, starved and very likely mad.

"It's necessary," he told himself. "It has to be."

Already the first of them had ridden under the trees. Tao-Lin in gold and vermilion, sparing no grief for the lover who had abandoned her, no glance for the world she was forsaking, her back straight and stiff as she spurred onward. The shadows retreated from her; a shimmer lay upon her, a moonlight sheen. Gwydion, Maura, Aidan, Morgiana, followed side by side, and the sheen grew to a spectral splendor, embracing the wolves that trotted in the Queen's wake, and the lady who rode her dun stallion behind. Cynan, perched on her saddlebow, gazed steadily back. She fixed her eyes firmly ahead. She had never been one for backward glances, had Thea Damaskena.

Jehan's horse halted of its own accord, snorting, tensed to shy. Alf's tall gray continued unruffled. Jehan would not, could not move or speak. Yes, let them go this way, calmly, without a word. No tears, no foolishness. Simply a man on a chestnut destrier, watching, and an enchanter on a gray mare with a moon-pale child peering out of his cloak, riding away into the luminous dark.

On the edge of it, as it began to reach for him, Alf paused. His mare half turned; he looked back. His hand raised, sketched a cross in the air. His smile was sudden and shining and laden with all there had never been time to say, and all there had. Jehan cried out, he hardly cared what, kicking his mount into a startled, veering gallop. The mists thickened. The stallion bucked, plunged, fought. Jehan cursed and wept and hauled the great beast back upon its haunches under the very eaves of Broceliande. Almost he could have touched the one he loved most in any world. Almost Alf could have touched him. Their eyes met. Jehan's blurred. The white figure shimmered and faded. When at last he could see, they were gone, all of them, and all their light with them.

"The magic has gone out of the world," he said. He threw back his head to rage at Heaven, dropped it to rage at earth and its fools of priests, and found his fist clenched upon something. With all his will he forced it open. And laughed in wonder through the flooding tears. In his palm lay a brooch of marvelous work, ivory and carnelian, malachite and silver: a white hound, red-eared, with wickedly merry eyes, and dancing with her among woven leaves a proud-winged falcon. Its eye glinted upon him, now silver-gilt, now ember-red. *All the magic, Jehan de Sevigny?*

He laughed again, with a little less pain. "Not if you can help it." He saluted the silent wood, a sweeping, exuberant, triumphant salute made all the stronger for its leavening of grief, and wheeled his stallion about. Now that he thought of it, he had a bishopric to take in hand. He rode toward it; and as he rode, though still he wept, he began to sing.